SHADOW VEIL ACADEMY

OMNIBUS EDITION: BOOKS 1-3

HEATHER RENEE

CONTENTS

DARING PROVOCATION

EXTRAS FOR THE READERS!

DELAYED ADMISSION

BOOK ONE

CHAPTER ONE

Blue light emanated from my fingertips as my irritation increased. Whatever new freakish thing that was happening to me was going to get me locked away in a crazy house or worse, hidden away by the government. The most frustrating part was the more I fought the light, the stronger it became.

Closing my eyes, I fisted my fingers and drowned out the sounds of the screaming children behind me on the bus. There were only two more stops until I arrived at my aunt's work, but I wasn't going to make it. Walking an extra half mile was more than worth it to calm my nerves before something worse happened than blue sparks from my hands.

Standing up, I pulled the cord so the driver would stop and made my way to the exit. Looking back, the two siblings were still screaming at one another, and their mother was so immersed in her phone, she didn't even realize the boy had his sister in a headlock.

This was why I didn't have a smartphone. They were as addicting as drugs. My trusty flip phone suited me just fine when I needed to make a call or text.

Once my feet hit the pavement, relief flooded through me and I unfurled my fingers. The bright blue had turned to a teal and appeared like paint on my hands. Figuring that was good enough, I began my walk to meet my aunt. She had called earlier, asking me to come help her with something.

Sometime soon, I would need to confide in her, but I had only known the woman eight short months. She had been absent before that, estranged from her sister, my mother. But when my parents were shot by a gang as they were walking to their car after a concert, Jules had shown up, saving me from being thrown into a group home when I suddenly became an orphan.

I was seventeen, eighteen within a couple months. There would have been no adoption for me, only a living hell from what I had gleaned from the social worker. Her empathetic eyes still haunted my dreams from when she told me of my parents' death with the policeman who had escorted her to my house.

Agony gripped my chest as I remembered the night. My mom had purchased three tickets, and we were supposed to go see most of my favorite nineties' bands all in one place, but I had gotten so sick. Like, locked-myself-in-the-bath-room-and-hugged-the-toilet-the-whole-evening sick.

They volunteered to stay home, but I practically pushed them out the door with my words, knowing my mom would have been disappointed. We had been looking forward to the night for weeks and there was no point in everyone's evening being ruined.

After that, I was left with more "what ifs" than I could handle.

What if I hadn't been sick?

What if I hadn't insisted they still go?

What if they had taken a taxi like most locals did when they went to the Moda Center?

Those questions still haunted me, but they came less frequently as more abnormalities kept happening to me, like the whole moving objects debacle I dealt with last week and my glowing fingers, which seemed to be getting harder to control.

The most important question that had run through my mind recently was, *What am I becoming?*

Finally, I made it to the studio and, before I entered, I checked my hands. Everything was back to normal, and I let out a sigh of relief. When I opened the door, the bell above my head jingled, announcing my arrival. Jules wasn't up front, so I took my time, glancing around to see what new pieces had come in since I was there a few days earlier.

My eyes landed on a skyscape painting of downtown Portland. Even though I'd lived in Oregon my whole life, the city showed me something new each time I explored it. It seemed to be never-ending and, until I lost my parents, I had been in love with my hometown.

The first few months after they died, I didn't venture out much, but Jules had been urging me to get out and prepare for college. Little did she know, I had no intention of continuing my education, especially with the oddities I seemed to be acquiring. My schooling had ended three months ago when I passed my GED instead of resuming my senior year after their deaths.

"Help!" Jules called from the back.

I ran to the storage area to find her about ready to be squished by an oversized sculpture she had no business carrying on her own.

My fingers grasped the underside of the art piece, and

Jules let out an audible sound of relief when the pressure lessened on her arms.

"Thank you. I really thought I had it, but it's heavier than it looks."

"Well, no shit. It's made out of plaster." I laughed.

"Language, child," she chastised, making me laugh even harder.

"Right. Because *you're* such an angel."

Focusing back on the task of moving the sculpture, we remained quiet until it was placed on its stand at the back of the art shop.

My head cocked sideways. "What is it?" The piece looked like a faceless head with hair sticking out everywhere.

"Uhhhh." She grabbed a paper off the counter behind us. "It's The Tree of Life by a local up-and-coming artist the owners found online."

"Alright, then." Turning away from the unique piece, I hopped up on the counter. "What did you need my help with?"

She rolled her eyes. "You really need a new phone. That thing is ancient. I left you a voicemail an hour ago saying you didn't have to come in."

I didn't bother checking my phone, because I knew she was probably right, but there was no way I was getting a new one. I loved my tiny dinosaur phone.

Instead, I changed the subject. "What time are you out of here tonight? I could stay anyway, then we can grab dinner when you're done."

"Not until late. It's end-of-month processing day and I also need to do payroll to send to the owners for review."

I slid off the counter, so I could still face her as she took a seat behind the counter, crossing her short legs that barely reached the ground and flicking her strawberry-blonde hair back. Her ever-changing grey eyes stared me down, seeming to see into my soul.

Depending on her mood, they would change from light grey, almost blue, to dark and stormy. She was leaning toward stormy then, and I decided to behave myself by not hassling her for working too much. Her five-foot-one frame might have been little compared to my five-foot-eight, but she was mighty in all other ways.

"I did want to talk to you, though. So, I'm glad you stopped by anyway." Her fingers brushed along the edge of the desk. "You didn't sleep very well last night."

She made it sound like a statement, but I knew she expected me to say something more. The majority of my nights were riddled with nightmares too real for my liking. My weird blue-teal fingers and slight telekinesis weren't the only abnormalities I experienced. The dreams had only gotten worse as my freakish abilities continued to grow.

When I didn't speak up, she continued, "Why don't you go visit with them? Take a walk, get some fresh air, and see if it helps."

I dropped my eyes from her, unable to keep her stare. "I can't, Jules. It hurts worse when I visit, and..." I trailed off, wanting so badly to tell her what was happening to me, but the right words failed me. "When will it stop hurting so much?"

She didn't answer my rhetorical question. We'd had the conversation before. Instead, she came back around the desk, and her arms wrapped around me as her calming lavender scent infused my body.

Pulling back, her fingers grasped my shoulders. "You have a purpose. You may not know what it is yet, but you're destined for great things, Raegan Keyes. Just give it time."

I nodded, wanting to offer a smile, but couldn't. "I'm trying. I really am."

"I know you are." Her hands released me as she took a step back. "And it's okay to lose your shit as often as you need. Grief never ends when you experience a loss like yours. You only learn how to channel it better as time passes. Remember, I'm here for you whenever you need to talk. You're not alone in this."

For the first few weeks, Jules had me on what felt like suicide watch. She rarely left me by myself, constantly asked how I was, offered to take me shopping, to go on vacations, and more. Anything to get my mind off the loss. Though, the best thing she did was approve my decision to test out of school early.

Guilt crept up on me as I thought about the apartments I had been looking at online that morning. As more strange things kept happening to me, I considered avoiding Jules as much as possible and not telling her what was happening. Even though we hadn't known each other very long, the grief we went through together brought us closer than I thought possible when she first showed up.

"Do you want me to close the shop today?" Jules asked. "We could go on a road trip, do whatever you want. The paperwork can wait an extra day."

As much as I wanted to say yes, I didn't want to get her in trouble. She might pretty much run the place, but she wasn't the owner. "I'll be fine. I'll take a walk and go visit my parents like you suggested."

Back to the joyful Jules I was used to as of late, she patted my shoulder as if I was a young child. "That sounds like a great idea. Nature can be your best friend, and I'm sure your parents would love the visit, but only if you're up for it. I'll pick you up if you need me, so don't hesitate to call."

Nodding, I moved in to give her a hug. "Thank you, Jules... for everything these last eight months."

"Even though I wasn't around before, there was absolutely no hesitation when I got the call. I will always be there for you, Rae."

When we pulled apart, I tucked my hands into my pockets in case my emotions made my fingers do the damn glowing thing again, but thankfully, I seemed to be keeping everything in check. As I walked out the door, I waved goodbye once more, then headed down the street.

Pulling earbuds from my bag, I put them in my ears before plugging into my iPod. Music was the only way I tolerated being alone. If there was silence around me, then my mind ventured to dark places I tried to avoid.

Taking in the quiet part of the city, I was grateful that Jules worked in a shop on the outside of Portland instead of downtown where most of the tourists were. When I arrived at the end of the street, I had the option to go left and head toward the city park, which was filled with acres of trees that called to me, or I could go right. That would take me to the cemetery I had avoided for the last month as more weird things kept happening to me.

Realizing quickly that I needed to put my big girl pants on and see my parents, I turned in their direction. The walk there took about an hour, but I didn't mind. Since I wasn't in school and didn't work much outside of helping Jules in the art studio on occasion, walking had saved me from going crazy in the house. There were too many memories for me to handle some days.

The closer I got to their resting place, the quicker my feet moved. Once the decision had been made to quit avoiding them, I became anxious to feel their spirits wrapped around me. Suddenly, I craved it like I needed my next breath.

After entering the cemetery, I started to run and continued until their gravesites came into view. I sat down in front of the headstones and ran my fingers over the engraved words, closing my eyes.

January 5th, 2019.

A day I would never forget no matter how much time passed.

"Hi, Mom and Dad."

I always spoke out loud to them. Even if they couldn't respond, a part of me needed to hear the words.

"I miss you both so much. I have to admit, I almost didn't come today, but between Jules and my subconscious, I knew I really had no choice. I'm sorry it's been so long."

The wind picked up, wrapping around me. Even though it was August, the chill bit at my skin. It was a welcome sensation, one I told myself was my parents acknowledging my presence, not just the ever-changing weather of Oregon.

"Something new happened since the last time I was here. Not that I'm excited to tell you about it, but you're the only ones I can talk to without fear of being thrown in a psych ward. Pretty sure Aunt Jules wouldn't do that, but you never know."

Glancing down at my hands, seeing how normal they looked like now, I partially wondered if it was all in my head. That would make more sense than what I thought was true. Maybe the trauma of losing my parents made me go crazy. I could understand that more than the thought of turning into some sort of witch like I'd only seen in the movies.

"When I get upset, teal light glows from my fingers, and I'm pretty sure I moved a pen across the table with only thought the other day. I'm scared as shit and feeling like I'm losing control of reality, and I don't know what to do."

Knowing they couldn't answer, I began chatting about happier things once I was able to get a few things off my chest. I knew I needed to steer clear of subjects that would darken my mood, and they didn't need my negativity. Before I knew it, the sun was beginning to set, and it was time to head back home.

Since the shooting, I tried not to stay out in the city at night, but some days it was unavoidable, and I knew I also needed to face my fears. I couldn't avoid the dark forever.

A half-hour later, the sun was fully set, and the moon shone behind the clouds casting a soft glow along the path I took back to the main section of town, in hopes of grabbing a bus ride home or possibly to the shop to help Jules with the paperwork. I sent her a text offering but hadn't heard back yet.

Adjusting my earbuds, I turned up my music since I was closer to town. I figured I was safer now that I was under the city lights and out of the trees, but I soon realized I was wrong.

Shadows darted in front of me, but out of sight quicker than humanly possible. Without conscious thought, my hands lit up and moved in front of me defensively. Turning slowly, my eyes searched for the shadows, but instead I saw a man picking up speed, making his way toward me.

My eyes remained on him, trying to make out his facial features, but the shadows appeared once more, distracting me. I glanced between the moving, potentially not-real figures and the stranger, trying to decide just how crazy I had officially become.

Lowering my hands, I silenced my music to focus on my surroundings and reached for my phone when both the shadows and the man slowed down. I took two steps backward and flipped open my phone, but before I could press the speed dial, I was engulfed in darkness.

Something pricked at my skin and coldness seeped into me, but what scared me most were the hard hands that wrapped around my arms, yanking me from the shadows as they dissipated into the night.

This isn't real, I chanted in my head over and over again.

My very cynical subconscious chose that moment to remind me that moving objects with my mind and glowing hands weren't supposed to be real, either. My subconscious could be a bitch sometimes.

Struggling against my attacker's hold, I recalled all of the action films I'd seen and hoped they had been good for something.

Stomping my heel down on his foot, I spun around, and raised my knee to his groin before backing up, but it did nothing to the stranger before me. He was barely fazed by my measly attack as his onyx eyes met mine.

"Oh, Raegan. Why do you fight me?" the man's voice cooed.

The accent was one I'd never heard before, and it chilled me to the bone that he knew my name.

"It's time to come home," he whispered, suddenly right in front of me even though he had been at least ten feet away just a second before.

"Leave me alone," I shouted as I shoved my palm into his nose.

His responding snarl wasn't a normal human sound and caused my body to freeze in fear.

He raised his arm up, striking my cheek with the back of his hand while the other wrapped around my arm again, more than likely leaving bruises. His face immediately blanched as he realized what he'd done. "You insolent child! Now they're going to be upset I marked you. Whatever. They'll get over it as long as you come with me."

Who the hell is "they"? I wondered as I struggled to get free of his tight grasp. His skin was a deep russet color, and his eyes were black like the shadows that were swirling around me once more.

"Leave her alone," another voice sneered from somewhere behind me.

"This doesn't concern you, Elf," the man holding on to me spat as he turned us in the direction of the new arrival.

The man in front of me was ridiculously tall, at least six-and-a-half feet, with the most striking honey-brown eyes I'd ever seen. The golds and browns seemed to swirl as he narrowed his gaze at us.

"I don't have time for games," the newcomer announced as he brushed his dark bronze hair back behind his ear that I was pretty sure was pointier than should be normal but wasn't positive in the darkening night.

He snapped his fingers and, just like that, my attacker was gone along with the shadows. Before I knew it, I was alone with the man I *thought* had saved me, but I couldn't be sure yet.

We stared at each other without speaking or moving. Afraid of being zapped out of existence, I waited for him to make the first move or me to finally find my lady balls and scream like hell.

"Hello, Raegan. I'm Enzo, and it's time to come to Shadow Veil."

H is face softened as a grin appeared, and my mouth dropped from how *not* human he appeared with a chiseled jawline, bright, almost-glowing honey eyes, and thick, bronzed hair that would put Thor to shame. I had no idea if the guy was friend or foe, but at least he was easy on the eyes. If I had to be kidnapped by someone, I'd rather it be the hottie before me than the creeper with the shadows following him.

As the adrenaline wore off, I thought I remembered my attacker calling him "Elf". He wasn't at all what I pictured as an elf since he was so damn tall, which made me believe I had misheard the name. I dismissed the thoughts and wondered silently why he intervened in the first place. There must have been a reason. I just needed to decide if I cared enough to find out before I ran from what I hoped was just another shitty nightmare.

"Did you kill that man?" I asked, choosing to ignore his previous statement about taking me to some shadow place.

He laughed. "That wasn't a man. And no, I didn't kill him. His body just disintegrated into millions of pieces, but if he's strong enough, he'll put himself back together again. Though, I really hope not."

Like humpty-freaking-dumpty? Yeah, because that was something normal people talked about every day. The rational part of me knew I needed to get away, but the curious part kept asking questions like an idiot.

"Okay," I said, drawing out the word. "Why are you here? What are *you*?"

His eyes seemed to darken to umber with his excitement. "I was here on vacation, if you must know, but now I'm here to bring you to Shadow Veil Academy, like I said before. And what I am isn't something you get to find out until you agree to come with me." He winked. "Then, I can tell you all of my secrets."

Screw that. I was getting away from the inhumanly handsome man as soon as I could.

"Thanks, but no thanks. Today isn't good for me to run off with a complete stranger. Rain check?" I replied, backing away slowly.

Within the blink of an eye, he stood before me just like the creeper before him had done, then placed his hand on my shoulder. "I know, and I can feel your suffering. Just hold still and I'll make it go away."

Before I could move out of his grasp, tingles ran through my body and every muscle within me relaxed instantly. My mind turned to mush as I struggled to remember where I was and what I had been doing.

"What did you do to me?" I mumbled, feeling unsteady on my feet.

My emotions were light, and a weight I didn't remember was lifted from me, but it wasn't right. I *wasn't* supposed to be happy. I needed the pain back. I needed to remember. But what was I supposed to remember?

I fought the swirling sensations running through me. I didn't want them. I wanted the agony back, or at least, I thought I did. It was something very important to me, but every time I was closer to figuring out what it was, the image slipped away.

"I wouldn't do that if I were you," Enzo warned. "It's going to hurt if you keep fighting me."

I ignored him, closing my eyes, trying to capture the memory that ran from me.

It was important.

I knew it, and I was stubborn enough to reach for the anguish it promised just to remember what Enzo had taken from me.

As I thought his name, a new memory showed up, one that wasn't hiding from me and easy to grasp on to.

I had seen him before.

I opened my eyes. "I know you, but I can't see how or why. What did you do to me? Why do I feel so calm when I know I should be furious right now?"

His hands cradled my face. "Because I am all you have left now, and it's important that you come with me willingly. We have to get to Shadow Veil before others come for you."

Shaking my head, I went back to ignoring him and gave my memory one last push before everything flooded back to me. Falling to the ground, I clutched my head as the suffering returned.

"I warned you," he chastised. "It doesn't feel good, does it? I can make it go away again if you quit being so damn stubborn."

I scrambled to my feet, moving further away from him.

"Don't you dare do that again. Those are *my* memories and you had no right to take them away."

My heart raced and hands shook. The swirling within me was now familiar, frighteningly familiar, as my hands began to glow brighter than ever before.

"Get away from me," I snapped. "I need to calm down."

Surprisingly, he actually listened and backed up.

"I can help you control it. Your power is growing too strong for you to control on your own without proper training."

His tone was more sympathetic that time, his face softening as the seconds ticked by.

"Why do I feel like I know you?" I asked.

Before he could answer, my aunt came stumbling through the tree line. "Raegan!"

I ran to her, instantly forgetting about Enzo behind me. "What's wrong?"

"Why are you asking me that? You're the one that called me, and all I could hear was struggling. I came as soon as you didn't answer me." Her wide eyes moved past my face as her whole body stiffened. "Get behind me."

When I didn't move, she sidestepped me. "What are you doing here, Elf? You have no business with my niece."

That was the second time someone had called him "Elf" and I was beginning to think it was his name, but the more concerning thought was that Jules might know him and she didn't seem to be afraid.

"It seems I do, Fox. Your niece can't control her powers, and I just saved her from being taken by a scavenger, so you're welcome."

Fox? Elf? I was so confused.

Jules stepped closer to me, and her fingers closed around my wrist. "I appreciate what you've done, but I'll take it from here." Her voice was tight and angry.

"She needs to go to Shadow Veil. A shifter has no

business training a hybrid not of their kind, and you should know that. You're just lucky I'm the one who found her."

Yep. That was enough for me.

"What. In. The. Actual. Hell? You two need to stop talking like I'm not here and explain what Elf, Fox, and Hybrid mean right now!" I tossed my deep auburn hair back and glared at both of them, waiting for answers that hopefully didn't create more questions.

"She doesn't know what she is?" Enzo sneered at Jules. "Do you understand how dangerous that is?"

"Yes, I do, but it wasn't my business until eight months ago. Her parents put a binding spell on her, and I was trying to figure out how to lift it before I told her."

Infuriated, I snapped my fingers between them. "Did you *not* hear me when I said to quit talking like I wasn't here? I'm pretty sure those words left my mouth like two seconds ago."

Jules turned to me. "I'm sorry, Rae. I never meant for you to find out this way, but you should have told me something was happening with you. I could have helped if I had known."

Thoughts raced through my head as more of the conversation started to sink in. Anger began to bubble within me and, this time, I watched in fascination instead of fear as my hands lit up. Apparently, I didn't need to hide it from these two, and being able to embrace it was more freeing than I expected.

"Raegan, you need to stop right now," Jules warned. "This is not the place for this conversation."

"Let's go home then, because I'm certainly *not* done talking." My tone was sharp as the thought of being lied to my whole life took over.

Who was I? Was Jules even my aunt? Who was I supposed to trust now?

Before I could ponder those questions for too long, Enzo's hand grasped my shoulder. "Home sounds like a great idea."

My body was sucked into thin air as my vision went black, but within half a second, I stood in my living room between Enzo and Jules. Nausea rose within me, causing me to run to the kitchen sink. I made it in time to dry heave over the counter before running cold water over my face.

"You could have warned her," Jules snapped.

"Would it have really made a difference?" he countered, but she didn't respond.

When I lifted my head up, I stared at my reflection in the kitchen window, taking in my appearance as they continued to bicker.

My normally fair skin was pasty and pale; my green eyes were brighter than I had ever seen before. Glancing down, I noticed my fingers were still tinged with color. Everything about me was starting to freak me out.

Turning around, I spotted Enzo leaning casually against the wall, waiting for me to get myself together. Apparently, he and Jules were done arguing and were awkwardly staring at me.

His swirling eyes seemed to see right through me, like he already knew my every secret. I didn't like it one bit. Even though my girly parts craved for me to move closer to him, I stood my ground, staying behind the counter.

I was done with him touching me and screwing with my psyche. Twice was two times too many.

He tossed his bronze locks, which were an inch or two longer than my shoulder-length hair, back out of his eyes. Seeing him standing in my house, I realized I hadn't been wrong about his height. He was taller than anyone I had ever met in person, making my five feet, eight inches seem miniscule.

Even though he was thin, his wide shoulders provided some much-needed bulk to his lithe frame. He wasn't overly muscled, and if he wasn't so imposing, I'd assume him to be weak, but he held himself as if he wasn't afraid of anyone. I guess if I could zap people out of existence, I'd have that confidence as well.

"Raegan, come sit down and I promise to answer all of your questions." Jules pointed toward the dining table, but I hesitated.

As much as I wanted answers, I was now uncertain that I could trust either person in the room. I knew my mother had a sister and I had so easily accepted Jules as that sister, but Enzo had called her Fox. I had no idea who she really was.

When I didn't move, Enzo stepped into my view and I decided he was going to be easier to deal with than Jules. He hadn't lied to me for eight months, and something told me he wasn't about to start lying to me now.

"How's that head of yours? The wheels seem to be turning a little fast in there."

I rolled my eyes at him. "How did you know I was in trouble tonight? Have you been following me?"

He raised a brow. "Straight to it, huh? No pleasantries? You're not even going to offer me a cup of tea?"

I narrowed my eyes, saying nothing in response. I wasn't going to play his games. He would be smart to figure that out quickly.

He let out an exaggerated sigh. "Fine. Business only. I got it." He paused, taking a seat at the table next to my aunt. His long, jean-clad legs edged out the other side of the table, and I couldn't help the small grin that appeared on my face. He didn't fit very well in our house.

When I finally took a seat, Jules reached a hand out to me, but I moved away. "I'd like to hear what Enzo has to say first, if you don't mind."

"That's understandable," she said with a smile that seemed forced.

Part of me felt guilty for pushing her away, but I needed answers to what had been happening to me, and I needed to know they wouldn't be given with a filter. Something told me the stranger across from me didn't pull any punches.

My gaze turned toward Enzo. "So, how did you know that creeper was attacking me?"

"It was pure luck." He shrugged. "I was passing through town on my way back to Shadow Veil, and I sensed a scavenger. I almost ignored him. I'm not supposed to engage in other supernatural business until I've finished school, but I don't always follow the rules." Tossing his hair back, he winked at me.

My girly parts got a little excited again, but I stomped that fire out without hesitation. No way was I hooking up with someone not human.

"Life's not near as fun when you don't push the boundaries," he continued with a smirk. "Anyway, then I felt your power. It wasn't controlled, and something told me it would be worth my time to check out what was happening. I let the academy know I found a stray before I stopped the attack, and they want me to bring you back now that the scavengers know you exist. Are you almost seventeen?"

Trying to ignore the fact he called me a stray, I responded, "I'm already seventeen. I'll be eighteen this October. Why?"

His brow pinched together, and he turned to Jules. "Is she not in the system?"

"I honestly don't know. I assumed Lara and Andy did what they needed to do, but when I learned Raegan was here instead of the academy, I thought she was exempt somehow. I was estranged from Lara for many years. When I realized there was a powerful magical block on Raegan and she wasn't showing any abilities, I assumed that was why she was never enrolled."

Listening to them talk was like being in a foreign country. I didn't understand a damn word coming out of their mouths.

"What are you people? Or more importantly, what am I?"

"I'm an elf. Jules over there is a fox shifter. You, on the other hand, are a hybrid. I'm not sure about the ratios, but you definitely have some elf in you. I'm not sure about the other half for some reason. But I would assume your mother was a fox shifter, right? So, your other half should be shifter."

I had no freaking clue, but I was hoping Jules could fill in that blank.

"Her parents were both witches. Full-blooded witches." She wouldn't meet my eyes, making me read between the lines and I was not at all liking what I was understanding.

"Are you saying those weren't my parents and you're not my aunt?"

"I'm sorry, Raegan. She might not have been your biological mother, but she loved you more than anything. That's evident by everything I see in this house. Your mom and I went to the academy together. We remained in touch for a long time until she moved out here with your father."

She paused, seeming to consider her next words carefully.

"I didn't know you even existed until I learned of her death and went to the house to clean up. I don't know how you ended up with them or why, but I do know they must have kept you a secret for a reason. The Lara I knew didn't do anything unless she had a purpose for the greater good."

Holy shit. I pushed away from the table and lowered my head into my hands. I knew I wasn't normal, but this was so far out of the realm of possibilities I had considered, I wasn't sure how to process it all.

"Raegan..." Jules warned. "How long have you been doing that?"

Lifting my head, I glanced at my hands. Sure enough, they were glowing again. "A month or so. Only when my emotions are heightened."

"That's the elf in you. Elves can do some badass shit. Be glad you're part elf," Enzo added, seeming to want to lighten the mood, but there was no making any of it better.

"How do you know so much about us?" I asked him.

"Elves are the original supernatural being. We created all others. One of our abilities is to be able to identify another supernatural when we encounter them. I could probably remove your binding as well, but I'd rather we did that at the academy. I like bending the rules, not breaking them entirely. Something tells me the council isn't going to be happy you've been hidden away."

Talks of taking me somewhere had been brought up one too many times for my comfort level. I had no desire to get more immersed in whatever world included creatures who preyed on weaker beings with magic and shadows.

"Enzo is right. I think going to the academy is going to be the best thing for you. When I thought you didn't have any abilities, I was all for you living a normal life until I could figure things out, but time is running out. All supernaturals are supposed to attend Shadow Veil when they turn seventeen. You're already a year behind."

"Let me make sure I understand what's happening here. I'm not human, neither are the both of you. Elves, witches, and shifters are real. My parents weren't *really* my parents, and Jules isn't my aunt. Now, I'm supposed to go attend some school that I've never heard of just because it's what everyone else like me does. Does that sum it up?"

"Yep," Enzo answered. "Now, be a good girl and pack a bag. I don't have time to waste. I need to get back to Shadow Veil before classes start, and I don't think it's a good idea to leave you behind. More scavengers will be back and you're defenseless against them until you have proper training."

Nope. Hard pass. No way was I going with him.

"I think I'll take my chances here. I appreciate you stepping in tonight, but I've learned my lesson. I won't be going out alone at night anymore. I'll be just fine."

He tsked at me. "Your power is growing and, without training that you can only get at the academy, you'll only continue to attract the scavengers. More will come, and they won't wait until you're alone in the dark. They don't take consequences into consideration when they're looking for their next fix. If one gets their hands on you, they'll keep you alive even after they've fed from you, just so your energy can rebuild before they suck you dry all over again. That's how they're able to stay on earth when they should have died long ago."

"So, they're like a magical vampire?" I cringed at my own question.

Enzo laughed. "You could say that, but don't repeat that in front of them. They despise vampires."

What in the actual hell? Vampires were real, too? I had just said the first reference that came to mind, and I... this was too much.

"Raegan, honey. I meant what I said when I told you that you weren't alone. I will go with you to Shadow Veil. I promise this is a safe place, and I will be with you for as long as you need me. I know it's hard right now, but I need you to trust me."

Glancing between the two of them, I knew I really didn't have a choice. As I peeked at my still-glowing hands and battled with the swirling sensations within my body, I also knew I would have eventually agreed anyway.

Though, it didn't mean I had to make it easy on either of them.

Standing from the table, I went to the window. City lights could be seen in the distance, and I let my mind focus on that, imagining the sounds of downtown Portland instead of the bickering behind me.

"I think I've had enough crazy talk for the night. I'm going to go to bed and hope that when I wake tomorrow, this will have all been a very shitty dream and my life can go back to the way it was."

Enzo snorted and muttered something that sounded a lot like an insult to my ears.

"If you have something to say, just spit it out," I snapped. When he didn't respond, I continued, "I realize my reaction to all of this may seem ridiculous, but I didn't know any of *this* existed until an hour ago. Excuse me for needing time to process. You don't have to make me feel worse by being so pompous."

Enzo stood from his chair, only needing three strides to reach me from across the room with his ridiculously long legs. "You're not taking this seriously enough. Those scavengers will be back, and I'm not going to wait around until you've *processed* the situation. In my world, that will get you killed."

His eyes flashed a darkness I hadn't yet seen within them. Gone was the friendly elf who had saved me and made jokes about tea when he arrived in my home.

Pressing myself against the wall, I swallowed hard and forgot whatever it was I wanted to respond with. Enzo was dangerous, and I needed to remember that. His sexy grin and somewhat endearing personality weren't things I could let distract me.

Taking a step back, his eyes were back to their previous color. "School starts next week on the second of September. You'll have plenty of time to consider your options before then, but it needs to be done at Shadow Veil. That's the only place you're safe now that a scavenger has found you."

Needing a moment, I remembered the shadows that encased me and the pain I felt when the creeper grabbed me. Glancing down at my arm, I lifted my sleeve up and found a red welt just above my elbow.

The mark caught Enzo's attention, and he hissed as he settled his hand over the bump. Something that felt a lot like ice stabbing me entered my arm beneath his touch. My arm instinctively pulled away, but his grip didn't falter.

"You've been marked. I need to remove it, or you won't last the night before another scavenger comes." Enzo's face relaxed, seeming to be sympathetic to my situation.

Clenching my jaw, I waited not-so-patiently for him to finish. When he released my arm, the welt was no longer visible, but where his hand had been, there was a red outline.

"It will fade by morning," he said when he noticed my stare.

Glancing at Jules, I took a moment to assess my current

situation. I knew I wasn't normal. I had known that for a while, but I was also stubborn as a mule. I had very little time to process. A night wasn't enough, but if I was honest and cut them some slack, I had been processing for weeks, ever since my hands began to glow.

Sitting back down at the table, I focused my attention on the saltshaker. If I could move it, then I'd go willingly, but if it did nothing, I was going to need more time and a hell of a lot more information.

Enzo started to say something, but I snapped my fingers at him, halting whatever words he wanted to say. Instead, I squinted my eyes and put all my effort into sounding like a lunatic within my head.

Move.

Come.

Slide, you stupid saltshaker!

It did nothing and I felt like an idiot.

"Do it again," Enzo said. "This time, don't try so hard. Magic should be effortless. It's a natural part of you. Even though it's suppressed, you should still be able to do basic magic like move an object from the bit that's leaked through the binding."

His words were encouraging and his expression sincere as everything in him seemed to be completely focused on me. My skin heated and heart raced as I thought about how it would have been to have his attention like this without all the complications. Even the smirk I could see hiding behind the twinkle in his eyes drew me to him.

As much as I wanted to argue with him, I knew there was a chance he could be right. When I'd had episodes in the past, I had never meant to do it. Maybe in magic, less was actually more.

When I tried again, I closed my eyes and visualized the

saltshaker, then thought about what I wanted it to do. Without looking, I opened my palm and called the item to me. Two seconds later, the cool glass was within my grasp, and I glanced down.

"Raegan, have you done that before?" Jules asked.

"Just once and by accident."

She nodded but didn't say anything else.

"We need to leave by sunrise. Are you going to make this harder than it needs to be for yourself?"

I grunted. Harder for me? Who was this guy?

Oh, right. He was an elf who could zap me out of existence.

"Can Jules come with me?" I asked. I might have been mad at her for keeping my parents' secret, but she was still my only family. Blood or not. I had kept a secret from her, too, and I wouldn't be a hypocrite by staying angry with her, especially when she promised she would come with me.

Enzo shook his head. "Not right away, but she'll be able to visit soon. First break from school will be eight weeks in, and she can come then."

"When will I be able to go home? How long am I expected to stay at this academy?"

It wasn't okay if this was going to be like a prison sentence. No way in hell. They could kiss my ass.

"School is on for eight weeks and then there's a one to two-week break for respite in which you can leave school or have visitors. Typically, first-year students aren't allowed to leave during breaks until the summer, but since you should be a second-year, I'm not sure what the council will say."

The council had been mentioned several times already, and I wondered who they were. I pictured them as old people, withering away while they told everyone around them what to do until someone with more power came along to stop them.

Whatever was within me made itself known then, reminding me that I wasn't normal and none of what was going on with me was getting easier. I needed to quit procrastinating and just deal with this shit head on.

"Okay."

Enzo leaned back in his seat, smugly. "Okay, what? I need to hear you say the words, Raegan."

"Okay, I'll go to this academy with you. Learn about witchcraft voodoo and whatever else. As long as you promise that when I'm done with it, I'll know how to make those scavenger dirt bags disappear."

"You've got fire in you. I think we're going to have a lot of fun this year."

"Not too much fun," Jules interrupted. "Raegan, you need to take this seriously. I know you weren't a fan of school during your last year, but this isn't something to be flippant about. Magic is dangerous, and if you don't properly learn how to control it, innocent people *will* get hurt. There is no doubt about that."

"I understand. So, what now? Do we run through a wall and take a train?" I was kidding, but my body tensed slightly, wondering if the books or movies had gotten any of it right.

"Not exactly. I'll transport us like I did when we came here from the park. We'll arrive on the outside of the school and have to walk through the security boundaries."

The train would have been better. I didn't like his teleporting. Well, more accurately, my stomach wasn't fond of it.

"If tonight is my last night of freedom for however long,

then I'd like to spend it without you lurking in my house. No offense." *But he has to go*, I finished silently.

He leaned forward, meeting my stare. "You got it, but I'll be close by, so don't even think about trying to run."

The thought hadn't crossed my mind, but now that he mentioned it...

No, I wouldn't run. My parents had done that for some reason—kept me hidden from a world I should have been a part of—and I wouldn't do that. Instead, I was going to put every effort into figuring out why they had done what they did.

Why was I their dirty little secret, and who were my birth parents?

Beyond learning how to control my glowing fingers and whatever else came next, figuring out those two things was my priority.

"I'll be here, and I'll be ready."

With a nod, Enzo disappeared, and then it was just me and Jules. We stared at each other for several minutes, neither seeming to know what to say. Both of us had omitted important information, but I didn't believe either of us meant any harm by it. We were just trying to protect each other, and it backfired. Lesson learned.

"Do you want to talk about it?" she asked.

"Not really. I have a feeling this is something I have to experience for myself and no amount of questions will make a difference, but I'm disappointed you can't come with me. What if I'm really bad at all of this?"

She reached for my hand. "You're going to do great. You're strong, Raegan. You've been through hell, and I know whatever comes next won't get in your way of showing the world what you're capable of."

"Thanks, Jules." I glanced around the living room. "Are

you going to stay here? It sounds like you have a family out there somewhere."

"I haven't decided, to be honest. Portland has grown on me, but I miss my pack. I was going to ask you after your birthday if you wanted to come with me back to New Orleans. I even had permission from my alpha to tell you about us, but Enzo beat me to it."

"I'm sorry I didn't tell you what was happening."

"I'm sorry, too." She smiled at me as an idea seemed to form in her head. "Why don't we go pack your stuff and then head out for the night? Go out to a late dinner, cause some trouble, whatever you want."

"Let's do it. Sleep is overrated anyway."

Plus, I could do without sleep for the night if it meant the nightmares stayed at bay. Maybe going to this academy and figuring out whatever was going on with me would make them lessen.

A girl could certainly hope.

THE SANDMAN HAD NEVER COME FOR ME THAT NIGHT. By the time me and Jules got home, it was after two in the morning and my mind was racing. I knew Enzo would be there in a few hours and didn't see the point of sleeping.

When the time came, Jules tapped on my door before popping her head in. "He's here. Are you ready?"

"Does it really matter?" I shrugged.

"Just breathe. I'll be there to check on you before you know it."

I grabbed my rolling luggage off the bed and headed toward the hall. Jules went ahead of me and, when she moved to the side, my eyes met Enzo's as he leaned against the wall in our living room, smirking at me.

"I thought for sure you were going to let me have some fun by chasing you down. I'm actually disappointed you didn't run."

"I don't run from anything. You'd be smart to figure that out sooner rather than later," I stated matter-of-factly.

Jules pulled on my arm, tugging me toward her. "I'm going to miss you," she whispered as her arms wrapped around me.

"I'll have my phone. I'll call as often as I can."

She pulled back, her mouth in a frown. "They won't let you keep it. No outside electronics allowed, but I'll get word to you, I promise."

I wanted to roll my eyes and say something snide, but it wouldn't change anything, so I kept my thoughts to myself. "Okay."

When I turned around, Enzo held his hand out to me. "Times up, Ginger."

The glare I shot him would have brought weaker men to their knees. I hated that nickname. Kids had used it incessantly when I was too young to defend myself, but I was older and could do something about it.

I strode over to him, my face mere inches from his and my palm hovering just over his junk. "Call me that again and you'll be missing what I assume is a vital organ, according to you."

He hissed. "You fight dirty."

"Your point is?" I quipped.

"Just making an observation." He flicked his gaze to Jules. "We need to go."

"I don't know you, Enzo. More importantly, you don't know me. If you hadn't saved my niece last night, I wouldn't be letting her leave with you right now, but you did, so I am. Do not make me regret that. I still know people at the academy, and if I find out a hair on her precious head has been harmed, I will find you."

"Is that a threat?" He winked.

"No, it's a promise. One you'd do well to remember if you know what's good for you, Elf."

"Understood, Fox." He nodded respectfully.

With one more hug and a quick goodbye to Jules, I turned back to Enzo. His hand waited for mine once more and, this time, I didn't hesitate. It was time to woman up and figure out who I really was.

Enzo's grip was firm and warm as his thumb stroked across the back of my hand, almost absentmindedly. Before I could process the movement, my world went black. Seconds later, my hand was released, and I bent over, this time not throwing up, but coming damn close.

Enzo waited patiently as I got myself together. When I did, I was severely underwhelmed. "*This* is the school?"

"Yep. Just wait until you get inside." His grin was so prideful, but I didn't get it. The building before me wasn't ancient like I had been picturing. It was modest in appearance and size. Maybe a few thousand square feet, nothing that should have been able to hold a school, let alone be impressive.

"Wait, I didn't grab my bag." I had been so distracted when he grabbed my hand that I hadn't thought about it.

"I grabbed it when you were saying goodbye to your aunt." His head gestured toward his left arm, where my luggage was held firmly in his grasp.

"Thank you," I said, taking a step toward the building before us.

His arm moved in front of me. "Wait a second." Lifting

his palm, he placed it on my forehead and a warmth spread through me. "There. Now you should be able to go through the shield without it messing with your head."

He pushed me through, not letting me consider his words. When I stumbled, his hand caught my wrist. "Where are we?" he asked.

"Uh, magic school?" I didn't understand why he was asking me that. Maybe he should have been more concerned with his head and not mine.

"Good. Just checking. And it's Shadow Veil Academy, not magic school. Don't be so *human*."

There was little doubt in my mind that I was going to punch him in the face at least once by the time I left this place.

When I glanced back at the school, my breath hitched. *Holy shit.* The monstrosity before me was not the modest home I had seen just moments before we walked through the invisible shield.

Three turrets spread out evenly amongst a mansion that was surrounded by a concrete border with iron gates placed throughout, the main entrance having an expansive arch over it.

As we approached the gates, I noticed a crest carved into the arch with the letters "SVA". The artwork was intricate and stunning within the stone, and I was already mesmerized by the beauty even though we hadn't even walked through the gates yet.

When we were within two feet of the front gate, it opened on its own and everything began to set in. This was no ordinary school, and I wasn't an ordinary student.

This was magic school, and I had no idea who I was or what I had gotten myself into.

As my shoes crunched on the gravel walkway, I was in awe. Everything around me looked to be straight out of a movie. The building had to be hundreds of years old, yet it was in pristine condition and seemed to have a faint glow surrounding its edges.

When my eyes glanced up toward the sky, I could see the shimmer of the shield over the property. It stretched far beyond what I could see from my vantage point and made me want to start exploring right away.

When we left Oregon, it was around five in the morning, which meant it was around eight in Massachusetts where Jules had told me the school was located just outside Salem. I also learned that the Salem witch trials were very real and a direct link to the history of the school. Creepy, but interesting.

"What do you think?" Enzo asked, slowing his pace to match mine.

My eyes focused on the gargoyle statues that were placed on top of the turrets and every twenty feet or so around the border of the school. I heard his question, but my mind was racing with everything I was seeing, unable to think of a proper answer.

"Yep. I thought you'd like it." He smirked, and I narrowed my gaze on him, my thoughts finally free of the surroundings.

"You don't know me, so don't be so cocky. Only an idiot wouldn't be fascinated by this place the first time they see it." Deciding I needed a break from him, I asked, "Where do I go now?"

Before he could answer, a peppy blonde dressed in a plaid pleated skirt, white collared shirt, and thin teal tie caught my attention.

"Hi, there! I'm Gemma. I've been sent to bring you to the headmaster's office."

Tension I didn't even realize I held was immediately released from my shoulders. I wasn't going to have to spend all day with Enzo. Even if Gemma was a bit over the top with her greeting, she hopefully wouldn't infuriate me like Enzo had.

"I brought her all this way. I can get her to the headmaster's office," Enzo answered, surprising me with the unhappiness in his voice.

"Headmaster Stone wants me to do it, so take that up with him if you have a problem with it," she remarked, losing some of her previous pep.

"Fine." He dropped my bag and disappeared into thin air.

"What the..." My head cocked sideways, trying to see any signs he had been standing before us just moments before, but there was nothing. Not even a whisper of wind.

"Don't worry. You'll get used to it. Elves like to disappear all the time like that." She glanced at her watch. "Come on. We're late."

Her hand clutched around my wrist as I scrambled to grab my bag, which was obviously too full, considering it seemed we were supposed to wear a uniform at the school. I wasn't sure I would be comfortable with the skirts, but I had some killer black pants that would work with the shirt and tie.

As she dragged me along the walkway, I realized I hadn't asked her what we were late for, but I didn't really care. Instead, I went back to checking out the school.

The creepiest part was the gargoyles. Their eyes, even though made of stone, seemed to follow me as I walked. They reminded me of an old sculpture my mom used to have of a wolf. The thing always creeped me out as a kid, but it had disappeared one day after I began having nightmares that it was chasing me through the house.

When we arrived at the main entrance to the actual building, there was a huge archway made from concrete just like the surrounding walls that encased two large wooden doors. Each door had the SVA crest I'd seen earlier, along with dark bronze handles.

The doors looked ridiculously heavy, but Gemma opened the left one with ease and gestured for me to go in first. When I stepped inside, the entrance before me was not what I expected. We were on a platform about thirty feet wide, and beyond that were several staircases and hallways with plaques above each opening.

Elves, Shifters, Vampires, Witches, and Hybrids were the names above the hallways. Magic, Combat, and History were the three names above the staircases, and I wondered if those led to the turrets I saw when I first arrived.

"I know it looks confusing, but it's more of an optical illusion. Magic is used to make the school a whole lot bigger than it looks. I'll show you to our dorm after we see Head-master Stone. His office is in the Magic wing."

When we were both on the stairs, they started to move like an escalator, causing me to flinch and possibly squeak, but I chose not to think about that. My focus was on the brick steps that were somehow moving without any sign of a mechanical function.

"How?" I asked as I glanced up at Gemma, hoping she'd know what I meant.

"The answer is almost always going to be magic. Things will seem less weird the longer you've been here. I'm on my second year like Enzo, and I still get surprised with some things, but it's not very often. By June, you'll be immune to most of it."

Ugh. Everyone I was meeting was going to be a year ahead of me. Enzo's previous words came back to me, though. There was a possibility I could get thrown in with the second-year students, but I didn't know how high that chance was.

If they looked back at my previous school records, they'd see I was a good student. Even though I was happy to finish early, that had more to do with my parents' death than the learning.

The corridor we ended up at opened into a wide dome-like area. There were skylights above us, letting the sun shine in, and several more hallways between three main doors.

The one that caught my attention first had "Head-master Stone" carved into the wood door with elaborate fili-gree decoration underneath the name. My fingers itched to reach out and touch the artwork.

Instead, Gemma tugged me along once more and knocked twice on the door. "Leave your bag by the door when we enter and stay standing until he addresses you," she whispered before the door opened on its own.

"Come in, Gemma," a deep voice called.

She gave one last smile before pulling me forward.

I did as she suggested and left my bag a couple feet in front of the door, pushing it against the wall so it was out of the way in case anyone else entered. The lights were dim in the office, and it took a few seconds for my eyes to adjust. When they did, I took in the massive floor-to-ceiling bookshelves that held much more than books.

Bottles of all sizes littered the shelves, along with herbs and plants that I assumed were needed for spells. My throat dried up, and it was hard to swallow as my nerves got the best of me.

I was in way far over my head.

"Headmaster Stone, this is Raegan Keyes. She just arrived, and we came straight here as per your request," Gemma said with respect as she stood up in front of his desk.

I tried to take her same posture, but how she stood ramrod straight while keeping her eyes on the headmaster was beyond me. When my gaze landed on him, I took in his appearance. He was exactly what I expected, and I actually felt a little relieved since everything else had taken me by surprise.

His hair was shoulder-length and silver along with a two-inch-long beard he rocked surprisingly well for an old guy. His eyes were a dark amber color, and the wrinkles around them told me he was well past retirement age in human years. He wore a black robe with silver trim, and the school crest was embroidered into the left shoulder area.

"Thank you, Gemma. Will you please wait outside? I'd

like to speak with Ms. Keyes privately before you show her to the dorm area."

Oh, shit. Private conversations with the principal were rarely good. My eyes flicked to Gemma, silently begging her not to leave. I didn't even know her, but having someone else in the room with me felt safer than being alone with the old guy before us.

"Yes, Headmaster." She bowed her head and backed up without even looking at me. The fact that she had been so peppy when she greeted me and then turned so submissive with the boss man told me I had every reason to be freaking out.

"Have a seat, Raegan," he said.

My head turned toward the door, but Gemma was already gone. Realizing I'd already committed to this and needed to comply for the time being, I took the offered seat.

"I hope Enzo got you here safely and there were no more incidents after the scavenger attacked you."

I nodded. "Everything went fine, thank you."

He finally smiled at me. His beard parted to show perfectly straight white teeth. "You don't need to be afraid of me. We mean you no harm. I only wanted to speak with you privately in case you were more comfortable. If you'd prefer Gemma to come back in, I can call for her."

A sigh escaped my lips. "No, that's okay. It's just a lot to take in." Relief flooded through me that I wasn't about to be chastised or something.

He leaned back in his chair and brought his hands together before settling them on his lap. "We've never had a student arrive late, so I'm not sure what to do with you. The fact that you know nothing about our world makes the decision that much harder."

"What decision?" I asked when he paused.

"Well, I have a few of them. The most important is whether or not you should be allowed to stay here, or if we should wipe your memories and keep your binding in place with a renewed spell."

My hands tightened on the arms of the chair. As much as I wouldn't mind being normal again, the thought of my head being messed with like Enzo had done previously pissed me the hell off. I wanted to scream "no" at him, but I knew better.

"If you stay, I also need to figure out where you come from and where you belong. Once we remove the suppression on your magic, I'll be able to recommend a better class schedule for you. Though, you have a decision to make as well." He paused, waiting for my reaction, but I gave him nothing. I wasn't interested in playing games, and I hoped he would get to the point.

"Do you want to work twice as hard as the rest of the students and take extra classes to catch up with your peers, or would you like to start fresh as a first-year? I'd like your opinion before I make my decision."

My fingers tapped against my thigh as I thought about everything he had said. There was a decent chance I wouldn't even be able to stay, but if I could, what did I want?

I had only known Gemma for five minutes, but she gave off a genuine vibe and, in a world where anything was possible, something told me that trait wasn't found very often. I would be better off sticking as close to her as possible if she'd let me.

"I'd like to enter as a second-year student. Enzo told me about the breaks every eight weeks. I will commit to studying as much as it takes and using the breaks to catch up if someone will be around to teach me."

"That's good to know, and I will take that into consideration. Did your guardians leave anything behind that would tell us about your birth parents?"

Pain erupted within me. Fast and unexpected.

Grief was a bitch like that.

Triggers could be anything, and today, it was a simple question.

Shaking my head, I hoped he didn't ask me anything else, because I wasn't sure I could speak without crying first.

"That will be all then. Use today to get settled. You'll be staying in the hybrid dorms with Gemma, and she'll show you around. If you have any issues, please come straight to me. Tomorrow, we will unbind your magic and see which classes you'll fit best in when we know exactly what you are."

Still afraid my emotions would get the best of me, I only nodded and waited for him to excuse me. Even though figuring out who I was and where I came from was high on the priority list for me, I knew my limits and needed a distraction from my history before I lost it completely.

"Gemma?" he called as his doors opened again. "Please, show Raegan to her room and whatever else she's up for seeing."

"Yes, Headmaster Stone."

She grabbed my bag for me as I followed her out the door. When it closed behind us, she whipped around, scaring the shit out of me. "What did he do to you?"

"What?" I asked, confused.

"Your eyes are all red like you were crying. What happened in there?"

"Oh, nothing. He just asked me a question that took me by surprise. My emotions got the best of me, but I'm fine. Really." Damn it. I was going to have to work on keeping my grief in check. I had no desire to share my business with strangers.

What I wanted most was to keep my head down, do whatever work I needed to do in order to protect myself from other supernatural beings, and stay as unnoticed as possible. All of that while trying to find the answers to the questions burning within me.

"Okay, then. Let's go see your room."

The fact that she didn't press me for more information told me my initial perception of her had been right, and I breathed a little easier knowing that.

We headed back the way we came, and I found it easier to handle the moving stairs than the first time. When we stepped off, Gemma took a hard right toward the hallway marked Hybrids. The segregation of the races seemed too old school, but maybe it was safer that way. I had no idea what these people were capable of.

The hallway we walked through was covered in tanned cobblestone. Each piece seemed to fit perfectly where it lay, and nothing was out of place, including the pictures that hung on the walls. I wasn't surprised that I didn't recognize the people in any of the portraits. I considered asking who they were but was more interested in seeing my room than taking a history lesson in that moment.

"There are three floors of hybrid rooms. We're on the second level, and your room is three down from mine. We use floating platforms to go up and down when needed."

Floating platforms? Hopefully they were comparable to the moving stairs. I really didn't want to throw up in front of what I hoped was my first friend.

"They're big, and nobody has ever fallen off. There are security measures in place to make sure of that." The smile she threw my way only made me feel a miniscule better.

As we arrived at the platform area, two others were coming down, a guy and a girl who couldn't keep their hands off each other. My eyes diverted as Gemma laughed, but I didn't ask about what.

"Hey, guys. This is Raegan. She's going to be living on our floor. Raegan, this is Jess and Ethan."

I waved, but they didn't separate far enough from each other to reciprocate.

"Hey." Jess giggled before Ethan's mouth devoured hers again and they kept awkwardly moving along, not at all watching where they were going.

When they left, we stepped onto the platform, and I was more than pleased when my stomach didn't lurch as the floor moved up. It felt just like an elevator without walls. As long as I didn't look over the side, my motion sickness would likely stay in check.

"You'll also want to get used to public displays of affection, at least from the shifters. They have a weird thing with touch, and they're not shy about it. Jess is part wolf shifter, and her boyfriend Ethan is part bear."

"Are the dorms co-ed?"

"Yep." She beamed as if I should be happy about that, but I didn't fully return the smile.

It wasn't that I was *unhappy* about the situation. Believe me, I appreciated a fine male specimen as much as most others did, but I also wondered if it would have been easier to settle in without worrying about male testosterone floating around.

When the platform stopped, we walked off the solid surface and walked two doors down. On the left side was a room with my name already on the door. There was a keypad above the handle that I assumed took a code I didn't have.

"Here." Gemma handed me a sealed envelope. "Don't worry. You can change the code at any time in case you think I peeked."

Tearing open the paper, I took the code out and punched it in, uncaring if she saw. I was going to change it, not because I was afraid she'd barge into my room, but because I wanted something I could easily remember. I wasn't stupid enough to leave it written down somewhere, and I didn't want to chance being locked out.

When the door swung open, the first things I saw were a queen-size bed, my own bathroom, and a mini-fridge. Nothing like what I had pictured but everything I wanted if I had to be stuck in a dorm room.

"You good here? I'll let you get settled and be back shortly to give a tour if you want."

I turned back to her. "That would be great. Thanks for helping me out."

"Us hybrids have to stick together."

Before I could ask her what that meant, she snuck out of the dorm and closed the door behind her. I tried not to worry about it as I dragged my bag to the bed and began to unpack.

When I was done, I settled on the mattress and thought about how everything had seemed much easier than I expected so far. It made me curious about whether it was the calm before the storm or maybe I had been meant for this place all along.

Only time could tell me which was true.

An hour later, Gemma came back to check on me and offer a tour of the academy. She had changed out of her uniform and was wearing bright pink pants, a tight dark tank, and black heels that extended her five-and-a-half-foot frame by a few inches, bringing her eyes level to me.

Her light blonde hair had been pulled back and braided, making her look like a completely different person than the prim and peppy girl who had greeted me earlier. The glittery makeup she added caused her hazel eyes to pop and added to the overall appeal.

"What happened to the uniform?" I asked.

"I only wear it when I'm officially working for the administration or going to class. I'm now off duty besides showing you around, but I'd do that anyway, so I put something on a little more my style." She glanced at my skinny jeans, flats, and loose tee. "You, on the other hand, could use some sparkle in your life."

"Hmmm. I'll think about it. How about that tour?" I changed the subject quickly. I didn't need a makeover. I didn't need to stand out. If my lack of "sparkle" helped me stay under the radar, then I was perfectly okay with that.

"Follow me." She grinned and began to chatter on about the layout and some of the history of the school. Most of it went over my head, but hopefully the information would make sense later when I was in class.

There were four hundred and eighty-six students enrolled in Shadow Veil Academy. Each student arrived when they were seventeen, and when they left the academy at twenty-one, they could choose to continue practicing their magic or venture off wherever they wanted without being bothered. Most students went back to where they came from, but we were free to find homes wherever we liked in the world.

The school sat on several-hundred acres, most of which was forest and space for those who needed room to run. I didn't ask about the different beings who had such a need, but I was certainly curious.

The building had been around for close to two-hundred years and was created as an escape when the elven world Elora fell. Apparently, all magical beings were created by elves, making them the strongest among us.

When we arrived at the main entrance, Gemma turned to me. "Outside or inside first?"

There was an ethereal beauty about the outside that had me itching to explore it, but the turrets and structure of the school had me equally captivated.

"You choose. Sounds like you've done this before, so I'll trust you on this one."

"Perfect. Inside it is." She tugged my hand and pulled me toward the entrance to the History section. "During first year, we're only supposed to focus on studies. Second year, we can take on additional duties for extra stipends. I welcome new hybrid students and give the tours. It's been a busy week, but I think you're the last of our new arrivals."

While we traversed the wide hallways, curiosity got the better of me, and I hoped she wasn't going to think I was rude. "What kind of hybrid are you?"

"Oh. Sorry. I rambled about the school and didn't really introduce myself, did I? I'm half witch and half vampire. Thankfully, my appetite comes from the witch side, but my strength and speed come from the blood sucker part of me."

I flinched at the last bit. She didn't hold anything back, it seemed.

"Too much?" She winked. "You'll get used to it."

I'd been told that one too many times in the last day. I didn't want to get used to it. I just wanted to survive. As much as I missed my parents, I wasn't ready to die yet, and the scavenger who attacked me had put the fear of death in me once the adrenaline wore off.

Gemma continued to ramble, and I continued to take in the surroundings. The interior of the school was made mostly of stone, and everything surrounding the main turrets seemed to have been updated with magical elements that made the impossible possible.

Every time I thought we had reached the top floor, another one would appear, but there was no way it was structurally possible. I opened my mouth to ask how, but realized I already knew the answer.

Magic.

That made me wonder, did the school's magic have limits? Who created it all and controlled it? The walls and rooms seemed to be a moving entity, making me feel like there was a greater power around us that I didn't know about yet. Gemma spoke so animatedly about the school that I didn't have the heart to interrupt her well-practiced tour with my very human questions.

When we reached the main level again, we headed toward an exit at the rear of the building. There was a barred-off door to my right before we made it outside. Three glowing locks were placed in the center of the door, but I couldn't see a place for a key. My arm instinctively reached for it, something about it enchanting me.

"What's that?" I asked as I pulled my hand back to my side where it belonged.

"That's nothing you need to worry about. Just know this isn't only a school. It is home to some of the most powerful beings in our existence, and some things are better left unknown. Consider this door forbidden and you'll be fine."

For the first time, there wasn't an air of excitement in her words. There was a darkness layered to them and damn if it didn't make me want to race through the locked door. It called to me like a siren, but when Gemma opened the back exit, the light caught my attention making me realize how dark the ancient school was, and I willingly followed her out.

"It's almost dinner time, so we'll start further out and make our way to the commissary."

Dinner? How had the day gone by so fast? I hadn't even eaten lunch. The thought never occurred to me, but as soon as she mentioned it, my stomach decided to roar to life.

She glanced over at me. "Did you not eat in your room when you were unpacking?"

"There's food in our rooms?"

"Girl, I have so much more to show you! Yes, there is a tablet next to the mini-fridge that you order from. Menu changes daily, and you can order as often as you like. Did you not snoop around your own space? Not to worry. I'll show you all the great things about living here."

"Okay, then." I had no other choice but to trust her and, thankfully, that didn't frighten me like I thought it would.

"We'll make this even quicker, so you can eat. You'll have plenty of time to explore the parts you really want to see later on." Her hand gestured left. "Out that way is the shifter forest. Don't go in there at night. Not all of them have a handle on their beasts yet. To the right of that is the feeding area for the vamps. They have donors who are treated respectfully, so don't think they're off murdering people, but I also recommend not venturing there unless you have a specific reason to."

I was beginning to think outside wasn't as peaceful as it had appeared when I first arrived.

"Now, to the fun parts. There is the training building just in front of us, beyond the trees. You'll likely have at least two classes there since you need to catch up. It's a massive dome structure that changes terrains to make you feel like you're wherever the teacher wants you to be. Desert, mountains, tropical forest. You name it, he can make it happen."

As dangerous as it sounded, I was also intrigued by it.

We kept walking, never venturing too far from the main building, and I realized she wasn't kidding about making the outside tour quick.

"Over there is the Courtyard of Tranquility. It's where magic users go to become one with earth. A lot of our power comes from magical elements beneath earth, and if you're ever struggling, I highly suggest you spend some time there."

My eyes stayed on the courtyard, even as Gemma kept walking. I fell a few steps behind her as I took in the iron fence and what lay beyond. There were fountains made from rock that appeared like mini waterfalls, along with flowers and weeping willow trees. Between all of that were open grass areas the brightest green I had ever seen.

That would definitely be high on my list of places to visit around the school very soon.

"... and here's the commissary," she finished, and I had missed whatever came before that.

The building before us was attached to the main structure but had its own entrance from the outside. I didn't recall seeing it from the inside, but there had been so much to see, I wasn't surprised I missed it.

"On a scale of one-to-ten, how overwhelmed are you?" she asked.

"A solid twenty," I answered seriously, causing her to laugh.

"Honesty. I like it. You'll fit right in with my friends."

She pulled me into the commissary and as soon as we entered, my mouth began to salivate so much that I lifted my hand to check for drool.

"The best part is when you look up," Gemma whispered in my ear.

My head tilted back, and she was right. The entire ceiling was made from a single sheet of glass. The sky shown through with clarity, but the brightness was muted so I could enjoy its beauty in its entirety.

My gaze was transfixed on colors reflecting from the glass, and I once again zoned out what was going on around me. That was until warm liquid poured down my arm, then splattered onto my flats as a body slammed into mine.

"Ugh! Walk much, Mutt?" a voice snapped at me.

My gaze met hers and skin prickled at the malice she threw my way. "Excuse me?" I replied. I wasn't sure I had heard her correctly, but if I had, she was going to get to know my fist really soon.

"Do you have a hearing problem as well as a walking one? Watch where you're going, *Mutt*."

That little bitch. I didn't do well with prissy girls like her who thought they were better than others. My arm cocked back, but Gemma grabbed it before I could do anything.

"Sorry, Lyssa," she mumbled before literally dragging me away from the wench and a friend who stood silently behind her with a smirk.

"What the hell?" I asked. "Who does she think she is?"

Gemma sighed. "The queen of this school. If you want to keep your head down, stay out of her way. She's pure elf and ridiculously powerful. Her parents are big donors to the academy, and it's best to avoid her at all costs, even when she deserves a solid beating."

Fury simmered beneath my skin. Lyssa, as Gemma had called her, was lucky I wanted to stay unnoticed, but if she spoke to me like that again, I wasn't sure I'd be able to hold my tongue.

After Gemma helped me wipe the hot chocolate off my arm, we headed to the buffet-style layout of food. Once she was satisfied I had enough food, she led me to a table where two other girls were already sitting. It was conveniently located far away from Lyssa's, which I noticed Enzo conveniently sat at. Maybe they were related, or they were together. It wouldn't surprise me in the least if it was the latter.

"Finley and Peyton, this is Raegan. With any luck, she'll be in classes with us as a second-year student. She's with me in the hybrid hall."

Finley, who had jet black hair cut in a perfect A-line

with rich chocolate eyes and pale skin, greeted me first. "Welcome to Shadow Veil." When she smiled, I also noticed her very prominent and *extremely* sharp teeth. Thankfully, it was only two of them, but they still made my muscles tighten in nerves for a second.

"Thanks," I replied, trying not to stare and seem rude.

"I saw your run-in with Lyssa. Hope she wasn't too much of a bitch," Peyton added, who was Finley's complete opposite with dark skin, light-colored long hair, and bright cobalt eyes.

"Eh. Nothing I can't handle," I replied.

"Did you already finish the tour?" Finley asked.

"Mostly, but I forgot to show Raegan how to properly use her room earlier, and she needed to eat before I could finish all of the outside."

After that, the conversation turned to upcoming events for the first week of school and classes they had requested and hoped they'd be approved for. Things like Herbs and Potions, History of Shifters and Witchcraft, Origins and Mythology, and a few others that intrigued me. All except the combat classes that were mentioned.

I might not *be* human, but I still *felt* very human, and going up against magical beings who had a shit ton more experience than I did wasn't something I was looking forward to.

Just as we finished eating, a shadow cast over me, causing Finley and Peyton to freeze in their seats. I was afraid to move, thinking there was some magical monster behind me, but then I heard a familiar voice, and my tension lessened.

"Raegan. I hope you settled in okay. No problems with the headmaster or anything like that?"

My head turned, glancing at the table he had previously

occupied and catching the glare being cast my way by Lyssa. "Other than the hot chocolate your friend the ice queen spilled down my arm, everything has been great."

"You're who she was bitching about?" His face tightened, but I couldn't tell if it was annoyance or rage that caused his change in demeanor. Surprisingly, I didn't care. "I'll take care of it."

My hand reached out to grab his wrist as he turned away. "No."

His brows shot up, and a look I couldn't read appeared on his face. "Excuse me? Did you just tell me no?"

"I don't need or want your help. I can handle myself, and Lyssa isn't going to be a problem for me. I'm only here to figure out who I am and how to protect myself. I'll be out of here as soon as that's done, and you can forget all about me."

His face pinched in obvious irritation and he opened his mouth to say something, but promptly closed it before regaining his composure.

"Alright, then. If that's how you want it." He pulled his wrist from my grasp, which I forgot I still held, and he walked back to the center of the commissary without turning back.

"How do you know Enzo? He's the hottest elf in this school and *never* associates with anyone other than those at his table," Finley whispered in a very nervous high-pitched voice that counteracted her attempts at being quiet.

"He's the one who told me I wasn't human. Some scavenger attacked me, and Enzo happened to be in the area. He snapped his fingers and the creeper along with his shadow friends disappeared into thin air."

"You survived a scavenger attack with no magic?"

Peyton's face paled in surprise. "Not many people can say the same."

I shrugged, not really wanting to talk about it, and was glad when Gemma changed the subject back to Enzo.

"I'd highly recommend staying away from Enzo, even if he saved you. Lyssa and he dated most of last year, but they called it off right before summer. It appears she's ready to have her man back, and you don't want to be in her way."

Letting out a groan, I ran a hand through my hair. I thought I was done with high school drama. I didn't want to be in anyone's way. I just wanted to do my thing and be done with it. I was even considering heading to New Orleans with Jules to get a fresh start if she went back home. Going back to Portland after learning my childhood had been a lie didn't seem appealing any longer.

When we finished eating, Finley excused herself for dessert at the donor building and Peyton announced she was going to the shifter forest. During dinner, I learned she was a wolf shifter from a very powerful pack in Wyoming. She had some serious points on her canines, too, but nothing as lethal-looking as Finley's.

"Want to look around the school some more or head back to your room?" Gemma asked when it was just the two of us.

"Room, please. Today has been the longest day of my life."

"You got it."

While we walked back, I had no problem remembering where the correct hallways were and how to get to the dorms. Gemma joined me inside mine and showed me how to order food directly to my room, which would come in handy on the many occasions I planned to stay locked away, studying to catch up and avoiding people.

If dinner had shown me anything, it was that I needed to try harder to stay unnoticed, especially from Enzo. I didn't need him to feel any obligation to me just because he brought me to the academy. I would be fine on my own.

At least, I hoped that was the case. I'd find out for sure the following day when my magic was released.

It was sink or swim time.

CHAPTER SIX

My foot tapped incessantly against the hardwood floor in the headmaster's office. He'd kept me anxiously waiting for the last hour, and I was going to combust if he didn't hurry the hell up.

"Well, Ms. Keyes, it appears we have everything in order. Just waiting on one person to arrive and then we're ready to go meet the council."

I was going to strangle him.

Ten more minutes passed in awkward silence. Gemma hadn't been able to join me, and after the first twenty minutes of forced conversation, the headmaster and I quit trying to force words. It had been the only thing I was grateful for that morning.

Finally, a knock sounded at the door and a breath whooshed from my lips. *About damn time*, I thought, at least until I saw who was entering.

"Oh, Enzo. I'm so glad you could join us. Since you'll be mentoring Raegan, I thought it pertinent you be present for the removal of her binding."

Crazy old magic man say what?

"Um, excuse me? Mentoring me? What does that mean?" I asked, trying to keep the attitude from my voice.

"Enzo is top of his class. If you're wanting to start as a second-year student, then you'll need the best available to catch you up to speed. Don't you think?" He raised a brow at me, challenging me to object.

"Oh. Yeah. Sure. That's just great." Not freaking great at all.

Enzo's hand slapped down on my shoulder. "I'm glad you agree. I was quite excited as well when Headmaster Stone asked me."

He peered down at me, and I could feel his eyes on my face, but I refused to meet his gaze. He was going to ruin my plans for staying off the radar. His ice queen of a girlfriend was not going to let this arrangement happen without retaliation. There was no doubt in my mind about that.

"Well, let's be on our way. The council will be waiting for us." Headmaster Stone shooed us out of his office.

I followed the two men down a hallway Gemma hadn't taken me through the day before. When we reached the end, a door with a significant arch and aging wood awaited us. There was no handle that I could see, but it opened within seconds of us being within proximity of it.

As I walked through the threshold, I peeked around for anything that could have made it open other than magic, but there were no mechanisms on the inside, either.

Before I could overthink the process, my attention diverted to the room before me. There was a glass cage large enough to hold ten humans set in the middle of the room, and four others stood around the enclosure. When they caught sight of me, mixed emotions were sent my way.

A man on the end smiled, but the woman next to him grimaced as if I'd ruined her entire day. The next male past her wouldn't even meet my eyes when the headmaster introduced me, and the fourth one looked as if he was about to piss his pants.

His face paled, and his brown eyes widened when they took me in. He averted his stare as soon as he realized I was watching him.

"Raegan, this is the council that makes final rulings for our supernatural community if there is ever a need. Starting on your left we have Alexander, Fiona, Bennett, and Desmond. The first three have been a part of the council for over fifty years with me, and Desmond joined us almost twenty years ago," Headmaster Stone said proudly.

He then gestured toward the cage. "We'll need you to step inside the glass case. We don't know what your magic will do once its released and it's safest for everyone, including you, if we can keep it contained until we know more."

My throat tightened, and my legs froze. I wasn't claustrophobic by any means, but I had no idea what was going to happen to me and being in the box made it seem a hell of a lot scarier.

Enzo leaned in closer to me. "Are you afraid? Would you rather run away?"

He was taunting me. The rational part of me knew that, but the not-so-rational part of me mentally said "screw you" as I stomped toward the open door like a child.

When Alexander closed it, my furious eyes met Enzo's. His smirk said I'd done exactly what he wanted, and I wasn't sure how I felt about that. Though, either way would have been a losing choice for me.

Desmond approached the glass with caution and laid one hand on the smooth surface. His mouth moved, but I couldn't make sense of the low words he spoke. My eyes glanced around the room and noticed the door I had come through was no longer present.

I was trapped in the cage.

My chest rose and fell in rapid succession until Enzo appeared in my line of sight. His eyes swirled, the normal honey color mixed with a deeper brown that entranced me, and I couldn't tear my gaze away. With each passing second that we remained locked in each other's stare, my fear of being trapped eased. When he seemed satisfied I wasn't going to absolutely lose my shit, he nodded his head and backed away so Desmond could continue.

The interaction was probably something I needed to dissect, but then was not the time. Once I was fully settled down and Desmond finished whatever he had been doing, all four council members placed their hands on the glass like he had done. Enzo disappeared behind the group as Headmaster Stone moved in to join them.

They began to chant in another language I didn't understand, and the words rattled on so quickly that I couldn't even guess at the pronunciations. My eyes grew heavy and my body weak. Whatever they were doing was quickly sucking my energy from me.

Falling to my knees, I cringed at the echo my thud made and shielded my ears. Every sound was amplified, including the chant from the council around me. When covering my ears wasn't enough, I curled into a ball and closed my eyes.

Images flashed before my eyes of a man I had never seen before. His eyes were familiar, but his face was foreign to me. His hand pressed to my forehead and pain ricocheted through my body, both in the vision and in real time.

My feet slammed against the glass as my hands still gripped my ears. A layer of skin felt like it was slowly being pulled away from me. When my eyes peeked open, everything around me glowed the teal color I was used to seeing on my hands, but this time, my whole body was lit up.

Panic ceased within me as another emotion replaced it, and my muscles ached as if I'd hiked the tallest mountain. I stood up as rage grew within me like never before. I was angry, and I didn't even know why. Magic flew from my hands as scales appeared on my arms and pain erupted in my back.

I hunched over, my hands settling on my knees as my shoulder blades dislocated and barbed wings about six feet in length burst from my skin. They were a blood-red color and covered in the same scales as my arms, but the insides appeared soft like leather.

"What the hell is happening to me?" I screamed, searching for anyone to help me understand.

"Dragon." The single word left Enzo's mouth in fascination as he continued to stare from across the room.

Minutes later, after I thought I'd lose my voice from all the screaming, the wings and scales disappeared, and what I presumed to be magic swirled all around me within the glass confinement. This time, the colors changed between white, teal, and burgundy. My eyes processed everything with a clarity I didn't think possible until finally, a sense of peace swept over me.

The magic began to disappear once I calmed and there was no pain or anger left within my body.

The door reappeared and the council backed up, watching me with trepidation, most of all Desmond, who I could then identify as a sorcerer. Whatever just happened had given me the ability to instinctively know what type of creature each person in the room was. Alexander, the vampire. Fiona, the wolf shifter. Bennett, the elf, and Headmaster Stone, another sorcerer, much more powerful than Desmond.

Enzo stepped forward, not seeming afraid at all. "How do you feel?"

My fingers brushed my hair back and, before I could answer, gasps and snarls came from the council behind him.

Enzo's eyes lit up with excitement, which confirmed whatever had happened wasn't good.

"What?" I asked when nobody said anything.

"Well, it appears as if you're not a hybrid like we thought," Headmaster Stone answered. "You have three races within you: witch, dragon shifter, and elf."

"How do you know?" I demanded.

Enzo pointed to my face. "Your ears. When you pushed your hair back just now, it showcased the lovely points that now grace your ears. Welcome to the cool kids club, Raegan."

No, no, no. This wasn't possible. Why couldn't I just be a regular hybrid like Gemma?

I didn't want to be different.

I wanted to blend in.

So. Damn. Bad.

"One of her abilities needs to be stripped," Fiona snapped. "We don't know what she'll be capable of otherwise. It's not safe for the other students."

I flinched at the harshness she directed at me, like I was the devil reincarnate. I hadn't done anything to anyone. I was just a girl trying to survive the shitty hand she was dealt, and a little understanding would have been nice.

"You're exactly right, Fiona. We don't know what she's capable of," the headmaster mused. "Which means we don't know whether this is a bad *or* good thing. It could be nothing, and she shouldn't be punished for the unknown."

"This isn't something to discuss with an audience, Alistair," Bennett said, glancing at both me and Enzo before turning back to Headmaster Stone.

"Yes, my old friend. You're right. Enzo, will you take Raegan to the uniform area and get her whatever she needs? I'll check in with you both this evening."

And just like that, we were dismissed while the old people chatted about my future.

Super freaking awesome.

Wrath began to build within me, and at the first signs of scales on my arm, Enzo shot a look at me that said I better get my shit under control before I proved them all right.

When we were halfway down the hall, Enzo stopped me and brushed my hair back. His cool fingers skimmed over my ears, down my jawline, and to my chin where his forefinger and thumb stayed, gently holding my face in place. My breathing stopped momentarily as I waited for him to say something or, better yet, *do* something.

"If they strip you of a race and give you the option of which, I'd be disappointed if you chose elf to lose." He dropped his hand and kept walking, not waiting for me.

Damn him and his sex appeal! My powers being unlocked wasn't helping, either. The moment his skin touched mine, I wanted to jump him. Well, my body did. My head, on the other hand, still wanted to throat-punch him.

I followed after him, and we went back downstairs to the main floor. He led me down two more hallways before we arrived at the uniform room. The men's options were on the left side and on the right were the women's.

Men wore black slacks as their only bottom choice and white collared shirts or dress shirts for tops, each with the SVA logo embroidered on them. Ties hung on the end of the racks, and I cringed when I remembered the women had them as well, only thinner in width.

Our shirts were similar to the men's, but more form-fitted. Then, there were the bottoms. Skirts galore in all different lengths spanned at least ten feet across. It wasn't fair that men could wear pants, but women couldn't.

I grabbed five shirts and a few ties, along with a sweater I found at the end. When I approached Enzo, who had stayed silent against the wall while I picked my items, he eyed my pile curiously.

"You forgot something," he said.

I glanced down. "Nope. Pretty sure I got it all."

"You're going to class without something to cover that pretty ass of yours? Not that I'm complaining, but the teachers might not appreciate the distraction."

"It looks like they're out of women's pants, so I'm just going to wear my black leather ones until they get more." My chin lifted defiantly.

"I think you're confused. The girls all wear skirts."

"I don't believe in double standards. Until I see *boys* wearing skirts, then I'm wearing my pants."

His laugh wrapped around me like silk, drawing me toward him. "Oh, this is going to be interesting. Alright, let's go then."

He led me back to my room and waited by the door. "Want to go grab some lunch?"

"With you? In public? No offense, but not a chance in hell."

His hand grasped at his chest dramatically. "Oh, how you wound me. Why not?"

"I doubt your girlfriend would appreciate that, and I'd rather not have her kind of drama in my life. So, let's keep whatever relationship we need to have strictly school-related. It would be easier on everyone."

"Whatever you say, little dragon."

He pushed away from my door and strode down the hall like he didn't have a care in the world. I, on the other hand, was about to lose my shit. Slamming my door shut, I waltzed over to the tablet where I could order food and found every bit of junk food available.

After I ordered, I threw myself on the bed and screamed into the pillow. Sparks flew from my hands, and I ran to the mirror as soon as I remembered the pointy ears I needed to check out. Slowly, I pulled my hair back and inspected my new additions.

The points weren't significant like the pure elf students I had already seen, but they were there, nonetheless. Thankfully, my hair was short, and I had no reason to pull it back. I just needed to keep my hands away from that area and maybe I could keep what we learned to myself. If Enzo valued his life, he'd do the same.

A ding came from the magical butler box, and my mouth began to drool at the thought of hot fudge brownies and vanilla ice cream. If my day was going to be ruined, I was at least going to get dessert. Lots and lots of dessert.

Tomorrow was soon enough to figure out what to do next. For the time being, I was having a pity party for one and didn't give a single damn.

CHAPTER SEVEN

The first Monday in September was the start of school. Having less than a week to prepare for the new world I had been thrown into was not enough, but Gemma and her two friends did everything they could to help me through it.

I rarely left my room. Learning how to manage the butler box, as I had officially named the thing that brought me food, was amazing. Gemma insisted it was a mini-fridge, but it was nothing like the ones I was used to, so it got a new name. It was capable of providing me almost everything I needed except fresh air, and I was beginning to believe natural air was overrated.

I hated drama, and Enzo was only going to bring me assloads of it, so I was avoiding him like the plague.

Yet, I couldn't stop thinking about the way his eyes held mine captive while I was locked in the glass box, or how his presence had been the only thing to calm me down when I was so close to absolutely losing my shit.

He was equally infuriating and intriguing at the same time.

I had casually inquired about his bitchface of a girl-friend and wondered if they were truly back together, considering he hadn't denied it when I called her his girl-friend the week before. Finley mentioned she hadn't seen much of either of them, but apparently, that wasn't abnormal since there had been so few days left of freedom. Not many people were hanging around the school.

As I dressed in my uniform for the first time, my stomach knotted and threatened to throw up the delicious fruit parfait I had eaten for breakfast. I still insisted on the pants instead of the skirt, even though Gemma also advised me it was a bad idea. The people around me were learning quickly that I was rather stubborn.

Once my crisp white shirt was buttoned, I slipped the tie around my neck. This I had no problem putting on as far as the technical part went, but the memories of watching my mom do the same act for my dad and then her teaching me were the hardest to overcome.

It made me want to call my Aunt Jules and see how she was coping with everything. She might not have been blood, but our shared grief was real, and she was now alone unless she had gone back to New Orleans. I hadn't received word from her yet, but I hoped I would this week.

When I was fully dressed, I took a long look in the mirror. My burgundy hair stood out most in contrast to my fair skin and the white dress shirt, the ends resting just at my shoulders. My fingers traced over the emblem embroi-dered just above my left breast before gliding along the silk teal tie.

Glancing down at my black leather pants and boots, I smirked. This was what they got for ripping me from every-thing I knew, even if it wasn't much of a life to be living.

A knock sounded at my door, and I rushed to open it, fully expecting Gemma to be on the other side, but the smile on my face swiftly fell as I met the swirling honey eyes of Enzo.

"Hello, little dragon." His eyes ran down my body, causing a shiver to come over me that I hopefully hid from him.

"What are you doing here?" I snapped.

"I'm your mentor. It's my duty to show you the ropes on the first day and give you your schedule. Aren't you excited?" Sarcasm dripped from his words, and I couldn't tell if he was enjoying this or was as equally disdained as me.

It was my first day, and if I was going to have to be at Shadow Veil for three more years, I really wanted to make the best of it. I decided to choose my battles wisely, and this was not one of them. If Enzo was my means to remaining a second-year student and not being behind, then so be it.

"You know what? I *am* excited. Let me grab my bag and we can go."

Before I turned away, I saw the shock that flashed across his chiseled face. Good. The more I could surprise him, the sooner he would learn I wasn't going to be messed with.

One of the few times I ventured out of my room after my magic had been unlocked was to grab the last of my school supplies. Gemma helped me pick out a bag and tablet. Apparently, there were no books, but we still needed bags for our magical possessions. I had simply nodded in agreement when she explained that, even though I had no idea what it meant.

With my black messenger bag strapped over my shoulder, I double-checked my tablet was still in it. When the cool metal touched my fingertips, I knew there was nothing more I could do to prepare for whatever I was about to experience.

"All set?" Enzo asked cheerfully.

"Yep. Unless I need something more than the bag and tablet."

"You also need a handsome mentor, so good thing I'm here or you'd be sorely lacking." He winked as I closed my door, waiting to hear the lock engage before walking away.

Other students were also leaving, their eyes on us as we moved through the crowd. Nerves slammed into me. I didn't want to be noticed, and I was already failing at that before I even got to my first class. Enzo was going to be the death of me.

"We need to stop by the office and have your schedule downloaded to your tablet," Enzo mentioned. "Once it's synced up, you'll receive notifications for class times and the quickest route to get there, depending on your current location. I highly advise using that until you've learned your way around the school. I won't always be with you, and there are some places you don't want to *accidentally* stumble upon."

For once, his voice was serious, as if he actually cared about what happened to me. It threw me off balance, but when I really thought about it, I shouldn't have been so surprised.

Our first encounter had been him saving me, then him calming me down, followed by not objecting to helping me catch up with my peers. There were many layers to Enzo, and the twisted part of me was looking forward to peeling them back and finding out who he really was, as well as myself.

That was if I didn't kill him first for causing me added grief.

"What are you doing with the mutt?" a high-pitched voice sneered as we turned left off the stairs.

I didn't bother turning around. I knew who it was, and she was Enzo's problem, not mine.

"Lyssa." Enzo's voice hardened as he twisted around. "If you want any sort of relationship with me, then you'll choose your next words carefully."

I couldn't see her face, because I refused to give her any of my attention, but my ears picked up the tremor in her voice.

"But you said that we..."

"I know what I said, but I won't tolerate anyone being put down. She's not a mutt, and I'm her mentor for the year. You're going to have to deal with it."

Before she could respond, Enzo grasped my arm and pulled me along. I ached to turn around and see the look on her face, but I knew better. If she was pure elf, then from what I had already learned from my friends, I didn't want to mess with her until I knew how to defend myself.

My poor attempts at practicing my magic with Gemma, Finley, and Peyton had been disastrous, and I was actually excited for classes, so I could learn how to manage it all.

When we arrived in the main office to get my list of classes, the scheduler lady frowned. "I'm sorry, Ms. Keyes. You don't have a schedule yet. It says here that you're to report directly to Headmaster Stone this morning. Alone."

I was so screwed.

"Are you sure it says alone?" Enzo asked rather rudely.

She turned her screen. "I'm not senile, young man."

I grinned at her smartass comment, then glanced at her desk, looking for a name. "Thank you, Louise. I'll head there now."

Spinning on my heel, I strode out of the door without

waiting for Enzo. He caught up to me within seconds, though. "Wait a minute. Have you spoken with the headmaster at all since last week?"

"No, so it's not really surprising he wants to see me. Previously, I was going on the assumption that no news was good news in this scenario. Now, it's time to find out if I was right."

Last week, when I found out that I had not two, but three races running through my blood, I went back to my room and lost my shit a little bit. Okay, a lot, but after I had some time to process it, I didn't dwell on it. One of my parents had to be a hybrid and the other a pure. I happened to get all three genes. There was no big deal. At least, that's what I kept telling myself over the last few days.

I couldn't even turn into a full dragon that I knew of. Just some badass scales and wings had appeared before, so it wasn't like I was going to take over the world with the extra abilities. Hopefully, the headmaster had been able to convince the rest of the council of that.

"I'm going to wait in the office for you, then. Don't be a pain in the ass and make me come find you, because I will, and there will be a scene when I do." He simply smiled at me, somehow knowing that I would do anything to avoid drawing attention.

"Whatever," was my lame reply before I headed toward the magic hall.

Since Enzo wasn't towering over me, students dismissed me easily in the busy hallways. I was just another face, and the ease I felt was more comforting than I thought it would be. I was going to have to work something out with Enzo. Like he said, he couldn't be with me all the time and I didn't need people staring, so the mentor portion needed to have its time and place. Not in public.

When I raised my hand to knock on the door, it opened, and Headmaster Stone's voice called out to me. "Come in, Raegan."

Bringing my bag in front of me to settle on my lap, I took a seat in the same chair I had when I first arrived at the school. The headmaster's smile put me at ease some, but I was still anxious to hear what had been decided about my future.

"How are you feeling?" he asked. "Anything out of the ordinary happen since we last met?"

I snorted. "I think our versions of *ordinary* are slightly different, but no, nothing I would worry about."

"Have you told anyone about what happened?"

I shook my head. I knew better than to open my mouth. Gemma, Finley, and Peyton seemed great, but I wasn't stupid. I didn't truly know them, and there was no way I was going to put a target on my back if the three races thing was truly a big deal.

When Gemma had asked me how everything went, I told her that I was part elf and witch. I didn't mention the dragon, because that was easier to hide than the elf ears, and witch seemed like the least threatening race.

"Very well. The council has come to an agreement, but I need you to be okay with it as well. Please keep an open mind and know your wellbeing, as well as that of the other students of this school, were at the forethought of every proposal that was considered."

My chest tightened. This didn't sound good at all.

"Dragon shifters are not common in our world. They exist, and we know where a lot of them are, but they very rarely socialize with us. We've never had a dragon student, and to train this side of you proves to be an issue because of that.

"I don't want to strip you of who you were born to be. Your dragon is a part of you, and we are not gods. We cannot decide who you get to be, but we do need to do something until we know more."

Ah. There was always a *but*.

"And what is that going to be?" I asked.

"I would like to ask your permission to place a binding on you, but not like the one that was previously done. This would only be for your dragon side, to prevent any surprise shifts should you be provoked in any way. Then, if all goes well this year, over the summer we will have private lessons for you in controlling your dragon."

No wonder it had taken him so long to reach out to me. Based upon the reaction of the other council members, I was sure there were going to be more drastic measures taken, but at least one person, if not more, had advocated for me, and I wasn't going to turn down what he was offering.

"I would be okay with that and I really appreciate you asking me instead of telling me how it was going to be. I didn't expect that."

His round cheeks raised as he smiled. "We're not bad people, Raegan. We want the best for all of our students and that includes you."

"So, when does this happen and how does it work?" I asked, wanting to steer clear of the heavy stuff.

Headmaster Stone reached into his desk and pulled out a vial before pushing it closer to me. The liquid was thick and blood red in color, just like my scales had been.

"You need to drink that, and then it's done." He lifted his other hand. "This is the reversal. I want you to know we have it and this isn't a trick."

The other bottle was filled with a crystalized-looking

substance, but I wasn't really concerned with that one. "Is that blood?" I nodded toward the first vial.

"No, but it is made with part of your dragon essence that was left behind after your shift in the box, so the color is that of your dragon-self."

The longer I waited, the more I was going to overthink things, which wouldn't be good for any of us. I had been offered a deal that was much kinder than the ones I had anticipated, and I needed to take it before anyone changed their mind.

My fingers closed around the small glass bottle as my other hand popped the cork out. Closing my eyes, I threw my head back and dumped the contents into my mouth all at once, swallowing it as quickly as I could.

Part of me expected some elaborate reaction: pain, sparks, smoke, anything other than the nothingness I experienced.

"Nothing is happening. Why didn't it work?" I asked, panicked.

"Magic doesn't harm when there is no need. Everything worked as it should have, I assure you. Now, when you find Enzo waiting at the top of the stairs, he's not going to remember you had a dragon side. Desmond will have found him and taken care of that. Enzo will take you to your first class as planned, and you shouldn't have any problems."

"Thank you." I stood and turned for the door, a little creeped out that they could take someone's memories like that.

"Raegan?" he called, and I swiveled back around. "Your schedule is now on your tablet, and if you have *any* issues, you come see me right away, okay?"

"Yeah, sure."

I didn't wait for him to say anything else. I didn't want there to be more. As the door closed behind me and my tablet dinged, I knew this was only the beginning.

The real magic started now, and I wasn't sure I was ready for it.

CHAPTER EIGHT

My class schedule wasn't nearly as awful as I was expecting, but the additional sessions I had to take with Enzo were the overwhelming parts. There were going to be too many hours of the day spent with him and not enough with my new friends or relaxing by myself.

Second Year Classes
8:30am – History of Shifters and Witches
9:45am – Herbs and Potions
11:00am – Defensive Magic
12:00pm – Lunch Break
1:00pm – History of Elora
2:15pm – Accelerated Elven Abilities

That was my regular schedule, and I was ready for it, but at the bottom of the screen, there was also my catch-up time that made me groan. On Mondays, Wednesdays, and Fridays, I would be in the Combat Hall's training center, learning offensive magic with Enzo from 3:30pm to 5:30pm. Following those sessions was an hour of tutoring to catch me up on the Herbs and Potions and Elven Abilities classes.

On Tuesdays and Thursdays, I would still be with Enzo for the same time, but we'd be working in the Magic Hall on mental protections and more elven magic.

My brain was already exhausted just thinking about the long-ass days I was going to have, not including the homework that would be assigned, plus my need to figure out who I was and who my parents were. I would likely rarely be able to leave my room.

When I arrived at my first class, Enzo left me at the door and, thankfully, didn't embarrass me by walking me all the way in like a child.

Seating didn't seem to be assigned, so I entered and breathed a sigh of relief when I laid eyes on Peyton. My wolf-shifter friend would at least be able to keep me company and hopefully help me catch up on anything Enzo wasn't already planning to help me with.

She waved me over, and I happily walked to her desk. That was, until I tripped and slammed my hands and knees into the hardwood floor. When I glanced back to see what I had tripped on, a girl smirked at me, and I recognized her from the table of elves Lyssa and Enzo had been at on my first day.

Great. Even if I was able to avoid the bitchface, I was still going to have to keep an eye out for her lackies.

Dusting myself off, I took a quick look around the class and, sure as shit, everyone had seen or heard my fall and was now staring at me. I kept my head held high as I finished making my way to Peyton without letting anyone see they had gotten to me.

"Are you okay?" Peyton asked when I took a seat.

"Yeah, it hurt my pride more than anything else. Who is that?"

"Tamra. She's not quite as evil as her best friend, but she's getting there. Don't let her bother you, though. There will be other drama from someone else soon, and they'll forget all about you."

Yeah, until Lyssa finds out just how much time I'll be spending with her boyfriend, I thought to myself.

A stout woman who appeared to be in her forties strode into class, and silence descended on the room. Even though she was on the shorter side, she commanded the room like a boss with a toss of her short, sleek brunette hair and perfectly tailored clothes.

"Good morning, students. My name is Professor Marteen. Welcome back to Shadow Veil Academy. Today will be a refresher on what you should have learned last year about shifters and witches. If you're unfamiliar with anything in the documents you'll have on your tablets shortly, I highly recommend you figure it out sooner rather than later."

She went on about stuff that only made surface-level sense to me, but I was typing notes on my tablet like a mad woman, so I could research things later. Apparently, our tablets had a catalogue of information on them, along with where exactly to find material one might need from the library.

After class was over, my relief was evident when Enzo wasn't waiting for me like a stalker outside the class door. Glancing down at my tablet, I found the next class and followed the instructions on how to get there. Herbs and

Potions was located under a dome-like structure at the top of Magic Hall. The sun shone through, warming me, and I immediately decided this would be my favorite class.

Morning classes were much of the same, refreshers and introductions, along with what to expect for the year. Nobody had done any real magic, which disappointed me, but my notes folder had many new pages in it, and I planned on doing what catch-up I could on my own after school.

Gemma was in Defensive Magic with me, which was perfect, because then we were able to go to lunch together and I didn't have to try to hunt anyone down or, worse, sit awkwardly by myself. I had made a few new friends in class, but nobody I would have felt comfortable joining without a previous invitation.

"How are you doing after three classes?" Gemma asked after we sat down to eat.

"Surprisingly well, but I have ridiculous amounts of studying in my future, so ask me in a week and I might have a different answer." I laughed.

After we finished our lunches, Gemma took me to find Peyton and Finley, who typically ate outside. I soaked in the rays of sun and listened to the other students chatter on about their classes and other dramas that had occurred. None of that kept my interest, so my attention wandered back to the sky.

When lunch ended, I said goodbye to my friends and promised to see them for dinner. My next two classes were with pure elves and elven hybrids, which meant none of them would be with me.

As I walked into the first afternoon class, I scanned the room of my History of Elora course and my heart sank when I saw Lyssa sitting at the back of the room. Besides the run-in with her lacky in my first class, I'd had no problems with any of the other students.

Everyone had been friendly enough, but I knew that wouldn't be the case in this class. I didn't recognize anyone else, so I chose the seat furthest from Lyssa in hopes it would help. Though, when I went to sit in my chair, I fell on my ass and didn't even bother to look back.

Lyssa didn't deserve any of my attention, and I wouldn't allow her the satisfaction of knowing she'd probably bruised my ass. My only hope was that she would behave herself while the professor was in the room, which turned out to be the case for the following hour as I became immersed in a world completely unknown to me. I devoured every bit of it until the bell chimed.

Enzo was in my last class. Convenient and likely not a coincidence. It meant I had no chance at running away from him after school and avoiding whatever he had planned for me. I was seriously rethinking starting as a second-year student as the day progressed.

"I didn't see you at lunch. How did classes go?" he asked as he took a seat next to mine.

"Great. Thanks for asking." My eyes stayed on the front of the class, hoping he'd get the point. This was an elven class, and I had no idea how many of Lyssa's friends might be lurking around. I didn't need to give her more reason to hate me by talking with Enzo when it wasn't necessary, even if I really wanted to.

He put off a vibe that drew me to him and calmed any lingering angst I had within me. Well, that was only true when he wasn't frustrating the shit out of me. It was a fine balance that was constantly teetering on the edge.

"Welcome, students!" a tall, thin man said cheerily as he entered the class. "My name is Professor Trinket. Feel free to laugh, I know you'll do it behind my back anyway." His grin was as friendly as his voice, and I was suddenly extremely interested in his class, just as I had been with the last.

His tall, thin frame leaned back against his desk as he continued to address the room with bright aqua eyes. "I know most teachers take it pretty easy on you the first day, but I don't plan on it. We're going to head outside and see what you've learned instead of talking about it. How's that sound?"

Most of the class cheered about this, but my heart sank. I didn't know anything about my abilities, let alone elven abilities, and I wasn't sure a learning curve was going to be allowed for me.

"Don't worry. We'll have you caught up in no time. You have the best tutor in all of Shadow Veil." Enzo winked. "If you're not comfortable within a few weeks, we can extend our hours after school."

Nope. Not going to happen. I was going to figure this magic thing out and hopefully lessen my time with Enzo, not increase it.

"Thanks, but I'm sure I'll be fine."

And that's when I bit myself in the ass by assuming.

Once we were outside, the professor pointed at me. "You there, in the pants with the red hair. What's your name?"

Seriously? Nobody had commented on my clothes all day. Why now, when the day was almost over?

"Raegan."

"Raegan, nice to meet you. Mostly because I'm nosy, why aren't you wearing the normal uniform? Can your legs not see the sun?"

Laughter erupted around the area, and my cheeks reddened as all eyes landed on me.

"No, Professor Trinket. I assumed that since the guys get to wear pants, as long as mine are just as nice, then there's no reason why I can't. It would seem very sexist to tell me I couldn't, and I didn't think Shadow Veil was that way."

Oooh's and aaah's went about the class, but I kept my attention on the teacher.

"So, do you also believe that the boys should be able to wear skirts?" he countered

"If that is what they'd be most comfortable in, then yes, I do. Everyone has the right to be themselves, don't you agree?"

He nodded at me with a smile still in place. "That they do, Raegan. Now that we have that out of the way. Who wants to demonstrate their elven magic first?"

Hands flew into the air, and very few students still paid attention to me, which was a relief.

"You handled that well. Most first-years would have caved, even with a cool guy like Trinket," Enzo whispered.

"Good thing I'm not a first-year then, huh?"

"Touché."

As I watched the others show their abilities, I paid attention to the words they used and their body movements. Before I realized it, I was mimicking them, and Enzo had to stop me from accidently throwing a magic ball at the student in front of us.

He eyed me carefully with a frown. "You're going to learn faster than I think I'm going to like."

Holding in my grin, I didn't respond. He couldn't have said anything else that would have made me happier.

Professor Trinket didn't end up calling on everyone, and

I was able to stay hidden behind other students to avoid being asked to show my lack of skills. When the final bell sounded through school grounds, nerves took over.

Enzo would soon be asking me to perform magic and, even though I had gotten into watching the other students in the last class, I wasn't sure how I felt about trying it myself with his full attention on me.

"Ready?" Enzo asked, the normal haughtiness missing from his demeanor.

"As I'll ever be."

He led the way to the training room within Combat Hall and showed me to the ladies' changing room. Inside was set up like a clothing store, except there were lockers along the walls instead of more clothes. I grabbed yoga-type pants off the shelves, then a large grey shirt with the school logo on it from the racks before heading to the changing room.

When I was done, I shoved my stuff into a locker and noticed a screen on the outside. I tapped it and a fingerprint showed up, so I pressed my pointer finger to it. The screen flashed once and then the lock engaged. Fancy.

Enzo was already changed and waiting for me. He wore loose black pants that hung low on his hips and a tank top with wide arm holes, leaving little to my imagination. Damn him! His bronze hair was pulled back, and he appeared ready for more than just training.

"First, we're going to practice basic offensive magic that you should have learned last year. You don't have any offense classes, so don't stress too much on this part. We will work on it three days a week until it comes naturally to you. With private lessons, it shouldn't take as long."

There was no sarcasm in his voice, no egotistical attitude. He was truly acting like a tutor. Hell, even a responsible one. It was weird, and nothing like my previous interactions with him.

He continued explaining a few other things, and then it was time for the real magic. No more talk. I needed to actually *do*.

We started with meditation and worked on tapping into my inner power source, which was much easier than I realized it would be. Whoever had put a block on my magic when I was younger did a hell of a job, because it was almost overwhelming now.

"Are you sure you weren't using magic before?" Enzo asked when I blasted him in the shoulder on accident.

"Yep. Pretty sure I would have remembered that and tried to defend myself against the shadow man if I knew I had access to this kind of power."

"True. You were pretty much a lowly human when I saved you from certain death." He smirked at me jokingly.

"I'd be so lost without you." I fake swooned and then laughed along with him.

I liked this Enzo. He was being respectful and actually teaching me without acting like an arrogant ass. Maybe hanging out with him after school every day wouldn't be so bad.

"Our time is almost up. Anything you want to ask me about from classes today?"

I shook my head. I wanted to look up some stuff on my own. My mom had raised me to be independent. I was going to stand on my own two feet whenever I could at Shadow Veil.

We went a few more rounds, exchanging harmless magical hits. Well, harmless from his side. I was still trying to control the amount of power I put into my thoughts. He was handling it like a champ, though.

After we said goodbye, I headed to my room and took the longest and hottest shower of my life. My muscles burned everywhere. When I was done, I considered ordering food in instead of meeting Gemma as planned, but when I finished getting dressed, I knew that wouldn't be happening.

"Raegan Keyes! Open this damn door," Gemma yelled from the hallway.

Rushing to the door, I opened it before she pissed off everyone in our dorm section.

"I was in the shower. Calm your tits, woman."

Her eyes widened and then laughter erupted. She couldn't contain herself as she pushed her way past me. "I'm stealing that next time I need it."

"Fine by me. What's with the yelling?"

"Well, you hadn't come to see me, and I'm hungry. Peyton and Finley are busy, and I don't like eating alone, so let's go."

Sighing, I threw myself back on my bed. "I don't wanna."

"Biatch, get your ass up before I get really hangry," she growled.

"What happened to the polite girl I met when I first arrived?" I teased.

"That's work Gemma, this is friend Gemma. You either love me or hate me, so learn to deal with it."

A smile spread across my face. "I think I'm going to love this version."

"Good. Let's go then." She grabbed my hand and yanked me off the bed.

No more protests came from me. I brushed my hair and dried it as quickly as I could, thankful for my short layers since Gemma continued to whine behind me about how she was withering away by the second.

The day had been a great one, and I was eagerly looking forward to the remainder of the week. Shadow Veil Academy might just be the best thing that had ever happened to me.

Two weeks into school, and the extra "tutoring" that was more like boot camp was causing my body to rebel. My muscles refused to move at the speed necessary to keep Enzo's much larger frame from slamming into mine, and it was driving me nuts.

Sexual tension filtered through the air of the training room we were using, and I was pretty positive Enzo was purposely kicking my ass just so he could touch me and get a rise out of me. Cocky bastard seemed to be well aware of our attraction, and it came out in full force when we were half-clothed and sweaty.

"You're not keeping your form when I kick at your feet," he reprimanded.

"Well, no shit," I snapped.

"Come on. You've come a long way already. Don't revert back to your weak human form or we'll have to start from lesson one again." The grin he threw my way as he tossed loose strands of hair back from his face told me he'd enjoy that too much.

"Not going to happen. Let's go again." Bracing my knees, I leaned forward on the balls of my feet and awaited the impact Enzo was sure to deliver, but it never came. At least, not from where I expected.

Air rushed from my lungs as my back suddenly slammed into the mats and I was staring up at the ceiling. Enzo straddled me, bringing his face into view.

"Never assume you know what your enemy will do. Always be prepared for several forms of attack," he said from above me.

Before he could move off of me, I hooked my ankles around his and pushed his body to my left to roll us over, effectively reversing our positions.

"Maybe getting you on the ground had been my intention and you hadn't caught me off guard at all." I smirked even though it wasn't true.

"Well, then I'd tell you good job, but you're lying, so do better next time, because it might be your life on the line." He was such a Debbie Downer.

Pushing on his chest, I made a move to stand up, but he once again had me on my back. This time, instead of straddling me, his entire body covered my own as he pinned my arms above my head. I was only wearing a sports bra and leggings, while he wore loose shorts and a tank. There was little left to the imagination in our current position.

"I didn't say you could get up." His voice deepened, barely above a whisper, and his eyes darted toward my tongue that involuntarily slipped out to wet my lips.

The golden specks of his eyes darkened, turning bronze like his hair, and as much as I was enjoying the close contact, my relationship with Enzo needed to remain professional. I needed him to get me caught up from missing an entire year of school, and I wasn't about to let my hormones screw that up for me.

"Enzo," I breathed heavily as I bit down on my lip, waiting for him to be fully distracted before making my move.

When his full attention was focused on my face, I freed my hands from above my head and trailed my fingers down his arm until I was within striking distance. Without skipping a beat, I twisted and jabbed my elbow into his chin before rolling a good five feet away from him.

"Oh, look at that? Our time is up," I said cheerily while getting up, as if the encounter hadn't made me rethink every bad thought I'd had about him. "See you tomorrow."

Only glancing back when I was at the exit, I found Enzo still on the floor and staring at the ceiling. We needed more boundaries, or this was going to be a long freaking year.

~

A COUPLE OF WEEKS LATER, SEPTEMBER WAS ABOUT over and I'd found a good routine. My first full month at the academy had been the most fun I'd ever had in school. I was still behind in a few of my classes, but my strength was growing, and Enzo began to praise my progress.

Our relationship had become more neutral since the training session that ended with both of us hot and bothered. Apparently, he didn't like the effects I had on him, either.

Even though I still had the occasional dirty thought about him, we'd both managed to keep things on a strictly student-and-tutor level. He even stopped bothering me outside of our elven class and private sessions, and I appreciated that he respected my space.

Gemma had also been great at keeping me from hiding in my room, which turned out not to be so horrible. Lyssa hadn't caused me any trouble in almost two weeks, so I was able to enjoy more of the school and the people without worrying about her causing any drama. I still avoided her and her lackies like the plague, but it seemed like they were avoiding me as well.

On the last weekend in September, I found myself with absolutely nothing to do for the first time since I arrived. I was caught up on my homework, and my friends were all preparing for a big test in a class I thankfully wasn't in.

I considered going to History Hall to do more research in my quest to figure out who my parents were, but I had no clue where to start. Every time I tried, I failed epically. Instead, I decided it was time to do some wandering around the campus and go back to check out the Courtyard of Tranquility. It had intrigued me before, but I hadn't had time to go inside it yet.

Making my way through the school, I took a different route, trying to explore other new things on my way. When I made it back to familiar territory, I had arrived at the door Gemma has said was forbidden to students.

Normally, I knew better than to push my boundaries, but the area piqued my interest more than I wanted to admit. I placed my hand on the door, and the magic keeping it closed vibrated beneath my hand. Closing my eyes, I tried to tell what kind of power was lying behind it, but before I could get very far with my thoughts, the door swung open from the inside, almost smacking me in the face.

"What do you think you're doing?" a guy snapped at me, his eyes dark and menacing.

"I... uh... I was just..."

"You were just what?" he snarled. "Stay away from here. This isn't a place for students."

I wanted to reply with any excuse so I didn't get in trouble, but before I could get the words out, power flooded out of the door and slammed right into me.

Hello, my sweet.

My eyes widened, and I scrambled further back. "I'm sorry."

"Don't come back here." With those final words, the door banged shut with an echoing thud.

Holy shit. Holy shit. Holy shit.

I had no idea what just happened, but when the door opened, I had been consumed with something sinister. Magic so heavy and thick, I couldn't breathe. Then, the voice. A woman had spoken in my head. I had no idea who she was, but her voice scared the piss out of me.

Shaking my head, I began to run for the exit. I needed some damn tranquility in my life after that encounter.

When I made it outside, I glanced around, all of a sudden feeling more paranoid than I had ever been. Keeping a brisk pace, I entered the courtyard I had been searching for and let out a sigh of relief as pure magic soaked into my being.

Courtyard of Tranquility was where I needed to keep my exploring to, not the creepy forbidden dungeon-esque area.

All of a sudden, the pure magic I was trying to soak in began to revolt against me. Pain pricked at my skin, and there was nothing tranquil about it. My skin was burning, and my insides began to cramp.

What the hell is happening to me?

Leaping for the gate, I threw my body out of the enclosed area and let out a sigh of relief when I hit the grass.

The ache immediately receded, but I was still having a hard time breathing, and I was pretty certain someone was trying to kill me.

So much for thinking it was a good idea to go exploring on my own.

Lesson freaking learned.

I picked myself up and hobbled back to the dorms. As I passed by the front of the school, I glanced up at the gargoyles again, convinced they were watching me. Hair rose on the back of my neck and I practically ran the rest of the way to my room.

LATER THAT AFTERNOON, WHEN GEMMA CAME BACK, she found me in my pajamas and hiding away while I nursed my mostly psychological wounds. The school grounds had kicked my ass, and I wasn't handling it well.

"The scary dude who yelled at me is going to haunt my dreams for days," I whined.

"You're lucky that's all he did. From your description, I'm pretty sure that's Ryn. He's been a guard here for a while, and nobody messes with him. I'm not sure where he came from, but he's not from around here." She shivered and rubbed her arms, proving my reaction to the situation was pretty on point.

I didn't tell her about the courtyard experience. Though, I was considering going to the headmaster about it since he was one of the few people who knew about my three races. Maybe whatever suppression he put on my dragon side had caused the reaction I had.

But I was also afraid.

I felt like I was on probation with the council already

and didn't want to give them another reason to send me packing or, worse, strip my memories like they had messed with Enzo's.

"Let's go have a girls' night. We can head into Salem and hit up a bar or something."

"Do you have fake IDs? No way we'll pass for twenty-one," I said.

"We have magic. We don't need fake IDs. We just have to make an illusion. Make the door guy see the right birth year. Have you done illusions yet with Enzo?"

Sighing, my mind flashed back to that day. He scared the shit out of me. When I entered the training room, I *thought* he was lying on the ground in a pool of blood. I screamed for help as my hands pressed into his stomach. That was, until I felt the vibration of his laughter beneath my fingers.

The bastard had thrown me right into illusions with no heads-up. After I had mastered creating one, he taught me how to catch one, a skill that came from my elven side and other races didn't have. That was when I forgave him for making me think he was dying.

"Yep. I can take care of that," I finally replied.

"Perfect. I'll message Peyton and Finley. They'll be pissed if we go without them."

"Alright, if you're going to keep my ass out all night in the bars, I'm going to need a nap. I'll come over to your room to get ready in a little while."

She was halfway out the door, excitement pouring from her, before I even finished my sentence.

My mind was exhausted from everything that had happened earlier in the day, so it wasn't long before I laid my head down and was out cold, but a peaceful rest wasn't what I received.

The nightmares I had experienced before I left had been few and far between since arriving at the academy. I still ached for my parents, but it wasn't in the depressive way that I was feeling before.

So, the new nightmare took me by surprise when it wasn't a rendition of how I imagined my parents' death. Instead, it was filled with the dark, menacing eyes of Ryn, and the woman's voice that had sounded in my head before.

Raegan, you have to come to me.

They're trying to kill me.

I need you.

Please save me.

When I was finally able to yank myself from the nightmare, my body was covered in sweat and shaking. The voice scared me most, but when she asked for me to save her, my heart hurt for the woman I didn't know. My mind began to wonder who she was and why she might have been trapped down there.

Or, maybe I was batshit crazy and she was nothing more than a spirit screwing with me. I'd have to ask the others if they knew about any areas of the school being haunted. Maybe that was why students weren't allowed behind the locked door.

I glanced at the clock to find that only forty-five minutes had passed, and I was even more exhausted than before. Instead of trying to sleep again, I ordered a few energy drinks from the butler box. I wasn't big on coffee, but energy drinks worked when I was in a pinch.

Downing the caffeine, I grabbed a couple of dresses I thought would work for going out and headed to Gemma's room. When she opened the door, her face twisted. "What the hell happened to you?"

"Gee. Thanks for making me feel better," I groaned.

"Stupid nightmares. The pale and pasty look will hopefully pass soon."

Pushing my way into the room, I saw Peyton half-naked and trying to shimmy into a tight sequin dress. "Stupid shifter genes give me wide hips. Hey, Rae, come help me squeeze into this thing. It *will* fit. I swear."

Laughing, I set my stuff down and went to help her, while Gemma finished doing Finley's hair into a fancy not-so-messy bun.

"What if it rips?" I asked when I began tugging on the thin material.

"Then Gemma can fix it. I just need to get it over my damn hips. Seriously, be thankful you're not a shifter. Shifting screws with your body composition, and not in a good way."

I cringed a little, because I was part shifter and hated not being able to tell them. I then began to wonder if I would suffer the same consequences, but remembered my entire body hadn't changed before. I'd only acquired the scales and wings, so maybe not. Maybe I'd just be a freakish hybrid, or tri-brid, if that was even a thing.

An hour later, the four of us were ready and walking across the academy toward the gates. I hadn't left the school grounds since I arrived, and nerves erupted in my stomach. Something was pulling me back, and I didn't know why or what. Apparently, the nightmare had screwed with me more than I realized.

"Are you alright, Rae?" Finley asked. "You're looking kinda pale again, and not in the hot vampire way like me."

I tried to laugh, but it didn't come out that way, more like a strangled cat noise. "Yeah, I'm fine."

When the gate opened and my feet officially left the inside of the school grounds, the agony I was experiencing got worse. I hissed at the pain but continued moving forward. I needed this girls' night, and I'd be damned if I was going to let some creeptastic stuff from earlier in the day take away my fun.

Gemma tugged me along, a worried look pushing her brows together. "Maybe we should reschedule?"

"No, I swear I'm okay. Plus, look at us. We can't waste all this on staying in for the night." I tried to joke, but it was forced, and I knew by their concerned glances that they didn't buy it.

We arrived at the shield, and I hesitated. Something was telling me it wasn't a good idea to go through and completely leave the school property, but being a stubborn person, I was determined to see just how bad it could get if I did.

Don't leave me, Raegan. I need you.

The voice had returned, and its presence urged me forward instead of backward like it wanted. When we pushed through the shield, I was bounced back while the three others went through just fine. I could see their mouths moving, but I couldn't hear anything they were saying.

There was a pounding in my head that wouldn't stop, and everything was on fire within me. I crawled away from the wall, and the closer I got back to the academy, the less severe the pain became.

My eyes glanced up at the school, curious how far I'd have to crawl to make it back, but instead of focusing on the distance, my eyes met those of a gargoyle, and there was no longer any denying that they were watching me. The flash of red within them proved I had been right before.

"Raegan!" Gemma's voice finally broke through the pounding.

Rolling onto my back, I gave up trying to move as several facts kept repeating in my mind.

Someone was inside my head.

Gargoyles were watching me.

I was trapped at the academy.

Worst of all, I had no idea what I was going to do about any of it.

Seconds ticked by slowly as my body returned to its normal state and the pain receded. Pushing up on my elbows, I glanced around and hoped nobody had seen me collapse. What I found was a very pissed-off elf running my way.

"What the hell happened?" Enzo demanded.

"We don't know. She wasn't feeling good, and when we walked through the shield, Raegan was kicked back," Gemma explained.

I still couldn't find my own voice as I tried to process everything.

"Where were you going?" Enzo asked as his hands roamed my body, likely checking for injuries.

"Just out for a girls' night. Nothing against the rules, Mr. Crabass," Gemma replied with the snark I loved so much.

Enzo mumbled something, but I couldn't make it out.

"I'm fine. You can go back inside, Enzo," I finally said.

"You're not fine. You need to go see the headmaster. The shield is meant to keep people out, not in." Without asking, his arms curled under my body, lifting me up as he pressed me against his chest.

"What do you think you're doing?" I snapped. "Put me down. Right. Now."

When he didn't listen, I started hitting his chest with my fists, but he didn't even flinch.

"Enzo." Gemma's voice deepened. "I know you think you run this school, but Raegan is *our* friend. If she doesn't want to go with you, we're not going to let you take her."

He turned around slowly, giving me a view of my friends. If looks could kill, Enzo would be ash.

Gemma stood with her hands on her hips, eyes narrowed, a fierce determination set in her jaw. Peyton and Finley flanked her, hands out at their sides, legs bent ever so slightly, seemingly ready to pounce at a moment's notice.

Enzo took three long strides toward them, the power radiating off him so hot that my skin began to burn and itch wherever it touched him. "I'll only say this once, so listen carefully. Raegan is *my* responsibility. I brought her here. I tutor her. I will keep her safe. Don't get in my way of that or you'll regret it."

Gemma stepped into his personal space, close enough that her chest was pressed against my side. "Are you threatening me?"

"No, I'm telling you facts. Either deal with it or push me and see what happens." Darkness seeped into his words, and I shivered despite the heat rolling off of him.

I reached an arm out to Gemma. "I'll be fine. I promise to come find you as soon as we're done with the headmaster."

Her eyes met mine and she shook her head. She didn't like it, and I didn't blame her. "First stop, Raegan. Not to your room. Not the bathroom. Not to get food. Right to my room. You don't want to see me if I find you elsewhere."

The last bit was directed at Enzo, but he didn't react. Instead, he twisted away from them and quickened his pace toward the academy.

Neither of us spoke, and students gave him a wide berth as he moved through the building. A teacher attempted to ask him what was wrong, but one wrathful look from Enzo had the teacher cowering and turning a different direction.

Good thing I wasn't really in danger. I'd have been sorely disappointed to not have anyone there to stop him from taking me.

"You don't have to be so rude to everyone, you know," I stated after the third student he practically shoved out of our way. "I'm not dying."

Dark eyes met mine. "How do you know?"

I gulped but didn't respond. Enzo was overreacting. I was certain of it, but I didn't push him further. If he wanted to go all caveman until he knew I was for sure okay, I wasn't going to stop him. When I thought about it more, it was kind of endearing. You know, in that this-guy-is-psycho-but-he-really-cares sort of way.

When we arrived in Magic Hall, Enzo closed-fist pounded on the headmaster's door and, before it connected a third time, the door opened. Headmaster Stone was on his feet within seconds, moving quicker than I had ever seen before.

"Bring her to me," he requested, then moved his hands back and forth like he was wiping down a table.

Enzo set me down on thin air, and I started to struggle, believing my ass was about to land on the ground, but the headmaster shushed me.

"You won't fall. Just calm down." Headmaster Stone's

hands roamed over my body, and the longer he stood there, the more severe the frown on his face became. "Where have you been today?"

My body tensed. I was afraid that if I had told him the truth, they'd kick me out without hesitation. I tried to think of a lie, but nothing came to me in my panicked state.

"Tell the truth, Raegan," Enzo said calmly when I didn't answer right away.

With a sigh, I gave in. "I went to the door Gemma told me was forbidden. As I was sensing the magic before trying to go inside—"

"You had no business trying to get *inside*. You should have known better." Enzo's eyes narrowed.

"Well, I figured if it was right out in the open for students to stumble upon, then it couldn't be *that* bad."

Headmaster Stone's hand cupped my elbow. "It's worse than bad, my child, and you shouldn't have been able to open that door. Something is wrong, but I'm going to fix it. Don't you worry."

He turned away, heading toward his wall of potions and oddities. Enzo continued to stare at me, a mixture of rage and curiosity written across his chiseled face.

"I'm sorry?" I said more as a question than a statement.

"Sorry doesn't keep you safe, Raegan. Gemma is a smart girl, and you need to listen to her when she tells you to stay away from somewhere."

I raised a brow. "Even if she tells me to stay away from you after tonight?"

"I said somewhere, not someone." A hint of a smile played on his lips, but before I could examine it, the head-master returned.

"Just a little cleansing spell and you should be better in no time." Reaching into a bowl, he scooped up something I couldn't see. He rubbed his hands together before pressing them to my arms and moving up to my shoulders then my temples.

Whatever was on his hands smelled like mint and vanilla, with a hint of sage. At first, I wanted to jerk away, but my body began to relax as the concoction seeped into my skin.

When the headmaster was done, he pressed my feet down and I slowly slid off his invisible table until I touched solid ground again. My body wavered, but Enzo was right there to catch me. My eyes met his, and I instantly regretted it as lust slammed into me.

He might have pissed off my friends, but he had done it in such an alpha way that my girly parts were fanning themselves and saying, "take me". Yes, I needed some mental help.

"You should be feeling like yourself by morning, but I don't suggest you try to leave the grounds again," the headmaster said with a hint of sorrow.

"Why?" I asked. "Am I in trouble? I promise I won't go near that door again."

He shook his head. "There are things happening within this school that the students don't need to worry about. Just know it's safer for you within the walls for the time being, as long as you stay away from the dungeon. Do you understand?"

"Yeah, I guess." I wanted to argue, but I also hadn't given them the full story and agreed with him that I needed to stay.

"Raegan, you need to know that arriving here as a late student and being unaware of who you are has caused the council to question some things about your history. We've come up with no paper trails as to where you're from or who your parents were. It's as if you didn't exist before Enzo found you."

"What does that mean?" I asked with a shaky voice. I had been coming up with the same answers in my failed attempts at research, but that hadn't surprised me. I hadn't known what I was doing. The council should have found something. I couldn't have been created from thin air.

He placed a hand on my shoulder and brought his kind face level with mine. "We're not sure, but we're going to figure it out. I swear, everything is going to be okay."

His words held promise, but his eyes told me he wasn't sure the words were true.

When he backed up, Enzo took my hand and led me from the room. His palm was warm within mine, but not like the heat I had experienced when he took me away from my friends. That had been dark and overwhelming. This was soothing and put me at ease for the first time that day.

"I have to go see Gemma," I said, wanting to keep my earlier promise.

"You need to see something first, and then I'll take you back to your dorm." Enzo tightened his grip on my hand as if he believed I'd try to run away from him.

Smart elf.

"If Gemma skins me because I didn't go straight to her, I will cut your balls off. Just so you know."

"We'll be quick, and she won't find us where we're going, so don't go threatening my jewels, woman." He flinched and used his other hand to cover his junk.

Good. He should be afraid of me.

We headed back downstairs and out of Magic Hall. When we were about halfway to our destination, I realized he was taking me to the library. I'd been there several times a week since starting classes and was well-versed in every crevice of the place.

Curiosity was getting the better of me, thinking that I had missed something and was about to learn some super-secret spy stuff about Shadow Veil. It was the perfect distraction to my shit-tastic day.

We ventured to the northern back corner of the room, and Enzo searched the shelves for a book. At least, I thought that's what he was doing until he found what he was looking for.

Using both hands, he pulled on three books at the same time, causing them to lean, but not fall. When the shelf began to groan in movement, he stepped out of the way. The shelf pushed in, then slid into the wall, leaving about a three-foot-wide opening into a dark hallway.

"What is that?" I asked.

"Something only the elves know about and, since you're one of us, it's about time you knew, too."

Once the wall finished moving into place and we entered the dank passage, Enzo turned around and tapped the wall in rapid succession. He urged me forward, and I heard the door close behind us. Claustrophobia began to choke me from the inside, but when we arrived at a cavern-like room just thirty seconds later, my chest eased.

The area was dome-shaped, reminding me of a cave. It was probably fifty feet across by thirty feet wide, and on the ceiling were tiny lights that looked like fireflies. Around the room, there were a few tables filled with maps, books, and magical items I didn't know how to identify. Though, they gave off a distinct elven vibe that made the room seem like it was pulsing in power.

"Welcome to what's left of Elora," Enzo said as I glanced around in fascination.

"Seriously?"

"Yep. I want you to see something." He tugged my hand, gesturing for me to sit at one of the tables while he grabbed a book from the shelf. "This book tells the beginning of all magical beings. If the council can't figure out where you come from, then maybe it will bring you a little bit of peace to learn about how it all started from those who were directly involved. Only Professor Trinket has access to this information, so you won't learn about it in most of your classes."

My fingers caressed the front of the ancient book. It was in perfect condition; no doubt, a spell kept it from aging. The leather-bound cover was engraved with a stunning tree I'd never seen before but reminded me of a cross between a cherry blossom tree and an oak tree. Underneath its roots were letters I couldn't read.

"What does this say?" I asked in a low voice of awe.

"Concentrate. Focus on the lines and call the words to you like you call the truth from an illusion. Your elven side will reveal the script to you. That is, if its strong enough."

My eyes flashed to his and caught a hint of laughter within them. There was the Enzo I was used to, the one who liked to push my buttons and capabilities.

"Can I take it with me?" I doubted it, but it couldn't hurt to ask.

"No, but you know where to come now when you want to learn more. Do you want to stay for a while and see what you can learn?"

Regrettably, I shook my head. "I really need to let my friends know I'm okay."

"Understandable." He took the book from my hands and carefully put it back where he had taken it from.

I followed him out of the room and instantly missed the

rush of power I experienced when we entered. Watching the wall close up when we were back in the library was almost painful. There was raw magic in that room that called to me almost as much as the woman's voice from the dungeon.

When we arrived back in my dorm area, Enzo insisted on taking me all the way to Gemma's room, but stopped us just outside my door.

"Raegan, I need you to take all of this seriously. You're not dealing with humans any longer. The magic here is real and, while it can be enchanting, it can also be extremely dangerous to you. The things in the dungeon are the worst of the worst, and you need to resist whatever is happening within you."

My eyes widened and my lips moved, but no words came out.

"I know you didn't go there for the fun of it. Something more is happening, and I don't expect you to tell me every-thing, but I meant what I told Gemma. I *will* keep you safe. If you won't talk to me, at least know you can trust me with your life."

Holy freaking swoon.

My heart was beating a mile a minute and doubled in speed when he placed his hand over my chest.

"The reaction you have to me isn't one-sided." His head leaned in and his rapturous eyes held me captive.

I couldn't move or breathe. I had daydreamed about tasting him but never thought it would happen. Almost as often, I thought about cutting his balls off, so I hadn't put much effort into trying to figure out my feelings for him. Though, as he moved closer, I knew without a doubt that I desperately wanted his lips on mine.

"Raegan!" Gemma screeched from her doorway, interrupting our perfect moment.

Enzo promptly backed up, winked at me, and then disappeared. *Asshole.* I hated when he did that, mostly because I couldn't.

Gemma's eyes watched me disapprovingly as I trudged my way to her room. She was going to lay into me, but I didn't really care.

The day had been filled with one shitty thing after another, but it had ended with something unpredicted, and I was beginning to realize that the unexpected wasn't always so bad.

CHAPTER ELEVEN

Finals week for the first quarter was upon us, and I was a freaking train wreck. On top of that, I was going to be off of school for two weeks, but most of it was going to be spent with Enzo still trying to play catch up, and I was running out of patience in dealing with him.

The only benefits to the break were that my birthday happened to be during it and Aunt Jules would be at the academy with me to celebrate since I still couldn't leave the school grounds. The last four weeks since my incident trying to leave the school had been interesting to say the least.

The day after, I was sure things with Enzo were going to be somewhat awkward, since he had tried to kiss me and admitted I wasn't the only one affected by our relationship, but the following week he didn't once mention what had happened. He pretended as if none of that night had transpired except for the time we spent in the hidden elven room.

I was tempted to broach the subject myself, but if he wasn't man enough to own his feelings, then I didn't need him. I had decided it was time to check out the rest of the eye candy in the school and had been eyeing a fellow witch named Embry in my History of Witches and Shifters class.

Peyton was more than encouraging of my slight crush, mostly on Gemma's behalf. None of my friends wanted me to get involved with Enzo more than I already was. He was trouble and everyone could see it, except me apparently, because more often than not, he intrigued me.

On the other hand, Embry was tall, dark, and handsome. Along with his tanned skin, he had striking indigo eyes that loved to wink whenever he caught me staring at him. I had yet to speak with him outside of class, but depending on how finals week went, I had considered approaching him soon.

"Ready for your first big finals week, Rae?" Gemma asked when she arrived at my door that Monday morning.

"Not even close. The professors have all been pretty understanding so far, but they can't baby me for finals. If I get a C or better on any of my tests, I'll be the happiest hybrid ever born."

"I thought you said you were catching on pretty well with the stuff Enzo was teaching you?" She frowned.

"I am, but second year stuff is a level above, and I'm just not there yet. Another few months and I should be, though."

She tossed a pillow from my bed at me. "Good, because I'll be pissed if we don't get more classes together next year because you failed. I might have to unfriend you if that happens."

I laughed. "You can't just unfriend me. It doesn't work that way."

Her brow quirked at me. "Have you not learned I tend to do things my own way?"

"This is true. Anyway, let's get this week started, so we can be over with it sooner." I grabbed my bag off my desk chair, then double-checked that I had my tablet and binder full of notes. They encouraged everything to be done on the tablets to save on resources, but some things needed pen to paper, and finals preparation was one of them.

Gemma tossed me a couple of energy drinks from my butler box that I had almost forgotten, and I threw her back a smile. "I don't know what I'd do without you."

"You'd probably have flunked out of school already and disappeared back to the dark depths of the human world, living a sad and pitiful life." Her face remained neutral for a few seconds before she broke out into hysterics. "I crack myself up, but seriously, you'd be lost without me. I know it."

We went our separate ways and, as I ventured the halls that were now so familiar to me, I couldn't keep the smile off my face. The last seven weeks had been insane, but also some of the best of my life.

I missed my old life, but not the one I left behind.

I missed my parents even if they weren't my birth parents, but that was a life I couldn't get back. This new one, however, was one I was happy to embrace after the last ten months of hell.

Being so lost in thought about the past, present, and future, I hadn't been paying well enough attention to where I was going and slammed into the back of someone as I turned into the classroom.

"I'm so sorry," I exclaimed right before tripping over my feet as I tried to back away. My arm shot out to try to catch my fall, but all I did was grasp on to the ass of the guy I had initially run into, causing him to come crashing down with me.

Thankfully, he was quicker than me and turned in time to catch himself before completely crushing me.

"Hey, Raegan," Embry said with a familiar wink, his face inches from my own. "A little nervous about the test?"

"Uhhh, I guess. How about you?"

"Well, I was feeling a little tired, but now..." He glanced between the two of us, still on the ground, practically pressed together. "I'm feeling a bit more awake."

Oh, shit.

Scrambling backward like a crab, I slid out from underneath him as quickly as I could and grabbed my bag that I had dropped.

"I'm so sorry."

He smirked as he also stood up. "You already said that."

"Yeah, well, I, uh, wanted to make sure you heard me," I stammered like an idiot.

His hands cupped my elbows. "Are you alright?"

"Yep. Just great. Gotta find my seat now. Bye." Rushing away, I heard his deep chuckle as I slid into my seat next to Peyton.

She opened her mouth to say something, but I held my finger over her mouth. "Don't say a word."

"But—"

"No."

"You're taking all the fun out of witnessing that, you know?" she whined.

"Yep, and I don't really care," I replied.

Pulling out my tablet, I was actually surprised Peyton was letting it go. The professor walked in, and I figured I was in the clear until the four of us were all back together, at least.

"So, I take it Enzo is officially being replaced?" she snickered.

Ah, I knew it was too good to be true for her to let the subject go so easily.

"Enzo was never mine to replace, so the answer to your question would be 'not applicable'."

"Right." She rolled her eyes at me and finished setting up her stuff for the test.

Her comments did make me question my attraction to Embry, though. He was the exact opposite of Enzo, so I couldn't see how my subconscious could be trying to replace one with the other, but it could have been that I was just refusing to consider it.

"Good morning, class. Your final test for the quarter is going to be seventy percent of your grade and will consist of two parts. For part one, you will have today and tomorrow to complete the actual test. The following three days will be spent writing an essay on your choice of topic. You can choose from any topic we have covered thus far in the class. Any questions?"

When nobody raised their hand, my tablet lit up and the test appeared. There were four segments and one hundred questions. Two segments per day. Fifty questions per day. No problem. I had this.

I had to have this.

Forty-five minutes later, I was done with the first fifty questions. I considered going on to the other parts to get a head start on the following day, but my brain was mush and I still had an hour tomorrow to complete them. So, I spent the rest of the time considering my options for my essay.

My first thought had been witches since I was part witch, but as I searched the walls showing pictures of the species we had covered, my eyes landed on the dragon shifters.

In my quest to find my birth parents and figure out who

I was, I had done an immense amount of research on drag-ons. When Headmaster Stone had told me they were rare, I figured it was the easiest place to start in my investigation.

I hadn't found anything I deemed helpful, but I had learned a lot about their history, especially the reason for them segregating themselves from the rest of the super-naturals.

Their blood was powerful, and many witches used it for dark magic. When young dragons began disappearing, the elders of their clans decided it was time to remove them-selves from the supernatural community. Some went into hiding, but most ventured to an off-the-grid area in Europe.

"That was seriously brutal," Peyton droned, inter-rupting my thoughts. "How far did you get?"

"Finished half, then thought about my essay subject. You?"

"Same for the questions, and essay is easy. They say to write what you know. I'll be writing about wolves. Well, one alpha to be exact."

My brow raised. "Oh, yeah? Anyone I know?"

As we gathered our things and headed for the door, she shook her head. "This guy was the original alpha. Every race has their first alpha, except the elves. They've been around too long to know the truth about their history, but the witches, shifters, and vampires all had to start somewhere."

My mind began racing with questions. In all of my research, original supernaturals never came up. I was intrigued with who they were and what roles they played. Like, was Headmaster Stone an original? Or were they all dead?

"Are any of them still living?" I asked as we traversed the hallway.

"Nope. Well, the dragon one might be, but the last living one that interacted in our community was a sorceress named Malina, but rumor has it, she went dark. Like Satan-level dark. The council caught her, and nobody knows what truly happened in the end for her. That was a couple decades ago, I think. Most of the others chose to die at some point. Nobody wants to live forever when everyone else they love has died."

"The originals were immortal?" My eyes were probably bulging out of my head, but coming from the human part of the world, I was sorely disappointed I hadn't learned about this yet.

"I gotta get to my next class and so do you. Search for Doyens in your tablet library. It's what they used to call the originals. You'll find what you're looking for, nerd."

She and the others liked to poke fun at me from time to time when I asked too many questions or still got fascinated by the magic around me, but I didn't have parents who taught me about any of it before I showed up at the academy.

I had been thrown into this world, and it was basically sink or swim for me. I was going to stay afloat no matter the cost, even if it made me a nerd in their eyes.

Halfway through the week, my emotional state was a wreck, but I was feeling good about my finals, so I tried to focus on that. I knew I hadn't knocked any of them out of the park, but so far, I was fully expecting to pass them all. A C-minus was still passing.

A couple of my classes finished early, and I was down to three classes for the last two days of the week. Plus, Enzo had canceled our tutoring sessions for the week, so I had a shit ton of extra time on my hands to focus on specific finals and the research I had been doing on the Doyens.

There hadn't been a ton of information available, but I was soaking it up and loving what I could find. Each bit I read about the witches and dragons made me feel like I knew a little more about myself.

Not knowing where I came from was a hard thing to grasp, but I was slowly coming to terms with everything I had been dealt.

I spent most of the afternoon in my room, but when it was time for dinner, I wanted to get out and enjoy the cool evening. Fall was upon us, and it was my favorite time of year.

Though, when I opened my door, I came face-to-face with Headmaster Stone. Startled, I did nothing but stare at him like an invalid.

"Raegan? Are you okay?" he asked, concerned.

Shaking my head, I blinked. "Oh, yeah. You just took me by surprise. I've never seen you in the dorms before."

"Well, I don't typically have a reason to come."

"But you do now?" Tension laced my voice.

"Unfortunately. I need you to come with me." His hand swept out, and his robe hung loose from his arm.

Without another word, I walked with him to Magic Hall. Instead of going to his office, he took me to the room where my abilities had been unlocked. Anxiety slammed into me as my hands began to shake; my heart rate increased when I thought back to the painful experience.

When we entered the room, it was completely different from the last time I had been there, and I learned it was normally a conference room for the council. There was now a long wooden table with the academy logo carved into the center set in the middle of the room. Oversized oak chairs with brown leather cushions surrounded the table, and all of the council members were already seated around it.

Headmaster Stone gestured for me to sit at the end of the table as he took the head seat. After I was situated, I took a few seconds to check out the council. Desmond's face caught my attention first. His skin was sunken, as if he hadn't eaten in weeks, with deep purple circles under his eyes. His head remained downcast with a frown on his face.

Fiona actually smiled at me this time instead of the scowl she had cast my way when I first met her. Alexander paid more attention to his nails than anything else in the room, and Bennett appeared more like Headmaster Stone, troubled by whatever we were about to discuss.

"Thank you for joining us, Raegan," Headmaster Stone began. "I wish it was under better circumstances or that it could have waited until after this week, but we've put it off for as long as we could."

"Put what off?" I asked him when he paused.

"When you opened the door to the lower levels of this school, a small amount of essence from a very powerful sorceress leaked out and entered your body. It's the reason you couldn't leave the academy grounds with the other students. While the shield is mostly meant to keep people out, there are some beings it's meant to keep in."

"Are you telling me there is another person riding shotgun *inside* of me?" My voice rose, and I tried to keep myself under control, but I was losing it more and more by the second.

Fiona leaned forward and caught my attention with sincerity written in her facial features. "Desmond has been fighting non-stop to try to counteract her, but somehow, she keeps growing stronger. We are hoping that maybe you've heard something or experienced anything out of the ordinary that could tell us why."

Well, that explained why he looked like death.

My mind thought back to everything that had happened since I ventured through the forbidden door. The woman's voice had gradually become stronger, but without telling Enzo why, I was able to get him to teach me how to shut out voices around me.

I hadn't known if it would work, because I only told him I was getting distracted in class, but it also happened to work in silencing the woman, for the most part. So, over the last couple weeks, I hadn't heard much out of her.

Then, there were the gargoyle statues. The sentient beings that shouldn't have been able to move and watch, but somehow could and only with me when nobody else was paying attention.

My hands rubbed over my face as I considered if it was truly in my best interest to tell them everything.

"It's okay, Raegan. You can trust us. Tell us what happened to you," Alexander's soothing voice sounded in the quiet room.

Lifting my head, my eyes met his and I was momentarily lost within their aqua depths. Tension left my body, and I was no longer afraid to tell the council *everything* they wanted to know.

My mouth opened, but the words wouldn't come. Instead, a sharp pain erupted in my head, and the woman's voice returned. This time, it was louder than it had ever been before.

Don't tell them, Raegan. They'll kill you, just like they tried to kill me.

Alexander's gaze hardened when I didn't speak. "She shouldn't have been able to disobey me. Bennett was right, and we're too late. Malina's too far rooted within her."

Malina.

I knew that name. I had been reading about the original supernaturals, and she was the first sorceress. The online library, which was like a massive Wikipedia for all things magical, told me about her dark years, and I remembered Peyton mentioning she had disappeared almost twenty years ago. Suddenly, it all started to make sense.

Malina wasn't dead like people assumed. She was locked in the basement of Shadow Veil. Worst of all, I was now connected to her somehow.

"Raegan." Bennett regarded me like a wild animal. "Do you know who Malina is?"

Deciding there was no point in hiding it, I nodded my head. I'd comply for the time being, but there were no promises I would tell them everything, depending on how they responded as the conversation progressed.

If Malina was truly in my head, I certainly wasn't going

to trust her, but she had made a valid point. I needed to watch my own back, because I couldn't count on anyone else to do it.

"A woman speaks in my head sometimes. She doesn't say much. Mostly cryptic stuff about power and not leaving her. Until just now, I didn't even know her name," I finally said.

Desmond narrowed his eyes at me, appearing to strain from the effort as sweat broke out on his forehead. With a loud sigh, his shoulders dropped. "She's telling the truth."

Headmaster Stone reached over and placed a hand on his shoulder. "You've done enough today, Desmond. Why don't you go rest?"

His mouth opened to say something, but even that seemed like it would take too much effort for the sorcerer. Instead of responding, he shuffled out of the room, barely lifting his feet as he walked out of the door.

Once he was gone, the attention of the room was back on me, but nobody spoke for nearly a minute as tension rose.

"Malina is getting stronger, and we don't know how. Are you sure there isn't anything you can tell us that would be helpful?" Fiona urged. "I know we weren't very accepting of you when you arrived, but it can't be a coincidence that this is all happening now. We want answers just as much as you do, and we'd like to work together."

Holding her stare, I considered her words. She was right about not making me feel good when I first arrived, but I hadn't held it against them. Honestly, I hadn't even thought much about the day since Headmaster Stone had told me I was allowed to stay.

I was a stranger who had no history. Could I really blame them for their initial reaction? No, I couldn't.

"There is a pull I feel toward her. I fight it almost daily. Some days it's weaker than others, but it's always there. Enzo helped me block her out for a while without knowing it, but when she really wants to get through, like when Alexander tried to force my hand—"

Another agonizing force swept through my head, and I fell out of the chair onto the floor. My hands cupped my ears as I tried to drown out the screeching noise. Only there was no blocking it out. It was coming from the inside.

You will obey me, child. You are no longer allowed to speak to the council about me. I own you, and if you try to disobey me, the consequences of your actions will be swift. I advise you not to test me on this.

Then, there was silence.

I could see the faces of the council hovering above me. Their mouths were moving, but no sound reached me. I lay on the floor, dazed from the power surging through me. The heavy oily darkness I had only experienced when I was inside the dungeon was flowing freely through me with no end in sight.

Panic surged through me as I thought of any way to stop it, but the magic was sucking the breath out of me. Paralysis took over, and all I could do was stare wide-eyed at the council as I was certain death was about to claim me.

Desmond came rushing into view, looking like he'd done a few rounds with death as well. He and the headmaster argued about something for a few seconds, but the determination on Desmond's face was unwavering. Whatever he wanted, he was going to get.

Finally, Headmaster Stone backed up, giving Desmond the space he had apparently demanded. His lips moved slowly, and I tried to focus on them. I was pretty sure he said, "I'm sorry", but what for I had no idea.

Then understanding smacked me in the face.

If I thought what Malina was doing to me was painful, I was sorely mistaken.

Desmond's magic fought with mine and Malina's. The war within me had my back arching and my body contorting in angles I was positive I'd be paying for in the morning. After what seemed like an eternity, sound filtered through my ears.

"The girl isn't strong enough to withstand them both, Alistair, and he's bleeding. Do something before that bitch kills them both." Bennett's angry voice was the first thing that registered with me and the furiousness that went with it scared me almost as much as Malina.

"Raegan can do this, and so can Desmond. He's not drained," Headmaster Stone replied.

"Yet," Alexander retorted from somewhere, but nobody replied.

The only sounds in the room were those of Desmond's grunting and my wincing as I tried to help him push Malina out of my body.

"I can't remove her essence completely. It's as if Malina is a part of her in a physical sense," Desmond heaved out the words with strained effort. "What do you want me to do?"

"Just do your best to make sure she's not hurting Raegan and be done. That's all we can do for now until we know more," Headmaster Stone said, his tone solemn.

They didn't win this fight, child. I don't want to hurt you, but you had to learn a lesson. I am in control here. You will do as I say or there will be more moments of pain. Don't think for one second that they can save you. I'm getting out, and it's in your best interest to remain in my good graces, or my need for you will no longer hold significance to the bigger picture. Now, go rest. I need you stronger than your current state.

The overwhelming feeling of Malina's presence lifted from my body, and a whoosh of air left my lungs as I reoriented myself. Hands grabbed at me as I got up off the ground, but I shoved them away.

"I can't help you. Literally, I will be incapable of assisting you or she will kill me." There was no emotion left within me. Malina had taken it all with her when she left my mind. Maybe the next day I could process the new information with more clarity, but right then, all I wanted was to be left alone.

"We'll figure something out. She is not stronger than the council," Alexander said, but he lacked the conviction in his voice to convince me he believed his own words.

"Yes, we stopped her once and we will do it again," Fiona agreed. "Raegan, you need to keep this between us. Even if people begin to ask questions, you can't say anything. Not even to Enzo."

Feelings, and not of the positive sort, started to swirl within me at once again being told what I could or couldn't do, but the deadness that had settled over me stomped out any emotion before it could grow into anything I reacted upon.

Glancing around the room, I saw the concerned faces of each of the five, no wait, four council members. Desmond had already disappeared again, and I wanted to question it, but I wanted to sleep more. Whatever Malina had done to me made me give zero fucks about anything at the moment.

I didn't bother saying goodbye. I simply walked toward the door, assuming they'd get the point that I was done.

Bennett's voice raised as he objected to my departure, but once again, Headmaster Stone had my back and let me go. One of these days, I'd have to thank him, but today was not that day.

My eyes grew heavy, and I barely made it back to the room. Dinner forgotten, I threw myself onto my bed and sank into oblivion.

For the first time in weeks, there were no nightmares. There was nothingness.

No feelings, no thoughts, nothing.

And it was so much worse.

FINALS WEEK ENDED, AND I PASSED ALL OF MY TESTS. Some of them just barely, but it was enough to lift the weight that had been settled on my chest since I chose to become a second-year student. A plus side to passing my finals, I didn't have to spend my first break training, so Enzo decided to take off.

Before he left for break, he and Gemma had wanted to celebrate my successes, but I'd brushed them both off, which was a lot harder than I expected. They were each persistent in their own ways.

Malina had done a number on me and, while I no longer felt dead on the inside, I was scared shitless. I wouldn't even pretend like I wasn't out of my mind after her threats. They were very real, and she had some sort of hold over me that shouldn't have been possible.

But, I did my best to push it all to the side, because the following day was my birthday and I was expecting Aunt Jules to arrive any minute.

Standing in the courtyard, I watched the shield, waiting for her to appear. It had been a long nine weeks without her after having spent almost as many months depending on her to keep me from losing my mind.

As excited as I was for her arrival, I was equally frustrated we wouldn't be able to leave the grounds. The furthest I seemed to be able to go without pain assaulting me was the large arch entrance to the school and the more I thought about it, the more pissed off I became.

Taking a quick glance back at the academy, I eyed the gargoyles. They hadn't given me any more creeper vibes since the day I tried to leave with my friends, but I was still convinced they were watching me.

"Raegan!" Aunt Jules' excited voice cut through my thoughts as I turned back toward the entrance. She was running toward me, and I wished so badly I could meet her in the middle.

Stupid freaking sorceress.

Yes, my ire toward the bitch riding shotgun in my body had escalated in the last week. No, I didn't want to think about whether that was a good or bad thing. I was dealing and that was enough for the time being.

When my aunt's arms wrapped around me, a sense of rightness settled over me. She might not have been my blood family like I believed in the beginning, but she'd been there for me when I needed her most and that was more important than blood.

"I missed you," I whispered into her neck as we embraced.

"I missed you, too."

We stayed that way for several beats. I was afraid to pull away and have something go wrong. So much had recently that I had become a glass-half-empty kind of girl.

Finally, Jules pulled back and rested her hand on my cheek. "Show me everything."

I laughed. "You've been here more than me. I should have *you* show *me*."

"It's been a couple decades for me. Indulge an old lady?"

"Right. Old lady." Shaking my head, I tugged her back toward my room, so she could put her things away. Jules appeared more like she was in her mid-twenties than her forties thanks to her supernatural genes. She wouldn't be considered an old lady for many more decades, possibly centuries.

She rattled on about what was different and what was unsurprisingly still the same. Apparently, the open platform elevator was new, and she got a kick out of that. Just like human parents talked about walking five miles in the snow, uphill both ways when they were young, Jules complained about the many floors of stairs she used to have to traverse to get around the massive school.

"Did you have one of these?" I asked her as I pointed to my butler box.

"A mini-fridge? No, but that would have been convenient on study nights." She opened it up and frowned when it was empty. "Do you not use it?"

Instead of answering, I ordered us two smoothies like we used to get on the weekends back in Portland to show her how it worked.

"You lucky bitch. I would have killed for this when I was a student here."

"Yeah, I call it my butler box. I don't think it has an official name, so I gave it one," I said with a smile.

"When do I get to meet Gemma and the others? I want to see everything you've been up to."

I hadn't told Aunt Jules everything, or really much of anything, that had been going on at the school. I highlighted the classes and my friendship with Gemma, Peyton, and Finley, but she had no idea I was three races, Malina was hanging around, or anything about Enzo, who was thankfully gone for the break.

Guilt poked at me, but I didn't need her worry on top of my own. There was nothing she could do to help me, so I didn't see the point in dragging her into the mess I'd found myself in.

"You can probably meet Gemma right now. Then, we can go grab some lunch and hopefully find the others, if you'd like," I said.

"I'd love nothing more. Show me the way." The grin that graced her porcelain face confirmed I'd made the right decision in letting Jules think everything was going well.

We grabbed Gemma from her room, and she hugged Jules like they were old friends. The two of them took over the conversation, mostly using the time it took to get to the commissary to talk trash about me and my stubbornness, as if I wasn't standing right next to them.

After we grabbed our food, we headed toward our usual table. I had been so involved in the conversation, I missed the signs of an ambush I should have seen coming from a mile away.

"Hey, Mutt. Thanks for screwing up my fall break. Thanks to your freakishness, I'm stuck here for two weeks while my parents attempt to help the council fix whatever evil you've brought into this school. Why don't you do us all a favor and disappear?"

Her voice was loud enough that everyone in the commissary stopped what they were doing to pay attention to our group. Thankfully, more than half the school was gone, but she'd done the damage she sought to do. The bitch had put a target on my back.

"I don't know what you think you know, but I didn't do anything. Maybe your parents lied to you because they couldn't stand the thought of having your pretentious princess attitude around for longer than necessary." I knew that was probably a lie, but I was pissed her parents had shared what should have been privileged information with their psycho daughter.

My words had struck a nerve with her, and her voice lowered. "You don't know a damn thing about me, so don't pretend and pass the blame just because you're jealous I still have parents. I know what you are and soon the whole school will, too."

After taking a step toward her, my plate was the only thing separating us, and I considered slamming it into her face. "Bitch, don't push me. If you know what I am, then you should know better than to threaten me."

I knew the moment the words left my mouth, I was going to regret them, but I couldn't stop myself. Her snide comment about having parents put me at my limit.

"Alright, that's enough." Aunt Jules stepped between us as a teacher approached.

"Do we have a problem here?" Professor Daye asked.

Lyssa turned on her sweetness. "We were just catching up. Nothing to worry about here. I was actually just leaving with my friends."

She turned to her lackies and called out a goodbye like we were actually friends. The teacher seemed satisfied, but I was still shaking with fury. Gemma grabbed my arm as Jules took my plate that was beginning to crack under my hold.

Instead of continuing toward our normal table, we left the commissary and went back to the dorms. None of us said a word until we were back in my room with the door closed.

"What the shit was that?" Gemma demanded first.

Aunt Jules set our plates down and took a seat, patiently waiting for me to answer, but I wasn't sure what to say. I had admitted there was something going on, but I couldn't tell them the whole truth, only enough that they'd let it go with minimal questioning.

"I went back to the forbidden door a few weeks ago. It was unlocked, and I might have opened it," I admitted, stringing a story together as I went.

"The door to the dungeon?" Jules gaped. "That's never unlocked. Ever. There's so many layers of magic over it, there shouldn't even be a possibility of it happening on purpose."

"Well, it did, and I was the sorry soul who found it. Apparently, when I opened it, I took in some of the dark magic from below, but Headmaster Stone fixed me right up, so there's nothing to worry about, okay?"

Gemma threw her hands in the air. "Are you screwing with me? Nothing to worry about? I know you haven't been around our world your whole life, but you're smart enough to know the consequences of dealing with dark magic by now. Why didn't you tell me? Is that why you couldn't leave the academy with us? Why you still won't?"

Hurt and betrayal weighed heavy in her words. I couldn't imagine how she'd feel if she knew the whole truth. It took every ounce of willpower not to confess everything to both of them right then.

Ignoring her third question, I answered the first two. "Yes, the day I couldn't leave with you was the day I found out what had happened. When everything was done, I wasn't given a choice. Headmaster Stone said if I told anyone, I could be kicked out of school." That was a lie, but hopefully one they wouldn't question.

It did give me an idea of seeing if Lyssa could be kicked out, though. She just opened a can of worms the council had been fighting hard to keep hidden. They weren't going to be happy, and that was the only positive to the screwed-up situation.

"Raegan, are you sure there is nothing else happening?" Jules pressed. "I can help you, but only if you tell me what's going on."

Plastering the biggest fake smile on my face, I said, "Everything is great. Seriously, you two don't need to worry about me. Lyssa is just a pain in the ass. School is good. I'm fine. Let's just enjoy the few days we have and forget about what happened."

Neither of them seemed convinced, but they let it go, thankfully.

As much as I wanted to confide in them, it would only put a target on their backs as well, and I didn't need Malina to take her temper tantrums out on anyone I loved. I wasn't sure I'd survive if anything happened to Gemma or Jules because of what I had done.

I was on my own, and when Enzo came back, our training needed to double, so I could be prepared for what came next. Something told me Malina wasn't even close to being done with me. I just needed to figure out what she wanted before she took it from me.

The following day-and-a-half passed in a blur while I spent as much time with Jules as possible. She was only at Shadow Veil for two days, and I took full advantage of it. Gemma hung out with us most of the time, but I didn't mind.

Having Gemma around left little time for Jules to question more of what happened with Lyssa and the story I had told them. I had a feeling neither of them believed me, but since it had been my birthday, they were letting me off easy.

I had taken full advantage of that while I could, but Jules was leaving, and it was no longer my birthday. I wasn't sure what to expect.

Standing as far away from the school as I would dare to go, I hugged Jules tight. "I don't want you to go. It's been good having you around."

"I know. I've missed you, kid, but I'll be back again in eight weeks." She pulled away, both hands grasping my face. "I know you're keeping something from me, but I also know you're a big girl. Just remember, when you need me, call me. I won't push you for anything more unless I have to. Please, don't make me have to."

Tension I hadn't even realized I'd been holding on to released from my shoulders. It wasn't that I wanted to deal with things on my own, I just couldn't tell everyone the whole story, so there was no point in even trying, in my opinion.

"Thank you, Aunt Jules. It really means a lot to me. Everything you've done. It's more than anyone would have expected."

"I love you, Raegan." She hugged me once more.

"I love you, too."

When we pulled apart, tears were in our eyes, but no more words were spoken as I watched her walk away and disappear through the shield.

"Are you okay?"

"Holy shit! Don't do that," I snapped. Gemma had appeared behind me, seemingly out of nowhere.

"Oops. But seriously, are you alright? I wanted to check on you as soon as I knew she was gone."

"You certainly didn't waste any time." I laughed. "But yes, I'm fine. I'll see her again soon."

Her eyes narrowed at me and finger raised in the air, a little too close to my face. "Well, now that I don't have to feel guilty for yelling at you... What in the actual hell is going on? And don't give me that half-assed explanation from before. I know you're lying or at least omitting. Now, spill it."

My cheeks lifted as a smile appeared on my face. "You're insane, you know that?"

She nodded proudly. "The fact that you're already aware of that should be the exact reason you fill me in on what the hell is going on with you."

"I can't tell you," I said honestly.

"Bullshit. You know you can trust me."

"Let me rephrase. I physically can't tell you. The words won't leave my mouth without my head feeling like it's going to explode." This was going to be a pain in the ass, I already knew it.

"Like someone spelled you so you couldn't tell me?" The look of confusion confirmed my previous thought.

"We can't talk about this here." My eyes glanced up at the gargoyles as I wondered if they only saw or could also hear, and if they could, how well?

Gemma grabbed my hand and dragged me back to the dorms. We made it all the way back to my room without saying a word. A few students tried to talk to us on the way, but Gemma shushed them as I laughed.

Nothing about my situation was funny, but my best friend trying to force her way into it was a little entertaining.

When the door was closed and we were seated on my bed, she turned to me with the most serious look on her face. "Secrets don't make friends, Raegan."

"I'm well aware of that, but thanks for the reminder. If there was anything I could do, I would."

She hesitated, and I knew that whatever she was about to say, she really didn't want to. "There have been some rumblings over break. Not just from Lyssa. There are people that believe you came here to purposely let something sinister out of the dungeon, and you almost succeeded but Ryn stopped you."

"That's not exactly how it happened," I stated, a little pissed off that a variation of the truth was out there, but it was making me look bad.

"So, you didn't come here only to wreak havoc on our

academy, and you're not some undercover spy who could kill me in a thousand ways?"

She didn't actually look convinced that I wasn't, and my level of irritation was rising as anger built up. Not at Gemma, but at Malina for putting a gag order on me.

You don't need to be angry. You can share with your friend what has happened. She will either join us or die. If she breathes a word of it, I will find her and make sure she suffers. Slowly. So, pass that along at the same time, dear.

Stupid psycho witch. Always there, always listening.

That's sorceress to you, and watch your language. I won't tolerate disrespect without consequence. That's your only warning.

There were so many things I wanted to say, but instead, I kept my thoughts to myself as much as I could, only slightly relieved I could confide in someone. Still, I hesitated. I didn't want Gemma dragged into my shit any more than I wanted to be involved in it.

"Rae? What's happening?" Gemma's concerned voice filtered through my haze from listening to Malina.

"The *lovely* woman riding shotgun in my head gave me permission to tell you, but there was an equally charming threat that went along with it if you breathed a word to anyone else." My voice dripped with sarcasm and I really hoped Gemma would just run for the hills.

"Well, tell your friend I said thanks. Now, divulge all of your secrets. You shouldn't have to deal with this alone, or maybe you haven't been... Is that why you and Enzo have gotten so close? Does he have something over you? I knew that bastard was screwing with you."

"Easy, killer. Enzo doesn't know the whole story, either. At least, I don't think he does. I haven't seen him all week.

Our whatever-you-want-to-call-it has nothing to do with this situation."

"Okay, so what does?"

After taking a deep breath, I summarized as best I could everything that had happened since I arrived at Shadow Veil Academy, which was a lot more than I realized. My three races were first, which made her ask more questions I didn't have the answers to, then the woman's voice that started, the draw I had to the forbidden door of the dungeon, the day I was able to go in, and what happened in the Courtyard of Tranquility.

Then, I explained the meeting with the headmaster after I couldn't go through the shield, and the gargoyles I was convinced were watching me.

"The gargoyles? Really?" she laughed. "There was this story when I was a child that the dragons created them for their lairs as guards and if we ever saw one, we needed to run as far in the opposite direction as possible or we'd face the dragon's fire."

"Well, I have no idea what it means, so your guess is as good as mine."

I continued to tell her about the last meeting with the council and what happened when Alexander tried to compel me to spill all my secrets, followed by learning who Malina was, and still having no idea what she wanted with me.

"Damn, girl. You've been going through all of this and *still* managed to pass your finals? You're superwoman. This is some seriously messed-up shit you've found yourself in. Now, people are saying all that stuff... I'll do what I can, but I can't really defend as good as I'd like to without telling your secrets."

Shaking my head furiously, I said, "Don't you dare try to

help. I have no idea if Malina could follow through on her threat or not, but I'd rather not find out. It's enough to know you know I'm not an evil wench sent here to do whatever it is they think I'm doing."

"I'll be honest, Peyton and Finley are a little on the fence. They reached out to me and asked what I knew. I did my best to defend you, but I didn't really know anything then. I still won't say anything to them, though hopefully they'll understand without me needing to. Try not to hold it against them if they don't, though. They're pure blood and were raised a little less understanding than us hybrids."

My mind was emotionally spent and, instead of questioning that statement, I decided it was the perfect evening for a girls' night in: movies, junk food, and alcohol, if available.

"Can you get us wine?" I asked, changing the subject.

"Duh. That's a stupid question, and you can now, too. As supernaturals, we're considered consenting adults at eighteen for all things. What do you have in mind?"

"A couple rom-coms, all the crap food we want, and wine until I can no longer think about everything we just talked about," I replied with a shrug.

"Done. You pick the movies, and I'll be back with the goods."

Gemma was out the door before I could even reply, and I was more than grateful for her. Almost even a little appreciative to Malina for not practically killing me when I needed to tell my best friend everything.

I'm not evil. You'll soon learn that. We're going to do great things together, child.

Ignoring her and the hope that she wasn't completely batshit crazy, I prepared for my much-needed girls' night and pretended my life wasn't a complete wreck.

THE FOLLOWING DAY WAS HALLOWEEN, AND EVEN though I was slowly becoming the outcast of the school, Gemma somehow convinced me it was a great idea to go to the big bash planned out by the lake I had never seen.

It was hidden within the shifter forest, but she assured me, it would be perfectly safe. There was little doubt that would be the case considering my run of bad shit happening as of late, but she really wanted to go. Since she had been there for me the night before, I agreed.

Standing in front of the mirror next to her, both of us dressed as flapper girls from the twenties with black and gold glittery dresses and fishnet stockings, I was beginning to regret it.

"Are you sure this is a good idea?" I asked.

"We look sexy as hell. We are *not* missing this party. Get your big girl panties on and get ready for your first supernatural party. It will be one you never forget, I promise."

I scoffed at her words, because I wasn't sure if it would be a bad or good thing that I never forgot it. Regardless, she wasn't letting me back out.

"We're fashionably late, so let's head out. The party started about two hours ago. Hopefully, everyone will already be well on their way to drunk and not even pay attention to you," she said, probably trying to be reassuring, but it didn't work.

We walked out of the room, and a few others were going in the same direction as us, but they gave us a wide berth. I tried to tell myself it was just a coincidence, but it didn't bode well for my confidence that everything would be fine.

Ten or so minutes later, we entered the forest, and the

music finally sounded a few minutes after that. Gemma moved along even faster as we got closer, but I pulled her back.

"If you expect me to arrive at this party in one piece, you're going to need to slow it down before I eat shit in these heels you stuffed my feet into, woman," I said.

"Beauty is pain. Come on." No mercy came from her as I stumbled my way through the forest, using the trees to keep myself from falling over.

When we arrived, Gemma promised to stay close, but I knew that was going to be an issue. Everyone loved her, and even though she was with me, it didn't stop them from trying to get her attention.

Thankfully, not everyone ignored me.

"Hey, Rae," Embry called from across the party with a big smile that showcased his perfect white teeth and dimples.

I waved back but didn't go to him when he waved me over. He was with his friends, and I felt relatively safer standing behind Gemma when she spoke with a few other students.

Sipping on some elven wine, I paid more attention to my drink than the stares of those around me. The only blessing was that Lyssa didn't appear to be in attendance, so at least nobody would call me out publicly. Hopefully.

A warm hand settled on my back, and I slowly turned to see who thought they knew me well enough to lay hands on me. Surprise rolled through me when my eyes met Embry's.

"Having fun?" he whispered in my ear as he leaned in.

"Sure."

"Sure? That's not really an answer. Come on, I'll loosen you up."

Before I could object, he pulled me away from Gemma.

All she did was give me two thumbs up. Shaking my head at her, I mouthed "help", but she only laughed, refusing to come to my aid. Traitor.

Embry led me to the dance area, which was a lot darker than where I had been standing before, so I decided it maybe wasn't such a bad idea. Less people would be able to stare at me.

We danced to a couple of songs, and I was finally relaxing and enjoying myself. Then, a slow song came on, and I tensed back up. It was one thing to dance *next* to Embry, but I wasn't sure I was ready to have his hands on me.

"One more?" he asked with his hand out.

His smile was sincere and, honestly, who was I kidding? Embry was hot with his dimples, dark skin, and bright eyes. I would be an idiot to tell him no.

Instead of answering, I put my hand in his and let him pull me close. His hands settled just above my ass, while mine wrapped around his neck. Inhaling as he started to spin us around, all I could smell was booze and trees, but I didn't care. Surprisingly, I was having fun.

When the song ended, his lips pressed to my neck and he pulled away. "How about we get another drink?"

Nerves slammed into me as I pictured Enzo and when he had almost kissed me. Was I ready to move on from the drama he brought me? I didn't know the answer to that question, but I was going to find out. I needed to decide my feelings for Enzo and move forward, because the sexual tension between us for the last two months was getting old.

"Sounds great," I said with a smile.

He grabbed two drinks and led me further away from the party, but not far enough that I couldn't still see Gemma chatting with Peyton and Finley who must have arrived while I was dancing with Embry.

"Thanks for the dances. Did you have fun?" he asked

"I did. Thanks for dragging me out there."

"Why do you sound so surprised?" He laughed.

"I just have a lot going on right now and didn't expect any of tonight to be enjoyable, to be honest."

He took a step closer and ran his knuckles down my arm before intertwining our fingers. "I'm glad I could help bring a smile to your face. You should do it more often."

My breath hitched. He was only inches from my mouth, and his eyes weren't looking anywhere other than my lips. I had mere seconds to decide if I wanted to back away. Instead of overthinking for those few seconds, I pressed forward, closing the gap myself, deciding that I only lived once and waiting on Enzo wasn't an option.

My body hummed as Embry's hands roamed my back before grabbing my ass and bringing me flush with his body. My fingers entangled in his hair as he angled his head to take the kiss deeper.

A groan slipped out from one of us, and I was having the best kiss of my life until a deep rumble sounded from behind me and my body froze. Embry pushed me behind him, but when my eyes found the source of the noise, I realized he should have been behind me.

"Enzo, what are you doing?" I asked defensively.

He didn't answer. Instead, he stomped over to us and Embry moved out of his way. I didn't blame Embry for being afraid. I would have done the same in his position, but I was a little disappointed he didn't even try to object at least once.

"Hey, I asked you a question," I said to Enzo and still didn't get a response.

Instead, he pulled me into his arms, then lifted me up to cradle my body against his chest before addressing Embry. "Don't touch her again, Witch. She is mine."

"Uh, no I'm not, asshole. You don't get to claim me like I have no choice. Now, put me down," I demanded with a rising voice.

His attention moved from Embry to me, and I immediately regretted yelling at him. Enzo's eyes were almost black, and his chest vibrated beneath me.

"Mine."

That one word was filled with a pain I couldn't identify and my heart hurt for him as my emotions warred with each other. I didn't want to give in to him, but I was afraid someone would get seriously hurt if I didn't.

"Okay," I replied and sincerely hoped I wouldn't regret it as he carried me away from Embry and the rest of the party. My only hope was that he had answers I needed, and he was willing to give them, or I was going to use any means necessary to force what I wanted to know out of him.

Still cradled in Enzo's arms, I stayed silent all the way back to the dorms. I assumed we were going back to mine, but when he passed the hybrid wing, my curiosity piqued.

"Where are we going?" I asked softly, feeling like I was talking more to a beast than a man with the tension I felt rolling off him.

"My room." His jaw ticked while his grip tightened on me.

"Can I ask why and what this is all about?"

He ignored my question, and I let out a huff while crossing my arms. I debated trying to get free, but I was genuinely curious as to what was going on with him. He hadn't outwardly expressed any feelings toward me since the night we almost kissed, so none of his actions or words were making sense.

The platform in the elven wing took us to the top floor, and I decided their dorms were considerably nicer than the hybrid ones. The décor was more modern, the floors shinier, and the common room was twice the size.

When Enzo stepped off the platform, I noticed there was only one door on his floor. "Are you by yourself up here?" I asked.

His nod was slight as he keyed in the code to open his door.

My gaze moved inside the massive suite Enzo called home. It was more of a penthouse than a dorm room, and I was immediately jealous.

Floor-to-ceiling windows took up half of the east wall, there was a full kitchen to my right, two more doors to my left, which I assumed led to the bedroom and a bathroom, and then a living room four times the size of my entire dorm.

After wiggling out of his hold, I walked toward the kitchen, and my hand glided over the smooth granite countertops while I admired the stainless-steel appliances he probably never used. Turning around, I went to the windows. His view overlooked the Courtyard of Tranquility, and longing slammed into me as I remembered the day I tried to enjoy its beauty not so long ago.

From above, I could see the tops of the weeping willow trees and acres of plush green grass lit up by antique streetlights guiding a path toward a small stream. My hand pressed against the glass as I once again wondered if I'd ever be able to experience it for myself.

"Raegan," Enzo whispered, his breath hot on my neck.

Afraid to turn around, I stayed facing the window. "Yes?"

"Did I scare you?"

Without hesitation, I turned around, no longer worried about his close proximity. I was more eager to see the expression on his face. "Why would you have scared me? Were you acting like a psycho? Yes. But I figured there was a reason for it, and I'd beat it out of you if I needed to."

The smirk I had a love-hate relationship with appeared on his face. "I love your spunk and that you say what's on your mind instead of what you think I want to hear."

"What's going on with you, Enzo?" I asked, ignoring his compliment. Talking about our feelings wasn't enough of an explanation for him appearing out of nowhere and scaring Embry half to death by acting like a caveman.

"I went to see someone during break and learned a few things. You can't trust anyone here. There are too many people that want to hurt you, and I will do everything I can to make sure nobody hurts my little dragon."

His hands cupped my face, but I backed up and pushed him away. "What did you just call me?"

His eyes widened as he realized the words he'd used, but it was too late, and he had some explaining to do. Last I knew, Enzo's memories had been wiped, and he was no longer supposed to know I was part dragon. He shouldn't have remembered the nickname he'd used for me a couple of times.

"Raegan, listen. You don't understand." He stepped closer again, but I moved away from the window, so I was no longer trapped.

"No, you listen first. I've had some screwed-up stuff happen to me while I've been here, and I don't have time for secrets. You either tell me what you know, or I'm leaving and going back to that party, so I can pretend none of this happened before I lose my shit."

My hands shook as I tried to figure out what was happening. Enzo claimed me in front of a whole party of students. He knew I was not only a hybrid, but also a dragon shifter, and he apparently had friends who knew things about me as well.

Enzo seemed to hesitate, but I didn't back down. My stare intensified until he blinked, muttering a curse, and I knew I'd won.

"Elves are the original power source. If prepared, there is a way to prevent a compulsion. They didn't remove my memories, they only tried to force me to remember them differently. Though, I knew it was coming and took precautions."

"What does that mean?" I snapped. I wasn't going to let him off the hook when he was barely answering my question. It wasn't enough for me to believe he wasn't one of the people I shouldn't trust.

"There is a concoction an elf can take to prevent their memories from being messed with. A little sage mixed with turmeric along with a few magic words will keep you protected for up to forty-eight hours. I knew the council would want as few loose ends as possible, so I let them believe it worked."

"Why? Why do it, and why tell me now?" There was a table between us at that point and I took a seat, making sure he knew I wasn't leaving until I had answers, no matter what I had threatened before.

"Things are changing. Malina is growing stronger, and you need to be protected."

My heart stuttered. "How do you know about Malina?"

"Hold on." Enzo moved to one of the closed doors and disappeared for a few seconds before appearing right next to me, holding out his hand.

Within his palm was a teardrop-shaped stone attached to a delicate looking chain. The pendant was blue with white streaks running through it, and a wire was wrapped around the top, keeping it secured to a silver chain.

"What is this?" I asked in awe, absorbing the energy pulsing from it.

"Kyanite Stone. Put it on," he insisted, but didn't give me time to grab it before taking care of the task himself.

The gem was cool against my skin, but the moment the clasp was done, the necklace warmed, and I felt like a weight had been lifted off me.

"This will keep Malina out for a little while, maybe a week. But, as she grows stronger, the stone will weaken faster."

"As much as I appreciate this gift, I'm only going to ask one more time, Enzo. How do you know about Malina?"

Instead of answering, he began pacing around his living room, mumbling about expectations and family obligations. I didn't understand anything he was saying, but I grew more nervous by the second. As much as a part of me wanted to walk away from him, I knew he was one of the few people in my life who could help me through whatever was happening to me.

"Enzo?" My voice was hard, catching his attention once again.

"I know someone who works in the dungeon. I can't tell you more than that, but I need you to trust me. I wish I never would have brought you here, but I hadn't had a choice. Now, I'm going to fix it. I promise."

My fingers toyed with the stone against my chest as I thought about his words. Was I ready to blindly trust him just because he knew a guy and had been tutoring me? I didn't even know if I was mentally capable of making the correct decision of whether or not to trust him.

With my girly bits still doing somersaults when he was around, I had no idea if it was my pent-up sexual tension telling me to trust him or my sensible head. Unfortunately, only time was going to tell, and with Lyssa having blasted my supposed evil intentions all over the school, I needed more allies than I already had.

"Fine," I snapped at him even though he wasn't really the person I was mad at.

"Fine, what?" He grinned.

"You win. Keep your secrets. Give me stones to keep Malina out. Tutor me. Whatever. As long as the school no longer thinks I'm the devil's daughter here to ruin all things Shadow Veil, then I'll try to be cooperative in whatever it is you have planned."

His deep laugh filled the room. "What makes you think I have a plan?"

"Well, you forced me here, had a necklace for me, and spilled some of your secrets. If you don't have a plan, then you're kind of an idiot and I should probably go."

His hand reached for mine, the table no longer between us. "I don't have a concrete plan, but I promise I have only the best intentions, Raegan. I meant it when I said I wouldn't let anyone hurt you. If you haven't figured it out by now, you've gotten under my skin."

I snorted. "Actually, no, I haven't noticed. Please, enlighten me on your feelings and intentions."

My body was suddenly pressed against the wall without a moment's notice, and Enzo's eyes bored into mine as he pushed closer, only clothes separating our bottom halves. His honey eyes swirled with gold this time as his fingertips traced along my jawline, down my neck, and around my collarbone before starting over again.

"I might not have a beast within me like shifters do to claim their mates, but you're mine, Raegan. I knew it the first time I laid eyes on you. Your soul called to mine like a siren. I tried to fight it for the longest time, but I'm done fighting it now. Consequences be damned."

Before I could question what consequences he was referring to, his lips pressed against mine, and when I gasped in surprise, he took the opportunity to deepen the kiss with his tongue. All coherent thoughts left my mind.

Lust, pure and strong, crashed into me, and I finally understood why other supernaturals weren't afraid of a little PDA. If Enzo was to kiss me like he was then in public, I wouldn't have given a shit about what others thought, either.

My hands snaked under his shirt, and I felt his muscles bunch and pull as my fingers traced every line they could find.

He, on the other hand, didn't touch me with his hands. They stayed right next to my head, keeping me locked in against the wall, but his tongue and body were doing enough damage to me that I didn't worry about it. I might have combusted if he put forth all of his efforts.

Vibrations from his pocket startled me, and I almost bit down on his tongue before he backed away just enough to pull a phone from his pocket.

"Hey, why do you get one of those?" I pouted, missing being able to text my aunt whenever I wanted.

"It's all in who you know, but it's not always a good thing, so don't be too upset." His brow narrowed. "I gotta go, but this right here isn't a one-time thing, Raegan, and I don't share. That witch better keep his hands off you."

The last bit was said with more jealousy than I anticipated, but I patted his chest. "I don't share, either, and I don't do drama, so keep Lyssa away from me."

As much as I wanted to see all of what Enzo could offer, especially after that kiss, it wasn't worth it if I had to worry about bitch drama.

"Don't worry. I already heard the rumors, and they'll be a distant memory by Monday morning. Lyssa isn't as bad as she acts. She just needs to understand that what we had is over and I've moved on, so she needs to as well."

He made it sound so easy, but Lyssa had that vengeful vibe going for her. No way was she ready to wave the white flag and admit defeat. That crazy bitch was going to fight for what she thought was hers until she decided otherwise. Not for any other reason or person.

He kissed me once more. "I really do have to go, but I'll take you back to your dorm first."

My first thought was to object. I was a big girl and could find my way home, but before I could say anything, my stomach was turned inside out. When I blinked, we were standing in front of my door, and a smirk was plastered to Enzo's face.

"You enjoy that entirely too much," I groaned as I got my bearings back.

Being a hybrid had its advantages, especially when I could practice both witch and elven magic, but it also meant I sometimes missed out on certain perks by not being pure blooded. Teleporting like Enzo had was one of the elf traits I wish I did have.

"I'll see you soon. If it's not tomorrow, then I'll meet you before school Monday morning. I can walk you to your first class," he said, leaning against my doorframe.

"Sure. Are you going to carry my books for me, too?" I teased.

He moved in closer and lowered his voice. "If you had books to carry, I certainly would."

Sexy bastard knew how to make a girl swoon. Too well.

With one last kiss, we said our goodbyes and I slipped into my room as he disappeared to wherever he had to go. I realized I never asked him what his text had been about, but I didn't really care. I wasn't a nag before arriving at Shadow Veil, and I wasn't going to start being one now.

I was mentally exhausted, and my body was feeling pretty heavy, so I didn't even bother to turn on my light or get out pajamas. Instead, I began stripping off my clothes and fell into bed in nothing more than my bra and underwear.

My arm stretched out, and I screamed when I made contact with another body. "Lumad," I said, for "light" in witch magic.

When my light came on, I was already halfway across my room, ready to fight, practically naked. But, when my eyes focused in on the blonde hair and thin frame of my best friend, I relaxed.

"What the hell, Gemma?" I asked as I began pulling my clothes back on, no longer half-asleep.

"What the hell is right. Where have you been?" she demanded.

"I was with Enzo. He showed up and—"

She moved off my bed, cutting me off. "I *know* what happened. He practically ripped you away from Embry while shaking with rage as he carried you away from the party before disappearing into the trees. Where did he take you?"

"Back to his place. What's the big deal?" I asked, concerned my friend was going a little crazy. "I know you don't like him, but your reaction is a little much, don't you think?"

I wasn't trying to be rude; I was just being honest. I didn't understand her hostility toward him. Unless there was something she wasn't telling me, she was overreacting.

"I'm sorry, Rae. There's just *something* about him. I can't read him most of the time, and when I can, his aura is all over the place. I don't like you with him."

Gemma's witch specialty was reading auras. It wasn't an ability I had mastered yet, but it was one she had done rather well since she was a kid. I understood better then why she was so hesitant about Enzo, but she also didn't know he was more powerful than he let on.

Him being able to prevent his mind from being messed with and knowing that I needed the necklace to get a reprieve from Malina was far beyond any second-year student I knew, but it wasn't my knowledge to share, even if Gemma did know about Malina.

"I know you don't like it, but I'm going to give him a chance," I said. "And it would make my life a lot easier if you did, too. I'm not saying you have to start giving him hugs when you see him, but a little less hostility would be cool."

She sighed. "This is really happening?"

"I think so."

"Fine, but if he starts hogging so much of your time that I never see you, then I make no promises as to my actions," she pouted.

"I promise that will never happen. If it helps, I give you full permission to kick my ass if it does." I reached my arms out to her. We'd both had a long night, and I could go for a hug from my friend before I crawled back into bed.

She met me in the middle and we hugged it out. "Why don't you stay in my room tonight?" I asked.

"Fine, but no boy talk unless we're talking trash. Like, did you see Silas rubbing his junk all over Abby tonight?"

And just like that, everything went back to normal. My only hope was our first day back from break went just as smoothly. Something told me that wasn't going to be the case.

The following Monday had been... interesting, to say the least. That was the only way I could have described it. The glares and sneers from the other students were minimal as long as I was with Enzo, but when I wasn't, it was made very clear I was still an outcast.

I didn't say anything to him, though. I was a big girl, officially an adult, and could handle my own problems. Or so I hoped.

Three weeks into the second semester, more than halfway through November, the little voice in my head kept warning me this was the calm before the storm.

Thankfully, that little voice was not Malina. Her voice hadn't been able to penetrate the magic of the stone Enzo had given me. He had taken the necklace and powered it back up twice already, even though it hadn't seemed to be dulling at all, but I could still sense her wrath brewing just beneath the surface, and the call I felt toward the dungeon continued to grow.

"What are we doing tonight?" Peyton asked at lunch.

Fridays were deemed mandatory "girls' day" and I

wasn't allowed to hang out with Enzo on those days. Even though our relationship was going slowly, we spent a lot of time together as he continued to tutor me, and it was nice to take a break from him, if I was being honest.

"Last week it was hiking through the forest, so I vote for something more relaxing this time," Finley answered.

"Dinner in the Courtyard of Tranquility?" Gemma suggested, and my entire body tensed.

I still hadn't tried to go there again, and I wasn't about to let my second attempt be in front of my friends. It had taken a solid week for Peyton and Finley to warm up to me after Lyssa had convinced half the school I was pure evil. I didn't need them to back away again.

Some might have faulted them for their lack of loyalty when I was going through a hard time, but I didn't. I was a stranger to them. I didn't hang out with them nearly as much as Gemma, and they didn't know my secrets like she did.

Trust was a two-way street, and I wouldn't be a hypocrite by judging them for their lack thereof.

"Nah, it's too cold at night now, even for us supernaturals," Peyton said, allowing me to relax some. "How about every other week we be lazy in one of our dorm rooms and the other weeks we get out to do something adventurous?"

"I think that sounds like the best idea I've heard all week," I finally piped in. "Who wants to volunteer their room first?"

All three of them raised their hands, and we broke out in unnecessary laughter. After lunch, it was decided we'd start in Finley's room, and I had to admit I was nervous. I had only been to the vampire dorms once before, and nobody made a move to suck my blood or anything, but it still creeped me out.

Eventually, someone was bound to snap.

When we parted ways, I headed toward my History of Elora class, which I was excelling in. Research had become my favorite pastime as of late, but the more I did, the more questions I had.

Sitting at my desk in the furthest corner from Lyssa, I swiped through the pages on my tablet as the professor droned on about the middle ages of Elora. The only subjects that ever truly held my attention were the creation of supernaturals and the ending of Elora.

My mind was convinced there was something I was missing, a connection I had to all of it, but there was still no word from the council on who my parents were, so I had no idea how any of it truly pertained to me. Except for the fact that Malina needed me for something.

At the end of history class, Enzo met me outside the door to walk to Accelerated Elven Abilities. It was the only class I was still behind in, but Professor Trinket cut me some slack since I was a hybrid. There weren't a lot of elven hybrids, so they really had no idea what to expect out of me.

"Are you sure you have to go with the girls tonight?" Enzo sulked.

"Very sure. Gemma is just now warming up to you. I'd rather not piss her off."

He scoffed. "You call that warming up? She lit my ass on fire two days ago when I was leaving your room."

I shrugged. "Fire is warm, isn't it? And it didn't actually burn you, so don't be so sensitive."

"You two have twisted minds."

I didn't bother disagreeing with him.

Glancing out the window, I noticed the rain coming down and wished the shield around the academy protected us from the elements as well. I wouldn't have complained about living all school year in seventy-degree weather.

"I seriously don't understand why the girls don't wear pants," I said randomly. "They have to be freezing this time of year."

Shortly after we learned I couldn't leave the school grounds, Gemma had taken my pants size and grabbed me several more pairs of black pants from town and a couple for herself, but I'd yet to see her wear them to class. I gave her another week, tops, before she caved.

"Most girls only care about what they look like, not how they feel. Another reason why I keep you around. You don't give a shit what other people think."

"Neither do you, Mr. Mysterious," I teased.

"Mr. Mysterious, huh? How'd I earn that nickname?"

Peeking up at the teacher, I made sure we weren't missing anything important. "Well, when I really think about it, I don't know a lot about you. I know you're full elf, but I don't know who your parents are. You never talk about your time before Shadow Veil. You don't really have any friends or even hobbies. You're always 'busy', but I have no idea what you're doing."

He looked away before commenting, seeming lost in thought. "You've never asked. I didn't think you wanted to know."

Ah, he was going to play that card. Game on.

"Who are your parents?" I asked casually.

"My father was Luca and my mother's name was Gemini—after her two different-colored eyes. They died when I was young."

Okay, maybe I shouldn't have started there, but I wasn't going to stop. My parents were dead, too. He knew I understood the pain.

"What's your favorite hobby?"

He hummed a moment before answering. "Fighting. More accurately, teaching combat."

"Seriously?" I said a little too loudly and caught the attention of the teacher.

"Ms. Keyes, Mr. Vaughn. Is there something more interesting you'd like to share with the class? I know my droning can be a bit much at times, but we are in school. If you aren't here to learn, what are you here for?"

His questions were rhetorical, but Enzo didn't seem to care. He stood up from his chair in the back of the class. "Sorry, Professor Trinket, but Professor Nyx beat you to this subject last year, and I already taught Raegan about power absorption."

The teacher cocked his head. "Is that so? Well, then. If you're such an expert at it, then why don't you come up here and teach the class?"

There was a challenge in his voice, and I pulled on Enzo's hand. "Just sit back down."

Professor Trinket was one of our more relaxed teachers, but he wasn't a saint and Enzo was pushing him too far.

"I'd love to," Enzo answered and pulled his hand from my grip. "Though, I'm better at doing than I am at speaking."

Enzo was already halfway down the steps, moving swiftly toward the front of the class, a grin firmly in place.

"Alright. Let's see what you can *show* us, Mr. Vaughn. Give me your best attempt at absorption."

Oh, this was going to be so bad. I knew Enzo held back most of the time, at least, when he was tutoring me and when we were practicing abilities in class.

When Enzo stood before Professor Trinket, the two of them wore identical smirks. Both of them were sure they could best the other and knock them down a peg. The class was eerily silent as everyone waited to see who would come out on top.

"An elf draws their power from deep within," Enzo began. "Before you can take another's ability, you must have full control of your own. Once you've strengthened your core, utilize your hands and send a tether to your target."

In a matter of seconds, Enzo was rubbing his hands together, and a dark grey, almost-black glow emanated around them. When he seemed confident enough, Enzo held his hand out, and I saw the moment Professor Trinket knew he was about to be bested. His eyes narrowed as he tried to fight Enzo's power, but there was no use.

Within a minute, the professor was on his knees, sweat beading on his forehead. "I think you've proved your point, Enzo."

"If you're sure," he goaded before pulling back his magic, then turned to the class. "Focus on your inner being and only when you've mastered your own power should you try to take another's."

Enzo waltzed back to his seat, grinning the whole way.

"You've just put a target on our backs. You know that, right?" I hissed when he sat down.

"Nah, Trinket likes a challenge. He'll be back for more. I know it."

I sighed and hoped he was right. I was finally feeling comfortable in my classes; I didn't need any setbacks. Hell, I couldn't afford any at this point.

Friday night and Saturday afternoon passed in a blur as I hung out with all three girls first and then spent

Saturday with just Gemma. That was until I received an email on my tablet from Enzo telling me to be ready for a training session that required "inconspicuous clothing".

Making up an excuse, I left Gemma's room and headed back to mine, letting her know I'd be in for the rest of the night. She was used to me preferring to spend my evenings studying, so I almost felt guilty when she didn't question me, but I was too intrigued to worry about it for long.

After I was dressed in my signature black pants and a grey hoodie, I brushed my hair and pulled it back into a small ponytail. It had grown a couple of inches since I'd arrived, and I was able to once again pull it back from my face. If Enzo wanted me to go for stealthy, then my hair needed to be out of my face.

A knock sounded at my door, and I took my time going to open it. Even though I was eager to know what he had planned, he didn't need to know that.

"Oh, hey," I said when I walked out of my room to join him in the hall.

"Ready?" he asked, and I noticed he was also wearing a hoodie, along with dark jeans that fit his lean legs just right to draw my attention.

"Yep. Let's go."

His hand wrapped around mine as he pulled me down the hallway, moving faster than normal. "Are you in a hurry?" I asked with a slight laugh.

"Sorta. Actually, hold on."

I didn't bother to object. I knew what "hold on" meant. Within the next second, we were outside of his room, and I breathed a sigh of relief when I didn't experience any nausea. I was finally getting the hang of teleporting with him, and my stomach no longer revolted against me every time he did it.

"Did you forget something? I thought we were going somewhere for training." When he told me to dress discreetly, hanging out in his room hadn't crossed my mind as a possibility.

He didn't answer, just opened his door and pulled me inside before closing it behind us, then led me into his dining area where a table for two was set with a candle lit in the middle. On each side of the candle were covered dinner plates and wine glasses filled with red liquid that looked like elven wine.

"What's all of this? I thought we were training." I was so confused. Had I read the email wrong? No, it couldn't be that. Enzo was dressed similarly to me.

"We've never had an actual date. I thought we could tonight."

A laugh built within me, but I managed to hold myself together. "And the dark clothes?"

"They should come in handy for part, but they were also just to throw you off. I thought you might tell me no if I asked you outright." Enzo oozed confidence with almost everything he did, but gone was the cocky guy I first met. In his place was another who was showing his true feelings, maybe even for the first time.

"Really?" I asked surprised.

"I guess. When you pointed out that you didn't know anything about me, it got me thinking. Now, we're on a date."

"I see. Well, let's get to it then. Whatever you've ordered smells amazing."

When I moved to pull my chair out, he beat me to it, offering me a smile when I narrowed my eyes at him. Something told me he was up to more than just wanting a date from me, and I wasn't ready to let my guard down just yet.

Before he stepped away, he lifted the lid to my plate and moved it to the opposite side of the table after doing the same with his.

Thick cuts of meat drizzled in a green sauce with the brightest-colored veggies I'd ever seen covered the plate. My inhale was deep, and I savored every smell that permeated the air around me.

Without waiting for him, I dug in eagerly. The green sauce was something with avocado and lime that made my tongue tingle with delicious flavors. Groans probably too inappropriate for a technical first date left my mouth as I continued to eat everything on my plate.

Glancing over at Enzo, I realized I was probably being rude. We were supposed to be on our first official date, and I'd paid more attention to my food than him.

"Why aren't you eating?" I asked.

His eyes heated, but another emotion flashed within them I couldn't quite read. "I'm rather enjoying watching you indulge. I take it you like the meal?"

Covering a yawn, I nodded. "Probably the best I've ever had. What's in this sauce?"

A food coma was going to hit me hard if I didn't slow down on eating.

"Eh. Just a few secret ingredients. Try the wine." He pushed a glass into my hand.

Smelling it first, it seemed sweeter than the wine I'd had the previous weekend with my friends, but it still seemed tantalizing in my current state.

As soon as the first taste hit my lips, a zap of energy ran through me. "Wow, that's some powerful stuff."

He drank his own drink, seeming to relax considerably. "I'm glad you like it. After we finish eating, I want to take you somewhere."

Ah, this was where the dark clothes came in.

"I'm going to guess somewhere we're not supposed to be?" I grinned.

"It wouldn't be memorable otherwise." He returned my smile and started in on his own food.

Once we were both done, we left his dorm and walked downstairs instead of teleporting like he normally preferred to do. When we finally made it outside, he zapped us to the tallest peak within Shadow Veil's shield. Bliss filled me as my eyes moved across the landscape before us.

The academy was further off in the distance, and I didn't even realize we could get this far from it. The shifter forest was between us and the school, stretching for miles I didn't know existed.

"We're going to have to come here more often," I insisted with awe ringing in my voice.

Warm arms wrapped around me as Enzo's lips pressed against my neck. He mumbled something, but I missed it, already lost in the beauty around us and his body pressing against mine.

This was so much better than the training session I assumed he had planned. I only needed to figure out how to turn more of our tutor times into moments like this one.

The rest of November flew by as I settled into a new normal. Monday through Thursday were spent focused on studying and training. Then on Fridays, I still had school, but it continued to be mostly spent with my friends. The weekends were typically spent with Enzo, without the stress of tutoring hanging over us.

The most exciting part about the last month was Headmaster Stone said if I passed my finals with Cs or better, then I could end my tutoring sessions and continue on as a normal second-year student.

I had taken to the course work with no problems over the last several months. The only things I still struggled with were my advanced elven abilities and remembering when it was best to utilize which race within me.

Enzo assured me the latter would come with time, but neither he nor Headmaster Stone could be certain I would ever be able to fully embrace my elven side. We still didn't know how much dragon was within me, because there still hadn't been any clues as to who my birth parents were.

When the time arrived for finals, Enzo and Gemma

both helped me with my studies, and I ended up getting only one C and the rest were Bs. We had celebrated as a group with lots of elven wine.

Second term break was upon us, and we weren't back in school until after the New Year. While all of my friends were heading home to see their families, I was still stuck at Shadow Veil Academy.

"I'm sorry, Raegan. We have been fighting Malina for weeks, but we can't break the connection she has formed with you. To be honest, we're barely keeping her contained any longer," Headmaster Stone said in our latest meeting.

We'd begun meeting weekly. They'd taken blood, hair, saliva, and even magic samples in attempts to locate my parents, but it was as if they didn't exist. Whoever had taken me went to great lengths to guarantee there would be no way to link me back to my family.

"I was really hoping to go to New Orleans with Jules, but I understand. She said she would come here, and Enzo will be around as well," I replied.

"Just know I'm really proud of how far you've come. The supernatural life suits you, and it's nice to see you settled in. You haven't had any problems, right?"

Hesitation took over as I thought about the only "problem" I'd had outside of Malina.

Lyssa.

She still attempted to screw with me on occasion, but she'd finally started seeing someone new, and it gave me hope that she'd officially be done with her games after break.

"Nah, just the usual teenage drama. Nothing to be concerned with," I said with a smile.

"Very well. I'll see you next week, then."

While leaving his office, I glanced back at him and

noticed the deep creases in his forehead that hadn't been there when I'd first arrived at the academy back in August. Malina was taking a toll on everyone.

Enzo met me downstairs just outside the entrance to Magic Hall. "Everything okay?"

"Yep. Same old, same old. No news on *any* fronts." I tried to keep the disappointment out of my voice but failed.

"I'm sorry, Rae." He gave my hand a squeeze.

"It's whatever. As much as I have enjoyed my time here, I'm getting a little stir crazy, so it would have been nice to be able to leave during break, but maybe next time."

Enzo had eased my cabin fever each week as best he could. He continued to teleport us to every corner of the shield, showing me all of the places I would have never found on my own. The only area we hadn't been back to was the hidden elven room in the library.

Each time I had tried to go back, there were too many other students around, but I was determined to venture back there during break when everything would be less crowded around the school.

"I'm going to go say goodbye to Gemma. I'll catch up with you later." Giving him a quick kiss, I stepped away to head toward the hybrid dorms. Except, before I could get too far, he called my name.

When I twisted back around, his eyes were on me, swirling with a deeper brown I'd come to associate with stress when it came to him. "Be careful, okay?"

Blowing him a kiss, I made my promise to be cautious. Sometimes, he was more overprotective than a parent. Outside of Malina, who hadn't really been a direct problem for me since Enzo gifted me with the necklace, there really was no reason to be concerned.

Arriving outside of Gemma's door, my chest got tight as

I knocked. We hadn't been apart all that much since I arrived, and I didn't realize how much I was going to miss her until that moment.

"Hey," she greeted me with a huge grin on her face. "Come to see me off?"

"You know it. I couldn't let you leave without one last chance to remind you of the things you shouldn't do when we're apart."

She laughed. "Yeah? And what's that?"

"Well, for starters, don't try any more magical enhancements on yourself. It almost killed you last time."

"You mean *you* almost killed me last time?" She rolled her eyes.

It was never a good idea to think about enlarging body parts when practicing magic. Part of casting spells was simply about pure intention. Gemma and I had learned that lesson the hard way when she accidentally made her boobs increase to at least ten sizes bigger than they already were. We ended up needing Enzo to reverse the damage we had both done after I tried to fix it on my own.

"Shush. Those are just details. Also, don't forget to bring me something from home," I added.

Gemma was from North Carolina, and I had never explored the east coast, but as soon as I figured out a way off the school grounds, we had plans to fly into New Orleans, then take a road trip all the way to her coven.

"I'm going to miss you, Rae," she said as she hugged me. "Are you sure you're going to be okay for two weeks here without me?"

"Enzo will be around, and I'll be working with the headmaster on some other stuff. I'm sure I'll figure out a way to survive without you somehow."

"Not likely, but I hope you do. I'd hate to have to bring

you back to life just to kick your ass for letting something stupid happen. Also, speaking of Enzo, are you sure it's a good idea to have so much alone time with him?"

A sigh escaped my lips. I knew what she was referring to, and I understood her concerns, but Enzo hadn't pushed me for anything more than what I had been ready for, and I wasn't worried about it. We'd had the sex talk, and he knew I was a virgin.

I wasn't saving myself for marriage or anything. I just hadn't met a guy I was serious enough about to want to deal with all the things that went along with sex. Enzo could possibly be that guy one day, but over the next two weeks was not going to be that time.

"Yes, *Mom*. I'm going to be fine. You have fun, but not too much fun, and hurry back to me."

"I'll be back by end of month. We can bring in the New Year together," she offered, and I gladly accepted.

Hugging her once more, I said my goodbyes and left her room. She still had a bit of packing to do, and the van taking everyone to the airport and bus stations was leaving soon.

After going back to my room, I ordered myself a warm brownie with vanilla ice cream drizzled in hot fudge. Nothing better than eating my feelings before preparing for almost two weeks without my bestie.

I HAD LIED WHEN I TOLD GEMMA I WOULD BE OKAY without her. Five days into the break, I was ready to kill Enzo and the council, poke their eyes out and feed them to the birds. Maybe I'd even sacrifice their bodies to the gargoyles who watched me in hopes they'd stop creeping me the hell out.

Pacing back and forth near the outside entrance to the commissary where I was supposed to have met Enzo, I decided I was giving him two more minutes before I ditched his ass.

Since break started, every time we made plans, he was either late or didn't show at all. We were supposed to have lunch before he had to go do something for the headmaster. Apparently, that wasn't going to happen.

Instead, Desmond appeared dressed in his signature cloak, a shade lighter than the headmaster's. "Ms. Keyes?"

"You can call me Raegan, you know?"

"Right, Raegan. Are you busy?" he asked politely.

"Not anymore. What did you need?" I asked, trying not to take my frustration out on him. It wasn't Desmond's fault my boyfriend was a jerk.

Even though he was weird as hell, Desmond seemed to be strictly on the side of Team Stop Malina. The other three, Alexander, Bennett, and Fiona, were too hot and cold to really tell what outcome they wanted. I often wondered if they were secretly ready to feed me to Malina just to see what might happen.

"I was hoping you'd come to the dungeon with me." His face remained neutral as his words sunk in.

He wanted me to go back to the place that got me into my current mess? Hell no.

"I'd rather not be subject to that kind of darkness again, but thanks for offering." I turned to leave, but he grabbed my arm.

"Raegan, I don't have a choice. I *need* you to come with me."

Lowering my voice, I narrowed my eyes at him. "Don't fucking touch me, Desmond. You might be stronger than me, but I'll happily go down with a fight."

He didn't bother to respond. Instead, he pulled his hand from his robe pocket and blew some sort of dust in my face before snapping his fingers.

Before I knew it, reality slipped away from me and my last thought was wondering how many ways I could kill Enzo for not showing up to our lunch date.

AWARENESS SLOWLY CAME BACK TO ME. SLOWLY *AND* painfully. I was laying on a bed, or at least I assumed I was from the soft surface I sensed beneath me. My head was pounding, and I didn't dare open my eyes as nausea rolled through me.

Feeling the blanket above me, my fingers traced over the nail polish Gemma had spilt on the edge of my comforter. I breathed a sigh of relief knowing where I was, then took my time trying to sit up. If I could do that without throwing up, then I'd attempt to open my eyes. Maybe.

What the hell happened? I thought as my stomach revolted from the throbbing circling my body. Instinctively, I reached for my necklace. It had become a bit of a habit of mine to rub on the stone when I was nervous or stressed.

"What the hell?" I said out loud, then opened my eyes and immediately regretted it.

Running toward my bathroom, I emptied the contents of my stomach into the sink, not making it to the toilet in time. After I washed my mouth out and pushed the agony down that was rolling through my body, my eyes focused on the mirror.

My skin was pasty, my hair was tangled, and there was a scratch on my forehead. Glancing again, I confirmed my necklace was no longer around my neck, and I could feel

Malina banging at my mental door, wanting to get through to me.

Much too slowly, I went back to my bed in hopes that maybe the chain simply broke and it was in the blankets. After I tore my bed apart and searched my floor, my heart sank. There was no necklace, and I was running out of time to keep Malina out.

Closing my eyes, I thought about the last thing I remembered. I was supposed to meet Enzo for lunch, and I was furious because he hadn't showed, but what did I do after that?

I couldn't remember, and I wasn't sure what freaked me out more: the fact that I couldn't remember or that I had no idea *why* I couldn't remember.

Raegan.

Shit, shit, shit. Malina was back, and I was *not* ready for her.

What do you want with me? I demanded as I sat down, trying to focus on pushing her out.

Why can't it be about what I can do for you, child? Have you thought about that? I'm not what you think I am. They've brainwashed you to believe I'm evil, but I only have the best intentions.

I huffed. No way was I buying the bullshit she was throwing my way.

So, you're saying history is lying? You didn't steal baby dragons and use their scales for practicing dark magic? Or the people you killed simply to gain more power? I didn't need anyone to tell me you were evil, Malina. I sensed it the moment I opened the dungeon door.

Opening that door was the greatest thing you've ever done, she snapped.

Don't make me ask again, Malina. What do you want?

I want what everyone wants. I want freedom, and you're going to help me get it. It's been almost two decades of darkness for me, and I'm ready to show the council they screwed with the wrong sorceress. Alistair made a mistake the day he locked me away, she hissed.

I'm not going to help you. You can torture me inside my head all you want, but I won't be a part of whatever it is you think you're doing.

Standing from my bed, I finally gave up trying to push her from my mind and began to pace. I refused to play her mind games, and I wasn't going to let her push me around.

Don't sound so smug, Raegan. You'll do as you're damn well told or those around you will pay the price. Your beloved Enzo is first on my list. Now, go practice your witch magic. I need you stronger. I'll be back soon, and you don't want to find out what happens if you disappoint me.

My hands grasped both sides of my head when the stabbing sensation returned, but only for a few seconds before it was gone almost as quickly as it had come. I needed to find that damn necklace and figure out how I got back to my room.

After brushing my hair and changing my clothes, I left the dorm area in search of Enzo. If he wasn't in his room, then Headmaster Stone would be my next stop. We had a problem, and one of them better be ready to help me fix it, because I refused to stand idly by while that witch tried to dictate my life.

E nzo was nowhere to be found, and I was beginning to freak the hell out. My stone was still missing. It had vanished into thin air, and Enzo seemed to have done the same.

"What do you mean, you don't know where he is?" I asked, and not for the first time since I waltzed into the headmaster's office that night. "Use some of your magic juju to find him."

"It doesn't work that way, Raegan. I'm sorry to disappoint you, but if Enzo doesn't want to be found, then we're not going to find him."

My hands tangled in my hair as my frustration increased.

"Did you not listen to a word I said? Malina threatened him. I'm missing time. I don't remember where I was for *several hours* today. Now, I don't have my necklace and Enzo can't be found. You think that's a coincidence?"

He leaned forward, face softening with compassion. "I understand you're worried, but it hasn't even been a day. I'm definitely concerned with you not remembering part of your day, but Enzo can take care of himself. He's more powerful than I believe you're giving him credit for. Maybe I can find you a similar stone like the one you lost to make up for your frustrations."

Something was going on. Headmaster Stone had always been on my side, but he was acting very nonchalant about everything I was telling him. I wanted to scream in his face, but as he continued to speak, I realized it wouldn't help.

Screw it. I'd figure it out on my own.

"You're right. I'm sorry for bothering you so late in the evening. Let me know if you find another necklace for me." Standing from my chair in his office, I forced a smile on my face and waved goodbye.

When I was back in the hallway, it took everything I had to keep from yelling at the top of my lungs.

Gemma was away.

Enzo was missing.

Malina was stronger than ever before.

And I was on my own.

Deciding I had no other options, I went back to Enzo's dorm. Something had to be there, and I was going to find my way in. I hadn't tried to get in before, because I assumed the headmaster knew where he was at, but I no longer had a choice.

I was about to be the crazy girlfriend who went through his shit.

Roaming through the halls, I tried to remain casual. Some of the teachers were still around who lived at the academy all year, but most of them knew I didn't have family, so not too many people questioned why I never left the school.

Headmaster Stone had kept my inability to go through a shield a secret from everyone except the council.

Gemma, Peyton, and Finley knew, but I had a feeling Peyton's and Finley's heads had been messed with, because neither of them had brought it up since the night they witnessed it.

Strolling into the elven dorms like I owned the place, I didn't see a single elf. Weird, but not overly concerning. I had been in such a hurry when I was there earlier in the evening that I hadn't thought much about it.

It was pushing close to midnight, half my memory of the day gone. Malina had stayed silent since our earlier conversation, which I appreciated, but it also made me nervous. There was a significant vibe of smugness coming from her, and I knew she had more than one something to do with my shit-tastic day.

Arriving at Enzo's door, just for curiosity's sake, I tried the handle first. No shocker, it was locked. Placing my hand on the panel to enter the code, I tapped into my witch magic. It was the strongest part of me, and what I felt most confident in.

I wasn't sure where to start, but a syphoning spell and a blasting one were at the top of my list. Since the former was more conspicuous than the latter, I went with it, begrudgingly so.

Focusing all of my energy on the power that controlled the door lock, I attached a magical tether to the object and began to pull on the energy within it. Since the keypad wasn't supernatural, everything felt off, but it was working. I just needed to drain the battery, and hopefully the locking mechanism would fail to work.

"What do you think you're doing?" a voice I could have gone the rest of my life without hearing snapped from behind me.

"It's none of your damn business, Lyssa. Go back to

whatever dark cave you crawled out of and leave me alone," I replied without turning around.

She was in my face within the blink of an eye. "Don't push me tonight, Mutt. Where is Enzo?"

"He doesn't concern you anymore. Why don't you run back to Drake and enjoy your vacation? It would make everything I'm trying to do a lot easier to accomplish."

She backed away, but only by a step. "I saw Desmond creeping around here earlier. I know we're not exactly friends, but if something has happened to Enzo, I want to help. Your aura is all over the place, and I know something is wrong."

I chose to ignore her while I finished my syphoning spell and heard the lock give way a minute later. She hadn't said another word and had lost the normal bitchy vibe she was so good at putting off. Also, something she had said tickled my memory, but I couldn't grasp it, which was fueling my irritation.

Damn it. I was going to regret this.

"Come in and tell me what you saw," I said as I pushed open Enzo's door.

She closed it behind her, and I began looking around his dorm, waiting for Lyssa to answer.

"What are you looking for?" she asked.

"Anything to tell me where Enzo might have been going or what his plans were. He was supposed to do something for Headmaster Stone today after we had lunch. He never made it to our meeting spot, and I haven't heard from him since this morning. Now, what did you see earlier?"

"We're supposed to be heading to the Caribbean tomorrow and I had forgotten my favorite swimsuit here, so I came back to grab it. When I did, I decided to check in on Enzo."

Taking a break from going through drawers, I rolled my eyes, which she saw and wasn't happy about.

"Enzo and I were friends for a long time before we became something more. Don't judge me before you know the whole story." Emotion I couldn't identify flashed across her face before she tucked it away and continued. "Anyway, the platform wouldn't go all the way up to his floor. It was jammed, so I waited at the bottom, assuming he was up to something. Enzo likes to push boundaries."

"Yeah, I'm well aware of that." I laughed. Ugh. Why was I laughing? She was not my friend, and we were not reminiscing. She was a means to more information, nothing more.

She flicked her platinum blonde, almost-white hair back, and offered me the first smile ever that wasn't more of a sneer. "When the platform began moving again, it wasn't Enzo that was on it, but Desmond."

Every time she said Desmond's name, my head pinged with a memory, but no matter how hard I pushed, I couldn't break through the block on whatever I needed to remember.

"What was he doing?" I asked when she paused.

"That's the thing. I have no idea. I hid behind a wall and didn't get to see. He's not the friendliest council member I've ever encountered. Always looks like he's in pain and ready to snap. Anyway, I peeked out from the wall in time to see him turn the corner, and I'm pretty sure he was alone, but he shouldn't have been up there. I know that for sure."

"Well, let's see if we can find what he was looking for, and maybe it will tell us what happened to Enzo."

"Really?" Her head cocked to the left and eyes widened. "You're not going to throw a fit about me helping?"

"Would you rather I did, so you can run back to your beach vacation? I need help and nobody else seems to believe me, so beggars can't be choosers. The only thing that matters is we find Enzo and soon. Something tells me he didn't just take off to screw with everyone."

She nodded but didn't say anything else as we went our separate ways in the suite. I took his room. I didn't feel comfortable with his ex, even if they were friends before, rummaging through his more private stuff, and I didn't think he would, either.

His closet was full of boring black pants, white dress shirts and a small dresser that held clothes not required by the academy. I pushed on walls and stomped on the floor just in case there was more to the closet than I could see, but nothing stood out.

Moving on to his nightstand, I found his school tablet. They were locked with facial recognition and if I tried to screw with it, I risked wiping out the whole thing. I wasn't that desperate yet, but I did take it with me.

Lyssa's head popped into the room. "Anything?"

I flinched, still surprised she was speaking to me without the normal hostility I was used to. "Nope. You?"

"There was a note in the garbage, scribbled down in what looks like a hurry. I can barely read it." She handed it to me. "I think it says, 'meet at ten near the water', but water could be way off."

Flipping the paper over, I looked to see if there was anything on it to tell us where he might have grabbed it from, but it was just a torn piece of plain paper.

Black ink was used, and it was smudged as if the paper had been rubbed against something immediately after writing on it. For all we knew, Enzo didn't even write it. We didn't do anything with writing in class. Everything was done on the tablets, so I wasn't familiar with his handwriting, but maybe Lyssa was.

"Are you sure he wrote it?" I asked.

"Well, I guess not. All men have shitty handwriting, so I guess it could be anyone. What do you think it says?"

"I think the 'meet at ten' part is right, but I'm not sure about the second part."

Frustration swept through me as I continued to stare at the note. Where was he going and who was he meeting? Was it ten in the morning or the evening? Had he been set up this morning and been gone all day?

"Do you have a phone?" I asked, wondering if we could try to call him.

"Of course, I do," she replied smugly, and I wanted to punch her in the nose.

"Well, would you like to maybe use it to call Enzo? Mine was taken when I arrived, and I don't have his number. Never needed it. You know, since we're usually always together."

Working with her was going to be more difficult than I really wanted to handle, but damn it. I was out of options, at least until Gemma came back or the headmaster pulled his head out of his ass.

Without replying, she pulled a phone from her back pocket and pressed a few buttons before holding it out, so I could see it was on speaker. Nothing happened for several seconds as I held my breath waiting for it to ring.

"The number you have dialed is not available or has traveled outside of the service area. Please try your call again later."

The operator's voice grated on my nerves. That had not been what I was hoping for. Even his voicemail would have been better than that.

"What about a tracking spell?" I was just learning about those in class, but Lyssa had been at this magic thing a lot longer than I had, so hopefully she was familiar with it.

"We could try it, but Enzo is normally shielded. Even his aura is kept a secret from others. If you haven't noticed, he does whatever he wants and doesn't usually like to talk about it. It's why we broke up last year. I got tired of his secrets and never knowing what he was doing."

Huh. That made sense. Lyssa probably nearly nagged him to death before he called it quits. I could picture that and understood better why Enzo happened to be traveling through the states far away from her last summer.

"We're out of options for the night. I'm going to go back to my dorm and try to remember what happened today. Come see me if you think of anything that could help." I turned to leave, but she grabbed my arm.

"What do you mean 'try to remember'? What happened to you?" Her voice was almost frantic, and her concern threw me off as I mentally chastised myself for not choosing my words more carefully around her. *Not my friend*, I reminded myself for the second time.

"I don't know. I was waiting for Enzo so we could eat lunch together, and the next thing I knew, I was in my room with a pounding headache." Along with Malina back in my head, but she didn't need to know the whole story. I'd already told her too much.

"The council is in on whatever is happening. They're the only ones powerful enough to screw with your memories. I could try and break through whatever blocker they have, but it would hurt."

I wanted to laugh. Maybe she didn't realize how powerful Enzo was, because he had been able to take memories from me when I first met him and certainly wasn't part of the council. Though, I had been able to painfully break through his spell. Regardless, now that I look back on it, he seemed to have let me. He gave me the choice, warned me of the consequences, and I chose to ignore them.

"No, that's alright. I'll try to work on it on my own. If I don't get anywhere, I'll let you know." No matter how nice that crazy bitch was being, she was still a crazy bitch, and I wasn't letting her in my head unless it was my only option.

"I'm going to go back to my room, then," Lyssa said. "I already called my parents and let them know I was going to be running late. I can stay for another day to help, but not much longer without raising suspicion."

"I understand. You don't have to stay at all, but I appreciate it. Let me know if you see anything around here before you leave."

She nodded and we said an awkward goodbye before closing Enzo's door and powering back up his lock.

Instead of taking the platform with me, she disappeared and teleported back to her room, or so I assumed. Irritation flooded through me once again that I hadn't been given that ability. Out of all the weird shit I could do, teleporting would have been the best gift.

After I arrived back at my room, exhaustion set in. The day had been mentally draining. I was ready for it to be over and wake up tomorrow to find out it had all been a nightmare. My hands reached for my necklace out of habit, and I bit back a curse when I didn't find it.

Just as I opened my dresser to grab pajamas, a knock sounded at my door. Hope soared through me that Enzo was there and I had been losing my shit for no reason, but when I opened my door, it was Lyssa's face that stared back at me.

"Here." She shoved a phone in my hand. "It's my old one and still works. I put mine and Enzo's numbers in there."

"I, uh, thanks." I didn't know how to respond. She had been nice enough earlier, but this was way more than I expected out of her.

"Whatever, Mutt. I gotta go." She turned on a heel and stomped down the hallway.

Ah. There was the Lyssa I was used to. A smile tugged at my lips. At least one thing was still normal in this scenario.

Even though her back was turned, I flipped her off like a child, then closed my door. Walking to my bed, I sat down and turned on the phone, which was thankfully an iPhone like my aunt had, so I was somewhat familiar with it.

Even though we had just tried, I pressed Enzo's name and put the phone to my ear. The annoying operator's voice came on again, and I was tempted to throw the phone in frustration but managed to hold in my anger.

After putting the phone on my nightstand, I finished getting ready for bed and decided I wasn't going to figure anything out while I was as exhausted as I was. Tomorrow would be a new day, and I'd hopefully not lose my shit and punch someone in the face.

Even though it sounded like a really great idea as I closed my eyes and drifted off to sleep.

S ix days had passed since Enzo disappeared. Six damn days, and I was beyond the point of no return with my irritation.

My only saving grace was that Gemma was due to arrive back at Shadow Veil within the next couple hours. If she didn't show, I couldn't be held responsible for my actions, and there was a high chance of the school burning down if I snapped.

Headmaster Stone had been brainwashed; I had no proof of it, but I was convinced of it. Some heavy magic was being thrown around and, somehow, he'd been caught in the crossfire. I had spent the last five days trying to figure out how to get his head back in the game, but nothing I tried had worked.

After finally being able to visit the "secret elven lair", as I liked to call it, I discovered a few new spells, but either I wasn't powerful enough to execute them or the magic suppressing the headmaster was a hell of a lot stronger than me. Either option was plausible.

Lyssa had left the evening after giving me the phone.

Neither of us had been able to get through to Enzo, and she had been checking in with me once a day. The more days that passed, the more I worried Malina had actually figured out a way to get her grimy hands on Enzo and had him locked away in the dungeon right underneath me.

A short time later, I was pacing the entryway. Waiting for Gemma was winding me up even more, so I decided to go for a walk, in hopes of releasing some of my tension. Without conscious thought, I ended up at the door to the dungeon.

The power behind it still called to me, but not like before. There wasn't a constant need to go beyond the barrier, but the connection to whatever was down there was blatant.

What if Enzo is down there? I thought.

My hands rested on the door as I considered trying to break through the locks. Would he kill me if I risked myself to go down there and find him? Absolutely. Would it be worth it? Definitely.

Screw the rules. The rules had gotten me nowhere in the last four months. I was taking a page from Enzo's book and pushing the mother-effing boundaries.

Hands placed on the door, I simply thought about what I wanted the door to do and connected with magic behind it. Each time I had been at the door, there didn't seem to be any difficulty getting past it. The council really needed to do something about the lack of security around something that was supposed to be dark and dangerous.

When the locks disengaged, I turned the handle slowly, glancing behind me to make sure nobody was coming. The coast was clear, and I slipped inside, leaving the door closed but unlocked for an easier escape if necessary.

Sneaking down the stairs, I pressed myself against the

wall and listened for anyone coming. I had no idea where I was going, but I was desperate to find Enzo.

My toes barely even touched the ground off the steps before I was busted.

"You again. What are you doing down here?" Ryn snarled at me so deeply, I would have thought he was a shifter until I saw his pointed ears.

Pushing my shoulders back, I held my head high. "I'm looking for Enzo Vaughn. I think one of your *guests* down here might have taken him."

"The prisoners in here don't ever leave, so nobody has taken Enzo. This isn't a place for you, and if I see you in here again, I'll have you thrown out of the academy."

Damn, he was actually sexy in a dark, twisted, this-guy-has-major-baggage-but-maybe-I-could-fix-him kind of way. Even still, he had no idea what he was talking about.

I laughed right in his face. I couldn't help it. I was past the point of giving a shit about anything. "Good luck with that. If I could leave this place, I already would have. I won't be going anywhere, no matter how many times I decide to venture down here."

My head snapped back and, if I hadn't been staring right at Ryn, I would have sworn he smacked me, but his hands never moved. "What the hell was that?" I screeched.

Both of his hands gripped my arms. "She's coming for you. You need to leave. Now, Raegan."

He pushed me up the steps, and I began taking them two at a time. As soon as the words left his mouth, I knew he was right. Malina's presence was everywhere around us, pulling at me and sucking the life out of my very being.

By the time I reached the top of the stairs, I could barely breathe, and my muscles felt like they were being ripped apart. When the door opened, I fell onto the ground and kicked it closed behind me, then stared up at the ceiling.

Shit, that hadn't gone how I wanted.

"Raegan!" Gemma's voice yelled from down the hall, followed by the sound of pounding footsteps. "What happened to you?" she asked as she dropped to her knees beside me.

"Oh, you know. Just the normal. Decided to go for a stroll in the dungeon. Had a nice chat with Ryn. Got bitch-slapped by Malina."

"Why were you—never mind, it doesn't matter. Let's get you to your room. More people are arriving today, and you don't want them to find you on the ground."

Gemma stood, reached out a hand to me, and helped to lift me up. My body ached, but I was able to walk on my own, for the most part. The wall only needed to help keep me steady every few steps.

Gemma switched her bag to the other side and looped her arm through mine when we got on the platform to go up to our rooms, which I was grateful for, because there were no sides on the platform and I really didn't want to be the first student to fall over the edge.

When we arrived at my door, she punched in the code I'd long ago given her. I made my way to my bed and fell on top of it. Tears built in my eyes, and a fire burned in my throat as I tried to hold them back. I wasn't sad or upset. I was pissed the hell off, and this was the result of what happened when I was pushed too far.

"Tell me what happened." Gemma held my hand as she snuggled in beside me.

"He just disappeared. It's been six days, Gem. I was getting desperate. I had to check if he was stuck down there, but Ryn found me before I could get anywhere. Then, when we were arguing, Malina's presence showed up."

"It's going to be okay. I'm here, and we're going to figure this out. I promise." Gemma's head leaned down, settling on top of mine.

Having her there helped to calm my raging emotions, but it wasn't enough to make everything okay. I needed to know where Enzo was and if he was alright. I had even resorted to reaching out to Malina, but the psycho refused to speak with me. Apparently, our mental connection only worked one way. Convenient for her, of course.

"What if he's stuck down there with her somehow?" I asked. "If she's powerful enough to get inside of my head and fly around the dungeon in some sort of spirit form, then I can't put it past her to have taken Enzo."

Gemma sighed. "I don't know. We just have to figure out a way to be stronger than her and hope that Enzo is doing the same."

She was right. Enzo wasn't new to dealing with the darker side of our supernatural world. He never told me exactly what he did when he went on his "errands", but I got the gist of it the last time he came back. He was covered in a film of dark magic and I had to help him with a cleansing spell.

Wherever he had been was not any place I ever wanted to venture, but if I had to for Enzo, then I'd find my lady balls and make it happen.

"You're right. I need to be bigger, better, and badder than the bitch downstairs. She has controlled enough of my life the last four months. No more. I'm done. I came here, so I could find out who my parents were and learn how to protect myself. I'm at least going to do one of those things."

A grin lit up her face. "There's my bestie. Now, show

me what Enzo's taught you and be prepared to have it amplified by a hundred."

My gut was telling me I would live to regret whatever it was I had just agreed to, but that didn't matter. I needed to be a stronger me in order to figure out how to rid myself of Malina and get Enzo back.

"Let me put my stuff in my room and change. We have less than a week before school starts. We need to narrow down your strengths before then, so we know what to focus on in what little time you'll have outside of classes," Gemma said, equal parts excited and serious.

Standing from the bed, I gave her a hug, holding on longer than necessary, but I had missed her, and I needed a moment. Thankfully, she understood without saying anything.

When she left, I glanced in the mirror, taking in my elf ears and the slight glow emanating from my hands. I needed both halves of me to beat Malina, maybe even the dragon side, too. I just had to convince Headmaster Stone it was a good idea if and when the time came.

On the last day of break, Gemma and I were training outside, quickly gathering a crowd. All of the students were back from break since school was back in session tomorrow, and they were enjoying our show.

"What next?" I asked Gemma with a huff after we finished creating shields. They might have sounded simple, but the process practically sucked the life out of me. I needed a bigger well of energy before I could do it without tiring.

"Elements?" she suggested.

Nodding, I held my hand out and called on my magic. Warmth filled my stomach, then heat transferred up my arm before scorching power erupted from my fingers and fire filtered through.

"Very nice, Rae. Twice as fast as it took you yesterday." Gemma applauded.

I hadn't become a pro, by any means, but intent went a long way toward how much success we had. Plus, Gemma wouldn't let me quit. Even when my arms were covered in burns, my muscles ached, and my eyes would barely stay open, she pushed me, reminding me what it was all for.

We swapped out elements until each one came naturally and the sun was setting. Hunger took over then, so we headed to the commissary.

"Muscles are screaming at me that I didn't even know existed," I complained when we sat down.

"Yeah, but you look like a total badass, so deal with it." She laughed.

Peyton and Finley walked by but didn't sit down. Things had been tense between the four of us. They wanted to know what we were up to, but Gemma and I had agreed it was better not to tell them. For many reasons, though mostly because we had no idea what we were dealing with and didn't want to put them in danger.

They didn't know that and were holding it against us, but it was better than having Malina screw with one of them as well.

Lyssa came by next and stopped at the table. "Anything?"

"No, you?"

She shook her head. "Maybe he'll just show up tomorrow."

"Yeah, maybe."

When she walked away, Gemma's body shook dramatically. "It seriously creeps me out that she's nice to you now."

"Agreed, but she has resources we might need later, so I'm not going to turn down her help."

"Smart girl." She went back to eating, and the rest of our dinner was spent mostly in silence as I reflected on everything that had happened over the last several days.

"Hey, I'm going to chat with Headmaster Stone. I'll see you later, okay?" I said when I finished eating.

"Do you want me to come with you?" Gemma asked.

"Nah, I'm sure it will be more of the same. I'll stop by your room when I'm done." Pushing away from the table, I headed toward Magic Hall.

The headmaster had been avoiding me, but I wasn't leaving his office this time until I spoke with him. I needed to know what they'd done to look for Enzo and what was going on with Malina. Even though his mind had been messed with, he still should have been doing his job, even if it was half-assed.

Malina still hadn't been back in my head, but I knew she was continuing to grow stronger. I could feel her in the hallways now, her power pulsing through the air, seeming to be searching for a way out.

It creeped me the hell out, but I did my best to ignore it. I needed to outmatch her and keep those around me safe. Besides getting Enzo back in one piece, that was all that mattered.

My hand lifted to knock, but I decided there was no use with the way the headmaster had been acting as of late. Instead, I opened the door and called out his name.

"In here, Raegan," he replied.

When I entered, his normally smooth grey hair was in complete disarray, and his office was torn apart.

"Uh, Headmaster Stone, what's going on?"

He shook his head and placed a finger to his lips, telling me to be quiet.

"Were you here about your class schedule?" he asked while nodding his head.

"Sure. I mean, yes. Did you get it worked out yet?"

"Yes, last night I was finally able to sit down and see about rearranging some of your classes. I have the new proposal right here." He slid a piece of paper across his desk, and I moved to pick it up while he went back to searching his office for something.

It read: Someone is listening. I need to find the orb they planted. It should be a small glass ball with either blue or purple light glowing from it.

Nodding my head, I set the paper down. "I think this is reasonable. Do you think I could borrow a few books for the new classes from you?" I asked, giving us an excuse as to why we would be moving about the room to whoever was listening.

"Yes, that's a great idea. I should have thought of it myself," he replied.

Soon, we were both scouring his office, moving books around and looking under chairs. Finally, he waved his hands. "Ah, here is the History of Witches book I was looking for." With a wave of his hand, the glass orb blinked once and then the purple light faded away.

"Is everything okay?" I asked again, needing to know his response before I went on a tangent. I wasn't sure we could speak freely just yet.

"No, nothing is okay, Raegan, but first I must apologize. I remember everything from the last couple weeks, but it was as if I didn't have any control over my body. I was finally able to break through this morning."

Damn it. I knew something was going on with him, but deep down, I had hoped I was wrong. That meant there was some really screwed-up shit happening.

"Where is Enzo?" I asked, hoping maybe he'd be able to finally give a solid answer.

"I don't know. All I do know is Malina has almost completely taken over the dungeon. Over the last five days, her strength has grown tremendously."

Shit, shit, shit.

That couldn't be a coincidence, and it was the worst-case scenario. There was no way I could ever beat Malina if she became stronger as I did.

Dread coursed through me as I struggled with what I needed to do next.

CHAPTER NINETEEN

Two months. Two mother-effing months had passed since Enzo disappeared. The council hadn't found a trace left of him on Earth, but I refused to believe he was dead. "No body, no death" was my latest mantra anytime someone tried to say it was a possibility.

"Rae, you look like shit," Gemma so kindly announced when she entered my room. "And you missed dinner."

Glancing at my nightstand, I nodded toward the plates without really paying attention to her. "I ordered in from my butler box."

"I could have joined you, so you didn't have to eat alone." When I didn't respond, she continued, "You're being kind of an asshole as of late with your attitude, if you ask me."

"Well, I didn't ask you, did I?" I snapped.

Guilt assaulted me, but I didn't apologize. I was angry at the world, and Gemma had been paying the price for that over the last several weeks.

I couldn't leave the academy; I could hardly even train for fear of Malina getting even stronger. Headmaster Stone had confirmed my connection to her was making her more powerful.

She had been visiting me more frequently lately, kindly reminding me I needed to excel in school or there would be a price to pay, but it seemed to me I was already paying that price, so I didn't see the point.

Gemma's face moved right into my line of sight. "Listen here, Raegan. I'm only going to say this once, and then I'm going to walk out your door and possibly never come back."

My head leaned back in surprise. She'd never spoken to me with such animosity before. .

"I have stood by your side for months as we tried to find Enzo, but I won't stand here and watch you wither away. Yes, I realize he means a lot to you and you feel responsible for his disappearance, but Enzo is a big boy. If anything, I'd have to guess he got himself into this mess all on his own and your guilt is severely misplaced."

I opened my mouth to respond, but her hand clasped over it.

"I'm not done. It's March, and you have less than three more months to figure out how to get yourself out of here. Why don't you focus on something for yourself for once and accept the help being offered from those around you instead of wallowing in self-pity that you can no longer do anything. I love you, girl, but I'm done feeling sorry for you. It's time to pick up your lady balls and bring back the Raegan I met last fall."

She removed her hand, turned on her heels, and stomped out of my room, completing her show by slamming the door.

Damn it all to hell.

My throat burned, but it was a feeling I was all too familiar with as I tried not to cry. My emotions were everywhere, and I went through a gamut of them every day. One minute I was angry, then depressed, determined, okay, or helpless. I'd done a bang-up job of nailing the woe-is-me act, and I'd finally pushed away the only friend I had left.

Lyssa still checked in from time-to-time, but Enzo no longer concerned her that I could tell. At first, it pissed me off, but then I realized it didn't matter. None of it mattered. I was a pawn in a game much bigger than me, and I was just trying to survive.

Almost a half-hour later, my door opened, and I assumed it was Gemma coming back, so I stood up, already calling out my apology to her. She deserved better from me after all that she had done.

"Oh, Raegan. What did you do?" Aunt Jules asked when she entered my room.

Shit. That definitely wasn't Gemma.

I'd been avoiding my aunt like the plague. I didn't have any good news for her, so I didn't see the point in talking about any of it.

"Why are you apologizing to Gemma?" she asked when I stood there dumbfounded at her arrival.

"I, well, you see... things are complicated," I sputtered.

"Explain." She crossed her arms and took a seat in my desk chair, giving me her best "mom" face. For having only been a mom to me for a little over a year, she had it down and it was rather intimidating.

"Jules, I don't think it's a good idea. Things are messy, and there is stuff going on here you don't need to be involved in. I can't lose you, too." My heart lurched as I said the last part, and I realized I had slowly been pushing away Gemma for the last month, because I was afraid to lose her, as well.

I was toxic to anyone around me, as long as Malina had her hold on me.

"Sweetheart, you don't know my past or where I come from. That's my fault, but I need you to understand there is nothing in this world that would scare me more than losing you. You're covered in a darkness you can no longer hide, and you need to tell me why that is."

That's when the dam broke.

When the first tear fell, there was nothing I could do to stop the rest. Word vomit followed, and I told Jules everything, even more than I had told Gemma or the headmaster. My stresses were no longer a weight I could bear on my own. When I was done, I began laughing hysterically, because I was officially a maniac.

"Raegan?" Jules asked with trepidation. "Why are you laughing?"

"Because just over a year ago, I was a normal high school student with plans for a future I can no longer have. Look at me, Jules! I'm a damn mess."

Her arms wrapped around me as the tears returned and I finished my first official mental breakdown. We sat on my bed together for several hours, changing the subject to stories of her pack and things that made New Orleans such a special place.

She had locked up my house and moved back home a couple months ago, claiming that while the magic of Portland would forever be in her heart, it just wasn't the same if I wasn't there.

"Why don't we go see if Gemma wants to come over and watch a movie with us?" Jules suggested.

"I doubt it. It's almost midnight, and I screwed up pretty big with her," I admitted ruefully.

"Honey, if the two of you are anything like your mom

and I were, there will be many more screw-ups by both of you, and you just have to remember that a heartfelt apology goes a long way. I bet you she's sitting in her room, waiting for you to pull your head out of your ass."

Taking a deep breath, I stood from the bed and checked in the mirror before I dared to enter the hallway. Makeup tracked down my face from my earlier tears, but it wasn't an ungodly sight, so I figured *screw it*. I didn't really care what anyone thought of me, as long as Gemma forgave me for being an idiot.

The steps it took to get from my room to hers were like trudging through wet concrete. Nerves slammed around in my stomach like it was a bounce house, but I knew I had to push through. I owed that to Gemma. If she chose not to accept my apology, I wouldn't hold it against her, but I had to try.

When I knocked, I heard her stomping feet coming toward the door. She still wasn't happy.

"What?" Gemma barked when the door opened.

"I'm sorry," I blurted out before she could disappear back into her room.

"For what?" she asked with less bite.

"For being an idiot. For pushing you away, so I didn't have to hurt so much if something happened to you. For not being honest with you. For everything else I can't remember right now and everything stupid I'll probably do in the near future."

She started to laugh, but the sound was mixed with tears. She pulled me into her arms before hitting me upside my head. "Don't be such an idiot again. Next time, I won't be so easy on you."

"I'll do my best."

We hugged for several more minutes while the tears

each of us had shed dried up. When we pulled apart, I remembered Jules was waiting on us. "My aunt made a surprise visit, and she's staying in my room. Do you want to come watch a movie with us? I don't want to leave her for too long since she just got here."

"Only if I can pick it." Gemma grinned.

And just like that, I had my best friend back, but I also had my aunt, which made the night even better. I had no idea how long Jules was going to be at Shadow Veil, and I didn't ask. I didn't want to know yet.

Instead, we spent the night pretending there wasn't an evil sorceress trying to break free and rain havoc down on the world.

TWO WEEKS LATER, JULES WAS STILL STAYING AT Shadow Veil, except we were no longer sharing a bed. Headmaster Stone had given her one of the empty dorms in Hybrid Hall and said it was hers for as long as she wanted. Apparently, her keeping me from going off the deep end into depression went a long way to bending some of their rules about no outsiders staying inside the school for extended periods of time.

Not much else was better except my outlook on things. Malina was still growing stronger, and Enzo was still gone, but I'd begun to accept that even though I had started to care deeply for him, I needed to move on. He wasn't my responsibility, and I needed to help myself before I could help anyone else. Most importantly, I needed to figure out how to remove the link Malina had to me.

Once I had accepted that, I breathed a hell of a lot easier and was able to excel in my classes once again. For a while there, I was afraid all the work I had done in the first half of the year was going to be for nothing.

"Raegan?" Headmaster Stone called from his door as I was headed to Defensive Magic with Gemma.

"Yeah?"

"I'd like to see you. You're going to have to miss this class, I'm afraid."

I glanced at Gemma, and she nodded. "I'll take notes and see you at lunch."

She gave me a hug and continued on, while I not-so-eagerly headed into the headmaster's office.

"What's going on?" I asked when he closed the door behind us.

"I have something I need to tell you, but I need you to listen to everything I have to say before you comment." He seemed more nervous than I was.

"Sure, go ahead." I'd been doing better lately. I didn't understand what he was so anxious about, but I was about to find out.

"We found Enzo—"

"When? Where is he? Why didn't you get me sooner?" Questions spit out before I could stop them, even though he specifically asked me not to.

Damn it. Just when I had accepted that I needed to move on... No, this was not happening. I couldn't handle this. I stood up to leave, because my heart didn't want to hear more. If Enzo wasn't in this room and he hadn't come to me first, then something was wrong.

"Raegan, I need you to stay in here and listen to me." With a snap of his fingers, my ass fell back into the chair without my doing. "I'm sorry, but you gave me no choice."

I tried to speak, but not even that was possible. My eyes glared at him, while I waited for him to continue, because apparently, I wasn't going to be allowed to do anything else until he was finished.

"Enzo showed up last night concealed with dark energy. He is currently in the box we used to unlock your powers. He needs to remain there until we can strip him of the darkness consuming him. He's slowly coming back to us, but we don't know if there is any permanent damage."

Damn it. I wanted to ask a million questions. Really effing bad.

"Desmond and Bennett have been with him around the clock, as have I, except to come see you just now. We are doing everything we can, but if it doesn't work, Desmond suggested we bring you in to see if it triggers his emotions in a more positive way. Right now, he isn't responding to anything with light or compassion. I know you've been through a lot trying to find him and are just beginning to come back around, but would you be willing to help him still?"

My first thought was, *Of course I would. Why wouldn't I?* But then, I remembered the hurt and fear I went through. Could I really go through that again if Enzo couldn't be saved? No, I couldn't, but in the end, it didn't really matter. I knew he was back at the academy, and whether I helped him or not made no difference in how much I was going to hurt again.

The wound was already opening, and my feelings for him hadn't changed. I missed the Enzo I had grown to know, and if I could help bring him back, then I needed to do my part. I may have started to move on, but I wasn't ready to give up when there was a real possibility of success.

I nodded, then Headmaster Stone snapped his fingers again, so I could speak.

"What would I have to do?" I asked.

"He'd stay in the box, and you'd simply just have to talk to him. Try to find any source of goodness within him. He won't tell us where he's been, but it's worse than I feared, I'm afraid."

"I'll do whatever you need me to do, and don't feel obligated to share any of the darker details with me."

Enzo deserved my help, but I didn't need the gory details of just how bad things were. If for some horrid reason we couldn't bring him back around, I wanted my memory of him to be as positive as possible, not tainted by what Malina had done to him.

He nodded in understanding. "If you want to take the rest of the day off, I'll excuse you from classes."

"No, I'll be fine, but I appreciate the offer."

At least, I hoped I would be.

Two days later, I received a summons from Headmaster Stone while I was at lunch with Gemma and Jules. I had told them all about my conversation with him, and they'd been the perfect listeners, but I could see the way they watched me. They were waiting for me to lose it again.

I had managed to hold myself together while walking toward the conference room, even though I knew I was moments from seeing Enzo for the first time in months. I had changed significantly since then and was calling on all the growth I had accomplished since last fall.

I was stronger and more capable. I was no longer letting my emotions guide me as I did my best to fight off the hold Malina had on me.

Another necklace like one Enzo had given me was

never found, but I had managed to grow enough in my abilities to block her out for the most part on my own. It was only those nights that she really wanted to stick it to me that I failed to tune her out.

Those were the evenings that the nightmares came, but the following day, I'd pick myself back up and move on, because that was all I could do. I would have to do the same thing after this.

I'd face Enzo and deal with the consequences if we couldn't heal him. There was no other choice.

Headmaster Stone waited for me at the door, his face solemn and lined with worry. "I'm sorry we have to ask you to do this. Just remember that he isn't himself. If he says something hurtful, it has nothing to do with you. It's the dark magic within him speaking. Malina likely did this, not you."

His pep talk wasn't necessary. Even though I already knew all of those things, I also knew seeing Enzo would crush me, regardless of how it ended.

"I understand, and I'm ready," I said.

When the door was only open half an inch, I could feel Malina's energy flooding out of the room. There was no denying she had a hand in this.

I slipped inside by myself and glanced around. Nobody else was in there except Enzo, but I refused to look at him until I was ready. There were a couple of chairs in front of his cage, so I took a seat. My eyes stared at the floor, but I could feel his burning into me the entire time. I knew that once I took him in, I wouldn't be able to turn away.

I had to be absolutely certain I was ready when I did.

Almost a full minute later, I whispered his name as my head finally lifted, but I didn't finish whatever it was that I wanted to say.

His eyes stopped all coherent thoughts from escaping my mouth. They were solid black, a complete contrast to the golden honey color I was used to, and my heart broke more than I thought was possible.

"Little dragon," he replied in a voice that didn't belong to the man I used to know.

I was in over my head. I couldn't do what needed to be done.

I couldn't be the one to save Enzo.

CHAPTER TWENTY

My body was frozen to the chair. I couldn't move nor speak as the evil permeating off Enzo filtered through the air in heavy waves.

"What's wrong?" He grinned. "Didn't you miss me? Or did you already move on in my absence? Malina mentioned you might have more than once."

Shaking my head, I tried to gain control of the situation before I spiraled out of control. My hands rubbed over my face as I pushed out a shield to help protect myself from whatever darkness he was throwing my way.

"Very well, little dragon. You've come a long way in your training without me." He clapped slowly, almost mockingly. "Which is good, because we have much to do, so why don't you be a doll and let me out of here?"

"No. Not until you tell me where you've been and what you want," I demanded, finally finding my voice once I wasn't being assaulted with his tainted energy.

His hand pressed against the glass. "I want you. I've missed you, and all I want to do is hold you." His eyes flashed the normal gold I was used to, but instead of the brown that normally swirled within the depths, black was still beneath the façade he was throwing my way.

"I don't believe you."

He snickered in my face. "You're right. You were never going to be good for me. That's why I've kept in contact with Lyssa this whole time. She was always the better option. I just needed to use you for a while, but now you're worthless to me. Just a mutt with no true purpose."

I flinched as if he physically assaulted me. His words hurt deep, but I brushed them off. I didn't know Lyssa all that well, but I sensed he was lying. He was trying to make me mad, so I'd do something stupid, but it wasn't going to work. Or at least, I hoped not.

I'd changed a lot, and he didn't know me anymore.

"Is that right? I could almost say the same thing about you," I chided. "I got what I wanted out of you when I needed it, and I'm only here because the headmaster forced my hand. I know you can sense my strength. I don't need you, either. So, let's cut the shit, why don't we?"

"Ah, there's my little spitfire." He cackled.

"I'm *your* nothing, Enzo. The sooner you realize that, the better it'll be for both of us." The version of him before me had no claim on me, and I needed to separate my feelings for the old Enzo from the evil imitation trying to hurt me.

He shook his finger, tsking at me. "That's where you're wrong. While I may not need you, you most certainly need me. Malina still wants you for some ungodly reason that's beyond me. If I don't take you to her, she's going to begin killing your friends one by one. Slowly. Torturously. Is that what you want?" he taunted.

"You know damn well that's not what I want." Crossing my arms, I stood up and marched closer to the cage. "But you know what I want more than anything? To stop evil like yourself from getting what they want."

Placing my hand on the cage, I lashed out at him through the glass. Letting my power build, I kept my palm where it was, wishing for nothing more than to hurt Malina the way she had hurt me. I knew it was her inside him, and I didn't want to physically injure him, but I needed to free him from her grasp.

Electricity sizzled along my skin as I began to lose control. It was exactly what Malina wanted, but I didn't give a damn anymore. I had zero doubts that the council was watching. If I took things too far, I trusted them to come rushing in to save the day.

Enzo's black eyes watched my every move with unabated fascination. It was as if Malina was staring back at me, wanting to see just how much I would hurt him in order to stop her. How far I might really take things against someone I cared about.

"Do it, Raegan. Kill me and make it all go away." His head lowered, so he was standing even with me.

I wasn't a killer. I didn't want anyone to die by my hands, but I wanted whatever was overtaking him to hurt like I had. To feel the anguish I had felt over the last couple of months.

Tears built up in my eyes, but not a single one fell. My throat tightened, burning as my chest ached with the effort it took to keep the worst of my emotions from spilling out. The hurt only fueled my magic, though. Without really thinking about the consequences, just what I hoped the end result would be, I lashed out at him like I'd never done before in any of my trainings.

"I hate you," I whispered.

"No, you love me so much that you think you hate me,

and that's okay with me, little dragon. Do what you have to do."

Malina thought I still assumed Enzo to be himself, but I knew better, and she was an idiot for underestimating me. Using both fists, I pulled back just enough to give me some momentum and slammed them down on the glass. "I. Hate. You," I repeated with clipped words.

Mist formed in the cage around him, a blood red just like the scales that were now showing up on my arms.

Damn. I had somehow broken through Headmaster Stone's spell that kept my dragon side locked down. My ire toward Malina was a lot stronger than I realized, and I needed to be careful not to actually harm Enzo.

He roared in pain as my power covered him until he was no longer visible. Glass rained down around us as the cage shattered and my magic warred with Malina's as I watched her spirit lift from Enzo's body into the air.

"Go back to your body. You're not welcome here, nor will you ever be," I snarled as I prepared for a fight.

"You're even better than I hoped, child," she cooed, her voice echoing around the room. "You might have gotten what you wanted this time, but I'll be back very soon" Black mist finished lifting from Enzo's crumpled body, and she charged toward me, apparently not quite as done as her previous words made it seem.

Her spirit form lashed out at me, latching on to my core and sucking power right from my main source. My shield had fallen when I lashed out, leaving me vulnerable to her attack, but it didn't make me weak.

"You're not welcome here. What part of that don't you understand?" I snarled as I fought back against her power.

Instead of answering mine, she asked a question of her own. "When are you going to realize I'm not going to take no for an answer? You will join me, and I will be free from this place. It's only a matter of when."

Pushing back, I dug deep for my dragon side. I had no idea why I did, but my instincts were telling me my elven and witch sides weren't going to be enough on their own to stop her from hurting me more than she already had.

Wings sprouted from my shoulder blades as I called on my third race for the first time. Red tinted my vision as I flapped the new additions to my back, pushing Malina's spirit away from me with pure force.

Agony like I'd never experienced before consumed my entire being as Malina forcefully withdrew from me, taking a part of me with her as she went.

"Ah, I feel honored you chose me as the reason to wake your dragon for the first time. Those wings are just what I needed to see to confirm your progress. Next time we meet, if you're still this difficult, I'll rip them from your back, one by one."

Her spirit circled around me once more, and I felt nails scratch across my left wing before she began to dissipate. The bitch might have had the upper hand for that fight, but I wasn't giving up. My gut told me a war was coming, and it wouldn't be the only time I faced her.

Once her presence was gone, I collapsed to the floor and heard the doors slam open. The council was coming, and it was their turn to deal with the mess before us. I was done, mentally and physically.

"Raegan, are you alright?" Headmaster Stone picked me up from the ground, stronger than I would have expected from such an old guy.

"Just get me out of here," I begged with a hoarse voice.

I wasn't ready to see Enzo in my current condition. I needed a clearer head before I saw him after what we had both been through, and he needed a thorough cleansing before we had our reunion.

"Where's Raegan?" I heard Enzo groan, and I ignored the pounding of my heart that was urging me to go to him.

"Please, Headmaster," I said.

He nodded and carried me from the room without another word. Instead of going back to my room, he carried me to his office and laid me down on a couch that seemed to come from nowhere. Closing my eyes, I gladly let my exhaustion take over.

"SHE NEEDS MORE TIME," AUNT JULES DEMANDED IN A soft but urgent voice. "My niece just did what the entire council couldn't do. It's the least she deserves."

"I understand that, Jules, but he's begging for her and we can't risk what he might do if she doesn't go to him. We don't know for sure that he's fully free of the darkness."

That last bit came from Headmaster Stone. From what I could gather in my shattered state, they were discussing me and Enzo. Deciding to see how far the conversation would get, I kept my eyes closed and breathing even as they continued.

"That's not her problem. Plus, I won't risk her being subjected to Malina's energy so soon after fighting her. Raegan has done more for you than necessary. I refuse to let you wake her before she's ready and demand even more from her. She's only a child," Jules said.

"It's been two days. If she doesn't wake soon, we're going to have to force her anyway, just to make sure she's okay. You can't keep her in here forever."

Shit. Two days since I busted through Enzo's cage? That was more than enough for me to hear.

"How about both of you let me decide for myself?" I suggested groggily.

"Raegan?" Aunt Jules' hands cupped both sides of my face as she leaned over from her spot next to the bed. "How are you feeling?"

"Like I was hit by a truck." Sitting up slowly, I realized I wasn't in my room, but in Aunt Jules'. "What's happened since I broke through the box?"

"Surprisingly, not much," Jules answered. "Malina has been quieter than usual, and Enzo has been back to normal, according to Alistair."

I glanced at him for confirmation. "He was out like you until yesterday, and he's been demanding to see you ever since. We won't force you, though."

Right, I thought. They wouldn't force me, but I was pretty much being volun-told based on the tone of his voice and what I had overheard. Not that I minded. Even though I was nervous, I wanted to see Enzo as well.

"What time is it?" I asked.

"Just after three in the afternoon," Jules answered before adding, "On Thursday."

"Can I get some food and shower first?" I glanced between the two of them.

Headmaster Stone nodded. "Of course. I'll leave you two. Just let me know when you're ready."

He stood from the chair at the foot of the bed and disappeared around the corner. When we heard the door click shut, Aunt Jules turned her full attention on me. "What happened?"

"They didn't tell you?" I asked in confusion.

"Well, they told me what they wanted me to know. I

want to make sure it matches what you remember." She grinned.

I couldn't fault her for not trusting them. Not that their intention was to keep her out of the situation, but there was a good chance they wanted the story of what happened to be spun in a different light than I recalled.

There was nothing good about what I remembered.

Starting from the moment the door to the conference room opened, to when the headmaster carried me out, I told Jules everything I could think of at the time. Even the part about me being part dragon, which she hadn't known. It had been the only part I withheld from her during my mental breakdown when she last arrived.

The reprimand on that subject wasn't as severe as it could have been, but considering I was recovering from magic overload, Jules took it easy on me.

When I was done, her arms wrapped around me. "I'm never leaving you again. It's like you attract chaos, and not in a good way."

"I'm going to be fine. I promise. It was just a lot all at once and, now that I've rested, I feel a lot better. As soon as I eat, I'll be back to normal," I promised, trying to minimize her worries.

"Do you want to eat in or go to the commissary?" she asked.

"Definitely in. I'll call Gemma while you order food."

Grabbing the phone I still had from Lyssa, I pressed Gemma's name in the favorites. Even though I finally had a smartphone, I still never used it for anything other than calls and the occasional text. Yes, I realized that made me sound like an old lady refusing technology, but I didn't care.

Within ten minutes, I had taken a shower, and our food arrived as soon as I got out. A steaming bowl of chicken alfredo and garlic bread was placed in front of me, with dessert waiting on the table. Gemma and Jules sat next to me on the bed with their own meals.

Even with the distraction of Gemma and food, though, Enzo hadn't been far from my mind. I knew I couldn't delay seeing him for much longer. My heart ached for him as I considered all he might have been through. I just needed to make sure I was at my best before I went to him.

"So, what are you going to do now?" Gemma asked after we filled her in.

"I'm going to go see him. Make sure he's okay, and then I don't know. We've both been through a lot, and that very well could have changed the direction we were headed in," I answered honestly.

"Fair enough," Gemma mumbled between bites of her pasta primavera. It was Italian night, and each of us had ordered a different kind of pasta. Jules was currently devouring spaghetti carbonara.

When we were done, I knew I had delayed the inevitable long enough. "Jules, will you take me to wherever Enzo is?"

"He's just in his room. Desmond put a boundary spell around it, so they'd know if he tried to leave just in case Malina still had a hold on him. He's been waiting for you."

"Oh." I guess I didn't need an escort, which meant I was going to have to face him on my own or admit I really wanted someone to hold my hand while I went. I didn't understand why I was so nervous, but I needed to squash the feelings within the five minutes it would take for me to walk to his dorm.

"We can still go with you if you'd like," Gemma added.

Hesitating, I almost said yes, but ended up shaking my

head. "I'll be fine, but thanks for offering. I'll let you both know when I'm done."

Putting my dishes in the butler box, I closed the door and heard the swoosh of air, meaning they'd disappeared just the same way as they arrived. That damn box was probably one of my favorite things about the academy. I hadn't done a dish in months, and I wouldn't ever complain about that.

Slowly, I made my way through the hallways. Students stared at me before leaning over to whisper to whoever they were with, probably having heard some horrid version about what happened already, but I couldn't find my give-a-damn to care and decided to ignore them.

When I arrived at the platform in Elven Hall, my hands began to shake, but I brushed it off and reminded myself this was necessary. No matter what happened in Enzo's room, he was back, and he was safe. I had done all I could do for him, and that would have to be enough, even if my heart continued to break.

Enzo's door was cracked open, and I wondered if he already knew I was coming. Not that it mattered, but the curiosity was there anyway.

"Hello?" I called as I pushed the door further open.

"Raegan?" Enzo responded with elation in his voice.

Joy filled me at the happiness radiating from him. He had been so full of hatred the last time I looked into his eyes that I wasn't sure I'd ever see the old Enzo again. The only problem was the hesitation I felt toward him. A part of me was afraid to let him back in, and I wasn't sure how much that part would affect how the coming conversation would go.

Within seconds, he was standing before me with the biggest smile on his face. When mine didn't quite reach my eyes, his darkened, but not the black I had seen before. The deep brown I was used to made its appearance.

"What's wrong? Are you not okay? They told me you were fine, which was the only reason I obeyed their stupid rules of me staying put. I didn't want to make anything worse for you." Anger dripped from his words at the thought of me not being alright.

"No, I'm fine. It's just been a while for us, and the last time I saw you... well, you weren't you, or at least, I don't think you were."

He reached for me, but I took a step back.

"I'm sorry, Raegan. I wasn't in control. Malina was there, but you pushed her out. I don't know how, but you did, and I couldn't be more proud of you." His eyes regained their golden sparkle, and I breathed a sigh of relief.

"Where have you been all this time?" I asked, reaching a hand out to him, which he gladly took.

"I was locked in the dungeon. Malina kept me hidden in her cell for weeks or what I thought was mere weeks, but apparently it was months. I was rendered unconscious for most of it and lost a lot of time. I managed to get out of the cell when you distracted her, but she took control of my mind before I officially left the dungeon, and there are some things I don't remember. Before I knew it, I was standing in front of the school, and the council took me in."

Maybe Malina had been the one to get to me when I lost time the day Enzo left. I had never figured out what happened before I woke up in my room with the massive pain in my head. It didn't matter much, though. It hadn't happened again, so I tried not to dwell on it.

"Did she say why she took you?"

He nodded. "It was motivation to make you fight for me. Every day you grew stronger, she went on and on about how soon she'd be free and the two of us would be her pawns. Then, within the last week, her plans changed. I don't know why, but suddenly I was no longer necessary to keep you motivated."

That was about the time I had finally let Enzo go. Since I was no longer fighting to find Enzo, Malina had figured out she lost her leverage. Bringing him back was a distraction I probably shouldn't allow, but I had a feeling that sticking together was also something she didn't want.

Seeing him now as I remembered him before he disappeared resurfaced all the feelings I thought I had managed to tuck away after months of suffering. I knew whatever nerves I had felt before coming to his room were unnecessary.

"What are you supposed to do now? I'm assuming she didn't just kick you out of the bird's nest without instructions," I said, trying to learn as much as I could before deciding what to do next.

"I think I was supposed to come back and hurt you. Well, Malina was by taking over my body, but you ended up being stronger than her, thankfully. I don't know what I would have done if I had hurt you."

"How long did she have control of you?" I cringed thinking it had been the entire time he was missing.

"For a day or two before I showed back up at the academy and until you came to visit me in the cage. I'm not sure I would have survived her darkness much longer than that. I'm still weak from it, if I'm being honest."

He took several steps closer, closing the gap between us, and I didn't back away. His hands wrapped around mine as he stared intently into my eyes. This time, the golden honey color sparkled, drawing me in like it had always done before.

"I know we have a lot to move past. I will do whatever it is that you need," he said with conviction. "All that time away made me realize you're all that matters. I have spent my entire life doing things the wrong way and for the wrong reasons, but for you, I'm going to be better. I'm going to make up for all of the bad I've done. I promise."

His words triggered a hundred more questions, but it wasn't the time to ask any of them. Instead, I met Enzo in the middle and pressed my lips to his for the first time in way too many months.

As I thought about all of the reasons I should have been more cautious, I realized I was done worrying so much. All that mattered was Enzo wasn't under Malina's control anymore and I had him back.

If I was wrong about him and everything else, I'd deal with the consequences when the time came. For the moment, I was going to enjoy the victory of having Enzo back where he belonged.

E very day after the first week of Enzo being back, Headmaster Stone, Desmond, and Bennett did daily scans on Enzo to test for dark energy, and all of them thankfully confirmed he was free from whatever hold Malina had on him. Even Gemma was impressed with how he was being toward me, and she didn't even really like Enzo.

So, after confirming I didn't have to worry about anything happening to him if we left the school buildings, I finally said yes to a date with him. We could go on a real date that didn't have to be held cooped up in his or my room, but still had to stay within the walls of the academy shield. As long as we were far away from the evil that continued to seep into me, I didn't care.

Malina's presence continued to grow stronger, and when I asked Headmaster Stone about it, he didn't really have an answer for me. The council had been working nonstop to contain Malina, but even the most powerful sorcerers, shifters, vampires, and elves couldn't stop whatever she was trying to accomplish.

But for tonight, I wasn't going to stress about it. There

was literally nothing I could do about Malina except wait for her to show her cards, so I might as well say "screw it" and live my life while I still had some freedoms.

"Do you need help getting ready for your date?" Gemma asked as she entered my room without knocking.

"Nope. All done." Glancing in the mirror one last time, I shook off my worrisome thoughts as best I could.

"Uh, are you sure?" she asked nervously.

"Yeah, why?" I was wearing jeans and a sweater with my hair down. It was going to be in the thirties that night. I didn't need to look cute; I needed to avoid hypothermia.

"Do you want me to do your makeup at least? Oh, and I also have these heeled boots you could borrow."

"Gemma, I appreciate the thought behind your words, but after everything that's happened, if Enzo isn't going to accept me for who I am, then I'll be glad he's back safe and sound, but nothing more will come from our relationship. This is who I am. I love who I am, and I'm not going to pretend to be someone else for a second first date." I considered the time he took me to the mountain peaks for our first date, but since so much time had passed, it felt like we were starting over, which hopefully wasn't a bad thing.

She let out a low whistle and clapped her hands. "You're seriously badass, and I want to be you when I grow up. The last time I went on a date, which was way too long ago, by the way, I went all out, and the jerk spilt his drink on my outfit. Didn't apologize or anything. I ended up ditching him when I excused myself to go clean up."

Grinning, I reached my hand toward her. "But that is who *you* are and there is nothing wrong with that. You enjoy all the dressing up, so own it whenever possible. You don't need to be me when you are already equally badass, my friend."

"Aww. Are we having a moment here? Like, a bestie moment that we can look back on when we're old and remember how awesome we were?"

"I believe we are. Now leave me alone. He should be here any minute."

She smirked at me and shook her head. "Nope, I think I'll stay. Give him a good talking to before he takes my little girl out."

"Oh, my gosh. You're ridiculous. Seriously, you need to leave." I began pushing her back toward the door in hopes of forcibly removing her from my room, but I was too late. A knock sounded, and Gemma's eyes lit up with mischief.

"Coming," I called out as I moved her out of my way.

"That's what she said," Gemma murmured as I passed her by.

Turning back to her, I flipped her off. "I kinda hate you right now."

"But you also kinda love me, so I don't care."

There was no winning this battle with her. Instead, I ran a hand through my hair, pretended I was completely ready for my date despite the jackhammers going off in my stomach now that Enzo had arrived, and opened the door.

Enzo stood on the other side with his signature grin I hadn't seen since before he disappeared. He wore jeans a shade lighter than mine with a hooded cream-colored Henley sweater and kept the top button undone. His hair was down instead of tied back like normal, and his eyes practically glowed as he smiled at me.

"Hello, beautiful." He leaned in and kissed my cheek.

I felt my face flush as I tried to keep him from coming inside. "Hi. Let's get going."

"You're not even going to say goodbye, Raegan? It's so unbecoming of you," Gemma called from behind me.

"Hi, Gemma," Enzo said, waving at her over my head.

"Oh, hi," she drawled. "Just a few things before you go. Please keep her out past midnight. Make sure to at least get to second base. Oh, and if she comes home with all of her clothes, you have failed at your date."

Pushing Enzo as hard as I could out the door he tried to step through, I turned back to Gemma. "I really do hate you right now." As I slammed the door shut, I heard her yell something about being the best part of my life, but I ignored her.

When I glanced at Enzo, his whole body was shaking in laughter. "Being in good with Gemma is much more fun than being on the outs with her."

"Yeah, you say that now. Just give it a few months. You'll change your mind," I complained, thinking of all the ways I was going to harm every hair on her head when I saw her again the following day.

Enzo brushed my hair back, his knuckles brushing over the slight points on my ears. "You really do look beautiful. I'm sorry she made you uncomfortable, but I promise we're going to take it slow tonight and only stick with things you're okay with."

"I really appreciate that." I pulled away a little and tugged him forward, so we could keep moving for two reasons: I didn't want to be in the hall when Gemma came out of my room. Also, he was making my girly bits go a little wild, so I needed a distraction from his overwhelming hotness.

"So, where are we headed?" I asked, mostly to distract myself.

"A surprise. Actually, one we need to hurry up for before the wind ruins it." He grabbed on to my hand and, within a second, we were outside on top of the tallest peak where we finished our original first date at.

Before I could really take in everything he had done, a gust of wind came tunneling over the mountain and almost knocked me on my ass. Enzo righted me as he waved his opposite hand. When he was done moving, the wind was gone, and it was about twenty degrees warmer.

"What did you do?" I asked as I saw his surprise was more than ruined.

"Put a shield over us, but I needed to be present to keep it active, so when I went to get you, all of this was left unprotected." He bent down, trying to salvage what was left of the candles and other assortments.

Kneeling, I began to help him and noticed a basket tucked next to the rocks. Delicious smells were permeating from it, making me drool a bit. I was more than excited to know that, while the chocolate and strawberries currently spread across the grassy area were ruined, not everything else was.

"Sorry, this wasn't how I wanted our date to start," he grumbled as we finished picking everything up.

"It's the thought that counts. You know how much I love it up here, and it means a lot to me that you thought to bring me here. Any time we can get away from the school is the best time."

Taking several steps closer to me, his hands trailed up my arms agonizingly slow before settling on my face and gently cupping my cheeks. His lips pressed to mine, and I eagerly pressed closer, happy to have a little bit of dessert before dinner.

My arms wrapped around his shoulders as my fingers became entangled in his silky-smooth hair. If I was a lesser woman, I might have even been jealous of his locks, but knowing he was all mine, I took full advantage.

Pressing my body closer to his, my hips made contact with the hard length of his groin, and I knew at least one of Gemma's suggestions for our date was definitely going to be happening, possibly even third base.

Enzo's mouth pulled away from mine and stalked down my neck, but then he pulled back to look into my eyes. The golden depths swirling and staring intently back at me were what I missed most while he was gone.

"We should eat before the food gets cold," he whispered.

"But I'm enjoying dessert," I hummed.

"As much as I am too, I also timed our date so we could eat dinner while the sun was setting, and I don't want you to miss it." His hands gently turned me around before wrapping around my waist, and he settled his chin on my shoulder.

My breath hitched as I took in the multitude of colors swirling together and the clouds moving through the sky as the sun set. Deep purples from the night began to emerge as the landscape before us deepened from orange to deep red, offset by the silver clouds floating across the horizon.

Dinner completely forgotten, we stood silently in each other's arms as the minutes ticked by. No words were needed to know this was a moment we would both remember. Energy passed between us everywhere our bodies touched, causing my skin to feel like it was on fire and the only way to put it out was to give more of myself to Enzo.

I finally had him back, and I didn't want to waste another moment, mostly because the threats from Malina were very real. I didn't know how to deal with her hurting those I cared about.

Life could be awfully short, even for supernaturals, and I decided as the final rays of the sun disappeared behind the mountains, I was done moving cautiously with Enzo. I wanted to give him all of me. There were no promises of a tomorrow in our current situation, and I wanted to have no regrets.

Turning around, I pressed my hand to his heart. It beat wildly beneath my fingers, and I knew without a single doubt in my heart that he was feeling what I was as I slid my other arm around his waist to bring him even closer.

"Are you sure?" he whispered before I even had to say anything.

"More sure than I've ever been of anything in my life."

His lips crashed down on mine in an all-consuming kiss that distracted me so thoroughly that I hadn't even realized we'd left the mountain top until the backs of my legs made contact with his bed and he gently laid me back on the soft surface.

"I'm going to worship every inch of your body before I'm done with you," he murmured passionately as he pulled my shoes off and made his way to the top of my pants.

Before he continued, a look of hesitation flashed across his face. "Are you absolutely positive this is what you want, Raegan? Once I taste you, I won't ever be able to let you go. You'll be mine for life, and I'm more than okay with that, but I need to know you are as well, because I can't lose you again."

Leaning up off the bed, I reached for him. "Enzo, I love you. I've known it since the moment you disappeared and my heart nearly ripped in two, but I refused to admit it, because I couldn't deal with the thought of losing another person I loved. Now that you're here, I don't want to miss out on a single thing with you."

His eyes darkened, and lines further creased on his face. "You love me?" He sounded so surprised, like nobody had ever told him those words before.

"Why wouldn't I? You have been there for me as often as was possible over the last seven months, pushing me beyond my limits and showing me what I was capable of, even when I didn't think I could. You're compassionate even if you can also be infuriating, and you have one of the sexiest grins in the world that makes my heart beat faster every time I see it."

His face softened, but he still didn't smile like I had hoped. "Nobody has loved me since my mother died, and I didn't think I would ever be worthy of it again, but I promise you, Raegan, I will be everything you need, and I will love you back just as fiercely."

No more words were spoken as clothes were stripped and hands moved everywhere. Just as he promised, Enzo worshiped every inch of my body until I was a writhing mess beneath him, begging for more. Begging for everything.

My body hummed with energy and when he slid into me for the first time, a lavender glow lit the room as our two beings became one, confirming I had made the right choice. Enzo was my happily-ever-after, and I was going to fight for as long as I could to show him he was worth all the love in the world.

More weeks passed after the date with Enzo, and I tried to enjoy the time we spent together, but after that night, things became complicated around the school. The first week he had been back was the calm before the storm, which was quickly turning into a hurricane right before our eyes.

Malina was constantly lashing out at me, breaking through on a daily basis, even with the new necklace Enzo had given me that was almost an exact replica of the one I had lost. When I had told him about the afternoon he was taken, his eyes darkened and body shook as he attempted to contain his rage.

I had finally convinced him that I was fine. Nothing bad had happened that I was aware of besides losing my necklace. We were back together, and he was safe, and that was all that mattered. It took him a while, but he finally accepted too much time had passed for us to try to figure out what happened to me on that day.

"If this bitch doesn't let up, I'm going to be physically

sick," Gemma complained as she took a seat next to us at lunch.

"What's wrong?" My body immediately tensed. Students had been leaving early, one by one, as Malina's strength continued to grow. School was closing a month early and next week was finals, but that didn't matter much to me. I still couldn't leave.

"Nothing that any of us can do about it." She rolled her eyes. "It's just too much darkness. The weight of it pressing down all around the school is making me nauseous. I'm so ready to leave next week."

I sighed, wishing I could say the same thing. Enzo squeezed my hand under the table, offering me his silent support. He was staying with me until the council figured out a way to get me out without giving Malina the opportunity she needed to escape.

I don't need the council to escape. Things are already in motion, which I know you can feel. I sense how the power draws you to me, she boasted inside my head. *You can fight it all you want, but your future is mine to control and my day is coming. I will show you what you were meant to be.*

My whole body shook as I pushed Malina's words out of my head. I refused to speak back to her any longer. There was nothing she was going to tell me that would be useful for what I wanted, so I didn't want to further fuel her drive.

"Everything okay?" Enzo asked.

Forcing a smile on my face, I nodded. "Of course. It's Friday and our last weekend before school gets out."

Neither he nor Gemma seemed excited or convinced I truly was, and I hated that Malina had ruined this year for everyone.

I had not-so-willingly come to the academy to learn how to defend myself and find out who my parents were. I might have failed at one of those things, but I knew I was more than capable of holding my own against another scavenger like the one who had attacked me the night I met Enzo.

Aunt Jules came rushing into the commissary and straight to our table. She had stayed at the academy, but I honestly hadn't seen much of her. She had been too busy working with Headmaster Stone on a secret project I assumed had to do with Malina, but she refused to tell me anything about it.

"I need both of you to come with me." A grin broke out across her face as she pointed at me and Enzo, and only some of my worry eased.

"What's going on?" I asked with trepidation as I started to stand.

"We don't have time for questions. Just come on," she pressed.

"Oh, hell no," Gemma piped in as she pushed away from the table. "I'm not getting left behind."

Jules groaned. "I don't care who else comes, I just need you to move your asses." She grabbed Enzo's and my hands, pulling us along and gathering stares from the other students as we moved through the commissary.

"Where are we going?" I asked while glancing back to make sure Gemma was keeping up with us. She was right at my heels, which I appreciated.

"To the front gate. I finished my project with the headmaster."

Hesitation slammed through me, even though I was curious as hell. The main entrance was painful if I moved too close to it. The stronger Malina became, the more powerful the enchantments on the shield had become, which meant my connection to her forced me to be even further away from leaving the confines of the academy.

Instead of continuing to question her, I let her pull us along. Enzo seemed intrigued about Jules' enthusiasm, but he held his tongue. He seemed to realize, like I had, that we weren't going to find anything out until we arrived where Jules was leading us.

The closer we came to the front of the school, the more my body tensed, and my muscles recoiled from the energy lashing out at me, but I ignored it, trusting Jules to make it worthwhile for me.

"How much farther are we going?" Enzo asked as he glanced at me.

Sweat had broken out on my face, and my jaw was tight as the pain became even worse than I had anticipated.

Jules glanced back. "Shit. I'm sorry, Raegan, but we're almost there. We have to be just close enough or it won't work."

"What won't work?" Enzo asked, and I was grateful, because if I opened my mouth, I was afraid all that would come out would be screams as everything within me began to burn.

She ignored his question and, about a minute later, came to an abrupt stop. We were about ten feet from the main entrance, and as I fought to stay upright, Enzo's hands wrapped around my waist.

"I got you," he whispered.

"Is she going to be okay?" Gemma asked, concern weighing heavily on her words.

"I hope so," Jules responded as she shoved a vial full of some red liquid into my hands. "Drink this, and then run for the shield. You only have a few seconds before it won't work. That's why we had to be so close."

"You're kidding me, right?" Enzo snapped. "You want to

risk having her entire body get shredded without testing it on anything else?"

Jules stepped right up to Enzo. "Listen, Elf. I appreciate everything you've done for my niece, but I love her, too. I would never ask this of her if I hadn't done everything in my power to make sure it would work, including making sure Headmaster Stone approved it. Now, back off and let her make the decision."

She turned to me and pulled me out of Enzo's grasp.

"You don't have to do this, but I know how much you want out and I wouldn't ask you to trust me if I didn't think it was worth it."

I nodded and managed to find my voice without crying out. "I know you wouldn't, and I'm thankful for you doing whatever it is you've done. I'm assuming I'll find out what that is when I'm done."

She grinned. "You know it, along with the biggest slice of chocolate cake to go along with the celebration."

"Throw ice cream in and we have a deal."

"Done," Jules said before turning to Enzo. "I need you to shield her as soon as she drinks the vial. Your strongest shield, more powerful than anything you've ever done before. I need her to basically be invisible. Can you do that?"

"Of course I can, but why didn't you ask the council to do it?"

That was a great question, and I was wondering the same thing.

"Because there is a power simmering beneath your skin that I sense from you. I believe if you were truly tested, your abilities could rival that of the council's. Plus, you have a connection to Raegan none of them have. It's motivation for you to do it right the first time in order for her to not get hurt."

He murmured something underneath his breath, but the pounding in my head was so severe at that point, I could barely even hear their normal conversation, let alone his mumblings.

My hands covered both of my ears. "That all sounds great, but can we get this moving along now before my head explodes?" Between the shield's power and Malina's incessant demands to get through, I was about ready to pass out.

"I'm so sorry, Raegan," Jules said. "I promise it will all be worth it in just a minute. As long as Enzo's ready, drink the vial, then run."

My eyes met his, and he nodded. "I won't let anything hurt you."

I smiled, or at least, I thought I did. Hard to say through all of the sharp pains assaulting my head and now chest, but I knew he meant his previous words. If it was within his power, not even a hair would ever be harmed on my body.

Pulling the cap off, I didn't even bother smelling the concoction. Instead, I readied myself for the short sprint I'd have to do from where we stood outside the shield. It wasn't far, in reality, but as I considered what could happen if it didn't work, it felt like miles away.

"I'm ready." After taking one deep and calming breath, I tossed the contents of the vial into my mouth, swallowed in one gulp, and began racing toward the border. My legs went numb as I passed through the open gate, and my vision blurred.

I wasn't going to make it.

My steps faltered, and I almost tripped as everything began moving in slow motion.

Adjusting my stride, I righted myself before I hit the ground and pressed forward but didn't make it very far.

Malina screamed in my head, causing me to fall to my knees.

YOU CAN'T LEAVE ME!

Watch me, bitch, I responded, even more motivated to complete my task.

Warmth filled me as I sensed Enzo's energy surround me, and I once again had faith I could accomplish getting to the other side of the shield.

Standing back up, the agony began to recede and, before I knew it, there was no pain at all. Turning back around, all I saw was the dilapidated old house that was the illusion of what the council wanted humans to see.

"I did it!" I cheered, knowing they could see me.

After months of being stuck at Shadow Veil, I was finally free. Even Malina's presence was severely muted. I could still sense her just beneath the surface, but it was fading, and I couldn't have been happier.

Jules, Enzo, and Gemma appeared within seconds. Each of them hugged me, offering their own congratulations, but when I met my aunt's face, I knew it wasn't going to be all celebrations.

"What's wrong?" I asked.

"Well, I'm ridiculously glad it worked. I swear, you have no idea how happy I am that all the time I spent with the witches in New Orleans when I was bored at my pack could be put to good use, but now I need you to go back. I was only given permission to try this, and then you had to return."

My eyes widened as any hope I had at real freedom was dashed. "Why?"

"Because there are still hundreds of students in the academy who need to finish their finals next week. If you leave permanently, the council believes Malina will tear the school down in an attempt to get free and find you. They can't risk all of them to give you your freedom. Not yet anyway."

Damn it. I could understand where they were coming from. If even one student was hurt because of my departure, then I wouldn't be able to live with myself.

"Can I just walk back in?" I asked, remembering the shield was mostly meant to keep evil out.

"Not without this." Jules handed me another vial. "Don't worry, I have several more where those came from, so as soon as all of the students are gone, we're busting you out of here. I promise."

Taking a few steps forward, I wrapped my arms around her and hugged tight. "Thank you so much."

"There isn't anything I wouldn't do for you, Raegan. Remember that next time you're in trouble instead of trying to shut me out." She smiled, but I could tell from the tone of her voice she was serious. It had hurt her more than I realized when I kept my struggles at the academy from her for so long.

My eyes met Enzo's, and he nodded his confirmation that he was ready for the second round. It was time to go back to my living hell.

Doing everything just the same as I had done before, it was a lot easier to get in than it was to get out, which surprised me for some reason. Probably because once I was back in, the further forward I continued to go, the less pain I was in.

That was only until my eyes caught on the main entrance of the school. Walls were shaking and gargoyle statues were falling from the rooftops, shattering into thousands of pieces as they hit the ground.

I had been outside the shield too long.

MALINA! I demanded. *I won't go as long as you leave the school alone, but if you continue, I'm out of here and I won't ever come back.*

Don't threaten me, child, she snarled in return. *I control you, not the other way around. You're lucky I need more time, or I'd gladly make this academy turn to rubble right before your eyes, just so you would feel the blame of all of those deaths. See what happens if you test me again.*

Malina pulled out of my head as soon as she finished her threats. Glancing around, the buildings began to settle, and students stopped screaming from within the school. She had kept her word, but I had finally pushed her too far, and for the first time, I truly feared how far she would go to punish me if I did it a second time.

CHAPTER TWENTY-THREE

Hours later, the tremors finally stopped from Malina's wrath and the students went back to the dorms. When it had all started, the council sent out emergency alerts to all of the students on their tablets, telling them to gather in the commissary.

When the four of us entered, everything was in chaos. All of the council members and teachers were present, answering questions and trying to calm everyone down, but the hysteria was constant until the building finally stopped shaking.

"Did anyone get hurt?" I asked Headmaster Stone when we finally pushed our way through to him.

He shook his head. "Not seriously. A couple of head bumps and bruises from falling items, but nothing to be concerned with. Are the rest of you okay?"

I nodded, but Jules spoke first. "Yes, everything went better than I thought until we realized Malina was retaliating."

"I promised her I wouldn't leave again if she stopped whatever it was she was doing," I said. "She mentioned not being ready yet, and then stopped. I haven't heard from her since."

"Very well," Headmaster Stone replied. "At least we know what she's capable of now. As soon as the students are settled again, the council is going to meet, and we will come up with a plan. Since it appears Ms. Reeves is more involved than I realized, the *four* of you are welcome to join us."

The last bit was said with a disapproving tone toward me for filling in Gemma without their permission, but I didn't really care. She had been there for me throughout every obstacle since I arrived. I wouldn't shut her out, regardless of what the council thought.

"Thank you, Headmaster. We appreciate being included," Enzo said from beside me.

Glancing over, I realized he almost always stood at my side, rarely in front of me or behind me. He treated me as his equal. As that revelation rolled through me, I knew without a doubt I had found the best partner I could ever ask for.

Headmaster Stone walked away, and the four of us filed out of the commissary, trying to avoid the crowds, but not doing a very good job. We were split up at the doors but found each other again at the dorm entrances.

"What do we do now?" Gemma asked.

"We prepare for finals and hope everyone gets off campus before Malina decides to strike again," I said.

At that point, I had zero faith that we would be able to beat Malina. The council didn't seem to have any ideas on what to do, and until the connection I had with her was broken, I wasn't all that keen on trying to kill her. A part of me figured there would be consequences to that action, and I had no desire to find out what those were.

"So, we just play defense for the time being?" Gemma quirked a brow at me, but I glanced at Enzo and Jules for confirmation.

"It seems like the best option at this point," Enzo answered. "Malina escaping is inevitable. All we can try to do is make sure the collateral damage is as small as possible."

Collateral damage meaning people. How many people would die in Malina's quest to free herself from the dungeon? That was a question I didn't have the answer to, and I wondered just how responsible I was for all of it.

I had been the one to open the dungeon door, but the pull was there before I did so. It hadn't been *all* my curiosity. Malina had a hold on me the moment I stepped foot into the academy. It might not have been as strong as it was right then, but it had been there, nonetheless.

"Let's go check our rooms and make sure there's no real damage. Then, hopefully the council will be ready for us," Jules suggested.

Since three of us had rooms in Hybrid Hall, Enzo came with us in case we needed help with anything if stuff had fallen over.

When Enzo followed me into my room, I was relieved to see only a few things had moved from their previous locations. The biggest disturbance was that my butler box was on the ground, but Enzo righted it for me while I checked my dresser and bathroom.

A few picture frames I had on the dresser had fallen to the carpeted flooring, but none of them were broken. My hand ran over my favorite picture of me with my parents two summers ago. I couldn't believe they had been gone for more than a year or how much life had changed since then.

I was no longer the naïve girl in the picture staring back

at me. Pride rolled through me as I thought of all I had overcome in the last eighteen months. My only "what ifs" were how different my life might have been if my parents had been honest with me.

What had been the point of hiding me away? What good did it do? Were my birth parents really that awful that I needed to be kept away from the world I was born into? All of those questions I had hoped to answer since arriving at Shadow Veil Academy, but I was no closer now than I had been then.

"Your butler box still works," Enzo said as he handed me a warm cup of hot chocolate with tiny marshmallows floating at the top.

"Thank you." I put the picture down and took the drink from him as I ventured to the bathroom. "My mirror is cracked, but other than that, everything seems to be fine. Hopefully the others were just as lucky."

"Let's go find out." He grabbed my hand, and I set the mug down before we went to Gemma's room.

She was just coming toward the door when we arrived. "Nothing broken, but there's a mess I'll need to deal with later."

Releasing Enzo's hand, I wrapped an arm around her back. "I'll help you."

We followed Enzo to Jules' room. The door was cracked open, so we let ourselves in. She was kneeling beside her bed.

"Shit." She hissed before placing her pointer finger in her mouth.

"Are you okay, Jules?" I asked, moving to her side.

"Yeah, there was a glass on my nightstand that broke. I was trying to pick up the glass and cut myself. Should be fine in a minute. How were the rest of your rooms?"

Glancing around hers, it appeared to have the most damage, including a hairline crack going up the wall next to me.

"Nothing we won't have cleaned up later when we get back," Gemma answered.

Handing Jules her small garbage can, I moved in to help her, but she pushed me away. "I got this. You go with Enzo and check his room. It's further up and might have damage that needs to be addressed sooner rather than later."

I hadn't even thought of that. After a quick hug good-bye, I pushed Enzo out into the hallway so he could zap us to his door. Knowing that those with the same ability couldn't just drop into any room was a really great thing most of the time, but I could have done without that perk just then.

"Ready?" he asked as he wrapped both arms around me.

Leaning up, I pressed my lips to his. "Now I am."

He winked, then the hallway disappeared, and we were standing in front of his door. Quickly, he entered his code, but the door would only open halfway. Enzo stuck his head through the small opening and managed to reach his left arm through. Something thudded on the ground, then the door fully opened.

"What was that?" I asked before entering.

"Maybe you shouldn't come inside," he said instead of answering me.

Pushing him out of the way, my hands covered my mouth as soon as I got a peek inside. Jules had been right. All of the windows were cracked, some even missing chunks of glass. There had been a piece of drywall blocking the door that had fallen from the ceiling and was now on the floor in front of me.

Stepping over it, I continued into the dorm with Enzo.

He went toward his bedroom while I went to the kitchen. The granite countertop was cracked down the middle of one side, and some of the smaller appliances he probably never used had fallen to the floor, but no other damage that I could see.

Venturing into the living room, I gave the windows a wide berth, wanting to avoid the glass on the floor. Paintings and pictures were on the ground, but there didn't appear to be any personal effects damaged.

"My bedroom is going to need some magical work, and the windows will need help, but not as bad as I feared," Enzo said as he joined me.

"You expected worse and still came with us to our dorms first?" I asked, surprised.

"Of course, I did. There was a higher chance of you needing my help than there being anything I could do to prevent any more damage here. What was done, was done."

"Can you fix this yourself?" I asked, looking back at the windows.

In some of my witch trainings, I knew I would have been able to do so with some more practice, but I wasn't ready yet for something of this magnitude. Hopefully, his elven magic would be sufficient.

"Yeah, I'll close up the windows and worry about the rest later. The council is ready for us."

Taking a deep breath, I watched in fascination as Enzo gathered magic into his hands while walking toward the windows. When he stood in front of each one, all he had to do was place his palms on the surface, and the glass slowly melded back together.

On the last one, he glanced back at me. "Do you want to try it?"

Shaking my head, I said, "We don't really have time."

But I would have loved to try it if we did, I thought to myself.

Disappointment must have been evident on my face, because he wasn't taking no for an answer. "The council will wait. You're an important piece in all of this. If you can't get it, we'll take off, but it won't hurt to try. I already sent a message to Jules, and she and Gemma will meet us there. We have an extra few minutes."

Giddiness filtered through me as I followed his previous steps and met him at the last window. "What do I do first?"

"Find your tether within, and pull on that magic. Gather healing magic in your hands. Even though you're not healing a physical being, you're still fixing the glass."

Closing my eyes, I focused on my inner energy, searching for the tether I had become so familiar with over the last few months. Once I latched on to it, my thoughts focused on healing and fixing as I drew the magic to my hands.

"Very good," Enzo said.

Peeking down, there was a yellow glow to my fingers, which surprised me since it was normally teal, but healing energy must have been different. As long as Enzo wasn't questioning it, then I wouldn't either.

"Now, place your palms on the window and gently push the magic into the glass. Not too fast or you'll overwhelm it and the whole thing will shatter."

Geez, no pressure there, I thought.

Stepping forward, I did as he asked, keeping my eyes wide open on the window before me. Gradually, I pushed the energy from my hands into the broken glass, but nothing was happening.

"A little faster than that, but not too much," Enzo urged.

Ugh. Magic was so precise. I almost pulled back, not

wanting to shatter the entire surface, but when my foot made even the slightest movement Enzo's hand pressed to my lower back.

"You can do this. Give it one more try," he whispered in my ear before backing away again.

Not wanting to disappoint him, and also really wanting to know if I could do it, I tried again. This time with a little more push on my part. The spiderweb cracks around my hand began to close, and a grin spread across my face.

"A little more and you'll have it," Enzo said as he watched intently.

Doing as he suggested, I gave just a bit more push, then tilted my head back in amazement as my energy filtered through the rest of the window. Within a minute, it appeared as if nothing had happened to it.

Removing my hands, I pulled my magic back in before sliding closer to Enzo. "Thank you for believing in me."

"You will always have me in your corner. Now, let's go see what the council has planned for us."

A piece of his bronze hair had fallen out of his hair tie and rested on his cheek. I brushed it back as he leaned in for a kiss, which I happily returned. We headed out of the room together, and he zapped us to Magic Hall.

We appeared right behind Gemma and Jules. When I placed my hand on Gemma's arm, she squealed. "Don't do that shit," she snapped, causing me to laugh.

I shrugged. "I was just trying to let you know we were here. My bad."

Headmaster Stone opened his door with a solemn look on his face. Something had happened, and it wasn't good for us.

"What's wrong?" Jules asked.

"I'm afraid there will be no meeting. The council is

divided, and we need to sort a few other matters out before proceeding. As soon as I know more, I will call for you," he replied in a confident voice that was betrayed by the worry lines around his eyes.

"If there is anything we can do, please let us know," Enzo offered.

The headmaster nodded, then slipped back into his office and closed the door behind him.

None of us said anything, because there wasn't much to say.

Malina had done exactly what I believed she wanted and only time would tell how much that was going to screw us. If the council couldn't work together, I wasn't sure what hope we had in making sure nobody else was hurt in Malina's quest for freedom.

When I looked around, I knew without a doubt if any of the three people at my sides were harmed because of the council's lack of cooperation, they would find out just how pissed off I could get.

/ CHAPTER TWENTY-FOUR

Five days had passed, and finals were over. The council still hadn't met with us, but we hoped that didn't mean there was nothing happening on their end. Earlier that day, students began to leave the academy and by tomorrow morning, it was supposed to be deserted.

Enzo assumed we wouldn't be able to leave until the council figured out how to keep Malina from ripping the school in half.

While laying on Enzo's bed and staring up at the ceiling, my mind was running wild with questions. "How is Malina so much more powerful than the council combined? I never really questioned it, because they continued to put forth so much effort, but now that it seems like they've given up, I don't understand."

Enzo stopped rummaging through his desk to turn toward me in his chair. "Malina is a Doyen, an original being, the last of her kind that we can prove. They can only die by another Doyen or willingly. Malina wasn't always evil. It wasn't until after the council was formed and the other originals chose to die that she grew greedy with her power. There was no one left to keep her in check."

"So, you're saying we have no chance at killing her, even if we can stop her?" I asked.

He nodded. "That's why she's been trapped underneath Shadow Veil all these years. She would never choose to die, and without another Doyen around, the only thing we can do is contain her. But, it seems as though she is even more powerful than she was last time she was free."

"How did the council beat her then?"

Enzo opened his mouth to answer, but I didn't hear anything he said. My palms pressed against my ears, though it was no use. The ringing in them was rising to screeching levels, and Malina was back.

Hello, my sweet. Did you miss me?

I couldn't even find the strength to respond to her. Everything hurt, and I was extremely grateful I was already lying down.

Enzo's face came into view. He was speaking, but I still didn't know what he was saying. He pulled his phone up to his ear, but then the bed started to rattle, and I knew the time had come. Malina was ready for her grand escape.

That's right. We're getting out of here, and I'll show you just how powerful you can be without all the rules of the council.

I won't go with you. I will fight you with everything I have.

We'll see about that, she replied mockingly, then disappeared from my thoughts, and the pain receded.

"I don't know. She can't seem to move. I'm bringing her downstairs before things get worse," Enzo's panicked voice sounded from across the room.

"I'm okay, but we won't be for long. Malina is coming

for us," I said as I slid my legs off the bed and slowly stood up.

"Now?" Enzo asked, still on the phone.

"Yes, we need to get the rest of the students off of school grounds."

"Did you hear that, Jules? Yes, do that, and we'll meet you out front when we're done here. We can't wait on the council to send out the alerts this time." Enzo turned to me when he hung up the phone. "Jules is going to start evacuating Hybrid Hall, Gemma is headed to the headmaster, and we need to clear out Elven Hall. We'll meet them out front when we're done."

"What about the witches, vampires, and shifters?" I asked rattled. We couldn't leave anyone behind if we had the ability to save them from Malina's ire.

"I'm sending a message now to the teachers I know in those halls. They'll take care of it. We need to go." He grabbed my hand, and we raced from the bedroom, heading straight for the door. As it closed behind us, Lyssa and Drake appeared in front of us.

"What's happening?" Lyssa demanded.

"Malina is coming, and everyone needs to leave now," Enzo said, and I wondered if either of them would really understand the importance of what that meant.

"Drake and I will take levels one through three if you two want to get the rest of the upper ones," Lyssa offered, and I was more grateful than ever that we had come to some sort of truce all those months ago.

"Thank you. Make sure they go outside the shield completely," Enzo insisted. "It will be safer for them out there than it will be in here for the time being."

Before waiting for her response, Enzo zapped us to the level below his. Doors were on each side of the hallway. We had no idea who was still on campus and who wasn't, so we just pounded on doors and kept moving.

As elves began exiting their rooms, Enzo yelled instructions at each of them. Finally, when we were almost done with the floor, the school alarm sounded, meaning Gemma had arrived at Headmaster Stone's office. Walls still shook around us, but nothing as bad as it had been for me in Enzo's bed. Malina must have made me believe it was worse than it was while she was in my head.

When we arrived on the fourth floor, students were already mostly gone. Most doors had been left open in their haste to escape the pandemonium.

"Let's go," Enzo suggested. "With the alarms and the shaking getting worse, students would have to be stupid to stay indoors. We need to get out and make sure they know to go outside the school grounds."

"She's not in my head anymore, Enzo. I don't know how much time we have left." Worry began to take over, and I hated that there was little chance we could stop Malina.

"We just need to keep moving and do the best we can. I'm sure the council is already working on getting everyone out as well."

Focusing on his strength, I nodded before he teleported us downstairs. Headmaster Stone was on the front steps, directing students just like Enzo thought, and I breathed a little lighter at seeing things in motion.

"We need to check on the dungeon," I suggested. "What about the guards? I've met Ryn a few times and he doesn't deserve to die if the council knows they can't stop her."

"Ryn quit a few months ago, and I'm sure the others are fine. They know what to do," Enzo said rather abruptly, causing me to wonder what he knew that I didn't.

Before I could question him further, arms wrapped around me from the back. "Oh, thank God you're okay," Jules said. "We got everyone out. It helped there was only half the number of students and they had just done this last week."

Turning around, I hugged her back. "Where's Gemma?"

"Right here," she said, coming toward us from the commissary. "A few students went there since that was where they were directed last time, but they're headed out the gates now."

Those I loved most were by my side, but we weren't in the clear yet. Walls were cracking up the sides, and stones fell crashing to the ground as everything about the academy became weaker.

"We can't just watch it fall," I said.

"We won't," Headmaster Stone replied from behind us. "All of the students are outside the shield. I've told the guards to lift the bindings. We can't lose this school. There is only so much repairing magic can do. We're going to have to let her go and figure out a way to disable her later."

Shit, it was just as Enzo thought before. I didn't like it, but it didn't seem like anyone did and there were no other plans set in place, so I just had to deal with it and hope it was the right choice.

Malina was just too damn powerful.

"Where is the rest of the council?" Jules asked.

"Around the academy. They'll be here soon, but so will Malina. We have no idea what she'll do once she's free, so prepare yourself. Best-case scenario, she will simply flee, and we will hunt her down later."

My mouth opened to ask what he thought the worst-case scenario was, but I didn't really want to know. Instead,

I focused on drawing from my well of power and brought forth my magic. My hands buzzed with energy ready to be thrown in whatever direction it was needed.

Headmaster Stone moved to my side. "If she tries to take you, use whatever means necessary to stop her, Raegan. I know your dragon side has been free ever since you broke the box when Enzo was in it, and even without proper training, your dragon is your greatest defense. Don't forget that."

"I won't."

He stepped away as Fiona and Bennett came racing toward us. They stayed just out of hearing range from us, but I didn't care. My attention was on the school doors. Malina would walk through them at any moment, and I wouldn't be caught off guard.

Enzo's hand wrapped around mine, and I worried my charged-up hands would harm him. Instead, the teal from my magic and the red from his made the same lavender glow we usually created whenever we had sex. It had happened every time since the first occasion, but I hadn't thought much of it before. Though, right then I was wondering if we were somehow connected because of it or what it might mean. Shaking the thoughts from my head, I decided later on would be a better time to analyze my relationship with Enzo.

"She's coming," he snarled as his grip tightened around mine.

My face pinched, wondering how he knew that and what I was missing, but then it smacked me right in the face.

The heavy oily feeling I remembered from my visits to the dungeon was flowing out of the academy in heavy waves.

The doors slammed further open, wood splitting from the force used as she stepped out of the school. She was tall, close to six feet, with creamy white skin and slick, straight black hair that fell halfway down her back. Her hollow silver eyes moved across the line of us waiting for her, then stopped when they met mine.

"Ah, my sweet Raegan. Look at how you've grown." Her hands lifted the bottom of the billowing blood-red dress she wore as she came down the steps. "I see your father in you. Well, one of them, at least. It's a pity you didn't get more of my genes, but the end result is still the same."

My knees buckled, but Jules and Enzo each had a hold on me, keeping me upright. She said... No, she had to be lying. Everyone said she had been locked away for twenty years. I was only eighteen. The math didn't add up. And multiple fathers? No, she was purely insane. That had to be it.

"No, you're not my mother. She was greater than you could ever dream of being," I snapped back. Even if my parents weren't blood, I realized I no longer cared who gave birth to me. They would always be Mom and Dad.

"Ah, your guardian was a powerful sorceress. It's why it took so long to find you. They hid you from me, but they made a mistake in doubting my ambitions. I created you, and you belong to me. I wasn't going to give you up that easily."

"You were locked away when she was born," Jules cut in. "You can't be her birth mother."

"Very observant, and also correct, but Raegan is special. She doesn't have a birth mother *or* father. I created her, and another sorcerer I had taken under my wing made sure she continued to grow until I needed her. That was, until he betrayed me and hid her from me. Then, I killed him and brought in Desmond to take his place on the council."

Holy shit. I was... I didn't know what I was, but I wasn't even born.

I was *made*.

By the most evil supernatural being that I knew of, no less.

"You killed Jakobi?" Headmaster Stone sneered at Malina before he turned toward Desmond. "And you've been helping her?"

"I wasn't the only one. She was going to get out with or without my help. I had to keep my family safe, Alistair," Desmond hissed with little remorse, making me think his family had nothing to do with his decision to betray the council.

Headmaster Stone was done speaking. His hands lifted, one directed at Malina, the other at Desmond. "You won't get away with this." Power slammed into Malina but did no damage that I could see. Then, he focused on Desmond, and the other council members turned on him as well.

Jules and Gemma moved into action, putting up shields and preparing for Malina's fight, but by the smirk on her face, she seemed to enjoy watching the council fall apart too much to do anything else just yet.

As much as I wanted to fall apart from her revelations about who I was and where I came from, I knew I couldn't. I needed to make sure none of my family was hurt and possibly even keep Malina locked away.

Now that Desmond could no longer sabotage things, there was a slight chance we could best her, and I wouldn't let the opportunity go without trying.

Instead of putting up a shield, I called on my dragon and grunted as my wings ripped free from my shoulder blades, taking half of my shirt with them, but mostly just exposing my back. Scales covered my arms, and my vision increased as soon as the transformation was done.

Being a dragon hybrid was badass.

Charging forward, I threw my most lethal magic at her, but she barely flinched.

"Your raw strength is not enough to stop me, but if you come with me willingly, I will make you the second most powerful being in the world. If you force my hand, I will simply continue to syphon power from you like I've been doing since you arrived at the academy."

She took a step toward me and smirked.

"I have one more secret. Would you like to know it? It might just help you make the right decision and prevent anyone from getting hurt."

Enzo moved in beside me, holding his hand out defensively, but not actually using his power. "We had an agreement, Malina."

"Oh, *Lorynzo*. You would say that, wouldn't you? I think your betrayal hurt the most. I trusted you, and you left me. That makes our agreement null and void."

"I did everything that was required of me."

Her gaze moved back to me, ignoring Enzo's pleas, which further confused me. "Did you know that elves are experts at deceit? They can change their appearance and hide their aura as if they didn't even exist. Your *Enzo* over there? He's a master at it, thanks to me."

My head swiveled between the two of them. I didn't want to believe Enzo could have had anything to do with Malina, but he had basically already admitted to being in cahoots with her. The rigid set of his jaw told me just how much her words were infuriating him.

"So what if you made him stronger? That doesn't make Enzo a bad person," I said, readying myself to attack her.

"But would him also playing the part of my guard *Ryn* and bringing you back to the academy for me make him a bad person?" she taunted.

The world froze around me as her words sunk in.

My first thought was it couldn't be true, but as I recalled each time I'd had an interaction with Ryn, I realized Enzo had never been on the school grounds.

Enzo had also told me earlier that Ryn no longer worked as a guard.

"Is it true?" I asked him, my words holding no emotion. I had given Enzo all of me, and if he had been lying to me this whole time, I wasn't sure what I would do.

"Raegan, you have to listen to me and not her. You don't understand. I—"

"No," I snarled. "I don't want to hear any more."

My wings spread, and I felt my body growing taller and wider. That had never happened before, but I didn't take a moment to question what was happening. Instinct took over as my fingernails turned to talons and I charged for Malina.

She had ruined my life, and I wanted her to pay for all of the agony I would be dealing with later. Much later when this was over.

Wings flapped behind me, pushing me forward with a force I wasn't sure could be stopped. Slamming into Malina, I knocked her on her ass and pressed my clawed hands to her chest. I had no idea what kind of magic I was using— witch, or elf, or even dragon. All that mattered was she hurt like I did.

As my fists began to pound into Malina's face, her shoulders started to shake with laughter. "You have come a long way, child, but you're not strong enough to beat me. You never will be."

Power slammed into me, knocking me back at least ten

feet onto the hard ground. Gemma stood above me, reaching a hand out to help me up, but I didn't take it. I was afraid if I touched her, I would hurt her, and that was the last thing I wanted.

Once I was back up, a gargoyle caught my attention, but its eyes were no longer pointed at me like I was used to. When I followed the almost-human glare, it was directed at Malina.

When my eyes landed on her, she had her hand around Enzo's neck, grinning at me. "Want me to kill him for you? He betrayed us both. I could do it so easily."

He wasn't even fighting back. Maybe he felt bad enough for all he had done that he was ready to die, but could I really be the one to say yes? To give permission for his murder?

No, I couldn't. If he was suffering that badly, then he deserved to live with it.

"Do whatever you want. He means nothing to me anymore," I said, remaining nonchalant. I had a feeling if I told Malina not to kill him, she would do so just to spite me for fighting back. "Look at him. He's broken anyway. Better to let him live with his agony than give him the freedom from his guilt."

She nodded at me. "I like the way that you think." With more force than necessary, she tossed Enzo's body to the side, and his head cracked against a fallen stone. "Now that we've gotten that out of the way, are you ready to leave?"

"She's not going with you, Malina," Headmaster Stone said from behind me.

I turned toward him, my wings barely missing his face since I forgot they were still extended. His face was already bruised, but he was not beaten. The rest of the council stood behind him with Desmond restrained. Their fight was over; one traitor dealt with, at least.

"Actually, I'll decide for myself," I stated loudly, "but not today. Malina, if you want any chance of me coming with you willingly, you need to leave. You need me, not the other way around. I have lost almost everything and everyone I care about. It doesn't matter to me if you kill me, but I think it matters to you if I come willingly."

Her brow quirked, but she didn't say anything.

"Show me that I can work with you and give me time. Only then will I consider voluntarily going with you," I finished.

"You have some facts straight, but that's not how any of this works, Raegan. I don't *need* you to come by choice. You're still useful to me locked away where I have access to your abilities. You're coming with me one way or another today."

Her gaze moved to Jules and Gemma, the only two people in my life I could still fully trust and refused to lose.

"You won't touch them," I growled. "They have nothing to do with this."

"But they do. You need to stop caring so much, and there's only one way to make that happen." Malina's hand twisted in the air as if she was trying to grasp something small. Then, Gemma's strangled voice sounded from behind me.

When my eyes landed on my best friend, she was kneeling on the ground, face turning red as she grabbed at her throat.

"You would rather make me wrathful than uncaring?" I yelled, trying to break Malina's attention on Gemma. "I'm a lot easier to deal with when I'm not pissed off."

Proving my point, fire heated within my hands, and

once I could no longer handle the burn, I threw the ball of energy at Malina. The flame hit the center of her chest, and I finally got my point across as I heard Gemma take several gasps of air.

Malina's eyes narrowed at me, and I was certain she was going to fight back, but before she could make a move, the gargoyle I had noticed before seemed to extend its wings. He was still perched on the upper railing but caught the attention of everyone present.

"No, it can't be," she murmured, her face turning ashen.

"What's wrong?" I taunted, glad to know the gargoyles hadn't been watching me for her, but now equally curious about who had been powering the statues.

"Nothing at all. I'll be in touch. Soon." With those final words and another glance at the gargoyle, she disappeared in a puff of red smoke. I turned to my aunt and best friend.

"Are you okay?" I asked Gemma, who was standing again.

"Yeah, I'm fine, but what about you?" she asked before her gaze glanced behind me, probably at Enzo. His betrayal would hurt more than just me.

"I'm sorry, but I need time. I'm going to leave, and I don't know when I'll be back," I said to both of them.

"Be safe and keep in touch," Aunt Jules said, holding on to Gemma, whose face crumpled in either pain or because of my statement. I couldn't be certain which, but I trusted Jules to keep Gemma protected and tried not to feel guilty over my sudden departure.

My wings flapped behind me as I prepared to leave, taking one last glance back. Headmaster Stone nodded, seeming to understand my desire to leave, but it was Enzo's eyes that gave me pause.

My heart still ached for him, but the deceptions were too deep. I couldn't forgive him for any of it.

"Raegan, I'm sorry," he pleaded.

"Sorry can't fix this. Nothing can."

With those final words, I bent my knees and pushed into the sky, flapping my wings as hard as I could, ripping through the shield above the academy and reveling in the pain it provided.

My heart couldn't be damaged any more than it already was.

DEADLY DECLARATION

BOOK TWO

As my subconscious forcibly led me back to the school late the following summer, I had never been more irritated. For weeks, I had argued with my subconscious, which was not fun, by the way, trying to convince my heart that going back to Shadow Veil Academy was *not* the right choice.

Staying as far away from the drama that place had brought into my life sounded like a much better idea.

But like a stubborn mule, my heart won. With one day to spare before classes started, I was a mere hour's flight from the place where my true self had been discovered and then torn apart by one psychotic sorceress. Just the thought of her brought out my dragon scales, which were getting harder to control as the days passed.

As I stood on the edge of a cliff overlooking the Atlantic, I ignored my phone vibrating in my back pocket for the fourth time. It could only be one of two people, and I'd see them both soon enough.

Jules and Gemma had called every day, twice a day,

while I had been gone. Even on the days I hadn't been able to find a charger, once I'd get my phone powered back on, I'd skim through their messages for anything important. I'd given them no indication of my intentions and had yet to return any of their calls, so as the new school year neared, their calls doubled.

During my time away, I'd grown more on my own than I thought I had during my nine months at the academy. Scavengers came for me whenever I stayed in one place for too long and every time, I sent them back to whatever hell they came from, just like Enzo had the first night we met.

My dragon side had become my more prominent race with each opponent I fought, and I didn't mind one bit. What I *did* mind were the opponents I couldn't see.

At least once a week for the last two months, I had sensed someone following me, my dragon picking up the same scent each time, but they never made themselves known and I couldn't tell *what* they were. That alone was scarier than a horde of scavengers.

The only thing I was happy about was that I knew the stalker wasn't Enzo. At least, not the versions of him I had known in the academy. My heart still yearned for the back-stabbing bastard, but as the days passed, I managed to push him further and further from my mind.

Spreading my wings, I shook the growing thoughts of him out of my head and took off. Burgundy scales covered my arms and legs, while my nails shifted to talons and my eyes turned to slits. I wasn't the prettiest sight being unable to turn full dragon, but I was still stronger in the semi-shift than in my human form with only my witch and elven powers to fight with.

As much as I didn't like the idea of going back, it was

time to face whatever was left for me at Shadow Veil Academy and figure out what came next with Malina. She, too, hadn't been far from my thoughts, and I wondered what had kept her away from me the entire summer.

Whatever or whoever it was, I needed them to be my new best friend and help me stop her. I refused to live in fear for the rest of my life knowing that the psycho wanted to use me for nefarious purposes. I would die before I ever let myself be a pawn in her games.

As I soared through the sky, I double-checked my shield was strong when I passed over Salem. My protective shield also served as a reflective device when I was covered in scales that kept me concealed from the humans. It was a handy perk I was pleasantly surprised to learn about when I flew over a body of water earlier in the summer.

The other awesome part about my partial shift was that my body didn't bulk out, so as long as my feet were bare and my wings could extend, my regular clothes didn't get ruined when I shifted. Tank tops and shorts, along with a fanny pack to keep flip-flops in, had been my best friend while I'd been gone.

I had tried a backpack first, but my wings got caught on the straps if they weren't positioned just right, and it wasn't fun trying to bend my wing back in or shake the bag off after it had been ripped from my back.

Within another ten minutes, the decrepit building that humans saw if they passed by—where the academy truly was—came into view. My heart pounded in my chest as all my muscles hardened. I knew the moment I walked through the shield and saw the school, the memories of my last day there would slap me across the face.

I wasn't sure I was ready to face everything just yet, but

if I was being honest with myself, I wouldn't ever be ready. The hurt ran deep, and moving forward was the only way I knew to get through it. It was how I barely survived losing my parents, and I'd use that strength to tackle what came next.

I had a small hope I'd be able to sneak into the academy and shower before seeking out Gemma, but that didn't happen. After I landed just outside the shield, I barely had time to get my sandals on before I was tackled to the ground.

"Holy shit, Gemma," I groaned while staring up at the blue sky. "Give a girl some notice before you throw yourself at her."

"Shut up and let me have my moment." She squeezed tighter, and I wrapped my arms around her as well.

I had missed my friend and didn't truly realize how much until then, as tears threatened to prick at my eyes.

"Uh, wanna loosen up?" Gemma barely breathed out.

"Oops, sorry. Dragon strength has a mind of its own." I shrugged as I let go and pulled in my emotions.

She stood up first with her hand reached out to me, and I gladly took it before giving her a proper hug.

"I missed you," I said when we pulled apart again.

"That doesn't get you off the hook for ignoring the majority of my calls. And the ones from Jules. Not cool at all."

"I texted to let you know I was alive when the messages started getting frantic. I needed time. Really, I still do, but I also know that nothing other than facing things head-on is going to make any of this better."

She looped her arm through mine and pulled me toward the shield. "It's your first day back. I don't want to talk about what happened when you left. I want to know about what happened while you were gone and why in the hell you're breaking every fashion code I believe in by wearing a *fanny pack*." The last two words were said with so much disgust, I couldn't help but laugh.

"Remember I have wings? They don't leave me with many options of being able to carry stuff with me."

"Yeah, I saw you land. I just happened to be heading to town for last minute school stuff, and I was cursing you in my head. Then suddenly, there you were. All dragon scales and wings. Kinda scared the piss out of me, actually."

Leaning my head on her shoulder, I sighed. "As much as I didn't want to be here, seeing you now made it all worth it."

"Duh. I'm amazing." She laughed.

We walked through the shield, and the academy appeared as if Malina hadn't caused any damage just three months earlier. The gargoyles were all back to their previous spots from having crashed to the ground, and the fallen bricks were placed where they belonged.

My eyes scanned the gargoyles, wondering if I would still feel their watchful eyes since Malina was gone. Nothing stood out to me, and I breathed a sigh of relief until we were in front of the main doors. The gargoyle who appeared to have moved back when I had been fighting Malina was still there, perched on the railing with its wings spread.

"Do you ever find those things creepy?" I asked Gemma as I nodded toward the roof.

"The gargoyles? No, but I grew up knowing them as protectors. How come?"

I didn't answer her until we were on the platform headed toward our dorms. "Did you notice how afraid Malina seemed when she left?"

Gemma scowled. "Unfortunately, I was a little busy trying not to die to notice much of anything else. How come?"

"Could just be crazy talk, but something tells me those gargoyles scared her. When she saw the big dude by the front door, that's when she left, but it didn't make any sense to me. Why would she be afraid of a statue?"

She smacked me upside the head as we stepped off the platform on our floor. "Raegan Keyes. No more. I just got you back. I don't want to talk about any of that. You and the headmaster can hash out whatever you need to, but today is for reuniting. Not stressing."

As we approached Jules's door, it flung open and her stormy grey eyes moved from my head to my toes. When she noticed there was nothing wrong with me, she raised a finger in the air. "You have so much explaining to do, young lady."

Shrugging, I nodded at Gemma. "She said I'm not allowed to."

Ignoring my smartass remark, Jules threw her arms around me as Gemma backed up. I hugged my aunt back with a fierce sense of love and a need to protect. She was hurting, and I could somehow sense it, probably from my dragon side. It reinforced my need to protect them all.

"I love you, Aunt Jules," I whispered as I squeezed tighter, "and I'm sorry for leaving you. If I can help it, I won't ever do it again."

"Damn right, you won't," she said as she pulled back, tears in her eyes.

"Okay, enough with the mushy stuff." Gemma grabbed both of our hands and tugged us toward my room. "We're going to eat junk food and drink wine and hear about all of the places you saw over the summer. Tomorrow, we can deal with the past and future."

"Didn't you have to go to town and grab some more school supplies?" I teased.

"Shush. I was more just going to distract myself. Peyton and Finley haven't been around much, either. Probably because I've been bitching about you being a pain in my ass so much."

We entered my room, and everything was different. The bed was moved, the walls were painted a pale blue, and pictures of me with my friends from the year before hung on the walls.

Tears gathered in my eyes, much to my surprise. I hadn't allowed myself to feel much besides anger while I had been gone. Rage was typically at the forefront of my mind, but seeing what they had done for me touched my heart and I couldn't help it.

As my eyes roamed over the pictures, I tried not to let thoughts of Enzo ruin the moment. He should have been in half of the pictures—some of them he even took—but there was no sign of him in my room and I think that's what they were trying to do. They removed his presence, so I could move forward, which I appreciated, but as thoughts of him continued to force their way through, I wasn't sure it would happen anytime soon.

"Thank you," I said as I turned around. "When did you guys do this?"

"Started about a month ago. Gemma thought something new and fresh would be good for you to return to. Was she right?" Jules asked with trepidation.

My eyes met the bright hazel ones of Gemma boring into me, eagerly awaiting my approval.

"This was more than I could have ever asked for. Thank

you both." I hugged each of them briefly before heading to my butler box. I had missed this magical perk the most. No offense to the two behind me, but they didn't feed me and clean up when I was done. The box was priceless, in my opinion.

Maybe I was overreacting, but it had been weeks since I'd had a proper meal. While I had been gone, I didn't have any identification or money. I scavenged for what I needed and stayed in the wild when I slept.

The last time I'd had a satisfying dinner was when I found a twenty-dollar bill lying on the ground in Denver and grabbed it up before anyone could claim it. I ended up treating myself to a steak, and it was the best one I'd ever had. Though, I probably only thought that because it had been so long.

Standing in front of the box, I glanced back at Gemma and Jules. "Don't judge me for this, and remember, I'm part dragon," I said before I began my order.

When I was done, I added, "I'm going to take a quick shower before I scare you two away with my stank."

Gemma plugged her nose. "I was trying to be nice by not saying anything, but thank you. The outdoor smell doesn't suit you."

I flipped her off and headed into the bathroom. As much as I wanted to enjoy a real shower, I was starving. So, I hurried up and was back in the room within five minutes.

Food had already begun arriving, and as I started devouring everything in sight without offering to share, Gemma decided to chime in about my appetite.

"Whoa, Bessie. You better watch all those calories, or you won't be able to fit through the door much longer." Her laugh was obnoxious, but even still, I joined in.

"There were only so many chickens I could steal or food

trucks I could raid without feeling ridiculously guilty for trying to survive. I'm practically starving right now."

"So, where did you go?" Jules asked as she began eating her own food without as much enthusiasm as I had.

"It feels like everywhere. I just kept flying until I was tired, and then I would land wherever I was. The Carolinas, Oklahoma, Minnesota, Colorado, Oregon, and a few others. I didn't stay long in one place because of the scavengers, but they were more annoying than an actual problem."

"You fought scavengers?" Gemma's eyes widened.

"Yeah, they're not nearly as scary when you know how to disintegrate them. Enz—" The name almost rolled completely from my tongue, and my heart stuttered before I recovered. "I learned it last year in my elven classes."

I tried to remain casual, but they had seen my slip and how it hurt me.

"I know we're not supposed to talk about it yet, but you should know Headmaster Stone allowed *him* to stay at the academy and remain part of everything. I tried to fight it, but Alistair said we didn't have all the facts. When I pressed for them, he also said it wasn't his story to tell," Jules stated with a splash of irritation in her voice.

One, two, three, four... I counted in my head until I calmed my racing heart. It was one thing to come back to the place where I had fallen for him, but it was a whole different situation to be faced with his presence every day.

Suddenly, I wasn't so sure I could stay. As much as I loved Gemma and Jules, my heart wasn't ready to face Enzo, and I was already mentally formulating a plan to flee the school before I ran into him.

While I had been gone, my mind had thought of a million scenarios and all of the things I would do if I ever saw him again, but none of it could prepare me for the reality of the situation.

As my mind and heart continued to battle things out, I leaned back against my bed and ate my chocolate cake. I was going to take Gemma's advice for the rest of the day and deal with the past and future tomorrow.

Or maybe never.

L ater in the evening, Headmaster Stone knocked on my door. Gemma and Jules were still with me, so I wasn't sure how he knew I was back, but he did, and he sure didn't give me much time to settle in before coming to find me.

"I'm sorry to interrupt, but I thought we should speak before tomorrow's classes," he said when I tried to tell him we were busy.

My mouth opened to argue with him, but Jules placed her hand on my shoulder, stopping the words from leaving. "I know you're still hurting, and we've avoided the topic for most of the day, but tomorrow won't be easy. You should be better informed, or it could be worse. I could tell you more myself, but it really should come from Alistair."

My chest swirled with emotions: fear, anger, sadness, and annoyance. I could have just left and avoided it all. A small part of me had been thinking of that option ever since I almost said Enzo's name out loud. The larger part of me refused to be a coward, and the more twisted part of me wanted a chance to see him again.

More because I wanted to punch him in the face than anything else.

At least, that's what I kept telling myself.

"Fine." Glancing back longingly at my second piece of chocolate cake I'd only taken one bite from, I waved goodbye to Gemma and Jules before following Headmaster Stone down the hallway.

We stayed silent as we passed by other students. Their stares were unnerving, because I had no idea how much they knew about me and what had transpired at the end of last school year. Was I going to be ridiculed for my part? I didn't even really know what my part was, but I felt to blame for Malina's escape.

Just by being alive, I'd made her stronger. Every day I had stayed at the academy and grown in my abilities, so had she. Somehow, we had been connected, and I still needed to figure out how deep that connection went. I no longer sensed Malina within my mind, but that didn't mean she didn't have a hold on me for future use.

The question that swirled through my mind most often was, *If I had the chance to kill her, if there was a way without a Doyen, would I also be killing myself?* And more importantly, was I okay with that?

I didn't have the answers yet, and she hadn't made contact with me, so I hadn't been pressured to figure it out. Though, since I was back at the academy, I really needed to.

Headmaster Stone opened his door and gestured for me to go in first. Fear slammed into me at the thought of being set up, causing me to hesitate before entering, but a heavy breath released from my chest when I saw the empty office. No Enzo in sight.

"Take a seat." He gestured to the same chair I had sat in so many times before, but this time felt different.

When he was settled behind his desk, our eyes met, and the stress he'd been through was evident in the deep wrinkles and dark circles on his face. His fingers stroked his beard as he seemed to choose his words carefully.

"How was your summer?" he asked.

"No offense, but I'd rather not make small talk. Though, to ease your worries, there were no huge developments on my end while I was gone. No Malina sightings, and she didn't reach out mentally like before."

"Well, that's good to hear." Pausing, he leaned back in his chair. "I wish I had better news for you, but I'm afraid we've made little progress where Malina is concerned as well. As much as I was hoping you had avoided her, I was also hopeful she had made contact."

My hand instinctively went to the replacement necklace I still wore. The one I told myself I only still wore because it kept Malina out, but deep down, I knew that wasn't true. It hadn't been recharged in months, and I wasn't willing to ask the only person I knew who could do it to do so.

"I haven't heard from her since the day she got out. I think her mental connection to me was only good when she was imprisoned. Not sure how or why, so maybe I'm wrong, but I would think if she could, she would have contacted me by now."

He nodded in agreement. "We kept her in a spirit form while she was locked away to weaken her. When you entered the dungeon, she likely attached a part of her spirit to you, but when she broke free, that connection was broken as she became whole again."

"So, you have no leads as to where she might be? You couldn't get either traitor to talk while I was gone?" I refused to say Enzo's name out loud. It hurt too damn much, so I had decided "traitor" was a good substitute for the time being. Much more appropriate than all the other names I had mentally called him over the last few months.

"Desmond has been a problem. He gave us just enough information to bargain his way into a comfortable holding cell, but none that told of Malina's plans for the future. Most of what he divulged just helped us piece together how we got to the point we did."

He paused, seeming to gauge my mood, but I was hopeful my face gave nothing away. The headmaster didn't need to know how much his next words were going to gut me.

"Enzo, on the other hand, has been invaluable with his cooperation. Though, he was out of the loop from Malina's plans at the end, so the tips he gave us mostly led to dead ends."

A growl rumbled in my chest. "Maybe there's a reason they led to nothing. Why would you even trust him?"

"Because I'm the headmaster of this school, and Enzo is my student. It's my job to give him the chance to explain. There are magical ways to make sure I'm not being lied to, and Enzo told me the truth. More than he needed to, actually. He *is* on our side."

My eyes rolled so far into the back of my head at that last statement, I was surprised I didn't get a glimpse of my brain. "Easy for you to say," I grumbled.

"I understand why you're angry. You have every right to feel the way you do, but I hope one day, preferably soon, you'll give him a chance to explain. The only thing Enzo asked of me when he explained himself was that he was the one to tell you why when you were ready."

Fury bubbled near the surface of my skin. I would never be ready to hear what he had to say. Regardless of his excuses, I couldn't risk my heart again. The pain he put me through was too great to experience again.

But what if the love you could experience is too great to miss out on? my bitch of a subconscious chimed in.

I needed to change the direction of my conversation with the headmaster before I lost my cool in front of him.

"Are you alright, Raegan?"

Apparently, I was too late.

Scales began to creep up my arms, but I counted to ten in my head and they receded. "Yes, it's a little harder to control the partial shifts, but I'm working on it."

"You reversed it rather quickly. I must say, I was concerned what would happen when you fully embraced all three races, but you seem to have handled it like a seasoned supernatural."

I shrugged at the compliment. "I didn't really have much of a choice."

"We always have a choice," he reminded me.

"So, what now?" I asked, needing to know why it was so important he speak with me.

He pulled a vial from his desk, one filled with a clear crystallized liquid I remembered from when he masked my dragon side. "You may have broken through the block on your shifter side, but it didn't completely go away. If you promise to work with Jules to learn more about shifters, then I would like to give this to you."

He dangled the glass tube between his fingers, and I briefly wondered how much more could have still been restrained from the previous potion he gave me. Not really caring about the consequences, I snatched the vial from his hand. "I promise."

As I chugged the liquid down, all I could hope was that there was an ability I had yet to discover that would keep my heart whole when I had to lay eyes on Enzo. I knew it was only a matter of time, and I'd need every possible advantage if I was going to make it through without losing my shit.

"I'm also going to need a favor from you tomorrow," he added.

Panic swelled in me at the thought that he would ask me to interact with Enzo in some way, and I was two seconds from vomiting up his magic concoction and saying, "thanks, but no thanks."

"Calm down. It's nothing you can't handle. We're simply hoping you can speak with Desmond. He's asked about you several times, but never really says why. We hope it means he has something to tell you that might help us with Malina."

Desmond I could tolerate. Plus, there was something about him that bothered me whenever he was around, something I felt like I should know, but I could never quite grasp the thought or make sense of the feeling.

"Sure, I'll come by before classes tomorrow. I'm assuming my schedule is on my tablet like before?"

"Yes, but I'm going to make adjustments to it now that we've spoken," he stated before reaching for his computer. "I should have it updated shortly."

A part of me wanted to ask why he was changing it, but it didn't really matter. My only hope was that it had more to do with my dragon abilities than it did with Enzo.

"Can I go back to my dorm now?" I asked, feeling like a child talking to their parent.

"Yes, but don't hesitate to come see me anytime. I want you to still feel at home here, Raegan. You thrived last year and did more work than any other student to catch up with your peers. I want you to continue to grow and not be weighed down with the past."

I nodded in understanding but didn't agree. "Easier to do when there's not an evil sorceress out there somewhere, hoping to use me as her personal well of power."

He didn't have a response to that, and I said my goodbyes. It was time to get back to my best friend and aunt. It was safer with them and all the junk food a girl could wish for. The following day would be a problem for future me, and I chose not to worry about it as I slipped back into my room, pretending like our evening hadn't been interrupted.

The following morning, I was up early after having slept six uninterrupted hours. It had been months since that had happened, and I was happier than I'd been in a long time.

I was the only one who could make my day bad. I didn't have to let the worries of others get to me, and I needed to make the most of being at the academy. There were a lot of positives in my life, and I needed to focus on those. Not the heartache Enzo brought me.

My class schedule was a replica of Gemma's, with the exception of two classes: Elven Advanced Magic and the time I was scheduled with Jules to work on my shifter side. Even though she wasn't a dragon, she agreed with Headmaster Stone's decision to have us work together, seeming confident she could help me with the sudden appearance of my scales when my emotions went wild.

She also had a slight concern about me feeling my dragon but not hearing her. Apparently, I was also supposed to have voices in my head. After what I had gone through with Malina, I couldn't say I was disappointed there were none.

Once I was dressed in my black leather pants, knee-high boots, and standard white, collared shirt with teal tie, I grabbed my bag and headed out the door. It was time to see what Desmond wanted, and he would hopefully have some insight to help me move forward.

As I passed by other students, I waved and said, "Good morning." Tension I hadn't even realized I'd been holding onto released from me when they didn't ignore my attempts to be social. I noticed more than a few other women wearing black pants as well, varying in fabric. I'd have to ask how that happened when I saw Gemma again.

The door to the headmaster's office was already open when I arrived, and another student was standing at his desk when I walked in.

My body froze on the spot as my mind tried to process what to do next. I needed to run. I wasn't ready. I wouldn't ever really be ready, but I definitely wasn't okay with facing him on the first day.

Headmaster Stone stood and smiled at me. "Good morning, Raegan. I was just finishing with Professor Melnier, so come on in."

The guy finally turned around, and I wanted to smack myself. It wasn't Enzo. Just someone who looked a hell of a lot like him from the back; not so much from the front. His skin was much lighter, a complete contrast to his darker hair that fell long around his face.

"Hello, Raegan." The teacher reached a hand to me, which I shook hesitantly. "I'm going to be your instructor for the advanced elven class."

"Nice to meet you," I replied.

"I need to get to class, but I'm sure we'll catch up later," he said to Headmaster Stone.

"Yes, very well. Let me know how the first day goes."

The two men shook hands as I moved out of the way so Professor Melnier could exit. In an attempt to get my pulse back to normal, I took several deep breaths and waited for the headmaster to let me know where I needed to go to see Desmond.

"Are you well this morning?" he asked with a pinched face.

"Yeah, I'm great." I forced a smile, trying to get back my earlier cheer. "Where is Desmond?"

"He's in the dungeon. We can head there now if you're sure."

"Yep. Let's do this. I'd rather not be late to my first class on the first day."

He eyed me skeptically but nodded in agreement.

When we stood in front of the previously forbidden door, I anticipated feeling some sort of anxiety, but none came. I was actually eager to get to explore the area without having to sneak around or get attacked by Malina.

"We have him in a room built specifically for his powers. There is an illusion that makes a wall appear complete on the inside, but from the outside, we can monitor everything he does. You won't be alone when you go in. I'll be right there if you need me," Headmaster Stone said as we traversed down the stairs.

"I'm not worried about him, but it's good to know in case something does happen."

When we approached the cell, I took in the two-way wall and my eyes landed on Desmond sitting chained to a chair inside the room.

"Being a little cautious?" I asked.

"We don't keep him like that all the time, only when he has visitors."

My brow raised. "Is that often?" I wouldn't think so after his betrayal, but it could have been possible for someone to still give a shit about him.

Headmaster Stone shook his head. "Mostly just someone from the council."

"Makes sense." I continued toward the door and waited for the headmaster to do his magical thing on the locks so I could open it.

When I walked in and Desmond laid eyes on me, a smirk appeared on his lips that grated on my nerves, but I kept my face neutral. He wouldn't get another moment of satisfaction from screwing with my life.

"Nice to see you again, Raegan," he mused. "What brings you here after all these months? I had hoped I'd see you again, but alongside Malina with me free, not chained like an animal." His voice was casual, as if we were longtime friends catching up.

Not answering, I took a seat about ten feet away from him and stared, really taking his appearance in. Gone was the haggard look of a man who had been fighting for the good of his people. Instead, before me was an unsympathetic piece of shit who got off on others' pain.

"You're going to ignore your elder when asked a simple question?" He tsked. "How unbecoming of you."

Crossing my ankles, I leaned forward and leveled my glower at him. "I'm not the same girl who entered this school a year ago, Desmond, partially in thanks to you. So, don't piss me off, because those chains won't protect you from my wrath if you do."

The grin on his face only grew wider. "You are so much like your creator."

"I'm nothing like her. I would never harm innocent people just for power," I spat.

"You think this is about power? Oh, child, you have so much to learn."

"Well, why don't you teach me? What was your part in all of this before she threw you under the proverbial bus? Why did you help her? And more importantly, why are you still helping her by keeping what you know to yourself when she hasn't once tried to come for you?"

He leaned back, seeming uninterested in my plethora of questions. His eyes roamed the room before a spark lit within them and met mine again. "I've already told the council everything I'm going to say about Malina, but if you do something for me, then I will tell you about the day Enzo disappeared."

My breath hitched and I regretted it immediately, because I had given away my feelings. Based on the growing gleam in his eye, he knew he had me. I had lost hours of my memory that day. I never figured out what had happened between the times I was supposed to meet Enzo for lunch and when I awoke in my bed, missing my original necklace.

"I can't give you whatever it is that you want," I finally said. He was going to want something ridiculous, like me letting him out, and knowing what transpired that day wasn't more important than keeping him locked up.

"Oh, but you can. I only want to see my family. Explain to them why I did what I did. While I have no regrets, they deserve answers, and the council refuses to let me see them. Get them to change their minds, and I will tell you what you want to know."

Well, that was nothing. They couldn't deny him his request if it meant more answers, right? Desmond wasn't demanding to be let out. He had accepted his fate and wanted to say goodbye. I didn't see anything wrong with it and stood to go confirm with Headmaster Stone that it wouldn't be a problem.

Desmond's arms crossed over his chest as he watched me walk from the room.

When I opened the door, the headmaster was already waiting for me, shaking his head at me. "We can't offer him that. He's asked for it before, and his wife refuses to see him," he said once the door was closed behind me.

"Shit, seriously?" My hands ran through my hair, trying to figure out another solution. "Did you ever tell him she refused?"

"No, we didn't want him to act out even worse. We just pretended to deny his request instead."

"What if I tell him you agreed, but he has to talk first?" I asked.

He nodded his head. "If you want to try it, you have my permission, but something tells me Desmond will get more enjoyment out of spilling whatever he knows than you will hearing it."

I sighed. He was probably right. I had gone all these months without knowing what happened that day. It really shouldn't matter now, but the curiosity was eating away at me.

"I'll be fine. I've been through worse."

Turning around, I went back into the room. Taking my same seat, I chose my words carefully. I didn't want to lie to Desmond—he would sense that—but I could omit and hopefully get what I wanted in the process.

"Headmaster Stone said he would grant the request only if you talked first. So, tell me what happened that day?" I requested.

He shook his finger at me. "How do I know you're telling me the truth?"

I quirked a brow at him. "Are you telling me a powerful sorcerer like yourself can't tell when someone is lying to him? Maybe we overestimated you."

Glaring at me, he sat up straighter in his chair. "Will the headmaster contact my family and tell them to come to see me?"

"Yes, he will." They wouldn't say yes, but Desmond didn't need to know that.

He paused, weighing my answer before finally nodding. "Very well, but first, I want food. Real food, not the crap they've been shoving in my cage. Have someone bring me my regular order and you can have your information today."

Ugh, this guy was a pain in my ass. Once again, I stood up, but Headmaster Stone was already entering the room. "It's been ordered, but you'll begin talking first before you receive it. No more demands, Desmond." He slammed the door closed, and I took my seat for the third time.

"The headmaster doesn't seem very happy today." Desmond gleamed. "That makes *me* happy, so I'll tell you what you want to know."

"Who took me from the commissary the day Enzo was taken, and what happened between that time and when I woke up in my room?" I asked, getting straight to the point.

"I took you to Malina, so she could syphon enough power off you to keep Enzo captured. We knew we were losing his alliance, and he needed to pay. Once she was done with you, I erased your memories and dropped you in your bed while Malina had her fun with your boyfriend."

Son of a bitch. I was going to kill him.

CHAPTER THREE

Scales pushed through my skin in rapid succession as my ire rose. Desmond had pretended to help me time and time again. Yeah, I had known he was a little weird, but never once did I suspect his betrayal. My skin crawled at the thought of him having access to my unconscious body.

"There's the dragon. I've been dying to get my hands on one of those scales since you first arrived at the academy, but Alistair had insisted on that part of you being restrained. Don't you see why I chose Malina?" His voice had begun to rise. "The council will only try to control you if you don't get away from here and find Malina. Only she can set you free!"

"I'm already free, you worthless piece of shit." I almost felt bad for my next move considering he was chained up, but I needed to let some of my anger out before the shift continued, and I couldn't control myself.

My fist slammed into Desmond's face, not once or twice, but three times before Headmaster Stone and Fiona rushed into the room.

"That's enough, Raegan," the headmaster said with a firm voice as they pulled me away.

Once we were out of the room, Fiona went back in to deal with Desmond as Headmaster Stone continued to pull me toward the stairs.

No words were shared between us until we arrived back in his office, with the door firmly shut.

"Are you okay?" he asked.

Glancing down at my arms, I confirmed my scales were gone. "Yep."

"Does that happen often? The rage and shifting?"

My eyes looked everywhere but at him. "Not really."

"I see. Well, Jules should be able to help you with that, regardless of how often it does *or* doesn't happen. You need to be in control of your dragon at all times or we will have bigger problems on our hands." He glanced at the clock on the wall. "It's almost time for class. Do you have everything you need?"

"Guess I'll find out when I get to my first class, which I'll be late for if I don't hurry up," I added, hoping to get out of answering any more of his probing questions.

"Very well. I'm sure I'll see you soon." He waved me off, and I didn't hesitate to make my exit.

My first class was Advanced Shifting and Magic. Everything I was taking seemed to have the word "Advanced" in it, which caused me a little bit of worry. At the same time, I was supposed to be a third-year student, so it wasn't too shocking when I really thought about it.

The class was located in the top level of Magic Hall, so I headed to the platform and crammed in with about ten other students. I squeezed into the middle of the group, still scared that I would fall off, even though Gemma had promised me several times that it wasn't possible.

I didn't believe her.

"Hey, Rae," a husky voice said from behind me.

My mind had begun to process my interaction with Desmond and whether or not it really mattered anymore. I was so deep in thought that I hadn't noticed anyone I knew on the platform. That was until someone called my name, making me flinch in surprise.

Turning my head, my eyes landed on Embry's smiling face. "Oh, hey. Where are you headed?" I asked.

"Advanced Shifting and Magic. You?"

"Same." There was a long pause as he continued to grin at me without furthering the conversation, so I did. "How was your summer?" The situation was quickly becoming awkward, and I wished the platform would move faster.

"Longer, thanks to you. How about yours?"

My gut twisted. I wasn't sure if I was supposed to have taken that comment as a compliment or an insult. My eyes scanned the crowd listening in on our little conversation. A few smiles were tossed my way, but most everyone tried to pretend they weren't eavesdropping.

"Uh, it was alright."

Before he could ask another question, the platform came to a gentle stop and I pushed forward as quickly as possible. I really needed to find out from Gemma what the other students knew about me before I interacted with more of them. The longer I was around people, the more weird vibes I felt from them.

Stepping into the classroom, I sighed when I noticed most of the seats were empty, and Gemma didn't occupy any of the ones that weren't. Apparently, everyone was running late on their first day or this was a common occurrence for third and fourth-year students. Either way, I didn't like it.

Taking a seat toward the back and at the end of the row, I sat my bag on the chair next to me in hopes nobody else would try to take it before Gemma arrived. I searched for the professor I was pretty sure I had never met, but I didn't see anyone resembling teacher material.

Magic pulsed around the room and, after a couple minutes, I started paying attention to the things I couldn't see and my body finally relaxed. It was one thing I had missed when I was traversing the states.

The academy lived and breathed pure magic and power. There was plenty of it around the humans, but it was dulled in most places unless there was a local pack or coven. Sitting in the class, I breathed in the magic peacefully before sensing a shift in the room.

My head snapped toward the door, but I didn't see anyone enter. I kept following the power signature I could sense and finally saw the rift in the air. Someone was concealed and sneaking into the room.

Instantly on alert, I sought out Embry, the only person I even remotely knew in the class, but he was busy flirting with a group of girls across the room.

Screw it. I could handle whatever it was on my own.

Standing from my seat, I found the rift floating by the professor's desk and kept my eyes on it while I moved toward the front of the room.

When I was mere feet from the source, Gemma called out my name, distracting me, and I lost sight of it.

"Sorry I'm late," she added from behind me when I ignored her.

Suddenly, there was a taller-than-average woman standing in front of me. She had to have been close to six feet in height with shoulder-length onyx hair, deep amber eyes, and a smirk I badly wanted to wipe from her face. I was seconds from punching her when I heard Gemma say, "Good morning, Professor Phox."

She paid Gemma no attention as she smirked at me. "How did you find me?" she asked.

"There was a shift of power in the room. I followed it until I saw the rift that your shield created."

"Very well. I've only had one other student spot me before I could surprise the class. You ruined my fun, and I'm not sure how I feel about that."

I grinned at her pout, because I was pretty sure it wasn't sincere. Something told me I was going to like having her as my first class of the day.

"I'm sure you'll figure out a way to screw with us later when I'm not paying attention."

Gemma stood next to us then, tugging on my bag. "We should take our seats. Did you pick a spot yet?"

"Yep, we're in the back."

Professor Phox nodded to me, and I showed Gemma where I had left my bag.

"What were you doing?" Gemma hissed when we sat down.

"Well, I thought I was stopping an intruder, but apparently it was just our teacher trying to pull a fast one on us. Why?"

"Dude. Nobody screws with the Phox. She's, like, legendary around here for making students cry and breaking them. By the end of next week, half of this class will be gone."

Tilting my head back, I rolled my eyes. Of course, I poked the bull. Why wouldn't I on the first day of a new year? Whatever. Professor Phox couldn't break me.

I was already broken.

"Just stick close to me, and you'll be fine. My cousin had

her and warned me over the summer what to expect and how to survive."

I nodded, not really knowing what else to say.

We both got our tablets out and, within a few minutes, class began. Sure enough, halfway through the hour-long lesson, a student was called to the front of the room.

"You, with the odd orange hair," Phox demanded. "Yes, come up here."

A girl I had never seen before moved from her chair and slowly walked to the front of the room while the professor tapped her foot, waiting impatiently.

"What's your name?"

"Bri," the girl squeaked out.

"You're a peregrine shifter, yes?" Bri nodded. "I want you to magic your clothes and shift, then do a lap around the room before shifting back and keeping your clothes whole."

Bri's eyes widened. "I can't do that."

"Then leave my class until you can," Professor Phox said without emotion.

"Excuse me?" Bri choked out.

The professor lowered her stance to be eye-level with the poor shifter. "Are you deaf or dumb? Either figure it out now or leave until you do."

Tears tracked down Bri's face as she raced from the room, leaving her stuff behind.

"Holy shit, you weren't kidding," I whispered to Gemma. The only positive thing to come from that was I now knew there was a spell to keep my clothes from ripping in a shift. If I was ever able to fully shift, I'd rather not ruin my entire wardrobe in the process.

We finished the class, paying complete attention in case

we were called on. Professor Phox didn't frighten me, but she certainly intrigued me.

~

WHEN LUNCH ROLLED AROUND, I STUCK CLOSE TO Gemma. We sat down at the same table we used the year before, and as my eyes spotted Peyton and Finley, I wondered what they might know and if they had even bothered to ask Gemma anything about me.

Before I could ask her, they tossed their trays on our table and glared at me. "Next time there's an evil sorceress harassing you, don't you dare leave us out," Peyton snapped with a flick of her hair.

"We should unfriend you, but Gemma explained, and what Peyton meant to say was we understand now that we know more. Just know if there is a next time, we'd love to have your back." Finley smiled and took the spot next to me.

"I would love nothing more than to have that happen, but hopefully there isn't a next time." I smiled, hoping it really would be that easy to move forward with them.

"Good, now let me eat before you begin to smell good." She traced her tongue over her pointed teeth, and I cringed. "Kidding, Raegan, but seriously, I'm starving and have to get some sustenance in me, stat."

As we ate lunch, I quietly caught them up on some of the things I had experienced over the summer. Once I had the confirmation there wouldn't be any awkwardness between the four of us, I breathed a little easier.

One hurdle down. Unfortunately, there were a shit ton left.

While we chatted, they seemed to be mostly interested in how I managed to defeat the scavengers and about my wings. Apparently, it was a well-known fact around the academy that I was part dragon, but nobody seemed to really be worried since I couldn't fully shift.

It was the little things I needed to be thankful for.

"Hey, Raegan," a voice announced behind me.

Swiveling in my chair, I saw a smiling Lyssa, who was looking rather nervous behind the grin she was trying to hold. "Hey, how's it going?" I asked.

"Not bad. I was wondering if I could talk to you about our elven class this afternoon really quick."

I nodded. "Sure, what's going on?"

Her face reddened into what I assumed was a blush, and I couldn't believe what I was seeing. Lyssa had never lacked confidence before.

She cleared her throat. "Um, can we speak in private?"

Glancing back at Gemma, she waved me along. "Lunch is almost over. I'll just catch up with you in your room after school."

Peyton and Finley both seemed as shocked as I was at Lyssa's behavior, but neither of them said anything.

Grabbing my plate, I turned back to Lyssa and stood. "Let me just put this away and we can talk."

"Thank you." She released a deep breath, which only made my unease rise.

Had something happened to Enzo? If it had, did I even really care?

Based upon my sweating palms and rapidly beating heart, apparently, I cared more than I realized or even preferred to truly acknowledge. Especially not out loud.

Once my lunch was disposed of, I followed Lyssa outside through the back door of the commissary. She led me to a grouping of willow trees that I knew had a bench underneath the branches, but the leaves were so thick that I couldn't see it.

"Lyssa, what's going on? I'm not stupid. Whatever you need doesn't have anything to do with class," I stated with a bit of attitude.

"I'm sorry, but I had no choice." Her shoulders shook, and sweat built up on her brow.

"No choice in what? What's wrong with you?"

"*Uscoto*," a deep voice whispered from behind the branches, releasing Lyssa from whatever hold had been placed over her.

"Please don't hate me. I didn't know what he had planned when he asked for my help, and by the time I realized it, I had no control." Lyssa pushed through the foliage, and I heard a grunt, followed by a slap. "Don't you ever ask for help again, Enzo. You're on my shitlist for the foreseeable future."

No, No, No. I wasn't ready for this. I knew it was coming, yet I had also hoped to avoid it for as long as possible. Half of a school day wasn't nearly long enough.

Lyssa stormed back toward me. "Feel free to run now. I would have never done that to you if the bastard hadn't spelled me."

Her advice sounded great, but the earlier part of me that had feared something awful had happened to him convinced me to stay put. "I just need to get it over with. If we both have to go to this school, I can't ignore him forever, no matter how much I wish I could."

"Give him hell, girl. He damn well deserves it, but I will say, it won't hurt to listen to him. I did, and while I don't condone his choices, I do understand them."

Without waiting for a response, Lyssa took off and I just stood there, unsure of how to proceed. Did I just waltz right through the branches and give him hell like Lyssa suggested, or did I make him come to me?

"Screw this," I huffed. I had survived three months on my own, all while being hunted by scavengers and who knew what else. Enzo didn't scare me, and I was going to face him head on. If I let him control my choices, then I wouldn't be able to move forward with my life, and that was all I wanted.

I wanted to be free of it all.

My hands surged forward as I pushed through the branches. When I saw Enzo standing there, I was taken aback by his appearance. His hair was wild, like he hadn't brushed it in weeks. I was pretty sure there were even some dreads poking through the oily bronze strands.

The circles under his eyes were almost as dark as his hair, and the previously vibrant, golden honey color of his eyes was a flat brown. My fingers twitched to reach out to him, but I restrained myself.

"When was the last time you slept?" I asked without emotion.

"I don't remember." His voice was rough, unrecognizable from what I remembered.

"Is this even the real you? Or was that Ryn's persona? Hell, was anything you did real?" My voice rose, and I took a step forward, but when his eyes lit up in a positive way, I moved back again.

"Everything I told you about me was the truth, Raegan. Since finding you that night with the scavenger, I never once lied to you. I only ever omitted the truth so I could protect you, but I failed, and I'm so sorry I wasn't stronger."

"It wasn't your job to *protect* me, Enzo. I'm a big girl, and I deserved the truth. You had no right to do what you did. People keep telling me that you had your reasons, but no matter those reasons, I couldn't fathom loving someone and keeping the secrets you kept. It leaves me with no choice but to believe it was all a lie. My only question is, how deep do those lies go? How long have you been involved in all of this?"

By then, I was pacing back and forth, trying to avoid staring at him. The more I saw the pain in his face, the more my heart tried to convince me he deserved my sympathy, but that wasn't happening. He did this. Nobody else. He made all of the choices that brought us to this point.

"Since the day I was born," he answered, his voice finally sounding somewhat normal.

"What does that even mean?" I snapped.

Instead of answering me, he reached behind the bench and pulled out a glass orb. "Do you know what this is?"

The only similar one I had seen before was a listening device, but I doubted it was the same thing, so I shook my head.

"It's spelled to light up if the person holding it lies. My name is Jason." The orb glowed a soft silver color. "Here, try it so you know I'm not lying."

When he pushed the circular object toward me, I reached for it, but immediately regretted it when our fingers brushed together and a shock of power passed between us. Doing my best to ignore whatever it meant, I focused on the orb.

"The sky is red." Sure enough, it lit up again, so I tossed it back at Enzo, afraid of touching him for a second time.

"For you to really understand, I have to go back to the beginning, and it's going to take a while. We'll probably miss our next class."

"Let's just get this over with. I'll have the headmaster

explain to the professor if necessary." I had no doubt Alistair would vouch for me, given the circumstances.

If this was going to take a while, I didn't want to pace for the entire time, so I took a seat on the very edge of the bench, hoping Enzo would get the point that I didn't want him too close to me. Thankfully, he did and sat on the opposite side but twisted his body so his legs were mere inches away from me.

"My grandfather was one of the creators of Elora. He lived a long life, doing good for his people in hopes of our world surviving for many generations to come. When my father replaced him on the original council, it was he who proposed the Doyens be created. He didn't believe our world was enough, and he thought with more power players, our kind could take over Earth."

I snorted. Men like his father disgusted me. Never satisfied, even if they had everything they could have ever dreamed of.

"Before the Doyens were created, my father had already married my mother. They'd been trying to conceive, but she'd lost several children through miscarriage. Malina had been created and grew close to my father. I don't know their exact relationship, but a deal was struck between them.

"She spelled my mother to carry a baby to full term, a protective spell to prevent another miscarriage, in exchange for my father's servitude. If he failed to uphold his side, Malina threatened to take me. My mother had no idea until the day I was born. Sure enough, my father had thought he could play the sorceress, so she wanted the child she had helped create."

Holy shit, Enzo was supposed to be me, or at least that was how he was making it sound. I wanted to ask all of the questions, but I could tell it was hard on him, so I let him continue while nodding my head and listening intently.

"My mother fought back and was killed in the process. I'm not sure how the rest of it worked out, but my father ended up raising me until he died a few years ago. Then, Malina sent someone to fetch me, so I could do her bidding. They explained how my father's debt was now mine, and she would let me out of the contract if I did her one favor."

"Bring me to her," I said, now understanding that Enzo hadn't just found me in Portland last year. He had been looking for me, and the scavenger attack had given him the perfect opening.

"Yes," was all he replied.

"Did you send that scavenger to attack me, so you could play the role of my hero?" I asked, needing to know or else I would always have too many "what ifs".

His only answer was a short nod as he looked away from me.

"How many times did you try to approach me before that little stunt?" My voice was thick with rage.

"Three. All three times, you rejected my request by either punching me, screaming at the top of your lungs, or, last time, you attempted to stab me in your kitchen."

"Why don't I remember these things?" I remembered feeling like I had seen him before when I first met him, but had long forgotten about it. I was pretty sure I knew the answer now, and I wasn't going to be happy about it.

"Because I made you forget, but every time I did, you grew stronger, which was why I couldn't convince you to go with me and you broke through my spell to remove your pain."

My fist swung out for the second time that day and

connected with Enzo's jaw. He held his chin, wincing at the power I put behind the punch.

"I hate you, and I don't want to be involved in whatever you've gotten yourself into. If you ever truly cared about me, you'll respect my decision and leave me the hell alone. For good."

"You can hate me all you want, Raegan, but it only gives me hope. You can't have hate without love, and I will fight for you for as long as it takes."

Turning away, I moved back through the trees, unable to speak any more words as I fought the burning sensation in my throat. I hated him even more, because he was right, and I had no clue what I was going to do about it.

There was no way I could have gone back to class after that interaction. My mind was racing, and I was pretty sure my heart was going to rip from my chest. It seemed like a good idea to no longer have one, other than the not living part. The organ had been nothing but a betrayer lately with its feelings.

My heart still cared, and I didn't want to. Not one damn bit.

Enzo hurt me in all the worst ways. He had taken my memories, brought me to the monster that was Malina, and kept secrets from me when I needed the information most.

I might have been able to forgive him had he confessed months ago, but to hear it from Malina that he wasn't who I thought... it had crushed me. Then, to know there was more made my skin itch with scales I'd managed to keep at bay.

With all of that, it made no sense why my body physically hurt as I stormed off further and further away from the canopy of the trees.

I SHOULDN'T CARE! I screamed inside my head as I

fought ridiculous tears that showed themselves whenever I was severely pissed off.

As I plowed my way into the school, I realized it was the last place I wanted to be and turned right back around. I needed to fly, and I needed to be free, even if it was just for the afternoon.

Racing toward the forest, I realized I should have gone back to change first, but I didn't care. I had other shirts. When I was within the privacy of the trees, it took no effort to call upon my dragon. As wings unfolded from my shoulders, I heard the tear of my shirt. Though, I tried to be easy, so the back of it stayed somewhat intact.

Once the shift was complete—well, as complete as I was capable of—I pushed off the soft dirt ground and flapped my wings until I was high enough to catch the wind. We were close enough to the ocean that the sea breeze often found its way over to the school, and I enjoyed the salty taste in the air as I soared.

That was, until something else caught my attention.

Couldn't a girl get some damn alone time?

Apparently, not. I also wasn't sure what I was going to do, because the scent I was picking up was the same one that had been trailing me almost all summer. Considering my options, I decided there really were only two: race back to the academy and ask for help or hunt the bastard down who kept following me.

The latter seemed like more fun and, after my conversation with Enzo, I needed the release.

Taking my time, I swooped around in a few circles before changing my trajectory. If the wind wasn't screwing with my senses, my stalker was hanging out closer to the trees and to my left.

Once I was near the treetops, I hooked a hard right and

decided to try to get behind whoever was following me. When I disappeared into the branches, I tucked my wings as close as I could without losing momentum, but none of it mattered when my eyes landed on the thing in front of me.

The thing was at least eight feet tall and covered in purple scales. But, the *thing* wasn't supposed to exist and was more like me than I wanted to admit.

Indigo eyes stared wide at me as I dropped to the ground, unable to keep my wings moving as shock took over. Stumbling, my back smacked into the rough bark of the tree trunk behind me.

"Who are you?" I asked, then mentally chastised myself. Animals couldn't talk, but maybe whoever it was would shift to their human form, so we could.

"My name is JayLeigh, and I'm here to tell you about your dragon history."

Holy shit. Dragons could talk. Okay, one deep breath at a time.

This was officially the worst first day of school ever—too much all at once—and I was going to lose my mind.

"I'm sorry. I'm doing this all wrong, aren't I? I was supposed to befriend you, and then show you I was like you, but you were always on the move and wouldn't ever speak to anyone, so I just continued to follow you. I couldn't go home until I at least made contact."

My eyes blinked rapidly. Her mouth only moved a fraction, but the voice projected as if she was a human standing before me. As she settled onto the ground, I took in her black talons and four-inch spikes running from the crown of her head down to her shimmering violet, barbed tail.

"Oh, I'm sorry. You probably don't want to talk to a dragon. Just a second." Her body began to waver and shrink right before my eyes. I blinked once, and the dragon was gone.

In its place was a badass chick. She had spikey, short blonde hair with vibrant indigo eyes that closely matched her dragon scales, and she was dressed in a black combat suit that formed to her muscular body perfectly.

"Is this better?" she asked as she took a step toward me.

"Uh, yeah." I drew my wings in as I tried to figure out what to say without sounding like an idiot.

"I really am sorry if I scared you," she said.

"No, you didn't. I actually thought I was going to be kicking some stalker's ass. So, you could apologize for ruining my fun, but not for scaring me," I answered. It was the truth, but I said it more so she knew I wasn't weak.

"Oh." Her brows raised. "You like to spar? We still can if you want."

This chick was crazy.

"How about we start with answering some questions. Who sent you to find me, and where did you come from? Everyone thinks the last of the dragons died twenty years ago and I was some freak show when it turned out I had wings like one of them."

She glanced around. "Is it safe to talk here?"

"I think so." I shrugged.

"Hold on." JayLeigh clasped her hands together and murmured something softly before pulling them apart and over her head. A thick cloud rose above her head before forming an opaque dome around the two of us. "Perfect, now there aren't any doubts if our words are safe."

Glancing up, I asked, "What is that?"

"You've never seen one of these?" She gaped. "What are they teaching you at this school? And for four years only? It's absurd, really. I went to Dragon School for eight years before following it up with Advanced Combat School for an additional two years."

"There is another school for people like us?" Maybe I could go there and get as far from Enzo as possible. It could be a win-win for everyone.

"Well, duh. I mean, mine isn't on Earth, but it's close enough."

"It's what now?" I stammered.

"Oh, you don't know. Which would make sense. You're not supposed to know. Nobody is unless they're a dragon, which you are, so I guess I could tell you." Words spewed from her mouth at a million miles a minute. It was hard to believe this girl was supposed to be well-versed in advanced combat.

"How about you start from the beginning?" I suggested, hoping she would continue to tell me things she maybe wasn't supposed to.

"I like you, Raegan." She grinned her pearly whites at me. "The beginning sounds like a good place to start, but I've been flying for a while. Mind if we sit?"

"Not at all, but where are we going to sit?"

"One second." She left the dome area and headed for a log that had probably been on the forest floor for years. With what seemed like little effort, she picked up the eight-foot trunk and carried it back into the dome. "There."

While she took a seat, I gawked at her, unable to move. I was beginning to understand why someone would send her to reach out to me. She wasn't at all what she portrayed on the outside. There was definitely more badass in her than I was giving her credit for, considering how much strength it would have taken to move the big-ass log.

Finally, I took my own seat and turned to her. "So, the beginning."

She nodded eagerly. "Yes, let's start there. Well, at least to the beginning of the end. Years ago, when the first Doyens were made, my grandfather saw the greed in most of them. He was grateful for his abilities and decided he wanted a safe place for dragon shifters. He had taken in the dragon Doyen as if he was another of his children and wanted to protect him. We are a rare bunch, and others often sought our kind out to use and harm."

I cringed, wondering what kind of *harm* had been done by Malina to steal whatever she had needed to make me part dragon.

"That's when a sub-realm of Elora was created using strictly dragon magic, not elven. So, when Elora fell, Drakken did not. Though, the dragons were trapped there for some time before they found a way to make another portal to Earth.

"Once they did, our present clan leader Marek Skye came back to Earth in hopes of finding other Doyens and the council still alive. When he arrived at Shadow Veil, so much time had passed that most of the other originals had either been killed or chose to die. All that was left was Malina and a new council that he knew nothing about. You keeping up so far?"

"Yep, I knew parts of it already, so I'm piecing it together as you go. I'll speak up if I have questions." My mind was absorbing every bit of info she was willing to give.

"Perfect. Anyway, fast forward a little bit and Malina betrayed Marek somehow. Nobody really knows what happened, and he shut down the portal until recently. I had just graduated from the academy, and he came to me asking a favor. I was top of my class, so it was no surprise that he would want my help, but I couldn't believe it when he wanted to send me to Earth."

Her eyes roamed over my body before she smirked. "But now I know why," she added.

"Care to tell me your theory?"

She shook her head. "That's not for me to tell. I'm sure Marek will fill you in when you meet him. So, are you ready?"

My eyes pinched together in confusion. "Ready for what?" I didn't think we were done talking yet. She didn't tell me much that I didn't already know.

She huffed as if it was obvious. "To go to Drakken."

My first instinct was to say "no way in hell," but as I took an extra minute to process it all, maybe it wasn't such a bad idea. I didn't belong at Shadow Veil Academy. I was different from all of the other students. More importantly, I would be as far from Enzo as possible.

However, there were good reasons for my first instinct. I was still very much human at heart. I had Gemma and Jules, who I had already abandoned for the entire summer. Could I leave them at Malina's mercy if she came back looking for me and I wasn't anywhere to be found on Earth?

No, I couldn't. No matter what JayLeigh was offering, I had responsibilities to deal with before I even considered it.

"I'm sorry, but I can't leave."

"What do you mean?" Her voice lowered, and I knew she hadn't been expecting me to reject her offer.

"There are people here who need me, and Malina is still out there. She's going to come back for me, and when she does, I won't let the people I love pay the price for my leaving."

She laughed. Actually full-on belly laughed, and I had to wait a solid minute before she was able to contain herself.

"Malina? You're worried about *her*? Don't be. We have protectors all around the academy. It's how we kept an eye on you last year, but when you left, Marek got nervous, and that also prompted his choice in sending me to find you."

"What do you mean by protectors?" I asked.

"The gargoyles. Do they not teach anything at this school?" She rolled her eyes.

"Nothing about dragons, because nobody thinks it's relevant," I snapped back.

"Hmm. That would make sense. Well, anyway. Yes, the gargoyles are there to help keep people at the school safe. They can't really fight. I mean, they are only statues, but they still have enough magic fused into them to zap someone out of existence when another life is in danger. Unless the people you care about are completely useless, you shouldn't have anything to worry about. So, let's go."

She reached a hand for my wrist, but I smacked it away. "Listen, JayLeigh. I appreciate you coming here to fill me in on the little bit of history you did, but I'm not going."

Her silver eyes turned to slits. "Why?" she practically growled as her dragon peeked through.

"Because I make my own damn choices, and you can't force me." I mentally punched myself in the face. I sounded like a child. Why was this chick bringing out the worst in me all of a sudden?

"Your dragon is fighting for dominance. Can you feel it? You'd know more about that if you'd just come with me."

She was pushing my damn buttons.

"If you seriously want me to consider this, then I need to speak with the headmaster and my aunt. You can't just show up and expect me to drop everything to leave for some place I've never heard of."

She grunted. "Well, actually, I can. You did it once before when you came here with Enzo."

My heart constricted as I remembered how easy it was

for me to trust him and leave for Shadow Veil Academy. "Yeah, and if you know so much, then you also know how that worked out for me."

"Touché." She stood up. "Well, let's go talk to whoever it is you need to consult with first."

As I straightened, she removed the dome around us and put the tree trunk back where it had been with ease. She moved with precision and confidence, traits one could only acquire from years of training.

"How old are you?" I asked randomly when we started walking back toward the academy.

"Twenty-two. What about you?"

"I'll be nineteen next month. So, you started training at age twelve? Seems a little young."

She laughed. "Well, it's not like we start out killing people. Damn, girl. Try to give the dragons the benefit of the doubt before you judge too quickly. I know this is all new to you, but we didn't stay hidden all these years because we're bad people. It's the exact opposite, if you ask me."

She was right. I didn't really know anything about them. So, I focused on what I did know about myself and from what she had already told me.

My dragon side had been my best asset, keeping me safest when I needed it most. When I was partially shifted, I'd never felt the urge to harm anyone, only to protect myself. From what JayLeigh had explained, dragons just wanted a peaceful existence.

It was what I had wanted when I first arrived at the academy, to learn what I needed to stay under the radar—not that it had worked out that way for me—so I understood the concept she described.

"I'm sorry," I said when we were exiting the forest.

"For what?"

"For judging you, or dragons, to be more exact. I'm going to try and keep an open mind, but you have to understand, I was raised as a human. My mind doesn't work the same as a supernatural's does all the time. Especially when I'm constantly having to choose between my elf, witch, and dragon sides."

She winced and gave her own apology. "You're right. I should have taken that into consideration as well. I've met very few others that aren't pure dragon. I sometimes forget life isn't as black and white as it is on Drakken."

We grinned at each other, seeming to come to a silent agreement. Of what, I wasn't sure, but I was no longer worried about her pressuring me. At least, for the moment.

"Do I need to try to hide you? I'm sure people will ask questions if you walk into the school looking like that," I said.

"Probably a good idea." She snapped her fingers and disappeared.

"What the hell?" Twisting around and looking up in the sky, she was nowhere to be found.

Then, I heard a laugh directly in front of me. I reached out a hand, and she swatted it away. "Hey, we haven't even had a first date. No feeling me up."

My face must have turned ten different shades of red. "Just follow me."

She continued to laugh behind me at my expense, and I chose to ignore her. Once we arrived at the main doors, she quieted, and I felt her grab on to the back of my ripped shirt.

"You really need to learn how to magic your clothes," she whispered, even though there was nobody in the front entry.

"Yeah, I'm getting there."

I headed straight for the Magic Hall platform. While I did, I pulled my phone from my pocket, once again grateful I didn't wear the skirt portion of the uniform previously required. I sent a text to Jules telling her to get to the headmaster's office ASAP.

Before I could slip the phone back into my pocket, she replied that she was already there and that I was in trouble for ditching class.

I smirked, because missing my afternoon classes on the first day was going to be the least of their worries when they met JayLeigh.

CHAPTER FIVE

When I waltzed into Headmaster Stone's office, I held my head high with confidence. That was, until I noticed Enzo was also in attendance. Why? Why did they do these things to me?

"Have a seat, Raegan," Aunt Jules said firmly.

"I'd rather stand. Plus, I have a guest of my own, but I think it's better if she makes her appearance only when we're alone." I didn't bother to even look at Enzo a second time. I was still pissed he had messed with my head and lied.

"Enzo is in trouble, as are you. He's not going anywhere, and your punishment will be given jointly, considering you chose not to attend your afternoon classes together," the headmaster said disapprovingly.

"Did Mr. Liar-Liar over there tell you how this all started? Oh, wait. He probably only *omitted* certain parts, so that's okay. My bad. I forgot." Sarcasm dripped from every word as I crossed my arms.

Suddenly, all three sets of eyes staring at me widened,

and I felt JayLeigh's body shaking from behind me before laughter ripped from her chest.

"This is like one of those soap opera shows the humans sometimes watch. No, this is even better, because I get to watch it live. But don't mind me. Keep going."

"Who the hell are you?" Jules snapped.

"She doesn't matter right now," I replied. "We can talk about her when we're alone."

Headmaster Stone came around his desk while I still avoided Enzo who was hunched over in the chair against the wall. I only knew that because my peripheral vision was on point, not because I had peeked another glance at him. Definitely not because of that.

"Raegan, you need to accept that we have forgiven Enzo and he will remain involved in the school, just as he was before. I'm sorry if you don't agree with it, but he did more good than he did harm in the end. I hope you can set your feelings aside one day and realize that."

Blood boiled just beneath the surface as I sucked in a breath.

"Oh, here it comes," JayLeigh murmured behind me.

"Put my feelings aside, you say? As if everything he did to me was *no* big deal and I just need to get over it. News flash, *Alistair*. That's not going to happen. Not today, tomorrow, or next week."

"That's not what he meant," Jules interjected, trying to reverse the downward momentum of our conversation.

"Really? Then how was I supposed to take it? Because it sounded a lot like I should just be okay with my memories being tampered with and lied to for months."

Enzo stood from the wall, distracting us from our bickering. "I'm just going to go. Raegan is right, and none of this should be taken out on her."

He walked painstakingly slow out of the room as we all watched him, but nobody said anything. My heart twitched, wanting me to tell him he didn't have to go, but for once, my head won out, and I said nothing.

"Happy?" Headmaster Stone asked.

"Very." Turning around, I addressed JayLeigh, "Can you do the dome thing again?"

"You know it." Her hands clasped together, then the dust-like fog hovered over our heads, once again making a half-circle.

"Who are you, and why can't I get a read on *what* you are?" Jules asked suspiciously.

JayLeigh glanced at me, and I nodded, encouraging her to tell them whatever she was comfortable with.

"My name is JayLeigh. I'm here on behalf of Marek Skye, King of the Dragons. You can't tell what I am, because I don't want you to be able to tell. I was sent to check on Raegan and bring her back with me to Drakken if I thought it was necessary. Considering she can't shift properly, I believe it's better for her to finish out her schooling at Dray Academy."

My eyes widened. "Are you saying there's a chance I could shift into a full dragon, even with my elf and witch side?"

"I don't know about your other two sides, but I do know your dragon is suffering being on its own. Dragons need clans and, from what I can tell, your circle is too small to satisfy its pack needs. The happier your dragon, the more she will do for you when you need her."

"You mean to tell me Marek Skye is still alive?" Headmaster Stone said in awe, completely disregarding anything else that had been said.

"Yes, he is, but you won't be seeing him. He refuses to come back to Earth," JayLeigh replied.

The headmaster turned to Jules and then me. "Do you know what this means? We can stop Malina. Raegan, you need to go with her and convince Marek to help us. Learn whatever you need to learn as quickly as you can, and we'll continue hunting down Malina. I'm close to figuring out her cloaking spell and should be done within a few weeks."

No, this was not going as I planned. They were supposed to be freaking out that someone had come for me, not pushing me out the door, possibly never to be seen again.

Glancing at Jules, I was hoping she wouldn't agree, but the glimmer in her eyes told me she was hopeful about something. Yet, I knew that whatever it was, it didn't have anything to do with me staying at Shadow Veil Academy.

"I agree with Alistair. We can handle things at the academy, and if you have the chance to get the training you really need, then you can't pass it up." She turned to JayLeigh. "How long would Raegan have to be gone?"

All attention went to the dragon. "Oh, well, I'd prefer the full year, but we could make it work in just a few weeks for the basics, most likely. Can't be certain since you're of mixed race, though. If you stayed the remainder of your school time, I'd definitely be able to make you as badass as me."

"Can I have some more time to think about this, or is this another one of those situations where I'm being volun-told?" I asked with resignation.

"This is completely your choice, Raegan," Headmaster Stone said, and Jules nodded in agreement.

Turning back toward JayLeigh, I asked, "How much time do I have to decide?"

"I have one more thing I need to do, so maybe another day. Two, at most."

"You're welcome to stay here while coming and going as you please," the headmaster said to her.

JayLeigh smiled, and I swore she looked as innocent as a five-year-old. "I appreciate that. I'll be back later this evening." She snapped her fingers and disappeared. Then, moments later, the dome around us dissolved and I heard the soft click of the office door as it opened and closed.

My body slumped into the chair in front of me. It had been a long damn day and it wasn't even dinner time yet.

Headmaster Stone paced in front of his desk. "I'm going to excuse you from classes until you've made your decision. I know nothing of Drakken, I didn't even know it existed, but I know of Marek and he was a good man if the stories told are true. Even if you can't figure out how to shift in the short time, figuring out why he sent JayLeigh for you could be equally as important."

"I get it. Can I go to my room now?" I asked, really needing to see my best friend.

"Of course." He nodded absentmindedly as the possibilities of everything swirled around in his eyes.

Just as I was about to open the door, Jules's fingers wrapped around my forearm. "You don't have to do this, and I will support you no matter what decision you choose."

She still had that twinkle in her eye, and I knew she wanted to say more. "But?" I prompted.

"No buts. I just need you to know I'm here for you and we'll figure things out as they come. You've been through a lot, and I apologize for not being more sensitive today with Enzo. I do understand it's different for you."

"Thank you. I really needed to hear that, because I was

beginning to think maybe I was overreacting, but what he did was wrong on so many levels," I said.

She nodded. "I have every faith you'll figure this out. Now, go see Gemma like I know you want, and I'll be by later tonight." She hugged me tightly before pushing me toward the door.

Glancing around, I wondered if JayLeigh had actually left the academy. When she was following me over the summer, I had sensed her, but I had never known *what* she was. I had assumed she was a creature similar to a scavenger, just one I had never met, but that was a mistake and one I wouldn't make again.

Now, I wondered if she had tricked me into picking up the scent just to throw me even further off. She liked to play coy, but something told me she had a bigger plan and there was more to the situation than she was letting on.

Classes were just about out for the day, so I hurried to my room where Gemma had mentioned wanting to meet me when I left her at lunch. When I entered the dorm, I went straight to my butler box and ordered my favorite fudge brownie and ice-cream, then an Oreo shake for Gemma.

Quickly, I changed out of my ruined shirt, which I was surprised neither Jules nor Headmaster Stone had said anything about, and into a comfy loose shirt and some yoga pants. Just as the familiar ding sounded from the box, Gemma burst into my room.

"Please tell me there is something sugary in that box, or I just may suck your blood instead."

"I missed your sweet ways of addressing me." I grinned at her, then handed her the shake. Sometimes, I forgot she was half-vampire since her witch side was prominent, but she wasn't shy about reminding others of her heritage.

She sucked down a long drink. "I love you almost as much as I love this shake. Third-year classes are nothing to joke around about. How did your afternoon go? What did Lyssa want?"

I moved onto my bed and patted the spot next to me. "You might want to sit down."

She winced. "That bad, huh? Are we moving from friends to frenemies with her? I can hate her again if you need me to, even though it's been nice not having to worry about her bitchiness."

"Lyssa was the least of my problems this afternoon. I never even made it to my other classes."

"Damn, girl. What happened?"

"Enzo. He spelled Lyssa to force her compliance in luring me toward his meeting spot without being able to tell me what was happening. I'm not mad at her, and I did let Enzo begin to explain what he wanted, but it only made things worse for him."

"Uh oh. How so?"

"The bastard seems to think now is the time to unload all of his deceits, and while I appreciate that he isn't continuing to lie or omit things from me, what he did have to say only dug his grave deeper. When I first met him, I recalled seeing him before, but I couldn't place where. I thought I was imagining it until he admitted he had screwed with my head before the night he saved me from the scavenger."

"Please tell me you kicked him in the balls." Her eyes narrowed, and I was grateful someone else was seeing the injustice of his actions.

"No, but I punched him in the face and stormed off."

"So, you've just been hiding here ever since?" she asked between sips.

"Not really. I decided to go for a fly, since that was what

I was used to doing over the summer, and the day turned even more interesting. Remember me telling you about the person or thing I thought was following me while I was gone?" She nodded. "Well, I met her today and she's not at all what I would have ever guessed."

"Keep going. Your day is way more entertaining than anything I've experienced in months."

Pushing her with my shoulder, I snatched her shake and took a long pull. "Don't take pleasure in my pain or I won't give you any more sugar."

She stole it back and waved her hand in the air for me to keep going.

"So, dragons are still alive," I said as she took a long sip from the shake, and it was the wrong thing to do.

Bits of Oreo sprayed all over my comforter as she choked. "Excuse me? As in, more hybrids like you or full-blooded ones?"

"Full-blooded."

She punched me in the arm. "You maybe could have led with that bit of information."

"Besides your spit all over my bed, it was worth it." I laughed. "Anyway, long story short, this chick from a dragon world called Drakken was following me. Her name is JayLeigh. You'd actually like her. Except for the fact that she wants to take me to another academy that's for dragons only. Headmaster Stone thinks I should go, so I can convince Marek Skye to come back to Earth and kill Malina. You know, because he's a Doyen, and I also forgot to lead with that."

"Ohmygod." Her words jumbled together as she shot up from my bed and started pacing. "You know what this means, right?"

"Well, I know what I think, but I'm curious how you feel about it all."

"We're going to Drakken together—I'm not getting left behind again—and then we're going to murder that bitch Malina. She's going to pay for trying to kill me."

I nodded my head at her demands. "I'm not sure I really have any say in who goes, but I'll see what I can do. Maybe I can make some ultimatums."

"Damn right, you will. They wouldn't have come for you if they didn't need you or want you for some reason. I bet you have more pull than you've been told. So, what now? You don't seem so sure about it all."

My shoulders shrugged. "I'm not. I know nothing about these people. To top it off, it's in another realm that none of us even knew existed before an hour ago. After everything I've been through the last couple years, I don't really want to deal with anything else, but I also know there may only be one way to stop Malina. And it's just been handed to me on a silver platter if I can convince Marek to help us."

Gemma sat back down on the bed. "It's because of everything you've been through that I know you can do this. You're one of the strongest people I know, Raegan. Most wouldn't have shown up here again, but you came back, owning what happened last year like a boss. Whatever happens, whatever you choose, I know you will make the most of it."

Tears pricked at my eyes. "Damn you. I thought you'd be totally against this, not lift me up and remind me of who I am."

"I like to surprise people. It keeps them on their toes." She grinned.

"So, I have to do this. I have to go to this Dray Academy

in Drakken and learn to be a real dragon and bring back their king to defeat Malina."

Her hand grasped mine. "No, *you* don't, but we will. I'll be there for you every step of the way."

"Thank you," I said as I brought my attention to my quickly melting ice cream. "Now, can we quit with the heavy and eat our weight in sugar before I have to talk to JayLeigh again?"

"Most definitely."

We spent the next hour devouring whatever we wanted. All the while, my mind raced with what I would have to do the following day. It was one thing to go across the United States to learn about the supernatural. It was on a whole different level of crazy to visit another realm and hang out with dragons.

I wasn't sure I was ready, but apparently, I was going to have to figure it out rather quickly.

JayLeigh never came back that evening, so I spent it with Gemma, Peyton, and Finley, trying to enjoy the last of my freedom for the next few weeks. I had no idea what I was supposed to expect at Dray Academy, but I had a feeling it wasn't going to be sunshine and rainbows.

The following morning, I slept in and only woke up when Aunt Jules came in my room to let me know JayLeigh was waiting in Headmaster Stone's office.

"How are you feeling? I heard you girls having fun last night, so I didn't want to come in and bother you," she said.

"You wouldn't have bothered us, but it was really nice having a carefree night. I haven't had one of those in way too long."

She smiled softly. "You deserved it. Want me to wait for you or meet you in the office?"

"Go on ahead. I'm just going to take a quick shower and I'll be there shortly."

She slid off the bed and waved goodbye as she closed the door behind her. When I heard it click shut, I trudged out of bed and into the bathroom. I had forgotten to remove my makeup the night before and looked like a raccoon, so I washed my face before hopping in the shower.

When the scalding water sprayed over my shoulders, a sigh of relief left my lips. There was nothing better than a scorching shower to wake a person up in the morning. Okay, maybe there was, but that wasn't an option for me at the moment.

Finishing up, I quickly got dressed in casual clothes: skinny jeans and a black tank top with my favorite boots. If I didn't have to go to class, I certainly wasn't going to dress for it.

As I headed down the hallway, I wondered how different the dragon realm would be and if I would stand out as being a hybrid. JayLeigh didn't seem any different than me, so I hoped not.

When I arrived at the office, I didn't bother to knock on the door since they were expecting me, and I was glad I didn't, because I walked in on a conversation I probably shouldn't have and couldn't decide if it was a good thing or not.

"I won't do this to her. She's made her point, and I'm going to respect her decision until she chooses otherwise," Enzo's voice sounded.

I kept the door cracked and didn't move a muscle as they continued.

"Enzo, you don't really have a choice here, and it makes me feel better knowing Raegan won't be alone. Don't you want the chance to prove to her you're on our side?" Headmaster Stone pushed.

"Of course, but not this way. Not when I know she won't agree. It will only piss her off further."

Well, at least he wasn't a complete idiot.

A throat cleared. "If I may chime in here," JayLeigh

began. "Enzo, you belong there almost as much as she does. If you won't do it for her, then do it for yourself. I don't know what I'm sensing within you, but I know Marek can figure it out and you don't want to miss this opportunity. I promise you that."

Shit. This couldn't be happening. Considering how much hesitation I had about going, Enzo joining me was going to make it even worse.

I knocked on the door as I opened it all the way and avoided the heated gaze I could feel coming from Enzo. When I entered all the way, I directed my attention to JayLeigh.

"I've decided to come with you only if I can bring Gemma." If Enzo was going regardless of what I wanted, then I at least wanted my best friend to help me through it.

"I'm sorry, Raegan, but I can't grant that request. To enter Drakken, a person needs to be all or at least part dragon. Unless there's something about Gemma I couldn't sense late last night when I checked on you, then she wouldn't survive trying to go through the portal." JayLeigh's eyes said she was sorry for the bad news, but I didn't understand.

If Enzo was coming, did that mean he was...

No, he couldn't be part dragon. Could he?

Without blowing my cover, I pretended like Gemma not being able to come didn't crush me. "So, it would just be me and you?"

"Actually, that's why I didn't come back earlier in the evening." Her eyes flicked to Enzo briefly. "I sensed something in the forest after I left you yesterday, and I came across caveman over there. He was throwing a tantrum like a dragon, but I didn't see any scales, so I decided to have a friendly little chat with him."

Enzo grunted. "I'd hate to see what you do when you're not being *friendly*."

An evil spark lit in her eyes as she grinned at me, and I wondered if whatever she had done was for me. Maybe having Enzo tag along wouldn't be the worst thing in the world. He might get his ass kicked every day, and that was something I could be okay with. Torture without death would leave my conscience relatively guilt-free.

"Anyway, it's small, but there is a trace of dragon within him, and I believe he'll make it through the portal. If I'm wrong... well, I'm leaving that risk up to him to take, but the invitation is there."

I choked on my own breath. "Are you saying he could die by coming with us?"

"There is a minuscule chance I'm wrong, and if I am, then yes, he could die."

My heart constricted at the thought of Enzo risking his life over just a trace of dragon within him that may not even be there. I might have been pissed at the idiot, but I still didn't condone him risking his life.

"No, he's not coming," I said firmly, hoping I was giving my best serious face.

JayLeigh's brow cocked. "Does his life matter to you? I was under the impression that it didn't."

Oh, she was trying to stir the pot. Not today, dragon.

"Any life matters to me. I'd say the same no matter who was trying to come. I'll be telling Gemma as well when I see her later."

"I see. Good to know. Anyway, Enzo is coming as long as he wants to. End of story. I'll be back at around six tonight to head to Drakken. Make sure you're ready. My dragon isn't known for her patience."

Before I could open my mouth to object once more, JayLeigh disappeared.

"Ugh, that little—" I began to say but was cut off.

"I wouldn't finish that sentence if I were you," JayLeigh's voice floated through the room before the door slammed closed.

"Her little disappearing trick is annoying," I grunted.

Jules laughed. "I don't think she's disappearing; that would be more of an elf thing. I think she's camouflaging herself with her surroundings, and it's pretty badass. You need to learn how to do that while you're gone."

Sighing, I crossed my arms. "I need to go unless you have anything else for me. I've already been gone the whole summer. I should get my stuff sorted before I leave. Again."

Headmaster Stone shook his head. "I don't have anything for you now, but I will have some items for you later that may help you while you're gone. Come see me before it's time."

I nodded and hugged Jules goodbye before heading out the door. I wasn't sure how many more times I would see her again before I left, and just in case something went south at this Dray Academy, I wanted to make every moment count.

Just as I was almost to the stairs to get on the platform, a familiar scent drifted my way. With a glare on my face, I spun around. "What do you want, Enzo?"

He still looked like hell with his ratted hair and dark circles under his eyes, but the heat in his gaze made the rest fade away as he moved in closer, almost seeming to stalk me like I was his prey.

"Thank you," he whispered when my back pressed against the cool stone wall.

"For what?" my voice squeaked, betraying my emotions.

Damn him for still affecting me when I was so infuriated with him.

"For giving me hope. You do care, and I'm going to prove to you it's okay. I know what I did was wrong. There will never be enough apologies I can make for that, but I will win you back and I'm going to enjoy doing it."

There was the cocky Enzo I had met a year ago. Though this one had more compassion in him, the confident elf that aggravated me all those months ago while I slowly fell in love with him was standing before me once more, and I wasn't sure how I felt about it.

"It's not going to happen. You and I are done. I will work with you when I have to, but nothing else. You're wasting your time."

His hand hovered over my chest, just enough that I could feel the heat pulsing off him, but not close enough to touch.

"The rapid beating of your heart tells a different story. I love you, Raegan, and I'm not going anywhere. I might have brought you to the academy under false pretenses, but you always belonged here. I never once lied about my feelings, and you saved me from Malina. Now, I'm going to help do the same for you. I'm going to make this right."

My breath hitched, and my insides turned to mush. Part of me wanted nothing more than to jerk my knee right up into his balls, but my heart ached to be closer to him. To accept his words and move forward. But that wasn't going to happen.

If—and that was a big *if*—I forgave him, there would be many more moments of groveling on his part. There was no making this easy for him after what he had done.

"Do whatever you want, Enzo. You're a big boy and you

can make your own decisions, but try not to be too disappointed when things don't go your way."

I patted his chest and then pushed him away before moving back toward the stairs. When I stepped onto the platform and turned around to press the button for the main floor, Enzo was still standing there with a grin on his face and a twinkle in his eyes.

Shit. I just gave him a challenge, and he wasn't even remotely afraid of it. I'd done the opposite of pushing him away, and I was in trouble.

He wiggled his fingers at me as the platform lowered and he disappeared from my sight.

A headache was forming in the back of my head, so I headed to my room and figured I might as well take a nap until lunchtime when I could meet Gemma and give her the bad news. She wasn't going to be happy, but at least it was only a few weeks and not months this time.

Although, it was going to feel like ages with Enzo along for the ride and me trying to avoid him at all costs.

~

SIX O'CLOCK CAME SOONER THAN I EXPECTED IT TO. Breaking the news to Gemma hadn't gone over well, especially when she started crying about being left behind again. I felt awful, but there wasn't much I could do about it. I wouldn't risk her life, and I had to go.

The more I thought about everything I could learn and accomplish in Drakken, I realized Headmaster Stone had every reason to be insistent about me going. If this Marek guy was friendly enough, he should understand why we needed him and hopefully break his vow to never return to Earth in order to stop Malina.

"Ready?" Jules asked when I grabbed my bag.

"Yep. At least this time when I'm leaving, I'll have my stuff with me. It wasn't all that fun taking off over the summer without my clothes or any cash."

She laughed. "I bet not. Where is Gemma? I figured she'd be seeing you off."

"Uh, she didn't take the news all that well. We already said our goodbyes, and she thought it was better if she didn't come meet JayLeigh with us, because she wanted to rip her eyes out. Gemma's words, not mine."

"Don't worry. I'll keep an eye on her while you're gone. She'll be okay."

I nodded. "Yeah, I know. I just feel bad."

We headed out the door, and I cast a glance at Gemma's door, wondering if I should poke my head in one last time.

"JayLeigh is waiting. I promise, I'll come check on her after you're gone and bring her dinner that's not made of pure sugar," Jules said.

A smile formed on my face as I squeezed my aunt tight. "Thank you. Seriously, I know you dropped everything to come take care of me in Portland, and you're doing the same thing now. It means more than I can properly describe to know that you're here, fighting to stop Malina and keeping everyone else safe."

"I wouldn't have it any other way."

Linking arms, we continued toward the headmaster's office. When we arrived, it was open and some guy was standing in front of the desk with his back to us. His hair was cut short at the sides and left a few inches long at the top. It was dark and silky-looking, making me want to run my fingers through it.

His form was on the thinner side, but I could still see the outline of muscles beneath the tight grey shirt he had on. As my eyes traveled south, I also appreciated the fit of his jeans as I checked out his ass. Whoever he was, I wished he was coming with us instead of Enzo. He would make for the perfect distraction from Enzo's persistence.

"Oh, good. Everyone's here. Can we go now? I'm starving and the food here sucks. No offense, Alistair," JayLeigh said when she saw us.

That's when the guy turned around and my jaw about hit the floor.

"Hi, Raegan," Enzo said huskily.

He was not playing fair, and this did not bode well for my ability to keep him at a distance.

Holy dragon babies! I thought he was hot before, but this new look was something else entirely. It had my girly bits going wild, just like the first time I met him.

Ignoring him as best I could, I turned to JayLeigh. "Yep, we're all here. Let's get this show on the road."

Enzo chuckled as I hurried right back out the door. JayLeigh had already mentioned we'd have to be outside for her to open the portal that would lead us to Drakken, and I was more than okay with the fresh air to cool down my insides.

Enzo caught up to me, putting his head close to mine as his voice lowered to a level of sultry that should be illegal. "I told you I would fight for you. The feeling you're experiencing right now that has your pulse racing and face flushed? It's because you still want me. I know you're afraid, but I won't ever hurt you again, Raegan. This is just the beginning for you and me, and I can't wait to show you how good it can be, again."

I was so dead.

CHAPTER SEVEN

E nzo strolled up ahead like he didn't have a care in the world. I, on the other hand, couldn't form a coherent thought. What a great way to start my journey to an unknown realm filled with freaking dragon shifters. Just great.

"Raegan," Headmaster Stone called from behind me. "I have the items I mentioned for you to take." He handed me a small pouch that was heavier than I was expecting.

"What's in it?" I asked as I tucked the pouch into my main bag.

"I'm not sure what you'll face in Drakken, but I thought I would at least give you a leg up during the training. There are a few potions in there for endurance, healing, and strength. If you need any of them, don't hesitate to use them."

My heart warmed at his kind gesture. It was something my dad would have done, and I was trying hard to control my emotions as memories suddenly assaulted me. Grief had a way of showing up when I least expected.

"Thank you. It really means a lot." Surprising him, I leaned in and gave him a quick hug.

"You're welcome. Now, hurry along. I'll be right behind you. I want to make sure everything goes well when the portal opens."

I nodded and jogged off to catch up with JayLeigh. She had a bit of explaining to do, and since I was pretty sure Jules and Enzo had already headed downstairs, I was glad we'd have a moment alone—as long as she had waited for me.

A sigh of relief escaped when I saw her spiky blonde hair as she peeked over the edge of the platform.

Deciding to get right to the point, I asked, "Why are you bringing *him* along?"

"Because he has a tiny bit of dragon in him and that only happened one of two ways. We need to know which. It very well could be the deciding factor in Marek agreeing to help, so you should be grateful I made this happen."

My brow pinched as I pressed the button for the main level and we began to descend. "Why do you seem so invested in making sure Marek helps? What's in it for you?"

She sighed. "You've never lived in a tiny realm with a small population before. Everyone knows everyone. Women are expected to breed more dragons, so we don't die out, and it's hard to earn respect if you want to be anything else. There are no strangers, and you can't even panty burp without your neighbor knowing."

Laughter, loud and obnoxious, ripped from my belly. "Panty burp? What the hell is that?"

She rolled her eyes. "Seriously? You don't say that here? It's when a girl loses gas. Don't tell me you've never done it."

I couldn't make the laughing stop. It turned into full-on

hiccups as I tried to confirm what she meant. "Do you mean fart?"

"I think I've heard it called that before. If it sometimes stinks and comes out of your ass, then yes, that would be a panty burp."

"Please, don't ever say that around me again, especially when we're around others. I don't think I could control myself. Gemma is going to love that one!"

My sides burned and cheeks ached from laughing. I had really needed the distraction in the moment. It brought my thoughts away from the feelings Enzo had conjured up within me, and I was more confident than ever about heading to Drakken.

When we made it back downstairs to go outside, I realized I never got a good answer out of her about why Enzo was coming, but I didn't really care anymore. If it was important, I'd find out soon enough. Enzo didn't seem to be able to keep anything to himself anymore, which I guessed wasn't always going to be a bad thing.

JayLeigh disappeared outside faster than necessary. Apparently, she really was ready to get off of Earth, even though she was just bitching about her supposedly tiny realm. Or maybe she was hiding something from me and didn't want me to ask any more questions. Both options were likely.

Jules was standing off to the side, so I headed over to her. Her gaze softened and she held an arm out when she saw me, but she seemed nervous.

"What's wrong?" I asked as I wrapped my arm around her.

"Nothing much. I'm excited for this opportunity for you. As much as I was looking forward to training, I wasn't the best fit. I just hope whatever they have planned for you isn't too much all at once. Three weeks isn't a long time."

"Whatever happens there, I can handle it." I tried to sound confident, but I knew what she meant.

Even though I was sure of my choice to go to Drakken, I wasn't entirely sure about trusting JayLeigh so completely. I was taking a huge gamble going through an unknown portal with her, but I wanted answers and nobody around me seemed to be able to find them.

She squeezed me tightly. "I know you can. Doesn't mean I don't worry. JayLeigh mentioned they don't have phones, but there is an email system of sorts, so you'll be able to check in. Make sure to let me know you arrived okay."

Pulling back, I nodded. "I will. Try not to worry. Everything is going to be fine."

She laughed. "Famous last words."

We joined the others, and they were discussing where to open the portal. We couldn't just do it right outside the academy. Students would see and this wasn't anything we were telling anyone about except Gemma. She'd have to think about something to tell Peyton and Finley, but I was sure that wouldn't be too hard.

"None of you can create a shield to make yourselves invisible? What do they teach you around here?" JayLeigh said, exasperated.

"Magic that each of our different races excel in. Unfortunately, all of the dragons left us before we could get their curriculum down," Headmaster Stone snapped, having shown up just in time to feel insulted.

"Right. Well, your elven ancestors left some things out as well, but not to worry. Dragons learned how to adopt the trick, and I have you all covered. Though, I can't hold the portal for long, so we at least need to be somewhere people won't see the three of us disappear into thin air."

"There's a clearing in the forest area nobody should be using right now since classes aren't in session," Headmaster Stone said, this time without as much animosity in his voice.

"Perfect. Let's go." JayLeigh grinned before spinning on her heel and heading toward the tree line.

Enzo followed after her first and the rest of us trailed behind. Within five minutes we were hidden within the canopy of trees and ready to go. I gave Jules one last hug with promises to reach out as soon as I could. She teared up a little but backed away and kept her head held high as if none of it bothered her.

"Okay, before we go, I need to go over a few things," JayLeigh began. "First, it takes a lot of energy to open a portal, meaning we only have one shot at this in order to leave today. Don't screw it up by distracting me or freaking out. Now, once we're cloaked, we won't be able to see each other. Raegan, I want you to grab my hand, and Enzo will take yours so we don't get separated. I don't need one of you ending up in neverland with the fairies."

She grinned and laughed at her own words, but none of us were joining in. Tough audience.

"Anyway," she drawled. "When we arrive, time will be different. You're going to be exhausted, even though it will only feel like you were in the portal for mere minutes. I'll show you to your rooms and, once you've rested, I'll show you around Drakken, then introduce you to Marek.

"My only warning is to not leave your rooms without me until you've been properly introduced to the other dragons. I'm sure you're aware, shifters have quite the temper, and not many of our residents are fond of change. The last time didn't work out so well for them, so they will act before asking questions. Understood?"

Nods came from me and Enzo, even though I really wanted to object. None of it sounded even remotely safe, making me question my sanity for thinking this was a good idea in the first place.

"Perfect. Let's get going then. The portal is only going to be a shimmer to you while we're on Earth, but once we walk through, it will be much brighter. Keep your eyes closed if you get motion sickness, because I will bite someone's head off if I get puked on. Literally."

I glanced at Enzo. "Are you sure you want to do this? You can still back out."

"Where you go, I go. I told you I'd help make everything right again, and if that means going through a portal that just might kill me, then so be it." He puffed out his chest, seemingly proud of the stubborn fool he was being.

Ugh. I really hoped he wasn't going to be all profound and mushy every time we spoke. It wasn't good for the steel wall I was trying to keep up around my heart. "No feelings allowed" was my new mantra.

"Whatever. It's your life. You can be an idiot if you want to be. Who am I to stop you?"

"You are everything to me and if you really didn't want me to go, then I wouldn't be, but there is a part of you that is glad I'm tagging along, and that is the part giving me hope."

Ignoring him, I paid more attention to JayLeigh as I should have been doing the entire time. She was creating something that was going to rip me from Earth and pop me into another realm. Keeping an eye on her should have been my priority instead of letting Enzo screw with my feelings.

Her hands were glowing a soft violet color as she moved them in a circular motion, pulling her arms further apart with each rotation. Ripples began to form in the air before her, transparent in color and shimmering just like she had said.

With a deep breath, JayLeigh turned back to us. "Okay, time to go invisible. I need the two of you to hold hands like Enzo is getting ready to transport you somewhere, assuming he is capable of that elf trait."

He grunted. "Of course, I am."

"Good. We're just going to act like we're disappearing for a little trip the good old-fashioned way. That way, if anyone can see us, they can think we just transported like elves do. Otherwise, they'd see the portal entrance and that could be bad."

"We should have just gone invisible before we left the office," I said, thinking this was entirely too dangerous if we were trying to keep JayLeigh's portal a secret.

"Yeah, well, we didn't. I'm not used to having to hide my abilities, so we're working with what we got. I've already been gone too long, and it's time to head back now." Her voice lowered and I could see the energy being sucked from her the longer we stood there. She hadn't been kidding when she said it would take a lot out of her.

Enzo must have noticed the same thing, because he immediately took my hand and pulled us closer to JayLeigh. Using his free hand, he held both of our bags since I was stuck in the middle of him and JayLeigh. "We're ready," he announced.

She placed a hand on his shoulder and grasped my free hand tighter than I was expecting for her size. I glanced back at Jules and Alistair one last time. She smiled at me, but it was forced. The headmaster stayed close but didn't seem as concerned until we must have fully disappeared, because a second later his eyes went wide like saucers.

"Stay close and, whatever you do, don't let go of each other or me," JayLeigh said, bringing my attention back to her as she took the first steps toward the shimmering portal.

It was wide enough that the three of us could step through at the same time and, with a massive deep breath, that's exactly what we did.

The time for turning back was gone as we were sucked into the portal. It pulled the air right from my lungs. My grip on Enzo's hand tightened, along with the one I had on JayLeigh's. Once I felt secure in the fact that we weren't going to get separated, I lifted my head and forced air back into my body.

Colors moved all around us in a kaleidoscope effect, which allowed me to calm down some and enjoy the ride. We moved around a lot, including flipping upside down, and I understood why JayLeigh warned us about the motion sickness, but thankfully, it didn't bother me.

When I peeked at Enzo, I was a little worried that wasn't the case for him. His face was turning a little green, and his eyes were clamped shut. I squeezed harder on his hand, giving him the reassurance that I was still there and everything was going to be okay.

More so because I didn't want to see JayLeigh bite someone's head off, not because I cared about making him feel better. At least, that's what I kept telling myself.

As we were nearing the end of the portal, the colors began to dull, and I kept my eyes focused on what appeared to be a black void we were headed straight for. JayLeigh wasn't freaking out, so I tried to remain calm, but then I remembered her previous words about Drakken's shield possibly not letting Enzo in and my heart began to race.

I wasn't sure how I would keep my shit together if he died right in front of me. The more I thought about what a stupid risk we were taking, the harder it was to breathe. Just as I was erupting into a full-blown panic attack, we were spit out onto a grassy knoll, and my legs buckled beneath me.

Scrambling to my knees, I crawled over to Enzo, who wasn't moving. Terror gripped at my chest as I shook his shoulders. "Enzo. Enzo, wake up!" I yelled.

No, this couldn't be happening. He couldn't have died. Not like this. Tears pricked at my eyes as my throat burned with emotion.

"JayLeigh, do something. Bring him back."

"Raegan—"

I cut her off. "No talking. Just fix him."

"He's not dead, you idiot. He just passed out. And now, I'm pretty sure he's only waiting to see how bad you'll freak out, because he's breathing just fine from what I can tell."

Enzo's eyes fluttered open, and a smirk appeared on his face. "Oops."

Without hesitation, I punched him in the jaw and stood up so I could storm off. Where to, I had no idea, but I needed a moment by myself before I did what the shield apparently didn't.

The only positive was that I now knew he wasn't always going to be so damn mushy, at least. He was also going to be a massive pain in my ass.

CHAPTER EIGHT

When I was no longer concerned with Enzo's wellbeing, I took my time taking in the new land we'd been dropped on. The sky above was a fiery crimson as if the sun was setting, but it was high above, telling me the deep red was just its normal color.

The ground beneath my feet was firm and covered in some sort of wild grass that was a deep forest green with half-inch-thick blades that seemed to crisscross over each other, creating the solid surface. Enormous trees were to our left that reminded me of the Redwoods from a trip my family took down the California coast when I was about ten. Most were so wide, a dozen people could hide behind them and none would be the wiser.

To the right was a town of sorts with a few clusters of average-sized buildings and a grander one right in the middle of them all. I assumed that was the academy JayLeigh had mentioned. Their population didn't seem very large, so I was counting on being right.

From where we stood atop a steep hill, the main structure appeared to be made from some sort of metal as the sun's rays reflected off its sides, shining in my eyes.

"What do you think?" JayLeigh asked once Enzo was up off the ground and grabbing our bags I had long since forgotten about. I was glad he didn't lose them in the portal when he was getting sick.

"It's incredible. The sky is something else," I answered. "Is it always this vibrant?"

She nodded her head. "Except for when it's our technical nighttime. The sky is pitch black then. No moon or stars. Our only light during the four hours it transpires comes only from sources we've created."

"You only get four hours of sleep *every day?*" Enzo gaped, and I was glad he asked. I was already feeling the exhaustion, and that was going to be nowhere near enough for me.

"Some do, some sleep when the sun's still up. Easy to cover windows, you know," she said sarcastically.

"Right." Enzo cleared his throat, clearly embarrassed for feeling like he asked a stupid question.

"So, where to first?" I asked with a yawn.

"We can head straight to King Marek's quarters, or I can show you to your dorms you'll be staying in while attending the academy for the next few weeks. If you need to rest, I'm sure the king will understand waiting to meet you." The challenge was evident in her voice, and I was going to accept.

"I'm fine to go now." I cast a glance at Enzo, who was finally getting some color back in his face.

"Well, I'm not going to let you go by yourself," he huffed.

Taking three steps in his direction, I got right in his face, poking a finger in his chest. "You don't *let* me do anything. I will do what I want and when I want while we're here. You have no say in my decisions. You made sure of that the day you met me and the lies began."

His eyes turned dark as I pushed him back, but they never left mine. He seemed to be taking caution with the words he wanted to say next, which was smart on his part. The exhaustion was making me a mega-bitch, and I didn't seem to be able to control it.

"Raegan, you know what I meant. I'd rather not have you go meet the king of dragons by yourself for the first time. We don't know these people, and I'd like to be certain you're not going to be harmed before we go our separate ways. Is that acceptable?"

"As long as you understand I'm my own person and will do whatever I want, then it's whatever. Just stay out of my way."

Enzo's eyes widened as JayLeigh began to snicker next to us.

"Raegan, are you alright?" he asked.

"Of course I am, why would you ask such a stupid question? You seem to be full of them tonight."

He rolled his eyes and glanced at JayLeigh. "What's wrong with her? Why are her eyes and skin changing?"

She stepped toward me as her own eyes changed from light green to a deeper emerald color that matched mine almost perfectly. "Stand down," she demanded as her height seemed to increase right before me.

Something whimpered that sounded like it was right behind me, but when I cast a glance back, there was nothing there. I quickly realized the sound had come from me.

"Raegan, get your dragon under control before you snap at someone who won't be so understanding. Not everything is going to go your way while you're here, and I promise you don't want to lose control around the wrong people." JayLeigh backed up as I regained control.

I hadn't even known my dragon side was that strong. Nothing had felt different except my emotions being stronger, but I had assumed it was the exhaustion. Maybe bringing my dragon side further out wasn't such a great idea after all.

JayLeigh's face softened. "Don't do that. There's nothing to be afraid of. This is why you're here. So you can control the beast inside of you and use all of your abilities. It will be easier than you think as long as you're not afraid. Your dragon will sense that and use it to overpower you, but if you stay strong and remain in charge, you should have a unified relationship."

My throat tightened, fear already coursing through me, regardless of her words. "Why do you talk about our dragon side as if it's another being? Anytime I've shifted before, I've still been me."

She tsked. "You've never shifted. You've utilized your dragon traits, but any toddler can do that. Until you've tripled in size and shot flames from your snout, you haven't shifted."

"Flames? Seriously?" I gaped.

"Yep, but enough of that. We need to get going. It's almost lunch time here, and I want to be in and out before the crowds descend from the academy."

Enzo still carried our bags, and when I tried to take mine, he refused, simply shaking his head and moving away from me until I quit trying. Fine, if he wanted to be my pack mule, who was I to stop him?

Instead of worrying about it, I focused on the buildings we were approaching. "None of these look like houses. Where do people live?" I asked.

"Well, there are a few choice places for the different dragons we have here. Most commonly, they live in the forest. The trees further in are twice the size of the ones you can see from here, and they've been made into homes. Second option is underground. That's more suited for the nocturnal ones, though."

"So, they live in tunnels?" Enzo asked.

She shrugged. "Not really. Metal buildings were placed underground with tunnels leading out of them. They're actually really nice homes if you don't mind fake light. Last, there are the nomads. They live in caves on the outskirts of our area and very rarely, if ever, come to socialize."

"I thought you mentioned that dragons need a pack or something?" I asked as we finally made it to the bottom of the steep hill.

"They do." She nodded. "There are around ten or so of them out there, keeping each other sane. What's the human saying? Misery loves friends? Well, that's them."

I laughed. "Misery loves company, but pretty close."

"Whatever. You guys talk weird half the time," she said, which made me laugh harder.

"Because *panty burp* is such a normal thing to say?"

She joined in with my laughter. "Okay, you might have me with that one."

Enzo nudged my shoulder. "Uh, should we be concerned?"

I glanced up to see what he was talking about, and my eyes landed on a colossal dragon, easily twice the girth and several feet taller than JayLeigh's. The scales were an obsidian color with silver undertones whose beauty I might have appreciated more if I wasn't all but certain that its intense cobalt eyes were glaring at us.

"Oh, that's just Onyx. He won't bite, or at least, I don't think he will." She winked.

I peeked again at the imposing dragon and was pretty sure she was wrong. The dude looked like he was seconds away from ripping our heads off. His nostrils flared before he whipped around, narrowly missing us with his spiked tail.

"Right," Enzo drawled.

We continued on, walking past structures with big glass windows that showcased products I assumed were for sale. Mostly weapons, which freaked me out a little. If this little slice of a realm was mostly blocked off from Earth and only dragons lived there, then what was with the artillery? Why did they have the academy, and what would they be teaching us when we arrived?

Something told me I probably shouldn't focus on the answers to those questions. I'd be better off learning what I could and walking away, but I wasn't so sure I'd be able to do that as time passed.

"The building up ahead is where the king stays. We don't call it a castle, more like a headquarters. The academy is on the first level of the building. There are only a few classrooms inside and everything else is outside, but within the walls of the headquarters property," JayLeigh explained.

"Where will we stay?" I asked since the academy was only one floor of the building.

"Most of the students have their own housing already, so you'll stay in the guest area of the headquarters. Adjoining rooms most likely on the second level."

My eyes flicked to Enzo who smirked at the information while I held in a groan. Three weeks was going to be too long to be in such close proximity to him. I had gotten up to speed at Shadow Veil within one year. Maybe I could shorten our stay in Drakken by working my ass off once more.

"When does training start?" I yawned again as I finished the question, silently cursing the time change. "Also, did we go backward or forward with a day?"

"Uh, you went forward." She didn't seem certain of her answer, but I couldn't tell why.

My mouth opened to question her, but a booming voice called out her name before I could.

"JayLeigh, my favorite niece. Back so soon, and with not one, but two guests." His voice lowered, giving way to his disapproval in Enzo's presence.

"Your highness." JayLeigh bowed. "This is Raegan and Enzo. I believe you'll be interested to meet *both* of them."

His fingers stroked his square jaw. "Indeed. If he made it through the portal, then you chose well, as usual."

Deep jade eyes focused in on me, a shade or two darker than mine. "Raegan, I'd like to speak with you before you settle in for the evening and then tomorrow, while JayLeigh starts your training, I will meet with your friend."

My eyes were so tired, I couldn't even see straight, and his frame began to blur at the edges, but I was curious if this guy would know anything about who might have played a part in my dragon DNA, so I nodded. "Sure, as long as you feed me before I pass out."

JayLeigh winced, and I didn't understand what I had said wrong.

"I will bring her food, King Marek."

Oh, shit. I wasn't used to a hierarchy. I probably wasn't supposed to demand things from the king, but what did they expect? I didn't know anything about Drakken or even dragons. It wasn't my fault.

"That's alright, JayLeigh. I anticipated the need for

sustenance, so I had food brought to my chambers. JayLeigh, if you'll take Enzo and show him where the eatery is, then their rooms, I would appreciate it." Marek kept his head high, peering down at her much shorter frame compared to his six-and-a-half-foot height.

Enzo's hand grasped my elbow. "Are you sure splitting up so soon is a good idea?"

I grunted. "If they want us dead, it will happen. No amount of sticking together is going to prevent that."

He seemed to consider that and nodded. "At least, let me know you're back before you go to sleep?"

"Yeah, sure." I waved him off and took a step toward Marek. "I'll follow you."

Once we were out of earshot from JayLeigh and Enzo, Marek began asking me questions. "What do you think of Drakken so far?"

"It's interesting, to say the least. The sky and big-ass dragons roaming around will take some getting used to if I'm here long enough to do so."

He raised a brow. "Eager to leave already?"

"I don't know," I answered honestly. "This place is messing with my head. JayLeigh mentioned something about my dragon, but I probably won't retain much of anything until I get food and rest."

"Well, then I'll keep things short," he said as we appeared at a side entrance of the headquarters. "This is my personal entrance. I will assign you a code that you may use for emergencies only during your stay in Drakken, along with one that will allow you to use the elevator to directly enter my quarters. I want you to feel comfortable here, so you can focus on JayLeigh's teachings. If anything doesn't agree with you, come straight to me."

His voice was deep and soothing, making me really wish

he'd stop talking, because I was close to falling asleep while walking if that was even possible. He also reminded me of Headmaster Stone with his insistence I come to him if there were any issues. Thinking of the headmaster made me remember my promise to Jules.

"Will I be able to use the email system JayLeigh mentioned to reach out to my aunt when I get back to my room?"

He shook his head. "The only communications system to reach Earth is in my residence. I'd offer to let you use it now, but it takes a while to connect. You should probably rest first while I take care of it and come see me before you meet JayLeigh after you wake."

I nodded, hoping Jules wouldn't be too pissed I didn't do it first thing like I'd promised. I hadn't known I'd be so exhausted from the travel, and there was no way I was going to last much longer without getting sleep. I only planned on chatting with Marek long enough to eat, and then I'd promptly find my bed.

Soon after we entered the headquarters, we arrived at an elevator that was made with etched glass walls and chrome trim. I followed him inside and observed as he pressed some numbers on a keypad before placing his hand on the screen. It beeped twice and then the doors slid silently closed.

"I'd hold on if I were you," he warned, but my reflexes were too slow.

The elevator shot up like a rocket, and my knees buckled, landing me on the ground with a hard thud.

"Shit, that hurt," I grumbled.

"Sorry, I should have said something sooner. Hopefully lunch will make up for it." He reached a hand out to me that I gladly took.

By the time I was on my feet, the doors to the elevator were already open and I was cursing the fact that even though this contraption had walls around it, it was no less dangerous than I considered the platforms at Shadow Veil.

We arrived inside his quarters, and the living area we entered was enclosed by floor-to-ceiling windows that reminded me of Enzo's dorm. My feet moved toward the walls to see out and really take in the land of Drakken, but then the smells of food hit my nose and I halted mid-stride. "What *is* that?" Drool was threatening to drip out of my mouth.

"That would be lunch. Come sit. We can talk while you eat, and then I will show you around my quarters before taking you back to yours."

There was no argument from me. I beat him to the already-set table I had somehow missed while entranced by the windows and took a seat. A plate was waiting in front of me, so I served myself, hoping there was no royal protocol I was supposed to abide by, and then dug in.

There were meats I didn't really want to know the source of, but they looked like beef and that was all that mattered to my brain at the moment. Those went on my plate first, followed by the fluffiest mashed potatoes I'd ever seen, soft breads, and some canary-yellow fruit that had the texture of melons, but much smaller and with no rind.

Marek leaned back, seeming to enjoy watching me fill my plate, and then even let out a laugh as a moan slipped out when I first tasted the potatoes. I had a serious appreciation for delicious food and didn't often hide the pleasure it brought me. I probably needed to work on that.

"So, you don't seem to hold back much, do you?" he asked.

Shaking my head, I wiped my mouth with a cloth napkin. "Not usually."

"And I assume you prefer others to be just as candid?"

"It typically makes things easier when I don't have to listen to people beating around the bush," I answered.

"Very well. Would you like to know what I have to say?"

With my fork already full of sliced meat, I nodded my head and took in the food.

"I'm your father."

With steak lodged in my throat, I choked and sputtered, not sure I'd heard his words right in my deliriously tired state.

"Crazy dragon king, come again?" I finally managed to spit out when my mouth was mostly clear of food.

"You are my daughter. My only child, to be more precise."

The walls began to close in around me as air no longer moved through my body. I tried to breathe and avoid passing out, but as my vision narrowed, my only hope was that I didn't land face-first in my lunch.

Marek moved from his seat faster than I could blink, catching me before I fell out of the chair. His fingers snapped in front of my face, bringing my focus back from the encroaching darkness.

"Raegan?" His brow creased. "Are you okay?"

My body swayed, but my vision began to come back, and I'd somehow avoided passing out after his bombshell statement.

"You're my…" I couldn't even finish the sentence.

"Yes, I was the last one with Malina before you were created. I had no idea what she was doing, or I would have stopped her. Don't get me wrong, I'm glad you exist, but what she was trying to accomplish, there was nothing maternal about it."

Holy shit, I thought I'd be spending the entire time I was in Drakken trying to figure out whose DNA ran through me, but it just landed on my lap within the first hour. It's not like it really mattered. He wasn't my actual father, more like a sperm donor, but to know I didn't come strictly from evil did make me feel a little better about my history and what it might mean for my future.

"Do you know what she wants? I've yet to figure that out besides her wanting to be free of her cage at Shadow Veil. I don't understand why she needs me if she's already so powerful." I had little desire to stay on the whole "father" topic now that I had the information, but I was more than happy to learn about Malina. Anything that might help us find and defeat her was worth discussing.

He took his seat again before speaking, and I appreciated the breathing room. "I can't be certain of her plans after spending the last two decades locked away, but before she hit rock bottom, she always talked a lot about trying to revive Elora. I used to think it was endearing and almost told her of Drakken, but something always held me back, even when I thought I loved her. When I caught her with one of my scales and some of my human hair, I knew she was just using me."

His face frowned as the memories seemed to resurface for him. The lines around his emerald eyes made me wonder just how old he was, because he didn't look over forty, but I knew that wasn't the case. He'd been around for centuries, at least. Unfortunately, this wasn't the time to ask as he ran his hands through dark, earthy-colored hair.

He had loved her, and she had broken his heart. It was no wonder he had fled Earth and never come back. If I had been able to run from Enzo and never see his face again after his betrayal, I might have done that as well. He was lucky I cared too much about Jules and Gemma to do so.

"What did you do?" I asked, trying to fill in what happened before he left for Drakken.

"I threatened to end her life if she ever used any part of me for her spells. I thought I had taken anything of mine she had, but here you are, proving I had missed something, or my discovery was simply too late. I only knew you existed when you showed up at Shadow Veil and the gargoyles alerted me to your existence.

"At the time, I didn't realize you had anything to do with Malina or even myself, but as more oddities kept happening, I began to put the pieces together. I trusted the council to be able to keep her locked away, but that didn't work out so well."

I shook my head. "No, it didn't, but back up a minute. Explain the gargoyles. My best friend Gemma told me stories, but you seem to know a whole lot more about them."

He took a small bite of food before answering, so I took it as a sign to resume eating my deliciousness as well, this time without as much enthusiasm.

"The gargoyles aren't the easiest thing to explain. They've been around since before my existence, so even I don't truly understand what they're capable of, but their allegiance moved to the dragons as the elves became greedy. When I decided to cut off contact with the other supernaturals, they became my eyes and ears. Like when you arrived, I knew immediately. As well as when Malina got out."

My memories ventured back to the day she broke free and all that had transpired. "Why was she afraid of the gargoyles?"

"Because she knows where their alliance is. She knew I would know she was free and that you existed, meaning I would come for her."

"Well, why haven't you come for her? Why send JayLeigh to follow me instead of coming yourself as previously promised?" Maybe Marek wasn't as badass of a Doyen as I thought, which was more than disappointing.

"That's complicated and something we don't really have

time for. I simply wanted to be open that my blood runs through your veins and you're welcome here in Drakken whenever you want, for as long as you want. I'd love if you'd stay here, but I know you have people back on Earth who you care about as well."

Another yawn slipped from my mouth. "You're right. I do have a family. One who needs protecting from Malina. She threatened to come back for me, and we don't have any way to stop her without you. We need your help."

His fingers tapped on the tabletop as his eyes glazed over. Clearly, his thoughts had taken his full attention. I finished the last of my lunch as I waited for him to respond to my statement, afraid his previous love for her was going to make the situation much more complicated than it needed to be.

He seemed to be interested in being a part of my life, but what life would I have if I was forced to hide away on Drakken, leaving Jules, Gemma, and the others to fend for themselves? He needed to figure out if running from the past was more important than protecting the future.

"Did you hear me?" I snapped, anger rising within me as I realized the very real possibility of him not assisting us. "We need you to stop Malina."

"Raegan, you have to understand, the people here need me. I can't leave them."

"So, you'll just leave your only heir to fend for herself against the most powerful sorceress on Earth?"

"That's not fair."

He was right, I wasn't being fair, but there was nothing fair about war, and Malina was promising a supernatural war if I didn't give in to her demands. She wanted her own world to run, and nothing was going to stop her from getting her way.

"Well, it's how I feel and if we don't get your assistance, then it could be Drakken she comes for next. Just remember that."

"It's certainly something to consider," he murmured.

Pushing my plate away, I stood up from the table, trying to remain civil. "Thank you for the lunch. Since I can't reach out to my aunt, I'd like to head to my room if you don't mind."

"Of course not. Let me show you the way."

Following him back toward the elevator, we didn't say another word to each other until we reached my room. While we walked, I enjoyed the smell of cut wood throughout the halls. I was pretty sure the entire house was made from the redwood-looking trees I had seen outside, and it was stunning, a complete contrast from the stone walls at Shadow Veil.

"Here you are. Enzo's room is one more door down, and there's a call button within your room if you need anything. We have several staff working at all times of the day, so even if it's dark out, don't hesitate to ask for assistance."

"Thank you." Opening the door, I stepped inside before half-closing it. "I guess I'll see you around."

"I'll check on you tomorrow or the day after. You're in good hands with JayLeigh," he said.

Smiling politely, I nodded and murmured goodnight before closing the door on him. If he wanted to be a pain in my ass about not helping, there was no way I was going to make getting to know me easy on him.

The only downside to closing the door on Marek was that the room was completely unfamiliar to me. Once the door was closed, I could barely see anything. There were blackout curtains on the windows, which I would have really appreciated if I was already in bed.

I had no idea where anything was, and as I felt around the walls for a light switch, my hip slammed into a desk.

"Damn it," I cursed.

Screw it. I was exhausted and could see the shape of the bed. I'd find my things and figure everything else out when I wasn't sleep-deprived. Taking my bra off and stripping down to my shirt and underwear, I pulled the silky sheets back and sunk into the plush bed.

A sigh escaped my lips as tension rolled out of me and I closed my eyes. The bed was heavenly, and JayLeigh was going to have a hell of a time getting me out of it the following day.

I reached for the other pillow I hoped to tuck between my legs for extra comfort, and a scream ripped from my throat when I came into contact with a very naked and muscular chest instead of a pillow. I fell out of bed, and then proceeded to trip over my boots, landing hard on the ground with legs tangled and a heel stabbing me in the ass.

"Lights on," Enzo's groggy voice sounded from the bed and, slowly, everything lit up around me. "Are you okay?" he asked, seeming to enjoy my current state of disarray once he could see me.

Scrambling to my feet, I stood before answering him. "Of course I'm not okay. I'm exhausted and overwhelmed and just want to sleep, but instead I find a mostly naked man in bed who doesn't belong there. To top it off, I now probably have a decent-sized bruise on my ass."

"Want me to check it for you?" Enzo winked while tossing a sexy grin my way.

He was standing on the opposite side of the bed, not at all deterred by my unhappiness. In my attempt to stop being distracted by his smile, I made the mistake of diverting my gaze toward his chest, which led my eyes further south to his boxer briefs that happened to be the only thing he was wearing.

"Take your time answering. I know it's been a while, and I don't want to rush your appreciation of my body. I'm fully okay with being your eye candy." I could hear the laugh in his voice, which drew my attention back to his face.

Still unused to seeing his short hair, I shook my head and turned away from him. It wasn't fair that his body was such a distraction. It seemed like the more I fought my feelings for him, the more they increased.

Stupid traitorous heart.

"Why are you in my room? No, better question, why are you in my bed with no clothes on?" I demanded as I grabbed my pants to get dressed again. The only thing I couldn't find was my bra, which wouldn't have been a problem if my boobs weren't showcasing my feelings as well.

"I had a feeling you wouldn't come to tell me you were back, so I decided to wait for you in your room and then got tired, so I went to bed and figured I'd wake when you turned on the lights. But you didn't, so really, this is all your fault." He smirked, playing the blame game.

Ugh, I really wanted to punch him again. Like really freaking bad.

My emotions were escalating by the second and, without warning, I felt a full-on breakdown rising to the surface. There was nothing I could do to stop the eruption, no matter how much I wished it wasn't happening with Enzo to witness it. Instead, he was going to take the brunt of my ire.

"No, all of this is *your* fault. From the very beginning, you could have left me alone. I would have been fine on my own. I *was* fine. Then, you came and forced your way into my world and everything since then has been complete shit."

Hot tears trailed down my face as every frustration decided to make itself known. There was no holding it back as every negative thought I'd had in the last few months came rushing out.

"Did you kill my parents, too? Did Malina force you to do that? Did you take every happiness away from me, so I would have no other choice but to depend on you?" I had never really believed he could have done those things, but those questions had made appearances in my head at the darkest of times when I had been alone over the summer and trying to cope with everything on my own.

"Raegan, I would never—"

My hand shot out, halting whatever he was going to say. "I don't want to hear it. I don't want to be this creation that Malina made to use against others. I don't want to be a damn dragon or be in a completely different realm from everything I've ever known. I just want to go back two years and be with my family, completely unknowing that you or any of this ever existed."

My body collapsed against the wall as everything I'd been through over the last year beat my body to shit. I had thought I was handling everything fine, but the last twenty-four hours had been too much. Whether it was the lack of sleep and changing worlds, or learning who donated my dragon DNA, or even Enzo's presence that I couldn't seem to escape, I'd never know, but I'd finally had enough.

All I did know was that once the floodgates opened, they wouldn't close, and I'd never even been able to put on my pants, which was making me feel all kinds of awkward, curled on the floor, half-naked, as Enzo cautiously made his way toward me.

"Raegan," His voice shook with trepidation, but I ignored him while sobs continued to escape from deep within me. "I'm going to sit next to you," he whispered.

His warmth covered my entire left side, causing my body to shake from the change in temperature and lean into him involuntarily. Not one to miss an opportunity, Enzo's hands slid under my frame and gently deposited me into his lap. I considered trying to get away, but I was done caring in that moment. I didn't bother to object, because if I was being honest... I still needed him.

I hated him, but I loved him.

I had never understood how that could be possible, but it was my life at the moment. No matter how much I wanted Enzo to disappear, I knew deep down, a part of me wanted him. I just didn't understand why, and there was no more energy left in me to fight him right then.

"Cry all you need to, little dragon. Even if you hate me more in the morning, I'm not leaving you alone right now. So, do what you need to and know I have you. I'll hold the both of us up for as long as you need."

His words made me cry harder, because it was like he understood exactly what I was feeling and confirmed it was okay to hate him for all he had done. The shit-tastic part was that it only made me love him all that much more.

CHAPTER TEN

The following morning, I woke up wrapped in Enzo's arms and back on the bed. I had no idea how long we had slept for, but it had been the best night's sleep I'd had in months. Though, I promptly ignored the "why" around that little fact and slid out of Enzo's hold, so I could use the bathroom.

Before Enzo had turned the lights out the night before, I saw the bathroom to my right, so I tiptoed in that direction. Once my hand grasped the door handle, I closed it behind me and whispered "lights on" like Enzo had previously done.

The area came into view, and I found another door at the opposite end, thinking it was a closet. I opened it up only to find another bedroom. My bag happened to be leaning against the bed, so I assumed it was Enzo's room and entered.

Grabbing my stuff, I took it back into the bathroom and left the door open, so I wouldn't get suffocated by the steam in the shower and didn't have to wake Enzo by opening my own door.

I turned on the shower first, which thankfully didn't require any kind of voice command like the weird techy lights, then proceeded to get undressed. The water was already scalding when I stepped in seconds later, just how I preferred.

The night before came back to me, and even though I had worried I'd be embarrassed for my breakdown, it was the complete opposite. The weight I had been carrying on my shoulders was lighter, and I felt like Enzo truly understood me. Even if I wasn't ready to forgive him, I knew we'd reached some sort of common ground and could move forward.

Whether that was going to be as friends or something more was yet to be decided.

As I was rinsing off the last of my soap that smelled a lot like the yellow fruit I'd had at lunch the previous day, I made the mistake of opening my eyes when I thought I heard a sound. Citrus found its way into my eyes and burned like a mother.

Twisting around, I tried to wash the soap out, but it was stinging worse with hot water, so I reached my hand outside the glass door in search of a towel. Cursing loudly, I realized I hadn't grabbed one and there was none waiting for me.

Blindly and slowly, I turned the water off and made my way out of the shower, keeping my arms out in front of me, because I couldn't see shit and didn't want to run into anything. I had high hopes of finding the cabinets I knew I had seen, but my sense of direction was completely thrown off and I had no such luck.

By the time I could partially see again and locate the towels, everything around me was wet and I was dripping water all over the floor, making my task even harder. I'd nearly fallen on my ass several times as I made my way to the corner cabinet. Before I could get it all the way open, a voice sounded in the room, freezing me in place.

"Were you looking for this?" I could hear Enzo's smirk in his voice as I made out the outline of his body through my blurry vision.

"Seriously? You've been watching me walk around naked in the bathroom, blind as a bat, and didn't say a damn word?"

He was going to pay. I didn't know how or when, but I was going to kill him. I took the towel regardless and rubbed at my eyes until I could see again, not great, but enough to get me by.

"Well, you weren't in bed when I woke up, and then I heard the shower. Not wanting to disturb you, I went out your door and into the hallway to go back to my room. You know, so I could remain the gentleman I am and give you your privacy."

I scoffed and rolled my eyes.

"But much to my surprise, you left the door open on *my* side, not yours, making me assume it was an open invitation to come in. So really, the confusion on my part is all *your* fault. I'm just an innocent bystander who happened to see a breathtakingly gorgeous woman walk out of the shower while water cascaded down the tantalizing curves of her delicious body."

The way his eyes roamed over my skin had all parts of me on fire. Every nerve ending was on high velocity in that moment, and I was actually shocked to find there wasn't any steam rising from my skin.

He was still wearing only his boxer briefs, hair mussed from the previous night's sleep, but in a sexy way I found irresistible. My heart was warning me that my next move was a bad one of epic proportions, but my head and hormones were in charge, and as my vision cleared up completely, I realized I *needed* Enzo.

Not just the emotional support he had given me the night before, but I craved a physical outlet. Even if it was a one-time thing, I was going to take what I needed from him and worry about the consequences later. Much, much later.

"Raegan," Enzo's voice cracked as I took a step closer to him. "What are you doing?"

"Taking what I want." I stalked closer, feeling more powerful with every step I took.

"I'm not saying no, and really, I should just let this happen and quit being an idiot, but are you sure?" He was flustered, and I was loving every second of it.

"Enzo," I whispered as I ran my fingers down his damp chest from all the steam around us.

"Yes?"

Leaning in closer, I nipped at his ear. "Shut up and give me everything you got. It might be your only chance." The last bit was a warning, which I hoped he understood the meaning of.

This was not me forgiving him. This was me taking what I wanted when I wanted it. Nothing more or less.

At least, that's what I kept telling myself, even as his lips crashed into mine and he wrapped my still-naked form around his body before carrying me to bed. By the time we hit the mattress, his boxers were gone and there was nothing separating us.

Nothing physical or emotional was holding us back. We acted in the moment, and it was the most powerful experience of my life. I let all of my inhibitions go and gave in to every ounce of love he was offering, drinking it in as if it was the last source of nourishment in all the worlds.

His left hand gripped my hair as the right roamed my

body. Everywhere he touched, sparks erupted between us. Not ones I could see, but the sensations of them were overpowering as I laid back and gave in to Enzo's passion.

"I love you, Raegan," he whispered when our bodies joined together for the first time in months.

He filled my entire being perfectly, like we were meant for each other on a deeper level. I tried not to get my emotions involved, but when the room was bathed in a lavender light that radiated from only us, I had a hard time ignoring the fact that it wasn't normal to glow *any* color when you made love to another person.

Instead of answering him back, I flipped us over and showed him that while I hadn't forgiven him, my love for him was still there. As much as I wanted to fight it, as much as I wanted to hate him for what he had done, there was something bigger at play between us and I was tired of constantly fighting it.

As we hit our climax, the room erupted in a way it'd never done before. Physical sparks came off our skin and bounced between us everywhere our skin touched, while the lavender glow I was used to brightened and mixed with a deeper midnight blue.

Once we came down from our high and everything around us went back to normal, Enzo's chest vibrated beneath me with a growl and his arms tightened around my lower back. "Mine."

Sitting up, I stared into his eyes and tried not freak out when they were slit like a dragon's. "Enzo, are you okay?"

"Mine. You are mine, and I will protect you until my dying breath." His voice was deep, much grumblier than I'd ever heard it before, and something told me it wasn't actually Enzo I was speaking with. At least, not his human counterpart.

Pushing myself up, I rolled over and off of the bed. When our physical connection was broken, he shook his head and a glazed look came over his golden eyes.

"That was..." He didn't finish, and he didn't need to.

"Yeah."

"Do you want to talk about it?" he asked.

"Not particularly. I need to shower again and meet with JayLeigh. While you get to go sit with daddy dearest for the better part of today. Good luck with that."

He sat up in bed as I walked toward the bathroom. "Uh, daddy dearest? What's that mean?"

Feigning innocence, I raised a brow. "Oh, did I forget to mention when I came back yesterday that Marek is my dragon DNA donor? I'm thinking of changing his name to Triple D. Think he'd mind?"

I was beginning to ramble, but I wanted to avoid the subject of whatever had happened while we'd made love, because it was too much for me to think about with so much else going on. I knew we had other obstacles to deal with, and DDD was at the top of that list.

"Yeah, you may have forgotten that." His eyes narrowed at me as he stood from the bed.

I saw the intention in his body before his feet hit the floor, so I quickly moved into the bathroom, closed the door, and turned the lock.

"Raegan, you can't hide from me." There was laughter in his voice, so I tried to keep the nerves out of mine.

"I'm showering in private. Completely normal and does *not* mean I'm hiding. Now, go away."

What I assumed to be his hand slammed onto the shared door, but not out of anger. More so to get my attention, which he fully had.

"You can run all you want, and I'll never tire of chasing

you. I'll let you pretend this morning didn't happen for now. Just remember, though, it will happen again. We're not done, nor will we ever be. You *are* mine, Raegan."

That was all Enzo speaking this time. Not a dragon hidden deep within him that I seemed to have pulled to the surface when we had sex, but my Enzo, who had loved me and hurt me. My Enzo, who was doing everything he could to put me back together and make things right.

My Enzo, who I knew I loved, but I couldn't decide if it was enough to let go of what he had done.

That was a problem for future me to worry about, though. Present me had to get ready before JayLeigh came to pound my door down and drag me to the academy part of the headquarters. My plan was to show her I was ready and willing to learn without needing to be forced.

I'd do anything to get back to Shadow Veil quicker, so we could stop Malina before she had a chance to put her plan in motion. If she wanted Elora back, then she needed Shadow Veil, and I wasn't going to let her have it without a battle.

THIRTY MINUTES LATER, I HAD FOUND MY WAY TO THE eatery and was enjoying a fresh salad with all the toppings, because apparently, we had slept for an entire day and missed breakfast.

Enzo appeared at my table with a plate of food and dug in without saying anything. I eyed him curiously, confused by whatever game he was playing, but decided to let him have his fun by himself and didn't say anything.

"Good afternoon, Newbies," JayLeigh said as she suddenly appeared in the chair next to me.

My hand went to my chest as I held in a scream. "You're going to give me a damn heart attack." Then, I remembered she had kept something pretty big from me, and I glared at her. "Did you plan on telling me we were related?"

"Oh, well, you see... he told you already?" she stammered, seeming rather surprised.

"Yeah, as soon as I sat down to eat with him. So, you're my cousin of sorts, I'm assuming, since Marek called you his niece yesterday?"

She nodded. "My mother was his adoptive sister."

I didn't miss the "was" part of that sentence, but she didn't seem to want to talk about it, so I let her change the subject.

"Marek wants me to bring Enzo to him, and then we'll go get you training clothes and weapons. We should still be able to get a solid eight hours in, assuming after almost two days of rest, you're up for it."

My eyes bulged, practically coming out of their sockets. "Come again? We slept through *all* of yesterday as well?"

"Yep, you're already on day three in Drakken, but your three weeks doesn't start until now, since you haven't actually trained any," she replied nonchalantly.

"Shit, I have to get a message to Jules. She has to be freaking out, alongside Gemma," I said, already standing up.

"Calm down before your head explodes. She was already freaking out. The gargoyles informed King Marek, and he asked me to step in, so I sent a message for you. She wasn't very polite in her response, and I haven't checked it again."

I glanced at Enzo. "You're done eating. Come on." Grabbing his hand, I drug him toward the elevators before I realized I had no idea how to get to Marek's room. Instead of waiting for JayLeigh, I started to push buttons, but nothing was working.

JayLeigh strolled up next to me and hip-checked me out of the way. "Humans have no patience. It's tragic, really. You should really learn to enjoy life more and embrace the better parts of you."

I rolled my eyes at her sarcasm and backed up as she pushed the necessary codes to get us into Marek's quarters. Remembering that I needed to hold on for dear life, I gripped the side rails but forgot to warn Enzo, who apparently hadn't been fortunate enough to experience the elevators yet.

Unlike me on my first time, he managed to keep himself upright, but his stance was unsteady, telling me it had affected him more than he was trying to let on.

When the door whooshed open, I waltzed into the room first. Marek was just coming out of the hallway and greeted me with a smile. "Glad to see you again, Raegan."

My hand waved in the air. "Yeah. You, too. Is the communications system working now?"

"Of course. Let me show you the way." Marek gestured back the way he had come from, and I followed without hesitation.

When we entered the office, I was surprised at how barren it was, but quickly realized this wasn't Marek's personal office. He must have moved the setup, so I wouldn't be in his personal space. There was a computer, desk, and chair in the room, but not much else that I could see.

"Nothing special to it. The screen is already up. We have one shared email for communication, so you'll see anything that's already been sent. Use it like you normally would," he said as I took a seat in the chair and placed my hand on the mouse.

"Thank you." I waited to open the last message thread until he nodded and slipped out of the room, closing the door behind him.

I started from oldest to newest and counted nine of them, making me cringe. I felt bad I had made them worry and hoped she wouldn't be too pissed.

The first one read: *JayLeigh, your message was not informative. I don't appreciate your sarcasm. Where is my niece? I don't care how long it takes me. I will find my way into Drakken and tear it apart until I get her back if you don't return her safely.*

Jules's words became more aggressive as the emails kept coming. Finally, she started writing directly to me, along with Gemma.

The final one read: *Raegan, you were supposed to be back two days ago. Without any word from you, Headmaster Stone is beginning to believe you could be dead, but I won't accept that. If I don't hear from you by the month's end, I'll resort to other resources and I will expose the dragons if I have to in order to come find you.*

I read the time stamp on the email, and it was sent September twenty-fourth. I didn't understand how so much time had passed, but I was going to find out really quickly.

W rath boiled just beneath the surface as I ground my teeth together and typed a quick response to Jules before going back to the living room. If time was going by faster there than in Drakken, I wasn't sure how close I was to the end of the month and didn't want to waste any more time.

Once I hit send, I pushed away from the desk and strode toward the door. When I yanked the door open, I reveled in the vibrations as it slammed into the wall. Stomping my way back to the living room, I made sure they'd know how irate I was before I even entered.

"Well, guess she figured out the time change," JayLeigh mused when I came around the corner.

"Yeah, asshole, I did. How could you not tell us? Did you forget that there is a psycho sorceress hell bent on getting her hands on me, and I just left my friends unprotected for who knows how long?"

"Oh, don't get your panties in a bunch." JayLeigh sighed. "I told you, the gargoyles have a handle on anything major. They'll be fine. Though, you won't be if you don't learn to bond with your dragon, and I knew you wouldn't come if I told you about the time difference."

"No shit, I wouldn't have come, and I'm ready to leave now. I won't stay here for months. There is too much to do on Earth. I've survived this long without my full dragon side. I'll be fine."

"Raegan, I know you're upset, but there has to be a way to make this work," Marek said. "What about a compromise?"

"The only way I see this working is if we take this little training session to Earth. Why can't I figure this out there and JayLeigh be put out instead of me?" I asked.

"Because you need the magic of Drakken for the highest chance of success. If it's not working after a couple weeks, then I promise to send you back with JayLeigh."

I still didn't like it. A couple weeks on Drakken was a several of months on Earth. So much could happen in that time, and I was too far away to protect those I loved most. I needed more from Marek if he expected me to rest easy while I was so far away.

"Fine, I'll give you those couple of weeks, but you have to send two of your top dragons to Earth to stay at Shadow Veil. I want to know that they have help with the absence of me and Enzo."

"Raegan, that's asking too much. The shifters here, not all of them see the other supernatural races as people worth protecting. There are things you don't understand about our history."

Taking three steps his way, I pushed my finger into his chest. "If you want me to behave, do all these dragon trainings, and be your heir, then I don't care what it takes. I want my family—the ones who have been there for me—to have the help they might need if they're in trouble. Gargoyles don't count. If that's not possible, take me back to Shadow Veil. Now."

His eyes narrowed at me, and the battle of wills began; he was about to learn just how stubborn I was. I didn't give a shit if he was a king or my DDD. I had family at Shadow Veil, and they meant more to me than anything I could learn by staying in Drakken, even if it meant we never received his assistance.

A heaviness settled in my chest as another presence made itself known within me. There was no voice, but there was power, and it was ridiculously strong. Stronger than I expected it to be.

Sweat broke out across my body as I fought to keep my stare. Another few seconds passed, and Marek finally nodded his head.

"Okay. I need a day to find volunteers I trust. I won't force anyone to go. In the meantime, you'll need to promise your cooperation. I expect you to do everything JayLeigh requests if we're doing this for you."

"How long until your volunteers would be at Shadow Veil?" I asked.

"No more than five days. They'd need a day or two to prepare and then the travel time to take into consideration."

I held back a groan. In Drakken time, that would be over a month on Earth. I wasn't sure how I was going to survive that long being unsure of their safety, but it was better than nothing, and I needed to remember that we still needed Marek. Maybe in the time I stayed, I could convince him to help us, even though he'd already said no.

"Fine. You have my promise that as long as it takes no longer than five days and there is nothing else you're not telling me, then I will stay as previously planned to train with JayLeigh."

He cleared his throat, seeming nervous about something. "There may be one other thing you'll want to know, but I need the rest of today to figure it out."

I tossed my hands in the air, annoyed with all of the revelations over the last couple days. "Whatever. I need to send a proper email now that we have this figured out. JayLeigh, give me a few more minutes, please."

"Sure thing," she chirped, seeming far too happy about the situation.

Trudging my way back to the room with the computer, I slammed the door behind me before practically falling into the desk chair. I couldn't believe the time difference was so severe. Stupid different supernatural realms.

When the screen came back up, there was already a reply from Jules. When I clicked on the email, there were no words, but an attachment, so I clicked on it. My fingers tapped impatiently on the desk for it to load. When it finally did a few minutes later, a smile formed on my face.

Even though it had only felt like a couple days for me, seeing Jules's and Gemma's faces brought me a little bit of peace. That was, until I heard their voices.

"Damn you, Raegan," Gemma started. "You know how hard it is to convince your aunt not to bring the cavalry to Shadow Veil and cause a scene? We thought you were gone for good, and all of a sudden at almost midnight, her phone dings with a message that says 'I'm alive. Don't do anything stupid. I'll be right back.' Well, right back was an hour ago and that doesn't work for us."

Jules nodded her head in agreement, eyes glaring at the screen. "Gemma's right. I don't know what's going on over there, but this is unacceptable. You're grounded for a year when you get home. No school parties, no boys, Gemma in moderation."

Gemma pushed Jules with her shoulder. "Hey, now. Don't punish me because she's an idiot."

"True. We'll figure something out. Regardless, you're in deep shit. We finally tracked down Malina or what we hope is her and not some distraction she cooked up, but now you're nowhere to be found."

Gemma cut in. "Yeah, it's doubly annoying because Malina keeps going from one major city to another, all except the one we have a trap in for her. Jules has half of New Orleans on the lookout for the psycho bitch."

Jules nodded. "There is enough power and magic in that city to keep Malina locked down, but we can't do anything unless she actually steps foot within range of the covens. If they leave, they'll lose their connection to their ancestors and their power won't be as strong."

Damn. I knew what she wanted now, but we still had no idea on how she planned to achieve it. Or what my role in it was. I was nothing but a mixed breed with limited powers from all three sides. She must have been searching for something within those cities, and it most certainly wasn't good for us.

"Anyway, we're headed to bed, but we expect an email back. You probably can't video chat, but your email better be long as hell with all the updates," Gemma said before blowing a kiss into the screen.

"We love you, Raegan. I hope you really are staying safe over there. It's been almost five weeks, and not knowing what's going on has almost killed me, but I know you're strong and you're handling whatever it is they're throwing at you. Just check in more often." Jules gave me her best motherly look before finishing her goodbyes, and then the video ended.

It wasn't nearly long enough, and I wished I could video

them back, but I didn't see a camera anywhere around, so I settled for an email, going through everything I could think of except anything to do with Enzo. That was staying with me until I figured more out.

I began with the portal and how it was traveling to Drakken, followed by the differences in landscape, and my conversation with Marek about him being my DDD. I could picture Gemma's reaction clearly and it made me laugh.

I continued with the conversation I'd just had with Marek and JayLeigh, forewarning them that within the next few weeks, there would be dragons at Shadow Veil to assist with whatever they needed. I ended with letting them know that I'd be training and couldn't promise how long it would be their time, but I'd check the communications system again as soon as I could.

As soon as I exited out of the email system, I headed back into the living area. Enzo and Marek were no longer present, and JayLeigh was leaning casually against the counter, eating some sort of round fruit.

"Ready?" she asked, tossing the core into the trash.

"Sure. Where did the other two go?" I asked.

"King Marek took your not-boyfriend to test his dragon side. Hopefully he comes back in one piece." When I glared at her, she raised her hands. "Just kidding, geez. You need to get laid and loosen up."

My face must have given away the fact that I had already been recently laid and it had done nothing to calm my bitchiness, because she began to laugh her ass off.

"Well, never mind then. Let's get going." She continued to laugh and make snide comments as we went down the elevator, but when we were in the halls and passing others, her face went from carefree to uptight.

"Why are you so serious now?" I asked when nobody else was around us.

"I have an image to maintain around here. There are very few women on the guard teams, and I refuse to look anything less than a badass around the others. If they think there is a weakness within me, they'll do everything they can to use it against me."

"Seriously? Your own kind treats you that way?" Drakken was becoming less and less appealing the longer I was there.

"It's complicated, and we don't really have time to get into it. You won't be attending conventional classes in the academy, but I do have a schedule for you. Some of it will be self-learning and practicing, and the rest will be with me. After the first week, I will reassess where you're at and consider integrating you in with another class for group training."

One week to prove my worth and another to kick the asses of however many dragons she threw my way. Hopefully within those first two weeks, I could bond enough with my dragon that Enzo and I could go back to Shadow Veil early.

Thinking of him made me wonder what Marek wanted with him and how in the world it was possible for Enzo to have any bit of dragon in him. Maybe one of his grandparents had been a hybrid from Elora before it fell. It was the only explanation I could think of that made sense.

We went down a set of stairs and through a door marked "Restricted." When we entered, another man was present and beating the stuffing out of a punching bag. Literally.

JayLeigh didn't pay him any attention and led me through another door that took us to an outdoor area. There were no training materials that I could see, and I wasn't sure what we were doing out there until JayLeigh stopped abruptly and began taking off her jacket.

"Are we shifting?" I asked.

"Yep. Well, you are. I just need more room to stretch. I could teach you all the defense training in the world, but it won't make a damn difference if you can't fully bond with your dragon. You need to bring her to the surface before you can move forward. Let's hope that happens within the next three weeks."

There was a challenge in her tone. She seemed to be well aware that I never backed down from one thrown my way. I'd find my dragon and figure out how to make her emerge, and it would happen before the sun set.

I was already wearing workout clothes since I hadn't been completely sure of what we would start with, so I went straight into my partial shift. My wings expanded with little effort after so many weeks of practice while I had been gone. By the time I shook the six-foot-long beauties out, my skin was covered in scales and my nails had turned to fierce talons.

"Impressive for someone with no training, but it's not good enough. Can you hear your dragon when you're in this form?" JayLeigh asked.

"No, I never even knew she was supposed to be a separate part of me. Nobody really explained to me what it means to be a shifter while I was at Shadow Veil. I just figured things out as I went."

"Hmmm. Okay, well, you need to draw her out. There are a few ways we can do this. Should we start with the least invasive or the most?" Before I could answer, she did. "Something in the middle sounds nice."

She pulled a knife from behind her back that I hadn't

seen and threw it at my head. The blade nicked my pointed ears, and I snarled at her.

"That was better. Your eyes are slits like they should be in a full shift. Sorry, Raegan, but if you can't draw her out on your own, I'm going to have to resort to violence." The grin on her face told me she wasn't sorry at all.

"Give me a minute," I said, then closed my eyes.

Come on, girl. I know we haven't officially met, but I don't want that psycho over there to throw any other sharp objects at us.

There was a stirring sensation within me that I recognized but had never really questioned before. Even with all of the learning I had already done at Shadow Veil, I still really didn't know how to identify certain things that happened within me.

Maybe all that would change once my dragon fully awoke.

The sensation that had stirred just moments before was gone again, so I opened my eyes to find JayLeigh standing near me with two more knives in her hand. "Did it work?"

"No, but I really don't think those are necessary." I nodded to the blades.

"Maybe. Maybe not. Only one way to find out."

She threw another one at me, but I dodged it, and just as a grin appeared on my face, the second knife lodged in my shoulder.

"Are you shitting me?" I screamed. "You actually hit me!"

"Well, duh. What did you think I was trying to do?"

"I don't know. Scare my dragon out?" I should have known better.

JayLeigh walked closer and yanked the blade from my

scales before replacing it with a cloth. "Your healing should kick in within the minute. I didn't cut you deep."

"You still cut me," I muttered.

"Don't be such a ninny. If you're going to pout about it so much, we can do hand-to-hand combat to piss off your dragon. I haven't kicked anyone's ass in a while."

I rolled my eyes. She was a cocky chick, but I secretly loved it. I just wished it wasn't directed at me personally.

Just as I pulled the cloth away to find there was no more blood, the door we had come through slammed open. The big guy we had seen before was headed straight for us, and I recognized his dark cobalt eyes.

My dragon senses heightened as his glare remained on me. Maybe JayLeigh kicking my ass wouldn't be necessary.

"What can I do for you, Onyx?" JayLeigh said with only a hint of irritation in her voice.

He ignored her question and moved to stand within two feet of me. "You don't belong here. You're a disgrace to our race. A dragon who can't shift should be put down."

I opened my mouth to say something, but JayLeigh cut me off.

"This doesn't concern you. Marek didn't ask you to train her, he asked me. So, if you don't have anything useful to say, get the fuck out of here before I make you."

He finally glanced at her, a smirk on his face. "I'd like to see you try, sweetheart."

"It wouldn't be the first time I kicked your ass. There's a reason I was welcomed into the guard."

He leaned toward her. "You're right. There is a reason, and you better thank the fates every day for your DNA or you'd be nothing more than a breeding whore."

She lunged for him, but he dodged her punch. "Leave, Onyx," she warned one last time.

His eyes met mine, and pure hatred filled them. "I'm not the one you should be encouraging to leave, JayLeigh." He spit at my feet. "Watch your back, human."

Onyx turned around and headed back inside while I used every bit of strength to hold in my rage. Ripping that asshole to shreds sounded like a great idea, but even if it was possible, I knew that wouldn't further my progression, so I bit my tongue and let him win. This time.

"I'm sorry, Raegan. He's always been a dick, so don't let him get to you. We'll figure out how to connect with your dragon, and nobody will be able to say anything to you again."

"And what if I can't? What if there are too many parts to me and none of them will ever thrive over the others?" I asked, because that was beginning to look like a very real possibility.

"I don't know, but however it works out, we'll figure out a solution. I promise. I've never failed at anything, and I won't let you be the thing that breaks my streak."

I had a hard time believing her, but I tried, even as she threw a sucker punch at me and our brawl began. Her in her human form and me in my half-dragon one, and she was still kicking my ass.

My dragon better hurry up and come on out or we were going to have major problems.

CHAPTER TWELVE

I had no idea what time it was when we finally stopped, because the days in Drakken seemed to be never-ending, but my body had been put through the grinder and spit back out several times over. Every facet of my being ached, and as JayLeigh skipped ahead of me toward the eatery, it made me want to stab her for being unaffected by our training sessions.

One thing was for certain, I healed way faster than I ever had on Earth. Even though I was hobbling behind at the moment, I'd be standing straighter within the half-hour. Other than that, no significant progress had been made, and I was ridiculously pissed I hadn't been able to coax my dragon out.

I'd tried everything from sweet-talking to yelling, and none of it worked. I could sense the beast just beneath the surface, but I couldn't pull her forward, no matter how hard I tried.

"You not hungry or what?" JayLeigh called from the door as she tapped her foot impatiently.

"Screw you," I mumbled. Our relationship had definitely taken a turn for the worse sometime between the tenth and hundredth time she'd kicked my ass.

"Oh, don't be such a poor sport about today. You actually did really well for someone with no proper training. You should be proud."

"Ha! I'll only be proud when everything inside me doesn't ache and I can fully shift. Also, jerk, I spent nine months training at Shadow Veil, so I'm not a complete invalid. This just isn't going how I wanted." I finally caught up to her, and she put her hand on my shoulder.

"Patience, Raegan. You're going to need lots of it to survive the next three weeks."

"Yeah, I'm sure I'll find that as soon as I find my dragon."

She laughed. "I wasn't sure what to think about this job when it was first assigned, but I'm glad it was me. This will probably be the most entertaining assignment I'll ever get."

I quit responding and kept walking. Anything I did or said only fueled her desire to poke at me, and I was done being screwed with for the day. I just wanted to eat, check for another message from Jules and Gemma, make sure Enzo wasn't dead, and then sleep.

JayLeigh had warned me earlier in the day, I'd be getting tomorrow's wake-up call at five in the morning and she expected me to be back where we were within a half-hour of that call. I wasn't looking forward to it, but going through the trainings was half the reason I'd come, so I just needed to deal with it instead of bitching about it.

We ran through the food line, and I piled my plate as high as I could without fear of dropping anything on the ground. When I took a seat, JayLeigh plopped down beside me.

"Do you know where Enzo is?" I asked.

"If he's not in here, then I'd assume he's still with Marek, but don't worry. I might have joked about it earlier, but Marek is a good king. He won't harm Enzo. At least, not intentionally."

Ignoring the last bit, because I knew she only said it to get a rise out of me, I nodded and hoped they'd be back in Marek's quarters, so I could use the computer and check on him all at once. Anything to get me to my bed sooner.

I barely even tasted my food as I gobbled it up, finishing before JayLeigh. "I'm going to head up to Marek's."

She raised a brow at me. "You sure you want to go on your own?"

"Do you really think anyone will mess with me within the headquarters of all places? I know they've all avoided me like a plague, but do I truly have a reason to fear for my wellbeing?"

After Onyx had made his appearance, threatening me and overall just being a dick, I began to ask more questions about the hierarchy in Drakken, but JayLeigh deflected most of them. Possibly because she truly didn't know, or else she wasn't allowed to tell me. My bet was on the latter.

"No, you should be fine. Just make sure you stay to the normal hallways and don't take any detours. I have some things to do or I'd go with you. Worst case scenario, just scream really loud if you encounter someone giving you a hard time."

I grunted. "Right. I'll be sure to do that."

"Hey, it's your life, not mine. Feel free to take on century-old dragon shifters by yourself if you want. I don't care."

My brain was done listening to her, so I spun on my heel and headed for the elevators. Things were beginning to look familiar around the academy, but only between the training area, eatery, and elevators. I previously had a bad habit of wandering where I wasn't supposed to at Shadow Veil, but I made sure to stick to the areas I knew at Drakken.

I wasn't stupid. Stubborn, yes, but never stupid.

Pulling out the code JayLeigh had given me earlier, I punched it into the elevator panel before holding on to the rail. Within seconds, the door was opening, and I entered Marek's home. Nobody was in the living room, so I finally took the time to glance out the window and get a good look at Drakken from the top.

The landscape seemed to go forever, filled with hundreds, if not thousands, of acres of forest where I wondered just how many dragons lived. There was a river that led to a lake much further outside of town, and I yearned to fly over it and take a dip. I'd have to ask JayLeigh about that the following day.

There weren't any buildings other than the ones I'd seen when we first arrived, so besides taking in the tranquility of their nature, there wasn't much else to see unless I set out on foot.

A few dragons were out flying over the town. I couldn't tell their colors as they were too far away and the sun was behind them, but I could gauge their size, and I shuddered at the thought of trying to defend myself from one of them on my own. Maybe I should have given JayLeigh's warning more thought. I had little faith that even staying in the populated areas would keep me safe if someone really wanted to hurt me.

I doubted any of the dragons would go up against someone like Onyx to protect an outsider.

Voices came from down the hall, and I turned around, hoping to see Marek and Enzo.

"You need to tell her. It might help," Marek's voice sounded.

"No offense, sir, but you don't know Raegan. This won't help."

With my hand on my hip, I glared in their direction until they came into the living room. They paused when they saw me, glancing at each other and seeming to know they were in trouble.

"What won't help?" I asked.

"Shit," Enzo muttered.

"Didn't you learn the first time around not to keep secrets from me, Enzo?"

He cleared his throat and met my hardened stare. "I wasn't going to keep it from you. I just wasn't looking forward to telling you about it."

"About what?" I pushed.

Marek took a step forward. "You two feel free to stay here while you talk. I'm going to go do my rounds with the patrols and make sure nothing went awry while I was otherwise occupied."

Enzo still stood in the hallway while I moved to the couch and took a seat on the plush cushions. When I was settled and Marek had shut the door behind him, Enzo finally took a few steps my way.

"You promise not to stab me for being honest?" he asked.

"Of course," I replied without hesitation. "I'm assuming this has something to do with the 'one other thing' Marek may have needed to disclose to me but needed today to figure out."

He nodded. "Yeah, he figured it out alright."

"Why do you seem so nervous? It can't be that bad, right?"

He grinned. "Well, it's not bad for me, but I'm not sure how happy you'll be with it."

"Oh," was all I could say as thoughts ran through my head. I couldn't think of any possible scenario that would make him happy and not me unless they were forcing us to get married or something ridiculous like that. That made me laugh out loud.

"What's so funny?" he asked.

"Oh, nothing. Now, tell me what's going on."

He took a seat on the chair opposite from me. His fingers ran through his much shorter hair than I was used to. I had thought I'd miss the length, but the more I was around him, the more his new look suited him. Almost too well.

"So, I had no idea this was possible. Apparently, it's a dragon thing, so you can't blame me for it," he began.

"Spit it out, Enzo."

"You know how whenever we have sex, that purple light appears?" I nodded, and he continued. "Well, I knew it wasn't a normal elf thing, but I didn't think too much of it with you being so unique."

Leaning forward, I glared at him. "What's your point? What does the glow have to do with us and what Marek knows?"

"Apparently, every time we have sex, we're solidifying a bond between us."

Holy shit, I wasn't that far off with the marriage thoughts.

"What do you mean, 'bond'?" I growled.

"Like a mate bond. Dragons mate for life. The bond isn't locked in right away after the first time they have sex, but as the relationship progresses, so does the connection. The stronger the emotional and physical aspects of the relationship, the quicker the bond sets in."

Moving to my feet, I began pacing the room, going in circles around him. I knew I loved Enzo, but I wasn't sure I could count on him. He had broken my trust, and even though I had needed him last night, it hadn't changed anything.

Though, the whole bond thing did explain why I had felt like I had *needed* him and why I was so much better after we'd been together.

"So, we're bonded," I said matter-of-factly.

He turned his head toward me since I had moved behind him and nodded.

"And I'm assuming because we're bonded, that's how you had a little bit of dragon in you that allowed you on Drakken?"

"That's what Marek believes. Though, he can't be certain as something like this has never happened before between a hybrid and a non-dragon. At this point, he can only go on assumption."

This was not good. I couldn't trust my own feelings anymore. Was I still attracted to Enzo because of a stupid bond or because I really did love him? I felt like any choice I might have been close to making was instantly taken away from me and I could no longer be sure of my own heart.

Tension and pain rattled through my body as I tried not to hyperventilate. Apparently, I had stopped moving, because Enzo appeared in my line of sight, his fingers grasping my jaw so I would look at him.

"I know what you're thinking. I can all but guarantee I had the same thoughts, but it doesn't matter if we are bonded or not, Raegan. I fell for you long before we had sex. I know my heart, and you're it for me. I'll give you space to digest the information, but I hope you can come to the same conclusion."

I opened my mouth to say something, anything at all, but I didn't know *what* to say. So much of my life was a mess, and this was too much at the moment. I needed information.

"We can deal with this when we're back at Shadow Veil or whenever you're ready," he continued. "Just don't push me away. If you really don't want the bond, then Marek believes it will dissolve on its own after time apart."

My eyes were lost in his. I wanted so badly to accept the bond and forget the past, but I couldn't. My head wouldn't let me, no matter how much my heart was rooting for it.

His thumb moved across my cheek, catching a stray tear I hadn't even realized had fallen. "Talk to me."

"I'm really tired of always feeling like I'm being pushed in a certain direction, like I have no control over my own life. Being a supernatural sucks."

His lips pulled into a grin. "Try talking to a dragon king about having sex with his only daughter."

My hands covered my mouth as I considered how hilariously awesome that conversation might have gone and wished I could have heard it myself. "You don't have me beat, but you did succeed in making me laugh."

He pressed a gentle kiss to my forehead. "Good. Now let's get out of here unless you need to speak with Marek."

I shook my head. "I do need to email Jules and Gemma, though. Shouldn't take long, but you don't have to wait."

He glared at me and growled. "I'm not leaving you."

"Enzo, you need to know I can't make any promises to you. One day, you might have to let me go or give me no choice but to disappear."

"I know, but until you really are done with me, I'm going to keep fighting for you like I promised. I'm going to keep on trying to make up for all of the wrong I've done and, as long as you're safe, then I'll be okay, even if you can't ever trust me again."

Pulling away, I turned my back on him and headed toward the office. I couldn't stand to look in his eyes any longer, especially after what he had learned and shared. I almost wished it had been something he had kept from me, because if it had been me who learned it first, I don't think I would have told him.

With that revelation, I realized I understood his past transgressions better than before.

Three days later, I was ready to give up on life. JayLeigh had been kicking my ass for fourteen hours a day. Seven hours on, then an hour break, followed by another brutal seven hours. I had muscles forming in every crevice of my body, and I was finally getting used to the torture, but it didn't mean I was enjoying myself.

On the third day, I was barely tolerating JayLeigh's training session. It seemed more like a fun game to her where she could experiment on all the different ways she might be able to piss my dragon off enough to come out.

Nothing had worked. The beast within had yet to make herself known, even after Enzo's life was threatened along with my own. Marek wanted to meet for dinner that evening if I still hadn't shifted as he had some theories, but I hadn't really spoken with him since the first day, and I wasn't looking forward to alone time with my DDD.

JayLeigh had gotten quite the laugh out of my nickname and wished she'd thought of it herself.

It was lunchtime and I wanted to go check out the lake I'd seen, but JayLeigh couldn't take us and it still wasn't a great idea for me and Enzo to be running around Drakken on our own. Onyx had made another appearance, this time verbally attacking Enzo before Marek had intervened.

Just when I thought he'd sulk away, Onyx snarled at his king, claiming he was bringing war to his people. Marek hadn't replied, but half the eatery had overheard, and it didn't seem like a good thing to have the two most powerful dragons in their realm arguing in public.

Something more was going on within Drakken, and nobody was filling in Enzo or me. The weapons, the distrust, the patrols I constantly saw flying over the town area and forests, and then brief mentions of war. None of it made sense, which had me itching to go back home.

If I couldn't bring my dragon fully forward really freaking soon, then that's exactly what I planned on doing.

After our allotted eating time was up, Enzo and I met JayLeigh outside the training room. She wanted to try something different, which I hoped meant less beating the shit out of me.

"So, we're going to head into the forest and then the caves. Most of that time, the two of you will somewhat be by yourselves," she said.

"Uh, are you trying to get us killed?" I asked.

"Not really, but I don't think I'm fooling your dragon by throwing sharp objects at you. You need real fear coursing through your body."

"So, you're using us as bait to dragons who would like to see us dead, in hopes they'll try to eat us, but not before Raegan's dragon hopefully wakes. Did I understand correctly?" Enzo asked, not at all happy with the new proposal.

"Pretty much. Isn't it better than me beating on the both of you for the next seven hours?"

I shrugged. "She has a point."

"Do we get weapons, at least?" Enzo sighed, and JayLeigh grinned, knowing she'd won.

"Sure. Go grab whatever you want, and I'll wait here while you talk trash about me," JayLeigh joked and leaned unconcerned against the door frame as we slipped into the training room.

"Do you think this is a good idea?" I asked.

"Not in the slightest, hence my request for weapons," he replied.

JayLeigh pretended not to watch us from the door while we took in the array of options before us. There weren't any guns, but there were blades galore. There were also several other items, but we had no idea what they did, so we left those be.

"I've never done any training with a knife unless you count all of the ones I've been dodging from JayLeigh," I grumbled.

"Stick with something smaller. You're fast, and if needed, you'll be able to move quicker than a ten-foot dragon, as long as you choose a blade you can actually handle," he replied.

Taking his advice, I pulled open a few drawers and tucked some smaller throwing knives into my pockets before covering them with my shirt. "Should I grab something that's more conspicuous?"

"Considering JayLeigh is sending you out as bait, I'd say it's not a bad idea. If we come across someone friendly and they want to know what we're doing, we can say we wanted to train in private against each other."

I nodded and grabbed a dagger that stood out most to me. I couldn't see the blade itself as it was tucked into a holster I was gladly going to use around my thigh, but the hilt was a golden bronze with green jewels embedded in it.

The two colors reminded me not only of Enzo's eyes, but mine as well.

"Good choice," Enzo said as I strapped it to my right leg.

By the time I was done, he had picked his out. It was a longer sword that I had no idea what to call, but he seemed to be able to move it with ease, and that was all that mattered.

JayLeigh must have disappeared for a moment while we were preoccupied, because she was no longer in workout clothes, she was dressed head-to-toe in a black one-piece that fit her body perfectly and had me wanting to cover Enzo's eyes.

"Um, did you leave something out?" I asked. "Why do you look like Catwoman?"

"I'll be staying behind in the shadows, and if I need to shift, it's easier to do it and keep my clothes when I'm wearing this. Don't worry, you'll understand soon."

My chest tightened. I didn't actually believe her words any longer, and if scaring my dragon out today didn't work, then I was over all of this. We had to get back to Shadow Veil and focus on Malina. If I wasn't becoming stronger in Drakken, then I was wasting my time, especially when Marek still hadn't changed his mind about helping.

"Okay, so what's the plan exactly?" Enzo asked as we went out the back door instead of through the main areas of the headquarters.

"Well, there really isn't one. We're just seeing how things go. It's the middle of the day, so people should be out, and there will be others you may run into that wouldn't ever be at the academy. Just make sure not to go into any of their houses if invited."

"And what if someone attacks?" I asked.

"Then defend yourself, obviously." Her tone made me feel like I'd asked the world's stupidest question.

Sure, let me just attack dragons who were fully trained in killing and seemed to hate anyone who wasn't just like them. Yep, it sounded like a great plan and I was going to die. Super fun.

Enzo's teeth ground together, but he actually held his tongue, which surprised the hell out of me. Maybe he saw some value in this little training exercise that I couldn't.

When we entered the forest, JayLeigh disappeared into the trees like a damn monkey. Just grabbed on to a branch and, poof, she was gone.

"I still can't decide if I like her or not," I grumbled.

"You like her, or you wouldn't still be here. She just pushes you beyond your boundaries; that's the part you don't like." He grinned, and I recalled all the times he had pushed me when I first arrived at Shadow Veil.

Not one time had he ever thrown a knife at me. Apparently, I should have been more appreciative of him back then.

About ten minutes into our little adventure, we came across two guys headed in our direction. They saw us and began whispering to each other but didn't move defensively or act like they were going to shift.

"Did you two get lost?" the blond one asked, attention mostly focused at the dagger on my thigh.

"No, JayLeigh said we could practice out in the woods, so we're just looking for a good spot," Enzo answered confidently.

The other one with dark hair glanced around. "Where is JayLeigh?"

Shit, that didn't sound like an innocent question.

"Not sure. She said she'd meet up with us shortly," Enzo replied again.

Blondie pushed the other one. "See? Told you there was nothing to worry about."

"What would you have to be worried about?" I asked curiously.

The two shared a glance before the first one answered, "We're supposed to be in class right now. JayLeigh is normally an attendance enforcer of sorts. We thought we were busted, but don't worry about telling her anything. We're headed there now. If you could just not even mention you saw us, we'll be on our way."

A smile formed on my face. These guys were truly afraid of JayLeigh, and it cracked me up. "I promise not to say anything, but I can't promise she won't see you on your way back, so I'd hurry up."

"Damn it, bro. I told you it wasn't worth it," Blondie said.

"Whatever. Let's just go before someone also sees us chatting with *them*." That last bit was said with more malice than I liked, but we let it go as they continued past us.

When they were out of hearing range, I turned to Enzo. "I don't understand it. We're missing a huge piece to all of this. We're all supernatural. Their hostility toward us doesn't make any sense. Nothing about how Drakken operates makes sense, either. They're tucked away safely in a realm that only dragons can enter. Why are they prepared for war?"

Enzo nodded. "Whatever the reason is, unfortunately, we may not figure it out before all of this is over. Or, we will learn their reasons and it will be worse than we could imagine."

I sighed. He was right. I had a feeling we were the

tipping point for something and all hell was going to rain down on us. We just didn't know when.

We kept moving through the forest and didn't come across anyone else directly before we made it to the boulders that housed the caves. This was the section that gave me the most pause. The dragons there were nomads. They lived by their own rules and didn't play well with others from what I understood.

As we crept past the entrances in the rocks, my hand stayed on the hilt of my knife and I felt the tingle of a shift just beneath the surface. Not a full-on shift like we were hoping for, but enough of one that I'd have some added protection if needed.

There was still no sign of my dragon other than the heavy presence she threw my way from time to time. Never any real connection as JayLeigh had described so many times. Enzo had come up with the idea that maybe she wouldn't come out until we were fully bonded, but all that got him was a book thrown at his head.

I had decided that we could be friends for the time being, but there would be no more sexy time until I could truly figure out what it meant to have a bond with someone, especially if they weren't a dragon. When Enzo had mentioned my girl hadn't come out to play because we weren't fully bonded, it had also given me the opposite idea.

Maybe she hadn't because we *were* bonded.

Enzo wasn't a dragon, and I had inadvertently given him some of myself each time we'd had sex. Maybe he was the reason I couldn't shift, and if I truly wanted to utilize my dragon, there was a decent chance I'd have to let Enzo go for good and figure out how to break what little bond we had already created.

I hadn't filled him in on those possibilities, because I

knew it would crush his heart. While he had broken mine, I had come to the realization that it hadn't been with malevolent intent and I needed to let things go before it changed who I was. Holding on to the anger wasn't good for me.

Enzo snapped his fingers in my face. "Earth to Raegan. Are you even paying attention?"

Shit, I hadn't been at all. Glancing around, I noticed we'd walk right into a dead-end between two boulders. Well, not exactly a dead-end, but the only way to continue past was to go through a cave entrance, and there was no way in hell that was happening.

"Sorry. Let's head back. I think this was a waste of our time, and JayLeigh is probably having too much fun laughing at us," I said.

He nodded, and we turned back toward the forest. This time, my guard was up and I was on high alert, so when a hand suddenly reached for my wrist from behind us, I let my reflexes take over. I spun around and knocked their legs out from underneath them with a swift kick.

I was feeling pretty proud of myself until I peered down at my attacker and realized she was just a little old lady and I was officially an asshole.

"Oh, my gosh. I'm so sorry!" Kneeling down, I grabbed her hand to help her up. When I did, a unique zap of power unlike anything I'd ever felt ran through my body. The shock caused me to pause, but before I could really process it, she shook loose from my grip and laughed.

"I should have seen that coming. Old age is getting the better of my visions." When she was on her feet again, she reached a hand to me, which I had no hesitation in taking. "I'm Ophelia, the last Dragon Seer."

My head snapped to Enzo, and he simply shrugged his shoulders, no help at all.

"Uh, I'm Raegan, and this is Enzo."

Her opaque eyes moved to Enzo as she took a few hobbled steps closer to him. "Yes, he who is but shouldn't be."

"What does that mean?" I asked as they seemed to share a moment that was freaking me the hell out.

"I'm a seer, dear. Not a fortune teller. Unless the world is ending, I don't interfere. I only prepare those I see the best I can without changing the timelines that shouldn't be affected. If I were to tell everything I saw, the future would never be correct, and I wouldn't really be a seer, would I?"

Shaking my head, I tried to make sense of what she'd just said. She was talking in circles and I had a feeling she did it on purpose, and often, while getting a kick out of it.

"So, how can we help you?" I asked, assuming she had come out from her cave for a purpose.

"We can help each other. Each of us has a path to follow. All you need to do is stay on that path, even when it is crumbling, and you will succeed."

"I don't understand what you're saying. I get that you can't outright tell me something, but you need to make more sense."

She eyed me carefully, and I wondered if she could actually see me. Her eyes were so clouded over, they were almost translucent. I couldn't even make out their true color. Her skin was tanned and aged, likely from living outdoors for how many decades old she was. Her hair was bright silver, though something told me it wasn't from age, but was her natural color even when she was younger.

"You are more than you understand. To succeed, you must let go of what you know and become what you were meant to be." She spoke more riddles, and as glad as I was that she wasn't trying to kill us, I was still frustrated as hell.

Even though I was certain she wouldn't answer, I still asked, "Who am I meant to be?"

She grinned a toothless smile, then surprised me. "A dragon."

My mouth opened to tell her I was already a dragon, but then realized, maybe I wasn't really. I couldn't shift into one, so what did that make me?

"You need to go. Find your path and follow it. Be prepared for obstacles and don't avoid them or you won't ever move forward." She pushed us back out of the boulders. When we hesitated, she pushed harder than I would have thought possible for her slight frame. "Go. Now."

Not needing to be told a third time, Enzo grabbed my hand, and we took off at a sprint back toward the forest. Once we were within the trees and hopefully closer to JayLeigh, we slowed down.

Neither of us spoke while we watched our surroundings, wondering if the previously mentioned obstacles were going to appear immediately, but nothing stood out.

Once I wasn't on such a high alert, I began to toss the seer's words around in my head, trying to make sense of them. Had I been correct in wondering if the bond with Enzo was holding me back? She said I had to give up something to become what I was meant to be, and he was the only thing I could think of that I could let go.

"Raegan, we have company," he whispered, and I followed his gaze.

Sure enough, there were two dragons coming our way, both already shifted with their heads down and eyes narrowed.

"Maybe they need directions?" I suggested, trying not to freak out.

"Maybe," Enzo replied while pulling his sword from its

sheath.

I did the same with my dagger and tucked in my shirt for easier access to the throwing knives. My dragon stirred as my heart rate increased, but there was still no real connection snapping into place.

The dragons stopped about fifteen feet from us. They were similarly colored in deep russets and golds, making me wonder if they were twins or at least related.

"You don't belong here," the one on the left snarled.

"Leave before you no longer have a choice," the other added.

"We were just on our way out. We didn't mean to intrude," I replied, taking a step to the right.

"Not just the forest. You need to leave Drakken. This is your last warning. You've already received one, and there won't be a third before we act."

So, these two were working with Onyx. Great.

Glancing around, I was waiting for JayLeigh to appear, but she hadn't made any attempts. Though, we weren't in immediate danger, so I shouldn't have been surprised.

"You don't think the king would notice if you killed us?" Enzo snapped. "You're signing your own death sentence if you lay a hand on us."

They both snarled at Enzo's attitude. "Don't disrespect us."

The one on the right brought his wing forward and swiped it at Enzo. He fell to the ground to avoid barbs at the wing points, but it had only been the distraction as the drag-on's tail quickly followed behind at a more rapid pace.

A scream ripped from my lungs as it connected with Enzo's head and he was rendered unconscious. The only reason I didn't lose my shit completely was because there was no blood coming from anywhere that I could see.

Without pause, I shifted as best as I was capable of and charged. My dragon was fighting to come through, but it never happened. I could feel a pressure like nothing before as I drew closer to the dragons, but it didn't matter.

She couldn't break through, and I was on my own until JayLeigh decided to make her appearance.

With the dagger raised, I pretended I was going to aim high, but at the last minute, I slid on the ground and sank the blade into the dragon's underbelly.

He roared and bucked while I held on to the hilt, pulling it out just as he backed away. The dragon who had hit Enzo came charging for me, teeth exposed and ready for the kill shot.

"You drew first blood. That makes you free game," he snarled right before grabbing my legs with his back claws that sank all the way to the bone as he tried to fly away with me.

"Not today, asshole," JayLeigh roared from above in her dragon form. She already had Enzo in her grasp as she swung her tail around to slam the dragon above me in the head, just as he'd done to Enzo.

He promptly let me go, and when the beast stumbled back, JayLeigh grabbed me gently with her other claw and flew up through the branches.

Glancing down, I made sure we weren't being followed before I gave way to the blood loss and passed out. My final thoughts were a jumbled mess as my eyes stayed open just long enough to wonder if Enzo was only unconscious or worse after the hit he had taken by a dragon a hundred times stronger than us.

The odds weren't in his favor, and my heart slowly broke as the world around me disappeared.

CHAPTER FOURTEEN

My legs were on fire. Literal freaking fire. When I opened my eyes, thinking my brain was exaggerating, I realized how very accurate my thoughts had been.

"What the hell is going on? Why are there flames covering the lower half of my body?" Panic was rising within me, and I was close to a full-on eruption until I saw Enzo's still-unconscious form lying next to me.

In a feeble attempt to get to him, I only hurt myself worse and JayLeigh's arms locked tight around my chest, effectively keeping me in my own bed. "He's fine, but you're not, so stay still unless you'd like to lose your legs."

Her voice was firm and her hold unyielding, even when I relaxed against her. I trusted she was telling the truth and Enzo was fine, so I focused on myself as a burning sensation moved throughout my lower half.

Marek stood over me, hands hovering just above my bare legs and covered in the flames he seemed to be creating. His face was tense as he concentrated on the task in front of him, which, from the looks of it, was a pretty big one.

I hadn't realized how bad the dragon had gotten me in the moment with adrenaline pumping through my body, but even after the healing had already begun, I could tell it was worse than I previously believed.

Gashes, several inches in diameter, covered my legs in eight different spots from all the places the dragon's talons had sank in, made worse when JayLeigh had hit him and he'd stumbled back.

"How long have I been out of it?" I asked, then flinched when Marek's fingers wrapped around one of the wounds.

"About an hour. I wanted to keep you under, but Marek thinks you'll heal faster when you're awake," JayLeigh replied as she loosened her hold and stepped away.

"What about Enzo? Why isn't he awake yet?"

"We kept him under. Neither of us thought he'd handle it well if he woke before you and saw your condition. He doesn't seem like someone who would be easy to calm down, but I would have had fun doing it." JayLeigh smirked, and I assumed it had been Marek who kept Enzo unconscious, based on her last statement.

Taking in my legs again, I took pleasure in knowing I could feel the pain radiating off them. Feeling nothing could have meant way worse, but then I frowned when I tried to move my toes and they wouldn't cooperate. The harder I tried, the quicker I realized I couldn't move any part of my lower body.

"What's wrong with my legs besides the obvious holes in them? Why can't I move them?" I asked while checking the rest of my body, which seemed to work normally.

"The damage was pretty extensive, Raegan," Marek finally spoke but didn't elaborate as he moved to another gash.

"And?" I pushed for more information.

"I was able to stop the bleeding relatively easily, but now I have to repair the nerve damage. It's more severe internally, and if I'm not careful, you won't ever walk again, so some silence and patience would give you the best chance of my success."

Well, alright then. DDD was on the cranky side, and I didn't feel like being wheelchair-bound for the rest of my life, so I shut my trap and let him do his thing. JayLeigh left the room and came back with food and pillows, so I could sit up easier.

By the time we were done eating and our mess had been cleaned up, Marek stepped back from my legs, but the fire remained on them. Though, it didn't burn nearly as much as when I had first woken.

"You'll need to stay here for the night, and I'll boost the healing flames every three hours or as needed. I've done all I can for the time being. Now, it's up to your body to do the rest," Marek said with a frown.

"Don't give me hope where there isn't any. What are the chances that my lack of feeling won't be permanent?" I asked.

His hands rubbed over his face. "I honestly don't know. You have a lot of magic within you, but there is nothing normal about the workings of your body."

I harrumphed. "No shit. I guess if I was going to connect with my dragon, I would have done it when my life was literally on the line. I could sense her, but she's blocked somehow."

"Yes, I would have to agree," Marek responded.

A decision settled firmly inside me at his reply. I didn't belong in Drakken. If Enzo and I stayed, there was a better chance we'd end up dead before I figured out what was going on with my dragon.

"If my legs are going to heal, when will we know?" I asked, already formulating my plan to get home.

"By morning. Why?" Marek asked.

"Because I'd like to go back to Shadow Veil. Our being here isn't helping anything. Yes, JayLeigh has beat my body into submission and I can kick a lot more ass now, but if my dragon hasn't come out yet, then I don't think it matters whether I'm here or not. Unless you have ideas I'm not aware of?"

Marek glanced between me and JayLeigh, then Enzo. He walked over to Enzo and pressed his palm to Enzo's forehead before turning to JayLeigh.

"I'd like to have some time with Raegan. You're off duty for the rest of the night."

Her brows furrowed. "Are you sure, King Marek?"

He nodded. "I don't need your services *here*." He put emphasis on "here," and I assumed JayLeigh was supposed to read between the lines.

"Ah. Yes, I understand. Well, you three have a good night and I'll report back in the morning." JayLeigh mock saluted us and disappeared out the door of the room we were in.

"I'm assuming we're in your quarters, just in a different room I haven't seen?" I asked.

"Yes, I didn't believe it would be safe for you in the infirmary. I really am sorry this happened to you on my watch."

"You're not my par—" I stopped, realizing he was technically my parent, so I tried to be sympathetic to his sense of responsibility. "It's okay. I'm choosing to believe I'll be up and walking around for breakfast tomorrow."

He grinned. "Yes, I hope so. There are other things I need to speak with you about before you leave, though. I will support your decision to go, but I hope once you're able to sort out whatever you need to, that you'll come back."

"As long as people aren't still trying to kill me, I would love that," I replied.

"Do you need anything? Would you like me to let you rest?" he asked, seeming nervous about whatever he wanted to talk about.

"Nope, I'm good." I grinned, enjoying the apprehension coming off him. It made him seem more genuine when he wasn't so in control and acting like a king.

He took a seat and rubbed his palms on his linen pants. "I can't prove this, but Raegan, I need you to know that I'm pretty sure I *am* your father."

I couldn't help but laugh. "Yeah, I think we already established that."

"No, you don't understand. I was bonded to Malina before I left Earth."

Air stuck in my throat as I tried to process his words. If he had been with Malina and thinks he's my real father, then she could really be my... I couldn't even think the word.

"How would you know? You left way before I was born." I was going to find any reason to prove his theories wrong.

"You're right, I did, and I know I didn't get her pregnant in the typical sense. I would have known almost immediately if I had, but she had more than one opportunity to take what she needed from me to create a child."

"So, you think I was still created, but you were the main ingredient?"

He laughed. "Yes, to put it not-so-eloquently. Considering you are struggling to connect fully with any side of you, I believe you were first only a dragon shifter, but

Malina snuffed your dragon out when she forcibly made you more than what you were meant to be."

His words triggered the memory of my conversation with Ophelia. When she told me I was meant to be a dragon, I had thought it was Enzo holding me back, but maybe I needed to give up the other supernatural parts of me to become what I always should have been.

"Can you take the other parts of me out? Is there a way to strip the elf and witch side of me?" I asked.

"There is, but it's not something I'm capable of. You'll need a powerful sorcerer to complete the task for you. So, I agree with your decision to leave, but I want you to come back. Just for a few days at a time, so you're not missing too much of Shadow Veil, enough that you can learn about your dragon."

I had an idea, and I wasn't sure he'd agree, but I knew one person who might. "What about if I promise to come back every other month if JayLeigh is allowed to come to Shadow Veil on the opposite months?"

He leaned back in his chair, considering the idea. "I'll speak with her, but I don't think that's a bad idea. I'd feel better if JayLeigh spent most of her time on Earth with you until Malina is found, but I don't know if that's such a good idea for multiple reasons."

Putting on my best pout face, I let water collect in my eyes to really sell my pleading as I stared at him. "You could come instead this time."

His face softened, telling me I had gotten to him, but he still shook his head. "You don't understand. I can't leave Drakken, or I will damn us all."

"That makes no sense, and if you don't want me to hate you for not helping protect my other family, then you'll need to explain." Yep, guilt trip. I had no problem going there if begging didn't work.

He sighed. "Fine, but then you need to leave it alone. Agreed?" I nodded and he continued, "Drakken is home to the last seer."

"Oh, yeah. I met her earlier, before I was almost dragon food."

His eyes bulged. "What did she say to you? She hasn't spoken to anyone that I know of in almost two decades."

I shrugged. "She basically told me I was meant to be a dragon and I needed to let go of something to become who I was supposed to be. I assumed she meant my bond with Enzo."

He shook his head. "Ophelia speaks in riddles. Don't begin pushing people away just yet. I think you need to see Alistair before you make any decisions. Tell him what we've discussed, and he'll know what to look for. Did she say anything else?"

"Just that I had a path to stay on and I needed to conquer my obstacles in order to move forward. Then, she basically forced us to go away, and that's when we were attacked. Pretty sure if she was a good seer, then she would have known it wasn't safe for us to go back into the forest."

He smirked. "Or maybe it was an obstacle you needed to face in order to move forward."

I rolled my eyes, seeing where he was coming from but not liking it. "Anyway, back to your story. Why can't you come with me?" I wasn't going to let him off the hook from explaining that tidbit.

"Right. Ophelia came to me when I arrived back in Drakken after I left Malina. She told me war was coming and that our walls would fall just like Elora's. Basically, what I took from it was if I left Drakken again, everything would crumble.

"I haven't considered leaving since, and we've been training an army for the day someone comes for us, just in case I misunderstood the prophecy. I thought it would be Malina, but then she was captured and we loosened up on things. Now that she's back, I don't know what to think, but I won't risk going back to Earth and letting Ophelia's vision come true. Drakken means too much to the dragons here."

Damn, crazy seer. That was probably why she stopped telling her visions. My DDD had taken his interpretation of her words and freaked the rest of the population out. No wonder most of the dragons hated me and Enzo. We could have been a Trojan horse, only in Drakken, to begin the war they were preparing for.

"I understand your concerns, but have you ever considered that if you don't come back to stop her, then she'll come for you anyway? You have what she wants. You told me yourself that Malina's purpose had been to restore Elora. Well, Drakken is the next best thing. If she wants a world to run and nobody can stop her, she will come for this place."

"That would be true if she knew Drakken existed, but nobody on Earth was aware of it before I had JayLeigh bring you here. Would I be wrong to assume those who know where you are kept your whereabouts a secret?"

"No, but it doesn't mean you're safe here," I countered, but his expression remained the same. There was no budging his decision.

Pain raced up my leg, effectively ending that part of our conversation. Without thinking it through, I let my reflexes take over and stuck my hands right into the flames that still flicked over my skin. "Holy shit, that hurts even worse," I screeched.

When I pulled my hand away, blisters bubbled in several places. "I thought these flames were supposed to be making me better?"

He pushed me back, so I was out of his way before he started moving his fingers through the fire again. "You have to know how to control the magic before you can touch it." He continued doing his thing, moving from one wound to another before settling back down.

"It's working, and you're actually healing faster than I thought, which is why you felt the discomfort. The quicker you heal, the more I need to power the flames to keep you mostly out of pain."

I nodded toward Enzo. "What about him? Can he wake up now?"

"He could if I wanted him to, but I wanted you to be able to speak freely without worrying about what you say in front of him," Marek stated.

"Haven't you learned I typically speak freely, regardless of who is around?" I grinned.

"While I am well aware of that fact, I'm also fairly certain your heart feels a different way. Enzo is your mate and, no matter how hard you fight it, you still care about him and what he thinks. You may not realize it, but every decision you've made since you've been here has been with him in mind. I've watched the two of you, and when he moves, so do you. Without even realizing it, the two of you are in sync."

That wasn't at all what I expected to hear. If anything, I felt I'd been keeping my distance from Enzo, especially since the morning I had practically forced myself on him. Though, the more I thought about it, I had *needed* Enzo.

Needed him in a way I'd never felt before, and it scared me more than I had wanted to admit.

He made me vulnerable, and I didn't like it. Not one damn bit.

"He screwed up pretty big," I said.

Marek nodded. "Haven't we all?"

Sure, I'd made mistakes in life, but I'd never lied like him. I'd never kept something from someone I loved that could put their life in danger. Regardless, I knew I'd already forgiven him. I accepted what had been done and let the anger go, but I wasn't sure yet if I was ready to move forward as if none of it had happened. To fully open my heart to him again.

"Let me ask you this, do you still love Enzo?" Marek asked.

"I do," I replied without hesitation.

"And you believe he is remorseful for what he did?"

"He wouldn't be alive if I didn't." Okay, that might have been an exaggeration, but it was close.

"Then, ask yourself this: which might give you more regrets? Giving him a second chance and possibly experiencing great love, or protecting your heart and maybe never knowing true love?"

My gut choice would be to take the chance at great love, but self-preservation was always there, reminding me of how much it would hurt if he screwed up again.

"I don't know," I answered honestly.

He moved around the bed I was on and went back to Enzo. "When you figure that out, everything else will fall into place." His palm pressed against Enzo's head again, and a groan left his lips.

"I'll be back to check on the healing flames shortly. Whatever you do, don't move from that bed or you'll regret it, but make sure you talk to him. Tomorrow, you head back to Shadow Veil, and you don't want to make love wait. It can disappear before you know it."

There was a sadness in his voice that told me Malina hadn't been the only love he'd experienced, and I felt for him. But, I couldn't ponder it for too long, because within seconds of the door closing, Enzo rolled over in bed with fury in his eyes.

A rumble began deep in his chest as he sat up and swung his legs over the side of the bed, eyes no longer meeting mine but staring daggers at the flames covering my lower extremities.

"I'm going to kill them," he snarled.

"Calm down. I know it sounds like a great idea now, but not if you expect to live long. These assholes have been preparing for a war for decades."

"What happened?" His voice was clipped with barely contained ferocity.

"Well, you got knocked out, and then I was almost dragon food. My dragon still didn't come out to save me, so JayLeigh did. She took us back here, and Marek is healing my legs. I should be up and walking in the morning." I tried to remain positive with my tone. He didn't need any added aggression in his current state.

"How do you feel?" I asked when he didn't move from the bed.

"I'd rather not answer that right now."

"Enzo, I'm fine. We're fine. Just take a deep breath." Marek had made the right call keeping him unconscious for as long as he had. If I couldn't get Enzo to calm down soon, I considered asking Marek to come back and knock him out again.

Enzo finally stood. "No."

"Huh?" I asked confused.

"Nothing is fine. Being here isn't right. I'm not okay with putting your life on the line in hopes your dragon side will come out. You don't need that part of you to be the best version of yourself. You're perfect as you are, and these people are only going to get you killed trying to change you."

I reached a hand out to him. "Come here."

Taking a step from his bed, he didn't need to be told twice. Warm arms wrapped around me, and I sighed when his heart beat rapidly against my cheek.

We held on to each other for several moments until I felt like he had calmed down enough to continue the conversation without blowing up.

"Enzo, we're going back to Shadow Veil Academy tomorrow." I paused as his eyes lit up, then fell.

"Why do I feel like there is a 'but' coming?" he groaned.

"Because there is." I laughed. "But I have every intention of coming back. DDD thinks Headmaster Stone can help me with what comes next."

"And what's that?"

He was either going to love the answer or hate it. "I'm going to ask him to strip my elf and witch sides, so there is nothing hindering my dragon from releasing."

He didn't say anything, so I added something I hoped would make things not sound so bad. "I was going to ask someone to break our bond, because I first thought that was what continued to hold me back, but after speaking with Marek, I think he's on to something."

His fingers stroked the tiny point on my ear as his other hand tightened around me, almost painfully. "I can't lose you."

The agony in his voice was real, and it broke my heart. I had kept him at arm's length long enough and decided it was time to put us both out of our misery. We'd each been through enough since his secrets were revealed. I wasn't just hurting him by fighting what I secretly always knew even when I hated him.

"I know and you're not going to, so long as you support my decision to embrace my dragon side. Would you still love me without my elf counterpart?"

He lowered himself, so our eyes were even. "Raegan, I'd love you even if you had horns sticking out the sides of your head. You're mine. You have been since the day I first met you. It just took me a while to figure it out."

When I didn't say anything, he pressed his lips to mine, gentle, yet so full of love.

"Can you forgive me for all of the wrongs I did?" he whispered, before kissing me again.

"I already have." This time, I pushed closer to him before realizing I couldn't get far when I had zero use of my legs.

Holding me fervently, Enzo moved in as close as he could without getting on the bed and disturbing my legs. He whispered words of love and passion between kisses, making me wish I had waited longer to officially forgive him.

Before things could get too heated, Marek knocked on

the door to warn us of his arrival, which I appreciated. As Enzo pulled back, I tried to calm my racing heart, but it was no use. Marek glowered when he walked over to check on me.

He pointed at me. "*You* are still bed-bound until sunrise." Then, he moved his intense glare to Enzo. "She needs her space to rest, so if I catch you preventing that from happening, I'll have no choice but to kick you out."

I so badly wanted to joke and say, "Yes, Dad", but that might have been taking things too far. Marek was trying, and I did give him credit for that, but I doubted I'd be calling him Dad in the affectionate sense anytime soon. Though, knowing he cared so much meant more to me than I realized it would.

I made a mental note to one day tell him about my parents who raised me. They'd given me a good life, and I hadn't ever needed for anything. Not all kids who were taken from their birth families were so lucky, but I certainly had been until they passed away.

"Yes, sir. I won't do anything to postpone us leaving tomorrow," Enzo replied, even though he didn't separate the distance from us. He might not get halfway in my bed again, but he wasn't leaving my side anytime soon.

Marek raised a brow at me. "Did you tell him you promised to come back?"

I nodded. "He'll support my decision to embrace my dragon side."

Enzo's chest rumbled next to me, but Marek raised a hand. "Before you lose your cool, I think that once people can see she's a fully transformed dragon, then they will accept her. Those who don't will be punished. We've already found the two who attacked you earlier."

"What about Onyx?" I asked.

"That is a lot harder situation. He is my second-in-command. I can't move against him until he physically does something to you or puts the other residents of Drakken at risk by his actions. We may not live like humans, but we did adopt some of their government practices, and Onyx has near equal power to me."

Shit. I had hoped DDD could just kick him out before we came back, but it sounded like an impeachment of sorts would need to happen first before the asshole could be knocked down a few pegs.

"What about you coming with us?" Enzo asked. "We still need your help to stop Malina."

"I've already discussed this with Raegan, and unfortunately, my assistance won't be available. I'm needed in Drakken."

"Are you fu—"

My hand covered Enzo's mouth before he could disrespect the dragon king. Marek might have been lenient with us thus far, but I wasn't willing to find out just how far that leniency would go. He was still in a position to control us, and I didn't want to find out what it meant to be on his bad side.

"It's okay. We'll figure it out," I said before removing my hold.

Enzo's eyes bored into mine before he finally nodded, seeming to trust I had a plan. I didn't really. I had willingly come to Drakken for two reasons: to figure out my dragon side and to bring back the dragon doyen. Neither of those things were happening, so we were going to be completely winging it when we got back.

I was beginning to think our only two options of

survival were to hope that Malina had either changed her mind in her desire to recreate Elora again, or maybe she'd start an attack so big that Marek had no choice but to come and stop her.

The first possibility was least likely, but preferable. The second was a horrible thought, but I didn't know how else we would get his help if my begging wouldn't work.

Marek moved closer to my legs and inspected the wounds again. "They're almost completely closed. You'll just need to remember there is still a lot of internal healing that needs to be done. Might be better for the both of you if you tried to get some sleep, and I'll continue to check on you throughout the night."

I nodded. "That's probably a good idea."

Marek did a few things with the flames before he said his goodbyes with promises to bring back food later. Then, it was just me and Enzo again. Without saying a word, Enzo moved the table between our two beds out of the way and pushed the mattresses together.

"If I can't get in your bed, then moving mine closer is the next best thing." He grinned.

"Always pushing the boundaries. It's like you can't help it."

"Life's not near as fun when you don't." He winked, and it reminded me of the first night we met. Well, the first time I remembered meeting him. He had been so carefree then, and I hoped to see that part of him more often, but the memory also gave me another idea.

"Can you remove the block from the times we met before the scavenger attacked?" I asked as he laid down next to me.

His hand cupped my cheek. "Raegan, I promise to

never lie to you again, but I'd rather leave the past where it belongs. There is nothing in those memories that will make a positive difference in the present or future. Removing the block will only hurt you like it did when you broke through it the last time, and possibly cause you to throw stuff at me." He smiled sheepishly, his eyes begging me to fully trust him enough to let the past go.

As I considered his words, I knew without a doubt that Enzo had been a different person when we first met—someone on a mission he was forced to complete—and I had no problem agreeing to his request. I didn't need to see that side of him and hurt myself in the process. It benefited no one.

"Okay. I'm trusting you." My hand settled on his that was still holding my face, and I closed my eyes, feeling a thousand-pound weight come off my chest.

Admitting out loud that I trusted him was something we both needed. Knowing I loved him and I had forgiven him was just the icing on the cake. Now, we only had to survive Malina's twisted plans and it would all be worth it.

THE FOLLOWING MORNING, I WOKE UP JUST BEFORE sunrise when Marek came back in. I'd half-woken each time he came back throughout the night, but he'd done his best to let us rest and I was able to fall back to sleep easily until something changed.

Finally, I was able to wiggle my toes, and a smile formed on my face. "So, I'm as good as new?"

"I'd say with another day or two of rest, yes, your legs will work as if the attack never happened," Marek replied.

Enzo stirred, and I realized he was no longer asleep.

"Good. Now, can we get out of here before it happens again?"

Marek didn't seem to appreciate his humor but held his tongue as he began extinguishing the flames that covered my legs.

While he worked, JayLeigh skipped into the room. "Good morning, lovebirds."

I shook my head at her. "Good morning to yourself. I take it from your cheery disposition, you had a good night?"

"I had a *productive* night." She smirked.

"That was either way too much information or not enough, and I'm afraid to ask you to elaborate," I said.

"Then don't. Anyway, who's ready to jump on back down to Earth?" she asked.

Enzo held his hand up as he got out of bed. "The sooner the better. I need a break from this place."

JayLeigh patted his shoulder. "Poor simple elf boy, can't keep up with the dragons."

I winced at her comment, because even though I knew the dragons were stronger in their physical form, Enzo was pretty damn powerful with his magic.

He glowered at her. "Want to find out if that statement is true?"

She cocked her head to the side, considering the challenge. "I do, actually, but it will have to wait. We have a portal ride to catch within the hour."

I groaned. It was one thing for JayLeigh and Enzo to spar in an attempt to pull my dragon out, but I had a feeling it was going to be something completely different when they were fighting for dominance.

"Oh, don't worry, Raegan. I won't damage his face too much. He'll still be pretty to look at when I'm done with him."

Enzo let out a deep laugh. "I can't wait to see you try."

"Enough, children," Marek said from my other side. "Raegan, can you move your legs?"

Glancing down, I realized while Enzo and JayLeigh had been distracting me, Marek had finished removing the flames. Not sure how I missed that, but I was glad it was done. Testing my mobility slowly, I moved a foot first, then attempted to lift my entire leg.

My muscles were weak compared to normal, and there was still discomfort, but not so much that I couldn't push through it. Sitting up straight, I gradually moved my legs off the side of the bed with Marek's assistance.

Within the blink of an eye, Enzo was at my other side, grasping my elbow to help me stand. Between them both, I was barely putting any weight on my legs. "I need you two to back off a little if I'm going to know how well I'm actually healed."

"Or I could just carry you until we're absolutely certain you're all better." Enzo grinned at me.

"Thanks for the laugh, and nice try, but I got this."

Enzo nodded and lessened his hold first. It had been one of the things that had made me fall for him to begin with. He never stood in my way, and he always encouraged me to do what I wanted. Right then was no different, except for the fact that Marek was still holding on.

I gave him my full attention. "I can do this."

He held my stare for several more seconds before he finally nodded and backed up a few inches. Not as much space as I was hoping for, but who was I to complain about having people in my life who cared.

When they were no longer holding on to me, I braced myself against the bed, getting a feel for where my weaknesses still laid. My left ankle burned from the weight of my body, and my right knee wasn't feeling too great, but other than that, I was confident I could walk if I took it slow.

Putting more weight on my right leg, I stood without holding on to anything, and then took a step forward. Where I moved, so did Enzo and Marek, which caused JayLeigh to murmur ridiculous comments from the corner about overprotective men.

Apparently, insulting her king was where she stopped with her quips.

Taking another few steps, I breathed a sigh of relief when each one became easier instead of harder.

JayLeigh grinned at me as I got closer. "See? All that ass-kicking for three days really strengthened your core. You'd be on the floor by now if it wasn't for me."

"Actually, I'd probably be in Advanced Shifting or Combat class right about now if it wasn't for you, but let's not play the blame game," I countered.

"Speaking of Shadow Veil, I replied to one of your aunt's emails. She's not happy with you or me."

"What did you tell her?" I growled.

"Well, I wasn't sure how much you wanted her to know, so I just said you were alive, but unable to reply to any messages and you'd be in touch soon-ish. When I checked the replies earlier, they weren't very friendly, so I told them to work on their manners, otherwise you wouldn't be responding at all. Seriously, you don't need that kind of language in your life."

My palm smacked against my forehead. "You seriously need to learn some peopling etiquette." Turning back to Marek, I asked, "How far is the other office? Can I reply to her now before we go, since the travel time takes longer?"

"It's just two more doors down the hall. If you feel up for it, then let's go."

He and Enzo continued to hover nearby, but it wasn't necessary. My strength continued to grow, and by the time I reached the other office, I was standing up straighter and breathing easier. Though I was still moving slowly so as not to set back any internal healing, I felt confident walking wherever I needed to on my own.

I didn't bother to read the previous messages. If something major had happened, I trusted JayLeigh enough to take things seriously and tell me. So instead, I typed out a quick reply, beginning with my apologies and once again telling them I was alive, then ended with the news of us returning home. Hopefully, it was enough to appease them for the next few days or weeks. I didn't even know what month it would be when we got back.

"Let's go pack up our stuff and go home," I said to Enzo when I was done, but he shook his head.

"There's nothing here we need to take with us now. Let's just get out of here and deal with it later, since you want to come back."

I considered the items in my room, and he was right. I had brought mostly training clothes, and I had plenty of those at Shadow Veil. When I nodded, he wasted no time picking me up and turning to JayLeigh. "Where is the portal?"

"Same spot we arrived in. Let's use Marek's private entrance instead of going through the main doors," she replied.

"Uh, you know I can walk, right?" I finally piped up.

"Yes, but you don't need to strain yourself. Save that energy for the portal. Plus, let me feel better by doing this for you." He lowered his voice to say the last part, and I conceded. As long as I went through the portal on my own, I'd be okay with him carrying me there.

That was what relationships were about. Give and take. Finding the perfect balance. We had a long road ahead of us, but I was confident we'd figure it out.

If we didn't, he'd be missing a pair of balls after I was done with him.

CHAPTER SIXTEEN

Gemma's tackle hug was even more aggressive than it had been when I'd arrived back from being gone all summer, which I guessed was acceptable since I had no idea how much time had passed since we'd left. It could have been the end of school for all I knew.

"I hope you don't ever have plans of returning there. This school year has been torturous without you here causing trouble like the last one," Gemma whined. "Ugh, and Professor Phox is way worse than you got to experience on the first day. I'm pretty sure every single person in our class has cried at least once. She's probably going to be gunning for you, too. She wasn't happy to find out you weren't coming back any time soon and nobody would tell her where you were. You are going to classes now, right? Everything is back to normal?"

My hands grasped her shoulders. "Gemma, my best friend, the most high-energy witch-vampire hybrid I know, calm down." I laughed. "I know it's been a while, but I'm not going anywhere any time soon. Let's cover one topic at a time, preferably after I've showered and eaten."

Jules wrapped an arm around both of our shoulders. "Come on. Let's get you settled, and we can properly catch up over dinner."

"What time is it? Or better yet, what day is it?" I asked.

"It's just after six and February fifteenth," Jules answered.

Damn, we'd been gone for six months Earth time, but it had only been two weeks on Drakken, including travel time, which I figured had eaten up at least a couple of days. Future visits were going to have to be much shorter.

I was going to have another crazy few months of catch up, and I no longer had an expert to train me. Enzo had been gone as well, so there was no way he'd already know the material. Though, we could at least study together. Thinking of him reminded me I had completely ignored him and JayLeigh once Gemma took my full attention.

I spun in a circle but didn't see them anywhere. "Where did the others go?"

"Headmaster Stone and Enzo took JayLeigh to show her where she'd be staying outside of the dorms. Enzo tried telling you, but Gemma was squealing too loudly in your ear for you to hear, I think," Jules said.

"Yeah, I missed that." I shrugged. They'd be fine on their own, and I didn't want to deny Gemma some needed attention, so it worked out.

Gemma grasped my arm as we headed for the academy. "Girl, why didn't you warn me the dragons were so sexy? The blond one that came to help us out... *yum* is all I have to say. The other students weren't allowed to know who they were, so Headmaster Stone assigned me as their liaison. Best. Job. Ever."

"Well, you'll have to tell me more about the blond beefcake later. I'm glad you had something to keep you busy while I was away. Sorry I didn't get to respond recently. There was an incident, but I'm okay and that's all that matters."

"What about Marek? I'm disappointed to see he didn't arrive with you as well," Jules said.

"I couldn't convince him to come. He has his reasons, and there isn't anything we can do to change them unless Malina forces his hand somehow."

Gemma huffed. "You mean, they'll come clean up the mess after Malina finally attacks for reals?"

My head snapped to her. "What do you mean 'for reals'? Did something happen?"

She winced. "You didn't get my last message?"

"No, I didn't read the other emails. I was in a hurry to get back here. What the hell happened?"

"Let's get to the room before we discuss this," Jules suggested, and I agreed with her.

Hopefully, the students had been kept mostly out of the loop with anything related to Malina. She didn't deserve to have any power behind her name. She wasn't someone to be feared, she was someone to be destroyed. Even if we didn't know how we were going to accomplish that particular task, I was no longer afraid of her.

I was going to figure out a way to remove her from this Earth, once and for all.

Something had crossed my mind before we left, and I wanted to speak with Headmaster Stone specifically about it. If I was the direct descendant of two Doyens, that had to give me some extra boost. Even if Malina hadn't birthed me or carried me in her stomach for nine months, she had created me. Used her DNA along with the others.

If the foreign parts of me, the ones not Doyen-related, were removed, maybe I had a chance at ending her myself.

Just maybe, Marek could save his world by staying put and I could save mine by becoming who I was meant to be, just like the seer said.

Gemma punched the code into my door, and as soon as we entered, she opened her mouth to likely ask several more questions, but I held my hand up.

"Shower first, then talking. I promise to be quick if you'll order food while I clean up."

She glared at me. "I feel like we just had this exact conversation six months ago. It'd be great if you'd quit disappearing, so we didn't have to do this again."

I gave her a quick hug. "I will do my best, but until Malina is dealt with, I make no promises."

"I'd really love it if someone would kill that bitch." Gemma pouted.

"We're working on it, and I have some ideas. Dig deep and find some patience," I teased as I skipped into the bathroom. As soon as the door was closed, I heard a thud, followed by Gemma's yelling.

"Yes, I threw a pillow at your door, and yes, it was supposed to have hit you in the back."

Laughing, I quickly stripped down and hopped into the shower before it was even warm. I hadn't been able to take a shower since before I was attacked, and while I wished I could enjoy the alone time, I didn't have a death wish. Gemma had even less patience than me.

So, I scrubbed and rinsed in record time, arriving back in the room fully dressed before the food was even ready. "See? You hardly had time to miss me again."

"Whatever," Gemma said. "Now, spill your guts out."

"Um, I'm pretty sure you have some explaining to do first. What happened with Malina?" I asked.

The butler box dinged, so Gemma waited to answer

until we were all sitting on my bed cross-legged with plates of pasta in front of us and bread in the middle.

"I'm going to let Jules answer. She retains that stuff better than me," Gemma garbled over a mouth full of food.

Shaking my head at her, I considered calling her out for just wanting to eat, but decided to let it go.

"There's not a ton to tell, actually," Jules began. "Malina is definitely up to something, but whoever she's working with has kept their mouths shut. You knew about her trips to the big cities from my first email, then there wasn't much to report, but over the last two weeks, she's been moving in closer to Shadow Veil."

"Did she come here?" I interrupted.

Jules tsked at my outburst. "I'm getting to that. She fell off the radar for a few days, and we thought she figured out we'd been tracking her, but then she reappeared again. Soon after that, our walls were tested with some pretty heavy magic. The council gathered, along with some of our best fighters and the two dragons, and they went beyond the shield to check it out."

I held my breath until the next words left her mouth.

"Nobody attacked, but a messenger did show up. He claimed to be there on Malina's behalf, stating she wasn't happy that you'd disappeared and if you didn't come home within a month to give yourself over, then she'd be decimating Shadow Veil, along with everyone within its walls."

My teeth ground together. "How long ago was this exactly?"

"Sixteen days ago," Jules answered.

I tried hard to block out the "what ifs" that plagued me, but it was hard. If we had waited any longer to come back, I would have been responsible for close to five hundred deaths if Malina followed through on her threat.

Considering it sounded like she was gathering an army of supernaturals who preferred the darker things in life, I had no doubt she intended to do exactly as she promised.

"Where is she now?" I asked.

"About a hundred miles west of us," Gemma answered, since Jules had taken a bite of her dinner.

"I need to go see the headmaster. We need to act before she has the chance to come closer or move up her timeline. If she can somehow tell I'm back, then she may do just that. I don't know how we were connected before, and even though she's not in my head anymore, Malina might still have other ways to get to me."

There was no time for dinners and catching up with friends. School was going to have to go out the door, too. The weight of the supernatural world was literally on my shoulders, and I was eating stupid fettuccini on my bed like a teenager.

I was still technically a teen at eighteen. Wait, it was February. I had missed my birthday, and I was nineteen, but that was beside the point. After the last year, well technically year-and-a-half, I felt like I'd aged well beyond my teens. The world was much bigger than my high school self had known, and I couldn't afford to sit around like I was. I needed to act before it was too late and I had nothing left to fight for.

Setting my plate on the nightstand, I moved toward my dresser for jeans and a sweatshirt instead of the yoga pants and tee I had originally put on. It was freezing outside this time of year, and I had no idea where I was going to find the headmaster at, but I needed to search for him sooner rather than later.

"Where do you think you're going?" Gemma asked with a huff.

"To find Headmaster Stone."

"Uh, we weren't really done here. You still have some explaining to do, too." Gemma did her best to glare at me, but after almost being eaten by a dragon, she didn't really scare me anymore.

My pants were already on and my arms halfway through the sweatshirt before I started rapid-firing information I'd not-so-accidentally left out of my replies back to their messages while I'd been gone.

"Marek is my dad. Enzo and I are back together. Marek can't leave Drakken or some world-ending prophecy may come true and destroy the dragon realm. I'm going to strip my elven side and possibly my witch one as soon as Headmaster Stone can do it. I was almost eaten by a dragon a few days ago and couldn't move my legs as they were covered in a healing fire, which was why you didn't hear from me. Oh, and some dragon seer lady told me riddles about my future, and now I need to go see if I understood any of it correctly by trying to kill Malina."

My hand was already on the doorknob as I rambled out the last bit and blew each of them a kiss. Gemma was the first to respond, but she was too late. I had already slipped out the door and was racing down the hallway as her curse words faded into the background.

I knew she was going to make me pay for dropping all those bombshells on her, but I didn't have a moment to waste. I'd spent too much time gone—not that I thought our trip to Drakken was a complete waste of time, but it had been too long.

I checked the headmaster's office, but there was no sign of them there. Then, I remembered that Jules said JayLeigh would be staying outside the dorms, so I headed for the nearest exit. My legs reminded me I wasn't completely healed, so I had to slow down, but I still moved as swiftly as I could without causing strain.

When I arrived outside, the sun was just setting and cast a purple glow across the sky. While I was enjoying the view instead of watching where I was going, I bumped into a hard chest.

Before I could apologize, a deep voice snarled at me, "What do you think you're doing?"

Backing up, I took in his appearance and ignored his attitude: vibrant blue eyes, blond cropped hair, wide frame packed with muscles, and taller than any other guy at Shadow Veil that I knew of. It could only mean one thing. He was a dragon, and a sexy one at that. Enzo was lucky I had already forgiven him or he'd have an even harder time convincing me with eye candy like that hanging around.

"Ah, you must be one of Marek's dragons. I'm Raegan, and you would be who?"

"I'm Talon, and I know who you are, but what I don't know is why you're out here instead of inside. You're supposed to be with Gemma." He narrowed his eyes, confusing me.

Then, it clicked; this must be the blond hottie she mentioned. I could tell by how pissed he was that she meant something to him and was disappointed I hadn't been able to hang around long enough with my bestie to get the details.

"Uh, I'm a big girl and do what I want. I was with Gemma, but then I needed—never mind. I'm not explaining myself to you."

He was hot, and I could see why Gemma was attracted to him, but he was annoying me and preventing me from my current task.

He continued to eye me like I was some alien, so I

pushed past him, deciding to deal with whatever just happened later. I didn't have time for his games, especially because there was a decent chance he could secretly hate me and I didn't have time for fighting dragons.

Talon called my name, causing me to pause, but I didn't turn around. "They're just past the tranquility garden if you're looking for JayLeigh and the others. I just left them to check on Ge—the students."

A smirk appeared on my face. Yep, I had totally guessed right. Dragon dude had a thing for my bestie. No wonder he was irritated I wasn't with her. He was either butthurt to be missing time with her or because I'd left her alone. Either way, she had some explaining to do when I was done.

I called out my thanks and moved toward the gardens. I still needed to try entering that place again, but I didn't have time right then. We had sat around too long wondering what Malina was going to do, and we needed to switch to offense. No more waiting. Even if I didn't have my full dragon capabilities, I was ready to act.

Malina had to be destroyed, and I was going to be the one to do it or die trying.

When I came around the back side of the garden, Enzo was already headed my way, which gave me some relief, because my legs were beginning to really scream at me. As I leaned against the garden wall, Enzo's eyes narrowed and he grabbed my arms to steady me.

"What's wrong?"

"Nothing. Well, everything. But nothing right now, except Malina is still breathing the same air as us," I responded.

"You shouldn't be out here running around. Why aren't you with Gemma and Jules?" he asked more calmly.

"They began catching me up on everything that's happened since we left, and none of it was okay with me. There's no good enough reason for why we haven't moved in on Malina yet. If the council locked her away two decades ago, then we should be able to do the same now. We still have the council. Plus, more help. Why are we sitting around waiting for her to act?"

His hands cupped my face as he brought his lips to mine in a demanding kiss. Passion instantly flared within me. I tried to retain my thoughts, but my need for a fight was quickly replaced with a need for Enzo.

"That's better," he murmured as he pulled back.

"What was that for?"

"You were losing it. I know you want to act now, but we have to be smart about how we approach the situation. I won't lose you, or anyone else here, just to finish this sooner. Alistair wants to meet with us tomorrow morning, including Talon and Sylas."

"Sylas must be the other dragon? I saw Talon on the way to find you. I'm pretty sure he and Gemma have something going on."

He shook his head. "That's of no interest to me. As long as neither of them are interested in you, I don't care."

A smirk appeared on my face. "You jealous?"

He pulled me flush against his body. "Do I have a reason to be?"

"Kiss me like before again and you should be safe."

He lifted me up and began walking back toward the academy. "I can do more than that."

I wanted to argue that I didn't need to be carried, but truth be told, he had my insides quivering and it was probably better that I let him take charge. I was running on adrenaline and passion, but exhaustion from the portal trip was just beneath the surface, waiting to take over. Though, I had just enough left in me to find out what Enzo had to offer.

BEFORE THE SUN EVEN ROSE THE NEXT DAY, I SNUCK out of Enzo's bed. He wasn't going to be happy about it, but

I had left Gemma and Jules in my room to get something accomplished and then hadn't really done that.

Damn sexy elf.

I headed toward my room with plans of ordering breakfast and taking it to Gemma. I knew Jules wouldn't have cared as much about my abrupt departure, but Gemma would need some coaxing to prevent her from being pissy with me for the foreseeable future.

As I opened my door, a smile formed on my face while I recalled my night with Enzo. Being with him and knowing our bond was growing stronger each time we made love was interesting, to say the least. I still wasn't sure how I felt about being tied together like that, but I was sure about Enzo.

Regardless of the past, I loved him. Even though I hadn't really comprehended the reasons for his actions when he told me the first time, I had listened, and his words stayed with me until I was ready to accept them. The stubborn side of me just hadn't wanted to admit Enzo really hadn't had a choice unless he wanted to die.

My thoughts were cut short, and my smile faded fast as I turned on my light. A rumble began in my chest as I took in the sight of a bloodied and gagged Gemma tied to a chair with some dude I'd never seen before holding a knife to her throat.

"It's about time you showed up. If you hadn't been out all night whoring around, your friend wouldn't have a scratch on her, but let's not make things worse. You're coming with me, or she dies."

He was of similar height to Talon, but with dark hair instead of light, and with his steely eyes slit like dragons, it wasn't hard to guess who he was.

"Sylas, you don't know what you're doing. You need to

let her go and walk away. Marek will kill you if you do any more damage," I snarled, pissed Marek had considered this guy trustworthy when he was nothing of the sort.

My eyes tried to stay on Sylas, but they kept moving to Gemma's face, which was cut in several places and battered all over, along with a bruise-colored handprint around her neck. Her eyes held only fury, though. She had fought hard and still wasn't giving up.

Sylas wouldn't get away with this.

"Marek is as pathetic as they come. He won't set foot on Earth, and I won't be going back to Drakken until Onyx is done with him, so he's of no concern to me. I have nothing to lose or worry about in this situation. You do, though, so don't test me or your friend will die."

"What do you want with me?" I asked, because he really did have a point. I wouldn't let Gemma get hurt further, and there wasn't anything I could expect Marek to do if he refused to come to Earth.

"Malina said you were smart. Guess she was right, which is disappointing. I had hoped you'd put up a fight like your friend here."

My teeth ground together. Of course, Malina was involved in this. The silver lining was that we didn't have another enemy to worry about.

"She's ready for you and doesn't want to wait until her deadline. It's time to do what you were created for," Sylas said.

And this was why I wanted to act first. Now, Malina had me right where she wanted me, and there wasn't shit I could do about it.

"Fine, but step away from her. I won't go with you until I know she's safe," I said, trying to keep my emotions in check. I could already feel scales trying to push through the surface of my skin, but I didn't want to show all my cards in case this idiot knew little about me.

He nodded before stepping around Gemma and heading toward me with the knife still out and ready for action. "We have a stop to make before we go to Malina. Move quickly and do as I say, or Gemma won't be safe for long. I'm not the only person here she needs to be afraid of."

Damn. Was Talon a traitor, too? She was going to lose her shit if that was the case. I made a mental note to help her with whatever revenge she deemed necessary when I got out of the situation I was headed into.

Sylas might have thought he had the upper hand, but going to Malina had been what I wanted last night, and even though Enzo had convinced me that being patient was better, I still had a plan up my sleeve that could easily be modified for my current predicament.

Sylas pushed back toward the door. "Walk. And if we see anyone, you better keep your mouth shut."

It wasn't even six in the morning; the likelihood of us seeing someone was slim to none, which was okay with me. I didn't need anyone else getting hurt on my conscience.

As I opened the door, Gemma screamed at me, but I couldn't understand anything she was saying with the gag in her mouth.

"I'm sorry, Gemma. Tell them I'll be back as soon as I can."

Sylas snickered. "Good luck with that."

I ignored Gemma's continued pleas and Sylas's snide comment as I walked out my door. When Sylas closed it behind us, he stood behind me with the knife pressing into my sweatshirt I still wore from the night before.

"One wrong move and I'll cut your organs out one by one. Do you understand?"

I nodded. "Where are we going?"

"To get Desmond. Malina isn't done with him, either."

Holding back my groan, I kept my head up as we continued onto the platform. I had a thousand questions I wanted to ask him but held my tongue. Malina would likely have enough to tell me and, without Marek, taking revenge on Sylas would be something I left to JayLeigh and Gemma.

Nothing good could come from letting Desmond out, but he was the least of my problems. If Malina wanted him, she could have him.

When we arrived at the door that led to the dungeon, Sylas yanked hard on my arm. "There will likely be two guards down there. If you say anything, I will kill them both. Keep your mouth shut and I'll just knock them out. Deal?"

"Whatever you say," I snapped, not appreciating the threats.

"Good mutt." He patted my head before opening the door and pushing me inside. "Stay behind me and keep up."

I did as he said, but that was only going to last for as long as it took to get us outside the academy. As soon as there were no more innocent people for Sylas to dangle over my head, I was going to do everything I could to make taking me to Malina difficult for him.

Bennett was on duty, and I hadn't seen him since before summer. His eyes widened in surprise. "Welcome back, Raegan. Alistair said you came in yesterday, but I didn't expect to see you until our meeting later today."

"Shut up, Elf," Sylas snapped before punching Bennett in the side of the head.

Bennett hadn't been expecting the hit, so he dropped like a sack of potatoes. His body lay awkwardly on the ground, but his chest still rose and fell. I had no idea how hard Sylas had hit him or how long he'd stay unconscious, but I kept moving just in case it wasn't long.

If we were still around when Bennett woke up, blood would be spilled, and I wasn't ready to have another's death on my hands.

"In a hurry?" Sylas jeered.

"Yep. Don't you know it's every girl's dream to be held hostage?" I drawled.

"You better not be up to anything. I don't care what Malina needs from you. I have no problem with crushing you if needed."

When we got to Desmond's cage, I glanced around for the second guard Sylas thought might be present, but I didn't see anyone. When I let out a sigh of relief, I realized just because I didn't see anyone, didn't mean they weren't there.

Pretending I didn't sense anything, I turned for Sylas. "So, what now? I don't have a key."

He shoved my shoulder. "It's a magical lock. Use your elf powers and break through. Malina seemed to think you'd be perfectly capable of it. Now, prove your use and unlock the door, or remember, Gemma will pay the price of your incompetence."

As I moved for the door, I shook my head, hoping Professor Phox was paying attention to me and not the idiot behind me. I knew she was there, but Sylas hadn't seemed to detect her. I hadn't seen the rift like before, but I recognized the power radiating off her from the first day of class.

"I don't need your help, but thanks," I said sarcastically, but hoped Phox knew I was talking to her and not Sylas.

"I wasn't offering, Mutt. Now, quit stalling."

My hand pressed to the lock as I syphoned the magic from the door. "Better watch out. I don't know if this thing will pop or not. I wouldn't want a chunk of metal to hit you in the face," I said to Sylas, even though I knew it wouldn't.

He grunted but backed up just like I wanted. When he did, Phox's presence moved in closer.

"You need to go before Desmond comes out. He won't be as oblivious as the dragon," I murmured under my breath, hoping she could hear me.

A heaviness pressed against my hand, and then the door popped open. Before I pulled on the latch, the weight of Phox's magic faded away. I hadn't needed her help, or at least, I didn't think I did, but I'd have to thank her later.

"Move it." Sylas pushed me out of the way as he jerked the door fully open.

I stood back, waiting for Desmond to come out, and made sure to keep my scales in check. I hadn't forgotten his previous comment about wanting to take one.

Desmond followed Sylas out of the room, half-asleep and not seeming all that excited that he'd been rescued from his cage.

"What the hell is she doing free?" Desmond snapped.

"What, are you afraid of getting punched in the face again?" I taunted, then pretended to lunge for him and enjoyed the flinch I caused in him.

Sylas grunted. "She knows what's at stake if she acts out. Don't you, Mutt?"

Ugh. I really hated that name. It was what Lyssa had called me when I first arrived at Shadow Veil, as well. This dude was really pushing my buttons and I wasn't sure how much longer I could keep myself in check.

"That's not good enough." Desmond took a few steps my way, stretching his arms and neck.

My body tensed, thinking he was preparing to hit me,

but instead, his hands wrapped around my face as he stared into my eyes and muttered, "*Dormito*."

Before I knew it, my knees gave out and the world around me faded away. The last thing I remembered before I lost full consciousness was the smirk on Desmond's face, and I couldn't wait to pound it out of existence.

When my consciousness returned, I took my time waking up. Even though he'd used a sleep spell on me, my memory was sharp, and I remembered everything that had happened, unlike the last time Desmond had knocked me out and kidnapped me.

Well, I guess he hadn't kidnapped me this time. I would have gone willingly just to get closer to Malina, but I wouldn't have made it easy on them as soon as we were outside the academy, so he had made the right call, unfortunately. Bastard was a fun-ruiner.

Since I had no idea where we were or how we had gotten there, my only hope was that Phox had been able to follow us and she'd call for backup. Having no clue how long I'd been out, I wasn't sure how much time I had to question Mommy Dearest before the cavalry arrived. So, as my breathing calmed, I focused on my surroundings.

Nothing stood out to me, which made me believe I was alone. That was, until I opened my eyes and Desmond's snarling face was inches from mine.

"Sucks being chained to a chair and defenseless, doesn't

it?" he taunted right before pulling his arm back and socking me in the jaw. "That was payback, you little bitch."

My mouth opened and closed, trying to relieve some of the pain as stars blinked in my eyes. He'd hit me hard, but I knew he'd also held back. It was the small things I had to be thankful for.

"Enough, Desmond. You can go now. I need a minute alone with my daughter." Malina strode into the room wearing another silky, floor-length dress like the last time I had seen her, but this one was emerald, almost the same exact color as my eyes.

As Desmond sulked out of the room, Malina took a seat in front of me and sighed. "I'm sorry about him. Let me make you more comfortable." She waved her hand in a zigzagging motion in front of me, and the chains fell away.

My arms stretched out, then my fingers rubbed my jaw, which was going to be sore for a while. The metal chair beneath me was even replaced by a cushioned one. She was either trying to butter me up or the chair was filled with poisonous spiders and one wrong move on my part would have me writhing in pain.

Either possibility seemed likely, considering the way she stared at me. A whole bunch of crazy was mixed in with the sparkle of her eyes.

"You left me, Raegan. That wasn't very nice of you. I offered you the world and gave you a few months to be free, then you disappeared. Where did you go?"

"If you have a dragon working for you, then you already know where I went," I replied smoothly. "I hadn't had much of a choice in the matter, though. It wasn't my intention to leave for so long."

Her brow raised. "So, you wanted to come to me, but Marek wouldn't let you?"

"Not exactly, but I'm here now, so that's all that matters, right?" I grinned, wondering if she could really be gullible enough to believe me.

"Yes, Daughter. Right here where you belong." Her eyes bored into mine, but I kept my face neutral, hopefully not giving away any inclination of my desire to wipe her from the face of the Earth.

"So, what do we do now? What do you need from me?" I asked when she didn't continue the conversation.

"Straight to the point. You don't want to ask me any questions about your history?"

Shaking my head, I leaned back in the chair, pretending to relax. "The past can't change the future, so what's the point? Even if I knew more about who my father might be or how I ended up in Oregon with my adoptive parents, it doesn't change what's happening now, right?"

She smirked. "No, I guess it doesn't. You're different than I thought you'd be. Why are you so agreeable to helping me now?"

"Because everyone else around me seems keen on holding me back. They're afraid of what lies beneath my surface, and I'm ready to set it free. Which brings me back to my original question. What do you need me for? It would also be nice to know what's in it for me if I comply?"

What I really wanted to know was whether Marek had been right when he told me of Malina's plan to create another Elora. There was a chance he was wrong, and any additional information I could glean from her would be helpful.

If Malina refused to bring me in on her plans, then anyone I cared about was still at risk, but if I could be involved from the inside, we stood a better chance at taking her down without Marek's help.

I still had hope that if Headmaster Stone stripped my other abilities, I could somehow tap into the Doyen blood that flowed through me. Then, if I was right, it would be the best way to take her down.

"Hmm, I'm not sure you're ready for the whole story. How can I know if you're trustworthy? You've only just arrived, and I don't know a thing about you. Do you believe I am a fool?"

"Of course not." *I just hope you are,* I added mentally.

"Then, before I answer any of your questions, how about you answer some of mine?"

I shrugged, finding that fair.

"Where is Marek?" she asked.

"In another realm called Drakken. You have to open a portal and need dragon DNA to get through. I wouldn't recommend going yourself unless you want to be shredded to bits." There was no hesitation in my answer. Sylas would have already given her that information, so I wasn't harming anyone.

Her eyes glowered. "How sweet of you to be concerned with my wellbeing."

Maybe I wasn't fooling her at all. She didn't seem happy with my answer.

She stood up, walking around behind me. I didn't bother to follow her, but I did take in the room I was in. There were no windows on the walls I could see, but there was light filtering through from somewhere, so I assumed one to be behind me.

The walls were painted a pale blue with white trim, and a king-size bed was to my left. Off to the right were two doors. One I assumed led to a closet and the other to an attached bathroom. There were no pictures on the walls, not even any decorations.

Finding nothing interesting to stare at, I picked at the fray on my jeans and noticed a decent-sized bruise forming where my pants had been ripped. Apparently, Desmond or Sylas hadn't taken any care with my body while bringing me to Malina. Both of them really needed to die along with her.

"Why aren't you fighting back?" she asked from behind me.

I stood, wanting to face her when I answered. If she wasn't believing me, I needed to be more convincing.

"Because I don't see the point. You're clearly stronger than me. You have bigger plans, and I'm curious about them. Why wouldn't I be? You seem like a smart lady, and it would be stupid of me to dismiss you completely, regardless of what others have said. I now realize the world is a lot bigger than I ever knew, and with so many secrets around me, I need to know all of my options."

Her eyes still narrowed at me, seeming to weigh my words for truth. There was a lot of it within them, so she would have a hard time ferreting out any lies. I just had to wait and see if she believed my version of the truth.

"I need you to prove your worth. You have to show me that you're on my side. Will you do that?" she asked, taking a step closer to me. The only space between us was the chair she created.

"I can try, but I make no promises without more information. While I'm curious about what you have to offer, it doesn't mean there aren't still people out there that I care about. If your plans will bring them harm, then we will have a problem."

She grinned proudly. "I expected nothing less from you."

Apparently, I had passed some sort of test, because she

relaxed and took a seat again. "I've changed my mind. You're going to stay here while I go on a little errand. I do need something from you, though, and if you fight me on it, it will only make things worse for you. Understand?"

My head nodded as I moved back to my own chair. "What would that be?" Hopefully she would answer this time, because I was pretty sure that had been the third time I'd asked since I woke up.

"I need your magic. I created you to share our power. You are part of me. We're connected like no mother and daughter before us. I may not be in your head anymore, but I sense you, no matter where you are. Well, at least on Earth. I knew the moment you left for Drakken and my plan was put into motion."

"And what would that plan be?" I asked, because needing my magic didn't really give me much information.

She raised a finger and shook it at me. "We're not there with our trust, dear daughter, but hopefully, one day, we will be. Let's see how this next part goes, and maybe I'll reward you with more information when I'm back."

My chest tightened as I realized getting anything other than what I already knew from her wasn't going to be nearly as easy as I hoped. She was being amicable now, but I wasn't sure how much longer that would last.

"So, what do I need to do to earn your trust?" I asked.

She moved slowly and stalked toward me, a gleam in her eye that told me I wasn't going to like what came next. "Stay very still."

Her fingers snapped, and suddenly the room I had thought was so boring, yet comfortable, disappeared from sight. In its place was a lab of sorts, except it was dingy and dark instead of bright and sanitary. Nothing about it was welcoming, and it had my blood running hot as I imagined what came next for me.

"Were you trying to trick me into a false sense of safety?" I snapped. "Not the best way to start our relationship, *Mother*."

She grabbed me by the hair and yanked me toward a chair with straps. "We have no relationship until you've earned it. Don't think for one second I bought anything you said before. You are, after all, *my* child. We only look out for ourselves."

I bit back the wince as she pulled me by the hold she had on my scalp, then shoved me into the chair. Desmond appeared and fastened me in before leaning forward.

"I've waited much too long for this moment, and I can't wait to hear you scream."

My head wasn't strapped in, and it wasn't him I had to win over, so there was no hesitation in my next move. My head slammed into his nose, and the resounding crunch followed by the flow of blood pouring from his face brought a smile to mine.

"Argh." He raised his hand to strike me, but Malina stopped him.

"I gave you one chance to get your hit in. No more unless I say otherwise," she spat.

"Do you really think treating her with any sort of kindness will help? You'll never be able to trust her," he retorted, which had been the wrong thing to do.

Her hand grasped his throat and squeezed with a force that gave me pause at its strength.

"You are nothing more than a rat. Don't question me again or I will replace you as quickly as I did the one before you. Do I make myself clear?"

Desmond's face was turning purple, and there was no

sign of air getting through for him to be able to talk. Instead, he nodded before crumbling into a heap on the floor as Malina let him go, tossing him aside like trash.

She turned toward me. "Hit him one more time and I might just let him have his fun with you. I don't have time to replace him, but I will if he disobeys me again. Don't make me have to dispose of you both."

I didn't bother responding. There was no getting the upper hand here. I had made a mistake in thinking it was a good idea to get closer to Malina. I'd only put myself in danger and possibly those I loved most, because they would come for me. And when they did... I wasn't sure how that would work out for either side.

"Now, be a good girl and shift for me," Malina demanded.

When I didn't immediately do as she asked, her hand struck me across the face. Apparently, it was okay for her to still hit me, just not Desmond. Super.

"There aren't many options here, Raegan. You either do as I ask without repercussions or be forced to comply while experiencing agony unlike anything before. Either way, you will do as I request."

I still had hope of getting away, but my chances lessened if I was injured, so I did as she demanded, hoping to not only avoid her wrath, but to figure out what she was up to.

When my body was covered in scales, she ripped the sleeve off my sweatshirt and brought my arm closer to her face. "You have so much of Marek within you," she spat as if it was a bad thing.

"What's wrong with that? Isn't that what you wanted?" I asked.

"No, what I wanted was a powerful dragon to help me

with my quest. All I got in return for my hard work was a mutt who doesn't listen very well."

My chest rumbled as I leaned forward as much as I could in the chair. She raised a brow at me, halting my next move. I was sick and tired of people calling me a mutt.

"Don't push me, Raegan," she said before ripping out one of my scales that I really hoped would grow back.

There was no stopping the scream that ripped from deep inside of me. I'd broken bones, been burned by fire, and nearly had my legs torn off, but nothing had ever hurt as much as losing a scale.

"Oh, I should have warned you that was going to sting a little. That's what you get for growling at me." She smirked before turning away.

Blood pooled on the top of my hand where my scale no longer was before dripping onto the ground. My heart pounded as I tried to rein in the fury that flowed through me. My dragon swirled just beneath the surface as well and, for the first time ever, I could feel her pain.

There was still no voice or true connection, but there was sorrow, and my heart ached for her. I didn't know this other part of me, but hopefully I would one day soon, and we would get our revenge on the bitch before us.

"Desmond, get the formula," Malina snapped while admiring my scale underneath a bright light on the table across from me. "It's been too long since I've held one of these. Previously, I wasted it on creating you. I won't make the same mistake twice."

I had no reply for her, because she was right. Her selfishness was wasted, and it would be her downfall. She had created something that never should have been, and it was going to destroy her.

I was going to destroy her.

CHAPTER NINETEEN

Sylas strode into the room, head held high and eyes only for Malina. When he stepped close to her, she raised her hand, caressing it down his cheek. "Is everything ready, darling?"

"Of course. Just say the word and I'll open the portal," he cooed.

Oh, no. Everything was beginning to make sense. Malina knew Drakken existed, and I'd just given her exactly what she needed to make it through the protective shields that kept non-dragons out. I wasn't sure how she intended to use the scale to trick the system, but I knew she would, and then she'd bring war to Drakken just like Ophelia prophesied.

Only, Marek hadn't left. So either the crazy old lady had gotten something wrong or Marek had misunderstood, but Drakken was about to have at least one unexpected visitor.

"When do I get to see this infamous realm?" Desmond asked with a slight whine.

Malina glared at him. "When I say so. This is just a test

run. Marek won't even know I'm there. Possibly. Just depends on how things go."

My eyes rolled as I shook my head. Malina turned toward me, smirking. "Have something to say, child?"

"Nope. You do whatever it is you need to, and I'll just sit here with the psychopath." My head jerked toward Desmond.

She patted my head. "Don't worry about him. He knows if he harms another hair on your head that he'll be nothing more than a lab rat."

Before I could reply, she went back to Sylas. "Are you sure you can't come with me?"

"Yes, I can't risk Marek seeing me, but Onyx will help you if necessary. I've made him aware of your arrival, and he's our biggest ally. That is, until he's no longer useful." The evil permeating off Sylas was thick in the air, and my skin shivered as his words sunk in.

Both Marek and Onyx were going to be betrayed. At least Marek knew people were turning against him, even if he didn't know who. Onyx, on the other hand, likely had no idea. I almost felt bad for him, but then memories of the way he treated me surfaced and I figured he deserved whatever was coming to him.

Malina took my scale and dropped it into a vial filled with a pale pink liquid. Everyone was silent as she did this, making me believe there was supposed to be some big show when she was done. As she swirled the vial around, the scale began to disintegrate and turn the liquid a maroon color.

She turned back to me and grinned. "This is why nobody can stop me and why they all fear me. Remember this moment. Learn from it." Lifting her head back, she poured the contents of the vial down her throat and then we all waited.

I was beginning to think she was all talk and no sparkle, but things changed within a few blinks of the eye. More accurately, Malina changed.

Her skin tightened as her head flung back and eyes closed. With a shake of her hair, she lowered her face and opened her eyes once more, looking directly at me. My body betrayed me and flinched at the sight of her dragon eyes. Then, as my stare moved down, I noticed scale impressions just beneath the surface of her skin, along with claws for nails. Not as long as mine were when I half-shifted, but present, nonetheless.

"In this form, Marek won't be able to sense I'm coming. I will be free to move through his lands that will soon be mine and do as I please. When I come back, there will be an army ready to descend on Drakken, and then I will have what I've always wanted."

Glaring at her, I held my head high, hopefully showing her she didn't scare me. "You're not going to win. There are too many powerful people willing to take you down."

She moved closer. "Yet, the most formidable of them all wouldn't get off his throne to stop me."

Damn it, she had every reason to be cocky. We'd done absolutely nothing to prevent her from growing stronger since her escape. If anything, I'd only made things worse by going to Drakken. Phox needed to show up soon with the others, so I could warn Marek, or things were about to get a whole lot uglier.

"Sylas, darling. Let's go," Malina said before turning to glower at Desmond. "I mean it. Touch her and I will use you to experiment on next."

"Understood," he replied gruffly.

Malina and Sylas left the room, leaving me chained to a chair and alone with Desmond. I wasn't sure how I felt about that, but hopefully he was going to take Malina's threats seriously and I didn't have anything to worry about.

He yanked on the top of the chair and drug me from the room once they were gone. "Time for you to go away. If I can't torture you, then I'd rather not have to look at you."

My mouth stayed shut as I paid close attention to the paths he was taking and our surroundings. We were in some sort of old industrial building on an upper level, I was pretty sure. There were several hallways, but none of them very long. I could see light streaming from around a corner, but we never made it that far.

Desmond opened a door and practically tossed my chair inside with me still secured to it. He must have used a spell, because there was no way the sorcerer was strong enough to accomplish the task on his own.

Cocky bastard hadn't even checked to see how I landed. Instead, he slammed the door shut, and I was surrounded by darkness. The only light that peeked into the room came from underneath the door, and it wasn't much.

My only saving grace was that when he had thrown me, the wooden back of the chair had cracked, giving me some room to maneuver. I was laying on my side, head touching the concrete floor, and my body ached from the impact. I needed to get out of there, though, and no amount of pain was going to stop that from happening.

Wiggling my ass around as much as I could, I heard the wood splinter even more, so I kept going. Only my hands and chest had been bound, so I used my legs to get me closer to the wall. Once I hit something solid, I used it to push myself over onto my knees.

My legs hadn't received the entire resting time they

needed, so my muscles were screaming at me, but I didn't care. If Phox and whoever else she might have told weren't around to break me out yet, then I had to assume I was on my own and Phox wasn't to be trusted.

Just as I was preparing to slam my body against the concrete floor again, the door opened, and I let out a groan, feigning injury. If Desmond had come back to check on me, I didn't want him to know I'd been trying to break free. I needed him to think I was weakened and use it to my advantage.

"Seriously? Did you not learn anything from all those ass-kickings I gave you? We're going to have to start over with your training," JayLeigh drawled from the doorway.

My head snapped up. "Well, don't just stand there. Get me out of this damn chair."

She grinned. "There's the spark I was looking for." As she bent to unbuckle the metal straps, she let out a low whistle. "No wonder you couldn't get out of these. This metal is old school and would have taken you hours to break free from."

I was still on my knees, and when the straps were undone, my body felt like it was going to collapse, but I didn't stop. Instead, I pushed up, and the chair fell from my back before JayLeigh could remove it. I faced her with a renewed determination flowing through me.

"How many did you bring with you?" I asked.

"Just four. Your people weren't prepared enough to face whatever army Malina's been gathering on such short notice. At least, not that I could tell. I didn't ask too many questions, just hopped in the truck when asked."

"Who's here? Enzo, Alistair, Phox, and you?"

She grimaced. "Enzo's not here, but Talon is. I know

Sylas turned on us and don't worry, he'll pay for that, but Talon is one of the good ones. I'd bet my life on it."

"Why isn't Enzo here?" I didn't particularly care about anything else she'd said.

"Well, Alistair thought it was best. You'll have to take that up with your headmaster later. Right now, I've been told to find you and get out, so that's what we're doing."

She tugged on my hand, and I followed her out, seriously confused about why Enzo wouldn't be present, but JayLeigh was right. We just needed to get out of there and warn Marek if it wasn't already too late.

"Malina left to Drakken. She took one of my scales, and Sylas opened a portal for her," I said, almost out of breath as we went down a flight of stairs.

"Shit, are you okay? That's like the worst kind of pain."

"Yeah, I'll be fine." Glancing down, I double-checked it had stopped bleeding. "But what about Marek? If we send him a message, will it get there in time?"

She nodded. "It should, and he's supposed to be checking it often since he has three dragons down here, but my guess is Marek already knows. A lot of the wrong people believe he has no idea what's going on, but Marek's smarter than that. He has a plan, even if the rest of us don't know what it is."

I groaned. "It would have been nice if his plan included coming back to Earth to kill Malina. Maybe he can just do it while she's there. I wouldn't be sad about that."

"We'll see. I don't know what's going on in his head, but I have faith he has it handled as much as any of us could in his situation."

Nodding, I paid closer attention to the door in front of us. Headmaster Stone was waiting there, dressed in full tactical gear, his white beard standing out starkly against the dark clothing and causing me to do a double-take, but Talon was nowhere to be seen.

"Let's go," the headmaster said. "Talon's waiting with the truck out front. We saw the two of you coming down the hallway from down here and got a head start."

"Someone please tell me why we're not blowing this place up right now?" I asked, full of irritation.

"Because finding you was more important, but don't worry, we'll be back," Headmaster Stone said as we all entered the waiting truck.

Nobody had followed us out, and I briefly wondered if it had been part of the plan to let me escape. That had all seemed way too easy.

"Wait, where's Phox?" I asked.

JayLeigh laughed. "Now, that's a woman I want to have my back at all times. She's evil and twisted and amazingly awesome. She said she'd meet us back at the academy. She wanted to screw with them a little bit, keeping the guards distracted while we got you out."

That explained the easy escape well enough.

A scream came from inside, and JayLeigh snickered. Phox was definitely having her fun as we drove away from the building.

"Where are we?" I asked when we left the industrial part of town and got on the interstate heading east.

"Just outside Greenfield, Massachusetts. We knew the general location of Malina's hideout, but we would have been searching for a while had Phox not followed you. The tracking we had wasn't as accurate as I would have liked," Headmaster Stone answered with a bit of irritation.

As I stretched my legs out, I remembered something that should have been one of my first questions. "Why didn't you bring Enzo?"

If they suspected he had anything to do with this, I was going to lose my shit. All the preaching about forgiving him, and just when I finally did... no way would I be able to keep my cool if they had proof he wasn't trustworthy.

"I wasn't going to risk him doing something stupid. Malina had some sort of hold on him at one point, and I haven't forgotten that. I fully believe he's on our side, but I won't deny that I'm worried Malina will be able to force his hand in some way down the road."

I considered the headmaster's words carefully and leaned back in my seat. I didn't have a reply to it, but I certainly had a lot of opinions about his statement, ones I would be sharing with Enzo as soon as we were back. If there was any reason to worry that he could turn on us again, even if he had no control of it, I needed to know how likely that was to happen and do everything I could to prevent it.

JayLeigh nudged my shoulder, and whispered, "Don't think too hard about what he said. The old man was just being cautious. Enzo is going to be fine. The two of you have a bond I've rarely seen on Drakken. He loves you, and you shouldn't ever doubt that."

"Right. Easy to say, a little harder to do," I murmured.

As the trees passed by, I stared off at nothing in particular and wondered just what taking down Malina was going to cost.

More importantly, was I willing to pay it?

CHAPTER TWENTY

When we arrived back at Shadow Veil, the sun was just setting, meaning I'd been gone for just over twelve hours. Nothing seemed amiss with the school, but as we drove through the gates, an ominous feeling settled over me.

"Where are all the students?" I asked.

"Inside. Nobody is allowed outside after sunrise until Malina is caught," Headmaster Stone answered.

Not a bad idea, but I doubted it would really keep anyone safe if Malina wanted access to them.

As soon as we pulled in, I carefully extracted myself from the truck, making sure not to put too much strain on my body all at once. Everything in me was sore, but mostly my legs and face. The bruising was already fading from my accelerated healing, but it didn't make it hurt any less just yet.

"I'm going to go find Enzo," I said, and JayLeigh laughed.

"I think he's found you."

Sure enough, when I twisted around, Enzo was stalking

toward us, indignation filling his eyes. Though, he didn't say a word. He simply picked me up and snarled at Talon who thought it would be a good idea to take a step in our direction. Not so much. When the dragon raised his hands in mock surrender, Enzo walked away with me in tow.

I'd seen his caveman side enough that I didn't bother trying to talk to him. As we passed by other students, I simply waved or apologized if Enzo growled at them being in his way. Gemma was nowhere to be seen, which surprised me, since I figured I'd be bombarded by her as well.

Just as we were getting on the platform to go up to Enzo's dorm, Peyton and Finley flanked us. "Where do you think you're taking her?" Finley snapped.

"Uh, ladies, now isn't really the time. I promise I'll catch up with everyone tomorrow," I said before Enzo could harm my friends.

"No. We haven't forgiven the bastard for what he did to you. What he did to all of us."

Shaking my head, I worried Enzo was going to completely lose his shit. His whole body vibrated beneath me.

"Seriously, you two need to go. I will be at breakfast tomorrow. I promise."

Enzo's snarls grew louder, and their eyes went wide.

"Are you safe with him?" Peyton asked.

"Yes, but you're not. So, please go," I begged.

With one last glare from Finley, Peyton drug her away and Enzo stepped on the platform. Still no words had been spoken from him outside the grunts and growls, but I knew he was just scared and would calm down as soon as I was safely tucked away in his room.

When we got to his door, his hands wouldn't remove

themselves from my body, so I punched in the code and he practically kicked the door in before I even had the handle all the way turned.

"Enzo, I'm safe now. You need to calm down and let me go," I said.

"If I let you go, I'm going to kill someone. It's better I hold on to you," he grumbled, carrying me to his bedroom and sitting on the bed. "Where are you hurt? What did they do to you?"

"My legs are sore. I'd really love to be able to stretch them out." Which I couldn't do if he refused to let me go. He stared at me for a long second before sighing in resignation.

"I'm not leaving your side. Today was too close. Malina had you, and they wouldn't let me do anything about it. Alistair spelled me. I couldn't leave the academy grounds, no matter how hard I tried. I want to kill that sorcerer."

My hands cupped his face. "Enzo, you don't have to leave me, but you do need to put me down. I'm not going anywhere, and Alistair isn't here."

His forehead pressed against mine as he took a deep inhale. "You're really okay?"

"Yes, I really am. Now, quit acting like a caveman."

Kissing me gently, he finally pulled back and laid me on the bed, but far enough over that he could lay next to me. He wasn't kidding about not leaving my side. Literally.

"What happened?" he asked, voice tight with barely controlled anger.

"Quick recap, and then I need food and sleep. Tomorrow will be soon enough to deal with the rest. JayLeigh should be taking care of the important stuff."

He nodded, so I summarized the key pieces I could think of since the moment I had slipped out of his room earlier that day. His grip tightened almost painfully on my hip when I explained a few parts, but other than that, he handled it better than I had imagined he would. At least, on the outside.

When I was done, I closed my eyes and he got up to order dinner, but I never got the chance to eat it. I was out before he even left the bedroom.

~

THREE DAYS HAD PASSED, AND I WAS BEGINNING TO feel the frustrations Jules and Gemma had when I was gone. Time working differently on Drakken was making it hard to know if JayLeigh had been successful in warning Marek before Malina's arrival.

She'd told me the night before that if we didn't hear from him by week's end, then she would go back home, but with Sylas still out there and Malina intending on coming back, she wasn't sure Marek would be happy with that choice.

He'd ordered her to not only continue training me, but to protect me as well. She hadn't realized that included babysitting within the academy, but now between her, Enzo, and Gemma, I never had a moment alone.

Though, I was down one overprotective aunt, at least. She'd reluctantly gone home to New Orleans to deal with pack stuff there that she was pretty tight-lipped about but had promised to be back as soon as possible.

Since Malina wasn't on Earth, I had decided to resume some of my classes and replace others with training time with JayLeigh.

I still hadn't seen Professor Phox since arriving back at the academy. Her classes had been canceled the last couple of days, but she was supposed to be back today, and I was eager to see her again. The more I thought about her, the more I wondered just who she really was.

She had talents others around the academy didn't appear to have, except she managed to stay under the radar, for the most part. There had to be a reason for that, and I was going to figure it out.

Enzo escorted me and Gemma to class that morning, complaining the entire way that it was pointless for me to continue, but what he didn't understand was I actually *liked* the classes. Well, most of them, anyway. I wasn't giving them up just yet.

"Enzo, darling dear, you're smothering like a mother. If you don't want to wake up with a knife in your chest, then give me some damn breathing room," I said as sweetly as I could, but failed at the end.

He'd somehow mastered the ability to walk next to me but turned just right, so anytime there was a loud noise or someone came too close, he was standing in front of me, blocking any potential threats.

"I'll take the knife to the chest as long as it keeps you safe." He shrugged, and I decided the only way to get past his suffocating ways was to ignore him the best I was able. I'd at least get a break during some of my classes.

That was a nice thought until we walked into Professor Phox's room and he followed us in. "Enzo, go to your own class," I snapped, and he smirked.

"I'm already here."

My eyes widened with anger. "What does that mean?"

"It means Headmaster Stone changed my schedule to match yours, and I'm in this class."

"You're in Advanced Shifting and Magic? A class for

witches and shifters? You've got to be kidding." So much for getting some space.

"Yep."

"You're not a shifter *or* a witch," Gemma piped in, stating the obvious.

Then he grinned, and it all clicked. Smart, cocky bastard.

"Technically, I *am* a shifter. I might not be able to shift now, but one day I could, and I want to know what to expect."

"Then you should have started with the first-year classes," I grumbled.

Gemma's hands flew up in the air. She was just as frustrated as I was with my constant guard dog. At least when she was with me, it was more because she wanted to spend as much time with me as she could before I up and disappeared again, not because she thought I was incapable of handling things on my own.

"Enzo, I'm going to say this once, and know that I say it with love. I'm being very serious right now. If you're in every one of my classes today, there will be no sexy time for you for at least a month."

His face paled. "You wouldn't dare."

I raised a brow. "Do you really want to take that chance?"

He mumbled several curse words under his breath and glanced around the classroom. "Fine. You can have this class, but only because Phox is the teacher and she helped bring you back to me before. I'll meet you right outside the door when it's over."

He leaned in to give me a kiss, and I patted his cheek. "That's a good boy."

The rumble from his chest rivaled any shifters, but I had gotten my way and I didn't care.

When he was out the door, Gemma and I took our seats in the back. As I got my tablet out, I couldn't help but notice the shaking of Gemma's shoulders.

"Let it out. I know you want to," I drawled.

Laughter erupted from her chest, causing the students who had already arrived to turn and stare. I sank lower into my seat as I waited for her to calm down, but before she could, we had another visitor.

Professor Phox's face appeared right in front of me, completely free of any emotion. "Glad you could finally join my class, Raegan."

"I'm equally glad to be here," I replied with a sweet smile.

Her lips lifted only a fraction. "We'll see about that."

Apparently, she was cool with saving my life, but not going to take it easy on me after missing seven months of lessons. Maybe I wasn't so glad to be back in class.

She moved to the front of the room and stood by the entrance, eyeing the clock.

Gemma nudged my shoulder. "Watch the door."

I did as she suggested, and when 8:30am came, Phox flicked her hand and the door slammed shut before the lock engaged. Poor Embry stood on the outside, staring through the window, eyes wide as fear took over.

What the hell has this teacher been doing to them all year? I wondered and even asked Gemma, but she shook her head, refusing to move her stare from the front of the room.

"Good morning, class," Professor Phox announced.

Glancing around, I realized only a third of the students who had been there on the first day were in attendance. "Do you think she'd notice if I slipped out?" I whispered to Gemma, but it wasn't her who responded.

"Yes, Ms. Keyes. I would notice, and good luck trying to get out. If you can break through my magic, then I'll pass you in this class without ever having to show up again."

Oh, a challenge. One that had my curiosity piqued and pulse quickening.

"Don't you dare, Rae. She will destroy you, and then Enzo will kill me for not keeping you in check," Gemma hissed, but I didn't listen.

I was already out of my seat and headed for the front of the room.

Phox kept her gaze on me but addressed the class. "Here is what you all should know *not* to do by now, but Ms. Keyes hasn't been present all year, so this can be our lesson for the day: How not to be an idiot."

Now she was just pissing me off.

I didn't bother to respond to her. I knew her type, or at least I hoped I did. Words weren't going to make the situation any better. Showing her that I was capable of great things was the only way to shut her up.

I'd managed to open the dungeon door last year, and I'd broken into Enzo's room. I couldn't imagine her magic was stronger than either of those, and I planned to prove it. Whether that was a good idea or not was to be determined.

Glancing up at Gemma, I second-guessed my decision to accept the professor's challenge. Her bottom lip quivered, and there was true fear in her eyes. I mouthed "I'm sorry" to her, but it didn't make anything better, and it was too late to back down.

I was going to open the damn door.

Placing my hands on the wood frame, the surge of magic that came back through burned my hands, and I instinctively pulled them back. Phox snickered from behind me, but I didn't bother giving her any attention.

Instead, I did a partial shift until scales appeared on my hands. When I had a little bit of protection, I moved for the door again. This time, the burn was more of a bite, but as soon as I tried to syphon the magic away, my blood began to burn just like my hands had.

Taking Phox's power in wasn't going to work. I had to filter it into something else, but I wasn't sure what. As I took a moment to come up with another plan, Phox tsked at me.

"You have two more minutes before I use you for something else that will make me much happier."

Ignoring her once more, I found something on the shelf to my right that should work and grabbed the round object. It was an orb, and I knew they could hold power, so I figured it was worth a try.

Placing my still-scale-covered left hand back on the door, I kept my right hand flat with the orb resting in my palm. When I peeked back at Phox, her brow was furrowed, and she looked a bit nervous. Good, she deserved whatever awful feeling was flowing through her after how she treated all these students.

Pulling on the magic of the door once more, I winced as it moved from one hand to the other and settled into the orb. There didn't appear to be an end to Phox's power, but I didn't stop until I broke through possibly only the first layer.

When I did that, I recognized immediately what I was sensing. The distraction was enough to stop whatever momentum I had created and turn back toward the professor. As our eyes met, I knew exactly what she was, and she knew I'd figured it out as well.

Professor Phox wasn't just any powerful shifter.

She was a dragon seer.

CHAPTER TWENTY-ONE

Phox strode toward me casually, but we both knew what I had figured out. Instead of getting in my face like I expected her to, she shoulder-checked me and moved to the door. Her fingers wrapped around the handle, and she opened it slowly.

"Very well, Raegan. You've proven your time away has been resourceful enough that you no longer need this class." She turned around to the rest of the students. "Lessons will resume tomorrow. Everyone is dismissed."

Nobody said a word as they gathered their items and carefully walked out the door. Each of them eyed me with a new curiosity.

Gemma was the last to arrive at the front of the room, and she carried both of our bags. There was a rigidness taking over her body that told me she wasn't happy. About what, I wasn't certain, but I was sure to find out based on the twitch in her eye.

Instead of glaring at me, her irritation was directed toward the professor, which surprised the shit out of me after all the times she'd warned me against doing anything that could piss off the teacher.

"Listen, Professor Phox. I've respected you and done everything you've expected of me, better even than most of the other students, but I won't stand by and let you bully Raegan. I'm not leaving this room until she does."

Phox glanced at me. "What does she know?"

"Everything."

She sighed. "So, it's accurate of me to assume that even if I dealt with her temper tantrum and kicked her out, she would end up knowing what we're about to discuss anyway?"

With a grin, I nodded.

"Fine." The professor slammed the door shut and waved her hand over it, effectively locking us in, or possibly keeping others out.

Gemma didn't flaunt the fact that she'd stuck up for me and won; her face remained serious and I realized I hadn't been the only one to grow over the last year-and-a-half. Everything that had happened to or around me had affected her as well. She'd almost been killed because of me, twice, and those situations had left lasting effects.

Behind closed doors, Gemma was still the bubbly blonde I met on my first day, but as I paid closer attention to her, I realized she was stronger now, and I should have noticed earlier.

We followed Phox to her desk and brought two chairs over to sit with her. She had some explaining to do, and I hoped whatever she had to say was finally going to piece everything together for me. For all of us.

"So, just to be clear, what did you learn when you broke through my magic?" Phox asked.

"Really?" I rolled my eyes.

"Just making sure I'm not giving unnecessary information. I've been bound to keep certain things to myself, and if my assumptions are wrong, then I'd be in deep shit for saying it first."

Fair enough, I thought.

"You're a dragon seer. The only one on Earth, I assume, since there is only one on Drakken. I met her, and her magic zapped into my body when we touched, which was how I recognized yours when I syphoned off the first layer of your spell on the door," I said.

Phox seemed perplexed about the information I'd given her. "She did that intentionally, and it means it's time for the dragons to come back."

"What's that supposed to mean?" Gemma asked.

"It means that no other was supposed to know what I was until the time was right. I knew with your dragon side that you had the highest chance of figuring it out, so I kept my distance, but Ophelia wouldn't have let you touch her if she didn't have a purpose for it."

I laughed. "So, you're saying the centuries-old dragon seer intended for me to knock her over, so I'd reach down to help her? And to think, I actually felt bad about that."

Gemma gasped. "You pushed an old lady to the ground? You previously left that part out."

I held my hands up, feigning innocence. "I did *not* push her. She grabbed my arm, and I defended myself."

"From a little old lady?" Gemma smirked.

"Whatever. It doesn't matter now. What matters is... how are we bringing the dragons back, and when can we do this, because Malina is in Drakken or almost there right this minute, and I'd rather not be left unprepared for when she comes back."

Phox leaned back in the chair and closed her eyes. She was a seer, after all, so I stayed quiet while she thought, hoping she had some sort of vision that would lead us to victory and not the one where Drakken would fall.

"This is what Drakken has been preparing for. Though, Malina has to be successful in her trip to Drakken. That doesn't mean lives will be lost, but we cannot stop her. Which is why it took so long for me to bring the others to your rescue when she had possession of you. I knew what she was going to do, and it needed to happen."

My chest rumbled. "You knew I was going to get kidnapped and tortured, and you did nothing about it?"

"Don't get your panties in a twist. I also knew you were going to survive, and you don't appear to have any permanent scars, so get over it. Life is hard, and then you move on. As I'm sure it's been explained to you, a seer cannot directly tell the future or interfere."

I rolled my eyes. "Yeah, I used to think it made sense. Not so much anymore."

"So, what do we do now?" Gemma asked as I continued to fume over Phox's revelations.

"Now, we wait for Malina to return. As long as she does, the future will stay as I've seen it, but things are always moving. Every decision a person makes has the chance to change their course."

So, there was a chance that Marek could stop Malina in Drakken, but it didn't sound like that was the best option for the many. Bringing her back and figuring out a way to stop her on our own land was best from what I got out of Phox's words.

"Am I a Doyen? Am I powerful enough to stop Malina on my own?"

Headmaster Stone had already refused my request to

strip my other abilities, because I was injured and my body needed time to heal before it went through a big change like that, but I was hopeful that I'd be back to tip-top shape by week's end.

"You are not a Doyen. They can only ever be those with original power gifted to them directly from Elora," Phox answered, but only one of my questions.

"What about stopping Malina?" I asked.

"Continue on your path. Follow your instincts and conquer your obstacles."

Shaking my head, ire began to build within me. "Do you ever tire of being a pain in the ass?" I snapped.

She grinned, but before she could respond, someone was pounding on the locked door.

I stood to see who it was, but Phox grasped my arm. "I mean it, Reagan. Follow your instincts. Nobody else's. Don't second-guess yourself, or we will all lose."

Her power raced through me. This time, it didn't burn, but it awoke something within me. A renewed strength and sense of purpose came over me as I felt my dragon stir stronger than ever.

After I nodded in understanding, she released me and removed the spell from the door. When she did, Enzo came tumbling into the room, purple-faced and fuming.

"What is going on?" he roared.

Gemma turned toward Phox. "He's always good for daytime drama. It's like watching the human soap operas."

I grinned. She and JayLeigh were so alike. If Gemma could let go of her resentment toward the dragon, then they'd likely be the best of friends. Maybe I needed to make that happen.

Enzo snarled, bringing my attention back to him. "Calm down before you hurt yourself. Phox is on our side. You know this, or you wouldn't have left me alone in her class. Now, quit acting like an idiot before she eats you for lunch."

"What's that supposed to mean?" he growled.

"It means you missed story time, and I need to catch you up, but not when you're acting like a child who didn't get his way. Let's go for a walk and, as long as you behave, then I can tell you what I know."

His eyes narrowed at me. "You're going to be the death of me, woman."

"Possibly." I shrugged before grabbing my bag, taking his hand, and pulling him from the room.

Before we exited, I turned back to Gemma when I realized she was still sitting. "Are you coming?"

She shook her head. "Some of us don't have cool dragon magic and we still have to go to our regular classes to grow stronger."

"Oh." I was more disappointed than I wanted to admit, but proud of her for continuing with the learning. She could have gotten a free pass on most of her classes if she really wanted, considering how involved in our current situation she was, but she wasn't taking the easy way out. No, my bestie was going to be a badass, and I couldn't wait to see her smash some heads in when the time came.

Enzo pulled on me, so I waved goodbye and went with him outside. We continued walking and were near the edge of the forest before either of us spoke. He had needed to cool off, and I'd needed the time to gather my thoughts.

Phox was very insistent that I listen to myself, which almost made me second-guess myself more, but I tried to focus on everything I had been working toward and what I wanted. When I broke it all down, I knew what needed to come next.

"So, what happened?" Enzo asked, considerably calmer than before.

"Professor Phox is a dragon seer."

He gaped at me, and I thought he was going to have something to say about that, but apparently, he wanted more information instead. I continued recapping what had been discussed before ending with what I wanted to do next.

"I'm going to request Headmaster Stone remove any foreign part of magic from my body this Friday. This means I will no longer have any elf and possibly witch magic within me."

I said the last part more to make sure he truly understood I wouldn't be like him anymore. While I doubted it would change his mind, I needed to be certain he truly knew what my decision meant.

"You're sure about this? Alistair made it sound like you could be seriously hurt in the process."

My hands cupped Enzo's cheeks. "I'm following my gut."

"Okay, then. I trust you."

With his words of acceptance, a determination settled within me. Having Enzo's full support fueled my fire even more. Come Friday, I was going to become who I was supposed to be, and I had never been more excited for anything in my life.

~

MY PREVIOUS ENTHUSIASM WAS TESTED WHEN Alistair fought me on removing any parts of my supernatural self.

"Raegan, I'm only looking out for your best interest. I've only done this twice before, and like I've said, it's not a pleasant experience. Are you sure it's worth it?"

"Headmaster Stone, with all due respect, I will not yield from my decision. I understand the consequences of my choice, and they are mine to own, so let me do that."

His face fell as he realized after an hour of trying to convince me otherwise, there was no changing my mind. "Fine, but when you cry for me to stop because you're writhing in pure agony, remember I tried to warn you and know I won't be able to halt the process. Once it's initiated, it has to be completed."

"I understand."

He turned to leave his office, grabbing supplies as he moved through the room. "I need a few minutes to finish preparing. Though, you're welcome to come in at any time."

Once the headmaster left the room, I turned toward Enzo who had remained silent, yet tense, during the entire conversation.

"Are you okay?" I asked.

"Honestly, no. I'm so far from okay I don't even know what I am, but I still support your decision and I'm not going to try to hold you back, so it doesn't really matter."

Grabbing both of his hands, I held them in mine. "It does matter, and I'm sorry for putting you through this, but it's my path and I have to follow it. I don't know where it leads, but I know it's the right choice."

He smirked. "Now you sound like a dragon seer with all your 'path' talk."

I shoved him away and stood from my seat. "Shut up and let's go."

He stood as well and grabbed my hand, spinning me

around into his chest as he lifted me up, so we were eye level. "I love you, Raegan, and no matter my fears, I believe in your choices. You can do this."

His lips crashed down on mine in an all-consuming kiss that had my toes curling. I kissed him back with just as much ferocity and squeezed tight around his neck. Our bond was stronger, but it had been held back by something. A part of me hoped stripping the pieces of me that didn't belong would not only wake my dragon but also help to solidify our connection.

When hands started roaming, a throat cleared, but we didn't pull apart. Then, something was thrown and hit right between us.

"What the hell?" Enzo snapped.

JayLeigh and Gemma stood side-by-side, giving each other fist bumps.

"Nice shot," JayLeigh said to her.

"Uh, when did this happen?" I asked, referring to their little womance they had going on.

Gemma tapped a finger against her chin mockingly. "Probably two nights ago when you were too busy shacking up with elf boy to spend time with your bestie. Talon was on guard duty and I was bored. JayLeigh had nothing better to do, either, so we figured why not. We talked a bunch of trash about you, and it brought us closer together. So, thanks for that."

A groan left my body as I realized how bad of an idea them being friends really was. For me, anyway. Based on previous conversations with Gemma, Talon had been keeping her so busy, I hadn't thought much more about trying to bring her and JayLeigh together.

Apparently, I wasn't needed to make that particular

friendship happen unless you counted me being their topic of conversation while bonding.

"I don't even want to know what was discussed," I said.

"Probably not." JayLeigh smirked. "There was a lot I witnessed while I followed you last summer. Things you probably didn't want other people to know, but oops, Gemma does now."

"Yep, time to go. Headmaster Stone is waiting." I grabbed Enzo's hand and headed toward the door not needing to hear anything else, but he paused when we passed by JayLeigh and Gemma.

"Care to fill me in later as well?" he asked the dragon.

She nodded. "I'd be delighted."

Letting go of his hand, I pushed away from him. "I hate you all."

Proceeding down the corridor without them, I did my best to ignore their laughs, considering they were at my expense, but I also smiled when they couldn't see me. Never once did I expect my life to turn out how it had. Knowing they all got along, even though they were opposites of each other in most ways, soothed a part of me that hadn't been settled in a very long time.

When we entered the council room, Fiona and Bennett were present as well. They'd still not filled Desmond's spot, but Alexander was off searching for potential candidates, so they'd hopefully be complete again soon.

The only person who wasn't going to be present that caused me disappointment was Aunt Jules. She'd try to make it back in time, but word of Malina and Drakken had spread through the masses. She was needed to assist with calming people down and gaining their alliance, should we need it.

Headmaster Stone approached me, handing me a vial

with a murky charcoal liquid in it without much of a greeting. "Drink this and then get in the box."

"That thing again? Really?" I hated that cage.

"It will help keep everyone around you safe, including yourself. I don't know how this is going to work exactly, so I'd rather err on the side of caution."

He had a point, so I downed the rancid-tasting liquid and strode over to the box. Before I stepped all the way in, Gemma yanked me back and pushed her finger into my chest.

"I've been through more hell during the last eighteen months since I met you than everything else combined before that. You have pushed me beyond my limits and frustrated the hell out of me."

"Uh, this is not helping me right now," I said, hoping she had a point with a positive spin.

She grinned. "*But* you have also shown me great strength and what true friendship is. So, if you die in here today, just know I will find your spirit and terrorize it for all time. You will never have peace."

Pulling her into a hug, I squeezed as tightly as I could. "I love you, too."

My body began to sway, and I knew it was time. Whatever Headmaster Stone had given me was working, and I needed to be in the box for him to begin.

Once Gemma was back with JayLeigh and Enzo, I blew them all a kiss and moved to the center of the cage. Bennett closed it up with his elf magic, then remained on my left, while Fiona took position on my right and Headmaster Stone stood directly in front.

My chest tightened with nerves, but I was trusting my instincts like Phox had said and praying she wasn't wrong.

Each of the council members placed their hands on the

glass and, as the process began, there was a ripping sensation coming from deep within my core. My head tilted back as the agony began, but all was forgotten as a voice spoke loud and clear within me.

I'm free.

CHAPTER TWENTY-TWO

The voice was firm, yet littered with exhilaration. I was trying to be as overjoyed as the dragon within me was, but my body was being torn to shreds. Anything she might have said after "I'm free" was lost to me.

If exorcisms were as real as supernaturals, then I was pretty sure I was experiencing what an innocent human would during one. Power was being pulled from all of my nerve endings, and it felt like a cow trying to fit through a mouse hole.

Screams tore from my throat as a fog swirled around me, cutting out my view of the others. My hands braced on the edges of the glass while I tried to take a few deep breaths and work through the pain.

It helped the tiniest of bits, but Headmaster Stone hadn't been kidding when he said this would be painful. Everything inside me felt like it was breaking.

It's going to be okay. Just don't—, the voice inside me whispered, but once again, the pain flared up and I didn't hear the rest of what she had to say.

My bones began breaking, and I fell to my knees, but

my head continued to rise as my body got bigger. Hopefully my dragon hadn't been telling me not to shift, because I had no control over whatever was happening to my body. The shift was coming whether I wanted it to or not.

The sound of glass breaking was heard clearly through my ears as the agony began to subside, but it was quickly replaced with panic.

I was no longer in my human form. I was a full dragon, and I had no control of my movements as my body slammed into walls and furniture. Alistair and Fiona just barely moved out of my way as I stumbled toward the window.

Enzo was yelling my name, but I didn't stop. A feeling of claustrophobia took over, and I needed to be free, to stretch my wings and truly be one with my dragon. It didn't matter that there was a wall made of stone in my way; all I cared about was getting outside as quickly as possible.

My head pointed and charged forward, and it wasn't until I broke through the wall that I saw the error of my actions.

I had no idea how to fly.

I got this, my dragon said, pushing forward to take control of the beast we were.

I had absolutely no problem taking a mental back seat while she drove. That was, until we came dangerously close to the ground and I had a minor heart attack before burgundy wings flapped, lifting us back into the sky.

Flying in this form was a completely different experience than in my half-shift. My eyesight was a thousand times better, as were my senses of smell and hearing. Remembering the spot Enzo used to take me all the time, I pictured it in my mind and urged my dragon to go there. It would give us a vantage point and some time to think.

She took her time soaring through the air, but I didn't

mind. There was no reason to be in a hurry, other than the fact everyone that had been in the room was probably freaking out. I'd probably have to apologize later.

When we landed on the mountain top, my dragon settled onto the ground, sighing in contentment.

This is better, she said.

I'm sorry you were trapped for so long. Were you always there, or not until I came to Shadow Veil? I asked.

I've always been there for you, but it wasn't until your magic started to show itself that I was able to really understand our predicament. I spent the last two years feeling like I was suffocating underneath your other magic.

I cringed, hating that she had felt that way, and even more so that the bitch of a sorceress had done that to us.

We're going to get our revenge. One way or another, we will stop Malina, I said.

You're right, but so are the others around you. We have to be patient. We only have one shot at this, and there is no room for error, she replied, standing up and stretching her wings out. *I've lived many lives, and she has power I've never seen before.*

You mean, you weren't born when I was? I asked.

In a way, I was. I don't remember most of my past lives, but a dragon spirit lives on forever. I've been around since the beginning of supernaturals.

Holy shit. I hadn't expected that answer, and I felt damn grateful to have been trusted with her spirit.

We should probably head back and deal with the chaos we left behind, huh? I asked.

She snorted, and smoke came out of her nose. *You get to deal with it. I'll be sitting on the sidelines for that particular conversation. None of them will want to talk to me.*

Damn it, she was right. I was on my own, but not really.

There was a serenity within me since my dragon was no longer confined. It was a bond different from mine and Enzo's that I knew could never be broken now that it was free.

She jumped off the edge of the mountain, and exhilaration filtered through from her to me as we freefell toward the ground, speeds increasing until the last moment when our wings moved and we were once again soaring.

Students were on the lawn outside the school, pointing and gasping at the sight of my dragon. They knew what I was, and I saw no point in hiding myself now that I could shift.

We landed a few yards in front of the crowd and, once our wings were put away, people crept closer. Only a select few brave ones came within touching distance, though nobody actually did.

When I saw Enzo pushing through the crowd with a laughing Gemma and JayLeigh behind him, I figured the show was over and it was time to clean up my mess.

Shifting back was easier than I thought, but still painful. Once I was back on two legs, Enzo's face turned a whole new shade of purple.

A slew of curse words spewed from his mouth as his shirt flew off and was suddenly coming over my head.

Oops, I hadn't learned how to shift and keep my clothes on, which meant I had just given a quarter of our school a nice peep show. I suddenly had multiple things to apologize for later.

Enzo picked me up, his body trembling with fury. He brushed past Gemma and JayLeigh without stopping as students around us catcalled and whistled at me.

My friends caught up to us, snickering at Enzo's expense.

"Don't worry, Raegan. Now, I can teach you all the things, and you won't lose your clothes near as often," JayLeigh said with delight.

Enzo's glare turned toward her. "She better *never* lose her clothes again in public."

"Or what?" she taunted.

"You don't really want to know." His voice was dark as power, thick and heavy, oozed off of him. I was pretty sure Enzo had finally hit his stress limit. I couldn't blame him. I'd pushed him quite a bit lately.

Even JayLeigh backed up a few inches, giving Enzo some space as he continued forward with me tight in his arms.

My dorm was closest, and he must have realized that as well, because instead of going to his like normal, he took the platform to Hybrid Hall. Most of the students were still in class, so there were no other interruptions on our way to privacy.

He set me down and then opened the door. Once we were inside, his palm pressed against the door, and the entire frame glowed.

"What did you just do?" I asked.

"Made sure nobody can bother us. I have very little control right now, and I need you alone. I don't know what happened, but when your dragon broke free, something within me snapped. Then, you were gone, and I might have added to your destruction."

Shit. I knew he was going to be pissed I took off, but I didn't realize it would have actually made him lose control. Enzo was almost always in control, and I didn't like being responsible for causing chaos in his life.

"I'm here now, and everything is going to be better from

here on out. I'm whole again, and we're going to find a way to defeat Malina."

His hands skimmed slowly over my arms and up my neck, before settling behind my head and gripping my hair. "No more talking."

With a single nod of agreement from me, that was all it took for him to move into action and for clothes to go flying through the room. As soon as our bodies became one, I knew the bond with Enzo was finally complete. The room was doused in a teal light that radiated from us brightly.

Burgundy and darker blues swirled within the teal, but I didn't pay attention to it for very long. Enzo stole every breath from me and had my full attention as he took us to heights I never knew possible.

OVER A MONTH LATER, WE WERE NEARING THE END OF April and school was finishing up. Word had come back from Marek that Malina arrived, but he couldn't track her down. Every time he thought he had her, she disappeared.

So, once again, school was ending early, but this time it was much more organized. A graduation had been planned for fourth-year students, and last year's class was also invited since they hadn't gotten one.

Enzo had eased up some as my training with JayLeigh came along. Since the days were shorter on Earth, it wasn't as strenuous as it had been on Drakken. Plus, having access to my dragon, who I learned was named Chelle, helped maintain my stamina considerably.

Apparently, dragons had their own names and *definitely* their own personalities. Chelle had been nearly as stubborn as me, but as we learned more about each other, we began to think and act more as one.

I'd mastered shifting and keeping my clothes. Talon had even taken a trip home to Drakken and brought back a couple of those awesome outfits JayLeigh wore that reminded me of Catwoman. Enzo's jaw about fell off the first time he saw me in it, which told me everything I needed to know, and I wore it more often than my academy uniform.

As I headed toward the upper atrium for another lesson with JayLeigh, I saw Gemma leaving one of her classes.

"Hey, you off to your next class?" I asked after we hugged.

"Actually, I'm done with my last two classes of the day for the remainder of the year, so I'm grabbing some food and then up to my room to finish one of my final assignments for Phox. Where are you headed?"

"To go train with JayLeigh in the atrium. Want to ditch the assignment and join us?"

She laughed. "Yeah, no. That crazy lady has kicked my ass enough over the last month. You have fun with that."

Not bothering to argue with her, we said our goodbyes and I went on my way. When I entered the training area, the glass ceiling was opened up and JayLeigh was tossing a dagger in the air.

"You're late." Without missing a beat, she threw the blade at my head, but I saw it coming and snatched it from the air.

"And you're a psycho."

"I won't argue that. Are you ready?" She grabbed another dagger from her hip holster.

"Yep. What are we working on up here?"

So far, I'd mastered shifting, communicating with my

dragon, throwing and dodging knives, evasive flying, and passed the basics in dragon history. Even though I wasn't taking the regular classes through Shadow Veil, JayLeigh had quite a knack for teaching, so I was getting in plenty of learning.

"Hand-to-hand combat. I thought you might prefer a better view from up here since you'll be on your back a lot."

She still acted as though she had little faith in me, but I had been working on hand-to-hand fighting with Enzo since I arrived at school. I wasn't worried about the day's lessons in the slightest.

"Alright, let's see how dirty dragons like to fight." I grinned.

JayLeigh needed no other sign to begin. She threw the other dagger in her hand, but this one wasn't aimed to hit me. It landed in the wall an inch past my ear. When she smirked, I wasted no time moving in.

She blocked every punch I threw, but I wasn't really trying yet. I was gauging her skills and how she'd fight against me now that I was full dragon, well, with a dash of witch as well.

Evidently, by the time I shifted during Headmaster Stone's spell, he hadn't quite finished, but it didn't matter if I still had my witch side since I got what I wanted out of the process.

Everything worked out how I had hoped, and the bonds I so badly needed with my dragon and Enzo were firmly in place.

After a solid ten minutes of staying even with her, I decided to up the ante. She was consistent with her moves, seeming to repeat most of them over in a different sequence each time. But still, they were all the same. I just had to figure out her pattern.

When I'd truly tested her defenses, I struck out hard and fast, landing a blow to her cheek.

"Oh, you think you're strong, do you? Watch this." JayLeigh countered with some leg kicks that were going to leave massive bruises, but they didn't slow me down.

I charged forward and went for her legs as well, but with my arms. Taking her by surprise, I was able to tackle her to the ground.

"So, how's that view you mentioned?"

She flipped me over just as easily. "I don't know, why don't you tell me?"

We began grappling on the floor, neither one of us staying on our back for long. Finally, I landed a solid punch to her kidney while she was on top of me, and we both laid on the ground panting, staring up at the sky.

"We could do this all day, and I don't think either of us would win," I said.

"You were keeping things from me and holding back before, my little protégé."

Rolling to my side, I sat up and reached for a bottle of water. She joined me and stole the water before I was done chugging.

"What next?" I asked.

"Well, no more of that, obviously. How about you pick?"

I'd never been able to pick before. She always just demanded I do whatever, and I did. I took mastering all skills seriously even if she drove me crazy on occasion. Okay, most of the time.

"How about—"

Before I could finish my thought, the doors blew open and Enzo frantically looked around until his eyes settled on us, still on the ground.

"What's wrong?" I asked.

He walked forward and kneeled before me, the bond between us flaring to life, but I ignored the distracting sensation, needing to know what was so important that he'd practically ripped the doors off their hinges.

"Malina's back," he ground out, and that was all it took for me to understand his ire.

JayLeigh and I were up on our feet within a second. "Like, she's back on Earth or back at Shadow Veil?" I asked, because there was a huge difference of urgency depending on the answer.

"Earth."

JayLeigh headed toward the exit. "I'll go see if Marek has e-mailed. Meet you in the headmaster's office when I'm done?"

Enzo shook his head. "Everyone is gathering in the council room where Raegan shifted. They just finished putting the wall back up, so we can use it again."

JayLeigh nodded in confirmation before taking off, and I cringed a little at the reminder of the council room. I had helped as much as I could on rebuilding until the construction crew kicked me out. Apparently, I was supposed to look before I threw things out the gaping hole I'd left, so I didn't hit anyone on the ground below.

"Is Jules back?" I asked. It had been weeks since she left for New Orleans, and I missed her like crazy. She was due back any day, and it would be nice to know she was close now that Malina was on Earth.

"Not that I've heard, but you can call her on the way. We need to get moving. Until Marek can confirm what happened in Drakken, we have to assume once she knows you escaped that she'll come for you."

"Go on ahead. I need to get out of these clothes and take a quick shower or nobody will want me present at the meeting." My body suit was covered in sweat, and I didn't imagine I was a pretty sight to see.

"I'm not leaving you now that she's back." There was true fear in his voice, so I didn't argue. Instead, I took his hand, and we hurried to my dorm.

Within fifteen minutes, I was changed into my favorite black leather pants with my school shirt and tie. It wasn't an official meeting, but Enzo was in his uniform, so I figured I should be, too.

I had called Jules on our way to my room, but she didn't answer, so I sent her a text instead. On the way to the council room, I sent another one since she hadn't responded to the first.

"Do you think Jules is okay on her own in New Orleans?" I asked Enzo as we traversed the hallways.

"New Orleans is probably the safest place for her, to be honest. The magic there is almost as strong as Shadow Veil's shield, and there are dozens of elders there from shifter packs and witch covens. Even vampires prefer the city."

Huh, that made me even more interested to visit my aunt's hometown. But first, Malina had to be dealt with. We had no idea what she was able to accomplish in Drakken. Whatever it was, it wasn't good for us.

"I just don't like not hearing from her. Would be nice to have a confirmation she was okay. I wouldn't put it past

Malina to figure out a way to use anyone I love as leverage against me."

Enzo squeezed tighter on my hand. "It's going to be fine. Malina won't lay a hand on anyone you love again."

His words didn't make me feel any better, but I did my best to put those thoughts aside. I needed to be completely present for the meeting. This was when we'd decide on how and when to act against Malina. A few people preferred to remain on the defense and let Malina bring the fight to us, but I wanted to move on the offense.

We had no idea how powerful she could get with every move she made. She was a Doyen, a being we really didn't know much about. We needed to act before it was too late. Plus, I still had faith there was a chance I could end her without Marek. His blood ran through my veins, and I was counting on it for our success.

As we entered the meeting, the council was already present, including Alexander. When my eyes scanned the rest of the room, I let out a squeal and ran toward the unexpected guest.

"I was just stressing about you. Why didn't you tell me you were here?" I asked Jules as I hugged her tightly.

"This was more fun. You hardly had time to chat while I was gone, and you were training. Surprising you sounded like a better idea. Alexander brought me back with him after his visit to New Orleans."

"Do you know if it went okay? Did he find any solid candidates to replace Desmond? We could use any and all help, especially now."

"Looks like the meeting is starting," she said without answering my questions. "Let's take a seat."

I shared a glance with Enzo, because Jules was acting strange. Something had happened in New Orleans, and I wondered if she'd maybe hooked up with the powerful vampire. I'd have to pry her for information later.

Once we were seated, I counted twelve people present, including myself and Enzo. The others were Alistair, Fiona, Bennett, Alexander, Jules, Gemma who'd just snuck in with JayLeigh and Talon, Professor Phox, and Professor Melnier, who I recognized as the guy I had mistaken for Enzo in the headmaster's office my first few days back.

When everyone was settled and greetings had been made, Alistair stood to speak at the head of the new table that had been brought in. It was the only piece of furniture in the room since the wall had just been repaired.

"Thank you all for gathering so quickly. I'd like to hear from JayLeigh before we begin deciding on how to proceed, unless anyone else has something pertinent they'd like to share."

My gaze went to Alexander. He'd been the only one away from the academy recently, but he remained silent, so JayLeigh began.

"I had a message from Marek. He was never able to track down Malina while she was on Drakken, but he could sense her power as she moved through the lands. It decreased by the day, and she was definitely receiving help from Onyx.

"Talon was able to present the evidence for Sylas's betrayal and Onyx's involvement in it all. There will be a vote held to remove Onyx from a position of power and decide his fate. It might have even been done by now, but there were no other updates since then."

"Did you ask Marek if he was willing to help now? His world is compromised. He should be just as worried as the rest of us," Fiona said.

"I did ask, but he hasn't responded yet. Drakken is

fragile right now. Even if he now wanted to help, leaving our world with no leadership could cause just as many problems for the dragons," JayLeigh replied.

"I beg to differ," Alexander cut in. "Coming back from the chaos of broken leadership is a hell of a lot easier than watching supernaturals die, because that's what will happen to those who go against Malina if we can't stop her."

JayLeigh grimaced. "I understand, but I cannot control my king. Though, I have every faith he will do what he believes is best for our people."

"Sometimes, a king needs to be challenged," Alexander added.

"Then, I welcome you to challenge the dragon king," JayLeigh retorted, effectively ending that part of the conversation.

"Very well, JayLeigh. Thank you for your updates, and please inform us as soon as you hear back from Marek." He paused, seeming to gather his thoughts. "We need to decide if we're going to wait for Malina or attack first. We have to keep in mind, if we bring the fight to Shadow Veil, yes, we might have a small advantage, but we risk an entire school full of irreplaceable history being destroyed."

Fiona stood. "What do we have going for us if we make the first move? We are short a council member and many more powerful supernaturals if we want any hope of restraining her again. Having Marek at our side to destroy her once and for all was our best shot."

Alistair's eyes moved to me. "We may not have Marek, but we have his heir, and it will have to be enough. We do not know the extent of Raegan's powers, but she has come a long way this year and I have faith she will be able to help restrain Malina, should the opportunity present itself."

"What about an army?" Professor Melnier asked as

Fiona sat back down. "We know Malina has been collecting a horde of supernaturals to stand with her. The twelve of us can't take them all on our own. The casualties would be too high."

Alexander glanced at Jules, and she nodded, seeming to give him permission for whatever it was he wanted to say. "While I was in New Orleans, I spoke with several leaders within the area. They would like to join us should we move in on Malina."

"How many of them?" Headmaster Stone asked.

"Almost all of them."

Several of the council members gaped at Alexander. I didn't understand the severity of the statement, because I knew very little about New Orleans, but I was obviously missing something big.

"Why would they do that? They've always kept to themselves," Professor Phox said.

"Because we have made an offer for Jules to join the council and she is one of them. Should she accept, they will do everything they can to stand behind her."

My head snapped toward my aunt. "You're going to accept, right?"

She raised a hand, pausing any further discussion. "That's not what we're here to discuss. Just know that no matter what I choose, you will still have their support."

"Then we attack first, as soon as we know Malina's location," JayLeigh said.

"Let's vote on the matter. Remember, there is no wrong choice. Follow your instincts, and whatever the decision is, we will *all* support it." Alistair snapped his fingers, and a clay bowl appeared with green smoke rising from it.

"What's that?" I whispered to Enzo.

"It's how votes are cast. Next, a pen and paper will

appear in front of you. You'll drop it into the smoke, and the votes will be counted. Nobody will know who chose what, just what the majority was."

Huh. That was interesting and I liked it. Nobody should have to feel guilty for their choices. We all had a right to our own opinions without judgement.

When the paper appeared, I had no hesitation with my answer. I quickly jotted it down and folded my paper in half while we waited for the bowl to make its way over to us.

My hands cupped the rough exterior when it was my turn, and I was surprised to find it cool to the touch. The green smoke had a slight smell that reminded me of pine needles, but I didn't want to take too long with it, so I tossed my paper in and passed the unique object to Jules, who was on my right.

Once all votes had been cast, Alistair covered the top of the bowl with both hands until no more green smoke could be seen. "When I lift my hands, the decision will be made and there is no going back. Blue will mean we stay and wait while red means we seek Malina out and bring the fight to her."

Every eye in the room was on the bowl as Alistair removed his hands. Tension filled the room as red smoke filtered through the top.

"It's decided. If you truly have a problem with the decision, please come see me and we will work something out. For now, we will let graduation pass, and once all of the students have left by week's end, we will head out to meet with the others from New Orleans before advancing on Malina."

"What if she's not where we think like before, when she had Raegan? Without Phox's information, it would have taken days to find her," Fiona said.

"Then we search for as long as it takes." With Alistair's final words, people began to disperse from the table.

A plan was set, and we just had to wait for a few key things to happen. My pulse was beating hard as the thought of Malina's terror finally coming to an end. Even if we couldn't kill her, hopefully we could at least contain her until we could convince Marek to do the job for us.

I'd hound him every day for as long as I needed if that was what it took.

Gemma and Jules met us outside the council room while JayLeigh and Talon disappeared to wherever it was they had their secret meetings.

"How about a girl's night before everything gets crazy?" Gemma suggested.

Glancing up at Enzo, I worried about his sanity if I said yes, but he nodded first. "Only if you stay in my dorm. It's safer than any of yours."

"Um, a room with views and a better TV? I don't think that will be a problem, as long as you're not there. No offense or anything, but you're not a girl," Gemma replied.

"And happily so. Raegan can let you in, and I'll stay away until midnight." When Gemma and Jules glared at him, he added, "Okay, one. Final offer."

Jules patted him on the chest. "You've come a long way." Then, she glanced at me. "Good job, Raegan."

Enzo opened his mouth to say something, but I covered it. "Just pretend it was a compliment and move on. It can only get worse if you don't." His tongue darted, licking my entire palm. "You're disgusting," I grumbled.

"And you're lucky I love you. Now, hurry up and go before I change my mind."

None of us needed to be told twice. Squished between Gemma and Jules, we made our way toward the platform.

Enzo had stayed behind, likely to discuss further strategy with the headmaster, because his mind was constantly on anything that had to do with keeping me safe.

Once we were settled in Enzo's room and Gemma quit gushing over how huge it was, we ordered food and put a movie on. While we waited for our treats, the movie was just background noise as I grilled both my best friend and aunt.

"You two have a lot of explaining to do," I began and turned toward Gemma. "You first. What's happening with you and Talon? He's like sex on a stick, and you've been completely tight-lipped about your relationship with him."

Jules laughed at my reference, but I paid no attention to her. Gemma had been avoiding the topic for weeks, and this was the first time I really had her alone without Enzo lurking around the corner.

"There isn't much to tell. He's only here for a short time, so I'm trying not to get attached." She shrugged, but I knew the words were forced and hurting her.

"You do remember why Enzo was able to go with me to Drakken, right?" I asked.

She nodded.

"Well, keep that in mind. If Talon is really the one and you two happen to bond, then there's no reason why you wouldn't be able to join him in Drakken."

"Didn't you and Enzo bond right away, though? You always had the weird glowing sex experiences. We don't have anything like that." For someone usually so blunt, I was surprised when her face blushed, but I could tell it'd been on her mind for a while.

"I would assume not everyone is the same. Give it time and maybe talk to JayLeigh. She'd know more than me.

Hell, she's the one who knew Enzo had the dragon bits in him."

A flicker of hope appeared on her face as she smiled. "Thanks, Raegan."

"I'm always available to you. Even if it doesn't seem like it with everything else going on."

When I was satisfied Gemma was feeling better about Talon, I moved the conversation to Jules. "So, are you going to accept? Why would you have any hesitation about taking the council position? It's a pretty big offer."

She huffed. "Exactly. My whole life would change. I have plans for a future, and if I accept, then I'll be tied down to Shadow Veil for decades. I want a mate and a life outside of this school, but my options for that will be severely limited if I choose to say yes."

Oh, damn. I hadn't thought of that. None of the council members had significant others, but I never questioned it.

"You're right," I said. "Take your time deciding and do what's best for you. You've already given up the last two years of your life. It's not fair to ask more from you. Was visiting home everything you hoped it would be?"

Her face lit up in a way I'd never seen before. "There is nothing like New Orleans. Regardless of what happens, we will make it there this summer. I have so many people I want you to meet."

She continued to tell me about the packs and covens, along with the shops owned by supernaturals. I could picture it all so clearly, and it was further motivation to make sure Malina didn't come out on top.

We all had a lot more life to live, and she wasn't going to take that away from any of us.

Not if I had anything to do with it.

CHAPTER TWENTY-FOUR

Within five days, all students were gone, including a very stubborn Peyton and Finley. They were appeased when Gemma and I had at least explained more to them than the other students, but still pissed they couldn't stay.

Once things were settled, all we were waiting on before we headed out to find Malina was a pack from New Orleans to arrive. The council felt more comfortable heading out in groups, so our search would go by faster.

The tracking spell that was previously used was put into action again and narrowed down Malina's location to somewhere near Portland, Maine, which made me laugh since I was from Portland, Oregon. I had always wanted to visit there; unfortunately, there would be no time for sightseeing on this trip.

"So, how much longer until shifters get here?" JayLeigh asked while a group of us were eating lunch outside.

"They're due to arrive tonight, so we'll leave first thing tomorrow morning," Enzo answered.

"About damn time. I was going stir crazy without anything to do. It's no fun sparring with Raegan anymore."

I smirked. We were on equal playing fields now, except when it came to flying. Her dragon had a hell of a lot more experience, which was more my fault than Chelle's, but we were catching on quick enough. We'd be an expert dragon team in no time.

That's right, Chelle chimed in.

She was always there, right beneath the surface, a steady presence to keep me motivated and moving forward. Even though it had been just over a month since we connected, I felt like I had known her all my life.

Gemma leaned up from where she had been laying on Talon's lap. "I'm up for some more training if you're bored. Talon has been working with me, but I know he's holding back." The way his face lit up as she smiled at him told me he felt just as strongly for her as she did for him.

My head shook hard. "No way. You don't want to voluntarily ask for that kind of punishment."

"If you can take her, then I'm sure I can handle it." Gemma glared, and I wasn't sure if she was truly offended or teasing.

My hands went up in mock surrender. "I'll be sure to remind you of this moment when you're crying because you can't walk after one of her 'lessons'."

She flipped me off, and then it suddenly clicked. My bestie wanted to keep up with dragons in case things continued with Talon, and I suddenly felt like an asshole. So, I added, "I'm happy to help, too. Might be better to start with someone who actually cares if you live rather than the psycho dragon."

She grinned from ear-to-ear. "I'd love that. Both of you

can teach me, so that I know Raegan isn't taking it too easy on me, either."

Stubborn girl.

Once we were all done eating, the guys took our stuff back inside while the three of us stayed at the table. Just as JayLeigh began to convince Gemma that there was no time like the present to begin training, a loud bang sounded at the front gates.

"What the hell was that?" JayLeigh asked as we all got to our feet to run that way.

"I don't know, but we're about to find out," I replied.

"Enzo's going to be so pissed." Gemma laughed.

Yeah, he was, but only if it was something bad. Plus, the noise was so loud that they had to have heard it inside, so I fully expected them to be right behind us.

We sprinted to the front entrance and didn't immediately see anything. Just as we began to turn around to search further down, a big-ass dragon appeared in our line of sight.

"Marek," JayLeigh whispered in surprise.

I hadn't seen him in his dragon form while I'd been in Drakken, so I didn't recognize him, but I should have with his burgundy scales just a few shades deeper than mine. The biggest difference between our two dragons was that his had three significant black spikes on his head, along with a near-perfect black stripe from the top of his head down to the end of his barbed tail, whereas mine only had two smaller spikes and no stripe. Though Chelle's head wasn't something to be feared, her tail was. She was quick to flick it and, while the barbs weren't long, there were more than a handful of them, making it easier to hit whatever target we aimed at.

Marek shifted when he got to the arched entrance and walked through to meet us, wearing the men's version of the bodysuit I loved. Instead of a one piece, his consisted of loose black pants and a tight shirt that showed just how powerful his human form was as well. "Are you okay?" he asked, looking between the three of us.

"Yeah, why?" I asked.

"Malina's last message I received said since I wasn't willing to give up my home without a fight then she'd take something else of mine away. I left Drakken as soon as I found out. She intends to kill you."

"That makes no sense. She needs me to get back and forth to Drakken. She took one of my scales to get through. I'd assume she needs more if she wants to do it again, unless she bonds with a dragon," I said.

JayLeigh shook her head. "She wouldn't need you if she was able to get her hands on a dragon she didn't care about. One who was easier to control. One without a team willing to fight against her."

Gemma growled. "Did that bitch steal a dragon while she was there?"

Marek nodded at her, seeming somewhat confused, since he didn't know who Gemma was. "Yes, she took Joren."

"Damn it," JayLeigh hissed.

Marek's face fell. "I know. Now, she's coming for Raegan, and you all need to prepare if you haven't already done so."

Enzo and Talon showed up just as Marek said that last part. Both looked rather furious that we'd taken off without them, but they were smart enough to hold their tongues and not yell at us in front of the dragon king.

"We're prepared, but half of our group was supposed to meet us in Maine," Enzo said.

"There's no point. I can all but guarantee she's already

headed here. She had a full day in Drakken for a head start. I didn't get her message until we realized Joren was missing. He lived alone, but still, it took longer than it should have."

JayLeigh grasped his shoulder. "Don't take the blame for this. Malina did this to all of us. We'll figure out a way to stop her."

"Yes, we will. So, come on. I'll show you to Headmaster Stone, and we can change our plans."

His face fell. "As long as it's not too late."

My arm hooked around his as I led him back to the academy. It was a small gesture, but it seemed to cheer him a little as he grinned at me. We needed more positive thoughts if we had any chance of making sure nobody ended up dead.

~

TWO HOURS LATER, THE FIRST GROUP FROM NEW Orleans arrived and the sun was just beginning to set. Enzo was off showing Marek to his room, and I was working with JayLeigh and Gemma.

While I hadn't been on board with Gemma getting her ass kicked right away, JayLeigh reminded me I was only increasing her risk of getting hurt by holding her back. The fight was coming, and we all needed to be ready.

Talon had promised to stay by her side the entire time, but shit happened, and if my best friend was killed in a battle that I felt partially responsible for, I wasn't sure I'd ever move past it. I needed her to be okay, so as I watched JayLeigh kick her ass up and down the field, I smiled instead of grimaced.

A vampire my aunt knew from New Orleans even ended up stepping in to teach her a few tricks about tapping into her speed she never used. My hope increased considerably when I saw how willing everyone was to help each other while we waited for Malina's pending arrival.

Enzo finally joined us, wrapping his arms around my waist from behind. "Did I miss anything?"

"Nothing much. Is Marek settled?" I asked.

"Yeah, though he'll be back out here shortly. I saw Alistair as well. The rest of the groups from New Orleans are on their way. Some are spreading out to cover the surrounding routes to Shadow Veil to be lookouts, and the rest should be here by morning."

"Good. Now we just have to hope Malina doesn't show before then with her own army. We're lucky Marek came when he did."

He nodded as we continued to watch the groups around us, all of which seemed excited to be back at Shadow Veil. Conversations filtered through the air about memories of the school most of them had attended.

When the sun fully set and the moon rose high in the sky, there was still no sign of Malina, but the tracking spell had confirmed whatever signature of hers we were picking up was moving in our direction.

"Why don't we take turns sleeping?" Enzo suggested when he caught me staring at Gemma curled up on Talon, pretty much dead to the world after her training sessions.

"Too much adrenaline pumping through me to sleep right now," I replied.

"At least make me feel better by resting? Even if you don't sleep, try to shut down your mind for a bit. It will only help you when you need to be focused later."

He was right. I was no good to anyone if I was exhausted from being up all night. "Promise, if I do fall asleep that you'll wake me if there is any news?"

His lips pressed to my forehead. "I promise."

Accepting that would have to be good enough, I leaned my head against him and closed my eyes, but it was a long while before any thoughts ceased. By the time I thought I had a chance at falling asleep, the vamp who had been helping Gemma blew by us and stopped in front of the headmaster.

"Five miles out, a horde of supes are heading right for the academy."

"Thank you, Zeke. Please, pass the information along to the other group leaders. We'll drop the shield and prepare," Headmaster Stone responded.

Marek was at our side in an instant. "Are you ready?"

"As we can be," I answered.

"Good. I'll be looking for Malina as soon as they arrive. I won't let her get her hands on you again, I promise."

I took his hand in mine. "I know you'll do your best, but you can't blame yourself for any part of what may happen tonight. This is all on Malina and we need to focus on taking her down, not what could happen."

"I'm sorry I wasn't here sooner. I could have stopped all of this, but I let the seer's words bring fear. I should have been a better leader."

JayLeigh appeared from thin air like she loved to do and punched him harder than was probably necessary in the chest. "Uncle Marek, if I ever hear you say anything like that again, I will cut you."

It was the first time I'd heard her speak to him with any sort of disrespect, and the wide eyes and shock that appeared on Marek's face was totally worth it.

"Yes, my precious niece. I'll do better," he finally answered.

"That's better. Now, let's go take our places. Not much

longer until they arrive." JayLeigh crossed her arms, waiting for the rest of us to begin moving.

Before we could get very far into the crowds, orbs of light flew through the sky, and everyone around us scattered to avoid them. Enzo grabbed my hand and we ran together. As soon as the orbs touched the ground, they blew up like grenades, and panic ensued.

"Well, I guess she doesn't want to chat first," Gemma grumbled from behind me.

When I glanced back to make sure everyone was okay, I saw Gemma tucked into Talon's side with a little bit of debris dusting her face, but no scratches. JayLeigh had gone into a partial shift, so I couldn't really tell if she'd been hit by anything, but I knew for certain she was pissed off from her glowing eyes and the rumbles coming from her chest.

There was a cut on my arm from a rock, but nothing that wouldn't heal within a few minutes. So, I disregarded it as our smaller group formulated a plan.

"Talon, Gemma, and JayLeigh, you three come in from the east side of the gates while Enzo, Raegan, and I take the west. Someone let out a sharp whistle the moment you spot Malina," Marek said, taking charge like the king he was.

"What about Jules and the council?" I asked. My head turned in every direction, but I'd yet to spot them.

"They were in Alistair's office when I came back outside, but I'm sure they heard the explosion and they'll be here soon," Marek answered.

No other words were spoken as we turned back toward the front gate, which was nothing more than a pile of stone, and saw the horde of people coming toward us. Glancing around at our own army, I took a small amount of peace from the fact that the chaos had died down and everyone was gathering into groups like we had.

Marek had surprised me earlier with the dagger I'd used in the forest on my last day in Drakken. He said it was mine now and to use it during the battle. There was no arguing from me when he'd given it to me, and his nod of approval when I'd pulled it from its sheath as we moved in told me he was pleased as well.

"Whatever happens, don't let anything separate us," Enzo said next to me.

"I'll do my best," I replied, unwilling to promise him something I wasn't sure I could do. If someone needed my help and Enzo was otherwise engaged, then I'd do what I needed to assist the others who had come to help us.

His teeth ground together at my response, but he knew better than to argue with me, especially as scavengers, vampires, elves, and shifters charged for us.

As I raised my dagger, I completed my half-shift, and Chelle was right there with me. Her mind was already processing the scene and the best course of action. Even though I was still mostly in my human form, Chelle had lived many lives, so I trusted her instincts explicitly.

Move right, she demanded, and I complied. *Scavenger to your left, bear to your right.*

We were one as I dissolved the scavenger and engaged the bear. Enzo was at my side, handling another elf, but I wasn't worried about him as I focused in on the bear.

He was easily seven feet tall in a half-shifted form, but he didn't seem to have nearly as much control over his beast as I did. The human part of him seemed to be fighting against the bear, and I wondered how many shifters were struggling with their other halves. If they were all like Chelle, then I'd bet most of those who were siding with Malina would be having one hell of a time staying in control.

My talons raked across my attacker's stomach, but not deep enough for a fatal injury. As he righted himself, I could see his body shrinking back to normal size and the bear part of him fading away.

"You're all going to die today," he snarled at me. "Malina will reign supreme, and we will all be free to live at the top of the food chain."

Swiping my dagger at him, I laughed. "You're an idiot." The dagger had only been the distraction, though, as my fist plowed into the side of his head.

The shifter swayed from the impact, so I took advantage of his disorientation and hit two more times. I wasn't aiming to kill if I didn't have to. If I could knock someone out, I would. Malina had poisoned these supernaturals' minds. Most of them likely deserved a second chance.

Once the bear was down for good, Enzo joined me and pressed his hand to the guy's head.

"What did you do?" I asked as we continued to move further into the battle.

"Keeps him in a deep sleep."

His words reminded me of a witch spell I'd learned the year before about deep sleeps, one Desmond had used on me when I was taken to Malina. I'd have to try it on my next opponent, considering I still had some witch left in me.

Gemma and Talon could be seen about twenty feet in front of us. She was bleeding from a hit to her head, but there was a fierce determination in her eyes that told me she probably had no idea it was even there.

When I gazed around their area, I caught where her focus had been, and it was on Sylas. The bastard had harmed the wrong girl, and he was going to find out how revenge felt by the end of the battle. I wished I could have helped her, but Talon was at her back, so I didn't worry about it for too long.

Marek was nowhere to be found. He seemed to have disappeared when I'd been fighting the bear, but all thoughts of him disappeared as my eyes landed on Desmond.

Red tinted my vision as I thought about all the wrongs he'd done, all of the selfish choices he'd made and needed to pay for. This would be one attacker I would have no mercy for, another who would learn that he'd crossed the wrong girl.

Witch incoming, Chelle said, reminding me that while my target was only a few yards away, I still had to go through several others to get to him.

The woman was tossing magical spells intended to hurt me like she had a never-ending supply. Thankfully, my badass dragon suit deflected most of them, but the ones that hit exposed skin burned like a mother.

"You will die for your betrayal to our queen!" she yelled as she barreled right into me, knocking me off my feet.

"First, crazy lady, Malina is no queen. Second, get the hell off of me!" With both hands braced against her gut, I pushed with all of my force.

The witch flew backward and landed in a tangled mess of arms and legs a few feet from me. As I stood, I retracted my claws, so the psycho wouldn't bleed out when I wrapped my hand around her throat.

She moved to throw another spell at me, but I kicked her in the ribs and bent over to grab her. As my grip tightened, I tapped into my dragon strength and lifted her up. Her arms flailed as she struggled to breathe, but I didn't loosen my hold until she was on the verge of passing out.

"*Dormito.*" I whispered the spell into her ear before

dropping her to the ground like a bag of rocks. She was stronger than I had previously given her credit for as I watched her fight the spell, but it wasn't enough.

When I was sure she was out, I searched for Desmond again, but I couldn't find him. Turning around, I saw Enzo was headed my way. He opened his mouth to yell something, but it was too late.

My eyes saw stars from the impact of whoever had punched me.

Reagan, I'm so sorry. I didn't sense him, Chelle cried in my head, but I shook her off. Nobody was perfect, and our attacker was good at what he did. She wasn't to blame. He was.

Before I turned around, my eyes caught the sight of Enzo being ambushed, confirming I was on my own for the time being, but that wouldn't stop me.

Desmond was going to die.

CHAPTER TWENTY-FIVE

Desmond's cold, calculating eyes watched me as I decided on my next move. Chelle was itching to shift and finish him, but that was too obvious, and I was afraid he had a plan for that. He had coveted my dragon scales, and I had no desire to give him access to them.

"Your mother isn't here to save you now," he taunted.

"I never needed Malina's help to stop you, and she's certainly no mother to me," I spat as we circled each other.

"Oh, that's right. Lara, the stuck-up sorceress, is the one you considered mommy. That bitch shouldn't have rejected me for her weak husband. It was one of my greatest pleasures when I got my revenge."

"When you what?" My skin stretched tight as fury took over, and I almost lost control of my half-shift.

"That's right. I killed your parents and now, I'm going to kill you, but not before I take what I need from you. I can't trust Malina, and you're my back-up plan. Now, be a good little dragon and shift."

Just as I had previously assumed, Desmond expected me to shift and I might have been able to hold back from doing so if he hadn't admitted to killing my parents. As rage continued to bubble up within me, I had no control left.

Don't worry, he won't live long enough to touch us, Chelle said as my bones broke and adjusted to our dragon form.

"That's right. Do as your told, Raegan," Desmond goaded as he backed away to avoid getting crunched by my larger form.

When I was fully shifted, we moved toward him, not wanting to prolong the inevitable. Desmond was going to die by my dragon. I refused to let him get away with murdering my parents and everything else he had done to the supernatural world.

His hands began to rub together, and I thought it was because he was excited, but I should have known better. It was too late by the time I realized he was cooking up a spell.

As his hands pulled apart and faced my dragon, there was a magnetic pull that was tugging painfully at my scales. Desmond had no mercy whatsoever as his power increased and five or more scales tore from my chest.

Chelle roared in pain as her head reared up and fire came out of her mouth. I would have loved to use that same fire on Desmond, but there were too many friendlies around us to risk burning them all. We were going to have to fight through the pain and crush him.

Hurts, Chelle barely managed to say.

I know, so let's knock him on his ass. Use your tail, I replied.

She did as I suggested, but our reaction was too slow, and Desmond evaded the blow.

"The more I pull, the weaker you'll be. Give up now and it won't hurt as much," he jeered.

"Never," my voice boomed from my dragon.

We stumbled forward, hoping to gain momentum, but Desmond was right. Several more scales had been torn from my body and we were slowing down, though I wouldn't give up until I had nothing left in me.

But, as despair began to filter through me as the agony rose and Chelle's continued apologies sounded in my head, I began to lose hope. Enzo still hadn't come to assist me, and I had no idea how he was faring against those who had ambushed him. My dragon knees buckled in pain as we lowered to the ground in obvious defeat.

"That's right. Bow to your master," Desmond said.

"You're nobody's master. You're a disgrace to all supernaturals," JayLeigh's voice sounded through the air, but she was nowhere in sight. She really needed to teach me that damn trick.

Desmond was knocked to the grass, and his spell broken. The force that had been tugging on my dragon was no longer present, but we were still weak and barely managed to stand back up on all fours.

JayLeigh's half-shifted form finally made an appearance as she dragged Desmond by the neck toward me. "You want to do the honors?" she asked.

"Hell, yes," I responded with a renewed sense of strength as adrenaline pumped through my dragon.

JayLeigh tossed the worthless sorcerer in front of me and, before he could right himself, my front foot landed on his chest with force.

"You won't win. Even if you kill me, you can't stop her," he wheezed.

"You killed my parents. This has nothing to do with *her*," I snapped as I continued to press my weight on him.

His eyes widened as his mouth opened to scream when my talons dug their way into his sides, but something didn't sit right with me. I was no better than him if I stood there and watched him slowly die.

There was no way I'd actually bite him, and the thought of stepping on him fully just creeped me out, imagining the feeling of snapping bones beneath me, so I glanced up at JayLeigh. "Finish him."

"Gladly," she said as she arched her sword and brought it down into Desmond's chest when I pulled my foot back to give her enough room.

There was no joy brought to me when Desmond took his last breath. Killing him didn't bring my parents back, but it did mean he couldn't harm another, which would be enough to help me move forward.

Alright, Chelle. I need my human form back, but I still need your senses. You ready to find Malina?

Find Marek, and you'll find Malina, she said, and I agreed. I hadn't seen him since the beginning of the battle and hoped he was still okay.

When I shifted back to my human form, I still tapped into my dragon strength, but not quite a half-shift until Chelle had time to recover from the loss of so many scales. She wasn't alright by any means and needed the time out from too many physical movements.

Before going to find Malina, I searched for Enzo. Behind me was a pile of bodies, most of whom I assumed were knocked out, but there was a lot of blood, so I couldn't be certain. Though, none of them were Enzo and that was most important.

He was nowhere to be found, and I was starting to panic, because he was the one who insisted we didn't separate.

"Do you know where Enzo or Marek are?" I asked JayLeigh when she stepped next to me.

"Marek was headed outside the walls last time I saw him, and I haven't seen Enzo at all since we originally separated."

Shit, this was not good. Too many of us were scattered around. I couldn't help them all, and as much as I wanted to make sure Enzo was okay, he was a big boy and my desire to find Malina won out.

"Let's search out Malina, then. I'm sure she's cowering around here somewhere while her army sacrifices themselves for her," I spat.

"They're not the only ones losing their lives," JayLeigh said with despair in her voice.

It would have been stupid of me to think we'd all survive this battle, but I wasn't ready to face the deaths of our own. When it was over, I'd mourn, but for now, I couldn't afford the emotional effects those thoughts would bring.

JayLeigh tossed me my dagger. "You dropped this."

Taking the blade, I tucked it back into its holster on my hip. "Thanks."

As we moved toward the crumbled gates, I caught sight of Gemma and Talon. Tension eased from my body when I saw them still together and keeping each other safe. My eyes made contact with Gemma's and she nodded toward her left. Glancing, I grinned when I saw Sylas's prone frame. I had no idea if he was dead since his eyes were closed, but I wouldn't feel sorry if he was.

I kept moving, not needing to be a distraction to her if I couldn't help. Hopefully it wasn't too much of me to hope that Talon would continue to keep her safe.

JayLeigh pointed over behind the academy building. "Over there. Let's hurry."

She took off at a full sprint, and I followed after her, barely keeping up in my still-weakened state.

I'm here if you need me, Chelle said.

You just keep resting until I really need you. Desmond didn't play fair, and you can't tell me you're not in pain, I replied, but she didn't respond. I was right, and there wasn't much else to say.

When we finally arrived at the back side of the school, my brain took a moment to really understand what I was seeing. Fallen gargoyle statues lay broken in pieces on the ground. The main tower of the school was blown to bits. There were craters in the dirt from more explosions, and bodies lay every ten feet or so all around the area.

So many deaths that could have been prevented if it wasn't for one covetous woman.

What surprised me most was seeing Enzo standing with Marek, but I didn't have time to think about why he was over there before Malina caught sight of me and JayLeigh.

"Ah, our dear daughter has finally joined us, and we're all together for the first time. How exciting is that, Marek?" Malina's voice was filled with false joy as she narrowed her eyes at the dragon king.

"Don't touch her," he snarled, taking a step toward me.

Malina sneered. "Be careful, old king. I'm not sure how much more you can take before you have no choice but to bow before me."

"I will die before that ever happens," he growled.

"So be it." Malina threw a spell at Marek, and JayLeigh winced at my side.

"What do we do?" I asked. "Just move in and fight?"

She shook her head. "Marek has a plan. I just need to figure it out."

"You sure seem to say that a lot. What if you're wrong?"

"Then, you'll be the new dragon queen and I'll owe you a life of servitude," she replied.

Hell no. I wasn't going to be the queen of anything. JayLeigh could hope all she wanted that Marek could handle things on his own, but I wasn't taking that risk.

Searching out Enzo once again, I couldn't get a read on him at all. He held his hand up for me to stay put, but there was no way I was doing so. Marek was in serious trouble, and I didn't understand why everyone else insisted on just standing around.

Racing forward, JayLeigh tried to stop me, but I shrugged her off. "He's the only real family I have left. I won't leave him on his own, no matter what you think."

I didn't wait for her response as I continued toward the fight. Malina saw me coming and changed her direction. "You want to play, Raegan? Let's see what you've learned in our time apart."

Tapping into my dragon strength, I apologized to Chelle for not giving her more healing time, but I needed her speed to evade the spells Malina shot out at me while I gathered one of my own.

I hadn't learned many offensive spells last year. That had been something I was supposed to accomplish in third year, but I knew enough to hopefully get by.

Firing off a few powerful orbs, Malina staggered back when only one of them made contact. "Impressive, but it's not enough. You'll never be enough. You were created for one purpose: to give power to me. Now, stand still while I take what's mine."

Before I could do anything, her hands raised in the air and a stabbing sensation started in my chest and spread across my body.

If she continues to do this for too long, we'll die, Chelle's sorrowful voice filtered through.

Not today, I replied.

Shifting into my dragon form was the only thing I could think of in order to break her concentration and while I did that, Enzo finally moved in as well, followed by JayLeigh. Enzo was still helping Marek while JayLeigh did her best to distract Malina without getting caught in the power-suck.

When I was fully shifted, Malina didn't stop, but I was stronger. Even though my chest still burned where I was missing scales, I moved against her spell, one step at a time, until I was within striking distance.

"I see Desmond had his fun with you. My little rat finally got what he wanted," Malina taunted.

"Too bad he didn't live long enough to enjoy it," I replied before whipping my tail around with force and striking her in the side.

She tumbled to the ground, and her spell was finally broken. Even if she wasn't down for the count, at least she wasn't growing more powerful.

Marek was up and moving with a purpose toward Malina, but she paid no attention to him as her glare remained on me.

"That stung, but it only pissed me off and confirmed what I should have admitted to myself long ago. You're too stubborn to be of any use to me."

She withdrew a blade from her hip and, when her fingers wrapped around the hilt, the tip of the dagger began to smoke, and she threw it toward my dragon.

I had no idea where my vital organs were in this form, but when the blade sank into an open spot with no scale for protection, I had a feeling it didn't matter. The spell she placed on the dagger moved quickly through my body and paralyzed me.

"Shift back," JayLeigh yelled as she quickly removed the dagger from my dragon's chest.

I tried to do as she said, but the process was slowed by the heaviness of the spell and I couldn't even sense Chelle when I reached out to her for help.

While I laid helplessly on the ground, I had the perfect view of Malina, so I saw the exact moment that Marek and Enzo attacked. Marek's clawed hands raked across Malina's chest, and shock covered her face.

"I might have loved you before, but I won't let you kill my daughter," he roared.

"She might as well be dead. That dagger will kill her dragon, and then she will never be whole again. She'll never be anything more than a shell of her former self. That's what she gets for being such a selfish child," Malina spat.

CHELLE! I yelled inside my head when Malina's words registered with me.

No, this couldn't be happening. She couldn't be dying. I'd only just gotten to know my other half, and I wasn't ready to let her go.

JayLeigh had told me to shift back, and I hoped that was supposed to help protect Chelle, so I focused harder on that while watching the scene before me play out.

Marek charged Malina once more, this time with death in his eyes. He was out to kill, and I prayed it would finally be over.

Marek landed on top of her, but she didn't go down easily, and even from where I laid, I could see how hard it was for him to harm her. A part of Marek still loved her, and this was killing that portion of him to fight against her.

JayLeigh tossed Marek my dagger and he caught it in

the air before plunging it into Malina's chest, twisting it and leaving a gaping hole.

She laughed in his face even as her face paled. "That might leave a mark, but you know that won't kill me. Are you man enough to finish the job, or will you die before your daughter?"

My dragon form was almost completely gone, but I still couldn't sense Chelle. I had no idea if she was gone, but before I fell into a pit of desolation, I put my focus on Marek. He needed help, and Enzo and JayLeigh weren't enough.

Fighting through the spell, I rolled onto my knees and missed whatever had happened but caught the sight of Marek laying on the ground.

Enzo and JayLeigh moved in on Malina at the same time, but she flung them away like tiny pests as she stalked toward Marek.

Standing, I took a few steps toward them, but I already knew I was going to be too late.

Malina smirked as she looked at me. "Say goodbye to Daddy."

Her hands were glowing with a power so severe it had me staggering back from its pulsing force. My only bit of hope left was when I saw Enzo racing toward Malina's back, but when he slid on the ground and landed next to Marek's prone body, I was thoroughly confused.

"I'm sorry, Raegan." His eyes met mine as he whispered the words.

Though, I didn't understand their meaning until he plunged a glowing blade of his own, one I'd never seen, into my father's chest.

I was going to kill him.

Rage built inside me as I proceeded to move forward.

Malina groaned as I glanced her way just in time to see her hand covering the wound Marek had left in her chest that had begun spilling blood.

"This isn't over, Raegan. I'll be back, and you will all pay for Marek's weaknesses." With those final words, Malina disappeared in a tornado of smoke to go lick her wounds, but I didn't give a shit about any of it.

My mind could only process the fact that the man I loved had killed my father. I didn't understand it, and as my hands transformed into claws made for killing, I wondered if I could really end Enzo for his actions.

"Raegan, stop," he begged. "I know you're upset—"

"Upset doesn't even come close, *Lorynzo*," I snapped, using the full name he hated.

"He's not dead."

Shaking my head, I didn't believe him. "Malina wouldn't have walked away if Marek was still alive."

JayLeigh approached me slowly. "Enzo is right. Marek can only be killed by Malina since they are Doyen, and she can only do that by stopping his heart with the power she was about to use on him. Enzo saved his life by doing what he did."

"Marek gave me this dagger and asked me to use it when I knew the time was right," Enzo continued to plead with me. "He didn't want to put the responsibility on either of you."

My stare went to JayLeigh. "If he's not dead, why isn't he waking up?"

"He will in time, but it will take days, possibly weeks, which is why Malina didn't stick around to finish the job. His heart has to be beating for her power to kill him."

"So, now what?" I still didn't quite know how to process everything my eyes had seen.

"Now, we finish the battle Malina started and recover from our wounds and losses. When we've done that, we do this all over again."

As I took in the bodies around me, I fought back tears from my broken heart at watching Enzo stab my birth father, and from still not being able to sense Chelle. Even if he wasn't really dead, I wasn't sure I could ever do this again. It took every bit of strength in me not to run away like before.

This time, I'd stay, but they were going to wish I'd left.

DARING PROVOCATION

BOOK THREE

New Orleans was possibly the most badass place in the universe. I'd yet to explore the many wonders of the world, but the two weeks I'd spent in the Crescent City, as it was often known, were the most relaxed I'd been in over two years.

After the battle with Malina had ended on a not-so-great note, it had taken a decent amount of the summer for us to get things settled around the academy and for me to not want to kill Enzo. Much of the academy had been damaged in the fight, and there had been more construction needed than simple magic could fix.

But when the dust settled and Jules told me what I would find in New Orleans, there had been no stopping me from taking a much-needed vacation and heading south.

"Do we have to leave?" I murmured to Jules.

"Well, I don't, but you do." She smirked.

I twisted my head toward her with a glare on my face. "If I have to, then so do you, and you only have yourself to blame. I didn't ask you to stick around so long and make yourself essential to everything we're dealing with. You did that all on your own."

She laughed. "So, you're saying because I was trying to be helpful, I'm doomed to see this through to the end?"

"Damn straight." I nodded curtly while Enzo chuckled from behind me as we strolled through the French Quarter.

"Good to know. Next time, I'll just be an asshole and leave you to figure things out on your own." She rolled her eyes, obviously not liking my thought process.

Instead of continuing to banter with her, I took in the magic around me. Humans took the uniqueness that was New Orleans for granted when they played tourist. The city was full of tranquility. Inside every shop was a piece of magic, and I'd visited them all, learning everything I could from the locals.

Enzo nudged me. "We'll be back. Hell, we can even live here when this school year is over if you love it that much. Just don't look so sad, because it makes me want to kill someone, and since Malina's not around...."

Plastering a smile on my face, I winked at him. "I'm fine. I promise. Just let me have this moment. Whether it's filled with sadness or happiness, I just want to soak it all in before we leave. It's good to just feel without having to act."

Recently, I'd had moments when I just needed to reflect and be left alone. Enzo was struggling with them, because he had an innate desire to fix everything, but sometimes a girl just needed to *feel*, be in the moment, and accept what was.

Over the summer, there had been a lot I'd accepted, half of which I didn't like, but I'd grown beyond my temper tantrums for the most part. A huge thanks to Chelle for that.

Her presence swirled within me, but she remained

silent, knowing what I meant when I wanted to be left alone. She had been gone for two full days after the fight with Malina, and I'd never been more depressed and miserable in my life.

When the power we shared had finally flared to life, I cried tears of joy for a solid hour while Enzo tried his best to figure out who he needed to kill. The poor guy always wanted to decimate something. Getting him into anger management was beginning to sound like a great idea.

"And now you're smirking. Oh, what I wouldn't give to know what you're thinking in that pretty little head of yours," Enzo grumbled from my side.

Ignoring him, I glanced up ahead to find Gemma and Talon turning into Café Du Monde. Even though it was nearing midnight, the place was packed, but Talon had a unique ability to make people give him a wide berth.

I watched in fascination as he simply stared at a group taking up two tables they didn't need and enjoyed the moment as the frat-looking guys scattered, mumbling apologies as they tripped over themselves in their haste. Talon hadn't even glared, but I was pretty sure one of them peed their pants.

I really needed to acquire his superpower.

Gemma waved us over as they took a seat, and we happily sat down. I'd had multiple beignets each day since arriving, and I wouldn't have minded at all if we spent the rest of the night sitting in the café, devouring all of the sugary perfection I could handle before exploding in white powdery dust.

"School's overrated. I think we should all just say 'screw it' and stay here. New Orleans seems like the only place Malina hasn't been, so maybe we'd be safe." Gemma sighed with wishful thinking.

"Where's JayLeigh?" Jules asked, ignoring Gemma's comment since we all knew it wasn't possible.

Malina was off licking her wounds and gathering resources while we were doing the same. It was a race to see who would be done first, because we couldn't risk an attack to the academy again. We were still trying to rebuild the damage her people had caused just a few months ago.

"I'm right here," JayLeigh's voice sounded right before she shimmered into appearance.

I'd long gotten used to her invisible act. She had tried to teach me, but I didn't have the patience for it. The act required a lot of concentration and focus, but I seemed to have a hard time with both as of late. Hopefully, I'd be changing that soon.

The group began to chat about how they wanted to spend their last night in New Orleans while I people watched, waiting until it was time to go see my new favorite person in this world.

Late at night in the Quarter, there always seemed to be more supernaturals than there were humans out. I smiled, loving how freely they roamed. Shifters, witches, and vampires were most common around the powerful city.

I'd yet to see an elf, but Enzo had said that wasn't surprising. Most of them lived in remote areas or other countries, and I made him promise we'd visit those countries one day. I was quickly learning that life was short, and I wanted to live it to the fullest while I still could.

We'd lost more than twenty good people in the battle against Malina, and I'd counted myself lucky that those closest to me survived. I'd been worried that we wouldn't be welcome in the city, since a decent number of those lost were from New Orleans, but they'd all been understanding.

Much more than I believed I would have been, had the situation been reversed.

The person I'd been most wanting to see came into my line of sight, and I waved the sorceress over eagerly. Enzo followed my gaze and moved over, so she could sit next to me.

"Good evening, Raegan," Amalia greeted me, then smiled at the rest of the group before taking a seat.

"Hey, Meme," I practically cooed. Leaving my grandmother after only just finding her was going to be excruciating on my heart.

My parents had kept me hidden from all things magical while I grew up, which meant I had never met any of my extended family. Blood or not, I still considered these people my own, and the day I met my Meme was one of the greatest of my life and a big reason I had no desire to leave New Orleans.

At first, I'd been mad that Jules hadn't told me about this part of my family, but I soon realized that there hadn't been a point. Well, after she forced me to listen to her reasonings, anyway.

I'd been stuck at the academy for the first year. Literally. There would have been no way for me to come find them, and knowing I had family out there and not being able to see them would have killed me. Then, I took off when I was finally free and wasted no time before disappearing to Drakken after I came back.

There hadn't really been time to bring it up, and she had been right in assuming I'd have dropped everything to come meet them, because that was exactly how we ended up spending part of summer break in New Orleans.

"Are you sure you can't come back with us?" I asked,

even though I knew my grandmother had never once in her centuries-old life left New Orleans.

She patted my hand resting on her shoulder. "I wish, child, but I have responsibilities here, just like you have them at Shadow Veil. We all have our part to play, but I will welcome you back into my home anytime you'd like."

Meme Amalia was leader to the witches and the hybrids who preferred their witch side. Her husband, my grandfather, was the previous leader until they had trouble with some vampires a couple decades ago and he was killed.

His funeral had been the last time my mother was in the city, and my heart hurt that she had spent so much time away from this mystical place and her family just to keep me safe. Meme assured me that my parents were at rest, though, and I tried to take some sort of peace from the knowledge, even if I was riddled with guilt.

Her wrinkled thumb rubbed between my eyes. "No sense worrying about what you can't change, child. You're too young to frown so much."

A grin formed as I leaned into Amalia. "I'm going to miss you, but we're going to be back soon. I want to find a place here and never leave, like you."

Both of her cool hands wrapped around my cheeks. "I want more for you than New Orleans. My city is wonderful, don't let anyone tell you otherwise, but there is more to life than magic. Be human. Make mistakes. Live your life, and when you're ready to settle down, you come back to me. There will always be a place for you here."

There was sorrow in her tone, and her soulful azure eyes pierced right through me. "Thank you, Meme."

A band began playing right outside the café, and whatever she'd been about to say was cut off. Instead, she squeezed my hand tighter, and we sat together with our group while their voices rose to be heard over the music.

Tomorrow was going to suck, but I'd be back just as soon as Malina was dead. Stopping her was all that mattered so I could keep those I loved most safe, but something told me my last year at Shadow Veil Academy wasn't going to be easy. I feared for the lives of those around me and wondered just how many of them were going to die because Malina was a selfish bitch.

Two days later, we were back at school, and the tension within me had never been worse. My Meme had held me tight as we both fought back tears. I ached to go back to her, as well as the aunt and uncle I had met, plus six cousins who were much too young to deal with anything I had going on.

Marek stood at the entrance when we pulled up, his smile inviting, and I realized I missed him more than I thought I would. "It's been quiet around here without you guys. I almost went back to Drakken," he said when I walked up the steps, which earned him a punch in the ribs.

"Kidding. I was only kidding," he moaned.

It had taken eighteen days for Marek to wake up after the fight with Malina where my mate had stabbed my father. I'd struggled majorly with accepting that what Enzo had done was for the best, but JayLeigh had managed to talk me off the edge, and Enzo lived.

He had explained the conversation with Marek and why he'd chosen to keep it from me, and while I didn't think keeping me safe and focused was the best excuse, I did understand. Enzo had been right. If I'd have known, my thoughts would have constantly been on Marek, and there had been too much going on during the battle for that to have been a good thing.

I might have still screamed at him and threatened to remove his balls several times once the entirety of the situation had registered with me, but I eventually calmed down and waited not-so-patiently by Marek's side for him to wake again. I wasn't ready to call him Dad by any means. I had already had a father, and calling someone else Dad felt disrespectful to the memory of the one who raised me.

By the time I'd turned away from Marek, Gemma, Talon, and JayLeigh were nowhere to be seen, but Enzo and Jules stood behind me.

"It's late, and tomorrow's the first day of school. You two should get some sleep," Jules said.

"I don't see the point in us attending classes," I groaned. Besides our history, there wasn't much I was going to learn that I couldn't figure out by working with JayLeigh, Jules, or Professor Phox.

"Because we're not going to let Malina dictate our lives. You will still do what you came here to do." Jules glared at me, and I held my hands up in surrender.

"Yes, ma'am."

She gave me a hug, then pushed me toward Enzo. "Go get some sleep, and I'll see the two of you tomorrow."

"Love you, Jules," I called over my shoulder as Enzo led me away.

"Love you, too," she replied before turning toward Marek. She obviously didn't want us to know about what they were discussing or she wouldn't have dismissed us so quickly.

I moved to turn back toward them, but Enzo swooped me up into his arms, his preferred way to walk with me.

"Let it go. We just got back from probably the best vacation I've ever had, and I want to end it on an equally good note. So, we're going to go up to our room, and I'm going to have my way with you. Got it?"

Well, I wasn't an idiot, so I simply grinned and nodded. There was still an ominous cloud lurking around me, and if he wanted to keep me distracted for just a little while longer, then I wasn't going to stop him.

Tomorrow would be soon enough to worry about classes and what progress the council made with Malina while we were gone. I had goals in life, and I'd be damned if I let that pain-in-the-ass sorceress screw with them any longer than necessary.

M orning came much too soon, but I had no idea what classes I was assigned, so I eagerly woke Enzo and got out of bed to get ready for school. While I dressed for the day, my hand hesitated on my normal go-to pants. I'd been stubborn for two years, refusing to wear the skirt, but it was still in the eighties outside, abnormally hot and humid for the time of year.

Screw it. I yanked out the skirt Gemma had given me just in case I was ever forced to wear one and put it on. The plus side to the skirt was I could hide my dagger underneath the material, and none would be the wiser.

Enzo was already in the shower, so he'd be nice and surprised when he came out. I was pretty sure I'd never worn anything other than pants around him before, unless we were headed to bed.

Over the summer, my hair had grown long enough to braid, so instead of spending the extra time drying it, I braided the mahogany strands and looked for my bag, which likely still had my tablet in it—I probably should have found it the night before, but oh well. Hopefully it wouldn't be necessary for the day, but I'd bring my charger just in case.

When Enzo came out with nothing but a towel wrapped around his waist, he stopped in his tracks and glared at me. "You need to change."

"What? Why?" I feigned innocence.

His heated gaze traveled up and down my body. "Because there's no way in hell I'll be able to focus on anything other than you in *that* all day now, and other guys shouldn't get the same pleasure unless I'm allowed to pummel them."

My hand patted his bare chest. "You're lucky you're adorable. Now get dressed, or I'm leaving without you, and if you *pummel* anyone, I'll wear the skirt every damn day."

He grunted, murmuring under his breath, but I didn't bother to decipher his complaints. Instead, I grabbed some granola bars and tossed them in my bag along with my charger before grabbing some juice. I was really craving a beignet and wasn't sure how I was going to go a whole day without one after having several of them each day for the last couple weeks.

More than that, I was missing my Meme. While I'd met other family members, she had been the one I'd connected with instantly. She reminded me so much of my mom, and I clung to that with ferocity.

We'd spent many of the nights I was with her exchanging stories about my mother, both the good and the bad. Laughter was more prevalent than the tears, but no matter the emotions I felt, I knew I had needed the family connection to truly begin moving forward.

Enzo's hand grazed along my thigh, halting me from my thoughts. "Keep inching higher and you risk losing a hand, *darling*," I said with a smirk.

"If that's how you want it, then fine. Just know, I'll remember this moment, and payback is a bitch," he grunted.

Shrugging, I moved toward the door. I might regret pushing his buttons later, but I didn't care at the time. That was a problem for future Raegan.

Just before the door shut behind me, Enzo snagged it and locked up our dorm. When he caught up to me, he tugged on my hand. Thinking he was going to continue to whine about my clothing choice, I rolled my eyes and huffed as I turned toward him.

"Raegan, this is serious, and I need you to listen to me."

I nodded, quickly realizing my assumptions had been wrong. "What happened?"

"Nothing, but something undoubtedly will, and we don't know when that might be. I know we slacked off for most of the summer, and I wasn't near as paranoid knowing Malina had to completely rebuild her resources, but she could have done so by now. We need to be prepared for an attack at any time."

I patted the thigh he hadn't previously tried to grope. "I'll have a weapon with me at all times, and I have Chelle. You don't need to worry about me."

Malina won't get away again, Chelle confirmed.

It had taken her weeks to process the fact that Malina had come very close to killing her. To say Chelle still held a grudge would be an understatement. It was much more personal than that for her, especially since Malina threatened to go after Drakken and all the dragons there as well.

"Raegan, we can't pretend she's not more powerful than us. We need to stick together. It's not that I want a guard around you at all times or to smother you, but we need to at least stick in pairs. All of us."

"So, you're saying you won't ever be alone, either?" I countered.

He nodded. "It applies to anyone Malina might be after."

Huh. He was taking this more seriously than I thought. I knew our situation was precarious, but Enzo was normally only concerned with me. This was the first time I'd seen him really worry about the bigger picture.

"Okay," I replied.

"Really? Just like that, with no argument?"

"Yep. If it's important to you that we all work together to stay safe, then it's important to me. That's how this whole relationship thing works. Give and take, supporting each other no matter the situation, is what it's all about."

He cupped my face as he gently pressed his lips against my forehead. "Being in New Orleans without the stresses of Malina and the council showed me what our future could be like. I'll do whatever it takes to have the possibilities I could so clearly see there."

No longer was I eager to find out my schedule and speak with Headmaster Stone. No longer did I give a shit about Malina and the threats that hung over our heads. All I wanted was what Enzo saw, and damn if it didn't piss me the hell off that we still had to wait for what we wanted.

He laced his fingers through mine as he pulled me forward. "Come on. We can't change what's happened, but we can do our damnedest to make sure Malina pays for what she's done and prevent her from doing more."

He was right, and as we passed by the other students in the halls, I knew we were doing this for more than just us. We were doing this for all of the supernaturals who would be affected, not just the ones in the present but those who would come after us as well. We had a legacy to leave behind, and I'd do my best to make sure it was one worthy of being remembered.

Headmaster Stone's door was open when we arrived, so we walked in, surprised to find him alone on the first day of classes. His face was creased with concern, but it seemed to be a permanent look for him since Malina escaped, so I tried not to worry about it too much.

"Good morning, Alistair," Enzo greeted him.

He stood from his desk and came around to shake both of our hands. "Nice to see the two of you back. I assume you had a nice visit?"

I nodded. "We did. Was there anything we missed while we were gone?"

"Lots of construction to ready for the arriving students and a few council meetings, but I'm assuming Jules already filled you in on those?"

My aunt had decided that she would be interim council member as long as she was able to still handle things in New Orleans as needed. She wasn't an official leader down there, but she was one of the liaisons for her pack, and they missed her dearly.

The council had happily agreed, and while we'd been gone, she'd taken several phone calls that I tried to ignore so we could enjoy our time away. I knew if there was something imperative, she'd have shared the information without me having to ask.

"Actually, no. We tried to keep the trip as close to a vacation as possible," I replied.

He moved back to his chair. "Well, have a seat and I'll fill you in, though I wish Marek was here. He was supposed to meet me about a half hour ago, but I haven't heard from him."

It was out of the ordinary for the dragon king to be late,

and I made a mental note to go look for him once we left the headmaster's office if I had time before class.

"I'm sure he just got caught up with something else," Enzo said, trying to ease Alistair's tension.

"Right. Well, Bennett has been helping me track Malina. She doesn't appear to be moving much. She's moved west instead of back up north, but the connection we have to her is poor at best. I'm not even confident it's her we're picking up."

"What about Marek? Being as they're both Doyens, has he been able to help now that he's completely healed?" I asked.

He had been down for a while, and none of the council were willing to ask for his assistance while he was on the mend. Marek hadn't even had enough energy to go back to Drakken, so he'd chosen an interim leader, which JayLeigh had gone back to announce to their people.

"He thinks he might be onto something but won't tell us. It's rather frustrating, but we've been compliant considering his position."

The headmaster's tone told me that their compliance wasn't going to last for very long.

"We'll talk to him today, before or after class, depending on when they start," I said, casting a glance at Enzo. He nodded in agreement.

"Speaking of classes, do you have a schedule for us?" Enzo asked, seeming to realize we weren't going to get anywhere until the whole group was together. That was supposed to happen that evening, last I'd heard.

"Ah, yes. I finished that up while you were gone. I hadn't uploaded anything to your tablets, because I had to confirm a few things, but it's all been sorted," Headmaster Stone said.

"What's been sorted? Aren't we going to class like all the other students?" I asked.

He shook his head while searching through the papers scattered on his desk. "Not exactly. Your training will be more specialized. You're only going to have three classes, and they'll be privately held."

I blinked rapidly as I tried to process what he was saying. "Why?"

"Well, we thought it would be best. If you're going to be so heavily involved, then we need to focus your trainings on subjects that will best help you succeed in defeating Malina. Otherwise, if you'd like to take normal classes like the rest of the fourth-year students, then we will have you sit out of the remainder of our dealings with Malina."

Damn, that was quite the statement, and not one I expected at all. I wasn't sure I liked it. Having classes with the other students was the only thing that made me feel like we were somewhat normal. Well, as normal as someone could feel with magical powers.

When the headmaster passed the paper across the desk, Enzo quickly snatched it and stood, pulling me with his other hand. "We appreciate everything you've done. We'll take a look at this and be wherever we're needed. Are we still meeting tonight with the others?"

"Yes, we are. Please let me know tonight if there are any issues with the schedule," Alistair replied.

Enzo nodded, and I followed him silently out of the room. He closed the door behind us and headed for the platform, but it was packed with students, so he pulled us toward the stairs, stairs that would take at least ten minutes to traverse depending on where he was leading us.

"What's going on?" I asked, wondering what I had missed in that meeting that had him losing his damn mind.

He didn't speak. Instead, he practically ripped the door off its hinges to enter the stairway only crazy people used and then pinned me against the wall.

"You were going to argue with him, so I cut you off to move things along. I'm sorry, but I couldn't wait any longer." His voice was low, and desire sparked in the air around us.

"Wait for what?"

Instead of answering me, his lips crashed down hard on mine in a demanding kiss. He gripped my thighs before picking me up, allowing me to wrap my bare legs around his waist. Maybe he had been right, and the skirt wasn't the best idea if we planned on getting anything done on our first day of the new school year.

"I couldn't wait a minute longer to get my hands on you," he murmured against my neck as he turned me into putty with every well-placed kiss.

"Back to our room?" I suggested, but he shook his head.

"We have class to get to." With those words, he pulled back and set me on my feet.

I was officially hot and bothered, and he was going to leave me in that state? Not. Happening.

Hands on my hips, I glared at him. "Seriously? All that buildup and then nothing?"

He leaned forward and stole a kiss before whispering, "Payback is a bitch, isn't it, *darling*?" Then, he darted from the area before I could beat him senseless.

As he rounded the corner and slipped onto a platform, he peeked his head out. "Meet you in the atrium!"

Well, at least he told me where I was supposed to be going for our first class. Though, I had no idea what we were going to be doing or if I should have anything with me besides my tablet.

Closing the stairwell door behind me, I went back to the

platform and contemplated heading back to our room to change, but I'd have Enzo zap us there if I needed to. I was more curious about who our first teacher was and what the headmaster thought was best for us to focus on.

The next platform was empty, and I was surprised until I realized it was already 8:25 a.m. and most smart students would already be in their classes, waiting for them to start at 8:30 a.m. sharp. My heart went out to those who had Professor Phox this year.

I'd been surprised when I heard she was sticking around but grateful as well. Hopefully, she'd forewarn us if anything life-threatening was about to happen. Though, the dragon seers seemed to do whatever the hell they wanted, so I wasn't counting on it.

When I arrived at the atrium five minutes later, the door was closed, and when I tried to pull on the handle, it was locked. *What the hell?*

Knocking hard, I waited until I heard footsteps approaching. "You're late. Try again tomorrow."

"Are you kidding me?" I screeched while throwing my hands up in the air at the sound of Phox's voice on the other side. Apparently, *I* was the poor student who had to deal with her. "Enzo took the schedule before I could see it and left me behind on purpose. Kick his elfy ass out, too, if you want to be fair."

His payback for me wearing the skirt was going to cost me so much grief.

The door cracked open. "Elfy ass? Really, is that the best you have?" Phox raised a brow.

I sighed. "It's the first day. Cut me some slack."

"This will be the only easy part of your day, Raegan. Now, get inside and prepare to be tortured." The grin on her face was menacing and had me hesitating, but I knew there was no way around it. Professor Phox really was the best person to be teaching me, so I straightened my big girl panties and entered the room, only to be surprised once again.

Standing in the center of the room were Gemma, Lyssa, Peyton, and Finley, while Enzo and Talon were just coming from a closet with an armful of weapons.

"What are you all doing here?" I asked.

Gemma grinned. "Lyssa wasn't happy about being left out and called Daddy to save the day. Peyton and Finley caught wind of it, and the three of them spent the summer training together. Lyssa's dad approved of their progress and made a call to the headmaster."

"Seriously? You three *want* to fight Malina?" I didn't understand why they weren't running far in the other direction.

"No, but we want to protect what this school stands for, and if Malina is threatening to take all of that away, then we will do whatever we can to stop her," Lyssa said with an air of confidence.

"All right, then. I won't argue with you as long as you all know what you're getting yourselves into," I said.

"Now, what we really need to talk about are those legs." Gemma whistled at me, then Phox glowered at her, and Enzo growled, effectively ending the conversation before it even began, thankfully.

Peyton and Finley laughed, and I caught a flash of fangs from Finley. Vampires weren't the most common supernatural I'd seen around the school, so it still freaked me out when I saw her fangs, even more so when she had a cup of blood in her hand.

Holding in my shudder, I accepted what was and decided I couldn't keep everyone I cared about in a bubble.

If they wanted to fight, then that was their choice, and I'd never hold them back. Though, it did just make the dynamic of training a lot more interesting. I was more excited than ever to see what boundaries I could push with my abilities next.

There had been no doubt that Professor Phox was an unyielding teacher in a normal classroom setting, but she was a straight-up tyrant in a private one. Since Enzo had yet to show me the schedule, I hadn't known what to expect when things got started, but it definitely wasn't what I thought.

We practiced spells for two hours straight, but not the normal 'mumble some words and hope for the best' kind. No, these were high-level sorcery spells that looked like something out of a movie. By the time class was over, I was able to string magic from one hand to the other, creating shields and weapons from thin air. They didn't last long, but with practice, that would change.

It wasn't necessarily a witch trait, Phox explained, but a supernatural thing, though it helped if you had witch or elven qualities. Even though I'd been completely stripped of my elven abilities, Phox believed there was still some natural witch magic left in me since Malina had created me, but since it wasn't a forced addition like the elven portion had been, my dragon had still broken free of her previous hold.

With that information, I understood better why Gemma, Enzo, Lyssa, and I had been able to accomplish creating the physical presence of our magic while Peyton, Finley, and Talon were only able to create sparks after the first class.

I wasn't too worried about the girls. The same determination that had been on their faces when I entered the room was still there when we left, but Talon was frustrated and pissed off. He and Gemma had taken off before I could get a chance to offer him help.

"Where to now?" I asked, hoping Enzo would pull out the schedule so I could steal it.

"Back to our rooms to shower and change; then, we spend two more hours with Phox before getting a lunch break," he answered without glancing at the paper.

"Seriously?" Peyton groaned. "What's the point of even changing?"

Finley snorted. "She's crazy. Besides giving us a false sense of hope that maybe the hard part is over for the day, she probably just wanted a break from us."

Phox appeared out of nowhere like JayLeigh loved to do, halting our walk back to the platform. "Or maybe I don't want to smell your disgusting body odor for the next two hours while I continue to make you my bitch. I guess you'll only find out if you're ballsy enough to come learn from the crazy professor again."

Phox disappeared, but we all assumed she was still around, so nobody said anything until we were on the platform. Then I let out a snort, which turned into a laugh, and then I was in full-on hysterics.

"Uh, babe? Are you okay?" Enzo asked as he placed his hand on my back.

Peyton and Finley joined in, while Lyssa looked just as confused as Enzo.

"I'm pretty sure it's a dragon thing. They all seem a little unhinged, if you ask me, and it's rubbing off on the others," Lyssa commented, which made me laugh harder for some reason.

When I finally regained my composure, I apologized. "Phox's goal will be to break us. I just had a vision of her standing over a pile of our broken bodies and saying, 'They just weren't ballsy enough to handle the crazy professor.'"

Enzo cracked a smile, but Lyssa didn't buy into the hilarity. While she had come a long way from her mean girl vibe, she still seemed to believe she was above some people. I wondered if she was only choosing to train with us to prove she was just as essential in keeping the academy safe.

Either way, as long as she kept up with the trainings and didn't talk down to any of us, then I was happy to have her help. We'd be idiots to turn down her assistance. I still wasn't sure who her father was or what he did, but everyone always made him sound so important, so we'd hopefully be able to use her resources if needed.

"Where are we meeting up next?" Finley asked when it was time for us to go our separate ways.

"In the garden of tranquility," Enzo replied casually, but my entire body tensed.

I'd yet to go in there again for many reasons, but mostly out of fear. Fear of being rejected and the pain it had previously caused. This time, I'd have an audience, and I wasn't sure I was okay with that.

Lyssa was with us until we arrived at her floor, just one below ours, but I didn't pay attention to anything they may or may not have been chatting about on the way up. Instead, I did my best not to have a panic attack.

When we no longer had an audience, Enzo's face appeared right in front of mine. "What's wrong?" Lines creased his forehead, and he shook with barely contained power.

"I can't go with you. I can't go to the next class," I murmured in hopes of calming him down some.

"What do you mean? Are you sick?" His hands roamed my body, seeming to be searching for something, but there was nothing to find. Nothing physical, anyway.

Whatever was wrong with me was on the inside.

Instead of asking more questions when I didn't answer, Enzo grasped my hand, surprising me by *not* picking me up, and led us inside the dorm. Once we were seated on the couch, he twisted both of us, so we were facing each other.

"Please explain whatever has you so scared, so I can fix it," he pleaded.

My head shook. "You can't fix this. Whatever is wrong is inside me. The gardens won't let me in without trying to kill me."

This caused his lips to turn up, but he did his best to hide his amusement at my statement. "I don't understand. The gardens only ward out evil, and there is nothing sinister about you, Love."

"Except for the fact that I was created by Malina," I countered. "The gardens were one of the first places I tried to explore my first year here. When I entered them, everything was fine for a moment until it wasn't. I couldn't breathe as my skin burned from the inside out. I used every bit of strength I had to throw myself back outside the gates before the torture completely consumed me."

"Why didn't you ever tell me this?" he asked softly, finally seeming to take me seriously.

"I never told anyone. I was ashamed. I'm made from evil, and those gardens proved it."

He cupped my face. "No, Raegan. There is nothing evil about you. Malina had a hold on you then that she doesn't now. Malina wasn't born evil, and neither were you. Her dark magic probably set the defense systems off in the garden, but I doubt it will happen a second time."

"But we can't be certain, and I'm not willing to let the rest of our friends see what I truly am: a creation of darkness."

He sighed heavily, giving in to the fact that there was no convincing me otherwise. "What if we show up before everyone else and try? If you still can't enter the gardens, I'll teleport us back here before going to class to tell the others we need to move the location."

His idea was a good one, and while I was still afraid of the outcome, I nodded in agreement. I needed to move past my fears if I wanted any chance of defeating Malina, and this was a bigger one than I realized.

"Perfect. Now move your ass into the shower before I toss you over my shoulder." He winked as he pushed me up.

When I stood, he followed right behind, but there was no time for fooling around. If he wanted to test his idea, then we needed to hurry, so I shut the door in his face when I entered the bathroom first and ignored his complaints as I took the fastest shower ever.

Instead of the skirt I'd chosen earlier, I dressed in workout clothes and decided to keep the braid I had recently become fond of. Enzo sped through getting ready as well. He had decided to keep his hair short after cutting it off last fall, and I wasn't complaining at all, especially when he decided to grow some facial hair. The scruff only added to his sex appeal that I already admired.

"Ready?" he asked as he tossed a shirt over his head.

"As I'll ever be," I replied, trying to keep my nerves in check.

Once we were outside of his room, he zapped us to the garden area, which I appreciated; my emotions were frazzled, and I didn't feel like running into anyone who might want to chat.

The iron gates of the garden entrance loomed before us, taunting me with their presence. The view of inside was still as stunning as before, but I knew that beauty packed a punch, and I wasn't sure if I was ready to handle the blow.

Enzo tugged on my hand. "Come on. I know you can do this. If anything starts to hurt, I'll be right by your side to bring you back outside the gates."

His words were sweet and sincere, but they didn't make me feel better. Thankfully, I was made of tougher stuff and decided to let go of my fears. Now that Malina no longer had her connection to me, I had to figure out what would happen.

"I got this," I said more to myself than Enzo.

His hand stayed on my back as we stepped through the gates. My body tensed as I felt a wave of magic flow through me, but nothing hurt like before.

"See? I told you it would be fine. There is nothing evil about you," Enzo said proudly.

"Yeah, that's what I would have thought the last time I was here as well."

Before I could really process the fact that everything was okay and the garden wasn't going to try to kill me, Gemma and Talon appeared.

"Hey," Gemma called out, waving enthusiastically.

When they entered the gardens, I gave her a hug while Enzo and Talon did some weird bromance handshake. They'd grown closer over the summer, finding a common interest in being overprotective brutes to me and Gemma.

Gemma and Enzo at least got along all the time now. There had been a long while when I was worried he might never live up to her standards for me, but all was forgiven at some point, and I didn't question it. Instead, I enjoyed a life filled with very little drama within my small circle.

"This class better be better than the last," Talon grumbled.

Gemma elbowed him in the ribs, or possibly the hip. Talon was quite a bit taller than her and made her look ridiculously short when they stood next to each other, even though she wasn't. He must have been at least six-and-a-half feet tall, which would make almost anyone feel tiny around him.

"Just because you're an overachiever at almost everything else, doesn't mean Phox's class before was bad. Quit being a baby, deal with the fact that you're not perfect, and accept that it's okay," Gemma droned.

Well, I guess we all knew what they chatted about during our little break.

Enzo decided to join in and began to stick up for his friend, but I paid their bickering no attention. Instead, I stepped away from the group and took in the gardens for the first time.

There was trickling water I could hear in the distance, along with willow trees I badly wanted to curl up and read a good book underneath. The sight of butterflies caught my attention, a couple of them fluttering their wings before landing on a grouping of yellow lilies.

Phox appeared at my side, but I didn't let her pull me

from the magic I felt pulsing from all of the living resources within the garden.

"I saw something," she said quietly, and gone was the tranquility I was beginning to soak up.

"Are you going to tell me what that was?" I asked calmly.

"I haven't decided yet. I need to speak with Ophelia. Technically, I need her permission to disclose any vision until she retires."

My head turned toward Phox. "And if she doesn't give consent?"

"Well, then you'll know how much I like to push my luck when I make my choice. I'll have to go back to Drakken, so I'll be gone for a couple of weeks."

"What about our training?" I asked. We'd only had one training session. It wasn't like we could do it ourselves when a portion of our class couldn't even do what she'd asked of us earlier in the day.

"Marek will take over the first one, and Alistair will share this class with Marek. You'll meet your other teacher later today after lunch."

I nodded. "Sounds like you already have it all worked out."

She smirked. "Well, not quite yet, but that's how it will work out when I tell the headmaster I have to go."

Laughing, I rolled my eyes. "Pretty sure that was just you telling me a vision."

"Eh. The small ones don't count. Anyway, no more slacking. We have work to do. I need to cram two weeks' worth of torture into two hours."

My groan was audible enough to draw Enzo's attention, and he was at my side in a split second. "What's wrong?"

"Nothing, Dear. Professor Phox just has exciting plans

for us." My voice dripped with sarcasm as Phox walked away laughing.

As I went with Enzo back to the group, I realized everyone else had arrived while I'd been talking with Phox, which meant whatever she had planned for us was about to start.

"Follow me, peasants." Phox waved her hand as she walked farther into the gardens.

We'd been going for a solid five minutes, and I began to wonder just how big the area was, so I asked as much.

Lyssa was the first to answer. "The gardens are about as big as Central Park, right around eight hundred acres. The entire outside of the area is cloaked, so you can't tell the true size unless you're inside it."

Huh. So, it was like the inside of the academy with all its levels and rooms you couldn't see from the outside.

Another ten minutes passed before we finally arrived in an open meadow area surrounded by looming pine trees, completely blocking out the rest of the gardens. The grass beneath my feet was thick and short like it was constantly landscaped, but I didn't even bother asking. Just like when I first arrived at Shadow Veil and the answer to all of my questions was magic, I assumed the care of the gardens was the same.

"Everyone, remove your shoes and take a seat," Phox announced.

Nobody argued with her, and we sat in a semicircle, waiting for further instructions.

"As some of you realized earlier, magic is a lot more than what you were born with. Even humans could tap into it if they knew what they were doing. In the mornings, you will continue to push your limits beyond the possible, and when you're here, you'll learn how to draw power from what's around when you're weakening."

Nobody said anything; we all just sat there in shock. There had to be some sort of twist. Professor Phox made it all sound so easy when I knew it would be nothing but.

"How are we going to learn to draw power?" Finley asked, finally breaking the minute-long silence.

"You're going to become one with nature." Phox smirked, and I knew this was where things would get complicated.

"And how do we do that?" Finley continued to push for more information.

"I get to bury each of you within the earth, and you have to work your way out before suffocating to death."

Phox certainly knew how to keep those around her on their toes. While I wasn't looking forward to having dirt in all crevices of my body, I was curious about how it felt to become "one with nature," so I raised my hand and volunteered first.

She wouldn't actually let me die.

At least, I hoped not.

But the look of terror on Enzo's face told me he didn't have the same confidence.

Oops.

P rofessor Phox made a hole in the ground with a flick of her hand. When I approached it, nerves finally began to slam into me as my hands shook and sweat broke out in all the normal places.

"Jump in," Phox said casually.

The hole looked like a gravesite, but shallower, about three feet deep and seven feet long. When I didn't immediately step in, Phox took the liberty of shoving me in.

"The dirt doesn't bite, but I do, so move your ass," she murmured.

Considering I was putting my life into her hands, I decided it was best not to counter back with my own smartass reply. Instead, I lay down and prayed I wasn't about to make the biggest mistake of my possibly short life.

"Alright, class. Pay close attention. Raegan has never done this before, and she's going to have to learn quick or suffer the consequences. Learn from her mistakes and you can suffer less. Got it?"

They weren't close enough that I could see any of them from where I lay, but I heard the rumble of Enzo's chest and knew he wasn't happy with any of it. Though, I was really proud of him for not interfering. His progress, while slow, was coming along nicely.

Phox turned back toward me and peered down with a sinister grin on her face. "Raegan, I'll only give you these instructions once, so listen up. As soon as I begin, take a deep breath, close your eyes, and when you're covered, send your magic through the dirt. Don't blast through it, or it will bury you deeper. You need to become one with the earth and move through it gently. Take too long and you'll suffocate, so make smart choices and good luck."

"That's it? You're not even going to tell me *how* to connect with the earth?" I asked with trepidation.

"Nope, you're a fourth-year student. You should already know how to bond with energies around you."

My eyes rolled as far back as they could go in my head. "Did you forget I missed most of last year?"

"Nope, and if you'd attended my class like you were supposed to, then you'd have learned this. Maybe this will teach you to show up for class more often."

Before I could respond, dirt started raining down on me, and even though I was pissed the hell off, I remembered her instructions and did as she said—one deep inhale and closed my eyes.

Once there was no more light shining through my closed eyelids, I could hear yelling from above, but I didn't focus on that. I knew I had a limited amount of time and needed to heed Phox's words carefully.

So, instead of letting my panic rise and claustrophobia set in, I focused my energy on becoming one with the dirt.

I'd love to say I could help you, but it wouldn't be in the way Phox wants, so I'm going to stay nice and quiet, Chelle chimed in.

She's trying to kill me, I complained.

I'd say she's trying to make you stronger.

Damn it, Dragon. You're supposed to agree with me and be my support system.

Her echoing laugh was the end of that short conversation.

Deep down, I knew Phox was only trying to help, but she was a complete psycho in the ways she did it, which made doubt filter in.

Once Chelle's presence completely receded, I knew what I had to do. I might not have taken most of Phox's classes last year, but I had a shit ton of training about connecting with my dragon, and I was going to approach this the same way.

My only hope was that it didn't take near as long as it did when I finally bonded with Chelle. Otherwise, they'd just need to dig a little further down, because I wasn't getting up without doing this the right way.

Sending my magic out was the easy part, but since I had never done it with dirt, I paid close attention to everything my power touched as it swirled around me. There were ants and spiders everywhere. Those freaked me out more than the cool dirt pressing against my skin, but I tried not to be concerned with the bugs. Instead, I went with the old mantra: they were more scared of me than I was of them.

The ground was definitely on its own frequency level, continually moving and changing around me. I never realized it before—everything always seemed so stationary—but the earth right beneath our feet was a constantly moving entity.

With a renewed determination, I made my first attempt to get out. Gentle movements and I could get out. Force would only push me down further. Those were the two things I needed to remember most. What I sensed below me was hot, and I was pretty sure Phox had chosen this spot because it was directly above some sort of hot spring or something similar.

Pushing out, I spoke to the dirt like I did with Chelle, trying to communicate as if it was a person above anything else.

Alright, little dirtlings. Unless you want our Earth to turn into chaos, you need to help me out here.

Okay, maybe that had sounded more like a threat, but whatever. Air was beginning to become precious, and I wasn't sure how much longer I could hold out, supernatural powers or not.

There was a shift in energy around me, but my body didn't budge, so I tried again.

Pushing out a little more energy of my own, I sought out that of the dirt. It was different from my own, but as I learned during my summer of running away, magic came in all shapes and forms.

Just as I was making progress, I made the mistake of opening my mouth even just the tiniest bit when air became harder to find within my own body. Dirt tumbled into my mouth, but my eyes had thankfully stayed closed, so nothing actually hurt. It just tasted like crap and filled my mouth with a mud paste.

Gagging on the taste, I forced the dirt down my throat and refocused myself. *Come on, I'm running out of time. Work with me here and show me just how powerful the earth really is.*

A shock rolled through my body as my energy pushed out and then fear rolled through me as I sensed bugs getting a whole lot closer.

Not funny, dirtlings. Get me out of here.

A full wave of panic was setting in, and I was ready to fail Phox's test and just break through. I knew I wouldn't actually die in the ground; I could just as easily shift and be free, but I wanted to do this the way Phox instructed.

I wanted to be a stronger me.

Air was now nonexistent within my body, and my head was becoming fuzzy, so I only had one more shot at success. Pushing through my panic, I sent my energy out one last time and found the earth's presence again.

Calming my mind, I reached out to it, moving around the magic it held, trying to approach the energy with a patience I didn't really have.

I need your help. Can you please assist me by lifting my body from the dirt? I asked, wondering if I'd actually get an answer and feeling like a complete loon for expecting one.

Thankfully, I was just thinking crazy, and the dirt didn't talk back, but it certainly did listen. Slowly, I began to move up as the earth around me shifted, so I wasn't actually pushing it out of my way, but we worked around each other.

I still hadn't opened my eyes, but light shone down on my eyelids making me really want to lift them. Though, I didn't dare since I could still feel dirt remnants around my face and really didn't want my eyes to experience the ground like my mouth had.

"Raegan?" Enzo's raspy voice sounded, making me pretty sure it was safe to at least open my mouth.

Turning my head, I used my hands to wipe at my face before opening my eyes fully. When I did, I caught the final moment before Talon and Gemma released their hold on Enzo and he ran toward me.

As Enzo helped me up, Phox clapped her hands. "Very well, Raegan. It's disappointing you didn't fail the first time, but I'm sure there will be others who do. Who's next?"

Gemma and Lyssa volunteered at the same time, but I didn't pay attention long enough to hear their arguments as to who would actually go next.

Instead, I brushed myself off the rest of the way and turned back around. I fully expected there to be a mound of dirt where I had laid, but nothing seemed disturbed in the ground beside the hole Phox had created. I had literally moved through the earth. Creepy, but cool.

"Are you okay?" Enzo asked.

"Of course, I am. I thought you were doing better about freaking out about my safety, but there's a chance you may need to start taking some anxiety meds before you give yourself a heart attack."

"She spelled the ground, Raegan. You weren't breaking through if you failed. She was going to hold you down there for as long as it took for you to get it right." His voice was hard, and I took a moment to understand his fear, because I now had it for my friends.

Though, the rest of them had been in school all year, and if they were volunteering, then I wasn't going to worry about them nearly as much as Enzo had about me. So, I took the time we had and walked him through what I had done and had him begin practicing.

He had some experience connecting with other energies, but I felt a sense of pride being the one to teach him something rather than it being the other way around like normal.

Sure enough, there were failures just like Professor Phox had wanted, but what had surprised me the most was Talon. He had seemed the calmest out of all of us and had gone last. So, I was actually pretty worried about him, but he'd been out of the dirt in under a minute with a bright smile on his face.

"I might not know a lot about magic, but I've been moving dirt in Drakken all my life," he announced when he got up.

Gemma laid into him for not telling the rest of us and helping out, but he just continued to grin, seeming to be overly happy he'd succeeded where others had not, instead of failing like he had the class before.

Before we knew it, class was over, and it was lunch time. We each went our separate ways again, and I showered for the third time that day while Enzo ordered lunch in our room instead of going to the commissary.

Once we were both cleaned up and food arrived, I asked about our next class.

"It's with Professor Melnier," he replied between mouthfuls of his turkey sandwich.

"Really? That surprises me."

"Why? He's like a thousand-year-old elf. He has endless knowledge of the Doyens." Enzo said the words so casually, but I was instantly intrigued.

"Why have we never consulted with him before?" I asked.

"Headmaster Stone did while we were in Drakken. It's why he sat in on the council meeting when we decided to go on the offense."

Huh. I remembered wondering why he was there, but it made more sense now. We'd had bigger things to worry about back then, so I hadn't thought to ask at the time, but I was wishing I had.

We finished eating and headed to an elven classroom I

hadn't been in since my first year. "Is Professor Trinket still around?" I asked before Enzo opened the door.

"Yeah, but I think he only has classes in the mornings, so it sounds like we'll be using his room in the afternoons. Professor Melnier doesn't actually teach here. He's only been helping out since Malina escaped," Enzo answered as he moved into the room with me right behind him.

Peyton, Finley, Gemma, and Talon were already chatting with the professor when we arrived, and Enzo said something about them, but I couldn't focus on anything other than my surroundings.

This was definitely not the room I remembered, but I certainly liked it better.

There was a forest-like theme going on, and literal trees were growing inside the room. Birds flew around the area, and I was pretty sure I'd seen a fox slip through the trees and wondered if it was Jules.

"Is this real?" I asked.

Enzo's brow pinched. "Is what real?"

My hands spread out in front of me. "All of this. The trees and animals and whatever else is happening."

"Uh, Raegan, I think you bumped your head. This is a normal classroom."

We arrived at the desk covered in vines, and my head was still swiveling around, trying to figure out why I could see something that Enzo couldn't even though we were standing right next to each other.

"What's wrong?" Gemma asked as soon as she laid eyes on me.

"I think I'm going crazy unless you see forest around us right now," I answered.

"Professor Melnier, what's going on?" Enzo asked when Gemma shook her head.

"Just a little test, and Raegan is actually the only one so far who passed. And please, call me Emmett."

"Care to fill me in on what sort of test would cause me to see a forest inside the classroom?" I asked.

"As soon as Lyssa joins us, we'll take a seat and I'll explain how this class will work," Emmett replied.

While we waited for Lyssa, I described to the others what I was seeing, and they were pretty irritated they couldn't join in. Emmett refused to answer even the most basic questions, which was rather frustrating.

About five minutes later, Lyssa strode into the room, moving slowly as her gaze moved about the room. "Where the hell are we? Was there some sort of gateway in the door when I walked in?"

"You see the forest?" I asked excitedly.

"Well, it's kinda hard to miss," she drawled.

"And this is why I didn't answer any questions until she arrived. I had a feeling she would need answers as well. Alright, everyone, take a seat."

Lyssa and I couldn't see anywhere to sit, but Enzo helped me find a seat that looked a whole lot like a rock to my eyes, and Lyssa sat on a stump.

"This class will include a few things, but to sum it up, I simply called it Advanced Combat Training. Here, you will learn how to create illusions depending on your magic levels, or you'll learn how to manipulate energies to bend them to your will along with defensive moves to withstand an attack of Doyen proportions."

"Why do only Lyssa and I see the forest?" I asked.

"You have a deeper connection with the earth's energy. It won't always be that way. Some days others will see something different and the two of you will be completely oblivious, but we'll work for as long as we're able for you all to be on a similar level for the tasks you'll excel at."

So, we had Advanced Magic, Energy Connections, and Advanced Combat Training for classes. Even though they were smaller in size and fewer students than taking normal classes, I was finally excited to be learning more and growing our powers together, especially with some of my dearest friends.

Emmett dropped his illusion on the classroom before he explained what we'd be working on for the afternoon. Most of it had to do with pushing our energies outside of our body, and I was quickly realizing that all three classes connected together. We couldn't succeed in one without doing so in all three.

I just had to hope there would be enough time to learn what we needed in order to not fail against Malina again. Otherwise, this would not only be my last year of school; it would also be my last year on Earth.

CHAPTER FIVE

Class with Professor Melnier—or Emmett, as he preferred to be called—was the least physically demanding of the three, but it had still been mentally draining. After two hours of attempting to force our minds to do things we'd never done before, I was pretty sure all of us were ready to sleep for a week.

When we were dismissed, Lyssa had taken off almost immediately. Gemma was asking Emmett something, and Enzo was chatting with Talon, but Peyton and Finley had practically collapsed to the ground. I stood above them and smirked.

"Still glad you decided to push your way into our shitastic situation?" I asked them.

Peyton lifted her head slightly and growled at me. "You could have warned us."

My hands went up innocently. "Hey, I tried to leave the two of you out of it. That was my way of warning you."

"I thought this was going to be easier than regular schoolwork. When Lyssa's dad said he'd take care of everything, I should have asked more questions. I now know where she gets her devious traits from," Finley droned as Gemma joined us.

"Seriously? Quit your crying. There's no time for rest. The guys have to go do some 'guy stuff', so we're having a girls' night," she announced as if there wasn't a choice in the matter for the rest of us.

I was all for hanging out, but I doubted Peyton and Finley would be awake longer than it took to shower and eat.

"What are they doing?" I nodded toward our men.

"Not sure. I heard something about Alistair before they saw me approaching and decided I didn't care enough to ask. My brain is too tired to do so."

I wondered if I should care. If there was something going on, I couldn't see either of them leaving us out, but then again, they were overprotective brutes. I wasn't going to put anything past Enzo and Talon when it came to my and Gemma's safety.

"Can we put this on hold for an hour?" I asked, deciding I at least wanted the opportunity to ask Enzo what they were up to before taking a long and scalding shower.

"Uh, sure." Gemma raised a brow at me skeptically, but Peyton and Finley didn't mind at all.

Finley stood first. "I need to go feed anyway or you ladies might begin to look like a good snack." Her tongue ran across the sharp points of where I knew fangs extended when needed.

Peyton pushed Finley as she got up as well. "You're not scary, Fin. Raegan is a dragon shifter. There's no beating that when her beast could eat all of us for lunch."

Huh. I had never considered myself notably dangerous, nor my dragon, but I could understand her viewpoint when Chelle's size was taken into consideration.

Dragons were once the most feared leaders. Your friend is smart to be cautious, because I would most certainly devour her should she cross you, Chelle said nonchalantly.

Seriously? Don't even think about eating my friends.

A shiver ran across my body as I tried to extract the image from my mind. Chelle just chuckled inside my head, and I decided we needed to have a serious talk soon about proper friend treatment and etiquette.

"Someone come pound on my door when we're ready to hang out. I'm going to go sleep for however long I have," Peyton said as she headed for the door, dragging her feet.

"I'll be in charge of her. Where are we meeting at, and should I invite Lyssa even though she took off without really saying bye?" Finley asked.

Gemma responded first. "Let's meet in my room. Less chance of the guys crashing our party if we stay away from Raegan's high-rise she calls a room. And yeah, invite Lyssa. We need to loosen her up."

With our plans made, I said my goodbyes and went over to Enzo, who was just parting ways with Talon.

"What's going on?" I asked.

"Not much. Talon asked for my help locating one of the outbuildings further out from campus. I guess Headmaster Stone wants something to do with it."

My brow raised. "And you don't know what that is?"

"Nope, didn't ask."

He wasn't lying. I could tell from the bond that had continued to grow and change over the summer, giving us the ability to read emotions from each other when we were together. Though, even if Enzo wasn't lying, he was definitely up to something.

"Alright. Well, if you figure it out, don't forget to tell me or there will be hell to pay," I said voice thick with a sweetness my words didn't portray.

"You're scary, you know that?"

"Peyton mentioned something similar just a moment ago. I'm thinking it's not such a bad thing as long as I can keep Chelle from eating my friends."

His brow pinched. "Do I want to know?"

My head shook. "Probably not. It's not something that can easily be forgotten."

"Okay, then. How about dinner before you take off? I heard Gemma mention girls' night."

"Sounds good to me."

Following him to the commissary, my stomach growled as I thought about what I wanted for dinner.

Peyton would taste the best if you ask me. Chelle chuckled.

Your jokes are not *funny.*

I find myself rather entertaining, so we'll have to agree to disagree, she replied with a soft laugh.

That we would, because I was going to need professional help getting those thoughts out of my head.

JUST OVER AN HOUR LATER, I WAS SPRAWLED ACROSS Gemma's bed and half-asleep before Peyton, Finley, and Lyssa showed up. Finley took pleasure in rushing across the room and dropping an elbow into my stomach.

"Wakey, wakey!" she screamed in my ear.

"Whatever blood you had contained entirely too much caffeine," I groaned while rolling out from under her.

"Possibly, but it's better than me being hangry."

"Touché. So, what's on the menu for girls' night,

because I didn't get my dessert with dinner," I whined to Gemma, who was at her butler box, punching a whole lot of buttons.

That girl loved food more than I did. Thankfully, our supernatural metabolisms kept us in top shape no matter how many chocolate cakes we ate.

"Well, since Phox seems to insist on trying to kill us, I figured we'd keep it low key and just pig out on sweets while playing some poker. We haven't done that in a while, and a movie night seemed too boring," Gemma said.

The mentioning of Phox reminded me of what she'd said earlier about having to head back to Drakken. I opened my mouth to say something to the others, but then realized there was likely a reason she hadn't announced it to us all at once. If she did indeed plan on leaving, then I'd let them find out when Phox was ready.

Lyssa sat down next to me. "Please, don't tell me I have to endure these nights often."

"Oh, come on. You were so much better last year in your attempts at being nice. Don't go back to being the bitch I first met when I arrived at Shadow Veil."

Her eyes widened in feigned offense. "I was no such thing."

"Lies, but it's okay. I get it now and we're all good, which means I'd like for you to be a real part of the group. Not just someone who trains with us because she's afraid of other people being better than her."

She flinched at my words, and I knew they held a truth in them. I felt bad, but I needed her to know she wasn't alone and didn't have to be something she wasn't or preferred not to be.

"You don't have to do this," I continued. "All of the

students respect you already. Being part of defeating Malina isn't necessary for you to be someone great."

"Yeah, *I* know that, but my dad doesn't," she said quietly, glancing around the room to make sure the others weren't listening. Gemma and Peyton were busy setting up food while Finley was shuffling cards, so Lyssa continued, "He's high up in supernatural dealings with the government. He demands I follow in his footsteps in order to carry on the 'Trich' family name. When he learned that you and I had become friends of sorts, yet I'd been sent home with the other students last year, he wasn't very happy."

Ire bubbled beneath the surface, and Chelle rumbled within me. Neither of us understood how a father could be so cruel as to insert their only child into a situation that had a high probability of getting her killed. Plus, she seemed to want nothing to do with it.

"I'm so sorry, Lys." I reached for her hand, but she yanked it away.

"I don't need your sympathy. I just need to make sure Malina dies and I graduate Shadow Veil. After that, I can deal with my father on my own and hopefully forge my own path. My future isn't set until I say."

Her voice was filled with a determination we could all learn from, and a grin widened on my face. She might not have wanted to be a part of our badass squad, but she was still going to give it her all in hopes of taking charge of her future. That was something to be damn proud of.

More than that, it was something to be respected, and I had a new sense of admiration for the feisty elf at my side.

CHAPTER SIX

E^{nzo}

Raegan was going to kill me, but technically, I hadn't lied to her. Talon was a sneaky bastard and well aware of the consequences to the bond between me and Raegan, since they came from her dragon side. So, when he asked for my help, he very carefully left out details that would raise suspicion to the importance of whatever he needed my help with.

After I dropped Raegan off at Gemma's dorm, I met Talon out by the main entrance. He looked like he was ready for war instead of a quick trip spent scouring the surrounding area for whatever it was the headmaster hoped to find.

He was wearing all black: boots, cargo pants, and shirt, along with multiple weapons strapped to his legs and hips.

My hand moved up and down. "Is all that *really* necessary?"

He shrugged. "Alistair told me not to shift, if possible, should we run into trouble. I thought some weapons would be nice. Not all of us can be pros at Enhanced Weapons magic on the first day."

"Alright. So, what is it we're doing exactly?" I asked, ignoring his pouting about our earlier class.

I was more curious about what Headmaster Stone wanted. Even though I had been okay with keeping Raegan out of the loop for the moment so they could enjoy their girls' night, I had every intention of telling her as soon as we were back.

I'd learned my lesson the first time I kept things from her, and I never wanted to go back to that dark place again.

"Well, four students arrived at school, but they never checked in for their classes. Marek thought he sensed something outside the school grounds a few days ago, but with all the comings and goings, he didn't think much of it, since whoever it was didn't leave behind any dark magic.

"We're supposed to go scouting for signs of either someone lurking or the students. Best case scenario, we find them in one of the outbuildings being idiots and ditching class. Worst case, we find some bodies."

My body tensed. This wasn't as simple as I thought it was going to be, and even if I told Raegan the truth right when we got back, she was going to be pissed for having been left out. But, if we were expecting bodies and she was already having fun with her friends... I had no intention of going back to get her.

"So, you need my help scouting since you're not supposed to be shifting per Headmaster Stone's request?" I asked after I took a minute to consider his words.

"Correct."

"And why can't you shift?" None of it was really making sense, and I wished I'd been involved in the original conversation.

"Because Marek is being paranoid. I don't know exactly. It's not often I question my king unless I want to risk his wrath. I know you haven't seen it yet, but his dragon can be insane. Now that he knows Malina has no problems killing him, I'm hopeful we'll see the real Marek when the time comes."

Nobody had really talked about the fact Marek hadn't used all of his abilities when we needed it most. I didn't say anything, either, because I should have known something was wrong the moment he asked me to kill him as a backup plan. Yet, I'd accepted it and done as I was told, which I regretted more and more as the days passed with Malina still alive.

We started walking through the front gates, and there were so many questions I wanted to ask about this other side of Marek that apparently existed, but I didn't. A part of me understood why the fight against Malina failed just a few months ago.

Whether or not his feelings had been returned or if the bond had been fabricated, Marek had loved Malina. His heart had been true, and I should have foreseen him having an issue with trying to end her.

Had Raegan chosen to go with Malina in the beginning and I'd been asked to destroy the love of my life in order to protect the greater good, I'm pretty sure I would have told them all to piss off.

As we crept further into the forest that was still within the cover of the academy's shield, I tried to remember where all the cool places to ditch had been my first year. Even though I'd already been working for Malina by then, my mission had been to fit in as well as I could and be the most sought-after elf at the academy.

I'd become the smartest kid in all of my classes and made friends with everyone on a surface level while keeping my fake inner circle small and exclusive. My biggest mistake had been using Lyssa in part of that disguise. I had known she was trying to do the same per her father's demand, but it wasn't fair to use her the way I did.

As soon as I had my first interaction with Raegan, I'd known I had to break things off with Lyssa, but when I did, it had been a disaster. She'd gone off the deep end trying to win me back in an attempt to make her father happy. Having her on our team worried me because of that, but Raegan seemed to see something in her, so I tried not to stress on it much.

"So, is there anything else we should be looking for besides checking the outbuildings for students?" I asked.

"Any traces of dark magic or signs people have been out here who shouldn't be."

Nodding, I focused on my own power and pushed it out as far as it would reach, which was about a half-mile. If there had been any dark magic practiced wherever we were searching, I'd find it.

About an hour later, we still hadn't found anything. We'd explored all of the outbuildings and walked almost the entire perimeter of the school grounds. The only exception was up in the mountains, but I refused to search there at night, which was quickly descending, or without more people. If someone was out there, we didn't need to be stupid and put ourselves in a bad spot.

"What if they're not within the academy's shield?" I asked.

Talon shrugged. "Only one way to find out."

"I'm not walking the several miles back, so you either need to be okay with me teleporting us or run fast," I said.

"I think if I can handle going through the portal from Drakken to here, I can handle teleporting." He puffed out his chest, making me really hope he threw up. Well, as long as it wasn't on me.

My hand grasped his shoulder, and in Raegan's words, I zapped us to the edge of the academy. When we arrived a second later, I stepped away from Talon as he swayed, but unfortunately, he recovered fast.

"I haven't been outside the academy yet. Where should we head?" he asked.

My eyes scanned the surrounding area as I thought about our options for a minute. The students would have been on foot. Even if they'd been lured away, it would likely have been close by.

"Let's go left. There are some farms down the way that might be the perfect spot for some kids to cause trouble."

Talon laughed. "You call them kids like you're much older than them."

I shrugged. "If they insist on acting like children by taking off, then that's how they'll be treated."

He eyed me curiously. "Where is the guy Gemma used to bitch about being reckless and completely wrong for her best friend? I assumed you to be a rule breaker."

"That was before I had Raegan and realized how easily I could lose her. I'm sure you felt that way when Sylas had Gemma. Don't get me wrong, I still like to have my fun and bend the occasional rule, but it will come in moderation until Malina is no longer breathing."

Talon's face turned a few different shades of red at the reminder of when Gemma had been used as bait for Sylas to take Raegan to Malina. Both of us had suffered that day, and it was one I hoped to never repeat again.

"Speaking of, did you figure your shit out with Gemma yet?" I asked since we didn't really have much else to talk about while searching the properties around the academy.

"Marek said there isn't anything he can do unless a bond kicks in. There's something stirring, but I don't know. It's weird."

"I get it. It was like that when I first met Raegan. Just keep doing what you're doing."

And that was it for our deep talk. Feelings weren't really my thing.

We came up on a farm with an old barn that's door was slamming against the side of it from the wind.

"Shall we?" I asked.

Talon didn't bother responding. It was the first sign of something out of place and, while it could have just been the wind that blew the door open, it also could have been someone leaving it open in haste while trying to escape.

We ran until we arrived and slowed down to check out the exterior. My magic wasn't sensing anything dark, but my guard would still be up until we cleared the whole structure.

Talon made a hand signal, telling me that he was going to go around the back, while I headed in through the open entrance. I wasn't sure splitting up was the best idea, but he was gone before I could object, so I went with it.

Creeping into the barn, my eyes scanned the area and confirmed quickly that people had been there recently. There were footprints in the dirt everywhere that hadn't been disturbed by time, and a pile of hay in the corner had a blanket over it with an imprint of at least two, maybe three, bodies.

Before I could look closer, there was a commotion followed by a grunt where I assumed Talon was, so I raced that way, no longer caring about stealth. Using what we'd learned from Phox earlier in the day, I called on my magic and, instead of creating a simple orb, I used my inner power to create a defensive shield.

The circular magic swirled with teal and deep purple colors as I held it in front of me with my left hand and readied another magical defense in my right. Phox had shown us we didn't have to carry physical weapons on us in order to protect ourselves, and I was going to put that theory to the test.

As I came around the final corner, my right hand readied to throw the power I'd gathered. Just as I lifted it, I realized there was no one there. Not even Talon.

"What the hell?" I murmured as I moved forward to the back door slower than before.

"Down here," Talon grumbled right before I almost stepped on him.

He was hidden beneath some metal sheets that looked like they'd been ripped from the roof. "What happened to you?" I asked as I began to pull the pieces off of him.

"The damn door was booby-trapped. There wasn't anything to see on the backside, so I was going to come in this way instead of going back around, but when I stepped inside, my foot hit a wire and all this shit came crashing down on me."

When he was fully uncovered, I saw scales covered his arms and knew he was pissed he hadn't seen the trap beforehand, but there was nothing we could do about it now. Unless there was someone hiding up in the loft I noticed when I first came in, the place was empty anyway.

"You good?" I asked.

"Yeah, what did you find?" he replied as he dusted himself off.

"People have definitely been here, and recently. The booby-trap confirms that, but I didn't see anyone. Let's check upstairs before we take off to tell the others."

He nodded, and we headed for a rickety set of stairs. We went up separately since I wasn't sure it would hold both of our weights at the same time and I went first in case it was another trap. Talon was still groaning about the cuts from the metal, and I didn't feel like hearing him cry about splinters, too.

When I got to the top, my body froze. I'd never seen anything like it, and my blood began to boil. I still hadn't managed to move out of the way when Talon got to the top step, but all he had to do was look sideways to see what had me immobilized.

My first scan counted three bodies, but on the second time around when I began to gather some sort of composure, I noticed another in the corner. None of them looked familiar, but they could have been incoming first-year students, or they had been helpless humans.

Whoever they were, they'd been slaughtered, and their blood was splattered on the walls around us. Three girls and a guy, none of which were old enough to die.

"Look at their necks," Talon said.

My eyes moved to the first girl, and then I confirmed with the remaining three: puncture wounds from a set of fangs.

"We have to get back *now*. They need to know about this. All of them," I ground out between clenched teeth.

A vampire had done this, and whoever they were, I was going to make sure they regretted hunting in our backyard.

These were pointless deaths, likely only made to send a message.

Well, message received, and we'd be sure to answer back.

There was a pounding on Gemma's door, and I groaned, because I'd lost the bet. The guys had come to break up our party a half-hour before I thought they would. Always the fun-ruiners.

"Pay up, bitches!" Gemma laughed.

She'd come within five minutes of guessing, but until we confirmed it was actually them, she wasn't getting anything from me.

While the others grumbled, I went to the door and opened it, expecting to see two overbearing men, but what I found were two very fearful ones.

"What's wrong?" I asked as Enzo pulled me into his arms and Talon pushed past us.

"Inside," he murmured in my ear.

Nodding, I let him lead me back in and waited not-so-patiently for them to tell us what had them so wound up. My mind instantly went to Malina, but no alarms had been sounded, and there wasn't chaos all around, so I assumed it to be something else.

"Is Jules okay?" I asked. While I cared about many of

the others around the academy currently not in the room with us, she was the only one I didn't think I could live without.

"Yeah, Jules is fine. We need you to listen to us in full before interrupting. You're going to be pissed, and you can yell later, but at least hear us out first," Enzo said gruffly.

Instead of saying anything, I made eye contact with Gemma and silently agreed we'd behave. It was the others he may have to worry about. We had no control of Peyton, Finley, and Lyssa, who were all still present.

Talon cleared his throat and began. "Headmaster Stone reached out to me earlier and asked if I would take Enzo to go check some of the outbuildings for missing students who didn't show up in any of their classes today."

My mouth opened to ask why we weren't included in said task, but Enzo squeezed tight around my waist, reminding me I was supposed to listen first.

Talon continued. "I approached Enzo after class and let him know I needed his help with something, but he didn't know the full extent of it until after we were already on our way to search for the students." This part was probably only said for my benefit, and it did help to know Enzo had no idea what he'd been agreeing to. "We didn't find anything within the academy grounds that would suggest they'd been taken or that someone had made it through our defenses."

"So, then what's with the pissed off and freaked out faces?" Lyssa asked.

This time, Enzo answered. "We didn't only search within the academy grounds like Alistair asked. We went beyond the perimeter to check the farms nearby. We came upon a barn that appeared to be abandoned with the main door swinging open. So, we went in to check for signs of the missing students."

"You didn't think it would be smart to come for backup before going into an unknown situation *outside* the protection shield?" I snarled. He wasn't the only one allowed to be protective. He'd made a stupid decision, and I planned on making sure he was fully aware of that.

"We had it under control, and we're fine, so there's nothing to be worried about when it comes to our safety," he replied coolly.

My eyes gave him the death glare before he continued and relayed to us what they'd found. I had a feeling they were leaving parts out, but all was forgotten when they got to the end of their story.

"Whoever they were, they were killed by a vampire," Enzo finished.

"How do you know there is only one psycho lurking around the school?" Finley asked, her face turning several shades of red. Her race already had a hard time fitting in. If this got around the school, it would only get worse for her kind.

"We don't, but we hope," Talon answered.

"We need to get back there with the headmaster and retrieve the bodies," I said. It didn't sit right with me to leave whoever they were in the barn for any longer than necessary. They deserved better than that.

Enzo nodded. "Agreed, but we can't all go. If our whole group left the school grounds at once, it would throw up too many red flags if people saw us."

Gemma leaned forward, her "don't mess with me" face firmly in place. "If we need to be discreet, then we will leave in smaller groups, but it's all of us or none of us, including the two of you. We're tired of being left behind. It ends now."

There was no bothering to hide the grin that formed on

my face. I loved my best friend so damn much. We'd both grown tremendously in the last two years, and I was proud of the person she was still growing into. She could have easily let it be the four of us who went—the guys would have been okay with that—but we were a "leave no woman behind" kind of group now.

Even if our group had just formed, we'd slowly been building our sisterhood over the last two years. Bringing us all together for the new classes was only going to make us stronger and a force to be reckoned with.

The five of us ladies would give Enzo and Talon all the hell necessary for them to realize that, and if they were smart, they'd learn quickly that we weren't to be messed with.

Enzo and Gemma had a stare down I hadn't witnessed since my first year at the academy. It used to stress me out, but not anymore. Instead of worrying about their disagreement, I had the sudden urge to grab some popcorn.

Then I remembered we had more important things to worry about than egos being upset. "Alright, Gemma has made a solid point and if Enzo had any kind of legitimate counter, then he'd have said so already.

"Here is the new plan: Talon, Gemma, and Lyssa will go to the headmaster and see if he'd like to come. The rest of us will head outside the gates and wait just beyond the barrier. If we see anyone, we'll let them know we're just running to town for some supplies. A group of four will not be out of the ordinary for us."

Enzo moved his glare to me next, but it didn't faze me, and he knew better. "Fine. Let's go."

Peyton and Finley were having a hard time holding in their excitement, so I let them go ahead and waited until everyone else left Gemma's room before grabbing Enzo's hand. "You've gotten a lot better, but when we are confronted with a problem, we finish it together or not at all. I won't waver from that, and you need to be okay with it one-hundred percent of the time."

His hands cupped my face. "I know, and thank you for reminding me." He paused, seeming to struggle with the words he wanted to say next. "I'm just afraid. I can't lose you."

"And you're not going to as long as you stand by my side."

His lips turned up into the smile I loved so much. "That I can do."

"Good, then let's go catch up with the others."

He nodded, but instead of moving toward the door, he pressed his mouth to mine and gave me a soul-branding type kiss. "I needed that first."

We both had needed it.

Taking his hand, we left Gemma's room and locked up behind us. The others were waiting at the platform for us before we split up.

"See you soon," Gemma said with a hug for me and then each of the other girls, including Lyssa, even though she was joining Gemma's group.

Lyssa tensed at the physical contact, but she returned the gesture, which was good. After her few comments about her father, I wanted to have a deeper conversation with her, but we needed more time than we currently had, so it'd have to wait, unfortunately.

Gemma, Talon, and Lyssa took one platform to Magic Hall, while the rest of us waited for another to go downstairs.

Peyton was practically shaking with excitement, but

Finley was bouncing between being happy to be included and fearing what we were about to see.

My hand wrapped around her elbow. "It's going to be okay. Whatever we find, none of it is a reflection on you."

"I'm a vampire. When one of us betrays the greater good, we are all marked as a threat. It's not fair, but it's my reality and I'm trying to deal with the fact I might soon be a target."

My head shook at what she had to deal with, and I felt ashamed to admit I'd been afraid my first year in school to even go into the vampire hall. I'd tried to blame it on my human side, but regardless, I'd passed judgement, believing what I thought I knew instead of fact.

It wasn't okay.

"We've got your back. You have a team behind you now, and no matter what we find or what people learn, we will stand up for you and any vampire who needs it. We won't let whatever this monster has done divide us."

She leaned her head against my shoulder as the platform arrived and whispered her thanks. Peyton stole her from me, and I was okay with that. They were closer, just like Gemma and I were, and there was no jealousy between the four of us.

We just had to make sure Lyssa had her place and we didn't let anyone feel like they didn't belong, because we were all equally important to our group even though we were polar opposites of each other.

I never would have thought a witch-vampire hybrid, elf, vampire, and wolf shifter were real just a couple years ago. Now, I was the dragon shifter who was friends with them.

When we arrived downstairs, we headed for the exit. It was nearing ten, so a majority of the students were already in their dorms. I had zero worries we'd run into problems on our way out, and I turned out to be right.

"See? That was easy," I said, poking Enzo in the ribs.

"Yeah. So far, anyway," he grumbled in reply while watching the barrier for the arrival of the rest of our group.

"What are we going to carry them in?" Peyton asked, and I was suddenly very interested in the answer as well.

"Talon should be grabbing something to respectfully cover them, and then I'll transport them back to the barrier one at a time. When we're all back here, we'll take them straight to the infirmary," Enzo answered.

By the time I was able to process the fact we'd be carrying dead bodies back into the academy, the rest of our group arrived and distracted me from being consumed by the sadness. There had already been too much death, and the reality was there would likely be much more of it before any of this was over.

"Marek and Jules stayed behind to let the council know and will keep an eye on the perimeter while we're gone, in case it's an elaborate trap for us to leave the school unprotected," Headmaster Stone said when they arrived.

He was wearing his normal robe attire, and he looked very much the leader I knew him to be, but it was his eyes that got to me. The depths continued to be riddled with despair as more and more of those he was charged to protect were harmed or killed.

"Then, let's go. Everyone, keep your eyes open and no talking. It's only about a ten-minute walk from here," Enzo said.

We moved like a team that had been working together for months, not days, each of us silently finding a spot to watch and doing our part to keep everyone safe.

When we arrived at the barn, the door was still open,

and Enzo halted us. "I'm not saying you girls can't come in, but we need to split up. Half of us need to go in and the other needs to stay outside in case whoever was here before has come back."

"We'll stick with our same groups we split into earlier. Those with me can spread out around the perimeter," Talon said, which made me feel better.

I wasn't keen on watching the headmaster fight a vampire if one had returned. He might have been powerful, but still, I wasn't sure that'd make a difference when someone was coming at him faster than the speed of light.

Enzo agreed and grabbed my hand before giving direction to the others. "We need to clear the bottom half before going to the loft, so we're not cornered. Peyton and Finley, use your senses to do just that and we'll go in behind you."

With Finley's speed and sense of smell, along with Peyton's strength and tracking, I wasn't worried at all about them going in first. That was why we made such a great team. We all had something to bring to the table.

Without hesitation, we all did as assigned, moving in different directions while covering as much as we could in the quickest time possible.

There was a sense of dread hovering over me. I wasn't ready to see the bodies, and knowing life had been taken in the barn we stood in was beginning to freak me out.

"Someone's been back. I had been doing scans for dark magic while we were out, and what I'm picking up now was not present before," Enzo whispered, and I instantly tensed.

"Are they still here?" I asked while connecting with Chelle in case a shift was in my near future.

"Not sure, but Peyton and Finley will let us know soon."

Another minute later, Finley blurred into appearance

before us, hair completely wild from moving so fast. "They were here within the last half-hour, but not anymore. Peyton is trying to track the scent; I think Gemma and Talon followed after her."

Damn it. We weren't supposed to be splitting up like this. That's when bad shit happened.

"Can we go after them?" I asked.

"They'll be fine. We need to get the headmaster in here and see if the bodies in the loft are the missing students or humans. Unless someone has pointed ears, you can't tell if they're supernatural once their dead. There's no aura or scent to go off like usual, and I don't recognize them, so we need Alistair to confirm."

Finley nodded before speeding off to get Lyssa and Headmaster Stone. Enzo began to make his way to the stairs before glancing back. "Honestly, if I didn't have to move the bodies, I wouldn't come up here, but I'll leave the choice to you. If you want to join me, feel free to do so, but we could also use someone to watch for the others coming back."

The prideful part of me wanted to say I could handle seeing the bodies. It wouldn't be the first time I had, nor would it be the last, but something about knowing they were innocent people who had been in the wrong place at the wrong time made it harder to fathom.

I wasn't prideful enough to do something that would scar me for life.

"I'll wait for the others down here, but if you need me, don't hesitate to ask."

He nodded and continued up the ladder. As I was exiting the barn, the others were coming in and Lyssa held the bags to cover the bodies.

"Where are you going?" she asked.

"Keeping an eye outside in case anyone comes back. Enzo already went up to the loft."

Finley and Alistair continued on, but Lyssa stayed with me after giving the bags to Finley. "Mind if I join you?"

"Not at all." I shrugged and kept walking. "What way did they take off?"

Lyssa pointed to the west, away from the school. That was good for everyone else at Shadow Veil, at least. "Are you okay?" she asked, her face creased with concern.

"Of course I am. Why?"

Her hand circled around in the air. "Your aura. It's changing so much, I can't really get a good read on you."

How had I forgotten she could read others?

"Just don't like the thought of pointless deaths, and us being separated isn't helping. I understand why Peyton took off to follow the trail, but that doesn't mean I like it."

Her mouth opened to respond, but Enzo appeared before us first.

"Two of them were the missing students, but the other two were humans," he said solemnly.

"So, we still have a chance to save the other students?" I asked.

"Possibly, but I wouldn't get your hopes up. What the killer did up there, it wasn't humane."

My skin crawled, and bile rose in my throat, but I held my shit together for the sake of the group. My friends were out there tracking the psycho, and until I knew they were safe again, I needed to remain in control.

We'll find whoever hurt those children and then let me finish what they started, Chelle sounded in my mind, and I had never agreed with her more.

CHAPTER EIGHT

Once we were back at Shadow Veil, Enzo, Talon, and Headmaster Stone took the bodies to the infirmary, while the rest of us went to the meeting room where the council wanted to talk about what had happened.

I was hopeful Marek and Jules would be present as well. I hadn't seen Marek since we first arrived back and Jules only in quick passing. Even though it had been just a couple days, I was missing my family, especially after seeing the bodies wrapped in the sheets.

It reminded me once again just how short life could be.

Gemma stepped next to me and looped her arm through mine. "I can't believe we didn't catch the psycho. We had been *so* close."

Thirty minutes had passed before Gemma, Talon, and Finley returned to the barn. Our plan had been to wrap the bodies while waiting, and then Enzo would still take them back to the academy, but if the others still hadn't returned once he had finished, we would go looking for them.

Thankfully, they'd shown up while Enzo was teleporting the last student.

"We'll get him next time," I said confidently, even though we had no idea who *he* was.

Finley swooped in on my other side, while Lyssa and Peyton squeezed in on Gemma's side.

"Damn right, we will. I don't need this dirtbag causing problems for my kind," Finley announced, seeming more self-assured about things than she had when we chatted earlier.

The five of us walked through the hall together like a force to be reckoned with. We didn't separate until we reached the platform to take us up to the council meeting room. Once we arrived on the correct floor, we moved back to our united front stance.

I'd had very few friends I could count on while growing up, but glancing around me, I knew I'd finally found my place in this world. I'd found my people.

Entering the already open door, I was surprised to see Phox still around. I thought for sure she'd have been long gone already, but she was standing there talking with Marek like she had nowhere else to be.

Jules came into our line of sight, and I hugged her first. "I'm glad you are all okay," she said once we pulled apart.

"Of course, we are. Nobody can touch all this awesomeness," Gemma replied with a smirk while gesturing to the five of us.

Apparently, our girl power was noticeable to more than just me.

"Regardless, there is a murderer out there and we all need to be cautious of where we go and when." Jules glanced back at Marek and Phox, then addressed me. "You should go see him. He's asked about you several times."

Nodding, I smiled at her and told the others to save me a seat before heading toward Marek.

Phox glanced over first and smirked. "I'm surprised you're not passed out after today."

"And I thought you'd be gone already. Looks like we're both disappointed tonight," I retorted in good fun.

"Touché. I'm leaving now, actually. I just needed to check in and confirm a few things before I took off. Now, that's done and I'm ready to go. JayLeigh's waiting for me, so you two have fun."

Marek grabbed her arm and lowered his gaze on the dragon seer. "Be safe," he warned.

She nodded curtly and disappeared.

"Why does she need to be safe?" Last I'd heard, things were okay in Drakken. If they weren't, then it was something he should have shared a hell of a lot sooner.

"No reason in particular. Sometimes we all need the reminder, though, especially with all that's going on around us. Don't you agree?"

He had a point, but I still felt like I was missing something. Maybe it had more to do with what Phox saw and not what may have happened. I tried not to stress about it since we had more pressing matters to discuss at the moment.

Marek reached a hand out to gently grasp my elbow. "How are you? Did you enjoy New Orleans? We didn't get to talk much the night you got back."

A sigh escaped me at the reminder of New Orleans. "It was the best. I wish we hadn't had to leave. It was nice being normal for just a little while, if you know what I mean."

He smiled lovingly at me. "I'm glad. I promise you'll make it back there again and hopefully to Drakken under better circumstances as well."

"How are things over there? Your proxy taking good care of the people?" I asked, because if things were falling apart there, he needed to go. We couldn't have both worlds going to shit at the same time.

"Things are fine. Ethaniel is doing a fine job in my place. He'll officially become my second-in-command once I'm back, since the position is now open."

That reminded me about their prisoner. "Is Onyx still breathing, or did he get the punishment he deserved?"

Onyx's betrayal to his king had cost more than one dragon their life and allowed Malina to enter a world she never even should have known existed. Hopefully, his followers had been dealt with as well, but only time would tell for sure.

"His sentencing is postponed until I'm back. While Ethaniel can handle many matters in my absence, this is not one of them," Marek said wistfully.

"Do you miss them? I don't want you to stay here if you're not doing okay."

"There's no doubt I miss my people, but for them, I haven't been gone all that long. A couple weeks, really. It will be fine. I'll go back as soon as I know you're safe."

The fatherly stare he bore into me chipped away at my heart. Not that I had intentionally kept him at bay; it was just odd to think of him as my dad. I had already had a father, an incredible one at that. I never wanted to replace the one I'd grown up with, but I also didn't want to miss out on getting to know the man whose blood flowed through my veins.

It was a fine line to walk, but I was slowly figuring it out.

Headmaster Stone walked in then with Enzo and Talon right behind him. With their arrival, I knew it was time to take my seat, so to help bridge the gap between me and Marek, I gave him an awkward half-hug with one arm and said we'd talk soon before I went to sit with Enzo next to our friends.

Gemma had saved me a seat as previously promised, and Enzo took the one next to me. The room quieted soon after, and the meeting began.

Headmaster Stone stood to address us. "As you all have heard, we had four students miss all of their classes today. All four of them ran in different circles of friends, but all of them were first-year students. Two of them were found tonight, brutally murdered by a vampire."

Apparently, not everyone was completely caught up to speed, because Fiona gasped, and when my eyes landed on her face, she was fighting back tears.

"Alongside the bodies of the students were two human ones. We do not know where they were from or how they were taken, but we will use some of our outside resources to make sure they end up where they need to tomorrow. Their families deserve closure."

"What about our students? What about the families of those confirmed dead and those still missing?" Alexander asked.

"I am personally taking responsibility for notifying the families. Their children were under my care, and I will take responsibility for what's happened," the headmaster said solemnly.

"Nobody blames you, Alistair," I spoke confidently as a thought began to form in my mind that should have been there a lot sooner. "Whoever did this is probably associated with Malina. She's run out of resources and is likely trying to cause a diversion in order to prevent her from being attacked first."

Marek nodded, but not many others seemed to agree with where my thoughts were headed.

"How could we not believe this was connected?" I continued. "Malina had the upper hand. She almost won, yet she hasn't shown her face since she ultimately failed. We took away her dragon connections, killed her righthand man, and captured many of those she'd recruited to fight for her."

Bennett spoke next. "Raegan may have a point. We were just saying in our last meeting how it makes no sense Malina hasn't been back since May. She's had three full months to plan her next move. This could be it, and she's hitting us where it will hurt most. If we continue to lose students, we won't have an academy to protect any longer."

"So, what are you suggesting? That we close the school in order to keep everyone safe until she's found? This institution hasn't been closed in over a century. I can't imagine sending all of these students home when they've only just gotten here," Headmaster Stone said as his shoulders began to droop in defeat.

Fiona stood next. "We don't need to send them home, but I think we need to finally open up to them and be more transparent. They should have the choice and know the risks if we really think this could be Malina."

I groaned. How could there be any doubt this was Malina's doing? There wasn't an ounce of uncertainty within me. Once the thought formed, everything else began to make sense.

"Easy, Rae," Enzo whispered in my ear, and I realized scales had appeared on my arm. Thankfully, I was pretty sure he was the only one who saw as I began to calm down.

Are you okay? I asked Chelle. The scales had been all her doing.

Harming our future is the most despicable act Malina

could have done. I should have connected it sooner, she replied, frustration filling her voice.

Don't blame yourself. Just focus on a way to stop her and help me convince everyone else it's the right lead to follow. Something tells me not everyone around this table is as certain as I am.

That I can do.

She went silent on me while we finished the meeting, and I was even more convinced most of the council didn't believe me when the discussion moved on to what to tell the students and nothing else about the murders specifically.

Jules, Marek, and Bennett seemed to be the only ones who were behind me, but I wasn't going to let that stop me from figuring out what to prepare for next.

Malina had the upper hand on us when she attacked the academy last time. We were still repairing the walls from her destruction, and I wouldn't let it happen again. The next time she stepped foot in the school, she would leave in a body bag.

Headmaster Stone asked our group to stay behind when all the council members left, but Marek and Jules had also stayed behind.

"Phox was needed elsewhere, and she won't be teaching your class for the foreseeable future. Marek will be filling in for her along with myself when he is needed for other situations. He will begin tomorrow and has already received your curriculum we'd given to Phox. Professor Melnier will continue his classes as normal."

Well, that could have been worse. I was more than happy to have Marek teaching our classes. Not only did I believe he had a lot to offer, I also knew he'd do it with less hope of tears from the seven of us than Phox did.

"Any questions?" he asked when none of us responded.

"No, sounds like we're in good hands. It's getting late, so we'll see you tomorrow," Enzo answered for us.

Nobody seemed to object as we were dismissed and headed toward the platform. Glancing at the clock in the hallway, I realized how correct Enzo's statement was when he mentioned it was getting late and let out a yawn. "How is it already after midnight?" I said, not really expecting an answer.

"We're going to be dead on our feet tomorrow after the day we've had." Peyton groaned.

"At least Phox won't be there to make things worse," Lyssa added.

"But I will be," JayLeigh's voice sounded from behind us, and we turned around slowly. "Phox asked me to watch over your group and make sure nobody was babying any of you. We don't have time for that kind of nonsense. So, I'll be your unofficial teacher's assistant while Marek is running the class."

Each of us held the same deadpan expression. This was not good news for any of us. JayLeigh was almost as bad as Phox, and I shivered when remembering her torturous training on Drakken. While it had been effective, it had also made me want to jump off a cliff.

"Oh, don't look so glum, plum. We're going to have the best time," she exclaimed before turning serious. "Now, get your asses to bed. I expect nothing less than your best tomorrow, so don't disappoint me. You won't like it if that happens."

Then, the crazy dragon disappeared. Though, none of us said anything, because we knew she was still present, and we weren't idiots.

She didn't need any more reason to make tomorrow or the days after harder on us. I had full faith JayLeigh would make us hate her by week's end, and she'd love every minute of it.

CHAPTER NINE

The following day went by torturously slow. JayLeigh had done her best to make the morning as strenuous as possible, but Marek had also done a good job of keeping her in check.

We'd learned Phox had pulled a lesson from something we shouldn't have even been trying to accomplish until at least a month later, but since we had already made progress, Marek decided to let us continue to work on the defense creation.

Anytime one of us was close to accomplishing something, JayLeigh would sneak up behind them and yell something totally random. Panty burp was a favorite of her, since people laughed every single time. She insisted that we needed to learn focus, and this was her way of helping us.

When we met with Emmett, it was a huge relief on our bodies. He split us into groups based upon what he'd observed the previous day about each of us. I was teamed with Lyssa and Enzo, while the rest were put together in a second group.

"You'll be fighting as a team and each of you will focus

on your own strengths. Where one is weak, another will be strong, and we will continue to work on balancing each other until the seven of you are the most feared group of supernaturals to face a Doyen," Emmett had said.

We all hung on his every word. He seemed to have faith in us that I hadn't seen from anyone else. Not that Marek hadn't been supportive, but he knew his role and was already resigned to the fact he'd have to kill Malina himself. He mainly talked about ways to protect ourselves, not to attack.

Emmett, though, had spoken of the ways he planned to teach us to incapacitate Malina and move on the offense instead. He had a passion for what he was doing, and it made me wonder about his past and how he ended up at Shadow Veil. There was a reason the headmaster had sought him out, and I wanted to know why that was.

"So, what are you doing for the rest of the night?" Gemma asked while we were eating dinner in the commissary after classes were done.

"I want to sleep. Yesterday was a long-ass day, and twelve hours of sleep sounds pretty damn nice right about now," I answered while glancing over at Enzo, who was paying more attention to Talon than my conversation with Gemma.

My finger tapped against my cheek. "But if you wanted to convince me to go do something stupid and reckless like skinny dipping in the lake or flying through Salem with you on Chelle's back, then I'm sure that could be arranged."

Talon smirked, and I knew he'd heard me, but Enzo still hadn't looked my way.

Gemma added to it. "Why don't we do both? Skinny dipping first, then shower and dress up to go clubbing in town. Let our hair down and see what trouble finds us."

Talon's chest rumbled. "Not a chance in hell." His arm reached out and smacked Enzo in the side of the head. "Do something about this, bro."

Enzo shrugged. "She's a big girl. I trust her. Maybe you just need to trust your woman some more."

My brow quirked up. "So, you're good if I show my goods off to whoever might be hanging around the water and then leave the protection shields to go have my fun with my girls?"

"Yep. Do whatever will make you happy, and I'll do what makes me happy." The grin that formed on his face told me the tables were about to be turned.

"And what makes you happy?" I asked, even though I knew I'd regret it.

"Beating the shit out of anyone who would dare ogle at your naked body and being your shadow as you have fun with your girls. I'm all for you doing whatever you want. Just know I'll be right there with you, making sure nothing happens that shouldn't."

"Possessive much?" I countered.

"Nope, but protective? You bet your sweet ass I am, and you love it."

Damn him. He was right. I loved everything about how much he wanted to keep anything from harming me. His alpha tendencies were a turn-on I would never admit out loud, for fear they'd only get worse, but I never wanted them to go away.

Gemma was doing her best to hold in her laughter, but I waved my hand. "Let it out, and just remember, yours isn't much better than mine."

Talon raised his hands in innocence. "How did I get looped into this?"

"You chose to be friends with Enzo. It's a package deal,

especially when you're dating my best friend." I shrugged. He really should have already known better.

Enzo's golden eyes bore into me. "We should head to bed."

"Seriously?" Peeking at my phone, it was just after six.

"Hey, you said twelve hours of sleep sounds nice. What my baby wants, my baby gets." He wasted no time picking me up and tossing me over his shoulder.

My laughter filtered through the commissary as I waved goodbye to my best friend without a bit of embarrassment rolling through me. When I first arrived at the academy, all I wanted was to be invisible, but since things had been good with Enzo as of late, I didn't really give a damn anymore. I had my circle, and what other people thought didn't get to me anymore.

The moment others learned I was a dragon shifter, all anonymity went out the window, and Enzo loved to give everyone a show, so who was I to keep him from doing what made him happy? I loved him for who he was. Possessive overprotective traits and all.

"There is blood rushing to my head that's beginning to make me dizzy, darling," I said with a grin.

Enzo wasted no time switching positions, and before I knew it, I was cradled in his arms like a baby. "Better?" he asked.

"Better would be allowing me to walk, but I'll take it."

"Yes, take advantage of the short rest now, because there won't be any when we get back to the room," he murmured softly in my ear before nipping at my neck.

"What happened to my twelve hours of sleep?" I fake pouted.

He winked before flashing my favorite smile. "You know better than that."

My heart melted just a little more, and I couldn't remove the grin from my face. Everything else around us might be going to shit, but moments like this made it all worth it. Our bond was solidified more and more every time we made love, which made not getting sleep the least of my worries.

THE REST OF THE WEEK WENT SMOOTHLY WITH classes, and we found a routine that didn't kill our bodies or minds. Marek was loosening up, and JayLeigh quit trying to challenge each of us every chance she had. None of us had learned how to do anything spectacular yet, but we were honing our skills and growing, which was something.

The council had decided to tell the students in smaller groups about what was truly going on so that there wasn't complete mayhem when they heard about the missing students. The two still gone hadn't been far from my mind, and I wondered how in the hell we were going to find them.

Each of the council members had gone to classrooms and given the information individually, so we weren't present, but we'd certainly heard about it in the hallways.

"What if the school gets blown up?"

"Are we all supposed to go evil if Malina takes over?"

"Should we just say 'screw school' and go home to never come back?"

"All vampires are garbage. The dirty blood suckers need to be burned from this earth."

The last one had hurt the most, but Finley hadn't been with me when I heard it, and I sincerely hoped she hadn't overheard anything similar. Enzo had been with me and stopped to have a "nice" chat with the kid who said it, but when I asked what he'd said, Enzo refused to respond. Just stated it was taken care of, whatever that meant. He likely threatened the kid, which I didn't mind if it taught him a lesson in being judgmental.

Then, we'd continued on to our classes like nothing ever happened. After five mentally exhausting days, we finally had a day off, but it wasn't really ours. We still had duties outside of learning, which meant no rest for the wicked.

"We learned the identity of the two humans," Headmaster Stone said after Enzo and I arrived in his office late Saturday morning.

"Should we get the others?" I asked, referring to the rest of our team.

"No, I can't have all seven of you in here every time I have something to say. I trust the two of you to relay what's necessary."

Enzo nodded. "We can handle that. So, where were they from?"

"One was from Boston and the other from Medford. They were only fifteen and sixteen years old. The girl had been at the park with her little sister when she went missing and the boy was thought to be a runaway."

My heart constricted. That vampire really needed to die a gruesome death. "Nobody else has disappeared, right?" I asked.

"No, the professors are required to take count in every class and send me the attendance first thing. I'll know the second someone isn't where they're supposed to be. We don't have any leads on the vampire, though, but we've been looking into your theory about how he could be connected to Malina."

My eyes rolled. *Could be connected.* There was no doubt about it in my mind.

"Have you heard from your grandmother, by chance?" Alistair asked, and my body froze.

Fear paralyzed every part of me as I thought about all the reasons he would ask me that. All of the bad reasons.

"No, she hasn't," Enzo finally answered for me. "Why?"

"I tried reaching out to her to see if she could ask the coven leader down there about potential rogue vampires we could look into. It's normal for her not to respond to me right away. She has her hands full down there, but I thought if Raegan reached out, then she may hear from her sooner."

Breath whooshed out of me when he said it was a normal occurrence, but the stress wasn't over. I'd be calling her as soon as we left the room.

"I'll see what I can find out," I finally said.

"I appreciate that. Now, how are the classes going? Are you finding them beneficial so far, or do we need to do something different?"

Enzo went on about what we were learning while my mind went dark. If anything happened to my Meme, I wasn't sure what would happen to my sanity. She was the last direct link I had to the parents who raised me, and I'd barely scratched the surface on getting to know her. I wanted years to spend with her still.

Enzo's hand tugged on my arm as he stood. Apparently, they were done talking and I'd missed it while I tried not to let the fear and potential wrath envelop my body.

"I'll see you two soon," Alistair waved as we turned for the door.

When it was closed behind us, I pulled out my phone and found the contact I needed. Pressing on her name, I held the phone to my ear while anxiously waiting for her to pick up.

"You've reached the voicemail for Amalia. Leave a message and I might call you back."

The grin that appeared on my face couldn't be helped. She was a spunky old lady.

"Hey, Meme. It's Raegan. I needed to ask you something important. Give me a call as soon as you get this. I love you."

Hitting the end button, my eyes met Enzo's as his hands wrapped around my face. "I know you've been through hell, but try not to think worst-case scenario. Go find Jules and confirm Headmaster Stone's theory about your grandmother always being too busy to call back. She has people down there who can confirm Amalia is fine as well."

Pressing my lips to his in a quick kiss, I decided I needed to see my aunt immediately. "Sorry, Love. I gotta go."

Before he could grab me, I ran toward the platform and hopped on just before it began to descend. Enzo was yelling my name, not at all happy I had ditched him, but he would forgive me later.

Another student was on the platform with me, and I smiled at her, but she just stared wide-eyed at me, not saying a word. Weird, but whatever.

Bringing my phone to my ear, I called Jules. "Where are you?" I asked when she answered on the second ring.

"In my room, getting ready to—"

"Don't move. I'll be there in five." I hung up before she could object and bounced on the balls of my feet, wishing the platform moved faster.

I was no longer afraid of falling off, but the slight thing next to me appeared to be petrified. "Are you okay?" I asked.

She gulped and nodded, her doe-like eyes getting even bigger somehow. "Not a fan of these things."

"You'll get used to them, maybe by your last year." I offered a smile, but she didn't return it, so I decided to leave her alone. If she wanted to be invisible, then she could be. I completely understood how that felt.

The platform came to my stop, and I waved goodbye to the girl even though she didn't really talk before I raced for Jules's room and focused my mind on what it might take to figure out if my grandmother was okay. At the moment, it was all that truly mattered to me.

Jules had left her door cracked for me, and I burst into the room without knocking, thankfully not out of breath due to all the training we'd been doing.

"What's wrong?" she asked immediately.

"Have you been in touch with your pack in New Orleans recently? Like the last couple of days?"

She shook her head. "Why? Did something happen down there?" Already on her feet, I could see the same tension filter into her that I'd felt earlier.

"I don't know. Alistair told me he couldn't get a hold of Amalia, and I haven't talked to her since we left other than a few shared texts. He thought it was normal, but in a time like this, it doesn't feel normal to me. I *need* to know those I care about are safe."

Hysteria was bubbling at the surface by the time I stopped talking, so I took a deep breath while Jules got her phone out. "Give me a second."

She placed one call that went unanswered, then another. Despair was choking me when the second one was also unsuccessful, but the third person finally answered, and I breathed a little lighter.

"What's going on down there?"

Waving my hands, I tried to ask her to put it on speaker, but she ignored me, plugging her other ear to focus on whoever was talking.

"When?" She paused. "How many?" Another pause. "Do you need me there?"

Damn it, this was going to be the death of me if she didn't tell me what the hell was going on.

"Okay. What about Amalia? Have you seen her?"

An even longer pause caused me to lose it, and I pressed myself against her side in an attempt to hear the person on the line, but by the time I did so, they were already done.

"Good. Keep us updated. We're doing everything we can here, but this helps to know. I'll call back if we learn anything else."

She hung up the phone and glared at me. "Girl, learn some patience."

"Is she okay? Do they know where my Meme is?"

Rolling her eyes, she nodded. "Amalia is fine. She's in the quarter helping with a turf war between the wolves and bears. A cub was found murdered, and the bears are blaming the wolves. Apparently, things are pretty tense, but no mention of vampires causing trouble."

My mind began to process the words, and as I really thought about what she'd said and realized I didn't have to worry about my grandmother, I put the connection together.

"We need to find out how many other packs or covens or whatever there is out there are having issues with losing their young. This isn't a coincidence, Jules. Malina is doing this. She wants to divide us before she attacks. We came together before and beat her. But if we have no back-up, then she will win."

Her eyes widened, and I knew that if she hadn't truly

believed me before, she did then. She would have stood by my side no matter what before, but there was no denying it now. If other supernaturals were having the same issues we were at the academy, the others had to see that I was right.

Malina was going to tear us apart from the inside if we didn't figure out a way to come together again, and I'd be damned if I let her win.

J ules called a meeting with the council for that afternoon, while I gathered the team and relayed the information I was convinced to be true. There was no doubt in my mind that when the other supernaturals were asked about their young, a majority would have regrettably suffered losses recently.

When I was done explaining to the group what I knew, the rage flowing through my and Enzo's room was thick.

"So, what are we doing now? Why aren't we with the council?" Lyssa asked.

"Jules thought it would be best if she met with them on her own. Not all of them believe our little group holds true value, and if the information is coming from her, well, it would have more weight to it, unfortunately," I answered honestly.

"That's bullshit," Peyton snapped, surprising me because she was usually the calmer one.

"While I agree, I also trust Jules. She will get the point across, and we will continue to work on a plan." I glanced at Enzo hoping like hell that he had one, because I didn't.

There was a knock at the door before anyone could say anything else. Tension rolled through me, because Jules shouldn't be done already if everything went well, and the council wouldn't want to meet with me if the meeting didn't go as we hoped.

When Enzo opened the door, I craned my neck to see who it was. Marek's head stood several inches above Enzo's as he glanced at me before saying something I couldn't hear from where I sat.

Enzo moved aside, and they both came to the table we were currently sitting around. Marek stood even though Enzo offered his seat, which made me laugh because both men ended up standing, stubborn in their own ways as usual.

Talon moved his chair back, facing Marek. "Is everything okay, King Marek?"

It still took me off guard to hear him referred to as King. I knew he was, but since we'd left Drakken, it wasn't often he was addressed that way. I wondered if we offended him by not doing so.

"I'm not sure. As you all know, Phox left here in a hurry a few days ago. I haven't heard from her since she left, but she gave me instructions to come find you today and tell you that it's important to believe in yourself even if nobody else does."

Shit, shit, shit. Was Phox trying to tell us that we wouldn't have the support of the council?

"Did she say anything else?" Enzo asked.

"Just that our future was at stake, and we needed to continue to train and prepare. It sounded as if she knew Malina would be showing her final hand soon and we needed to be ready at a moment's notice," Marek replied.

"What about the vampire? We can't let the psycho roam from place to place killing children," Finley snarled.

Standing up, I began to pace behind the table. "I think if we can track the vamp, then he might lead us back to Malina. Do you think we should go back to the barn and search it for anything the idiot might have left behind? Anything that would be helpful in conducting a locating spell? I doubt Malina has a protection over one of her pawns that would prevent us from tracking him magically."

"I can handle that part," Marek replied. When I eyed him curiously, he continued, "We've adapted to much while living in Drakken. I have more magic up my sleeve than I've yet to reveal."

There was a slight grin on his face, and it warmed my heart in a surprising way. Ever since he'd faced Malina, there had been a cloud of doom hanging over him, but giving him something to contribute to the team that didn't require physical violence had brought him true joy.

For a powerful dragon king, he sure hated war. It was something he'd hopefully overcome before we faced Malina again, because we couldn't afford to have our most-needed team member hesitate. If we lost again, so would all supernaturals.

"Did Phox say what the rest of us should do while we wait for her to return?" Talon asked.

"Not specifically, but from what I understood, until we can nail an exact location down for Malina, she wants us to do what we've been doing and hopefully, the council will send out the warning about the children."

Frustration tugged at my body. If the council didn't listen to Jules, I was going to lose my shit on them.

Enzo came to me and wrapped his arm around my waist, which immediately calmed the dragon within me.

Chelle wasn't happy about what we were hearing, either, but until we knew more, there wasn't a damn thing we could do about it, no matter how much we wanted to.

We had no idea where Malina was and scouring the states looking for her wasn't the best use of our time. No, the only thing we could do was warn as many people as possible about the foreboding threats to their children and keep preparing. I might not like the plan, but Marek was right.

We'd wait for Phox and I'd just have to hope that Ophelia would give her the permission she needed to help us. Otherwise, we would all be screwed.

My phone buzzed in my pocket, so I stepped away from Enzo to answer, assuming it would be Jules with bad news, based upon what I'd just learned. Though, to my surprise, Meme Amalia was on the screen instead.

She was already talking when I answered the call, so I let her finish, enjoying what I was hearing.

"No, that's *not* what I said, damn it. Does the little old lady have to do everything around here? Don't you dare answer that or I'll give you a pig nose. That's right, run off and do your damn job, so I can talk to my granddaughter."

"Uh, hi, Meme," I said while trying to hold back my laughter.

"Hello, Dear. Sorry about that. It's complete chaos around here, and everyone is acting like we've never been threatened before."

"Did something else happen besides the cub's death?"

She sighed. "There have been children taken from each race. It's taken days to convince the group leaders this is not an attack by the people of New Orleans. Something smells fishy to me, and its name is Malina."

"That's what I already told Jules. She's meeting with

our council now, but I'm not convinced they'll believe her," I said, resigned.

"Didn't I tell you I needed to talk with my granddaughter? That means go the hell away and do as you're told before I bend you over my knee and spank you like I did when you were a child!"

I couldn't contain the laughter any longer, and everyone in the room turned to look at me like I was crazy, but I didn't care.

"Meme, who are you talking to?"

"The wolf alpha. He thinks he's in charge here, but I have no problem putting him in his place. I used to change his diapers, for Christ's sake. Anyway, the council will believe her, or they'll be seeing me, and they don't want to make me leave New Orleans. Everything is going to be okay. We know who and what we're up against. That's the most important part."

I didn't respond, because I didn't know what to say. We've known for over a year what we were up against, but she still hasn't been stopped. We were too far apart to keep each other safe, and no sane parent would be willing to help us and leave their children unprotected while others were going missing.

"Raegan, stop it. I can't even see you, and I already know you're pacing and fidgeting while thinking of all the ways this won't work. I have a plan brewing, and as soon as I get the race leaders to stop acting like toddlers, I'll be putting it into place. Just have patience."

Ha, patience. Something I've struggled with all my life. But I trusted her, so I promised to do my best.

"That's my girl. I'll be seeing you soon, and text me the moment something changes. I can check those quicker than voicemails. Then, I'll call you as soon as I can."

"Will do. I love you, Meme."

"Love you, too, Dear. Talk soon."

The line disconnected as my emotions warred with each other. Hearing her voice had been good for me, and hearing her act like a crazy tyrant over men who could possibly squish her was even better, but there was an ominous feeling in my gut that wasn't going anywhere anytime soon.

When I turned back to the team, all eyes were on me. "What?" I asked.

"Care to fill us in, Love? We only heard one half of the conversation." Enzo smiled, stating the obvious.

"Oh, yeah, sorry. Amalia had already come to the conclusion that Malina was at fault for the children as well. She's working on something down there and, like everyone else has said, apparently we're just supposed to stay put and prepare to act at a moment's notice."

"Your grandma is life goals. I heard everything she said, and she is one badass old lady. I've never heard a race leader talk like that to another without starting a war," Finley said with a spark in her eye that had been missing lately. I was sure her vampire hearing came in handy most days, and I was glad it brought her some joy in this instance.

"We can learn all we need about being a feared old lady from her *after* Malina is dead. As much as I don't like it, we've had plenty of people we respect, Marek included, tell us we need to stay and keep preparing. Which means training in our classes and behaving. We might not like it, but hopefully it's short-lived."

Gemma groaned. "I never thought I'd say this, but I miss normal school. Where homework wasn't talks about impending wars with crazy powerful sorceresses and whoever else is stupid enough to follow her. This was not at all how I pictured my last year at Shadow Veil."

Talon took her hand and whispered something in her ear that had her blushing, so I left the consoling up to him. He seemed to be better at it than me.

"You guys go enjoy the rest of your day. As soon as we hear from Jules, we'll let you know," Enzo finally said when we realized there was nothing else to really discuss until we knew what direction the council thought was best.

It was either going to make things easier or harder, but whichever way it went, I already knew what needed to be done, and we were doing it with or without the council's permission.

It wasn't until after dinner when we heard from Jules and, even then, it wasn't exactly the news we were hoping for. She sent a text saying they were still discussing things and she'd see us the following day.

"Try not to stress about it. There's nothing you can do to change what they may be thinking," Enzo murmured in my ear as I read the text.

"Sure, there is. I can go in there channeling my inner Meme and tell them all how it's going to be."

He grinned. "While I'd love to see that, I don't think that would further any of your plans."

My shoulders shrugged. "But it would make me feel better."

"How about chocolate cake and ice cream?"

My stomach growled. I'd barely eaten anything for dinner, and chocolate always made me feel better, even if it was a temporary fix.

"I won't say no to that."

Trusting him again had been the best thing I'd ever done. It had taken a while, especially after watching him stab Marek, but instead of taking off like before, I had stayed and listened. While the reasons had pissed me off to no end, I was able to truly put things to rest once Marek had woken up.

Enzo was a good man. Stupid sometimes, but loyal to a fault. I knew without a doubt in my mind that he loved me, and that was more than enough.

A few minutes later, he brought me a heaping bowl of chocolate ice cream with chunks of mint and a cake drizzled in hot fudge. "You are the greatest thing to ever walk this Earth," I murmured as I took my first bite.

"Thanks, Love." He chuckled.

My eyes peeked up at him. "Oh, I was talking to the cake."

He threw a pillow at me from the couch, and I let it hit me in the head while I protected my goods from being spilled. "Don't mess with me when I'm enjoying my dessert. That's grounds for break-up."

He lowered his face to mine, eyes smoldering. "There's no breaking up here. You can have your cake and eat it, too, Love."

My eyes went from the yummy dessert to him several times before I took one more overwhelming bite of sugary greatness. "You win," I mumbled with a mouth full of food before setting the plate down.

"I win every day I fall asleep next to you."

My body melted faster than the ice cream I was leaving behind as Enzo carried me to our room. I knew without a doubt, no matter how bad things got, I was still the luckiest girl in the world.

CHAPTER ELEVEN

E nzo

A COUPLE OF WEEKS HAD PASSED, AND OUR TRAINING sessions were getting more complex, but also more manageable. Watching Raegan disappear for the first time had nearly given me a coronary, but Professor Melnier had been just the teacher needed to focus her on the task.

He'd also taught Talon how to do illusions so real that even the teacher didn't know when he was in one. When I thought there was nothing special left for the rest of us to learn, Emmett showed us otherwise.

"It's not just dragons who are capable of pushing their mind beyond normal restrictions. You each have a place in this team, and before I'm done with you, you'll know exactly what that is."

Peyton and Finley had struggled the most since magic had never been their thing—brute force and speed was more their calling—but I watched in fascination as Raegan worked tirelessly with them when the professor wasn't, so that nobody felt left behind.

"Yes, Peyton, just like that. Now, use your hand to twist. Yep. You got it. Just a little bit more." Raegan paused, watching every move Peyton made closely, and when her fading form began to solidify again, Raegan was right there cheering her on to keep trying.

"I don't mean to sound like a tiny fairy, but you just have to believe, Peyton. Believe in yourself and what you're capable of," Raegan said.

Peyton flipped her off, and I just shook my head. My mate had the kindest soul I'd ever known, and I was damn proud of her.

Lyssa strode up next to me. "Never thought I'd see the day a dragon would be teaching a wolf how to manipulate magic."

"Neither did I, but I wouldn't change a thing about it." I grinned as Peyton finally disappeared completely. It only lasted for a few seconds, but it proved she was capable of more than she previously thought.

"You wouldn't?" Lyssa asked.

"Huh?" I had been so distracted watching the celebrations, I'd forgotten what I'd said.

"You wouldn't change any of what's led us to this point?"

"Oh, well, I guess some things, but I don't mess with fate, Lys. We all have to go through bad shit to get to the good stuff. This isn't Utopia. Sure, I wish I hadn't screwed things up so badly with Raegan to begin with, but I can't change what's already happened, so I don't dwell on it."

She remained pensive, and I knew she wanted to keep talking, but a part of me wanted to walk away. I tried to keep my distance from her so that Raegan would never have doubts, but when I took two steps toward Raegan, she narrowed her gaze at me and motioned toward Lyssa.

I read between the glares and stepped back, but the moment was already gone.

"I'm going to run with Finley," she said, then disappeared. Finley seemed to be her favorite, because the vampire was good company without the deep stuff, and that seemed to be just what Lyssa needed.

It was nearing dinner, so I went to break up Raegan's training session before they decided to go all night, but just as I moved to do so, a hand wrapped around my arm.

"Wait for it," JayLeigh whispered with a sadistic smile on her face, and since I was a curious bastard, I let her have her fun.

Just as Raegan vanished into thin air, Phox took her spot, and Peyton screamed like a banshee when the dragon seer's form appeared instead of Raegan's. "What did you do with Raegan?"

Raegan was rolling on the grass, laughing her ass off just ten feet to the right. "Sorry, Pey. I swear I did *not* plan that, but I sure as hell enjoyed it."

"Screw you both." Her chest rumbled.

Phox feigned offense. "Now, Peyton, I know you only had one class with me, but I'm sure you've heard the stories. Do you really want to growl at me?"

Peyton blanched and shook her head, then Raegan nudged Phox. "Leave her be and tell us what happened."

JayLeigh and I moved in closer. Phox had been gone for almost three weeks, and this was a moment we'd all been looking forward to: knowing whether Ophelia had given her permission to share the vision that caused Phox to leave in the first place.

JayLeigh's face fell and my gut told me it wasn't just the vision we had to worry about any longer.

"Maybe we should gather the others and take this inside," I suggested.

"Gemma and Talon will be here soon, and we don't have time to track Lyssa and Finley or anyone else you consider necessary," Phox said. My head cocked to the side as I tried to determine if she was being snide or if it was just her personality. Likely, it was the latter, so I let it go.

"So, what is it?" Raegan pushed.

"Ophelia is dead. I'm the only dragon seer left in any of the worlds."

Everyone remained silent as we processed the information. I wasn't really sure what it meant, though we knew it had to happen at some point. From what we'd learned, there was always a predecessor and successor, and the two could not co-exist for long or their visions would begin to meld and confuse their minds.

"When?" I asked.

"While I was there. She left me with some books and little direction as to what they were for, then said it was time. She died in my arms with no warning whatsoever." There was a flash of emotion in her face I'd never seen before, and for the first time, I could really tell how much Ophelia had meant to Phox.

Raegan's jaw twitched, and I couldn't tell if she was fighting back tears or frustration. Probably both, because we needed all the help we could get, and we'd just lost the most experienced seer.

Talon and Gemma slid in next to me and caught on quickly to what had happened. Phox continued to speak of the happenings in Drakken and feared they weren't prepared for what was to come.

"So, what did you see that you needed permission to share with us? I mean, we appreciate all the updates, but what about Malina?" Gemma asked.

"What day is it?" Phox asked.

"September Twenty-Sixth. Why?" I asked.

She sighed like I was an idiot. "Time is everything in my world." Then, she disappeared.

All eyes turned toward JayLeigh, but she held her hands up in mock-surrender. "I have no idea what she knows. I just met her this side of the portal when I felt the energy shift. She asked where you all were, and I led her here."

Something shady was happening, and I was worried we weren't going to find out until something drastic happened.

Moving closer to Raegan, I wrapped an arm around her shaking form. She was pissed off and I didn't blame her. So was I and made sure JayLeigh knew it. "So, we've waited weeks for Phox to come back with information, and now we're expected to wait some more when we have no idea what could be coming for us around the next corner?"

JayLeigh patted my shoulder. "You're a smart little elf." Then, she disappeared as well, but Raegan wasn't accepting that.

With cat-like reflexes, Raegan moved and yanked on JayLeigh's invisible form. How she knew where the dragon was, I had no idea, but literal sparks flew between them as Raegan forced JayLeigh's body into visibility again.

"How the hell..." JayLeigh gaped.

"No, *what* the hell?" Raegan snapped. "I'm done with the games, JayLeigh. I refuse to continue to play them. Not for Malina, the council, you, or Phox. We've done nothing but work our asses off, and for what? To be treated like we're children who need to have more patience? Well, excuse me, but fuck that."

Ah, there was my little spitfire dragon. Raegan's emerald eyes were beginning to split, and I knew Chelle was close to the surface, but Raegan maintained control, and I was damn proud of her.

Before the shock wore off from JayLeigh's face, Phox reappeared. "Raegan, come with me. The rest of you, we'll see you tomorrow."

"Tomorrow? What do you need my mate for that will take all night?" I snarled, not at all okay with her demands.

"It's not what I need, Elf, but what everyone else needs. Now, go blow shit up in the forest for a release if you need to, but your mate is required elsewhere." Phox leveled her stormy eyes on me. Being the shifter she was, I knew she was trying to throw alpha power at me, but it didn't work. I would never obey her, and she was no queen.

Turning Raegan toward me, I made sure I had her complete attention. "Do you want to go with Phox?"

"If it means one step closer to destroying Malina, then yes."

"Do you want to go by yourself?" I asked.

"No, I'd always rather have you at my side, but I trust her enough, and if it's the only way to hear what she has to say, then I'll be fine." Raegan's chin tilted up as she held my stare. There wasn't an ounce of fear rolling through her. I, on the other hand, was about to lose my shit.

It wasn't often I let her out of my sight for more than a few hours, but for a whole evening? It hadn't happened in almost a year.

"Okay, but come back to me soon," I all but begged.

She caressed my cheek. "Go with Talon, take Phox's advice, and let some aggression out. Morning will be here before you know it."

Gemma scoffed. "Just because you don't get your man, doesn't mean I have to go without as well."

Talon grinned. "We won't be long, and I promise to make it worth the wait."

"Well, I've had enough." JayLeigh gagged. "The four of you are repulsive."

Peyton grunted. "Try hanging out with them every day, all day."

"Hey, we're not *that* bad," Gemma said, and continued defending us, but I stopped listening.

Phox stepped forward and whispered something in my mate's ear that had her stiffening before Raegan met my stare. "We have to go. Keep your phone on you, and I'll call you as soon as I can. Be safe and I love you."

Before I could respond, they both disappeared, and there was no reaching out to grab Reagan like she had done with JayLeigh. No, they were gone into thin air like they'd transported.

My chest rumbled, and the air grew chilly around me. My elf powers gave me a link to the elements, but not really any control over them. Marek had been trying to teach me how to tap further into the resources, though all my trainings had really done was amplified my connections when my emotions were escalated, still with no control.

"Come on, bro. Let's go let off some steam." Talon gripped my shoulder until I calmed down and the weather around us went back to normal.

I still wasn't okay by any means, but I had a better handle on the rage within.

Talon said bye to Gemma while the girls made plans that had him grinding his teeth. "You owe me for leaving her with JayLeigh. That dragon is a bad influence."

My laugh was dark. "While I'd love to agree with you, none of them are bad on their own. It's only when they're together that they feed off each other and we have to watch our balls."

"Ain't that the truth."

We ventured into the forest like Phox had suggested. Not that I wanted to listen to her after she'd taken Raegan away, but blowing up a few boulders *did* sound like a good use of my unexpected free time.

We headed toward a creek, and I decided to see what I could do with the water and the new magic I'd learned. "Feel like experimenting?"

Talon smirked. "As long as we're still blowing shit up, then hell yeah."

Moving toward the water, I dipped my fingers in and felt the power rolling through the stream. Marek had taught us that everything had its own magic, whether it was created by paranormal means or nature. We just needed the patience to access it.

Using the magic Phox had taught us on the first day combined with what I learned from Marek, I wrapped my energy around the water source and drew it toward me. Deciding to show off, I created a trident with the liquid.

"Overachiever," Talon grumbled as he half-shifted and tossed a ten-foot boulder into the sky like it was nothing.

Focusing on the rock, I waited until the perfect moment to fling the water weapon at my target.

The trident sliced right through the rock, and the weapon exploded, but only water rained down on us, making me think it didn't work.

That was until the boulder landed with a thud then split into two perfect halves.

Before I could inspect the damage, clapping sounded

from behind us, and my entire being changed when I heard the cackle that went with it.

Slowly, I turned around and came face-to-face with Malina, though I wasn't sure if it was actually her, because I couldn't sense the evil that normally permeated from her.

"You've come so far, Lorynzo. I can't wait to see what else you've learned," she cooed while flicking her long dark hair back.

"How did you get in here?" Talon snapped while I continued to watch her. There was something off, but I couldn't place it.

"Shadow Veil isn't as safe as you believe it is, dragon. Come with me, and I can show you just what I mean." Malina's hands began to move in a pulling motion as if she had a tether directly tied to Talon.

His face turned every shade of red as he fought her pull. He was already half-shifted, so I assumed he'd finish and bring his dragon out, but no such luck.

"Did you really come here for him, Malina? This doesn't seem like you to sneak around. Or has time weakened you and you're no longer so sure of your abilities," I said, hoping to draw her attention.

It worked. A little too well.

One hand continued to tug at Talon, but the other flung out toward me, and an invisible force knocked me back a good twenty feet.

"You're an idiot if you think I've weakened in the slightest."

Getting up, I didn't bother to dust myself off. "Then why are you hiding? You're holding back. I can sense it. Maybe you're just scared."

She laughed as she waved her hand, opening a portal next to her. "No, I'm just smarter than the rest of you, and I know what and when things need to be done in order to get what I want. You all just lack the patience and power to do the same. Now, I'm going to take this dragon and be on my way."

"That's not going to happen," I growled.

She raised a brow at me. "And who's going to stop me?"

There was no point in responding to her question. It was what we'd spent the prior weeks training for. What Emmett believed we could do.

Only, we weren't facing her together as a team, and I wasn't stupid enough to believe I could defeat her on my own, but hopeful enough that I could at least prevent her from getting hands on Talon.

Drawing on the water and air around me, I pulled as much energy into my core as I could in the shortest amount of time and, without pause, created another trident and threw the weapon toward Malina's form.

She twisted to avoid a direct hit, and the tip grazed her arm which only served to piss her off more. I hadn't done enough damage to break the hold she had on Talon, but there was a weird spark when my magic collided with her.

"I don't have time for you," she roared, walking closer to Talon and further from the portal.

Charging for her, I had no idea what I intended to do, but I couldn't just stand there any longer. She paid me little attention, and I soon realized why.

Just as my body should have smashed into hers, her form shimmered, and I moved right through her.

"Portal," Talon managed to say through gritted teeth.

Taking one look back, I realized there was someone trying to come through, a vampire with disturbing red eyes and a scar across his cheek I'd seen before. Knowing he had to be dealt with later, I focused on destroying the portal, so neither he nor anyone else could sneak in.

Gathering enough power to take a building down, I threw it toward the opening and enjoyed the shouts of the vampire as my power pushed him back and the portal closed.

But my celebration was short lived when I turned toward Talon again. Malina was ripping scales from his arm, and I didn't understand how she could do that when I couldn't touch her and she wasn't touching him. It was like she was suctioning them off.

An idea formed, and I hoped Talon would forgive me because we were running out of time.

Without pause, I aimed for my target and fired off several rounds of magic toward my friend. When his form crumbled to the ground, his half-shift disappeared.

"Maybe you're smarter than I gave you credit for," Malina snarled, "but I have what I came here for. Taking him would have just been an added bonus."

"We're coming for you, Malina. You can't hide forever."

"Who said I was hiding?" She winked, and then her body disintegrated into a pixelated dust before completely disappearing.

There had been only one way Phox was going to get me alone, and she knew it. She used my desire for more information against me and I played right into it like a fool. I had assumed she was taking me somewhere private to tell me about her "surprise information", but instead, we ended up in Marek's room.

"Phox, nice of you to knock," Marek said before noticing I was standing there, too. "Is everything okay?"

She shrugged. "I need you to keep Raegan's dragon contained for another thirty or so minutes."

My body tensed. This was no surprise. This was a kidnapping.

Taking two steps back, my hand reached for the door, but Phox yanked me back toward her. "Marek, tell her she can't leave."

"I need more information than that before I demand my dau—her to do anything. You know I don't like to take people's free will."

My heart fluttered at him almost calling me his daughter. I knew he would have if I wasn't there, and he'd only corrected himself because we really hadn't talked about what our relationship was or could be. One day, when there wasn't chaos all around us, we'd have to air things out.

"What about if it prevents her from getting taken by Malina?" Phox countered.

Marek's eyes widened as he mumbled an apology to me before uttering his next words. "Raegan, you will sit on this couch and not leave it until I say you're allowed to. Any attempt to fight my command will only resort in pain for yourself. *Please* don't fight it." He was practically begging me when he finished, and I tried to be pissed at him as my legs involuntarily took me to the couch, but I didn't have the energy.

"One of these days, I'm going to kick your ass, Phox. More importantly, I'm going to enjoy the hell out of it," I grumbled. Suddenly, the love-hate relationship I had with her was strongly leaning toward hate.

"I eagerly await the day. Now, who wants to know what I know?" she asked with too much enthusiasm.

"What's going on? Why would Malina have a chance at taking Raegan?" Marek asked.

"Well, she's on the grounds of Shadow Veil right now. A version of her anyway. She has managed to create a magical replica of herself that we can't physically touch, but defensive magic will weaken the temporary form."

"And where exactly is she at?" I asked.

"She's headed for Enzo and Talon in the forest. It was the best place I could send them with the least number of casualties."

Every muscle in my body fought to move, but with every centimeter I gained, anguish tore through my chest.

"I'm sorry, Raegan. Please, stop fighting it," Marek pleaded.

"Let. Me. Go," I snarled.

Phox slapped her hand over Marek's mouth. "Nobody will die today if we do not interfere. You have to trust me."

He glared at her but nodded his head. "You better keep talking," he demanded once his mouth was free.

"Well, I've had a few visions. Even more since Ophelia passed on."

Marek stopped her. "What? When did this happen?"

"Umm, a few days ago? Hard to tell with travel time. She was ready to go, and it was her choice, so don't feel sad for her. We will properly celebrate her life as soon as this is over."

I knew Phox was crass, but she seemed to have little remorse for the elder dragon seer's death, and I suddenly questioned how much we could trust her. Something happened in Drakken, and she had changed for the worse.

I knew death had a way of changing those left behind, and with Phox being so closed-off, I doubted we would get anything that was actually helpful in understanding just how Ophelia's passing was really affecting her.

"Fine, keep going," Marek grunted.

Deciding there really was no choice but to listen to her, I held my tongue about Ophelia. Though, I was still fuming from knowing Enzo was going to be near Malina without any backup. We'd been training for this. There wasn't any reason why our team couldn't have descended wherever Enzo was and stopped Malina right then.

Phox rested her hand on my shoulder. "Raegan, calm down. I know it doesn't seem like it, but I'm helping you. Talon and Enzo are fine. If you want to win the war, you have to let Malina win this battle. I promise."

"I will calm down when you tell me what the hell is going on and Enzo is back safe inside this school."

She let out a frustrated sigh and walked to sit in front of me, while Marek took the seat next to me. "So, I left here because I had a split vision: two different potential futures. One where we were attacked at the academy and another where the fight was taken to New Orleans."

"Which is the one where we win?" I asked.

"I don't know, but I can tell you that if you fight within the academy, it will fall. Even if you stop Malina, you will have nothing left to protect."

Marek leaned forward. "What are you saying, Phox?"

"I'm saying that there will be several battles between now and then. You will not win them, but there is a chance to still defeat her."

My chest physically hurt. Worse than when I found out Enzo had been working for Malina. Worse than when my parents died, because this time, it sounded like I could lose everything, and that scared the hell out of me.

The door opened, and Jules came twirling in without looking up from her phone. "Hey, have you seen my—" Her voice cut off when she noticed Marek wasn't alone. "What's going on?" she asked after recovering from the surprise.

"Malina is apparently on school grounds right now beating the shit out of my mate and Talon, but since supposedly they won't die, it's totally okay, and I've been forced to sit here and do nothing. Oh, and we will lose every fight headed for us. Except maybe not the final battle, which should take place in New Orleans. Otherwise, everything goes to shit regardless of who wins." My head turned toward Phox. "Did I miss anything?"

She shrugged. "You got the important pieces."

"What the hell? Why didn't anyone call me?" Jules asked as she squeezed in next to Marek.

His hand reached out to hers, and I could see the

tension between the two of them. Had I missed something? Possibly. Or maybe it was just the shitastic situation we'd found ourselves in. Either way, I didn't have time to dissect whatever may or may not be going on between them.

"You're here now, so don't get your panties in a bunch." Phox glanced at her watch. "They should be almost done and making their way back to us now."

My chest heaved as I tried once again to get free of Marek's power. Damn him and his Doyen abilities.

"If Malina should be gone, why can't we go to them?" I asked when my attempts to get free failed once again.

"Because there is a process, and you need to wait. It will be good for you. Something you should learn sooner rather than later," Phox deadpanned, and I wanted to rip her head right off her body.

Deciding I wasn't going to get any more out of Phox, I let Marek catch Jules up more gracefully than I had and went inside my head.

Chelle? You there?

Yes, I'm here, but I can't help you get free. If I could have, I would have done so the minute you sat on this couch. I can't even force a shift on you. Marek's power is much stronger than me.

It's okay. What should we do?

See if Phox will tell you about Malina's magic. She mentioned something about only magic being able to defeat the form Malina was currently in.

Ah, I had forgotten about that piece once I learned Enzo was in trouble.

Sitting up straighter, I kicked Phox to get her attention and was glad I could at least move my legs even if my ass was glued down. She snarled at me but didn't make a move to retaliate. "What is the magical form Malina created that you mentioned earlier?" I asked.

"Oh, yes. This is an old form of magic I haven't actually seen before, but basically, it's like an astral projection of herself. She isn't, or wasn't, actually at Shadow Veil, but she can wield magic as if she was."

"What did you mean before about defensive magic being the only thing to weaken her form?" Marek asked next.

"Well, think of that version of Malina like a video game character. She will weaken with every hit, and when she disappears, she only has to channel enough power to come back again."

"How many times can she do this?" Jules piped in.

"Thankfully, not much. While it is an effective way of staying alive for small intrusions like today, if she tried this in a battle, her physical form would need to be close by. She would be defenseless and would weaken quickly against too many attackers."

Well, cheers to small blessings.

A few more minutes ticked by, and the room remained awkwardly silent. Phox had nothing else to reveal, and I had nothing else to ask until Enzo and Talon were safely back.

Shit. Talon. Gemma. I had to call her.

"Someone needs to get Gemma. She should be here when they get back."

Phox smirked. "Actually, Gemma already found them, and Finley should be arriving in three, two..."

The door burst open, splintering in the process. "Raegan, you have to come now."

My eyes met Marek's, and he released me with a nod of his head. Before I left the room, I turned to Phox. "If either of them was more than moderately hurt, I will do whatever it takes to kick your ass until you know what pain feels like because right now, I'm pretty sure you have no heart."

Without giving her the chance to reply, I raced after Finley and followed her to the infirmary. "Did you see them?"

She nodded. "Talon has some scratches and Enzo was dirty from being tossed around it sounded like, but they seem fine. Pissed beyond reason, but okay. What's up with Phox?"

"We'll talk about that as a team." Tension left my body in waves. They weren't dead. Malina hadn't won. Phox was wrong. Which meant maybe she was wrong about the other things, too.

When we arrived in the room they were being kept, Gemma was darting around the bed, tucking covers and moving Talon until she seemed absolutely sure he was as comfortable as he could be.

"Babe, I'm fine. She only took a few scales, and they'll grow back."

My body flinched when I heard that, because I knew how painful it was, even when they grew back, but I didn't dwell on it too long. "Where is Enzo?"

"I'm right here, Love." His voice never sounded sweeter.

Spinning around, I ran right into his arms and wrapped myself around him as close as I could. "They wouldn't let me go to you. Phox knew what was happening, and the bitch did nothing to stop it."

I might have begun to like Phox at some point, but she had crossed a line, and I wasn't sure I could trust her again. Visions aside, I should have had a choice to be there for Enzo.

"It's okay. I'm glad she kept you away. Otherwise, Malina's plans might have changed. She only came here for dragon scales, and she got them. Now, we just need to figure out why she wanted them."

Shit. Malina *had* won. Even if this wasn't a battle of normal circumstance, she'd invaded and taken what she wanted, then escaped with her life.

Wiggling out of Enzo's hold, I glanced up at him. "I know where she's going, and we have to warn the dragons. The last time she had me, she took a scale and used it to insert enough dragon DNA into herself that she could go through the portal into Drakken."

Enzo let out a string of curses, and I wasn't sure how we were going to stop her, but Marek better have a plan in place, because I doubted Malina was going to just look around this time.

This time, she was going to make a statement.

Enzo grabbed my hand and zapped us to Marek's room. Since the door had been broken by Finley, we didn't have to knock. Instead, we stepped carefully over the splintered pieces, and I was surprised to see Phox and Jules still present.

Phox wore a smirk that told me she likely already knew what I was about to say, so I disregarded her and focused on Marek.

"What's wrong?" he asked.

"Your people are in danger. We have to go to Drakken right now."

Phox stood, stealing Marek's attention. "It's as I said earlier. You will lose, and it's imperative for that to happen so things can come full circle. I know it's difficult to understand, but you must trust me. I'm not saying lives won't be lost, but Drakken will be better for this. Trust that you've prepared them for this exact situation and know that one day soon, it will all make sense."

Taking a step further toward Marek, I was fuming. "You're not just going to take her word for it, *are you?*"

His face pinched, and Jules took his hand. "Trust yourself. Do what you *want* to do. It hasn't led you astray so far, and you're the only one who has to live with the choice."

He nodded before closing his eyes. Standing there, my foot tapped on the ground. Enzo placed his hand on my shoulder, his hold being the only reason I didn't lose my shit and go off on Phox. She was either making things up as she went, or she was withholding something important.

Something that could help us to trust her.

Either way, I really wanted to take my frustrations out on her face.

Marek finally stood. "We will stay put. As you said, my people have been preparing for this day for decades."

Phox grinned. "Very well. I'll be in touch soon." Then, the seer disappeared.

"Are you sure? Malina took scales from Talon. More than a few of them. And who knows how many she took when she was in Drakken before? She could be bringing an army to Drakken right now," I said, trying to make him see how dangerous the situation could be.

He smiled softly at me. "I know it's hard for you to understand, but a dragon seer is bound by duty. Yes, I believe Phox toes the line of those responsibilities, and I'm also certain she's omitting something useful, but she isn't lying. Whether any of us like it, this is a path we must follow for the best chance at success when it matters most. Now, let's gather the council and get in touch with your grandmother."

"No." My hands went to my hips and I glared at him.

"What do you mean 'no'?" He tilted his head, seeming genuinely surprised.

"I mean no, we're not going to ignore the threat to Drakken. I won't just stand by and let innocent people die.

Phox wasn't even sure that we'll stop Malina. Why should we listen to her now?"

Marek walked toward me, and Enzo stepped away. He'd remained my silent support, which I appreciated, but I also wished he would speak up and agree with me.

"Raegan, your spirit is strong. Your love for others is unbreakable, even complete strangers. I'm not trying to disregard that, but I have lived for a very long time, and I know how these things work. Phox can't be certain we will defeat Malina, because people still have free will. If I chose to go to Drakken now and fight Malina, then Phox's vision would change once again.

"But by heeding her advice, no matter how poorly it was given, I am allowing that possibility of us winning to remain. Choices will need to be made along the way and every choice has a consequence. Some of them will come with a heavy burden, and some won't, but one thing is for certain, all of them will either lead to our success or failure."

Tears of frustration brimmed in my eyes. "I don't like it. It's not right to leave them on their own."

He hugged me tightly, and the tears finally fell. He'd never hugged me before—probably because I'd subconsciously been keeping him at a distance—but his arms around me felt right. It felt like a piece of me I didn't know was missing clicked into place, and my heart filled with a joy I shouldn't have been feeling when people were about to die.

"I know, and I will minimize the damage as much as I can. I already sent a message to Ethaniel when I learned Malina took the scales. Now, we just have to hope he gets it in time. I've made the choice to be here, and here I will stay until the task of removing Malina from this existence has been completed. I've failed you before; I won't do it again."

Pulling back from our embrace, my brows pinched. "How have you failed me?"

"How about we chat more later? I'd rather not be rushed to have this conversation, and I believe we need to be on our way."

Glancing at Jules behind him, she smiled with tears of her own. "The council has already called a meeting, but the team doesn't need to attend. Raegan, why don't you go fill them in and we'll meet later?"

"Yes, you and I have some catching up to do," I said while looking between her and Marek.

There was a blush to her face that told me my earlier thoughts had been accurate. There was something going on between her and my DDD, and while it might not have been something I'd have ever predicted, I didn't mind it. Everyone deserved happiness in their life, and if they'd found it with each other, then so be it. There was no reason to hide their feelings, especially not for my sake.

Enzo had already begun working to repair Marek's door. Just like when he'd repaired his windows my first year, he pieced the broken wood back together with his elf magic before straightening the hinges. "There. Nobody will ever know a vampire burst through here not too long ago."

Marek nodded. "Thank you. We'll see the two of you soon."

With that, we all went our separate ways, and the knot that had been growing in my stomach since the moment Phox came back finally began to unravel.

"Are you okay?" Enzo asked.

"No, but I will be," I answered honestly.

"Is there anything I can do?"

My head shook. "Nothing more than what you've already done. Let's get dinner with the team and then wait for Jules and Marek to finish. I doubt we'll learn anything new, so I'm not going to worry about it for now."

Marek was right about one thing: we all had free will, and I could only be pushed so far before I stopped caring about what other people wanted me to do and did what I believed was right.

If I had known how to open a portal, I'd have left a note and gone to Drakken myself. Visions or not, every life was worth defending, even if it put mine at risk.

DINNER WITH THE TEAM HAD BEEN TENSE AND NOT AT all how I thought it was going to go. Talon had been just as irate as I was when he learned Marek wasn't going back to help defend Drakken. He'd stormed off, and Gemma left to calm him down.

Lyssa had been understanding of the situation, while Peyton and Finley didn't really voice any opinions other than they were excited to be going to New Orleans. Gemma and Talon never made it back, so we called it an early night and headed to our dorm.

"Do you want to talk about it?" Enzo asked as soon as we sat down on the couch.

"Not really. I mean, I know I need to chat with Jules. There's a lot more going on around here than I think we're aware of, and if we're just expected to sit tight and obey, then the council is going to see just how rebellious I can become. They need to be more forthcoming."

"I hate to be the bearer of bad news, but I'm not sure you're going to get what you want. It's why I didn't argue with Phox earlier. Yes, we might be essential in defending against Malina, but ultimately, the council could do this themselves along with Marek. They don't need us, and there is no changing their minds when they've made a decision."

My chest rumbled. "So, you're saying we're doing the dirty work they'd rather not do themselves while they also choose not to be transparent with us?"

"Essentially."

I'd been around this supernatural community for over two years now, and I still wasn't sure I liked it. The only time I'd ever really thrived and enjoyed myself was when we were in New Orleans. School life officially sucked, and I was ready to move on.

I've been thinking about it as well, Chelle chimed in.

And what did you come up with? I asked.

Well, I agree. Marek made some valid points, and I think we need to trust the bigger picture.

Damn her for agreeing. I hated feeling like I was just throwing a fit for not getting my way, but again, I didn't grow up in this world. Maybe it was possible for me to dig a little deeper and let this play out how Phox saw.

"What did Chelle say?" Enzo asked with a smirk.

"How did you know I was talking to her?" I asked instead of replying.

His finger traced between my eyes. "You get this crease right here whenever you're checked out. It's adorable and helpful to know I'm not being ignored when you don't answer me back."

My face warmed as he kept up with the soft touches. "What did you say?"

"I told you your phone was ringing and almost grabbed it, but Jules hung up."

Grabbing my phone, I glanced at the screen and saw a missed call, followed by a text.

Jules: Making plans to head to New Orleans, so I'll be busy for another couple hours. Breakfast tomorrow morning?

Me: Sure, but if you don't show up, I will find you.

She didn't answer, but I didn't worry about it. She knew I'd follow through on the threat if she canceled on me.

"Should I call my grandma? Amalia should know war is coming for her territory," I said. I didn't care what Phox thought, I'd warn my Meme with or without permission. If she tried to force me to do anything differently, the seer would learn quickly how fierce my dragon was.

"War isn't coming tomorrow. Let's deal with it in the morning," he suggested, and I wanted to object, but he was probably right.

Jules would have more information for me, and letting Amalia know everything at once was probably better. As much as I didn't agree with everything that happened, I also didn't want to be the reason things moved faster than necessary.

"Do you think we'll get to finish school this year?" I asked, because it had been on my mind a lot as of late. There were no tomorrows promised with our given situation, and as frustrated as I'd been, I missed the beginning days of my time at Shadow Veil Academy.

"I do. Something tells me Malina going to Drakken is the start of something that won't end until one of us has been defeated, and I refuse to believe that someone will be us. She's running out of resources, and if she doesn't start making moves quicker than before, then she won't have any help to do so."

"It's not going to be the same, though." I sighed, resigned to the fact that the foreboding battle meant lives would be lost.

"No, nothing will ever be the same after this. Not for us or any of the supernaturals. Whatever is coming will change everything, no matter who wins. War affects everyone, even if they're not on the battlefield."

He was right, but my biggest concern was for those who would be coming with us. Losing any part of our team would gut me. Losing Jules, Marek, Headmaster Stone, or anyone else who had helped me get to where I was would equally destroy me.

As much as I wanted Malina gone, I wasn't sure I was mentally prepared to pay the price it could cost me.

CHAPTER FOURTEEN

Early the next morning, I slipped out of bed and left Enzo a note. We'd been up late into the night, so he was still out cold, allowing my escape to go unnoticed.

Once I was outside our dorm, I headed straight for Jules's room. When I arrived, her door was just closing, and I smirked.

Raising my hand, I knocked instead of barging in.

"Did you forget... oh, hey, Raegan. I didn't think I'd see you this early," Jules stammered.

"I bet you didn't. Who was just here?" I asked casually.

"Nobody."

"Lies. Now move out of my way and keep the details to yourself. I may not call him Dad, but I still don't want to hear anything about whatever the two of you have going on. Well, other than whether or not he makes you happy and you do the same for him."

Her whole face lit up when she grinned. "You're ridiculous. It's not like that. Too much is going on for us to start something new right now."

"So, what you're saying is there is something going on, but both of you are too selfless to act on it?"

She gave me her best aunt-mom face. "Raegan."

My hands went up in surrender. "All I'm saying is that nobody cares and you're just causing yourself more grief than necessary by not exploring what could be. Tomorrow isn't promised."

She adjusted her robe and nodded before going to her butler box. "Coffee?"

And that was the end of that conversation. As awkward as it was to think about my aunt and my dragon DNA donor together, I also remembered Jules wasn't my aunt by blood, so there wasn't anything wrong with their feelings. I just wouldn't be calling her Aunt Jules anymore if they actually got together.

"Yes, coffee, please. Oh, and a chocolate muffin, too," I finally answered.

She ordered food, then excused herself to get dressed while we waited. Breakfast came while she was still busy, so I set the table and began to whistle a random tune until she finally emerged.

"Someone's a little eager this morning," she mused, seeming happy to finally be talking about something other than herself.

"Well, can you blame me? I need to know we're all on the same page. It's been driving me crazy."

Her hand covered mine on the table. "You can rest easy. Between what I had to say, followed by Phox, and then Amalia, we're all on the same page, and we will be moving forward with the plans that Phox proposed to us last night. The council sends their apologies for not taking you more seriously before."

Ha, I bet they did.

"So, what now? I know Phox pushed for us to go to New Orleans, but how do we make that happen? It's the only place Malina hasn't been. I don't see why she would all of a sudden."

"Marek has an idea for that. Something he's been working on that he hasn't revealed yet. A theory he'd like to test once more before telling us about it."

Sipping my coffee, I wondered when he would have had time to work on said theory but decided it didn't matter as long as it was successful.

We continued to talk about how the council meeting went, and I learned they wanted us to leave within the week. My stomach twisted with equal parts dread and excitement.

Just when we were almost finished, there was a knock at her door. "Expecting anyone?" I asked.

"Nope, but then again, I hadn't been expecting you at the crack of dawn either."

She stood to answer the door, and as she did, Enzo's voice boomed from the other side. "I know you're in there, Raegan, and yes, you're in trouble."

She raised a brow at me. "You left him sleeping in bed, didn't you?"

"Maybe." I grinned.

She shook her head and opened the door. "Break anything in my room and I'll break your nose, elf."

"As long as she's here and in one piece, then we don't have anything to worry about. I'll dish out her punishment later in private."

Jules shuddered, and I sighed. Last time he'd "punished" me, I'd been left hot and bothered on the stairs. I'd have to avoid that at all costs.

"I thought we were going to come see Jules *together?*" He glowered at me.

"Well, I couldn't sleep, and you looked so peaceful, I didn't want to disturb you." That was a lie and he knew it, but he let me get away with it. Really, I had just wanted some alone time with my aunt, and he'd given it to me for as long as he could handle.

"Whatever you say, *Dear*. Now that I'm here, I'm assuming since Raegan hasn't stormed in on the council members that everything went as we hoped?"

Jules nodded. "Yes, we're all in agreement about what to do next."

"Good. Well, I have something to add, but I was waiting to see what the council thought of the situation before I mentioned it." Enzo took a seat, and I eyeballed him.

"Something you failed to tell me first?"

He grinned. "Yep. You would have been the first to know, but you weren't there when I woke up."

Damn him. He had a point, so I couldn't argue. I considered doing it anyway but decided hearing what he had to say was more important than being a pain in his ass like I loved.

"Anyway, when Malina was there yesterday, she'd opened a portal in hopes of taking Talon. As I mentioned before to Raegan, we at least stopped her from doing that, but while it was open, a vampire almost came through from wherever it originated. A vampire I've seen before."

My hand had just reached for my chocolate muffin, but it stopped mid-air as my head slowly turned toward him and my eyes shot daggers his way. "Excuse me? This was something you could have told me *last* night. Me leaving this morning had nothing to do with it."

"You were already stressed, and I knew more information was only going to make it worse. Now that we know what we're doing, I figured I'd share." He shrugged casually like I wasn't about ready to choke him.

"Well, are you going to tell us who the vampire was?" Jules asked, clearly annoyed with our stand-off.

"I don't know his name, but we saw him in New Orleans once when Amalia was showing us around the quarter the second day. The guy with the nasty scar on his cheek."

That dude had been hard to forget, because he'd frightened the shit out of me. His scar should have healed cleaner than it did with his supernatural abilities, but it hadn't, and Meme refused to talk about it when I asked.

"So, what was he doing?" I asked, no longer upset that he'd withheld information. Honestly, I wouldn't have slept at all if I'd known so it was probably better, but I wouldn't tell him that. He could figure it out on his own.

"He mostly seemed to be watching us, but when I thought he was going to try and come in, I blasted the portal with a shit ton of energy, and it closed on him. Shortly after that is when Malina left, but she didn't open another portal, she just sort of disintegrated."

Jules stood and grabbed her phone off the counter. "We need to call Amalia. That's Vincent. He's never caused problems in the quarter before that weren't easily dealt with. Though, he's made it known he wasn't happy with the hierarchy many times before."

"Do you think he's the one who took the students?" I asked.

Jules nodded. "It's certainly probable. If Malina was able to convince him she'd put him toward the top of the food chain, I'd bet everything I own that he gladly became her errand boy." She pressed a few buttons on her phone and then rested it on the table.

"Everything okay, Jules?" Amalia answered the video chat, but it wasn't her face that came into view. All we could see was greying hair and the top of her ear.

"Yeah, but we're on a video call. Look at your screen," Jules said.

We all held our laughter in as she began to curse her phone. "This old lady doesn't do technology. You're lucky I even have this mini-computer. Anyway, what do I owe the pleasure of seeing your pretty faces?" When Enzo snorted, she added, "Yes, Enzo, you have a pretty face, too. Though, it's a little more manly now with the beard you're trying to grow, so good on you."

My stomach ached from the laughter that erupted from my body. I loved this woman more than chocolate, and that was saying something.

"Uh, thanks, Amalia." Enzo backed away from the camera and let Jules and I take over when we stopped laughing.

"We think we know who the vampire is that took the students from up here and he's from the quarter," Jules said.

"Do I need to be sitting down for this?" Amalia asked.

"Probably not. You won't be surprised. Enzo said he saw Vincent with Malina last night. We didn't know this information when we spoke with you before."

Amalia narrowed her eyes, and then lowered her voice as she stepped into an alley from the looks of the brick behind her. "I'll send some people I trust to check out his normal hideaways. I know you're still missing two of your own, so have Alistair send me their photos and we'll see what we can turn up. If he brought them back to New Orleans, we'll find them."

"Thank you. How did everything go this morning with the other leaders?" Jules asked.

"Hasn't happened yet. I was actually headed to the meeting spot now, but it will be fine. You all just let me know when you'll be here, and I'll make sure we're ready. Malina made a mistake messing with our young. I made sure it didn't divide us, and she'll stand to regret her decisions by the time I'm done with her. So will Vincent."

My lips turned up. "Thank you, Meme. One of us will let you know when we have more information. Let us know if you find Vincent."

"I will, darling. Now, I need to go. Love you all."

Instead of hanging up, she simply stuck the phone in her pocket, making us laugh some more, but I didn't want to frustrate her, so I hung up on our end and handed Jules her phone. "What now?"

"Now, we prepare. Everything is set in motion, and it's time for final trainings and making a game plan everyone can agree to," she answered, and Enzo grunted.

"Good luck with that," he added.

I was thinking the same thing but didn't add to it. There was no point. We were doing this. One way or another, we'd be facing Malina soon.

I'm ready. Like Amalia said, she's going to regret the day she came after you, Chelle said in a menacing tone that had my whole body shivering.

Letting my dragon out when she was so pissed off didn't seem like the best idea if I wanted to maintain any type of control, but I'd use her when the time was right. We'd do this together.

"Alright, you two. I need to get ready if we're all done here. Seeing as how I was so rudely interrupted this morning, I need to do a few other things," Jules said.

"Right. That's why you weren't dressed yet," I laughed, needing to give her more shit about Marek, even though she previously said nothing was going on.

She rolled her eyes. "*Anyway*, it's Monday. Go meet with your team before class starts. You don't have much time left for polishing your skills. Marek will be pushing you hard, as will Emmett, on the things you've already learned. There's no point trying to teach anything new at this point."

"Agreed. We'll get going and catch up later." Enzo tugged on me, but I pulled back my hand and gave Jules a hug before we left.

"I'm so thankful for everything you've done for me, and I hope you know how much I love you," I whispered in her ear as I held her tight.

"I love you, too, and I'd do it all over again just to keep you safe. Everything else aside, that's the most important thing to me."

We parted ways with emotions high. Considering we were leaving soon, and we truly had no idea how things were going to work out, it was best to make sure we said everything that needed to be said every chance we had. The thought reminded me, I still really needed to speak with Marek. We had some things to clear up sooner rather than later.

Enzo dropped his arm over my shoulder once we entered the hallway. "You okay?"

"Yeah, it's just getting real now. This is it. Everything else before this was just a trial run, but according to Phox, there will be a clear winner this time around, and there's a chance it won't be us. That's some scary shit when it feels like I've only just found all of you. I'm not ready for any of it to go away."

He squeezed tighter. "And it won't. We're going to beat Malina. I won't let her take anyone else away from you if I have any control over it."

A smile formed on my face, because I knew that's what he needed. Enzo needed to see me strong or he'd lose his shit, too, and we couldn't afford for both of us to fall apart. So, I straightened my shoulders and kept walking by his side. All the while, I knew he had no control over any of it. Whatever was going to happen would ensue regardless of what we wanted.

Even though I was dying a little on the inside, I made a mental vow to remain as positive as I could for the next week or so before we left. I'd take the time to make sure those closest to me knew what they meant to me, and most of all, I'd make sure Enzo was happy and mentally prepared for what we'd be facing.

He didn't need my stress on him. I already knew he would worry enough for the whole damn school.

CHAPTER FIFTEEN

Sixteen days had passed, and it was just about the middle of October. Fall had officially set in, and the trees were beginning to shed their colorful leaves while the breeze blew through. The weather was crisp, students were enjoying the brief glimpses of sun we still saw, and on the outside, everything seemed great.

Though, if one looked deeper, past the fall décor and school festivities, they'd see the tension lying just beneath the surface of anyone who actually gave a damn.

We had expected to receive word back about an attack on Drakken the week prior, but there had been no communication from the dragons. That was either the best thing ever or the worst.

The council had met with the students again, warning them of our departure and offering an early break to those who wanted it. Nobody was going to be forced to stay at the school if they didn't want to be there, but thankfully, most of the students were made of stronger stuff.

Only a handful went home, mostly those who lived

closest to New Orleans. The majority of that group had wanted to be involved in whatever way they could to protect their families, but just a handful of fourth-year students were chosen to be a part of the front lines with us. They were training separately from our group after their normal classes.

My birthday was at the end of the month, not that my twentieth birthday was really anything to celebrate, but I'd completely missed my nineteenth when Enzo and I were in Drakken. It would be nice to not be fighting a psychopath during it, but I wasn't holding my breath.

Phox had told us we'd have three days to get to New Orleans from the time we heard news of the attacks in Drakken. It wasn't much of a warning, but knowing it was close helped us to prepare for a moment's notice.

"Are you gonna tell me what has you looking so pensive over there?" Gemma poked at my side.

We were done with Marek's class and waiting for the guys to bring us lunch before heading to Professor Melnier's room, but they were taking their sweet time. Though, the sun was just poking out from the clouds, so we were lying in the grass enjoying its warmth, which made waiting for sustenance more tolerable.

"I was actually thinking about my birthday and how I missed it last year. Does that mean I'm not actually turning twenty this time around?" I teased, keeping the mood light. I'd done an award-winning job at not bringing the heavy stuff into any conversation except for the few chats I'd had with those closest to me. Even then, I had mostly just done my best to make sure they knew I was there for them and how much they meant to me.

I'd accomplished that with everyone but Marek. I was

well aware of the fact we were running out of time before we left, but I was being a chicken-shit and didn't deny it at all.

Gemma laughed at my birthday comment. "Not a chance in hell, but good try. Your teens are almost a thing of the past. Don't worry, we celebrated your birthday last year by thinking you were dead and drank enough bottles of alcohol for all the guests you might have had if you actually had a party."

I cringed, remembering how badly that had gone when JayLeigh failed to tell any of us there was a massive time difference while on Drakken compared to Earth. Hence, the reason it was taking so long for us to hear back about Malina.

"Let's worry about any sort of plans when it's closer," I said, trying to brush off any thoughts of a party. If we were all still together on my birthday, then that would be celebration enough. It was the only thing I would be asking for.

"So, two weeks away isn't close enough? I'll check in next week then." She rolled her eyes, but thankfully let the subject drop.

Finley showed up and sat on the grass next to us while licking her lips. "They're giving me the good shit since it's getting closer to leaving," she hummed.

"Yeah?" Gemma laughed and I joined in.

"You seem as happy as someone who just got laid," I joked.

"Maybe I did." She shrugged as she stretched out next to Gemma.

"You have a new beau we don't know about?" Gemma asked first.

Finley nudged her teasingly. "Yeah, like I've had any

time for men since I started training with you crazies. I might as well be considered a nun, and that's *not* a good thing."

I felt for her. Supernaturals were very physical beings. I'd been lucky to have Enzo this whole time. Otherwise, I might have been just as sexually frustrated as her.

"Food's here, so no more girl talk," Enzo called from a few feet way.

After walking in on our period schedule talk the week before, he'd learned his lesson about not announcing himself when he joined us.

Half his plate was already gone, and there was nothing left on Talon's. "A little hungry?" I teased to both of them.

"We're growing boys. What did you expect?" Talon replied while handing Gemma her food.

He was right. We should have known better and just gone with them. That way, we could have been eating a lot earlier, but enjoying the outdoors had seemed more appealing at the time.

We dug right in, because we only had another ten or so minutes left before heading to our next class, and we needed every bit of energy we could consume.

I was only four bites in when JayLeigh appeared. She'd been tamer as of late, but she was strictly Team Phox while I was still irritated with the dragon seer, so we hadn't seen much of her while they worked on whatever it was they did.

"Good afternoon," she said with more friendliness than usual.

"What's wrong?" I asked immediately.

"Why does something have to be wrong?" she asked instead of answering me.

"Because you didn't insult one of us as soon as you

arrived, or give us shit for being lazy and eating, or something equally asinine."

She narrowed her eyes, glancing at each of us. "Fine, but just remember I tried to do this nicely."

"Do what nicely?" Enzo leaned forward, instantly on guard.

"Tell you that Drakken was attacked and we just got word. There were multiple casualties, and it's time to pack up. We have a sorceress to murder."

Shit. Why couldn't she have just shown up to give us hell? I would have much preferred that.

Each of us stood, but JayLeigh stopped us before we could head to our rooms and get our stuff. "Headmaster Stone wants everyone to meet in the council room before you go anywhere. I was sent to collect your team. Do you know where the dog and elf are?"

"Who are you calling a dog, lizard?" Peyton snarled from behind as she and Lyssa joined us.

JayLeigh winked, trying to lighten the mood with her teasing. "Ah, I thought I smelled a wet mutt getting closer. Your friends will fill you in. It's time to get your hands dirty, kids. I'll see you soon. Don't make the council wait long."

When JayLeigh disappeared, Peyton and Lyssa glanced at us expectantly. Gemma filled them in while I snuck in a few more bites of food before we had to race off to join the others. I had no idea what to expect next or when we'd have time to eat again, and I wasn't going to risk Chelle getting hangry.

"Alright, let's do this," Lyssa said. "I need to call my dad, though, so I'll be right behind you guys."

My eyes met hers, worried as to why she had to do so right then. "Everything okay?"

"Yeah, he's been working on something that still needed tweaking and asked me to let him know when time was up. I promise I won't be long," she answered.

Finley threw an arm around her. "I'll wait for you."

"Alright, try to make it quick. We'll make sure they don't start without the two of you," I said, then the rest of us took off as Lyssa pulled out her phone.

I kept glancing back at them, but as we moved through some trees, no matter how hard I tried, I couldn't see them any longer.

"They're going to be fine," Enzo reminded me.

"I know, I just don't like separating, especially when we know the battle at Drakken is over. Malina could be back at any moment, and Phox said there was a possibility of the fight coming to Shadow Veil. We can't be too careful."

He nodded. "You're right, we can't, but if it was happening today, Phox would tell us."

"Would she, though?" I countered.

Gemma grunted. "I'm with Rae. I don't think she would, simply for the entertainment of watching us scramble around like ants."

Talon shushed Gemma, which was his first mistake, followed by his second, which was disagreeing with her. "Phox is good people. I didn't know her well before she was sent here, but if Ophelia trusted her, then we should, too."

Even Enzo flinched, anticipating what came next.

Gemma's heel stomped on Talon's toes and, as he bent over, her elbow connected with his kidney. "Don't shush me. You ever do it again and it will be your balls I aim for next, and I won't miss."

"Yes, Dear," he grunted, hobbling just a few steps behind us as we kept moving.

Enzo was a smart man and kept his mouth shut, not even looking back at his friend, which had me surprised but smirking.

When we entered back into the school, Talon was walking upright again. Gemma pretended that none of it had transpired, which was even funnier because Talon was still tense, awaiting the next attack that never came.

Sometimes, instilling fear in others was just as good of a punishment as the act itself.

We arrived at the door to the council room and I glanced back, hoping to see Lyssa and Finley right behind us, but no such luck. When we entered, all of the council members were present, along with Jules, Marek, JayLeigh, Phox, and Emmett.

Marek's face was downturned and his body tense, as to be expected, so I went to join him and offer my condolences. Growing up without family outside my parents hadn't prepared me for what loss felt like. It was a blessing and a curse to have never felt the loss of anyone close to me until my parents.

Now that my family expanded beyond blood, I feared for so much more than myself, but regardless of what I felt, I did my best to remain focused on the task at hand. Stopping Malina from destroying any more lives with her selfishness was key.

"Ethaniel is taking care of that, but with Onyx loose, I fear that their battles aren't over yet," Marek said as Enzo and I walked up.

My body froze. Onyx was free? Of course, Malina would have gone there to get him. He was her greatest ally, and we were so screwed if we had to fight him. He had been Marek's right-hand man. He probably knew almost everything about his king, and it would put us at a huge disadvantage.

"This changes nothing. I'm not afraid of Onyx. His arrogance has always been his greatest weakness, and we can take advantage of that," JayLeigh said.

My chest was tight, but I did my best to hope she was right. Deciding I'd heard enough, I pulled Enzo back to our group and was relieved to see Lyssa and Finley were standing there, too.

"What happened?" Gemma asked.

"Malina has Onyx," I answered.

"What does that mean for us?" Peyton asked.

Talon's chest rumbled. "It means Malina just gained a partner with too much information. We'll need to watch our backs even more, because Onyx is ruthless. He won't hold back; he's crossed too many lines to have mercy on any of us and risk losing. He knew his fate when he was caught before. He'll see this as a second chance to gain the freedom Malina enticed him with originally."

My few short interactions with Onyx had already allowed me to come to the same conclusion, and I hated the doubt of our success that filtered through Gemma, Peyton, Finley, and Lyssa's faces. This was a blow to our confidence and likely exactly what Malina was hoping for by going to Drakken first.

Taking a page from JayLeigh's book, I repeated her earlier words. "This changes nothing. We've been training for weeks—hell, some of you for years. Every class, every lesson, it's all prepared us for this moment. It's why Shadow Veil was created. Not only to learn about our history, but to give each of us the best possible chance of protecting everything being a supernatural stands for."

Enzo nodded at my side. "Raegan is right. Let's hear

what the council has to say, and then go from there. We're ready for this."

Not everyone seemed to buy into our confidence, but they didn't say anything else, so we took our seats at the table and waited not-so-patiently for the meeting to begin. Precious time was passing by and sitting idly was not what I had in mind.

When Headmaster Stone saw everyone was in attendance, he stood at the head of the table and waited for silence.

"You all know why we're here. It's time to head to New Orleans before Malina decides to come to Shadow Veil. After speaking with Marek, we'd like to ask the dragons to fly to New Orleans, while the rest of us will use a portal to get there. It will take a lot of magic to make happen, but Phox said she can handle it with the assistance of the council."

"Why are we separating? What purpose does it serve to have them fly to New Orleans?" Enzo asked.

Marek answered first. "It's what I've been working on. Malina has been tracking shifter magic, specifically dragons. I tested that theory several times as I monitored the use of each dragon present. I had a feeling she'd been doing it ever since she realized Raegan had used a portal to come to Drakken."

Well, at least some things were beginning to make more sense. Though I had a feeling he was withholding some of what he learned, I trusted him enough to know he'd have told us more if it was pertinent to the current situation.

"So, the dragons are going to be used as bait?" Gemma asked, not at all happy with that possibility.

"Not exactly, more like a beacon. Malina doesn't have enough resources to attack by air. Yes, she may have Onyx, but he was the only dragon to go with her that I know of. As long as we don't stop along the way, then we will simply be leaving a trail for her to follow."

As much as I wanted to ask more questions, I knew they'd be pointless. Phox was guiding them, and they trusted her. I just needed to figure out a way to do the same.

The seer has long been a respected position within the dragon history. Phox will not lead you astray, and even if she tried, I would not let her. Yes, we are missing pieces to this puzzle but I have faith we will know what we need to know when the time is right, Chelle said, reminding me of what I once seemed so sure of.

Thank you, Chelle. I don't think I could do this without you.

Yes, you could, and you would. I'm merely here to support you when needed.

Enzo squeezed my hand, drawing my attention back to the meeting. Bennett had been saying something, and I'd completely missed it.

"Marek, JayLeigh, Raegan, Enzo, Gemma, Talon, Peyton, and Finley will all head out tonight. Those of you named that aren't dragons will ride on the back of one. I'd advise you dress warm," Headmaster Stone said.

"What about Lyssa?" I asked when I realized her name hadn't been called.

"I'll be with my father, but I'll meet you all there. He should arrive by morning, and we'll use the portal," she answered.

Judging by the relaxed expression on Lyssa's face, she didn't seem fazed about the situation, but there was an underlying harshness in her tone that told me otherwise. I hated that she had to deal with it on her own.

Headmaster Stone nodded in confirmation to Lyssa's

reply and then dismissed us. My gut twisted with anxiety and foreboding, but I tucked those feelings away as quickly as they came.

There was no room for doubt when we were headed for war.

CHAPTER SIXTEEN

Before I could make it to the platform with our group, my name was called. I knew the voice and assumed I also knew what he wanted, but I wasn't ready, so like a coward, I pretended not to hear him.

Enzo nudged me. "Marek is standing behind us, and I know you heard him."

"What? I didn't hear anything. I think you're mistaken. Come on, we have stuff to do." I pulled on his hand and placed one foot on the platform, but he quickly spun me around before yanking me back.

My body was flush with his, but there was nothing sexual about it. I was losing my shit and Enzo was calming me down, because whether or not I talked about it, he knew I had my issues with Marek. Even if I didn't understand what those were, Enzo knew me well enough to know when to be there.

My eyes stayed focused on Enzo's chest. I had zero idea what was wrong with me. I was being ridiculous. I'd talked to Marek a million times. He may just want to tell me where we were supposed to meet up before flying out. At least, that's what I told myself as I took a few deep calming breaths and drew on the bond with Enzo.

"Go see what he needs. I know what you've been doing the last couple weeks and if you don't talk to him before we leave, you're going to be distracted later," Enzo said, and I simply nodded.

Of course, he had known what I was up to, but like the perfect mate I thought him to be, he hadn't previously called me out on it.

"Okay, wait for me in our room. I'll be there as soon as I can."

He pressed his lips to my forehead. "We're not going anywhere without you, so take your time."

When Enzo stepped onto the platform with the others who had waited, a piece of me went with him like it always did when we were apart. As soon as they disappeared from sight, I plastered a smile on my face and turned for Marek.

"Come with me," he said before turning and walking toward the stairs.

With my head held high, I followed him and tried to figure out what I was so damn afraid of. There was something about Marek that frightened my soul. Not that I thought he would ever intentionally hurt me, but there was a part of me that refused to care for him. Refused to let him in when I'd already let so many others in.

Marek held open a door for me, and I entered the hallway before moving to the side since I had no idea where he wanted to go to chat.

Then, he surprised me by taking a seat on a bench and patting the spot next to him. "Join me."

My body moved on autopilot as I tried to figure out what the hell we were doing there.

"I think we've been avoiding each other, and I'm sorry I

didn't reach out to you sooner," he began, voice already thick with emotion that had my body tensing.

"Avoiding? We've seen each other pretty much every day," I said.

"There's a wall between us, and I know why mine is there, but I don't think you've figured out why yours is, but I might have some insight if you'd like it," he continued as if I hadn't said anything.

When I didn't respond, he added, "I hope you don't mind, but I took the liberty of asking Jules about your growing up and your parents. It was important to me to know that if I wasn't there for you that you had been loved and cared for. The moment I learned of your existence, a part of me died instead of coming to life."

My head cocked to the side, not understanding how this was helpful. "What do you mean?"

"I've taken care of people my whole life. I'm a king. The need of others has always come before my own, hence why I never came back to Earth until you entered my life. You, the one person I should have put before all others. A beautiful soul I helped to create. I failed you."

Instinctively, I reached out to him. "No, you didn't. I had a great life. My parents were the best a kid could ask for."

"I know that now, but I didn't then. All I knew was Malina had you within her grasp. Malina had won, and I'd lost the only thing I ever wanted."

My throat burned with emotion as I tried hard to figure out what to say, but every time I opened my mouth, no words came.

"I would never want to replace your father. From what I've heard, he was a great man, but I need you to know that you are my daughter in my heart, and I have loved you from the moment I knew you walked the earth."

And that's when it all clicked for me. Tears fell freely from my eyes as the hiccups began, and I didn't bother to hold them back. I needed the release and gladly took it.

By accepting Marek into my life, I'd subconsciously thought I would be giving my parents less value. I'd loved them and respected them too much to ever consider another my parent, but as I sobbed into Marek's chest and relished in the parental feelings pouring from him, I knew there was enough room in my heart for all three of them.

I'd wasted so much time being scared, and now we were off to fight a battle nobody was sure we'd win. My heart ached for everything I might lose and for everything Malina had taken from me. I wanted her to pay for taking my parents, most of all. Even if it had been Desmond who had pulled the trigger, she'd given him the gun.

I stood to lose Marek as well, because only one of them was going to survive when they faced each other, and I wasn't sure I could survive losing another parent I cared about.

"Shhhh, sweet girl. It's going to be okay. I know you don't trust Phox, but I do. Everything will be fine, and we'll have plenty of time to continue this conversation. I just needed you to know that I understood, and it's okay. Most importantly, I need you to know what you mean to me."

Wiping at the tears that continued to fall, I gathered my composure before grabbing his hands and meeting his eyes. His eyes were so similar to mine that I couldn't deny we were related. "Thank you for everything you have done to make things right, but you need to hear a few things as well. You did not fail me. I had seventeen years of normalcy before I lost my parents. Seventeen years of feeling loved and cherished and knowing what a family should be, so I could one day have one of my own.

"When Malina took that away, you did what you could to save me and even broke a lifelong vow to come warn me of her plans. Without you, I wouldn't be here, and I wouldn't have had a second chance at a family. While it may be unconventional, it's still mine, and I have you to thank for that, Dad."

His grip on my hands became unbearably tight, but I took the pain because it was full of joy instead of anguish. I'd given Marek what he long ago deserved. I wasn't replacing the father who had raised me; I was gaining another man in my life who would love me unconditionally like a real parent was supposed to.

He finally loosened his hold on me and cleared the tears from his face. We were both hot messes, and while it might not have been the best time to finally open up, it had been the right time.

Standing up, I offered him a hand. "Come on. We have a batshit crazy sorceress to kill before we can enjoy all of the things life has given us."

His massive hand engulfed mine as he stood and towered over me. "Your heart and light are as big as all the oceans, Raegan. Never let anyone dull it, no matter what. It's what will keep our world moving forward to better things."

We hugged for the second time, and it was even better than the first. I thought of my parents and knew they were smiling down on us with approval. I would love them for as long as I lived, and it was the best feeling to know I could love all three of them at the same time without guilt.

Marek took me back to my room, insisting I have an escort to make sure nothing happened, which was equal parts adorable and annoying. There were too many overprotective men in my life, but I didn't complain. Instead, I appreciated their presence and counted myself lucky to have so many people in my life to care about.

Enzo was at the door just as I turned the handle. "Everything okay?" He glanced between me and Marek a couple times before finally settling on my face, eagerly awaiting my answer.

"Everything is great. Are we packed?" I asked, not really wanting to get into anything heavy before we took off. I'd fill Enzo in as soon as we landed in New Orleans.

He hesitated, clearly not liking that I'd chosen to avoid the topic, but let it go. "Yep. I packed for both of us since I didn't know how long you'd be. JayLeigh said we needed to meet her out front within the hour."

Marek gave my shoulder a squeeze. "I'll see you two out there."

Turning around, I gave him another hug and watched him go. When I went back inside the dorm, Enzo was eyeing me cautiously.

"What happened?" he asked softly.

"Nothing bad, but I'd rather not talk about it now. I promise you'll be the first I let know when I'm ready, though."

He nodded and smiled. "As long as it wasn't bad, take all the time you need. He might be able to kill me, but I wouldn't hesitate to retaliate if he'd hurt you, even if it was just emotionally."

"And that's why I love you." After kissing him quickly, I darted toward our bedroom to make sure he'd gotten everything I wanted. There wasn't much I needed to bring with me besides some extra clothes. I didn't have a weapon of choice, not when I knew I had my dragon simmering just beneath the surface.

Regardless, I noticed the dagger I sometimes carried was tucked into the bag right next to my training suit, which would be my go-to attire for the imminent battle.

"Everything looks great. Let's go," I said when I turned back toward Enzo.

He stared as if he really wanted to say something heavy but stopped himself before grinning and grabbing the bag. "Better fly steady on the way down there."

Enzo had never ridden on the back of Chelle before. It hadn't been something that ever really crossed my mind as a thing to try, but he seemed eager to give it a go, and I wished we'd thought to practice previously.

"Just don't do anything like tug too hard on her scales and I'll make sure she doesn't barrel roll. You just might pee your pants if she does."

His face blanched, and I laughed before leaving him to ponder the fact that his life was going to be in the hands of a dragon.

After recovering from whatever thoughts raced through his head, Enzo caught up to me at the door where I waited for him.

"She wouldn't actually kill your mate, right?"

Chelle chuckled inside my head. *How much should I torture him?*

Not much. Just enough to make him behave on the trip, I replied while grinning at Enzo.

"She said probably not, but she's kind of hungry, so don't test her patience. It's worse than mine," I finally answered him.

"Shit," he murmured as we headed down the hallway toward the platform.

When we got downstairs, the front doors were just opening, and a man nearly as tall as Enzo entered. His dark eyes briefly flicked to us before he turned his head up and continued forward as if we were beneath him and not worth a second glance. I'd never seen him before, but since Enzo didn't seem alarmed, I didn't say anything until we were outside.

"That was Lyssa's dad. He must still be pissed at me, but he's always been arrogant, so who knows. Hopefully, he'll give Alistair whatever he's been working on and then be gone. We don't need him in New Orleans and, more importantly, Lyssa doesn't need him in her head. He'll only make her doubt herself and the progress she's made."

The man was lucky we had somewhere to be, because I wanted nothing more than to go turn him around and punch him in the throat in hopes of destroying his vocal cords. He didn't deserve a daughter like Lyssa.

Before I continued picturing all of the things I wanted to say to him, Enzo led me to where the rest of our group was already waiting. JayLeigh had shifted and Finley was climbing on top of her, not an ounce of fright showing.

"This is how it's done. Taking control and showing the dragon who's boss," Finley said proudly when she reached the top.

JayLeigh snorted and turned, purple scales reflecting off the moon that was high in the sky. "I'm sorry, what was that?"

As Finley opened her mouth to reply, JayLeigh bucked her off and everyone went silent as the vampire flew through the air, but like a stealthy cat, she landed on her feet.

"This is going to be fun." Finley grinned and then moved for JayLeigh again, still no fear whatsoever.

Talon began to shift, and Marek was speaking quietly with Peyton, probably giving her tips on where to hold and sit.

This was it. We were leaving. If Phox was right, there was no turning back, but I tried not to focus on that and thought about seeing Meme again instead as I shifted, enjoying the trepidation rolling off Enzo as he watched my dragon come into view.

CHAPTER SEVENTEEN

The trip had taken nearly thirteen hours to complete, and all of our dragon forms were exhausted, but according to Marek, everything was going as planned. JayLeigh had cocooned us all in some sort of speed enhancement bubble, very similar to the one she created when we needed privacy.

The enclosure had served to increase each dragon's speed, as well as keep our passengers safe. There was no chance they'd fall off with the cocoon around us, but JayLeigh hadn't told them that until after Chelle had her fun.

Poor Enzo almost had a heart attack when Chelle appeared to spiral out of control and he damn near fell off. I had probably enjoyed it more than I should have, but it was all in good fun and certainly woke up the group when we were halfway to our destination.

When we reached the outskirts of New Orleans, my eyes scanned the swamps for Meme. She said we were to meet her on the east side of town, a few miles out in the swamps. Apparently, it was wolf territory, but I didn't worry about it. Based on the phone conversation I'd heard a few weeks back, the alpha knew better than to mess with my Meme.

Marek found the landing spot first, and we followed his lead. Coming in, I could see cabins set up all along the wooded area and wondered how large their pack was. We hadn't made it out this far when we'd visited over the summer, but now I wished we had.

Mind if I take over as soon as we land? I've missed Amalia, I said to Chelle.

Of course not. Just know I'm right here whenever you need me.

As soon as Enzo disembarked from my dragon, I shifted back to my human form and then began laughing at the daggers Enzo's eyes were shooting at me.

"What's wrong with you?"

"Did you not remember me almost dying on the way here?" He threw his hands in the air, clearly exasperated with me.

"Oh, you were fine. Don't tell me you've been simmering about that the whole second half of the trip." I couldn't help but laugh, which only made the situation worse.

"There will be payback. I don't know when and I don't know how yet, but when it happens, it will be epic."

My thumbs rubbed at the side of his face, trying to smooth the stress lines out. "Calm down. I promise she won't ever do it again."

"Damn right, she won't. I won't ever ride with her again," he grumbled.

Meme was walking toward us, so I patted his back and let him continue to stew. He'd get over it sooner or later.

"Raegan," Meme called, her arms open and waiting for me.

"Hi, Meme. I missed you." My arms wrapped tightly around her slight but strong frame.

"I missed you, too. Next time you're here, I hope it will be on better circumstances. We have news for you, but let's wait for the others. I do hate to repeat myself."

A small smile lifted on my lips. She really was the best.

Once Marek and JayLeigh were shifted back to humans, Amalia led us to the wolf den, as she called it.

"Everyone, this is Jones. Jones this is everyone," she announced when we entered what appeared to be his home. It was massive and ridiculously oversized unless he had a shit ton of pups running around somewhere.

Meme took a seat at a large round table located in a spacious area off the living room. "Jones has been helping me track Vincent. We searched all of his known hideaways, but it didn't appear he had been to any of them in ages, so we expanded and found one of your students. She's a bit of a wreck, but one of my covens has her."

"Does Headmaster Stone know this?" I asked her.

"He does. I let him know the moment we located her, and his horde should be here shortly. He's the one who recommended she go with the witches, so she can be around people who best understand her. Alistair said he'd notify the family and they'd likely be there to get her soon."

"But no sign of the vampire?" Finley asked.

Meme shook her head. "But we'll find him. He can't hide forever."

Jones moved his chair out and leaned back while reaching his arms behind his head. His arms were thick with muscles, dark skin, and hair cropped short with a slight curl to it. His bronze eyes moved about the room before he spoke.

"My wolves have a better lead now that they have a fresh scent to go off. It won't be long, I promise. All of you are welcome to stay here or head into town. We have temporary housing set up for those arriving by portal, but there are enough rooms in the pack house for those of you already here if you can share."

Ah, the big house made more sense. Though it was technically his, it seemed it was also a place for anyone who was a guest of the pack. Drakken had been like that, but since it was also a school, I hadn't thought too much about it while we were there.

"We appreciate the hospitality and we will stay here, so our group can be close together," Marek said.

The two men continued to exchange information, mostly about territory boundaries and what to expect if we ventured out. The rest of us weren't too concerned with it, so when Meme stood and gestured for the rest of us to do the same, we gladly followed.

She led us to a kitchen and on the counter were a few dozen beignets.

"Amalia, I think I've officially fallen in love with you," JayLeigh practically purred as she pushed her way through to grab one first.

"I don't think you could handle me," Meme quipped, and the rest of us laughed, because she was probably right.

For once, JayLeigh didn't respond, because her mouth was otherwise occupied.

"So, now what? We keep searching for Vincent and the other student while we wait for Malina to hopefully follow our trail?" Gemma asked.

"That's all we can do for now, but we need to stick as

close to the swamps as possible. It was part of the agreement with the local council. They would assist in the fight and provide resources, but we had to stay outside of town. There is too much history there and innocents to risk any of them getting hurt," Meme answered.

Wiping my face, I turned toward her. "Where did you find Samantha?" I asked, referencing the witch student who had been found.

"About a mile outside the wolf territory. She was left in a neutral zone, which makes me think it was intentional. Vincent would have known exactly where he left her, and that makes me believe the girl was bait for something else. Or, we have another surprise in store for us."

I groaned. I didn't want any more surprises. I just wanted this to be over and all of the people I cared about to be safe.

Enzo's hand tightened on my shoulder as he addressed Amalia. "What can we do?"

"The six of you can go find your rooms and get settled. Once the rest of everyone arrives, we'll need help getting them to the tent area out back and making sure everyone has what they need. Then, we wait. We have plenty of others searching for the last student and Vincent, so don't you go venturing around in parts unknown. It will only get you shot at."

Peyton's eyes widened at the last part. I didn't blame her. New Orleans was a totally different world, and she'd never been there, but hopefully we'd have time to show her all of the greatness it held before we left.

With that, each of us grabbed another beignet before JayLeigh took the whole box. "Those will not go to waste."

I almost objected, but figured I'd let her have this one. We hadn't been getting along the best since Phox held me hostage, and I wanted to fix that. The trip down had given me a lot of time to think about all of the things that had happened recently, and while I was still pissed at Phox for the way she went about things, I was beginning to accept it.

Between Chelle and Marek, they'd both convinced me that it was just the way things were done. I no longer wanted to waste time holding on to anger. Instead, I wanted to use my energy to figure out solutions to whatever information Phox was allowed to give us.

Enzo and I took the first room, while Peyton, Finley, and JayLeigh took the largest so that Marek could have his own. Once our bags were settled, Enzo turned toward me. "How are you holding up?"

"I'm doing better than I thought. I had a lot of time to think on the way down since Chelle was in charge, and it was good for me."

"Me too, and I have something I'd like to ask you." He tugged on my hand and pulled me onto the bed. Sitting across from me, I'd never seen him so nervous, so I was beginning to freak out.

"Whatever it is, just say it. I can handle it," I snapped, thinking something bad had happened and he didn't know how to tell me.

As long as nobody died, I could handle it.

"Geez, cut me some slack, woman, or you'll make me regret what I'm about to do before I even do it."

My face pinched in confusion, and I opened my mouth to speak again, but he covered it up. "Just give me a minute. Nothing is wrong."

When I nodded, Enzo removed his hand from my mouth and took both mine in his again. "Raegan Elizabeth Keyes, I have loved you for the last two years without fail. You are the light I needed in my life when I didn't think there was any chance of happiness left for me. I need you to know I will always stand by your side and support you in any of your choices.

"I will fight for you whenever necessary and without hesitation. Hell, I will fight *with* you, but I know it will only make us stronger. I know I've screwed up in the past, but I need you to know that the day you forgave me was probably the second-best day of my life."

Tears were streaming down my face, and my heart felt like it was going to explode. I didn't know why he was telling me all of this, but I was soaking it up.

"What was the first best day of your life?" I asked.

"The day you say you will officially be mine forever." He moved to kneel before me. "I know we're bonded, but I want you to be mine in every way possible. Raegan, will you do me the great honor of allowing me to call you my wife?"

My head nodded before he could even finish the question, and the tears came so strongly that I couldn't even talk, but words weren't needed thankfully.

He pulled me toward him, and we tumbled onto the ground, but it didn't matter. My lips found his, and passion flared between us like never before. In the midst of chaos, Enzo had brought me more joy than I ever could have imagined.

Even though we had no idea what the following day would bring, it didn't matter. He was mine and I was his. No matter what happened, Malina could never take that away from us.

We didn't leave our room for the next hour, and surprisingly, nobody had needed us, but when we heard shouts from outside, our bubble burst.

"Sounds like the rest of our group is arriving," Enzo murmured in my ear.

"Jones and Marek probably have it under control. If not, Meme will give them snouts. We're fine to stay here," I replied, really not wanting to move.

His chuckle was soft on my neck. "And what if she needs us and we're not there? Then *we'll* end up with the snouts."

Shit. He was right, and as much as I knew my Meme loved me, she was devious in all the best ways. I didn't want to test her.

Flinging the covers off of us, I found our clothes and began throwing them at Enzo. Once we were both dressed, we headed outside to find a gaping hole in the sky, much bigger than any portal I'd used before.

"Why is it so big?" I asked Finley when we were next to them.

"Well, Phox was having issues, so JayLeigh went to help and they decided the bigger the portal, the shorter time they had to leave it up."

"So, they're just going to shove the whole group through at the same time and hope for the best?" Enzo asked.

"Yep. Sounds like it." Finley pointed to the far right. "Peyton, Gemma, and Talon are over there. I was supposed to be with the wolves, but one of them growled at me, so I decided to just watch instead."

She sounded so offended, like none of us had ever snarled at her before, but I knew better. She probably thought the wolf was hot and he'd slighted her. He was lucky she hadn't bit him. Would have been an entertaining way to start our time in New Orleans.

The crowd was pushing through the portal, and I stood on tippy toes, trying to find any sight of Lyssa. Knowing her dad had been around and we hadn't been there to have her back had been bugging me. All I could hope was he'd left what was needed and took off. We didn't need his kind of arrogance to win the battle.

Enzo pointed. "There she is. Shit, this is going to be interesting."

I still couldn't see. There were too many people in front of us, and I wasn't as tall as Enzo, so I started moving through the crowd in the direction he had pointed.

When I finally bumped my way through the shifters, Enzo apologizing behind me, I saw what had him worried.

"Don't push Richard. He won't care if you're a dragon, and it's more trouble than it's worth to deal with him right now."

Richard. That was his name. I wondered if he'd mind me calling him Dick instead. I'd only known him as Lyssa's dad thus far, and that would have been okay with me to never know anything about the douche, but apparently that wasn't going to be an option for this trip.

Dick's fingers gripped Lyssa's elbow tightly and by the pursed look on her face, she was either really pissed about it or in pain, maybe both, so I intended on doing something about it.

"Tread carefully, Raegan," Enzo reminded me.

"I got this."

Plastering a massive smile on my face, I moved swiftly toward Lyssa, completely disregarding Dick. "Lyssa! I'm so glad you're here." Pulling her toward me, I yanked her from her dad's grasp as he let out a scoff. *Tough shit, Dick.*

"We're having a team meeting, so come on, let's go," I said, still completely ignoring Dick, but he wasn't having it.

He yanked her back to him. "Lyssa has business to attend to. She won't be assisting with your little group any longer."

"Excuse me?" I snarled.

He moved Lyssa behind him and lowered his head to mine. "*My* daughter is coming with me. Now go away."

"Listen here, Dick. Your daughter is a grown-ass woman and can decide for herself. If you'd take five minutes to really appreciate the amazing person she has become, then you'd know that. But no, you're too busy with your head shoved up your ass to realize all you've done is make her hate you."

Enzo hissed, and Lyssa's eyes widened in fear as Dick's hand raised to strike me. My body was ready for the hit. I wanted him to do it in order for me to retaliate without recourse, but it never happened.

His hand froze mid-air and Headmaster Stone appeared. "Richard, what do you think you're doing?"

"I'm teaching this worthless girl a lesson in manners. I

don't know what you're teaching them at Shadow Veil, but this is unacceptable. Lyssa will not be going back to that decrepit place you call a school."

Headmaster Stone moved until he was right in Dick's face. "I'm teaching my students everything they need to know in order to keep pompous supernaturals like yourself from ruining their lives. Lyssa has already been offered a job at the school, because she has excelled so much. Just because your child wants more than what you've offered, doesn't mean she is unworthy of your love. You'd do well to learn that, because while your resources are helpful, they are not necessary."

Dick was outnumbered by a powerful sorcerer, dragon, and elf; plus, we were beginning to draw the attention of the others. Something told me that was the last thing he wanted, so he turned to Lyssa. "Is this what you want? To be one of them, working in the trenches instead of with me at the office?"

For the first time that I'd seen, she met his eyes and didn't waver. "Yes."

He straightened his shirt and leaned in to whisper, but loud enough for the three of us to hear as well. "You're going to regret this. I won't take you back for the embarrassment you've caused me. Good luck being a nobody."

She didn't even flinch until he was several feet away. It was then that I saw how much he had truly hurt her. Moving toward my friend, I wrapped my arms around her, but it wasn't what she needed. Though, I didn't realize that until she didn't hug me back and things became weird as I stepped back.

"Let's go to that meeting," she said as if nothing life-changing had just happened.

"Umm, I'm really sorry, Lyssa. There isn't a meeting. I

just wanted to get his hands off you," I said, wondering if I'd just ruined things for her instead of making them better.

"Thank you, and I appreciate what the three of you did, but if I'm not needed, I'd like some time alone."

Headmaster Stone nodded. "Take whatever time you need."

When Lyssa passed by me, she paused and my whole body tensed, waiting for what she had to say. "I really do appreciate you sticking up for me. I've never had anyone in my life not be afraid of my father, and to know he would rather disown me than let me be my own person is something I should have realized long ago."

I smiled. "Good thing I'm kind of a badass then, huh?"

"I'll let you think whatever you want." She winked and then continued on.

Relief rushed into me that I hadn't just done something completely catastrophic.

"Raegan, that really wasn't good for the situation," Headmaster Stone said as soon as Lyssa was gone.

Apparently, I wasn't out of the woods with any repercussions.

"Why? He was manhandling her, and anyone could clearly see she wasn't happy," I said standing by my decision.

"Yes, I realize that, and I hadn't known how controlling Richard had gotten until I saw him with Lyssa last night. I intended on doing something about it myself, but not until *after* we were done here."

Shit. I wanted to apologize, but I didn't because I also believed the sooner Dick was out of Lyssa's life, the better. Though, I wished maybe I'd have known more about what he was offering before I did.

"What are we losing by him walking?" Enzo asked.

Alistair shrugged. "Maybe nothing, but what he had been working on could be a game changer. He brought in vests that are magic-proof like the bullet-proof ones the humans use. He's already handed them out, but if he demands them back, then there isn't much I can do about it."

Double shit. I might have saved Lyssa for the moment, but how many lives did I put at risk by doing so?

"Uhhh, we might have an even bigger problem," Enzo said.

Turning to where he stared, I saw Meme laying into Dick.

He was yelling. She was yelling. People were staring.

It was bad. So, so bad.

We walked closer, and I could barely understand a word they said, because they kept talking over each other and then, suddenly, there was silence. Each glaring at the other, both seeming to refuse to back down. We stopped moving, not wanting to intrude and ruin whatever Meme was doing, but it was damn hard, because if he harmed her, I wanted to be near enough to kill him on the spot.

Finally, Meme leaned in closer. "Do we have a deal?"

"Yes, but just remember, I won't forget this."

She smirked. "Neither will I."

Dick stormed off, and Amalia turned toward us and waved. "Hey, how's it going?"

"It's going. What was that all about?" I asked.

"Not much. Just two old friends catching up. I've been around a while, and I know a lot of things about a lot of people. Richard was smart enough to see what that could mean for him if he raised a finger at my granddaughter again or anyone she cares about again."

"Did you blackmail him, Meme?" I laughed.

Her hand went to her chest innocently. "That would be unladylike. Of course, I did."

"So, he's going to leave the vests for everyone to use?" Headmaster Stone asked.

"He most certainly is. The only thing he's taking with him when he leaves is the tiniest bit of pride I left him with."

I seriously had the best grandma in all the worlds.

"Well, now that's over. We have a hundred people to get settled and then a meeting to attend. Let's get moving," Headmaster Stone said, and we all got to work.

Meme directed Enzo and me to the tents where we could help people find beds. We weren't entirely sure how long we'd be here before Malina finally decided to show up, but it was supposed to be within the next three days.

The temperature was dropping, but the oversized canvas tents slept eighteen people, and each one had a small stove tucked into the back. Between that and the body heat, people should sleep just fine.

When we were done, Enzo took my hand and led me to the tree line. "Are you doing okay?"

"I sure am. How come?" I didn't think I'd been putting off any warning signs that I was about to lose my shit, but lately, it seemed Enzo was more aware of me than I was.

"Well, we went from celebrating an engagement to challenging a powerful elf to helping close to a hundred people find beds. Kind of one extreme to the next, and I feel like an idiot for proposing to you when we have so much chaos going on around us."

I laughed, and by the pinched look on his face, I knew that hadn't been what he expected, but it was just our life. Nothing had been normal since we met, so why should his proposal be?

"Enzo, everything about what you did earlier was perfect. I don't need extravagant gestures, large diamonds, or anything else some people deem necessary for such celebrations. I just need you and your love. Most of all, I had needed to hear those words more than I realized."

His hands rubbed over his face. "I didn't even get you a ring yet. What kind of husband am I going to be?"

Pulling his hands away, I made sure to have his full attention before I spoke. "The kind that knows his wife. The kind that understands love is more important than material things. The kind that is perfect for me."

His lips pressed to mine, and things quickly escalated from frantic to passionate. We weren't far enough into the trees that nobody would see us, but neither of us seemed to care. It wasn't like we were going to get naked. At least I didn't think so...

Many minutes later, a throat cleared from behind us, and we pulled apart only enough to glance at the new arrival.

Phox stood there, hand on her hip and not looking at all pleased with us. "What do you two think you're doing?"

"Making out." I shrugged, because my give-a-damn was still broken even if I wasn't mad at her anymore.

"I see. Well, your presence is requested, so quit dry-humping each other in public and head back to the pack house."

Enzo lowered his head, obviously not comfortable with the conversation, but I didn't care. Enzo was mine, and if people objected to a little PDA, then they could kiss my ass. If we didn't have moments like these, the hard ones would be too unbearable and none of us would survive.

Phox still stood there, glaring at us until we finally moved. Instead of disappearing like she normally did, she followed us the entire way back to the house, as if we were children being escorted to the principal's office. Ridiculous, but true.

When we arrived back at the house, there was a large gathering of people, none of whom looked pleased. My stomach tightened as I wondered just what bomb we were going to be dealing with next.

CHAPTER NINETEEN

P hox went straight to the back of the room, leaving us front and center as a majority of the group we walked into turned to stare. Why they did so, I had no idea, but I was certain we were about to find out.

"They shouldn't be here. We can't trust them," a lanky man from the center said with disdain.

"Uh, excuse me?" I replied, really confused about what the hell was happening.

The same man pointed a finger at me and then Enzo. "You're *her* daughter, and he worked for the sorceress. You shouldn't be allowed here. You're both going to get us all killed. You're the reason *she* broke free. The council should have disposed of you when they had the chance."

Enzo snarled and moved next to me. "You mean that the council should have killed an innocent child before she was even able to defend herself? You're a disgrace to the shifter race if that's the way you feel. Raegan is no different than any of you."

"And what about you?" someone else called from further back.

"If you have a problem with my being here, then take it up with someone who gives a shit. I'm not going anywhere, and if you really knew a damn thing about me, you'd realize how lucky you are that's the case." Enzo shook next to me, his rage barely contained as sparks fell from his clenched fists.

Jones stepped forward. "I declared my territory a neutral zone until Malina is dealt with, and I will not tolerate hate in my home. Everyone needs to understand we are working toward the same thing, even if we come from different backgrounds. So, before we judge, how about you ask Enzo why he worked for Malina? Or ask Raegan who actually raised her?

"Did you all forget she is the granddaughter to Amalia? For those of you who knew Lara, do you for one second think she could have raised a daughter that would turn against the many for personal gain? I know Lara wasn't around for a long time before she died, but I trust Amalia, and if she accepts them, then so do I. Anyone who has a problem with that can leave."

Silence descended upon the room, and I held my breath as I waited for more hate to be thrown our way. I understood why they were afraid. Technically, I was Malina's daughter, but Lara had raised me, and she was one hell of a mother. It took me a while, but I had finally learned that blood didn't define who I was. Only I could do that. Unfortunately, that wouldn't make a difference to some, and I wasn't going to hold that against them.

The older gentleman who first began yelling at us left the room, but nobody else. He didn't go out the front door, so I didn't think he went far, but I also didn't really care.

Amalia stood up on a chair. I hadn't even realized she was hiding back there and was surprised we hadn't heard her yet. "I have always led our people with respect and love. I have always done what was right for the greater good as opposed to what was best for my family. However, like Jones said, I won't tolerate hate, either. I won't make a big deal of it, because as far as I can see, what's done is done, but the next time someone accuses Raegan or Enzo of being untrustworthy, then you will know my wrath."

Heads nodded in agreement, and I was glad to see the problem we walked in on was not going to be another battle we had to face.

Enzo held my hand in his as we moved further into the room. My Meme waved us over, but I stayed just a little bit further back, reverting to the times when all I wanted to be was invisible.

"Now that Alistair and his people are here, it's time for us to ready for battle. If anyone needs anything, please don't hesitate to ask. We don't know when Malina will arrive—" Jones was cut off as Phox stepped next to him.

"Actually, we do," she said confidently.

"Who are you?" a female from the front called out.

"My name is Phox, and I'm a dragon seer. Certain decisions hadn't been made yet, so I couldn't tell you exactly when or how, but as long as nothing veers off course in the near future, I can now tell you that Malina and damn near two hundred supernaturals will be in this very swamp within the next forty-eight hours."

"If you're a seer, then tell us what we need to do to win," the same woman said.

Phox rolled her eyes. "It doesn't work like that. If I tell you what needs to be done and even one person changes course because of the information I've given, then I could damn you all. Yes, I realize that's unfair, blah, blah, blah, but you just have to deal with it. At least you have a two-day heads up instead of nothing at all."

A grin appeared on my face as I realized how right Phox was, and I wished I had been able to put it together sooner. I had been childish and unfair, but when she'd kept me from going to Enzo, she'd become enemy number one. In my twisted thought process, everything was her fault even though he hadn't been hurt, but thankfully, I'd realized that was completely wrong.

Voices began to rise, as to be expected when someone refused to give important information, but Amalia quieted them all down with a snap of her fingers. "Silence." Then, she nodded to Jones to continue.

"Two days is more than enough time to strengthen our defenses, and thank you to Phox for giving us that invaluable information. For those of you living in the city, I advise you to go home and gather whatever you might need. Anyone who shows back up tomorrow will be counted on for the battle.

"If you choose not to come back, we understand, and it won't be held against you. This will not be easy, and we will lose loved ones, but the risk of loss is greater if we do nothing. If anyone has any major concerns, come see me, Amalia, or any of the other race leaders."

When the meeting was dismissed, Lyssa and Gemma joined us. "That guy was lucky I didn't stab him. If Talon hadn't been next to me, I certainly would have," Gemma said.

Enzo glanced around. "Where is Talon now?"

"He and Marek left to go check out a few things around the territory. Said they'd be back soon. Peyton and Finley are out scouting for weaknesses in the area as per Emmett's request, and I said we'd meet them after we were done here."

I hadn't seen Emmett in a while but was glad to hear he was settling in already and not wrapped up in any drama. There seemed to be too many damn alpha-type men around New Orleans.

"Well, I'd like to gather our team and make sure we're all on the same page. Should we bring in Marek and Amalia?" Enzo asked, but I shook my head.

"They have enough going on right now, and it's why we trained for the last month. I know it doesn't seem like a long time, but really, we've been growing together and toward this moment for the last two years," I said, doing my best to keep the nerves out of my voice.

Did I fully believe we were as ready as we could be for this battle? Yes, I truly did, but I also knew shit happened, and like Jones had said earlier, we would lose loved ones. It was a thought that had been nagging at me for weeks now, and I wasn't ready to face that, no matter how battle-ready we were.

"It's almost dinner time. Why don't we grab food to go and eat somewhere where we don't feel like everyone hates us?" Gemma suggested, and I couldn't agree more.

While it seemed Jones's little speech helped some, as people left the room, they gave our group a wide berth, and I hated that there was doubt in their eyes as to the reasons we were in New Orleans.

Before we could funnel out of the main living area, Amalia stopped us. "Where are you kids going?"

"Not sure yet. Probably to one of our rooms after we grab some dinner," I replied. "Did you need our help with something?"

Her head shook. "Just making sure you weren't running

for the swamps after Daryll made his stink. Don't worry, he'll be dealt with later. I also wanted to make sure you knew I wasn't letting what he said go. He's allowed to have his own opinions, but he *will* also listen to the truth before he goes spewing lies about my family."

Wrapping an arm around her, I pulled her into my side. "And that's why you're the best."

"I have my own tent set up out back. There was no way I was staying in a pack house." She shuddered, as if the thought truly repulsed her. "Why don't you and whoever else you want to invite come join me for some sandwiches and a few cold beers?"

Glancing around at the others, I knew by the gleam in their eyes that hanging out with Meme was more appealing than anything else. I couldn't blame them; she was one entertaining old lady who I never planned to cross, because she was also scary as shit.

"That would be perfect. We'll follow you," I said.

We made our way to the exit and were stopped several times when people wanted to ask Amalia something, though she refused to do business just then. None of it was concerning her coven, and she had dinner with her granddaughter. Every time she said my name or granddaughter, a smile came to her face that was so similar to my mom's, it took my breath away.

I missed my parents more than I had truly been able to process with how insane my life had become over the last two years. The more I was around Amalia, the more I thought about them. I had thought it would bring sadness, but instead it was just bringing closure. Much needed closure. My only regret was that I never got to say goodbye.

When we finally entered Amalia's tent, I smirked,

because the crazy lady had somehow managed to acquire one of the large canvas tents just for herself.

"A coven leader needs her privacy," was all she had to say when Enzo joked with her about it.

She pulled bread from a bag and then condiments from an ice chest next to it, so I immediately went to help her as she set all the items on a plastic table. "Peanut butter and jelly sandwiches?" I confirmed.

"You know it. It's delicious and easy and typically will leave your belly full, so why not?" Meme quipped.

I wasn't about to argue, so instead, I started laying out bread and waited for whatever she needed next.

By the time we were done preparing meals, Meme had roped Gemma into cutting enough fruit for an army, Talon had gone back to the house for anything salty per Meme's request, and Enzo had been sent to collect the rest of our team.

Within twenty minutes, we were all together: me, Enzo, Gemma, Talon, Peyton, Finley, and Lyssa. Even Jules and JayLeigh joined us, which surprised me, but they said Marek, Emmett, and Headmaster Stone were off doing something while Phox was meditating. Another thing that shocked me.

We sat around in camping chairs, laughing while eating PB&J sandwiches, and not once was the impending battle mentioned. Yes, we were supposed to have been meeting to make sure we were all on the same page, but once the mood began to lift, it seemed none of us wanted to dim it with talks of war.

Overall, the day had been good, and knowing that a decent amount of those I loved most were sitting around me, I decided it was time to share more good news.

Squeezing Enzo's hand, I grinned. "Should we tell

them?"

Having said it loud enough that the others heard me, Gemma was instantly in my face. "Tell me what? As your best friend, I'm supposed to have secret privileges, so you better spill now. Wait, are you pregnant? Oh my god, you're pregnant!"

My head whipped back and forth while everyone else's eyes went wide with fear. While a child is always good news, we weren't nearly ready for that, and I'd never be able to help fight Malina if I was pregnant. That thought was likely many years from becoming a reality.

"No, calm down before you officially freak everyone out. I'm definitely not pregnant, crazy lady," I said and heard several audible sighs of relief.

"So, what is it, then? Did you finally get smart and kick Enzo to the curb? I mean, he doesn't even have a dragon," JayLeigh said, then winked at me.

"Actually, the complete opposite. At some point after all of the chaos, Enzo and I are going to get married. We may be bonded already, but there will be an official celebration to go along with that at some point. Possibly far off in the future."

Honestly, I was only twenty and in no hurry to get married, but at the same time, since we were bonded anyway, it didn't really make a difference.

"Probably sooner rather than later," Enzo added, and everyone else just laughed.

We stayed in Amalia's tent for the next couple hours, just enjoying each other's company. We all knew what was coming, and we had less than forty-eight hours before chaos descended. I refused to spend the remaining time living in constant stress and fear, and this was the perfect way to make sure that didn't happen.

The following day was a whirlwind of pandemonium. More supernaturals showed up from the quarter and based on the last count by Jones, there were just over one-hundred-fifty of us. Not as many as Phox predicted we'd face against Malina, but it would have to do.

The unfortunate part was that we still needed a backup plan in case we failed, meaning not all of those willing to fight were able to come. Someone needed to stay behind and protect those who couldn't fight, just in case. As fond as I was of the power of positivity, I was also a realist, and I understood why people stayed in the quarter.

We'd just finished eating dinner and were sitting out in the lawn under the stars. It was peaceful and tense at the same time. Groups mingled together, but there was no laughter like the night before.

Most talks centered around strategies and who would be where and when, including our own conversations between the seven of us.

"So, Peyton, Finley, and Lyssa will defend the perimeter of our group while Raegan hopefully draws Malina's attention, and the rest of us will be on her six. Best case scenario, we keep Malina as far from the main fight as possible since we don't know what kind of control she has over those she's bringing to fight against us," Enzo said.

"What if one of us goes down?" Finley asked.

It was something none of us wanted to think about but certainly needed to talk about.

"Then whoever is closest to them needs to get them out of the fight as quick as possible. There will be a triage tent set up behind the house. Finley, if you want to do your best to take point on that, followed by Gemma as your backup, that would be best. Unless Enzo is in the area and he teleports them," I said.

Finley was the fastest as a full vampire, and Gemma was a close second since she'd been working on her vampire side instead of just her witch one. Though, Enzo being able to transport people with his elf powers would always be best if he wasn't needed elsewhere.

Each of them nodded, and the talks continued until it was time. We hadn't known exactly when we would be facing Malina, but Phox hinted at it being sometime tonight, so none of us slept as we waited for word from the scouts or Phox.

She had at least promised to come to Marek or us, whoever she found first, and let us know when the wait was over, which I appreciated. We still hadn't really talked, but there seemed to be a mutual understanding between the two of us that left me feeling good.

We each had our roles and even though they conflicted sometimes, it didn't necessarily mean she was less supportive of me or I was of her. It just meant we needed to be accepting of differences, to agree to disagree at times.

When Marek appeared just before nine that evening,

my shoulders stiffened, but apparently, he was just coming to check on us.

"There's no word from Phox. She's still off meditating on the future, so you might as well try to get some sleep," he'd suggested.

"Sure, we can certainly try," I said with a smile.

He offered me a hug, which I gladly accepted. When I returned the embrace, we'd each held on longer than normal and I worried about where his head was.

Based on a few comments he'd made, I worried he was prepared to die, and that scared the shit out of me. I wasn't ready to lose another parent when I had just finally accepted having another one. Really, I wasn't ready to lose anyone.

When Marek left to go back to the council members and local leader meeting, I moved off to the side of our group for a moment to myself, but Enzo joined me. Though, I didn't mind. My head would probably drive me insane on my own.

"How's my fiancé doing?" he asked softly.

My heart filled with warmth when he whispered in my ear. "She's sort of a mess, but ready nonetheless."

"I'm pretty sure we all are, but the important part is we're ready. Adrenaline will kick in when the fight starts, and you'll forget all about the nerves."

I nodded, not really believing that would be the case for me, but he didn't need to know that then.

"Hey, Enzo. Can I borrow you?" Talon called from behind us.

Enzo's arms tightened around me, but I pushed him back. "Go. I'm not moving from this spot until it's time."

He kissed my cheek before giving me one squeeze and disappearing.

While I stood there, I enjoyed the breeze blowing in, moving the branches and bringing the unique scent of the bayou swirling around me. The fog rolled in through the trees from the bog, and the salty marsh flooded my senses as I took a deep breath.

Closing my eyes, I focused on those things instead of the dark thoughts that wanted to come through and tried to relax for just a moment as the sounds of cicadas filtered through the noise around me.

A hand pressed against my shoulder, one that wasn't Enzo, but still familiar enough. Realizing my time for relaxing was over, I opened my eyes and turned toward Phox.

"Is it time?" I asked.

She nodded. "But I wanted to see you first."

My head tilted. "Why is that?"

"Because you are the most important piece in the fight, and I need you to understand that not everything is as it seems. You need to believe in yourself. Everything you thought possible can be if you just try. Don't forget what Ophelia told you as well. You need to not be afraid to become what you were meant to be. Even when everything is crumbling around you, continue on your path."

My hands clenched into fists. Seers were a huge pain in the ass. I remembered Ophelia's words; more specifically, I recalled how confused I had been when I heard them. Phox wasn't making any more sense than the first seer, but before I could question it further, she spoke again.

"I need to inform the others, but follow your path, Raegan, and know I did everything I could to give you the outcome you want, but even those who can see the future can't predict it."

She disappeared from sight, and Enzo rejoined me. "Is everything okay?"

"We're about to find out. It's time to join the rest of the main group. Malina will be here soon."

His jaw tensed, but he nodded in understanding, and we went back to our team.

Apparently, the news had already arrived to everyone else as well, because emotions were high and there were very few smiles going around.

"So, we gonna do this?" Gemma asked, trying to remain positive for the rest of us.

"We don't really have a choice now, do we?" Finley quipped.

Nobody answered her rhetorical question, but we all started to move toward the rest of the supernaturals who had arrived over the last twenty-four hours. As we moved forward, Jules and Gemma stood at my side with Enzo and Talon at our backs. Finley, Peyton, and Lyssa filtered in on the sides while JayLeigh and Marek followed behind at a slightly slower pace.

I held the hands of the two women who meant the world to me while praying we all made it out together.

"It's going to be fine," Gemma said.

Jules nodded before adding, "I agree. We're ready for this. We've come too far to lose now."

We stayed together for as long as we could, but when I saw my Meme, I couldn't help but break away and go to her.

She was pointing fingers and moving her hands animatedly as she told people what to do. I loved it. She was life goals, and I hoped to be half as awesome as her when I got older.

"That's right. The wolves spotted them about a mile out. I want a perimeter set up on the east and west sides.

We know they won't come from the north, so I'm not as worried about there. For the south, we need our best crews.

"We can't let any of Malina's people get close to town, so don't be stupid and hold back, no matter who your adversary is. You showed up, and we need everyone to give it their all or there was no point in your coming to our aid," Meme finished bluntly.

"You know we'll do everything we can," a vampire I hadn't met officially said.

"Good. Now go. We're running out of time." She shooed him away like he was a child and turned toward us. "Oh, good. You're all here. I want the dragons to shift, including Raegan. We need to make the first few hits in the battle count. If we can put any kind of dent in their confidence, it will go a long way, but if we start off easy, testing their strengths, we will lose."

"Hard and fast, I like the way you think." JayLeigh grinned, already going into a half-shift.

Gemma snorted. "That's what she said."

Her comment was barely a whisper, but I'd been close enough to hear it, and so had Talon. His hand wrapped around her mouth before she could say more. It was the perfect thing to ease the somber mood that had grown around us.

"Anyone have any questions?" Amalia asked.

Heads shook and she nodded. "Good. Raegan and Enzo, you're coming with me. Gemma and Talon, you two head with JayLeigh to the opposite side, so we can come from different angles. The rest of you, do as you've discussed, and your team will be reunited soon."

Taking a few deep breaths, I reached out to Chelle. *Are you ready for this?"*

It's what I was born for. Malina doesn't stand a chance this time.

She had enough positive juju emanating off her for the both of us, and I had never been more grateful for her presence.

As everyone else began to disperse, our smaller group went off to the side so I could shift. We didn't need anyone getting hit by my tail on accident, which had happened more than once.

As I readied for the shift, I calmed my mind and let Chelle fully come forward. With a few more deep breaths, I let the change come. The process had become second nature to me and was no longer an out-of-body experience.

When the scales appeared on my skin and my bones shifted, so did my mind. I went from worried and stressed to motivated and secure in what needed to be done. That was the best part about being a shifter.

Our other half was always there to be strong when the human part was losing its shit. I wasn't sure of how the relationships with others' dragons were—I'd learned it was more of a private thing—but I was pretty sure I was damn lucky.

Chelle had come into my life when I needed her most, and I would forever be grateful for her companionship.

As I will of yours, she said softly, picking up on my thoughts.

Once the transformation was complete, she stretched her wings out and waited for Amalia's instructions.

Enzo moved in closer once we were settled and rested his hand on our chest. Chelle couldn't communicate with others—she was only in my head—but she could hear everything that was going on, and Enzo was aware of that tidbit. So, it didn't surprise me in the least when he began speaking to her.

"Chelle, I have a feeling you value your own life enough not to be reckless, and I'm even more sure that you love Raegan almost as much as I do. So, I probably don't need to remind you of this, but she's stubborn. More so than anyone else I know, so if things get bad, I need you to force her to leave. I can't lose her, and you need to help make sure that doesn't happen."

His voice was thick and rough, telling me how hard those words were for him to say. I knew then that he'd been just as worried as I had been about losing, and my heart cracked. Not only mine, but Chelle's, too.

A loan tear fell from her dragon eye as she nodded. I was more than capable of saying something while in dragon form, but it wasn't me he needed to hear from then, and I knew that.

Amalia approached us and waved a hand for us to follow. We went through a few trees and around the area where everyone else was heading. "We're going to be part of the big upfront attack, but I want the dragons to come from the sides and throw the attention off."

When we arrived at our waiting spot, it wasn't long before my dragon ears picked up the sound of the approaching army. "They're almost here," I whispered.

Enzo crept forward and Amalia followed, also lowering her voice. "When I drop my hand, we move in, not a moment before. Disable as many as you can before seeking out Malina to give the rest of the packs and covens the best chance."

That was what made Amalia such a good leader in New Orleans. She was looking out for everyone and not just the end game. We could have easily hung back until Malina made an appearance, but unnecessary lives would have been lost if so.

I was happy to be on the front lines, making as big of a dent as possible in the twisted souls who thought Malina was their best chance at happiness. Even if they managed to win, they were going to be sorely disappointed, because there was no doubt in my mind that she had little to no intention of following through with any of her promises she may have given in order to win their allegiance.

The first signs of supernaturals began to break through the south tree line, and we readied. My eyes focused in on the groups on our side, searching out the rest of our team. I found Gemma standing next to Talon's dragon at one end and JayLeigh further down the line of people. Peyton was in her wolf form waiting patiently by Finley's side.

Jules, Marek, and Lyssa were missing, and I hoped they were just on the opposite side of us, waiting to make the same move Amalia wanted.

As I took one last look around, I was forced to do a double take. Out in the crowd, a few rows from the front, was Richard the Dick. "Is Lyssa's dad actually helping?" I asked quietly.

Amalia nodded. "He snuck back in last night to collect the items he'd donated before leaving town like the coward he is. Though, his plan failed when I happened to catch him, and we had another nice little chat. I don't anticipate anything great from him, but at least he's here."

That was true, but I wondered why I couldn't see the vests and asked as much.

"It's what Talon needed me for. It wouldn't work on your dragon form, but he gave me one earlier. It's a clear encasing, so nobody knows we have them on."

I decided to test that theory and thumped him with my tail, gently, but enough to tell if it worked. He stumbled, but I hadn't actually made contact with him.

"Easy, Rae. The shields only last for so many hits." He winked, and I took a step back, afraid to waste any of the power behind the magical tech.

Amalia snapped her fingers and raised her hand again. Each of us watched her intently until the moment it dropped.

The wait was over, and our fate would soon be decided. Whatever path I was supposed to be on was either about to hit a dead end or be something I hadn't yet let myself dream of.

CHAPTER TWENTY-ONE

A group of no less than fifty stormed through the forest toward us. All the while, I could sense another batch of Malina's army waiting just beyond the tree line. When shifters began to fight other shifters and vampires started snapping heads, I inched closer.

Amalia's hand pressed against Chelle's leg. "Not yet."

"Why not?" I asked sharply as we watched several of our people go down.

"If we move too soon, then our efforts will be wasted. Just be patient."

If dragons' eyes could roll, I was certain mine did. Didn't everyone know by then that I had no patience? Asking me to stand by while other supernaturals were being defeated did not sit well with me, but I trusted Amalia and stayed put.

Enzo brushed closer to my other side, silently providing me with the strength and support I desperately craved. Even Chelle lowered her head toward him, needing the something extra he provided us both.

Another tortuously long minute passed, and the second wave of Malina's people began to break through. My insides tensed, but Chelle didn't make a move until Amalia gave the signal.

Finally, her hand fell and the three of us charged forward.

"Don't let the second group combine with the first. We need to keep them separated if at all possible," Amalia yelled as I sprinted ahead, moving faster than both of them in my dragon form.

Making a big first impression, Chelle charged into the incoming horde like a bowling ball and plowed into the enemies before us. Her spike-tipped wings spread out, taking down those that dared to come near us, while her tail swung in well-thought-out circles and took several people off their feet at once.

None of them were down for the count, but many of them were at least knocked out for a few minutes from the force in which she used. Enzo moved in behind us, and I noticed those who were already out, he was touching each of them on the forehead.

I had no idea what he was doing, but I assumed it was something similar to when we'd put as many people to sleep as possible during the last battle. We weren't heartless opponents. A decent amount of the supernaturals fighting against us likely didn't deserve to die.

Malina could be quite persuasive with her words and threats, and I didn't want to damn someone without having solid proof they were another Desmond.

"Raegan, on your left," Enzo yelled, and I didn't even bother to look.

Well, Chelle didn't anyway. Her head dipped and the

vampire running full speed toward us with a sword raised met his fate with a spike on the top of Chelle's head.

Even though I had just been thinking that not everyone deserved to die, self-preservation definitely came before mercy.

He's not dead. Vamps need their heads severed for them to die. He'll come back, and we'll be ready when he does, Chelle said as she swatted away a wolf who had been creeping up on my Meme.

How I didn't know about how vampires died was beyond me, but I went with it since I'd missed a decent amount of school the year before. Instead, I focused on the incoming shifter, a massive grizzly bear that was foaming at the mouth and roaring as he ran straight for us. The beast dipped low at the last second—a move I would have used myself against a larger opponent—and swiped at Chelle's front legs.

The sting of contact told me blood had been drawn, but Chelle wasn't fazed for even a second. She adjusted her stance and took a few steps back before using her tail to distract the bear while swiping out with her six-inch-long talons.

The bear ended up catching hold of Chelle's tail, but she landed her mark as well, and he howled in pain as her talons raked down his side.

When he let go, Enzo appeared before us and pressed his palm to the bear's forehead before disappearing again.

Do you know what exactly he's doing? I asked Chelle.

He's rendering them unconscious and taking away the memory of the last day or two so that if their magic is on the stronger side and they will wake before the battle is over, they'll at least be disoriented and hopefully not continue to fight.

Oh, that was genius. I had forgotten Enzo had the ability to take memories away. I knew he didn't like to use it after how things transpired with us, but this was as good of a time as any to resume that particular skill.

We continued forward, following Meme through the horde and keeping as many of the second-wave attackers at bay as possible. Chelle glanced back and it seemed to still be a pretty even fight with the first group and our people.

I caught a glance of Gemma and Talon. Gemma was bleeding from her cheek, but Talon's dragon was right at her side and she wasn't slowing down, so I tried not to worry.

Malina still hadn't made an appearance, but that didn't surprise me in the slightest. She was playing a game, and while I hadn't quite figured her out completely, I knew enough to be certain of the fact that the army she'd acquired was nothing more than a means to an end.

Meme turned back toward us. "I don't think there is a third wave. When we get through most of the second, I want you to shift back. Your dragon is too vulnerable against Malina. You're going to need to draw on your witch side now."

Chelle nodded for me as we continued to work our way through the crowd. Since Chelle had broken free before Headmaster Stone finished removing all parts of me, I'd learned from Emmett that a part of my heritage from Malina was still alive and well. Most importantly, since it was a natural part of me, my witch side hadn't affected my dragon like the forced elf aspect had.

The magic part of me had been buried deep when we started training, but just as when I had fought to bring my dragon out, I fought to keep the parts of me that belonged. I may not have been proud to have Malina's blood running through me, but being the creation of two Doyens had to be good for something.

A group of vampires came out of nowhere, moving faster than we could track. There were at least five or six of them blurring around us, and Chelle was severely outnumbered. Their daggers must have been laced with something, because with every cut, she began to weaken.

Within moments, I realized I was going to have to shift back sooner than Meme requested if we didn't get some help.

Chelle's tail swung out blindly and finally connected with one, but her hit wasn't as strong as it should have been. Plus, the contact had only knocked him down and not out of commission.

JayLeigh's dragon appeared in front of us, and she did her best to help, but more and more of Malina's people descended on us. Fear started to seep through both of us for the first time since the fight initiated, but we weren't giving up.

Do whatever it takes to get them off you, Chelle. We can't let them win, I said to her when I sensed her holding back for some reason. We weren't so far gone that she was willing to start killing people at random, but if she didn't change her tactics soon, it would be too late to change her mind.

When she didn't respond, I worried she hadn't heard me or was choosing to ignore me. Then, my worry turned to horror when she stopped moving and let the vampires and various shifters jump all over her.

Agony bled through every bite and slash they made, and I attempted to force a shift on her, but she overpowered me and did something I never expected.

Her body began to tremble and heat up. Once JayLeigh

saw was what happening, she retreated, and I started to lose my shit.

Chelle, what are you doing? I screamed inside her head. I was not ready to die and definitely not by the hands of a throng of crazy supernaturals.

Will you shut up so I can concentrate, please? she hissed in return.

She had yet to lead me down the wrong path, so I did as she demanded and waited, then waited some more even as I felt her growing weaker by the second.

Then, when I thought she would pass out from blood loss, a light surrounded us so bright, she closed her eyes and cut off my vision to what was around us. As the light grew stronger, it also became hotter until I was pretty sure we were going to turn into ash.

Screams sounded from all around us, but I held my tongue, because even though I was pretty sure we were burning alive, Chelle's strength seemed to be increasing. Or, maybe it was mine; I couldn't be sure.

I'm going to shift back, and then you're on your own. Possibly for the rest of the fight. The vampires, most of those from the second wave, should be gone now, she said, sounding out of breath.

What did you do? I asked.

I turned into a fireball and probably gave our mate a heart attack, but it was the only way we were going to survive the attack.

Before I could ask any other questions, the transformation back to my human form began, and I felt Chelle fading away. She'd used a lot of her own energy but had somehow recharged my human form.

She was hovering in the back of my mind, and I let her

rest while I focused on my surroundings. I was no longer blinded and weakened.

Enzo was on me in a split second, hands moving rapidly over my body. "I thought you were going to explode. JayLeigh told everyone to retreat, and when I wouldn't listen, her dragon grabbed me and pulled me away forcibly. How the hell did you do that?"

"No idea. Chelle apparently has a few surprises up her sleeve, but she's resting now, so we'll have to ask her later. Is everyone okay so far?"

I swiveled around while waiting for his reply and noticed Malina's people were gaining the upper hand with the first group. My eyes continued to search for the rest of our team while Enzo answered.

"The vests from Richard seem to be doing their job, but we're not out of the woods yet. Chelle attracted the attention of Malina, and she's headed our way. We still have a long way to go before we're in the clear. Try to stay focused on what's in front of us and not behind."

The request was easier said than done. I couldn't find Gemma or Jules, not even Talon's dragon, and I wondered if he had the same ability to become a fireball like I had. If he did, he better use it soon and make sure my best friend stayed alive or I wasn't sure what I would do.

Marek appeared between where Malina was headed and us. Meme joined him and just as I took a step forward, I heard a scream so horrific my blood ran cold.

Enzo's head turned before mine and he grabbed my arms trying to get me not to look. "Don't, Reagan. There's nothing you can do from here."

"Enzo. Move." My eyes glared at him before I ripped myself from his grasp.

Turning around, I saw Talon's dragon on the ground

just at the tree line, blood pouring from a long cut on his neck, and Gemma kneeled unprotected next to him. Several beings were moving in on her, and I'd never make it there in time, but I could sure as hell try to make sure whoever was near paid with their life.

My best friend's heart was broken, and mine was about to be shattered.

CHAPTER TWENTY-TWO

I didn't care that I wouldn't make it in time. All that mattered was that I tried, because regardless of the fact that Malina was close by and I probably shouldn't turn my back on her, Gemma was my best friend. I would never be able to live with the "what ifs" if I didn't attempt to save her.

Enzo snarled as I raced into the heart of the battle, but instead of trying to stop me, he picked me up and teleported us to her just as the nearest of her attackers moved in.

We appeared out of nowhere and threw them off a little, but they recovered quickly, and we were outnumbered. While Enzo fought against the closest two, I moved for Gemma, shaking her shoulders.

"You have to help us," I begged when I had her attention.

Her lip quivered, and my heart crumbled at the sorrow emanating from her. "He's gone."

JayLeigh appeared from nowhere. "Not if I have anything to do about it. Keep those bloodsuckers off of me while I work on him."

Hope sparked in Gemma's eyes as she nodded and

turned to jump right into the fight without questioning JayLeigh. Peyton and Finley showed up, and all three of them worked with Enzo to keep the attackers at bay.

Before I could join the fight, I watched in detached fascination as Gemma snapped the neck of a vampire and blasted a fox with so much of her own magic, I smelled burnt fur.

They'd messed with the wrong dragon, and regardless of whether or not they were officially bonded, Gemma was going to defend Talon as if they were.

"Raegan, I need your help," JayLeigh called, and I didn't hesitate to go back to her since the others appeared to have everything under control.

"Hold his neck here where my hands are." She pulled one bloodied hand away, and the dragon scales immediately began to separate again.

My hand replaced hers, and blood oozed through my fingers as my stomach turned, but I did exactly as she asked and didn't lessen the pressure as I fought through the queasiness.

"I need him to shift back to his human form or this will never heal. It's too big of a wound for the level of my healing abilities, and it's in a sensitive spot. I don't want to do more harm than good." Her hands rubbed together, and I didn't have to wait long before finding out what she was doing.

She pressed her palms to the dragon's chest and shocked him like her hands were a defibrillator. He didn't budge, and I worried she wasn't going to be able to wake him, but JayLeigh wasn't one to give up easily.

She started over and tried again, but still nothing.

Gemma joined us and caught on quickly to what JayLeigh was trying to do before pushing her out of the way. "Move."

Gemma was beyond furious and covered in blood. I was legitimately afraid of her.

I had no idea if it was a great idea to remove my hands from Talon's wound, but she glared at me until I did. JayLeigh moved closer to me as we both backed up to watch Gemma do her thing.

Her hands pressed together, and she thrust them forward without actually touching Talon, then she screamed at the top of her lungs. Golden magic poured from her hands and straight into Talon's chest.

People all around us paused for just a moment to simply stare at what was happening, though I had no idea *what* was actually happening, but I was equally enraptured.

Once the magic stopped, Gemma stepped forward and snarled. "Shift."

Talon's form began to shimmer, but we were out of time to watch. The battle still went on around us, and the others needed our help.

My hand raised at just the right time when a panther lunged for me. Her claws sliced down my forearm, cutting deep enough that I lost movement in my fingers, but that didn't mean I was completely defenseless.

Raising my left hand, I created a shield like Phox had taught us and pressed forward in an attempt to keep the shifter away from Gemma and Talon.

My name was called, but I couldn't turn and risk the panther getting the upper hand on me, so I continued to dance with her as she tested my reflexes. I might not have been able to fight back, but I wasn't incapable of protecting myself and others, either.

A hand gripped my injured forearm from behind, but instead of pain seizing through me, I experienced relief.

"Hold still," Meme grumbled as I sidestepped the

panther for the fifth or sixth time.

"Well, unless you want your face to look like my arm, then I kinda need to move," I replied with a grunt as the oversized cat slammed against my shield.

"Don't sass me, child." She tightened her grip, and then all pain disappeared. "There. Now, end the kitty and get back to Marek. I'm headed there after I give Talon a boost as well."

Without waiting for my reply, she turned toward Talon. I dropped my shield and lunged for the panther. Even though Chelle was still taking her timeout, I didn't need her to half-shift and use my partial talons to scratch across my attacker's face.

Hitting my mark, I blinded her and then blasted the cat back with some of my own magic when I heard Gemma and Enzo beginning to argue.

The panther scurried away, and I could have easily chased her and finished the job, but she wasn't my concern at the moment.

Turning back to the others, Gemma was crouched over a naked Talon, practically foaming at the mouth and swiping out at Enzo as he tried to get closer.

"You can't take him away from me," she screamed.

"I need to get him off the field. I will take you to him as soon as he's at the triage tent, but you're not helping him by preventing any of us from getting close," Enzo said softly, trying to reason with her.

I knew it wouldn't work, and I hoped Gemma would see reason if I intervened. So, I tried a different approach as Peyton and Finley continued to ward off any new attackers and Meme left our small group to go heal others, or so I assumed.

"Gem, I need you to listen to me," I said firmly as I

lowered to her level, but still several feet away. "Talon is your mate and he's hurt. I can see from the visible wounds that he needs more help than Amalia was able to give him in the short time she had. Don't you want to help him?"

She nodded her head but didn't look at me. Her eyes were glued to the cuts still seeping blood. The only promising thing was that the one on his neck was no longer bleeding.

"Okay, if you want to help him, how do you plan on doing so on your own?" I asked.

"Killing everyone who comes near him," she snarled.

"What if more than one person comes? We can't stay here and help you the rest of the battle. We have to stop Malina, remember?"

Her eyes met mine, filled with tears. She was certainly on a rollercoaster of emotions. "I can't let go, Raegan. The bond, I feel it."

Oh, shit. While I was happy it had finally snapped into place for them, it wasn't exactly the best time.

"I understand, babe, and so does Enzo. He even gets it better than me, because he was in your shoes not too long ago. So, let him help you and Talon. You can trust him, I promise."

She glanced down at Talon, who was beginning to shake, then back at me before giving the slightest nod and collapsing next to her mate.

Enzo stepped in without pause, because we didn't know how long her compliance would last, and scooped Talon's broken form into his arms. I had no idea how he'd ended up so beaten, but I refused to ask and have Gemma relive the moments so soon.

Instead, I held her as tightly as I could until Enzo returned less than sixty seconds later. He took her from me, and I glanced around at my surroundings. Peyton and Finley had done an amazing job keeping us from being interrupted, but my mind instantly worried about Lyssa and Jules. I hadn't seen either of them since the start.

Jules was finally spotted in her fox form running with Amalia. They were headed toward Marek and Malina, which made me ache to go that way as well, but I really wanted to lay eyes on Lyssa first. My heart started to pound as I dodged and punched several supernaturals in my attempt to move through the crowds.

The battle was beginning to calm down, but it was far from over. There was less chaos and more one-on-one fighting. Though, from the looks of everything around me and all the blood soaking into the ground, I couldn't tell which was better, the former or the latter.

Finally, after making it halfway across the field and dodging several attacks, I found Lyssa fighting side-by-side with Headmaster Stone. Both of them were bloodied, but I didn't see any noticeable wounds, so I hoped most of the blood wasn't theirs.

She made eye contact with me for a split second and nodded, telling me she was okay, and that one movement allowed me to move on to where I was truly needed.

Nothing had been going as planned. Our group was majorly split up, but everyone was doing their part and they were moderately safe. I tried to take solace in that fact.

As a witch began throwing magic my way, Enzo appeared and wrapped his arm around my waist. I waved bye to the witch and happily let him take me where we needed to be.

"Are you okay?" he asked, clearly out of breath from the quick movements of his chest.

"I am. What about you?"

"Fine. And Talon will be, too. Gemma getting him to shift saved his life along with Amalia showing up."

My chest loosened at hearing those words, because I had no idea how I would have consoled my best friend if she lost her mate just after the bond solidified.

We moved toward Marek and Malina, who were dancing around each other in the beginnings of a fight while several people surrounded them, none of whom were on our side. Before we could get close enough, another wave of Malina's people arrived, or so I assumed when they raced past Malina and straight toward us.

Red eyes and pale faces snarled as they separated and surrounded me and Enzo, along with Amalia and a few of her people. Just when I had thought we were on even footing, Malina showed us that was not the case.

Vincent, the vampire we'd assumed to have taken the students and humans at the beginning of the school year, sauntered his way through the crowd. "Ah, the infamous Raegan. Your *mother* has told me much about you."

"Hmmm, funny. I know nothing about you."

His eyes narrowed, obviously not happy that he received no recognition in return. "Well, you're about to know plenty."

He spat on the ground, and it was like a green light for the others as chaos descended on us.

Chelle, how are you doing? I could really use your help, I practically begged, but received no response. My dragon was still healing, and I was on my own.

Realizing we had no chance in hell of fighting them, Enzo and I both created shields and did our best to simply protect ourselves. He was yelling something at me, but I couldn't understand him over all of the hissing from the damn bloodsuckers.

Several sets of teeth sank into me, and I howled in pain as the venom spread into my muscles, making it harder to move. Normally, I could burn off the venom within a reasonable time, but there were so many of them, I could only withstand a few more bites before my body succumbed to the poison and began to convulse.

"I'm so sorry, Raegan," Enzo shouted in my ear as he did his best to cover me. At that point, there had to be close to twenty vamps on us and there was nothing we could do. It was even worse than when Chelle had been attacked, and no burst of power was going to save us this time.

Any last shreds of hope were completely dashed a moment later when the sky opened up and Onyx's dragon appeared in a portal with several more behind him.

This was it. Malina had won, and there wasn't a damn thing we could do about it. The only saving grace was that I was at least going out with Enzo, and we'd done everything we could to stop my psycho egg donor of a mother.

The pounding of dragon feet sounded closer, and I expected at any moment we were about to become a snack for the traitor, but then something else happened.

The weight above us lessened, and the sting of venom began to dissipate. Instead of attacking us, Onyx was saving us. Why? I had no idea, but I didn't have time to question it.

Onyx and the dragons he brought with him began throwing vamps around like they were play toys before moving on to help those ahead of us.

Once we were no longer being buried alive by vampires, I checked on our team. Just because we suddenly had more help, didn't mean things were going to go our way.

Marek and Malina were still going at it with their fight, and my Meme was doing her best to prevent others from intervening. Those who had been helping her before were no longer around, and she wasn't faring well.

As we finally joined in, Malina decided she hadn't made my day bad enough and she really wanted to stick it to me.

"There's my dear daughter. I thought you were avoiding me," she said sweetly while glaring at me.

Marek took the moment of his distraction to regain his composure, but before he could move back in, Malina made her next move.

"You've surrounded yourself with all the wrong people, Raegan, and I don't approve. You need to learn a lesson in what happens when you disappoint your mother. So, remember this moment and learn from it."

Her arm stretched out and her fingers curled in, but not quite in a fist. I had no idea what she was doing until Enzo began to choke behind me, but it wasn't just him who couldn't breathe. Meme was falling to the ground, and so was Jules, who was only halfway across the field and had been coming toward us.

"I wonder which would hurt you most but not completely ruin you," Malina pondered out loud. "I could kill all three of them and crush your soul entirely, but I'd like to show you I have some mercy in me. So, you choose? Who is going to die today?"

Marek moved toward her, but she tsked. "One step closer and they all die. All I have to do is close my fist and it's bye-bye to three of your loved ones."

Silently, I pleaded with him to hold off. There had to be some way to negotiate with her.

"What do you want?" I growled.

"I want you to choose, and we don't have all day," she snapped.

My head shook. "There has to be something else. Do you want me to go with you willingly? Fine, I will. Just let them go and end this chaos."

Her lips lifted and eyes crinkled. "You're in no position to offer anything other than a name. The name of who will die. Now, choose and let's finish this before I decide for you. I promise I'll enjoy that option more than you will."

My eyes glanced from Enzo, to my Meme, to Jules. All people I didn't believe I could live without. I wouldn't choose, but at the same time, if I didn't... I couldn't even imagine losing them all at the same time.

Amalia, stronger than even I knew, managed to break through Malina's spell just enough to piss off the sorceress by tossing the tiniest ball of magic at her. While I had assumed it to be weak, Malina didn't seem to care if the hit hurt or not.

"I guess she's decided for me," Malina winced and shoved her other hand toward my Meme.

Amalia's eyes met mine as the life began to fade from them. I ran toward her, tears already streaming down my face. "No!" I cried as I scooped up her limp form.

Malina cackled from behind me, and the battle continued on as if nothing had happened. Anger rose within me and scales sprouted on my arms, but Chelle still wasn't around. This was all me, and I was okay with that.

Amalia's body began to glow underneath me, and I held her for just a moment longer, wanting to be with her until she was completely at peace. The only bright light was that she would now be with her daughter, my true mother.

But instead of feeling like Amalia was letting go and moving on, I felt like I was struck with lightning.

Her power slammed into me, and my jaw clenched as I tried to take it all in without making a scene. I didn't need anyone coming to my rescue while Malina was hell bent on killing those I loved.

Amalia had once said everything that was hers would one day be mine, and I never understood what she meant by that or why she had once taken my blood, but it all made sense in that moment. She'd chosen herself to die just so that I could beat Malina.

As my body grew stronger, I knew this without a doubt, and I knew exactly what I needed to do in order to accomplish the task set before me.

After gently laying my Meme on the ground, I stood up and realized my entire being glowed a deep teal color. Enzo's attention faltered, and another got a solid hit in, but he resumed his fight while I continued toward Marek and Malina.

She had him pinned against the ground, taunting him with my weaknesses. "She could have been great, but they took her from me and made her not much better than a feeble human. If I didn't need her power to take over Drakken, I'd have killed her the first chance I had. Instead, I'll take great joy in your death."

Marek pushed Malina back just enough that her feet collided with my legs. The power radiating off of me must have drawn her attention, because she turned away from Marek, completely forgetting about him as she glared at me.

"How?" she murmured, but I wasn't listening.

Malina needed to die, and there was no mercy left in me, nor patience to care what else she might have to say.

My hands reached for her and wrapped around her neck while she was still caught off guard. Her own power fought against mine, but it was in that moment that I knew exactly who I was, and I wasn't worried at all.

I was the first natural-born Doyen.

I was a witch.

I was a dragon.

Most importantly, I was going to kill Malina.

That's when the burning sensation began, and several people started to call my name, screaming even with a fear greater than my own. Though, none of it stopped me.

I had one task to complete, and I wouldn't fail. Not this time.

Malina's hands scratched me, but Marek had already weakened her, and I'd just been powered up by Amalia's sacrifice.

Her soulless eyes begged me to stop when words failed her, but I had no sympathy for the woman before me. She wasn't my family; she never had been. There would be no tears shed when she died.

The only problem was that when I was certain the task had been completed—that Malina was finally dead—I couldn't stop.

Power continued to flow through me, both incoming and outgoing, and I couldn't control any of it.

When I finally dropped Malina's lifeless body to the ground, my head tilted up toward the sky, and the glow around me heated just like I had felt when Chelle used all her energy to save us.

Is that what I had done? If so, I lacked control and may have taken it too far.

Was I paying the ultimate price just to make sure the rest of those I cared about were safe?

As the power finally began to wane, I knew the answer to that question, and while I wasn't happy with the outcome, I was okay with it.

Even as Enzo screamed for me, I sent my love to him and said goodbye.

CHAPTER TWENTY-THREE

E nzo

When the portal opened up and Onyx came waltzing onto Earth, I thought for sure we were about to lose, and the weight of the world crashed down on me. I'd failed my mate. I hadn't been able to save her, and that killed me.

Then, hope sparked when Onyx chose to fight with us and not against us for whatever reason. Nobody had time to question it, but Malina must have pissed him off in some way, and I wasn't going to complain.

Though, that hope was quickly dashed when Malina's magic took hold of me.

She'd cut off all air supply to me, Amalia, and Jules, putting Raegan on the spot to choose between three of the people she loved most in the world.

The decision would cripple my mate if she had to damn one of us to death.

Malina knew this, and the bitch took advantage of Raegan's caring heart, something Malina had never had.

My eyes began to blur as spots appeared within them, and I was dangerously close to passing out. Frustrated beyond anything I'd ever been in my life, I hated most that there was nothing I could do. My legs had even given out, but I was frozen in place, standing limp as Raegan hurt.

Amalia, a much stronger and wiser being than I ever would be, somehow broke through Malina's hold and shot just enough magic at the evil sorceress to piss her off.

Raegan's cry of pain as life faded away from Amalia was nothing I ever wanted to hear again, but I didn't have a moment to process it for fear Malina would go for her next.

As soon as the hold was released from me, I moved to stand in front of Raegan, and Marek charged for Malina. Jules joined in, and I kept anyone at bay who thought they could get close enough to my mate to harm her while she grieved her grandmother.

It didn't matter that we were in the middle of a battle. She deserved a few moments, and I'd damn well make sure she got it.

That was true until a blast of heat slammed into my back and I wondered what the hell was happening. Before I could turn around, another bear shifter charged at me. I was getting sick of fighting off these beasts.

They had no damn coordination, but they were huge and obnoxious. Their size alone was the only reason they stood a chance against any basic-trained supernatural.

Trading blows with the mammoth was working, and I knew we were supposed to be having mercy on these supernaturals—we were the good guys, after all—but my gut was screaming that my mate needed me. Being by her side was more important to me than being compassionate to someone who would sooner rip my head off than show the same courtesy.

Gathering up enough magic to bulldoze an elephant, I slammed my hands into the bear's chest and cringed as his hair burned and he toppled to the ground.

Though, that guilt only lasted a split-second when I laid eyes on Raegan. She was headed straight for Malina, and Marek was in no position to help her.

I screamed out her name and tried to go to her, but the power radiating off her was so bright and strong, there was no getting through unless she wanted someone to. Marek was even at a loss as I watched him circle Malina and Raegan, seeming just as helpless as I felt.

Raegan glowed the teal color I'd long ago associated as uniquely hers, and as her hands wrapped around Malina's throat, there was a moment of pride in my mate.

She was going to do it. She was going to get vengeance for her family, and Malina would be no more.

I wasn't sure how Raegan was capable, but when Malina stopped fighting back, I knew the important part of the battle had been won.

Jules strode next to me, also seeming at peace. Like every other time there was the tiniest bit of optimism, though, it was dashed away just as fast.

"What is happening?" I snarled.

"I don't know. Malina is dead. Raegan should be coming down from the magic, not growing."

Marek came over to us with tears in his eyes, and I knew it wasn't good. He was going to tell me something that would break me so badly that I would never be able to come back from it.

"I was supposed to kill Malina. It was never meant to be

her. It shouldn't have ended this way," Marek murmured with his shoulders slumped.

"What are you saying?" Jules said with a quiver, but I already knew what he was saying, and my jaw locked tight with rage.

"Raegan is absorbing Malina's power right now. She won't survive the transference," Marek replied, his head cast down, unable to meet either of our stares.

Jules began to sob, but I didn't.

There was so much hatred within me that I didn't believe I was capable of tears.

My Raegan, the beautiful soul who had brought light into my life when I didn't think I was deserving of it, she was dying right before me and I couldn't stop it.

Phox appeared at Marek's side, and they began to talk, but I didn't hear a word they said as I pushed through the power surrounding my mate and did whatever I could to get to her.

Her head was tilted up to the sky, and her knees buckled as she fell to the ground and closed her eyes. When her form went limp, there was still a glow around her, but I was finally able to move through the magic pulsing off of her.

My hands reached out when I was close enough, but I had to pull them back; her temperature was running so high, her skin burned mine.

"Raegan, don't do this. You can't leave me." I pounded my fist into the ground, and thunder sounded in the sky with each strike as I begged her to stay, then proceeded to pray to any God who was listening to not take away my mate.

Even if Malina was gone, the world would never be bright without Raegan's soul in it.

I wanted to go with her. I didn't have any reason to stay on this Earth without her. My heart was shattering beyond repair as the seconds ticked by and the light around her continued to dim.

Marek came to my side, saying something, but I couldn't hear him above the roaring in my ears. There was a storm raging inside me, and nothing would ever be able to control it besides death now that my mate was gone.

Giving into the grief, I let Marek push me aside while he, Jules, and Phox surrounded Raegan's lifeless form. They continued to speak amongst themselves, but I had other plans.

I was going to join my mate one way or another.

Gemma raced toward me with a smile on her face until she saw mine. I didn't have to open my mouth for her to know what had happened. She crumpled to the ground as I continued forward, relishing in the physical storm my emotions were creating.

There was nothing left in me to comfort anyone else. Gemma was better off on her own.

Even though Malina was dead, the battle continued, but we had the upper hand. Onyx had given us that, though it meant nothing to me any longer.

The closer I made it to the fight, the more set in my decision I had become. Whoever wanted to end me, I'd gladly let them. They'd be doing me a favor while thinking they'd somehow accomplished something great.

You don't want to do this, a voice sounded in my head.

Assuming it was my subconscious, I ignored it and pressed forward.

I'm warning you, don't go into that fight.

"Shut up," I snapped out loud.

Peyton and Finley were there, acting as if they were

having the time of their life, regardless of the fact they were covered in blood and cut up from their attackers. They had no clue what had happened, and I realized how true the old saying was that ignorance was bliss.

Fine, we can do this the hard way, the voice spoke again as pain raced up my spine and my body arched forward until I was involuntarily on my hands and knees.

A roar tore from my throat as bones inside me broke. My eyes snapped closed as I embraced the pain, hoping it wouldn't last long. The quicker it ended, the quicker I would be with Raegan again. I had no idea who was doing what to me, but whatever it was, with the amount of agony I was feeling, it could only mean one thing. Death was coming, and with it, would be relief from my heartache.

You're about to be really surprised, the voice snickered, and fear raced through me.

If I wasn't dying, then what the hell was happening?

I'm taking over, so just quit fighting me and everything will go by a lot faster, the voice answered.

Who are you?

I'm Jayce, and we're about to become well acquainted.

The world around me shook as I transformed from man into something else, something I didn't want any longer. All the times I wished I could have been Raegan's equal in every way, and now that she was gone... I just couldn't handle it.

Stop fighting me, Enzo. We have to go save our girls, Jayce grumbled as the shift finished and he did his best to navigate us back toward Raegan's body.

What do you mean? I watched her die. The tiniest flicker of hope flared within me as I let the dragon take over, but I tried to ignore it. There had been too many of those moments in the last few hours taken from me and I couldn't survive being let down again.

Did you forget we're supernatural and laws of life and death don't apply to us? It just requires a sacrifice of equal value.

I almost asked what he meant about the sacrifice, but decided I'd find out when we arrived back. Wings flapped at my side, a sleek silver color with random flashes of red that matched Raegan's perfectly. I tried to focus on that instead of anything else until Jules was at our side.

I'm going to force you to shift back now. It's going to hurt, but it shouldn't be as bad as the first change. We don't have time for me to be gentle.

Just do it, I replied, not at all caring about the pain. Nothing could be worse than what I had been experiencing earlier.

When the shift was complete, I realized I was completely naked, but didn't really give a damn. Marek held Raegan in his arms, and I had the sudden urge to be the only one holding her tight.

Sloan, a witch I recognized as one of Raegan's distant family members, approached me. I growled at her when she stood in my way, but it didn't faze her.

"Nobody wants to see your junk. Let me give you some clothes, and then you can be on your way," she said.

When I nodded, she placed her hand on my shoulder. Within the blink of an eye, I had on a plain white tee and loose black pants.

She didn't wait for my thanks, which was good, because my manners were long gone at that point. So, I continued forward and sank down onto the ground, coming in on the middle of a tense conversation.

"She won't like it," Jules said.

"Yeah, well, she's not here to decide, is she?" Marek responded with snark as he brushed Raegan's hair back with his hand.

"What's going on?" I asked, wishing my dragon had been more forthcoming with information.

"Marek has a choice to make. As you already know, a Doyen can only be killed by another Doyen. Well, it works the opposite way as well," Phox said.

"He can bring her back?" I asked for confirmation, because if he could, I didn't understand why he hadn't done it already.

"Yes, he can, but it requires him to give up his life force in exchange for Raegan's," Jules answered as tears ran down her face.

Raegan had mentioned something about Jules and Marek becoming closer, so I quickly understood her struggle. If they'd been more involved than we realized, Jules was going to have to give up one love for another.

"Are you going to do it?" I asked, because he had to already know. Regardless of how hard the decision was, he likely knew the moment he realized what was happening.

Marek's eyes met Jules's, and he nodded ever-so-slightly.

Jules stiffened but didn't say anything.

"Marek, you know how much I respect you, but we're running out of time. If Raegan spends too much time in the in-between, she won't come back the same person," Phox said.

He nodded and stood, pulling Jules up with him. Their embrace wasn't something I could watch, because I was self-ishly excited to be getting my girl back. Yes, I cared for Marek. He'd been ever-present in our lives for almost a year now, but Raegan would always come before anyone else for me.

Once his goodbyes were said, Marek leaned back down and took Raegan from me. "Tell her how sorry I am. Tell her how much I loved her, please. I need to know that she'll understand my love for her outshined any other, even if it was only for a short time."

Tears pricked at my eyes. "She knew, and I'll remind her, but you need to know she loved you, too."

A smile played on his lips as he gazed at her. "I knew that the moment she called me Dad."

Raegan hadn't filled me in on the specifics of her previous conversation with Marek, but it sounded like it had come at just the right time.

"It's time, and you need to back up," Marek said.

With a strength I didn't know I possessed, I left my mate's body once more and placed my hand on Marek's shoulder. "Thank you."

He nodded. "Just take care of my daughter."

D eath was a strange thing. I've never given it much thought, so when I'd realized it was coming, I decided to just accept my fate, because all that mattered was that Malina would no longer be able to hurt anyone I loved.

The transition from Earth to afterlife was easy. Once my body was done burning up from the overwhelming power that coursed through me, I felt nothing.

Literally nothing.

There was no sadness or happiness or anything in between.

When I arrived wherever it was I ended up, two people greeted me. Two people I wasn't sure I'd ever see again.

"Mom? Meme?" I stammered, still unfeeling of emotions, but knowing this was a good thing, or so I hoped.

"Hi, baby girl," my mom cooed, opening her arms to me.

Instinctively, I went to her and held her tight, then did the same to my Meme. "Where are we?" I asked as I glanced around. There was nothing around us. Just pure white floors and walls. No windows or any identifying objects.

"You're in the in-between. I've been here waiting, and your mother came to collect me," Meme answered.

"Waiting for what?" I asked.

"To say goodbye." She smiled, and still, I was so confused. I knew I should have been crying or yelling or something, but I just stood there.

"Aren't I going with you?" I continued with more questions.

"It's not your time, yet. Soon, you'll be pulled back to Earth, and it will be your job to help restore peace between the races, along with watching over Drakken," Mom answered.

"Drakken doesn't need my help. They have Marek," I replied.

Both of them frowned as Mom continued, "Marek won't be there when you get back, baby girl. He will have traded his life for yours, because it was him who was meant to die today. Not you."

A few tears fell down my face, but there was still no feeling associated with them. If I could have been anything, I knew I would have been epically pissed off, but this place had taken the ability from me.

"Why do I feel this way? What's wrong with me?" I asked.

"You don't belong here. Your emotions haven't come through, because you haven't been accepted into the after-life. You'll have them back when you return to your body as long as you do so soon," Meme replied and reached a hand for me. "Dealing with the aftereffects of this battle will not be easy, but everything I owned is now yours, and I want you to live the life you wanted in New Orleans. Don't worry about us up here. This is how it should be, and we're happy, so long as you are safe and thriving."

A flickering of something sparked within me, and my chest pained. It was the first feeling of anything since I became aware of where I was.

Mom and Meme glanced at each other. "It's almost time," Mom said.

"Time for what?" I asked, feeling like all I had been doing was asking questions. When the tiniest bit of emotions began to filter back into me, I realized how much I didn't want to leave.

"You need to go back to Earth. The longer you're here, the higher risk you may not get your emotions back," Mom answered.

My head shook as I squeezed my eyes closed.

Love. Sadness. Heartache. Sorrow. Joy.

So many emotions were starting to swirl within me, and I wasn't sure how to handle them, or if I even understood everything correctly.

"So, you're telling me that I died and we're in the in-between, but I'm not allowed to stay? Instead, my dad is going to die so that I can live, and I'll never get to see any of you again? If that's the case, then no. I don't want to go back. It's not right."

By then, tears were freely trailing down my face, and I was beginning to get angry.

My mom sighed. "Oh, Raegan. I'm so sorry we didn't properly prepare you for this life. We thought we were doing right by you when we hid you away. Your dad and I never expected Malina would get free, and we had no idea who your biological father was, but I hope you know how much we love you. Your happiness is most important to us even now."

"Where is Dad? Why isn't he here with you two?"

Mom grinned. "You know your dad. He doesn't do goodbyes well and we'd already said our goodbyes in our own way. He didn't want to make things worse for you by falling apart in front of you."

My heart twisted, and more tears fell as I crashed into my mom's arms. She wound them tight around me and Meme joined in. Suddenly, everything I knew I should have been feeling earlier began to storm inside me.

My body tingled, and I felt the urge to run, but I didn't know where I was supposed to run to.

Mom pulled back. "We don't have any more time left, baby girl. It's time to say goodbye and try to be thankful for this moment. It's one I have wished for ever since we had to leave you."

I swiped at my tears, but it was futile. They weren't going to be stopping anytime soon, so I finally just let them fall.

Mom held my hands, and warmth seeped into my body as I felt her love surround me. "Raegan, I have loved you from the moment you were placed in my arms, and I have always known you were special. You're going to do great things in this world. Don't let what Malina has done close off your heart. You have the capacity to love so big, and I promise, the risk is worth it. Don't worry about us and follow your heart. It will always lead you in the right direction."

She hugged me once more before passing me to Meme, who wore my favorite smirk. "Your mother has always been better with the mushy stuff than me. I'm pretty sure she got it from her father, because I won't take any credit for it."

I snorted through the tears, because there was nothing better than Meme's crass disposition.

"Anyway, you already know how I feel, but most importantly, I need you to know that nothing you could have done today would have resulted in any better ending. Everything that transpired happened for a reason, and remember, those who are no longer with you are at peace with their decisions.

"I don't need you pissing me off up here with any 'woe is me' crap, you hear? I want to look down on you and see the badass granddaughter I know you can be. Let this battle strengthen you instead of weakening you, because if you don't, then our deaths won't mean as much. You don't want that, right? Of course, you don't. Now, it's time for you to go, so give your Meme a hug and run before I decide to never let you go."

Through a torrential downpour of tears, I told them both how much I loved them, but I doubted they understood the words coming out of my mouth. It didn't matter, though. I was confident they knew, regardless of shared words.

Finally, I was pushed away, and I did as Meme said. I ran as fast as I could through the white room. The further I moved away from my mom and Meme, the darker my surroundings became and the heavier my muscles were.

Before I knew it, I was lying on the ground and shivering. Voices began to filter through, and hands touched me, but I didn't respond. I took a moment to take in everything that had happened as I did my best to remember everything about my time in the in-between.

I'd seen my mom again. I'd been able to give her a proper goodbye, along with my Meme. It had been everything I needed, yet my heart still ached, because I knew that as soon as I opened my eyes, nothing was ever going to be the same again.

I did my best to heed Meme's last words, to not let what transpired dim my outlook on life, but it was hard when I had just begun to accept my parents' death and let others into my world. Now, some of those people were gone, and everything hurt so damn bad.

"Raegan, can you hear me? Please say something. These tears are killing me," Enzo whispered into my ear as he laid on the ground with me.

My chest shuddered as I took one more deep breath and opened my eyes. Enzo's face was the first thing I saw, and the tears in his eyes almost tore my heart out.

He gathered me close and squeezed so tight I couldn't move my arms to return the gesture. "I thought I had lost you. Having you here now... there are no words other than I love you and I'm never letting you go again."

"I love you, too," I whispered into his shoulder as I peeked over, needing to see who else was still with us.

Behind him stood Jules, Gemma, and JayLeigh. All three wore varying expressions of grief, and I felt a strong desire to run as far from their pain as I could.

But I wouldn't. We had all suffered through this together, and we would find a way back to happiness together, too. I refused to let Malina take anything else away from me, no matter how much it hurt to face things head on.

Enzo finally released me, and I turned around to see what had most of Jules's attention.

Immediately, I scrambled to my hands and knees, so I could crawl to Marek who was mere inches from me. His hand was outstretched, and I took it in my own, holding it to my heart.

Quietly, I told him everything I wished I could have said and more, though I took some solace in the fact that we had our brief discussion before New Orleans.

A smile appeared through the tears as I thought about my two dads meeting for the first time, and I pictured the epic tear-fest they would have. For the first time since I learned of his sacrifice, I had some peace with the decision.

Enzo helped me up and guided me toward Jules and Gemma, who both hugged me at the same time. We cried together without words before I pulled away and turned to JayLeigh.

She wasn't a warm and fuzzy type of person, but I didn't give a damn. We were all hurting, and she could deal with my hug. She patted me awkwardly on the back before taking a step away and bowing.

"Queen Raegan," she said, then winked at me.

My head shook. "Too soon, JayLeigh. Way too soon."

"I know, but all those dragons behind me will be looking for leadership after what they've gone through, and you're going to be the first place they look as Marek's only heir."

She had mostly only ever been a pain in my ass, so why I was surprised she continued to be one then was beyond me. I simply nodded and went back to Enzo.

He held me close as we glanced around the battlefield. There was no more fighting. No more screams. Just people standing around, looking as lost as I felt.

So many lives had been lost because of the selfishness of one woman, and my heart began to hurt all over.

"What now?" I asked, because nobody seemed to be intent on moving.

"Now, we pick up the pieces and move forward, and we do it together in hopes of making the future a brighter one for all," Jules answered as more people came closer.

Peyton, Finley, Lyssa, Headmaster Stone, some of the council, and more. Each of them was bruised and worse off than I had ever seen them, but they were alive, and I tried to focus on that fact.

Jones approached me first out of the group, his head down as he did so. "I'm very sorry for your losses, and I would like to invite you and whoever else you want to stay here as long as you'd like, but more importantly, stay long enough to witness how we do a proper sendoff for those who move on to the other side."

"I would be honored to stay in New Orleans. Though, we will be staying in Amalia's home while we're here if that's okay."

I knew I didn't really need his permission, but since he seemed to be the man in charge now, I at least wanted to show him the respect he deserved after today.

"Of course." He gave a slight bow and walked away to a waiting group of wolves.

I didn't quite know how we were going to move forward, but I knew without a doubt that we would somehow. Even if it took us years to do so.

The lives lost would be honored to the best of our ability, and we couldn't do that by letting the grief take over. Just like Meme requested, I'd make sure her death meant something and make her proud from the other side.

Seven months after the battle that changed more lives than I could count, I stood on a stage at Shadow Veil Academy and received my certificate of completion. It was a bittersweet moment for me as I glanced out into the crowd, wishing I could see the faces of those who had been taken from this world too soon.

After the fight ended, Enzo, Jules, Gemma, Talon, and Lyssa stayed behind with me in New Orleans to help settle the quarter and plan the celebration of life for those lost, with a special tribute to my Meme.

She had touched lives all over New Orleans, and it would be many lifetimes before she was forgotten. There had been a parade down the main streets that tourists took as something just for fun while the rest of us mourned, remembered, and celebrated those who had given their all to stop Malina.

The coven Amalia had belonged to headed up the tribute, and I made a promise to myself that I'd be more involved with my witch side when we moved to New Orleans.

It wasn't going to be a permanent move, but it was a "for the moment" choice. Enzo and I decided that life was short, and we needed to experience the world, so our intention was to explore every bit of it that we could.

When we'd come back to school, it took well over a month for the cloud of sorrow to lift. We'd received notice that Vincent's latest hideaway had been found, along with the body of the last missing student.

On top of her death, there had been thirteen others, including Alexander, one of the council members. Jules had made the decision then that she would join the council on a longer but still temporary basis, and Professor Emmett Melnier had filled the remaining spot.

Jules had taken Marek's death nearly as hard as I had, and joining the council had given her something to focus on while we all healed.

"Raegan Keyes," Headmaster Stone called, probably not for the first time based upon the snicker that ran through the crowd.

My face blushed as I moved forward in the line and took my certificate while shaking his hand. "Thank you."

"Don't be a stranger around here, Raegan. I know you have plans, but I expect to see you back for a visit at some point," Headmaster Stone said with a warm smile.

"I will be sure to do so." I grinned back at him and then exited the stage through an archway of teal and silver balloons.

Gemma was waiting for me under a banner that was set up for pictures and read "Congratulations, Graduate". Pain struck through me as I watched waiting families ready to take pictures. There were happy moms and dads with their kids, something I'd never have for myself.

Gemma strode toward me, her eyes wide and full of happiness. "Can you believe we're done?"

My head shook. "Actually, I can't. Though, I do hope that the rest of my life is only a fraction as stressful as the last three years have been."

"Girl, you and me both, but something tells me that life on Drakken is going to be just as crazy as here."

About a month after we had returned home from New Orleans, the four of us and JayLeigh went back to Drakken. While we were there, Talon had asked Gemma to move to Drakken with him, and she'd immediately said yes, but with the stipulation I visited at least once a year. I had happily agreed, as long as she did the same on Earth.

During our second visit to Drakken, Enzo and I had received a much warmer welcoming, and I had been surprised to find Onyx there. Even though he had come to our rescue when we needed it most during the final moments of the battle, I wasn't sure the dragons would ever trust him again.

Apparently, he had turned over a new leaf when he overheard Malina talking about how she planned on killing all of the dragons as soon as she was finished with Marek. That hadn't sat well with Onyx and worked out in our favor. He'd been tempted with power and realized it came with a price he wasn't willing to pay.

While he wasn't put back in a leadership role, he was welcomed back as a resident in Drakken. Now that it was public knowledge dragons still existed, some of them had decided to venture to Earth, but outsiders would never be allowed in Drakken.

It was too much of a risk to the small population of dragons to lower their shields and allow those without dragon DNA in. I didn't blame them and fully supported the decision.

Ethaniel had stepped in permanently to run things in Drakken, but JayLeigh was next in line to the throne if she wanted it since I had declined. As much as I loved my dragon side, I wasn't "Queen" material, and I didn't want to spend the rest of my life tied to one world. Instead, I wanted to explore everything each of them had to offer.

For the time being, JayLeigh had temporarily declined the role when I pushed that she should have been next in line after me. She wasn't ready yet, either, but Drakken was her home and she would one day settle down. Until then, she took pleasure in warning Ethaniel that she could be lurking around any corner, so he'd do well to be on his best behavior.

Though, the most interesting thing we had learned when we went back was about Enzo. Phox had found us while we were there and said she had some information we'd be interested in.

My stomach had twisted, and I shook my head. We hadn't needed any more surprises; all I wanted was some normalcy for a little while. The conversation came back to me clearly because it had made Enzo so incredibly happy, while at the same time making me realize how close I had come to losing him.

"So, has anyone questioned why elf boy can suddenly turn into a dragon?" she remarked.

"Well, I assumed Jayce came with the bond I have with Raegan. I never thought I needed to question it," Enzo replied.

Phox groaned, clearly disappointed in our lack of query. "No, your bond would have only ever allowed you into Drakken. Nothing more, nothing less. For some reason, the dragon spirits thought you worthy of being Raegan's equal in more ways than one. When you should have died after having been hit with the dragon's tail that day in the forest, the spirits saved you by giving you Jayce."

"What? I *should have* died that day?" Enzo gaped.

"Well, duh. You were bleeding internally from being hit by a dragon. It really shouldn't come as a surprise. The three of you were too far from the castle to get to Marek in time and without the spirits' mercy... Anyway, don't screw it up."

"Wait, how do you know all of this? You weren't even in Drakken at the time." I immediately regretted questioning her.

Phox rolled her eyes. "Have you not learned anything? I won't even justify your idiocy with an answer. Just know Enzo is now officially a hybrid." She turned to him. "You are half-dragon and half-elf. The only of your kind. Be worthy of the beast within you, and hopefully our paths won't need to cross again for many years to come."

Gemma's fingers snapped in front of my face, and I shook my head to clear the memory.

"We're still on to go to dinner with the others, right?" she asked with some irritation, telling me it wasn't the first time she had done so. Apparently, I had no attention span left in me.

"As far as I know. Where is Talon?" I asked, since he was the only one in our group not graduating.

"He's changing. I might have jumped on him when I exited the stage and knocked over the vase of flowers he was holding that proceeded to cover his pants in water. Oops."

My head shook as laughter took over while I pictured poor Talon covered in petals and water. Enzo snuck up behind me, and I flinched as his arms wrapped around me.

He pressed a light kiss to my neck and whispered, "Congratulations."

I responded with a kiss of my own before greeting Finley and Lyssa, who had joined us as well. "Where's Peyton?" I asked.

"Uhhh, she won't be joining us tonight. Her and her new bae decided they needed some 'alone time'," Lyssa answered using finger quotes around the last part, which had Enzo groaning. He hated that we had no filter around him.

"See? I told you we could have gotten out of it," Enzo grumbled some more, but I elbowed him in the ribs.

"We're all going our separate ways soon. We're *not* missing this dinner." My glare held until he conceded.

"Yes, Dear."

With Gemma and Talon heading to Drakken within the week, I would be trying to get as much time in with her as possible. Lyssa was staying at Shadow Veil and would be working toward becoming one of the teachers. The choice had surprised me, but in a good way.

Peyton and Finley were supposed to head off on a girls-only trip, but I had a feeling Peyton's new boyfriend was going to put a kink in those plans, so I had invited Finley to join us in New Orleans if she wanted. Nothing had been decided, but I hoped she would accept the offer.

We moved through the crowd of people and stood in front of the school, waiting for Talon. He apparently took longer to change than most girls.

"Hey, I'm glad I caught you," Peyton said excitedly as she approached us with her boyfriend Linc practically wrapped around her waist. Her eyes were bright with bliss, and my heart was truly happy for her.

Hugs and more congratulations went around before

Gemma shoved her phone at Talon, who had finally arrived. "Take our picture."

"Ours, like mine and yours? Or ours, as in you and your friends, because if it's the latter, I'm going to feel a little left out." Talon pouted adorably.

Gemma patted his chest. "You'll get over it. Now be a good mate and take the picture. If you make it look good enough, maybe we can do a group one, too."

Enzo snagged the phone. "I'll do it, and then we will do a group one no matter what."

Gemma shrugged, then grabbed my hand. She, Peyton, Finley, Lyssa, and I each wrapped an arm around the person next to us as we stood in front of the school. Enzo backed up several feet and took a few pictures for us.

When he handed the phone back, we all approved and even invited Linc into the group picture. He might be new to the group, but if he was important to Peyton, then he was important to us. Though, I did push them to the end so that if things went south later on, we could also crop him out.

Evil, yes. Smart, definitely.

We headed off to dinner minus Peyton and Linc, and warmth settled over me. Even though Marek and Amalia weren't physically present, I had no doubt they were hanging out with my parents and watching over us.

A MONTH LATER, WE WERE SETTLED INTO AMALIA'S home back in New Orleans. It was still hard to consider it mine, because I refused to change a thing about the place. It was perfect as it stood, and I discovered something new about my grandmother every day.

For example, she had a crazy obsession with frogs.

There were there little frog figurines found throughout her house in odd places. The weirdest one yet was the cheese drawer.

Finley had indeed joined us, and Lyssa was due to visit within the next week. I couldn't be more excited to have another one of my girls close, even if it was for a short time.

After the sun set on a warm and humid evening, I was sitting out on the balcony that was attached to the bedroom we had claimed as our own and enjoying the slight breeze that blew in.

Meme's house had five bedrooms, and I couldn't fathom taking hers anytime soon. Plus, the view of the French Quarter from ours was pretty fantastic.

Lights twinkled off in the distance, and music could be heard just enough that it had my fingers tapping to the beat. Down in the street, there were still kids running about, most of whom were supernatural and enjoyed pulling pranks on Enzo at every chance.

Considering he was the only elf, or half-elf, this side of New Orleans, he took it all in stride, and thoughts of how he would be as a father began to filter through. Well, up until he snuck up behind me and scared the crap out of me.

"Whatcha doing, mate?" he said with a laugh.

"Well, I *was* thinking nice thoughts about you, but now I'm plotting your death."

He shrugged. "So, nothing new?"

"Nope. Where have you been?" I asked since he hadn't surfaced in a few hours. The house was huge, and I gave up trying to keep track of him half of the time.

"I was in the attic. Leesa asked me to look for some books she thought would be helpful for the upcoming ceremony. I found one, but not the other two she requested."

Leesa was the new coven leader, and she was having a

hell of a time picking up where Amalia had left off. Apparently, my grandmother didn't accept help all that often, and nobody knew how to do her job. I had no doubt in my mind that she was enjoying the hell out of how frustrated people were in their attempts to replace her.

"Well, are you done for the evening or do you need help?" I asked, really hoping he would say he was finished.

"Depends. What did you have in mind if I'm done?" He smirked and leaned closer before trailing a finger up my arm and under my chin.

"I was hoping I could persuade my mate to stay in, close the windows, and have his way with me. Though, he was busy, so I figured I could ask you."

His eyes darkened and a rumble sounded in his chest as a few scales appeared on his arms. Even months later, it was the most beautiful thing to me when his dragon side came out. Jayce had been a gift none of us expected, but we all appreciated, especially Chelle.

"Mine. Always mine," he growled in my ear as he picked me up from the chair and strode back inside, waving his hand to close all of the windows with a loud bang.

Placing a gentle kiss to his neck, I whispered, "Yes, my love. Always yours. Forever and infinity."

Enzo was my happily ever after, no matter where we ended up, who we were with, or what we were doing. None of it mattered as long as we were together.

EXTRAS FOR THE READERS!

I've included a few additional scenes. Some of which you might have seen floating around before, but none of which are still available anywhere else.

So, without further ado, enjoy a short story, a bonus POV from Enzo, and an extended epilogue!

Thank you for enjoying Shadow Veil Academy!

"What if we make bullets shoot out of our fingers and create real life finger guns?" Gemma teased as we sat in the corner of our Defensive Magic class.

We needed to think of a new defensive trick we hadn't learned in class and write an essay on why it would be helpful in a fight. Extra credit was given if we could actually perform the spell. Gemma had come up with some interesting ideas, none of which were appropriate for school.

Shadow Veil Academy was all for the students having fun, but there were limits on said fun.

"Okay, Texas Ranger. I'm sure Professor Inferna would love that one," I drawled.

"You're just jealous you didn't think of it first. I'm still voting that we go with the 'Enhance Your Assets' idea. Seriously, Raegan. Think about it. Plus, I wouldn't say no to a magical boob job. My girls need some love."

Shaking my head at her, I flipped through the screens on my tablet, trying to find something that wouldn't get us kicked out of school. Gemma kept mumbling about her "girls", but I ignored her. I needed to get an 'A' on the assignment and was going to make sure we did something useful, not cosmetic.

I was a first-year student taking second-year classes in order to catch up with my peers. Not much had gone right since I arrived a couple of months ago, but I was handling the course work well for the most part as long as I didn't get too distracted, which was really easy to do given who my tutor was.

"Ohmyfuckinggod," Gemma whispered not-so-eloquently and so fast I hardly understood her.

My head snapped up to see what happened, and the laughter that ripped from my throat couldn't be helped. "What did you do?" I asked when I regained most of my composure.

"I don't know! I was trying to figure out the enhancing spell, but I was going to use it on this dagger instead to try and enhance our weapons. I must have still been thinking too hard about my tatas and then... THIS!"

My eyes tried to process what I was seeing, but all I could see were boobs. The biggest ones I'd ever seen on someone the size of Gemma who maybe weighed one-hundred-twenty pounds and was 5'6". Her shirt was being stretched to max capacity, and I realized her chest was only getting bigger.

"Do something," she hissed as her hazel eyes widened in fear.

I'd known Gemma for a few months and she'd never been afraid of anything during that time.

Serious worry for my friend began to set in, so I thought back to all the magic I had learned. I was a hybrid. I had elven and witch abilities within me, but none of my training had included anything remotely close to the situation before me.

Changing weapons? Yes. Human body parts? Not so much.

"Come on." Grabbing her hand, I dragged her from our seats and out the door, thankful that it was within mere feet of us, and we'd only caught the attention of a few students.

Without saying a word, I led her toward History Hall. I knew who we needed and where he was. The only problem was I wasn't sure he was going to be a willing participant in making it better without me owing him and that made me more nervous than I wanted to admit.

"Raegan, they won't stop growing," Gemma's panicked voice echoed through the empty halls.

Thinking back to my elven magic classes, I tried to think of anything that would help at least slow whatever she had done with her witch magic. Stopping in the middle of the hallway, I brushed my auburn hair out of my face and concentrated on my friend.

"I have no idea if this will work, but I doubt it can make it worse," I said, trying to hide my smile as her shirt was beginning to pop buttons.

"Don't you dare enjoy this right now." Her glare should have worried me, but I knew her well enough by then that I disregarded her attitude and got to work.

"I'm going to have to touch them..."

"Just do it!" she demanded.

A chuckle slipped from my lips. "That's what she said."

"I fucking hate you right now."

Ignoring her anger, I placed my hands around her boobs, awkwardly trying to cup the massive monsters growing before my eyes as I thought about the words I needed to say. There was a dwarfing spell we had done on our weapons in elven class the week before that I was hoping would counteract whatever Gemma had done.

"Shrivato enchota devatter."

Warmth filled my hands, and a teal glow surrounded them. Grinning, I pulled away as the light began to fade, and I hoped the spell was starting to work.

Her boobs weren't getting any bigger, but they weren't getting smaller, either. Gemma's hands moved to where mine had been, and her face pinched.

"Holy shit, it burns! What did you do to me?"

"Uhhh, I thought I was making your boobs smaller, but I guess not. Back to plan A. Let's go." Grabbing her hand once more, we ran through the halls. Thankfully, everyone was in classes, so the trip from Magic Hall to History Hall took half the time it normally did.

"Stay here and maybe face the wall in case anyone comes out," I suggested, but all I received in return was her middle finger in my face.

I opened the door to Enzo's class. They were in the middle of some sort of project where everyone was split up around the room in groups, so nobody paid attention to me as I slipped in. I found him with two other guys in the back of the room and waved him over.

He took his sweet time, even though I continued moving my hand in hopes he would move his feet even just a bit faster.

"Miss me so much you had to interrupt my studies?" He winked, running a hand through his shoulder-length bronze hair.

"If I say yes, will you promise to help me with something?"

His eyes narrowed. "What did you do?"

"It wasn't me this time. I promise. Well, I might have made it worse, but I didn't start it. You see, Gemma was trying to create a spell and it backfired."

"Where is she?" he demanded before I could tell any more.

"In the hallway."

His hand wrapped around my wrist and he pulled me toward the door. Enzo was my tutor and one of the top students at the academy. He was smart and sexy and a serious pain in my ass, but I knew we could count on him.

He might like to push my buttons, but deep down in the depths of his soul that rarely saw light, I knew there was a speck of goodness in him. Okay, maybe I was being dramatic, but the sexual tension between the two of us was driving me insane and leading me to think ridiculous things.

When we entered the hallway, Gemma was curled up on the floor, shoulders shaking. My heart lurched. The situation was no longer funny, and I was afraid I had *really* done something to make it worse.

Enzo flew into immediate action and asked for a step-by-step playback of everything that had happened. When I finished with the important pieces, he let out a string of cuss words.

"You can't mix witch and elven magic. They're fighting against each other and it's causing her massive amounts of pain right now. I need you to reverse your spell, so I can fix hers."

Holy shit. I almost killed my best friend. She was half witch and vampire while I was half witch and elf. I didn't even think about my elf magic clashing with her witch spell.

Pushing him aside, I placed my hands back on Gemma's boobs, this time without a smirk on my face. The area felt like it was on fire and my hands burned, but I didn't let it deter me as I recited my previous spell backward two times.

An audible sigh of relief left Gemma's lips, but she still wasn't getting up off the ground or opening her eyes.

"How are you going to fix her? You're pure elf," I said, panic continuing to rise within me.

"I'm going to walk her through fixing herself. Just back up a little and give her some space."

I wanted to protest. I had no desire to leave her side, but I had come to Enzo for a reason, so I reluctantly walked away and gave them the space he suggested.

Pacing the hallway wasn't helping, so I stopped and stared out the window. History Hall looked over the shifter forest. I longed to go explore it, but I'd been warned too many times that it wasn't the safest place for non-shifters or those who didn't have a complete handle on their magic. I still had a while before I'd feel confident using my magic to defend myself, should the need arise.

Minutes later, a warm hand cupped my shoulder and I practically jumped out of my skin.

"Sorry," Enzo said as his hand fell away. "Gemma's got a handle on her spell now and she should be better in a minute."

Tension eased out of my body as his words registered with me. "Thank you. Seriously, I don't know what we would have done. Well, I mean, we could have gone to the headmaster, but that would have gotten us in trouble and that didn't sound like fun."

"I'm happy to be of service for any of your needs. You know that." He smirked, and I wanted to smack the look right off his chiseled and irresistible face.

Taking a step back, I put some much-needed space between us. "Right. Well, thanks again. You can go back to class now."

He closed the space between us, even nearer than before. "What about payment for my services? What do I get for helping your friend?"

A swift knee to the balls, I thought.

My gaze didn't leave his. I wasn't going to let him push me around with all his sexiness. He knew what he did to me, but I wouldn't let him win. I knew how to play just as dirty as he did.

"What would you like?" I lowered my voice and batted my eyes at him.

His lips opened to respond, but I had caught him off guard and no words came. Enzo took too long to recover, and showed how I affected him. Then, by the hardened look on his face, I knew he was aware he had lost this battle.

He hadn't expected me to respond that way, and I was jumping for joy on the inside for having taken control of the situation so quickly.

"Well played, Rae. Don't worry, I'll collect one of these days, but it will be on *my* time." His fingers brushed along my jaw, causing my girly bits to go off like Pop Rocks.

Before I could reply, he turned away and headed back for his class. When I was able to get myself together, I went back to Gemma who was now standing up and giving me her best glare.

"Don't let him touch you like that again," she ground out. "We talked about this. Enzo equals trouble."

"Enzo also equals you not having monstrous tatas, so he's not all bad," I countered.

"I'll give you that. I would have never figured that out on my own, but I still say you need to keep your distance. I see the way he looks at you, and it's not good. It's like he wants to lock you away and never let anyone else near you. Creepy, if you ask me."

Looping my arm through hers, we began the walk back to class. "Good thing I wasn't asking you, huh? How about we get back to our class and show those spells who's boss?"

She rolled her eyes at me, but didn't object.

On the way back to class, I considered her words about Enzo. I knew she was only trying to be a friend and she had known him longer than I had, but there was something about him I couldn't let go. Something he was hiding, and I wanted to figure out.

He was an itch I had to scratch, even if it might break my heart.

The boom that sounded from the front gates wouldn't have normally affected me so severely, but considering Raegan wasn't at my side when it happened, my chest beat rapidly, and my body began to move before my brain really processed what was happening.

With everything that had transpired as of late, my thoughts instantly went to worst case scenario and the dishes I'd been holding flew across the room as several choice words were yelled.

"Move your ass, Talon. We need to know what that was and where the girls are. You know damn well they didn't stay put," I grumbled.

My Raegan was as stubborn as they came and while it frustrated the hell out of me most days, I loved her all the more for it. Except when her stubbornness was amplified by being around JayLeigh and Gemma. Those three took their "girl power" to the extreme.

"Do you think *she's* here?" Talon snarled as we raced for the exit. "If she is, I hope Sylas is with her. I will kill that bastard first chance I get."

Not that this was the time, but we were hardly ever without Raegan or Gemma, so I had to ask considering he was nearly as enraged as I was at the moment. "Did you bond with Gemma?"

He kept pace as he shrugged. "I don't know, man. It's different with her, but it's not what I expected. Maybe because she's a hybrid? I figured I'd ask Marek when I went back home and figure it out then. She's his daughter's best friend. I doubt he'll deny helping me figure it out since it would make Raegan happy for Gemma to visit Drakken."

I nodded as we came around the corner and the gates were finally within sight. As my eyes focused on what was waiting, I realized Talon wasn't going to have to wait until he was home to ask Marek about his issue. Instead of walking in on an attack like I'd fully expected, Marek was shifting back to his human form and all three girls stood before him.

"Slow down," I said. "It's just Marek. Let's give them a minute."

We moved to a brisk walk and even though I was no longer worried for Raegan's safety, my eyes never left her back. She was my everything. My entire world and if anything ever took her away from me again, I wasn't sure how I would contain the wrath simmering just beneath the surface.

I'd screwed up before. I had known it from the first day Raegan was on campus, but fear of losing her had made me keep my secrets. Secrets which caused me to lose her anyway.

I thanked the fates every day for bringing her back to Shadow Veil after Malina revealed my part in her despicable plans.

The summer Raegan was gone was a dark one. The

darkest I'd ever experienced and there had been times I considered going back to Malina just so she would end my life, but there was a tiny voice inside my head that told me to be patient.

The day she forgave me in Drakken was one I'd never forget. I'd seen the changes in her when she came back to the academy and the way I still affected her, but like I'd said before, my girl was stubborn, and I didn't exactly deserve her forgiveness.

So, when I realized there was true hope to earn it back, I made a vow to do whatever it took, protect her at all costs, and to make sure Malina died because letting that bitch use my bonded mate was not something I'd ever let happen.

Talon nudged me with his shoulder, pulling me from my thoughts. "Should we even interrupt?"

I smirked. "Of course we should. They fully expect it, so why not?"

"True. You are slightly psycho when it comes to Raegan."

There was no point in denying it. I never once tried to hide it and he saw the worst of it when Headmaster Stone refused to let me go with them to rescue Raegan when Sylas and Desmond had taken her.

As we got closer, I heard the tail end of what Marek had been saying. "...she's coming for Raegan and you all need to prepare if you haven't already done so."

Rage rolled through me because I knew who *she* was without needing to hear ewhat they'd been saying before. Talon wasn't faring any better as he pulled Gemma into his side with a grunt.

Lifting my head, I met Marek's stare. "We're prepared, but half of our group was supposed to meet us in Maine."

"There's no point. I can all but guarantee she's already

headed here. She had a full day in Drakken for a head start. I didn't get her message until we realized Joren was missing. He lived alone, but still, it took longer than it should have."

JayLeigh grasped his shoulder. "Don't take blame for this. Malina did this to all of us. We'll figure out a way to stop her."

Raegan nodded next to me. "Yes, we will. So, come on. I'll show you to Headmaster Stone and we can change our plans."

His face fell. "As long as it's not too late."

Raegan pulled away from me and went to Marek. She looped her arm through his and he seemed to relax a bit more as she led us to Alistair's office.

Even though Malina was now headed for us and we'd no longer be on the offense like we'd intended, having Marek present gave me hope that within the next twenty-four hours all our problems would be solved.

WELL, THAT HOPE WAS QUICKLY DASHED ONCE I showed Marek to his room after our meeting with the council. The meeting itself had gone fine. They'd been prepared for this possibility and things were already in motion to bring those willing to fight with us to Shadow Veil.

What didn't make me feel any better was the talk that Marek wanted to have with me. I'd almost made it out. One foot was already out the door of the room I'd showed him to before he spoke again.

"There's actually something I'd like to ask you if you could wait," Marek said, and my shoulders tensed.

I didn't have any guesses as to what he could want, but I

knew it wasn't good if he chose to wait until we were alone to bring it up.

Turning around, I closed the door and took a seat at the table he stood next to. "Does this have something to do with Raegan?" I asked once he was seated across from me.

"No, but it is something she can't know until after the battle."

My hands instantly went up as my head shook. "Not going to happen. Keeping secrets from her almost ruined us. I won't do it again."

I didn't care if he was the dragon king and could probably kill me in an instant, I wouldn't keep something else from Raegan. I didn't often make the same mistakes twice especially when it hurt those I cared about.

"It's not a secret necessarily and it may not even happen. It's just a backup plan and I need you to do something for me should it appear as if Malina is going to win. If she kills me, you will never be able to stop her, and we can't let that happen, no matter what."

Damn it. I didn't like how he was talking, but I unfortunately understood why he asked me because I was beginning to see where he was going with the conversation.

"What do you need?" I asked resigned and hopeful I was wrong.

Reaching into his jacket, he pulled out a dagger. "I need you to keep this and stay near me as much as possible during the battle. I'm confident Raegan can handle herself against anyone Malina might bring with her and I'll make sure JayLeigh is watching her if not."

"You're asking me to leave my bonded mate who has barely scratched the surface on her abilities to watch over you, a powerful dragon king, a Doyen?"

His face drew tight. "I understand it doesn't make sense,

but Malina is powerful and I won't take any chances in letting her best me. I need you to kill me before she does if the situation arises."

"How am I supposed to kill you? I thought Doyens couldn't be killed by anyone other than another Doyen. And what good would that do us if you were dead anyway? Besides making Raegan hate me, I'm not seeing the point."

He needed to have a damn good reason or I was walking away before he could say anymore. I wouldn't risk losing Raegan just because.

"I have died three other times before. Each time I've come back because I wasn't killed at the hands of another Doyen, but it takes days, sometimes weeks, for my body to regenerate and Malina can't end me if my heart's not beating."

"So, you're telling me that if I kill you that you'll come back to life and Raegan won't hate me or even kill me herself for taking her father away?"

Shock registered on his face as he leaned back. "She considers me her father?"

I shrugged. "I don't think she'll be calling you Dad anytime soon, but you are her family. One of very few members she has left, and I don't know that I can hurt her like that. Why can't we tell her if it's only a backup plan?"

His hands rubbed over his tired face. "Because then she'll spend the entire fight worried about me and not herself. I've seen how much Raegan cares about other people, and I don't want her putting my safety before her own."

I laughed. "But mine isn't as important?"

"You of all people should understand what I meant by that." He didn't find my joke as funny as I did, apparently.

"I do understand, and while I would risk my life for

Raegan any day of the week, I don't know that I'm willing to lie to her and risk losing her as a favor to you. You may not know her well enough, but that's a choice you made when you decided to never come back to Earth. I trust—"

His resounding snarl cut me off mid-sentence as he narrowed his eyes at me. "I've given you a lot of freedom in the way you speak to me, Enzo, but no longer will I be disrespected. I would have been there for Raegan if I knew she existed. My choices are mine to own, but *you* don't get to put them into question. Do you understand?"

The full force of his power weighed down on me and I was smart enough to know when I'd pushed too far, so I calmed my magic that so badly wanted to lash out at him for outpowering me and sat up straighter.

"I understand just fine, but you need to understand as well. You're asking me to risk losing Raegan. We might be bonded, but if I hurt her again, even without malicious intent, she'll kill me, or worse, she'll leave me to wallow in my own misery for the rest of my pathetic life."

He slid the dagger to the middle of the table, ignoring my concerns. "You have two choices, Enzo, and I won't force you to do either one. You can take this dagger and keep it to yourself as I've asked until the time comes where it might be necessary for you to use it or you can walk out the door, tell Raegan what we've discussed in order to prevent secrets from being between the two of you and see what happens.

"Either way, you're risking her because you know damn well what she'll do with that information. As her bonded mate, I'll let you make that decision, but just remember, sometimes it's better to ask for forgiveness than it is permission. So, make your choice and let's move forward."

Marek stood from the table, leaving the dagger for me to

stare at as he walked away. My eyes wouldn't move from the blade, even when I heard the door open and close. He was giving me an impossible choice and the hesitation was killing me.

If I took the dagger and didn't tell Raegan, there was a chance I would never even have to use it and she'd be none the wiser.

Or I could take it and tell her, but Marek had been right. She would only then put herself at risk to keep him safe.

I wasn't willing to wager her life to save his even if he was the only one who could stop Malina.

If I didn't accept the dagger, I'd have to hope Marek would be able to hold his own against the sorceress. All the while, pretending the previous conversation never happened.

Then guilt slammed into me.

If Marek died at the hands of Malina causing Raegan to lose another parent when I could have prevented it, I'd forever be the reason for her pain.

Damn him for asking this of me. I'd just gotten Raegan back and as I swiped the dagger from the table, I risked losing her again. My only hope was she'd give me enough time to explain should it be necessary for me to use the blade.

Even I knew what a stupid choice I was making, but I was trusting Marek and if he was this worried, then I'd do whatever it took to keep Raegan safe, even if she hated me for it.

Even though I'd promised Headmaster Stone I'd come back to visit, it had somehow been two years since I'd stepped foot in the academy. After so much time, I was standing in front of the gates, with Enzo by my side, feeling like it was the first time all over again.

Enzo nudged me. "Raegan?"

"Hmm?"

"Are you okay?" he asked, trailing his finger over the scales that appeared on my arm without me realizing.

"I don't know. A part of me is freaking the hell out. Like it's five years ago all over again, even though I know Malina isn't in there."

He frowned. "You haven't thought about her in a long time. What's going on with you?"

"Nothing. I'm totally fine. Forget I said anything." I forced the dragon scales to disappear and took a step toward the gates of Shadow Veil Academy.

And then, I was on my ass.

"What the f—" I grumbled until a mess of blonde hair covered my face.

"Rae Bae!" Oh, gods. Talon had decided he wanted to take an extended vacation on Earth last year, and I loathed the nickname Gemma had made up for me after spending an extended amount of time with humans.

"Hi, Gem," I murmured as I pushed her off me.

Gone was the worry I'd been feeling, and in its place was contentment at having my bestie with us as well.

Enzo and Talon were already waiting for us at the gate. They'd formed an adorable bromance, and I was glad they got along so well, because, really, they didn't have a choice. Gemma was my soul sister for life.

She cocked her head to the side. "There's something different about you."

"And there's something wrong with you. Come on. Lyssa is waiting." I grabbed her hand and pulled her toward the guys.

Enzo gave me a once-over, overprotective brute likely checking to make sure I hadn't received any injuries from Gemma's over-the-top greeting.

"Can you believe Lyssa is going to be the youngest council member?" Gemma asked with glee.

We'd stayed in touch with Lyssa, Peyton, and Finley over the years, but we hadn't seen them as much as we would have liked. After our stay in New Orleans, Finley had taken off and was going through a wild phase she never told us much about.

Peyton and Linc had gotten married only a year after they got together, and we'd had back-to-back weddings, hers then mine.

I hadn't made Enzo wait as long as I thought I would to officially become his wife. He was it for me and I'd been stupid to wait at all.

Lyssa had stayed on at the school and made quite the

name for herself. Now, it was time for Jules to move on, and Lyssa was taking her place.

"Raegan!"

Speaking of... My aunt's voice rang across the school grounds, and I spotted her running toward us.

Even though Enzo and I hadn't been back to the academy, I'd still seen Jules on many occasions. She liked to meet us in New Orleans or whenever we were somewhere tropical.

I'd spent the last few years doing what I'd always dreamed of with the people I loved most. I couldn't have asked for anything more.

Jogging toward her, I met Jules in the middle. "Hey, Aunt Jules."

Her arms wrapped tight around me and mine did the same to her, holding on for a solid minute before Gemma pulled us apart.

"My turn," she whined.

"How was the trip over?" Jules asked once pleasantries were exchanged.

Enzo tucked me into his side, but his concern wasn't necessary. Whatever feeling had me so preoccupied when we first arrived was long gone once I got my hands on my best friend and aunt. Though, I wouldn't tell him that and hurt his feelings. He might be a brute, but he was also a sensitive guy when it came to me.

"It was good. I'm glad we could make it." I smiled and truly meant it.

"Lyssa will be, too. The arrival of you girls has been all she's talked about. Peyton and Finley won't be here until tomorrow, though. Peyton had to track Finley down in Africa somewhere. I think. Honestly, I can't keep up with that girl."

I laughed. "We don't even try anymore. As long as she's happy."

"She sounded almost *too* happy last time I chatted with her, if you know what I mean." Gemma winked, and I shook my head. She hadn't grown up at all.

"Let's head inside. I know there are a lot of people who can't wait to see you," Jules said, looping her arm through mine. Gemma did the same on the other side.

I glanced back at Enzo and offered him a smile. He waved me on and grinned back. Gods, I loved that elf.

Gemma and Jules chatted on and on while I took in the academy. Not much had changed since I was last there, and I was a little disappointed. Well, that was until we stepped onto the platform with no sides and I remembered how scared I used to be of them.

"It really does seem like just yesterday," I muttered, and Jules patted my back.

We headed up to the headmaster's office, and I hoped Talon and Enzo would be on the lift after us. I'd lied to myself earlier. I still wasn't okay. Enzo being out of eyesight threw my emotions out of whack, and I had no clue what was happening to me.

Holy hell. Had I subconsciously been avoiding this place all these years to avoid whatever was happening?

"What's going on with you?" Jules asked as we stepped off the platform.

I growled at her. "Will everyone stop asking me that? I'm fine!" My hand covered my mouth, and my eyes widened. "I'm so sorry. I didn't mean that."

Jules gave me a once over and pressed her hand to my head. "Well, you don't have a fever."

Lyssa came out of Headmaster Stone's office and rushed

toward us. She threw her arms around me and Gemma, pulling us in tight. "I missed you both so much."

"It's only been a few months," Gemma murmured against Lyssa's shoulder.

"Yeah, but for me, during those few months, I've been working my ass off with no play while the two of you do whatever the hell you want."

I grinned at her, once again feeling normal, which was totally not normal. "You could have come with us."

Her eyes lit up with elation. "No, I couldn't have. This is where I'm meant to be."

"Will Dic—I mean, your dad, be here to see the ceremony?" I asked. I still hated that man with a fiery passion.

She nodded. "He's changed, Rae. Cut him some slack."

Like hell that would happen, but I didn't tell her that. She didn't need to stress about anything. This was her special weekend.

She released us and I noticed Headmaster Stone behind her. His beard was shorter, but other than that, he still looked exactly the same with his black robes and white hair. When he opened his arms, I didn't hesitate to walk into them, and guilt instantly assaulted me.

The feeling was so heavy that tears built in my eyes, and I held on just a bit longer in hopes of getting myself in check. It didn't work.

"I'm sorry," I mumbled as I pulled back.

"Oh, Gods," Jules said at the same time Enzo came around the corner.

"What happened?" he snarled and pulled me closer.

I shook my head. "Nothing. It's just me. I guess I'm more emotional about this place than I realized I'd be."

He squeezed me tighter, and I heard Jules and Gemma

whispering about something but couldn't make out the words before the rest of the council made an appearance.

"How about we get you to a room and relax?" Enzo suggested, and I didn't disagree with him. Jules handed him a paper which I assumed held our room number and code, and we headed back toward the platforms.

I hated that I wasn't sticking around to visit with everyone after only just arriving. It had been too long since we'd all been together, but I needed to figure out what the hell was wrong with me.

"Looks like we're in our old room," Enzo said once the platform was headed up.

I nodded but didn't reply.

He held my hand and stayed quiet, making me appreciate him even more than I already did. I thought back to what I'd eaten, where we'd been, and who we'd been around in the last few days, but nothing stood out. There was literally nothing I could think of that should have had me acting so erratically.

We made it to the room, and Enzo held the door open for me. My eyes instantly searched the area, and I took in the floor-to-ceiling windows and couches that were just the same as before, but instead of going to sit down, I spotted the butler box.

Oh, how I'd missed that contraption.

Without hesitating, or even asking Enzo what he wanted, I ordered damn near everything on the menu. Salty and sweet everything was what I needed. Maybe that was what was wrong with me. I hadn't eaten enough for my dragon.

Speaking of... Chelle had been quiet lately.

You around? I asked.

I am.

Odd and short answer. I didn't like it.

Do you know what's wrong with me? I asked.

There's nothing wrong with you, Raegan. You're perfectly healthy.

Well, I don't feel healthy. I feel like a damn nut-job.

She chuckled. *I promise I would tell you if there was anything wrong. Just enjoy this time with your friends.*

I felt her presence fade away and tried not to worry. I trusted her to tell me if she knew something. Then, my food began arriving and all else was forgotten.

First, I ate half a small cake, then fries covered in cheese, followed by ice cream and a burger. All while Enzo watched me with a Cheshire grin on his face.

I wiped my mouth with the back of my hand. Super lady like. "What?"

"Nothing. I'm just enjoying how much you're loving the spread. I should have thought to feed you sooner. It's like you're eating for two."

Holy fucking shit.

"What did you just say?" I asked.

"Uhhh, nothing that should cause your dragon scales to appear again. Are you sure you're okay?"

I began counting the days since my last heat. Yes, heat, because dragons were more dog-like than human.

"It's not possible. I mean, I know we do it a lot. Like every day, but still..." I let my words trail off.

"What are you talking about, Rae? You're making me nervous." By then, Enzo was on his knees in front of me. His hands cradled my face.

"I think you were right," I said, still unable to say the words out loud.

"Right about what?"

I glanced down at my stomach, then at all of the food before going back to him. "I'm eating for two."

His brows pinched together for only a millisecond, and then I saw the recognition—the exact moment when he realized he was going to be a dad—and the flood gates opened again because his joy was also mine.

He picked me up and swirled me around the room, tears falling from his eyes as well. "I love you so fucking much, Raegan." He sat me down, then kneeled before me again, pressing his lips to my stomach. "And I love you, little bean. I will protect you with my life, and nobody will ever hurt you."

Our combined bliss was almost too much to handle. Almost, but not quite. "We're going to be parents," I said with the biggest grin I'd ever had.

"We're going to be the best damn parents to ever walk this earth."

I snorted, trying not to laugh. "I guess this explains the mood swings."

"Love, you can have all the mood swings you want while you're growing our child. I will be, and do, whatever you need as a thank you for this gift you've given me." His fingers splayed across my stomach, and I set my hand on top of his.

"I couldn't have done it without you, but I'll take the pampering and the credit anyway."

He leaned down and kissed me softly. "I'm going to have to be careful with you now."

"Not *that* careful." I winked and kissed him again, more joyous than I'd ever been.

LATER THAT NIGHT, WE LEFT OUR ROOM AND I KNEW the moment Jules and Gemma laid eyes on me that they'd already pieced together I was pregnant. My erratic emotions had clearly taken care of that. We all spent the night celebrating—everyone else drinking and me switching between bouts of laughter and tears.

The following day, Peyton and Finley arrived, causing the celebrations to begin all over again. Finley seemed to step away from me when she found out I was pregnant, as if it was contagious, and Peyton held a longing in her eyes that had me tearing up. Hopefully soon, we'd be celebrating for her as well.

On our third day at the academy was Lyssa's ceremony, and I tried to avoid any baby talk. It was her special day, and she deserved all the focus on her.

"Are you ready, ladies?" Enzo asked as he peeked into the bathroom.

Gemma was curling my hair and on the last section. "Just about," she answered.

"We need to be downstairs in ten minutes," he added.

Gemma's head whipped around, and she glared at him. "We'll be there in five."

He disappeared with his hands up as she removed the curling iron then sprayed my hair with some gloss stuff I'd never normally use. "There. Now your hair will glow like your face has been the last two days."

My head shook. "Not today, Gem."

"Whatever, Rae Bae. I'll talk about my niece or nephew all I want. Lyssa understands." She bent over to my stomach and laid her hand across. "Oh, yes, Lyssa does. She's going to love you, too, but not like Auntie Gem. Nope. Nobody else will love you like me. Not even your mommy and daddy."

I shoved her away. "Hey, now."

She shrugged. "I speak the truth. Plus, I didn't say it would be less, just different."

"Come on before Enzo comes back in here," I said, letting the subject drop. Again, the day was about Lyssa.

We all headed downstairs toward the council room where I'd first shifted into not only my hybrid-dragon form, but my full dragon as well. Gods, we'd done so much damage that day.

There was a long table at the front of the room at which all of the council members sat, including Jules and Lyssa. I waved to them and found our reserved seats up front with Peyton and Finley.

They each smiled at us as we took our seats. I noticed a dozen or so other people in attendance, but I didn't recognize a single one until my eyes met that of Dick, also known as Lyssa's dad. He stood in the back, arms crossed and eyes focused on me. Apparently, the mutual dislike hadn't lessened for him, either. Good.

Before I could do anything to ruin her special day, Headmaster Stone stood and began speaking.

"Several years ago, one of our own lost their life in the fight against one of our greatest enemies. The council has had many changes and, while we love having Jules as part of our group, we knew her stay was temporary. We've had our eye on a potential replacement for the last two years, and I know she will do us proud."

Headmaster Stone gestured to Lyssa and she stood.

"Lyssa Trich, do you swear to uphold the values and laws of the council, making your decisions based on what is best for the people and not yourself?"

She nodded. "I do."

He continued on, asking her more questions, all to which she eagerly agreed. Then came the fun part.

"Jules, will you please join Lyssa?" Headmaster Stone asked.

My aunt did just that and placed her hands on Lyssa's shoulders right before silver and teal magic began swirling from the headmaster, then between the two of them.

They each closed their eyes, and a hum moved across the room. Chelle even reacted to the magic, but I managed to keep my scales in check.

"Jules Timmons, I now release you from the council." Headmaster Stone thrust his arms forward, and magic slammed into Jules, knocking her back several steps.

"Lyssa Trich, I now accept you into the council." He repeated the same step, but instead of being shoved back, Lyssa's head tilted up, and she soaked every ounce of magic into her being.

Headmaster Stone turned to the rest of us. "Thank you everyone for joining us. Please head to the magic hall meeting room where we will have dinner and spend the rest of the evening celebrating these two incredible women."

Enzo squeezed my hand. "I bet you didn't think we'd be doing so much celebrating when we came back here."

"That I didn't, but I wouldn't have it any other way."

ANOTHER YEAR LATER...

HAVE KIDS, THEY SAID. IT WILL BE FUN, THEY SAID.

They all *lied*.

While I loved my little dragon, I was no longer

enthused with her throwing of food and toys, an action she thought was a hilarious game. She was more stubborn than me and her father combined, but when it came down to it, I wouldn't change a thing about my curly-haired monster.

Amalia Cecile Vaughn, named after my Meme, was born just four months after we'd found out I was pregnant. Along with my expedited pregnancy, our daughter also grew ridiculously fast. Phox had come to visit after Amalia was born and let us know that she would be full grown by the age of five, a side effect of raising a dragon on Earth, apparently.

We didn't want her to grow too fast, so we were headed to Drakken by the end of the month. Unfortunately, with everything happening so fast, leaving Earth to spend decades away wasn't as easy as we'd have liked.

Though, Gemma and Talon were more than excited about this revelation, and if I was being honest, I couldn't wait to have my bestie as my neighbor, either. Of course, I'd miss a lot about Earth as well, but once Amalia was old enough, there would be frequent visits in our future.

"How's my beautiful wife doing today?" Enzo asked when he entered our New Orleans home that we'd been staying in since Amalia was born.

I sighed. "I have banana in my hair and a new bruise on my thigh from a flying My Little Pony. How do you think I'm doing?"

He swooped down and picked up Amalia from her play area in the living room. "Did you give momma a hard time today?"

She let out a little yawn. "Love the momma."

"Let's try to love the momma a little more gently before she runs away, princess."

Ha, I was tempted on some days, but there was no way

I'd ever miss a moment of this. Mashed food and bruises aside.

"I think it's someone's bedtime," I said, thankful this was the one thing she'd always done well. Our little dragon princess loved to sleep.

I took her from Enzo, and he grabbed my arm before I could walk away. "Meet me in our room when you're done?"

Even after all these years, butterflies still swirled inside me when he looked at me with those seductive eyes. "I'll be there before you know it."

He grinned. "Not too quickly." Then, he smacked me on the ass as I walked toward the stairs to go to Amalia's room. We'd given her my Meme's room, since I'd known neither Enzo nor I would ever be comfortable sleeping in it. She had all the space to grow and play, and I knew her teenage self would appreciate it when we came back for visits and eventually to live.

Her hand cradled my cheek. "Love the momma."

"And the momma loves you." I kissed her forehead and squeezed tight. Tomorrow, she'd be a bigger version of herself, and I cherished the moment of holding her close for as long as she'd let me.

"I hurt the momma." Her little lip quivered when I pulled back.

"I'm sorry, baby girl. Momma isn't hurt. I was just teasing. Just try to stop throwing your stuff. It also makes a mess." I really needed to watch what I said around her. Even though I saw the physical changes in her daily, her words were still limited, but apparently, her mind understood more than she was able to speak.

I never wanted her to feel guilt for being a child. A dragon child, nonetheless.

"Nigh-nigh, momma," she whispered and yawned once more.

I settled her into her toddler bed and tucked the blanket tightly around her before giving her a soft kiss to the forehead and brushing her hair back. "Goodnight, my beautiful girl. Sweet dreams."

She was already fast asleep before I stood back up. Gods, I loved that girl more than I ever thought possible.

I turned on her nightlight, then closed the door and walked to the other side of the house where our room was. Soft music was playing, and the lights were low. Curiosity got the better of me, and my feet moved quicker than I intended since Enzo had asked for extra time.

When I entered the room, flower petals trailed from the door to our bathroom, where the lights were off but candles were lit all over the counter and on the sides of the bath.

"What is this?" I asked while he was still leaning over the running bath.

Enzo turned toward me. "This is my way of saying thank you for being the most amazing wife and mother I could have ever dreamed of." He straightened and took two steps closer, kissing me senseless for several moments. "I love and appreciate you more than I tell you, and you deserve to know it every day."

His fingers moved down my arms and to the hem of my shirt.

"I think I could be okay with this sort of appreciation," I murmured as he lifted my shirt above my head.

"I figured you might be." He smirked and then kissed my shoulder blade before reaching around to undo my bra.

Piece by piece, he undressed all while leaving well-placed kisses along my body until I was quivering where I stood. While the bath seemed very tempting, I no longer had any interest in having it all to myself.

Enzo lifted me up, but I held on tight. "You're only allowed to set me in that water so long as you're joining me."

"Are you sure? I did this so you could relax," he replied, fighting a grin.

"Right. You didn't at all mean to seduce me at the same time. Either way, your appreciation is noted, and now I expect you to love me like there's no tomorrow." My nails dug into his neck until he nodded.

"Yes, wife. Whatever you want, whenever you want, because we have all of the tomorrows we need."

He set me down into the bath, and I watched him with abandon as he got undressed while I leaned back in the oversized jetted tub that we'd had installed a couple years ago. Best investment ever.

When Enzo joined me, I brought his mouth to mine and kissed him with all the love I had in my soul for him and our little family.

He would forever be my always, and I couldn't wait for whatever life threw at us next, so long as he was by my side.

Elite Supernatural Trackers

A complete Urban Fantasy series featuring witches, demons, fae, and more

Royal Fae Guardians

A complete Urban Fantasy duology featuring fae and magic users

Raven Point Pack Series

A complete Paranormal Romance series featuring wolves and witches

Shadow Veil Academy

A complete Urban Fantasy series featuring shifters, elves, witches, and more

Blood of the Sea Series

A complete Paranormal Romance series featuring vampires

Standalone

Marked Paradox - A complete Fantasy fae story